Different Seasons

Different

THE VIKING PRESS   NEW YORK

Stephen King

Seasons

Library of Congress Cataloging in Publication Data
King, Stephen, 1947–
  Different seasons.
  I. Title.
PS3561.I483D5   813'.54   82–70145
ISBN 0–670–27266–3   AACR2

Grateful acknowledgment is made to the following for permission to reprint copyrighted material:

Beechwood Music Corporation and Castle Music Pty. Limited: Portions of lyrics from
  "Tie Me Kangaroo Down, Sport," by Rolf Harris. Copyright © MCMLX by Castle
  Music Pty. Limited. Assigned to and copyrighted © 1961 by Beechwood Music
  Corp. for the United States and Canada. Copyright © Castle Music Pty. Limited
  for other territories. Used by permission. All rights reserved.
Big Seven Music Corporation: Portions of lyrics from "Party Doll," by Buddy Knox
  and Jimmy Bowen. Copyright © 1956 by Big Seven Music Corp. Portions of lyrics
  from "Sorry (I Ran All the Way Home)" by Zwirn/Giosasi. Copyright © 1959 by
  Big Seven Music Corp. All rights reserved.
*Holt, Rinehart and Winston, Publishers, Jonathan Cape Ltd., and the Estate of Robert
  Frost:* Two lines from "Mending Wall" from *The Poetry of Robert Frost,* edited by
  Edward Connery Lathem. Copyright 1930, 1939, © 1969 by Holt, Rinehart and
  Winston. Copyright © 1958 by Robert Frost. Copyright © 1967 by Lesley Frost
  Ballantine.

Contents

"Dirty deeds done dirt cheap."
——AC/DC

"I heard it through the grapevine."
——Norman Whitfield

*Tout s'en va, tout passe, l'eau coule,
et le coeur oublie.*
——Flaubert

It is the tale, not he who tells it.

Hope Springs Eternal

For Russ and Florence Dorr

Rita Hayworth and Shawshank Redemption

There's a guy like me in every state and federal prison in America, I guess—I'm the guy who can get it for you. Tailormade cigarettes, a bag of reefer if you're partial to that, a bottle of brandy to celebrate your son or daughter's high school graduation, or almost anything else . . . within reason, that is. It wasn't always that way.

I came to Shawshank when I was just twenty, and I am one of the few people in our happy little family willing to own up to what they did. I committed murder. I put a large insurance policy on my wife, who was three years older than I was, and then I fixed the brakes of the Chevrolet coupe her father had given us as a wedding present. It worked out exactly as I had planned, except I hadn't planned on her stopping to pick up the neighbor woman and the neighbor woman's infant son on their way down Castle Hill and into town. The brakes let go and the car crashed through the bushes at the edge of the town common, gathering speed. Bystanders said it must have been doing fifty or better when it hit the base of the Civil War statue and burst into flames.

I also hadn't planned on getting caught, but caught I was. I got a season's pass into this place. Maine has no death-penalty, but the District Attorney saw to it that I was tried for all three deaths and given three life sentences, to run one after the other. That fixed up any chance of parole I might have for a long, long time. The judge called what I had done "a hideous, heinous crime," and it was, but it is also in the past now. You can look it up in the yellowing files of the Castle Rock *Call*, where the big headlines announcing my

3

conviction look sort of funny and antique next to the news of Hitler and Mussolini and FDR's alphabet soup agencies.

Have I rehabilitated myself, you ask? I don't even know what that word means, at least as far as prisons and corrections go. I think it's a politician's word. It may have some other meaning, and it may be that I will have a chance to find out, but that is the future . . . something cons teach themselves not to think about. I was young, good-looking, and from the poor side of town. I knocked up a pretty, sulky, headstrong girl who lived in one of the fine old houses on Carbine Street. Her father was agreeable to the marriage if I would take a job in the optical company he owned and "work my way up." I found out that what he really had in mind was keeping me in his house and under his thumb, like a disagreeable pet that has not quite been housebroken and which may bite. Enough hate eventually piled up to cause me to do what I did. Given a second chance I would not do it again, but I'm not sure that means I am rehabilitated.

Anyway, it's not me I want to tell you about; I want to tell you about a guy named Andy Dufresne. But before I can tell you about Andy, I have to explain a few other things about myself. It won't take long.

As I said, I've been the guy who can get it for you here at Shawshank for damn near forty years. And that doesn't just mean contraband items like extra cigarettes or booze, although those items always top the list. But I've gotten thousands of other items for men doing time here, some of them perfectly legal yet hard to come by in a place where you've supposedly been brought to be punished. There was one fellow who was in for raping a little girl and exposing himself to dozens of others; I got him three pieces of pink Vermont marble and he did three lovely sculptures out of them—a baby, a boy of about twelve, and a bearded young man. He called them *The Three Ages of Jesus*, and those pieces of sculpture are now in the parlor of a man who used to be governor of this state.

Or here's a name you may remember if you grew up north of Massachusetts—Robert Alan Cote. In 1951 he tried to rob the First Mercantile Bank of Mechanic Falls, and the holdup turned into a bloodbath—six dead in the end, two of them members of the gang, three of them hostages, one of them a young state cop who put his head up at the wrong time and got a bullet in the eye. Cote had a penny collection. Naturally they weren't going to let him have it in here, but with a little help from his mother and a middleman who used to drive a laundry truck, I was able to get it for him. I told him, Bobby, you must be crazy, wanting to have a coin collection in a stone hotel full of thieves. He looked at me and smiled and said, I know where to keep them. They'll be safe enough. Don't you worry. And he was right. Bobby Cote died of a brain tumor in 1967, but that coin collection has never turned up.

I've gotten men chocolates on Valentine's Day; I got three of those green milkshakes they serve at McDonald's around St. Paddy's Day for a crazy Irishman named O'Malley; I even arranged for a midnight showing of *Deep Throat* and *The Devil in Miss Jones* for a party of twenty men who had pooled their resources to rent the films . . . although I ended up doing a week in solitary for that little escapade. It's the risk you run when you're the guy who can get it.

I've gotten reference books and fuck-books, joke novelties like handbuzzers and itching powder, and on more than one occasion I've seen that a long-timer has gotten a pair of panties from his wife or his girlfriend . . . and I guess you'll know what guys in here do with such items during the long nights when time draws out like a blade. I don't get all those things gratis, and for some items the price comes high. But I don't do it *just* for the money; what good is money to me? I'm never going to own a Cadillac car or fly off to Jamaica for two weeks in February. I do it for the same reason that a good butcher will only sell you fresh meat: I got a reputation and I want to keep it. The only two things I refuse to handle are guns and heavy drugs. I won't help anyone kill himself or anyone else. I have enough killing on my mind to last me a lifetime.

Yeah, I'm a regular Neiman-Marcus. And so when Andy Dufresne came to me in 1949 and asked if I could smuggle Rita Hayworth into the prison for him, I said it would be no problem at all. And it wasn't.

When Andy came to Shawshank in 1948, he was thirty years old. He was a short, neat little man with sandy hair and small, clever hands. He wore gold-rimmed spectacles. His fingernails were always clipped, and they were always clean. That's a funny thing to remember about a man, I suppose, but it seems to sum Andy up for me. He always looked as if he should have been wearing a tie. On the outside he had been a vice-president in the trust department of a large Portland bank. Good work for a man as young as he was, especially when you consider how conservative most banks are . . . and you have to multiply that conservatism by ten when you get up into New England, where folks don't like to trust a man with their money unless he's bald, limping, and constantly plucking at his pants to get his truss around straight. Andy was in for murdering his wife and her lover.

As I believe I have said, everyone in prison is an innocent man. Oh, they read that scripture the way those holy rollers on TV read the Book of Revelation. They were the victims of judges with hearts of stone and balls to match, or incompetent lawyers, or police frame-ups, or bad luck. They read the scripture, but you can see a different scripture in their faces. Most cons are a low sort, no good to themselves or anyone else, and their worst luck was that their mothers carried them to term.

In all my years at Shawshank, there have been less than ten men whom I believed when they told me they were innocent. Andy Dufresne was one of them, although I only became convinced of his innocence over a period of years. If I had been on the jury that heard his case in Portland Superior Court over six stormy weeks in 1947–48, I would have voted to convict, too.

It was one hell of a case, all right; one of those juicy ones with all the right elements. There was a beautiful girl with society connections (dead), a local sports figure (also dead), and a prominent young businessman in the dock. There was this, plus all the scandal the newspapers could hint at. The prosecution had an open-and-shut case. The trial only lasted as long as it did because the DA was planning to run for the U.S. House of Representatives and he wanted John Q. Public to get a good long look at his phiz. It was a crackerjack legal circus, with spectators getting in line at four in the morning, despite the subzero temperatures, to assure themselves of a seat.

The facts of the prosecution's case that Andy never contested were these: that he had a wife, Linda Collins Dufresne; that in June of 1947 she had expressed an interest in learning the game of golf at the Falmouth Hills Country Club; that she did indeed take lessons for four months; that her instructor was the Falmouth Hills golf pro, Glenn Quentin; that in late August of 1947 Andy learned that Quentin and his wife had become lovers; that Andy and Linda Dufresne argued bitterly on the afternoon of September 10th, 1947; that the subject of their argument was her infidelity.

He testified that Linda professed to be glad he knew; the sneaking around, she said, was distressing. She told Andy that she planned to obtain a Reno divorce. Andy told her he would see her in hell before he would see her in Reno. She went off to spend the night with Quentin in Quentin's rented bungalow not far from the golf course. The next morning his cleaning woman found both of them dead in bed. Each had been shot four times.

It was that last fact that militated more against Andy than any of the others. The DA with the political aspirations made a great deal of it in his opening statement and his closing summation. Andrew Dufresne, he said, was not a wronged husband seeking a hot-blooded revenge against his cheating wife; that, the DA said, could be understood, if not condoned. But this revenge had been of a much colder type. Consider! the DA thundered at the jury. Four and four! Not six shots, but eight! *He had fired the gun empty . . . and then stopped to reload so he could shoot each of them again!* FOUR FOR HIM AND FOUR FOR HER, the Portland *Sun* blared. The Boston *Register* dubbed him The Even-Steven Killer.

A clerk from the Wise Pawnshop in Lewiston testified that he had sold a six-shot .38 Police Special to Andrew Dufresne just two days before the double murder. A bartender from the country club bar testified that Andy had come in around seven o'clock on the evening of September 10th, had tossed off three straight whiskeys in a twenty-minute period—when he got up from the bar-stool he told the bartender that he was going up to Glenn Quentin's house and he, the bartender, could "read about the rest of it in the papers." Another clerk, this one from the Handy-Pik store a mile or so from Quentin's house, told the court that Dufresne had come in around quarter to nine on that same night. He purchased cigarettes, three quarts of beer, and some dishtowels. The county medical examiner testified that Quentin and the Dufresne woman had been killed between 11:00 P.M. and 2:00 A.M. on the night of September 10th–11th. The detective from the Attorney General's office who had been in charge of the case testified that there was a turnout less than seventy yards from the bungalow, and that on the afternoon of September 11th, three pieces of evidence had been removed from that turnout: first item, two empty quart bottles of Narragansett Beer (with the defendant's fingerprints on them); second item, twelve cigarette ends (all Kools, the defendant's brand); third item, a plaster moulage of a set of tire tracks (exactly matching the tread-and-wear pattern of the tires on the defendant's 1947 Plymouth).

In the living room of Quentin's bungalow, four dishtowels had been found lying on the sofa. There were bullet-holes through them and powder-burns on them. The detective theorized (over the agonized objections of Andy's lawyer) that the murderer had wrapped the towels around the muzzle of the murder-weapon to muffle the sound of the gunshots.

Andy Dufresne took the stand in his own defense and told his story calmly, coolly, and dispassionately. He said he had begun to hear distressing rumors about his wife and Glenn Quentin as early as the last week in July. In late August he had become distressed enough to investigate a bit. On an evening when Linda was supposed to have gone shopping in Portland after her golf lesson, Andy had followed her and Quentin to Quentin's two-story rented house (inevitably dubbed "the love-nest" by the papers). He had parked in the turnout until Quentin drove her back to the country club where her car was parked, about three hours later.

"Do you mean to tell this court that you followed your wife in your brand-new Plymouth sedan?" the DA asked him on cross-examination.

"I swapped cars for the evening with a friend," Andy said, and this cool admission of how well-planned his investigation had been did him no good at all in the eyes of the jury.

After returning the friend's car and picking up his own, he had gone home. Linda had been in bed, reading a book. He asked her how her trip to Portland had been. She replied that it had been fun, but she hadn't seen anything she liked well enough to buy. "That's when I knew for sure," Andy told the breathless spectators. He spoke in the same calm, remote voice in which he delivered almost all of his testimony.

"What was your frame of mind in the seventeen days between then and the night your wife was murdered?" Andy's lawyer asked him.

"I was in great distress," Andy said calmly, coldly. Like a man reciting a shopping list he said that he had considered suicide, and had even gone so far as to purchase a gun in Lewiston on September 8th.

His lawyer then invited him to tell the jury what had happened after his wife left to meet Glenn Quentin on the night of the murders. Andy told them . . . and the impression he made was the worst possible.

I knew him for close to thirty years, and I can tell you he was the most self-possessed man I've ever known. What was right with him he'd only give you a little at a time. What was wrong with him he kept bottled up inside. If he ever had a dark night of the soul, as some writer or other has called it, you would never know. He was the type of man who, if he had decided to commit suicide, would do it without leaving a note but not until his affairs had been put neatly in order. If he had cried on the witness stand, or if his voice had thickened and grown hesitant, even if he had started yelling at that Washington-bound District Attorney, I don't believe he would have gotten the life sentence he wound up with. Even if he had've, he would have been out on parole by 1954. But he told his story like a recording machine, seeming to say to the jury: This is it. Take it or leave it. They left it.

He said he was drunk that night, that he'd been more or less drunk since August 24th, and that he was a man who didn't handle his liquor very well. Of course that by itself would have been hard for any jury to swallow. They just couldn't see this coldly self-possessed young man in the neat double-breasted three-piece woollen suit ever getting falling-down drunk over his wife's sleazy little affair with some small-town golf pro. I believed it because I had a chance to watch Andy that those six men and six women didn't have.

Andy Dufresne took just four drinks a year all the time I knew him. He would meet me in the exercise yard every year about a week before his birthday and then again about two weeks before Christmas. On each occasion he would arrange for a bottle of Jack Daniel's. He bought it the way most cons arrange to buy their stuff—the slave's wages they pay in here, plus a little of his own. Up until 1965 what you got for your time was a dime an hour. In '65 they raised it all the way up to a quarter. My commission on liquor was and is ten per cent, and when you add on that surcharge to the price of a fine sippin whiskey like the Black Jack, you get an idea of how many hours of Andy Dufresne's sweat in the prison laundry was going to buy his four drinks a year.

On the morning of his birthday, September 20th, he would have himself a big knock, and then he'd have another that night after lights-out. The following day he'd give the rest of the bottle back to me, and I would share it around. As for the other bottle, he dealt himself one drink Christmas night and another on New Year's Eve. Then that bottle would also come to me with instructions to pass it on. Four drinks a year—and that is the behavior of a man who has been bitten hard by the bottle. Hard enough to draw blood.

He told the jury that on the night of the tenth he had been so drunk he could only remember what had happened in little isolated snatches. He had gotten drunk that afternoon—"I took on a double helping of Dutch courage" is how he put it—before taking on Linda.

After she left to meet Quentin, he remembered deciding to confront them. On the way to Quentin's bungalow, he swung into the country club for a couple of quick ones. He could not, he said, remember telling the bartender he could "read about the rest of it in the papers," or saying anything to him at all. He remembered buying beer in the Handy-Pik, but not the dishtowels. "Why would I want dishtowels?" he asked, and one of the papers reported that three of the lady jurors shuddered.

Later, much later, he speculated to me about the clerk who had testified on the subject of those dishtowels, and I think it's worth jotting down what he said. "Suppose that, during their canvass for witnesses," Andy said one day in the exercise yard, "they stumble on this fellow who sold me the beer that night. By then three days have gone by. The facts of the case have been broadsided in all the papers. Maybe they ganged up on the guy, five or six cops, plus the dick from the Attorney General's office, plus the DA's assistant. Memory is a pretty subjective thing, Red. They could have started out with 'Isn't it possible that he purchased four or five dishtowels?' and worked their way up from there. If enough people *want* you to remember something, that can be a pretty powerful persuader."

I agreed that it could.

"But there's one even more powerful," Andy went on in that musing way of his. "I think it's at least possible that he convinced himself. It was the limelight. Reporters asking him questions, his picture in the papers . . . all topped, of course, by his star turn in court. I'm not saying that he deliberately falsified his story, or perjured himself. I think it's possible that he could have passed a lie detector test with flying colors, or sworn on his mother's sacred name that I bought those dishtowels. But still . . . memory is such a *goddam* subjective thing.

"I know this much: even though my own lawyer thought I had to be lying about half my story, he never bought that business about the dishtowels. It's crazy on the face of it. I was pig-drunk, too drunk to have been thinking about muffling the gunshots. If I'd done it, I just would have let them rip."

He went up to the turnout and parked there. He drank beer and smoked cigarettes. He watched the lights downstairs in Quentin's place go out. He watched a single light go on upstairs . . . and fifteen minutes later he watched that one go out. He said he could guess the rest.

"Mr. Dufresne, did you then go up to Glenn Quentin's house and kill the two of them?" his lawyer thundered.

"No, I did not," Andy answered. By midnight, he said, he was sobering up. He was also feeling the first signs of a bad hangover. He decided to go home and sleep it off and think about the whole thing in a more adult fashion the next day. "At that time, as I drove home, I was beginning to think that the wisest course would be to simply let her go to Reno and get her divorce."

"Thank you, Mr. Dufresne."

The DA popped up.

"You divorced her in the quickest way you could think of, didn't you? You divorced her with a .38 revolver wrapped in dishtowels, didn't you?"

"No sir, I did not," Andy said calmly.

"And then you shot her lover."

"No, sir."

"You mean you shot Quentin first?"

"I mean I didn't shoot either one of them. I drank two quarts of beer and smoked however many cigarettes the police found at the turnout. Then I drove home and went to bed."

"You told the jury that between August twenty-fourth and September tenth you were feeling suicidal."

"Yes, sir."

"Suicidal enough to buy a revolver."

"Yes."

"Would it bother you overmuch, Mr. Dufresne, if I told you that you do not seem to me to be the suicidal type?"

"No," Andy said, "but you don't impress me as being terribly sensitive, and I doubt very much that, if I *were* feeling suicidal, I would take my problem to you."

There was a slight tense titter in the courtroom at this, but it won him no points with the jury.

"Did you take your thirty-eight with you on the night of September tenth?"

"No; as I've already testified—"

"Oh, yes!" The DA smiled sarcastically. "You threw it into the river, didn't you? The Royal River. On the afternoon of September ninth."

"Yes, sir."

"One day before the murders."

"Yes, sir."

"That's convenient, isn't it?"

"It's neither convenient nor inconvenient. Only the truth."

"I believe you heard Lieutenant Mincher's testimony?" Mincher had been in charge of the party which had dragged the stretch of the Royal near Pond Road Bridge, from which Andy had testified he had thrown the gun. The police had not found it.

"Yes, sir. You know I heard it."

"Then you heard him tell the court that they found no gun, although they dragged for three days. That was rather convenient, too, wasn't it?"

"Convenience aside, it's a fact that they didn't find the gun," Andy responded calmly. "But I should like to point out to both you and the jury that the Pond Road Bridge is very close to where the Royal River empties into the Bay of Yarmouth. The current is strong. The gun may bave been carried out into the bay itself."

"And so no comparison can be made between the riflings on the bullets taken from the bloodstained corpses of your wife and Mr. Glenn Quentin and the riflings on the barrel of your gun. That's correct, isn't it, Mr. Dufresne?"

"Yes."

"That's also rather convenient, isn't it?"

At that, according to the papers, Andy displayed one of the few slight emotional reactions he allowed himself during the entire six-week period of the trial. A slight, bitter smile crossed his face.

"Since I am innocent of this crime, sir, and since I am telling the truth about throwing my gun into the river the day before the crime took place, then it seems to me decidedly inconvenient that the gun was never found."

The DA hammered at him for two days. He re-read the Handy-Pik clerk's testimony about the dishtowels to Andy. Andy repeated that he could not recall buying them, but admitted that he also couldn't remember *not* buying them.

Was it true that Andy and Linda Dufresne had taken out a joint insurance policy in early 1947? Yes, that was true. And if acquitted, wasn't it true that Andy stood to gain fifty thousand dollars in benefits? True. And wasn't it true that he had gone up to Glenn Quentin's house with murder in his heart, and wasn't it *also* true that he had indeed committed murder twice over? No, it was not true. Then what did he think had happened, since there had been no signs of robbery?

"I have no way of knowing that, sir," Andy said quietly.

The case went to the jury at 1:00 P.M. on a snowy Wednesday afternoon. The twelve jurymen and -women came back in at 3:30. The bailiff said they would have been back earlier, but they had held off in order to enjoy a nice chicken dinner from Bentley's Restaurant at the county's expense. They found him guilty, and brother, if Maine had the death-penalty, he would have done the airdance before that spring's crocuses poked their heads out of the snow.

The DA had asked him what he thought had happened, and Andy slipped the question—but he did have an idea, and I got it out of him late one evening in 1955. It had taken those seven years for us to progress from nodding acquaintances to fairly close friends—but I never felt really close to Andy until 1960 or so, and I believe I was the only one who ever did get really close to him. Both being long-timers, we were in the same cellblock from beginning to end, although I was halfway down the corridor from him.

"What do I think?" He laughed—but there was no humor in the sound. "I think there was a lot of bad luck floating around that night. More than could ever get together in the same short span of time again. I think it must have been some stranger, just passing through. Maybe someone who had a flat tire on that road after I went home. Maybe a burglar. Maybe a psychopath. He killed them, that's all. And I'm here."

As simple as that. And he was condemned to spend the rest of his life in Shawshank—or the part of it that mattered. Five years later he began to have parole hearings, and he was turned down just as regular as clockwork in spite of being a model prisoner. Getting a pass out of Shawshank when you've got *murder* stamped on your admittance-slip is slow work, as slow as a river eroding a rock. Seven men sit on the board, two more than at most state prisons, and every one of those seven has an ass as hard as the water drawn up from a mineral-spring well. You can't buy those guys, you can't sweet-talk them, you can't cry for them. As far as the board in here is concerned, money don't talk, and *nobody* walks. There were other reasons in Andy's case as well . . . but that belongs a little further along in my story.

There was a trusty, name of Kendricks, who was into me for some pretty heavy money back in the fifties, and it was four years before he got it all paid off. Most of the interest he paid me was information—in my line of work, you're dead if you can't find ways of keeping your ear to the ground. This Kendricks, for instance, had access to records I was never going to see running a stamper down in the goddam plate-shop.

Kendricks told me that the parole board vote was 7–0 against Andy Dufresne through 1957, 6–1 in '58, 7–0 again in '59, and 5–2 in '60. After that I don't know, but I do know that sixteen years later he was still in Cell 14 of Cellblock 5. By then, 1975, he was fifty-seven. They probably would have gotten big-hearted and let him out around 1983. They give you life, and that's what they take—all of it that counts, anyway. Maybe they set you loose someday, but . . . well, listen: I knew this guy, Sherwood Bolton, his name was, and he had this pigeon in his cell. From 1945 until 1953, when they let him out, he had that pigeon. He wasn't any Birdman of Alcatraz; he just had this pigeon. Jake, he called him. He set Jake free a day before he, Sherwood, that is, was to walk, and Jake flew away just as pretty as you could want. But about a week after Sherwood Bolton left our happy little family, a friend of mine called me over to the west corner of the exercise yard, where Sherwood used to hang out. A bird was lying there like a very small pile of dirty bedlinen. It looked starved. My friend said: "Isn't that Jake, Red?" It was. That pigeon was just as dead as a turd.

I remember the first time Andy Dufresne got in touch with me for something; I remember like it was yesterday. That wasn't the time he wanted Rita Hayworth, though. That came later. In that summer of 1948 he came around for something else.

Most of my deals are done right there in the exercise yard, and that's where this one went down. Our yard is big, much bigger than most. It's a perfect square, ninety yards on a side. The north side is the outer wall, with a guard-tower at either end. The guards up there are armed with binoculars and riot guns. The main gate is in that north side. The truck loading-bays are on the south side of the yard. There are five of them. Shawshank is a busy place during the work-week—deliveries in, deliveries out. We have the license-plate factory, and a big industrial laundry that does all the prison wetwash, plus that of Kittery Receiving Hospital and the Eliot

Nursing Home. There's also a big automotive garage where mechanic inmates fix prison, state, and municipal vehicles—not to mention the private cars of the screws, the administration officers . . . and, on more than one occasion, those of the parole board.

The east side is a thick stone wall full of tiny slit windows. Cellblock 5 is on the other side of that wall. The west side is Administration and the infirmary. Shawshank has never been as overcrowded as most prisons, and back in '48 it was only filled to something like two-thirds capacity, but at any given time there might be eighty to a hundred and twenty cons on the yard— playing toss with a football or a baseball, shooting craps, jawing at each other, making deals. On Sunday the place was even more crowded; on Sunday the place would have looked like a country holiday . . . if there had been any women.

It was on a Sunday that Andy first came to me. I had just finished talking to Elmore Armitage, a fellow who often came in handy to me, about a radio when Andy walked up. I knew who he was, of course; he had a reputation for being a snob and a cold fish. People were saying he was marked for trouble already. One of the people saying so was Bogs Diamond, a bad man to have on your case. Andy had no cellmate, and I'd heard that was just the way he wanted it, although people were already saying he thought his shit smelled sweeter than the ordinary. But I don't have to listen to rumors about a man when I can judge him for myself.

"Hello," he said. "I'm Andy Dufresne." He offered his hand and I shook it. He wasn't a man to waste time being social; he got right to the point. "I understand that you're a man who knows how to get things."

I agreed that I was able to locate certain items from time to time.

"How do you do that?" Andy asked.

"Sometimes," I said, "things just seem to come into my hand. I can't explain it. Unless it's because I'm Irish."

He smiled a little at that. "I wonder if you could get me a rock-hammer."

"What would that be, and why would you want it?"

Andy looked surprised. "Do you make motivations a part of your business?" With words like those I could understand how he had gotten a reputation for being the snobby sort, the kind of guy who likes to put on airs—but I sensed a tiny thread of humor in his question.

"I'll tell you," I said. "If you wanted a toothbrush, I wouldn't ask questions. I'd just quote you a price. Because a toothbrush, you see, is a non-lethal sort of an object."

"You have strong feelings about lethal objects?"

"I do."

An old friction-taped baseball flew toward us and he turned, cat-quick, and picked it out of the air. It was a move Frank Malzone would have been proud of. Andy flicked the ball back to where it had come from—just a quick and easy-looking flick of the wrist, but that throw had some mustard on it, just the same. I could see a lot of people were watching us with one eye as they went about their business. Probably the guards in the tower were watching, too. I won't gild the lily; there are cons that swing weight in any prison, maybe four or five in a small one, maybe two or three dozen in a big one. At Shawshank I was one of those with some weight, and what I thought of Andy Dufresne would have a lot to do with how his time went. He probably knew it, too, but he wasn't kowtowing or sucking up to me, and I respected him for that.

"Fair enough. I'll tell you what it is and why I want it. A rock-hammer looks like a miniature pickaxe—about so long." He held his hands about a foot apart, and that was when I first noticed how neatly kept his nails were. "It's got a small sharp pick on one end and a flat, blunt hammerhead on the other. I want it because I like rocks."

"Rocks," I said.

"Squat down here a minute," he said.

I humored him. We hunkered down on our haunches like Indians.

Andy took a handful of exercise yard dirt and began to sift it between his neat hands, so it emerged in a fine cloud. Small pebbles were left over, one or two sparkly, the rest dull and plain. One of the dull ones was quartz, but it was only dull until you'd rubbed it clean. Then it had a nice milky glow. Andy did the cleaning and then tossed it to me. I caught it and named it.

"Quartz, sure," he said. "And look. Mica. Shale. Silted granite. Here's a place of graded limestone, from when they cut this place out of the side of the hill." He tossed them away and dusted his hands. "I'm a rockhound. At least . . . I *was* a rockhound. In my old life. I'd like to be one again, on a limited scale."

"Sunday expeditions in the exercise yard?" I asked, standing up. It was a silly idea, and yet . . . seeing that little piece of quartz had given my heart a funny tweak. I don't know exactly why; just an association with the outside world, I suppose. You didn't think of such things in terms of the yard. Quartz was something you picked out of a small, quick-running stream.

"Better to have Sunday expeditions here than no Sunday expeditions at all," he said.

"You could plant an item like that rock-hammer in somebody's skull," I remarked.

"I have no enemies here," he said quietly.

"No?" I smiled. "Wait awhile."

"If there's trouble, I can handle it without using a rock-hammer."

"Maybe you want to try an escape? Going under the wall? Because if you do—"

He laughed politely. When I saw the rock-hammer three weeks later, I understood why.

"You know," I said, "if anyone sees you with it, they'll take it away. If they saw you with a spoon, they'd take it away. What are you going to do, just sit down here in the yard and start bangin away?"

"Oh, I believe I can do a lot better than that."

I nodded. That part of it really wasn't my business, anyway. A man engages my services to get him something. Whether he can keep it or not after I get it is his business.

"How much would an item like that go for?" I asked. I was beginning to enjoy his quiet, low-key style. When you've spent ten years in stir, as I had then, you can get awfully tired of the bellowers and the braggarts and the loud-mouths. Yes, I think it would be fair to say I liked Andy from the first.

"Eight dollars in any rock-and-gem shop," he said, "but I realize that in a business like yours you work on a cost-plus basis—"

"Cost plus ten per cent is my going rate, but I have to go up some on a dangerous item. For something like the gadget you're talking about, it takes a little more goose-grease to get the wheels turning. Let's say ten dollars."

"Ten it is."

I looked at him, smiling a little. "Have you *got* ten dollars?"

"I do," he said quietly.

A long time after, I discovered that he had better than five hundred. He had brought it in with him. When they check you in at this hotel, one of the bellhops is obliged to bend you over and take a look up your works—but there are a lot of works, and, not to put too fine a point on it, a man who is really determined can get a fairly large item quite a ways up them—far enough to be out of sight, unless the bellhop you happen to draw is in the mood to pull on a rubber glove and go prospecting.

"That's fine," I said. "You ought to know what I expect if you get caught with what I get you."

"I suppose I should," he said, and I could tell by the slight change in his gray eyes that he knew exactly what I was going to say. It was a slight lightening, a gleam of his special ironic humor.

"If you get caught, you'll say you found it. That's about the long and short of it. They'll put you in solitary for three or four weeks . . . plus, of course, you'll lose your toy and you'll get a black mark on your record. If you give them my name, you and I will never do business again. Not for so much as a pair of shoelaces or a bag of Bugler. And I'll send some fellows around to lump you up. I don't like violence, but you'll understand my position. I can't allow it to get around that I can't handle myself. That would surely finish me."

"Yes. I suppose it would. I understand, and you don't need to worry."

"I never worry," I said. "In a place like this there's no percentage in it."

He nodded and walked away. Three days later he walked up beside me in the exercise yard during the laundry's morning break. He didn't speak or even look my way, but pressed a picture of the

Hon. Alexander Hamilton into my hand as neatly as a good magician does a card-trick. He was a man who adapted fast. I got him his rock-hammer. I had it in my cell for one night, and it was just as he described it. It was no tool for escape (it would have taken a man just about six hundred years to tunnel under the wall using that rock-hammer, I figured), but I still felt some misgivings. If you planted that pickaxe end in a man's head, he would surely never listen to *Fibber McGee and Molly* on the radio again. And Andy had already begun having trouble with the sisters. I hoped it wasn't them he was wanting the rock-hammer for.

In the end, I trusted my judgment. Early the next morning, twenty minutes before the wake-up horn went off, I slipped the rock-hammer and a package of Camels to Ernie, the old trusty who swept the Cellblock 5 corridors until he was let free in 1956. He slipped it into his tunic without a word, and I didn't see the rock-hammer again for nineteen years, and by then it was damned near worn away to nothing.

The following Sunday Andy walked over to me in the exercise yard again. He was nothing to look at that day, I can tell you. His lower lip was swelled up so big it looked like a summer sausage, his right eye was swollen half-shut, and there was an ugly washboard scrape across one cheek. He was having his troubles with the sisters, all right, but he never mentioned them. "Thanks for the tool," he said, and walked away.

I watched him curiously. He walked a few steps, saw something in the dirt, bent over, and picked it up. It was a small rock. Prison fatigues, except for those worn by mechanics when they're on the job, have no pockets. But there are ways to get around that. The little pebble disappeared up Andy's sleeve and didn't come down. I admired that . . . and I admired him. In spite of the problems he was having, he was going on with his life. There are thousands who don't or won't or can't, and plenty of them aren't in prison, either. And I noticed that, although his face looked as if a twister had happened to it, his hands were still neat and clean, the nails well-kept.

I didn't see much of him over the next six months; Andy spent a lot of that time in solitary.

*   *   *

A few words about the sisters.

In a lot of pens they are known as bull queers or jailhouse susies—just lately the term in fashion is "killer queens." But in Shawshank they were always the sisters. I don't know why, but other than the name I guess there was no difference.

It comes as no surprise to most these days that there's a lot of buggery going on inside the walls—except to some of the new fish, maybe, who have the misfortune to be young, slim, good-looking, and unwary—but homosexuality, like straight sex, comes in a hundred different shapes and forms. There are men who can't stand to be without sex of some kind and turn to another man to keep from going crazy. Usually what follows is an arrangement between two fundamentally heterosexual men, although I've sometimes wondered if they are quite as heterosexual as they thought they were going to be when they get back to their wives or their girl-friends.

There are also men who get "turned" in prison. In the current parlance they "go gay," or "come out of the closet." Mostly (but not always) they play the female, and their favors are competed for fiercely.

And then there are the sisters.

They are to prison society what the rapist is to the society outside the walls. They're usually long-timers, doing hard bullets for brutal crimes. Their prey is the young, the weak, and the inexperienced . . . or, as in the case of Andy Dufresne, the weak-looking. Their hunting grounds are the showers, the cramped, tunnel-like areaway behind the industrial washers in the laundry, sometimes the infirmary. On more than one occasion rape has occurred in the closet-sized projection booth behind the auditorium. Most often what the sisters take by force they could have had for free, if they wanted it that way; those who have been turned always seem to have "crushes" on one sister or another, like teenage girls with their Sinatras, Presleys, or Redfords. But for the sisters, the joy has always been in taking it by force . . . and I guess it always will be.

Because of his small size and fair good looks (and maybe also because of that very quality of self-possession I had admired), the sisters were after Andy from the day he walked in. If this was some

kind of fairy story, I'd tell you that Andy fought the good fight until they left him alone. I wish I could say that, but I can't. Prison is no fairy-tale world.

The first time for him was in the shower less than three days after he joined our happy Shawshank family. Just a lot of slap and tickle that time, I understand. They like to size you up before they make their real move, like jackals finding out if the prey is as weak and hamstrung as it looks.

Andy punched back and bloodied the lip of a big, hulking sister named Bogs Diamond—gone these many years since to who knows where. A guard broke it up before it could go any further, but Bogs promised to get him—and Bogs did.

The second time was behind the washers in the laundry. A lot has gone on in that long, dusty, and narrow space over the years; the guards know about it and just let it be. It's dim and littered with bags of washing and bleaching compound, drums of Hexlite catalyst, as harmless as salt if your hands are dry, murderous as battery acid if they're wet. The guards don't like to go back there. There's no room to maneuver, and one of the first things they teach them when they come to work in a place like this is to never let the cons get you in a place where you can't back up.

Bogs wasn't there that day, but Henley Backus, who had been washroom foreman down there since 1922, told me that four of his friends were. Andy held them at bay for awhile with a scoop of Hexlite, threatening to throw it in their eyes if they came any closer, but he tripped trying to back around one of the big Washex four-pockets. That was all it took. They were on him.

I guess the phrase gang-rape is one that doesn't change much from one generation to the next. That's what they did to him, those four sisters. They bent him over a gear-box and one of them held a Phillips screwdriver to his temple while they gave him the business. It rips you up some, but not bad—am I speaking from personal experience, you ask?—I only wish I weren't. You bleed for awhile. If you don't want some clown asking you if you just started your period, you wad up a bunch of toilet paper and keep it down the back of your underwear until it stops. The bleeding really is like a menstrual flow; it keeps up for two, maybe three days, a slow trickle. Then it stops. No harm done, unless they've done

something even more unnatural to you. No *physical* harm done—but rape is rape, and eventually you have to look at your face in the mirror again and decide what to make of yourself.

Andy went through that alone, the way he went through everything alone in those days. He must have come to the conclusion that others before him had come to, namely, that there are only two ways to deal with the sisters: fight them and get taken, or just get taken.

He decided to fight. When Bogs and two of his buddies came after him a week or so after the laundry incident ("I heard ya got broke in," Bogs said, according to Ernie, who was around at the time), Andy slugged it out with them. He broke the nose of a fellow named Rooster MacBride, a heavy-gutted farmer who was in for beating his stepdaughter to death. Rooster died in here, I'm happy to add.

They took him, all three of them. When it was done, Rooster and the other egg—it might have been Pete Verness, but I'm not completely sure—forced Andy down to his knees. Bogs Diamond stepped in front of him. He had a pearl-handled razor in those days with the words *Diamond Pearl* engraved on both sides of the grip. He opened it and said, "I'm gonna open my fly now, mister man, and you're going to swallow what I give you to swallow. And when you done swallowed mine, you're gonna swallow Rooster's. I guess you done broke his nose and I think he ought to have something to pay for it."

Andy said, "Anything of yours that you stick in my mouth, you're going to lose it."

Bogs looked at Andy like he was crazy, Ernie said.

"No," he told Andy, talking to him slowly, like Andy was a stupid kid. "You didn't understand what I said. You do anything like that and I'll put all eight inches of this steel into your ear. Get it?"

"I understood what you said. I don't think you understood *me*. I'm going to bite whatever you stick into my mouth. You can put that razor into my brain, I guess, but you should know that a sudden serious brain injury causes the victim to simultaneously urinate, defecate . . . and bite down."

He looked up at Bogs, smiling that little smile of his, old Ernie said, as if the three of them had been discussing stocks and bonds with him instead of throwing it to him just as hard as they could. Just as if he was wearing one of his three-piece bankers' suits instead of kneeling on a dirty broom-closet floor with his pants around his ankles and blood trickling down the insides of his thighs.

"In fact," he went on, "I understand that the bite-reflex is sometimes so strong that the victim's jaws have to be pried open with a crowbar or a jackhandle."

Bogs didn't put anything in Andy's mouth that night in late February of 1948, and neither did Rooster MacBride, and so far as I know, no one else ever did, either. What the three of them did was to beat Andy within an inch of his life, and all four of them ended up doing a jolt in solitary. Andy and Rooster MacBride went by way of the infirmary.

How many times did that particular crew have at him? I don't know. I think Rooster lost his taste fairly early on—being in nose-splints for a month can do that to a fellow—and Bogs Diamond left off that summer, all at once.

That was a strange thing. Bogs was found in his cell, badly beaten, one morning in early June, when he didn't show up in the breakfast nose-count. He wouldn't say who had done it, or how they had gotten to him, but being in my business, I know that a screw can be bribed to do almost anything except get a gun for an inmate. They didn't make big salaries then, and they don't now. And in those days there was no electronic locking system, no closed-circuit TV, no master-switches which controlled whole areas of the prison. Back in 1948, each cellblock had its own turnkey. A guard could have been bribed real easy to let someone—maybe two or three someones—into the block, and, yes, even into Diamond's cell.

Of course a job like that would have cost a lot of money. Not by outside standards, no. Prison economics are on a smaller scale. When you've been in here awhile, a dollar bill in your hand looks like a twenty did outside. My guess is that, if Bogs was done, it cost someone a serious piece of change—fifteen bucks, we'll say, for the turnkey, and two or three apiece for each of the lump-up guys.

I'm not saying it was Andy Dufresne, but I do know that he brought in five hundred dollars when he came, and he was a banker in the straight world—a man who understands better than the rest of us the ways in which money can become power.

And I know this: after the beating—the three broken ribs, the hemorrhaged eye, the sprained back, and the dislocated hip—Bogs Diamond left Andy alone. In fact, after that he left everyone pretty much alone. He got to be like a high wind in the summertime, all bluster and no bite. You could say, in fact, that he turned into a "weak sister."

That was the end of Bogs Diamond, a man who might eventually have killed Andy if Andy hadn't taken steps to prevent it (if it *was* him who took the steps). But it wasn't the end of Andy's trouble with the sisters. There was a little hiatus, and then it began again, although not so hard or so often. Jackals like easy prey, and there were easier pickings around than Andy Dufresne.

He always fought them, that's what I remember. He knew, I guess, that if you let them have at you even once without fighting, it got that much easier to let them have their way without fighting next time. So Andy would turn up with bruises on his face every once in awhile, and there was the matter of the two broken fingers six or eight months after Diamond's beating. Oh yes—and sometime in late 1949, the man landed in the infirmary with a broken cheekbone that was probably the result of someone swinging a nice chunk of pipe with the business-end wrapped in flannel. He always fought back, and as a result, he did his time in solitary. But I don't think solitary was the hardship for Andy that it was for some men. He got along with himself.

The sisters was something he adjusted himself to—and then, in 1950, it stopped almost completely. That is a part of my story that I'll get to in due time.

In the fall of 1948, Andy met me one morning in the exercise yard and asked me if I could get him half a dozen rock-blankets.

"What the hell are those?" I asked.

He told me that was just what rockhounds called them; they were polishing cloths about the size of dishtowels. They were heavily padded, with a smooth side and a rough side—the smooth side like fine-grained sandpaper, the rough side almost as abrasive as industrial steel wool (Andy also kept a box of that in his cell, although he didn't get it from me—I imagine he kited it from the prison laundry).

I told him I thought we could do business on those, and I ended up getting them from the very same rock-and-gem shop where I'd arranged to get the rock-hammer. This time I charged Andy my usual ten per cent and not a penny more. I didn't see anything lethal or even dangerous in a dozen $7'' \times 7''$ squares of padded cloth. Rock-blankets, indeed.

It was about five months later that Andy asked if I could get him Rita Hayworth. That conversation took place in the auditorium, during a movie-show. Nowadays we get the movie-shows once or twice a week, but back then the shows were a monthly event. Usually the movies we got had a morally uplifting message to them, and this one, *The Lost Weekend*, was no different. The moral was that it's dangerous to drink. It was a moral we could take some comfort in.

Andy maneuvered to get next to me, and about halfway through the show he leaned a little closer and asked if I could get him Rita Hayworth. I'll tell you the truth, it kind of tickled me. He was usually cool, calm, and collected, but that night he was jumpy as hell, almost embarrassed, as if he was asking me to get him a load of Trojans or one of those sheepskin-lined gadgets that are supposed to "enhance your solitary pleasure," as the magazines put it. He seemed overcharged, a man on the verge of blowing his radiator.

"I can get her," I said. "No sweat, calm down. You want the big one or the little one?" At that time Rita was my best girl (a few years before it had been Betty Grable) and she came in two sizes. For a buck you could get the little Rita. For two-fifty you could have the big Rita, four feet high and all woman.

"The big one," he said, not looking at me. I tell you, he was a hot sketch that night. He was blushing just like a kid trying to get into a kootch show with his big brother's draft-card. "Can you do it?"

"Take it easy, sure I can. Does a bear shit in the woods?" The audience was applauding and catcalling as the bugs came out of the walls to get Ray Milland, who was having a bad case of the DT's.

"How soon?"

"A week. Maybe less."

"Okay." But he sounded disappointed, as if he had been hoping I had one stuffed down my pants right then. "How much?"

I quoted him the wholesale price. I could afford to give him this one at cost; he'd been a good customer, what with his rock-hammer and his rock-blankets. Furthermore, he'd been a good boy—on more than one night when he was having his problems with Bogs, Rooster, and the rest, I wondered how long it would be before he used the rock-hammer to crack someone's head open.

Posters are a big part of my business, just behind the booze and cigarettes, usually half a step ahead of the reefer. In the sixties the business exploded in every direction, with a lot of people wanting funky hang-ups like Jimi Hendrix, Bob Dylan, that *Easy Rider* poster. But mostly it's girls; one pin-up queen after another.

A few days after Andy spoke to me, a laundry driver I did business with back then brought in better than sixty posters, most of them Rita Hayworths. You may even remember the picture; I sure do. Rita is dressed—sort of—in a bathing suit, one hand behind her head, her eyes half-closed, those full, sulky red lips parted. They called it Rita Hayworth, but they might as well have called it Woman in Heat.

The prison administration knows about the black market, in case you were wondering. Sure they do. They probably know almost as much about my business as I do myself. They live with it because they know that a prison is like a big pressure-cooker, and there have to be vents somewhere to let off steam. They make the occasional bust, and I've done time in solitary a time or three over the years, but when it's something like posters, they wink. Live and let live. And when a big Rita Hayworth went up in some fishie's cell, the assumption was that it came in the mail from a friend or a relative. Of course all the care-packages from friends and relatives are opened and the contents inventoried, but who goes back and re-checks the inventory sheets for something as harmless as a Rita Hayworth or an Ava Gardner pin-up? When you're in a pressure-cooker you learn to live and let live or somebody will carve you a brand-new mouth just above the Adam's apple. You learn to make allowances.

It was Ernie again who took the poster up to Andy's cell, 14, from my own, 6. And it was Ernie who brought back the note, written in Andy's careful hand, just one word: "Thanks."

A little while later, as they filed us out for morning chow, I glanced into his cell and saw Rita over his bunk in all her swimsuited glory, one hand behind her head, her eyes half-closed, those soft, satiny lips parted. It was over his bunk where he could look at her nights, after lights-out, in the glow of the arc sodiums in the exercise yard.

But in the bright morning sunlight, there were dark slashes across her face—the shadow of the bars on his single slit window.

Now I'm going to tell you what happened in mid-May of 1950 that finally ended Andy's three-year series of skirmishes with the sisters. It was also the incident which eventually got him out of the laundry and into the library, where he filled out his work-time until he left our happy little family earlier this year.

You may have noticed how much of what I've told you already is hearsay—someone saw something and told me and I told you. Well, in some cases I've simplified it even more than it really was, and have repeated (or will repeat) fourth- or fifth-hand information. That's the way it is here. The grapevine is very real, and you have to use it if you're going to stay ahead. Also, of course, you have to know how to pick out the grains of truth from the chaff of lies, rumors, and wish-it-had-beens.

You may also have gotten the idea that I'm describing someone who's more legend than man, and I would have to agree that there's some truth to that. To us long-timers who knew Andy over a space of years, there was an element of fantasy to him, a sense, almost, of myth-magic, if you get what I mean. That story I passed on about Andy refusing to give Bogs Diamond a head-job is part of that myth, and how he kept on fighting the sisters is part of it, and how he got the library job is part of it, too . . . but with one important difference: I was there and I saw what happened, and I swear on my mother's name that it's all true. The oath of a convicted murderer may not be worth much, but believe this: I don't lie.

Andy and I were on fair speaking terms by then. The guy fascinated me. Looking back to the poster episode, I see there's one thing I neglected to tell you, and maybe I should. Five weeks after he hung Rita up (I'd forgotten all about it by then, and had gone on to other deals), Ernie passed a small white box through the bars of my cell.

"From Dufresne," he said, low, and never missed a stroke with his push-broom.

"Thanks, Ernie," I said, and slipped him half a pack of Camels.

Now what the hell was this, I was wondering as I slipped the cover from the box. There was a lot of white cotton inside, and below that . . .

I looked for a long time. For a few minutes it was like I didn't even dare touch them, they were so pretty. There's a crying shortage of pretty things in the slam, and the real pity of it is that a lot of men don't even seem to miss them.

There were two pieces of quartz in that box, both of them carefully polished. They had been chipped into driftwood shapes. There were little sparkles of iron pyrites in them like flecks of gold. If they hadn't been so heavy, they would have served as a fine pair of men's cufflinks—they were that close to being a matched set.

How much work went into creating those two pieces? Hours and hours after lights-out, I knew that. First the chipping and shaping, and then the almost endless polishing and finishing with those rock-blankets. Looking at them, I felt the warmth that any man or woman feels when he or she is looking at something pretty, something that has been *worked* and *made*—that's the thing that really separates us from the animals, I think—and I felt something else, too. A sense of awe for the man's brute persistence. But I never knew just how persistent Andy Dufresne could be until much later.

In May of 1950, the powers that be decided that the roof of the license-plate factory ought to be re-surfaced with roofing tar. They wanted it done before it got too hot up there, and they asked for volunteers for the work, which was planned to take about a week. More than seventy men spoke up, because it was outside work and

May is one damn fine month for outside work. Nine or ten names were drawn out of a hat, and two of them happened to be Andy's and my own.

For the next week we'd be marched out to the exercise yard after breakfast, with two guards up front and two more behind . . . plus all the guards in the towers keeping a weather eye on the proceedings through their field-glasses for good measure.

Four of us would be carrying a big extension ladder on those morning marches—I always got a kick out of the way Dickie Betts, who was on that job, called that sort of ladder an extensible—and we'd put it up against the side of that low, flat building. Then we'd start bucket-brigading hot buckets of tar up to the roof. Spill that shit on you and you'd jitterbug all the way to the infirmary.

There were six guards on the project, all of them picked on the basis of seniority. It was almost as good as a week's vacation, because instead of sweating it out in the laundry or the plate-shop or standing over a bunch of cons cutting pulp or brush somewhere out in the willywags, they were having a regular May holiday in the sun, just sitting there with their backs up against the low parapet, shooting the bull back and forth.

They didn't even have to keep more than half an eye on us, because the south wall sentry post was close enough so that the fellows up there could have spit their chews on us, if they'd wanted to. If anyone on the roof-sealing party had made one funny move, it would take four seconds to cut him smack in two with .45-caliber machine-gun bullets. So those screws just sat there and took their ease. All they needed was a couple of six-packs buried in crushed ice, and they would have been the lords of all creation.

One of them was a fellow named Byron Hadley, and in that year of 1950, he'd been at Shawshank longer than I had. Longer than the last two wardens put together, as a matter of fact. The fellow running the show in 1950 was a prissy-looking downeast Yankee named George Dunahy. He had a degree in penal administration. No one liked him, as far as I could tell, except the people who had gotten him his appointment. I heard that he was only interested in three things: compiling statistics for a book (which was later published by a small New England outfit called Light Side Press, where he probably had to pay to have it done), which team won the intramural baseball championship each September, and getting a death-penalty law passed in Maine. A regular bear for the death-penalty was George Dunahy. He was fired off the job in 1953, when it came out he was running a discount auto-repair service down in the prison garage and splitting the profits with Byron Hadley and Greg Stammas. Hadley and Stammas came out of that one okay—they were old hands at keeping their asses covered—but Dunahy took a walk. No one was sorry to see him go, but nobody was exactly pleased to see Greg Stammas step into his shoes, either. He was a short man with a tight, hard gut and the coldest brown eyes you ever saw. He always had a painful, pursed little grin on his face, as if he had to go to the bathroom and couldn't quite manage it. During Stammas's tenure as warden there was a lot of brutality at Shawshank, and although I have no proof, I believe there were maybe half a dozen moonlight burials in the stand of scrub forest that lies east of the prison. Dunahy was bad, but Greg Stammas was a cruel, wretched, cold-hearted man.

He and Byron Hadley were good friends. As warden, George Dunahy was nothing but a posturing figurehead; it was Stammas, and through him, Hadley, who actually administered the prison.

Hadley was a tall, shambling man with thinning red hair. He sunburned easily and he talked loud and if you didn't move fast enough to suit him, he'd clout you with his stick. On that day, our third on the roof, he was talking to another guard named Mert Entwhistle.

Hadley had gotten some amazingly good news, so he was griping about it. That was his style—he was a thankless man with not a good word for anyone, a man who was convinced that the whole world was against him. The world had cheated him out of the best years of his life, and the world would be more than happy to cheat him out of the rest. I have seen some screws that I thought were almost saintly, and I think I know why that happens—they are able to see the difference between their own lives, poor and struggling as they might be, and the lives of the men they are paid by the State to watch over. These guards are able to formulate a comparison concerning pain. Others can't, or won't.

For Byron Hadley there was no basis of comparison. He could sit there, cool and at his ease under the warm May sun, and find the gall to mourn his own good luck while less than ten feet away a bunch of men were working and sweating and burning their hands on great big buckets filled with bubbling tar, men who had to work so hard in their ordinary round of days that this looked like a *respite*. You may remember the old question, the one that's supposed to define your outlook on life when you answer it. For Byron Hadley the answer would always be *half empty, the glass is half empty*. Forever and ever, amen. If you gave him a cool drink of apple cider, he'd think about vinegar. If you told him his wife had always been faithful to him, he'd tell you it was because she was so damn ugly.

So there he sat, talking to Mert Entwhistle loud enough for all of us to hear, his broad white forehead already starting to redden with the sun. He had one hand thrown back over the low parapet surrounding the roof. The other was on the butt of his .38.

We all got the story along with Mert. It seemed that Hadley's older brother had gone off to Texas some fourteen years ago and the rest of the family hadn't heard from the son of a bitch since. They had all assumed he was dead, and good riddance. Then, a week and a half ago, a lawyer had called them long-distance from Austin. It seemed that Hadley's brother had died four months ago, and a rich man at that ("It's frigging incredible how lucky some assholes can get," this paragon of gratitude on the plate-shop roof said). The money had come as a result of oil and oil-leases, and there was close to a million dollars.

No, Hadley wasn't a millionaire—that might have made even him happy, at least for awhile—but the brother had left a pretty damned decent bequest of thirty-five thousand dollars to each surviving member of his family back in Maine, if they could be found. Not bad. Like getting lucky and winning a sweepstakes.

But to Byron Hadley the glass was always half empty. He spent most of the morning bitching to Mert about the bite that the goddam government was going to take out of his windfall. "They'll leave me about enough to buy a new car with," he allowed, "and then what happens? You have to pay the damn taxes on the car, and the repairs and maintenance, you got your goddam kids pestering you to take 'em for a ride with the top down—"

"And to *drive* it, if they're old enough," Mert said. Old Mert Entwhistle knew which side his bread was buttered on, and he didn't say what must have been as obvious to him as to the rest of us: If that money's worrying you so bad, Byron old kid old sock, I'll just take it off your hands. After all, what are friends for?

"That's right, wanting to drive it, wanting to *learn* to drive on it, for Chrissake," Byron said with a shudder. "Then what happens at the end of the year? If you figured the tax wrong and you don't have enough left over to pay the overdraft, you got to pay out of your own pocket, or maybe even borrow it from one of those kikey loan agencies. And they audit you anyway, you know. It don't matter. And when the government audits you, they always take more. Who can fight Uncle Sam? He puts his hand inside your shirt and squeezes your tit until it's purple, and you end up getting the short end. Christ."

He lapsed into a morose silence, thinking of what terrible bad luck he'd had to inherit that thirty-five thousand dollars. Andy Dufresne had been spreading tar with a big Padd brush less than fifteen feet away and now he tossed it into his pail and walked over to where Mert and Hadley were sitting.

We all tightened up, and I saw one of the other screws, Tim Youngblood, drag his hand down to where his pistol was holstered. One of the fellows in the sentry tower struck his partner on the arm and they both turned, too. For one moment I thought Andy was going to get shot, or clubbed, or both.

Then he said, very softly, to Hadley: "Do you trust your wife?"

Hadley just stared at him. He was starting to get red in the face, and I knew that was a bad sign. In about three seconds he was going to pull his billy and give Andy the butt end of it right in the solar plexus, where that big bundle of nerves is. A hard enough hit there can kill you, but they always go for it. If it doesn't kill you it will paralyze you long enough to forget whatever cute move it was that you had planned.

"Boy," Hadley said, "I'll give you just one chance to pick up that Padd. And then you're goin off this roof on your head."

Andy just looked at him, very calm and still. His eyes were like ice. It was as if he hadn't heard. And I found myself wanting to tell him how it was, to give him the crash course. The crash course is you *never* let on that you hear the guards talking, you *never* try to horn in on their conversation unless you're asked (and then you always tell them just what they want to hear and shut up again). Black man, white man, red man, yellow man, in prison it doesn't matter because we've got our own brand of equality. In prison every con's a nigger and you have to get used to the idea if you intend to survive men like Hadley and Greg Stammas, who really would kill you just as soon as look at you. When you're in stir you belong to the State and if you forget it, woe is you. I've known men who've lost eyes, men who've lost toes and fingers; I knew one man who lost the tip of his penis and counted himself lucky that was all he lost. I wanted to tell Andy that it was already too late. He could go back and pick up his brush and there would still be some big lug waiting for him in the showers that night, ready to charley-horse both of his legs and leave him writhing on the cement. You could buy a lug like that for a pack of cigarettes or three Baby Ruths. Most of all, I wanted to tell him not to make it any worse than it already was.

What I did was to keep on running tar out onto the roof as if nothing at all was happening. Like everyone else, I look after my own ass first. I have to. It's cracked already, and in Shawshank there have always been Hadleys willing to finish the job of breaking it.

Andy said, "Maybe I put it wrong. Whether you trust her or not is immaterial. The problem is whether or not you believe she would ever go behind your back, try to hamstring you."

Hadley got up. Mert got up. Tim Youngblood got up. Hadley's face was as red as the side of a firebarn. "Your only problem," he said, "is going to be how many bones you still got unbroken. You can count them in the infirmary. Come on, Mert. We're throwing this sucker over the side."

Tim Youngblood drew his gun. The rest of us kept tarring like mad. The sun beat down. They were going to do it; Hadley and Mert were simply going to pitch him over the side. Terrible accident. Dufresne, prisoner 81433-SHNK, was taking a couple of empties down and slipped on the ladder. Too bad.

They laid hold of him, Mert on the right arm, Hadley on the left. Andy didn't resist. His eyes never left Hadley's red, horsey face.

"If you've got your thumb on her, Mr. Hadley," he said in that same calm, composed voice, "there's not a reason why you shouldn't have every cent of that money. Final score, Mr. Byron Hadley thirty-five thousand, Uncle Sam zip."

Mert started to drag him toward the edge. Hadley just stood there. For a moment Andy was like a rope between them in a tug-of-war game. Then Hadley said, "Hold on one second, Mert. What do you mean, boy?"

"I mean, if you've got your thumb on your wife, you can give it to her," Andy said.

"You better start making sense, boy, or you're going over."

"The IRS allows you a one-time-only gift to your spouse," Andy said. "It's good up to sixty thousand dollars."

Hadley was now looking at Andy as if he had been poleaxed. "Naw, that ain't right," he said. "Tax *free?*"

"Tax free," Andy said. "IRS can't touch cent one."

"How would you know a thing like that?"

Tim Youngblood said: "He used to be a banker, Byron. I s'pose he might—"

"Shut ya head, Trout," Hadley said without looking at him. Tim Youngblood flushed and shut up. Some of the guards called him Trout because of his thick lips and buggy eyes. Hadley kept looking at Andy. "You're the smart banker who shot his wife. Why should I believe a smart banker like you? So I can wind up in here breaking rocks right alongside you? You'd like that, wouldn't you?"

Andy said quietly: "If you went to jail for tax evasion, you'd go to a federal penitentiary, not Shawshank. But you won't. The tax-free gift to the spouse is a perfectly legal loophole. I've done dozens . . . no, hundreds of them. It's meant primarily for people with small businesses to pass on, or for people who come into one-time-only windfalls. Like yourself."

"I think you're lying," Hadley said, but he didn't—you could see he didn't. There was an emotion dawning on his face, something that was grotesque overlying that long, ugly countenance and that receding, sunburned brow. An almost obscene emotion when seen on the features of Byron Hadley. It was hope.

"No, I'm not lying. There's no reason why you should take my word for it, either. Engage a lawyer—"

"Ambulance-chasing highway-robbing cocksuckers!" Hadley cried.

Andy shrugged. "Then go to the IRS. They'll tell you the same thing for free. Actually, you don't need me to tell you at all. You would have investigated the matter for yourself."

"Your fucking-A. I don't need any smart wife-killing banker to show me where the bear shit in the buckwheat."

"You'll need a tax lawyer or a banker to set up the gift for you and that will cost you something," Andy said. "Or . . . if you were interested, I'd be glad to set it up for you nearly free of charge. The price would be three beers apiece for my co-workers—"

"Co-workers," Mert said, and let out a rusty guffaw. He slapped his knee. A real knee-slapper was old Mert, and I hope he died of intestinal cancer in a part of the world where morphine is as of yet undiscovered. "Co-workers, ain't that cute? Co-workers! You ain't got any—"

"Shut your friggin trap," Hadley growled, and Mert shut. Hadley looked at Andy again. "What was you sayin?"

"I was saying that I'd only ask three beers apiece for my co-workers, if that seems fair," Andy said. "I think a man feels more like a man when he's working out of doors in the springtime if he can have a bottle of suds. That's only my opinion. It would go down smooth, and I'm sure you'd have their gratitude."

I have talked to some of the other men who were up there that day—Rennie Martin, Logan St. Pierre, and Paul Bonsaint were three of them—and we all saw the same thing then . . . *felt* the same thing. Suddenly it was Andy who had the upper hand. It was Hadley who had the gun on his hip and the billy in his hand, Hadley who had his friend Greg Stammas behind him and the whole prison administration behind Stammas, the whole power of the State behind *that*, but all at once in that golden sunshine it didn't matter, and I felt my heart leap up in my chest as it never had since the truck drove me and four others through the gate back in 1938 and I stepped out into the exercise yard.

Andy was looking at Hadley with those cold, clear, calm eyes, and it wasn't just the thirty-five thousand then, we all agreed on that. I've played it over and over in my mind and I *know*. It was man against man, and Andy simply *forced* him, the way a strong man can force a weaker man's wrist to the table in a game of Indian rasseling. There was no reason, you see, why Hadley couldn't've given Mert the nod at that very minute, pitched Andy overside onto his head, and still taken Andy's advice.

No reason. *But he didn't.*

"I could get you all a couple of beers if I wanted to," Hadley said. "A beer does taste good while you're workin." The colossal prick even managed to sound magnanimous.

"I'd just give you one piece of advice the IRS wouldn't bother with," Andy said. His eyes were fixed unwinkingly on Hadley's. "Make the gift to your wife if you're *sure*. If you think there's even a chance she might double-cross you or backshoot you, we could work out something else—"

"Double-cross me?" Hadley asked harshly. "Double-cross *me?* Mr. Hotshot Banker, if she ate her way through a boxcar of Ex-Lax, she wouldn't dare fart unless I gave her the nod."

Mert, Youngblood, and the other screws yucked it up dutifully. Andy never cracked a smile.

"I'll write down the forms you need," he said. "You can get them at the post office, and I'll fill them out for your signature."

That sounded suitably important, and Hadley's chest swelled. Then he glared around at the rest of us and hollered, "What are you jimmies starin at? Move your asses, goddammit!" He looked back at Andy. "You come over here with me, hotshot. And listen to me well: if you're jewing me somehow, you're gonna find yourself chasing your own head around Shower C before the week's out."

"Yes, I understand that," Andy said softly.

And he did understand it. The way it turned out, he understood a lot more than I did—more than any of us did.

That's how, on the second-to-last day of the job, the convict crew that tarred the plate-factory roof in 1950 ended up sitting in a row at ten o'clock on a spring morning, drinking Black Label beer supplied by the hardest screw that ever walked a turn at Shawshank State Prison. That beer was piss-warm, but it was still the best I ever had in my life. We sat and drank it and felt the sun on our shoulders, and not even the expression of half-amusement, half-contempt on Hadley's face—as if he were watching apes drink beer instead of men—could spoil it. It lasted twenty minutes, that beer-break, and for those twenty minutes we felt like free men. We could have been drinking beer and tarring the roof of one of our own houses.

Only Andy didn't drink. I already told you about his drinking habits. He sat hunkered down in the shade, hands dangling between his knees, watching us and smiling a little. It's amazing how many men remember him that way, and amazing how many men were on that work-crew when Andy Dufresne faced down Byron Hadley. I thought there were nine or ten of us, but by 1955 there must have been two hundred of us, maybe more . . . if you believed what you heard.

So, yeah—if you asked me to give you a flat-out answer to the question of whether I'm trying to tell you about a man or a legend that got made up around the man, like a pearl around a little piece of grit—I'd have to say that the answer lies somewhere in between. All I know for sure is that Andy Dufresne wasn't much like me or anyone else I ever knew since I came inside. He brought in five hundred dollars jammed up his back porch, but somehow that graymeat son of a bitch managed to bring in something else as well. A sense of his own worth, maybe, or a feeling that he would be the winner in the end . . . or maybe it was only a sense of freedom, even inside these goddamned gray walls. It was a kind of inner light he carried around with him. I only knew him to lose that light once, and that is also a part of this story.

By World Series time of 1950—this was the year the Philadelphia Whiz Kids dropped four straight, you will remember—Andy was having no more trouble from the sisters. Stammas and Hadley had passed the word. If Andy Dufresne came to either of them, or any of the other screws that formed a part of their coterie, and showed so much as a single drop of blood in his underpants, every sister in Shawshank would go to bed that night with a headache. They didn't fight it. As I have pointed out, there was always an eighteen-year-old car thief or a firebug or some guy who'd gotten his kicks handling little children. After the day on the plate-shop roof, Andy went his way and the sisters went theirs.

He was working in the library then, under a tough old con named Brooks Hatlen. Hatlen had gotten the job back in the late twenties because he had a college education. Brooksie's degree was in animal husbandry, true enough, but college educations in institutes of lower learning like The Shank are so rare that it's a case of beggars not being able to be choosers.

In 1952 Brooksie, who had killed his wife and daughter after a losing streak at poker back when Coolidge was President, was paroled. As usual, the State in all its wisdom had let him go long after any chance he might have had to become a useful part of society was gone. He was sixty-eight and arthritic when he tottered out of the main gate in his Polish suit and his French shoes, his parole papers in one hand and a Greyhound bus ticket in the other. He was crying when he left. Shawshank was his world. What lay beyond its walls was as terrible to Brooks as the Western Seas had been to superstitious fifteenth-century sailors. In prison, Brooksie had been a person of some importance. He was the librarian, an educated man. If he went to the Kittery library and asked for a job, they wouldn't even give him a library card. I heard he died in a home for indigent old folks up Freeport way in 1953, and at that he lasted about six months longer than I thought he would. Yeah, I guess the State got its own back on Brooksie, all right. They trained him to like it inside the shithouse and then they threw him out.

Andy succeeded to Brooksie's job, and he was librarian for twenty-three years. He used the same force of will I'd seen him use on Byron Hadley to get what he wanted for the library, and I saw him gradually turn one small room (which still smelled of turpentine because it had been a paint closet until 1922 and had never been properly aired) lined with Reader's Digest Condensed Books and *National Geographic*s into the best prison library in New England.

He did it a step at a time. He put a suggestion box by the door and patiently weeded out such attempts at humor as *More Fuk-Boox Pleeze* and *Excape in 10 EZ Lesions*. He got hold of the things the prisoners seemed serious about. He wrote to the major book clubs in

New York and got two of them, The Literary Guild and The Book-of-the-Month Club, to send editions of all their major selections to us at a special cheap rate. He discovered a hunger for information on such small hobbies as soap-carving, woodworking, sleight of hand, and card solitaire. He got all the books he could on such subjects. And those two jailhouse staples, Erle Stanley Gardner and Louis L'Amour. Cons never seem to get enough of the courtroom or the open range. And yes, he did keep a box of fairly spicy paperbacks under the checkout desk, loaning them out carefully and making sure they always got back. Even so, each new acquisition of that type was quickly read to tatters.

He began to write to the State Senate in Augusta in 1954. Stammas was warden by then, and he used to pretend Andy was some sort of mascot. He was always in the library, shooting the bull with Andy, and sometimes he'd even throw a paternal arm around Andy's shoulders or give him a goose. He didn't fool anybody. Andy Dufresne was no one's mascot.

He told Andy that maybe he'd been a banker on the outside, but that part of his life was receding rapidly into his past and he had better get a hold on the facts of prison life. As far as that bunch of jumped-up Republican Rotarians in Augusta was concerned, there were only three viable expenditures of the taxpayers' money in the field of prisons and corrections. Number one was more walls, number two was more bars, and number three was more guards. As far as the State Senate was concerned, Stammas explained, the folks in Thomastan and Shawshank and Pittsfield and South Portland were the scum of the earth. They were there to do hard time, and by God and Sonny Jesus, it was hard time they were going to do. And if there were a few weevils in the bread, wasn't that just too fucking bad?

Andy smiled his small, composed smile and asked Stammas what would happen to a block of concrete if a drop of water fell on it once every year for a million years. Stammas laughed and clapped Andy on the back. "You got no million years, old horse, but if you did, I bleeve you'd do it with that same little grin on your face. You go on and write your letters. I'll even mail them for you if you pay for the stamps."

Which Andy did. And he had the last laugh, although Stammas and Hadley weren't around to see it. Andy's requests for library funds were routinely turned down until 1960, when he received a check for two hundred dollars—the Senate probably appropriated it in hopes that he would shut up and go away. Vain hope. Andy felt that he had finally gotten one foot in the door and he simply redoubled his efforts; two letters a week instead of one. In 1962 he got four hundred dollars, and for the rest of the decade the library received seven hundred dollars a year like clockwork. By 1971 that had risen to an even thousand. Not much stacked up against what your average small-town library receives, I guess, but a thousand bucks can buy a lot of recycled Perry Mason stories and Jake Logan Westerns. By the time Andy left, you could go into the library (expanded from its original paint-locker to three rooms), and find just about anything you'd want. And if you couldn't find it, chances were good that Andy could get it for you.

Now you're asking yourself if all this came about just because Andy told Byron Hadley how to save the taxes on his windfall inheritance. The answer is yes . . . and no. You can probably figure out what happened for yourself.

Word got around that Shawshank was housing its very own pet financial wizard. In the late spring and the summer of 1950, Andy set up two trust funds for guards who wanted to assure a college education for their kids, he advised a couple of others who wanted to take small fliers in common stock (and they did pretty damn well, as things turned out; one of them did so well he was able to take an early retirement two years later), and I'll be damned if he didn't advise the warden himself, old Lemon Lips George Dunahy, on how to go about setting up a tax-shelter for himself. That was just before Dunahy got the bum's rush, and I believe he must have been dreaming about all the millions his book was going to make him. By April of 1951, Andy was doing the tax returns for half the screws at Shawshank, and by 1952, he was doing almost all of them. He was paid in what may be a prison's most valuable coin: simple good will.

Later on, after Greg Stammas took over the warden's office, Andy became even more important—but if I tried to tell you the specifics of just how, I'd be guessing. There are some things I know about and others I can only guess at. I know that there were some prisoners who received all sorts of special considerations—radios in their cells, extraordinary visiting privileges, things like that—and there were people on the outside who were paying for them to have those privileges. Such people are known as "angels" by the prisoners. All at once some fellow would be excused from working in the plate-shop on Saturday forenoons, and you'd know that fellow had an angel out there who'd coughed up a chunk of dough to make sure it happened. The way it usually works is that the angel will pay the bribe to some middle-level screw, and the screw will spread the grease both up and down the administrative ladder.

Then there was the discount auto-repair service that laid Warden Dunahy low. It went underground for awhile and then emerged stronger than ever in the late fifties. And some of the contractors that worked at the prison from time to time were paying kickbacks to the top administration officials, I'm pretty sure, and the same was almost certainly true of the companies whose equipment was bought and installed in the laundry and the license-plate shop and the stamping-mill that was built in 1963.

By the late sixties there was also a booming trade in pills, and the same administrative crowd was involved in turning a buck on that. All of it added up to a pretty good-sized river of illicit income. Not like the pile of clandestine bucks that must fly around a really big prison like Attica or San Quentin, but not peanuts, either. And money itself becomes a problem after awhile. You can't just stuff it into your wallet and then shell out a bunch of crumpled twenties and dog-eared tens when you want a pool built in your back yard or an addition put on your house. Once you get past a certain point, you have to explain where that money came from . . . and if your explanations aren't convincing enough, you're apt to wind up wearing a number yourself.

So there was a need for Andy's services. They took him out of the laundry and installed him in the library, but if you wanted to look at it another way, they never took him out of the laundry at all. They just set him to work washing dirty money instead of dirty sheets. He funnelled it into stocks, bonds, tax-free municipals, you name it.

He told me once about ten years after that day on the plate-shop roof that his feelings about what he was doing were pretty clear, and that his conscience was relatively untroubled. The rackets would have gone on with him or without him. He had not asked to be sent to Shawshank, he went on; he was an innocent man who had been victimized by colossal bad luck, not a missionary or a do-gooder.

"Besides, Red," he told me with that same half-grin, "what I'm doing in here isn't all *that* different from what I was doing outside. I'll hand you a pretty cynical axiom: the amount of expert financial help an individual or company needs rises in direct proportion to how many people that person or business is screwing.

"The people who run this place are stupid, brutal monsters for the most part. The people who run the straight world are brutal and monstrous, but they happen not to be quite as stupid, because the standard of competence out there is a little higher. Not much, but a little."

"But the pills," I said. "I don't want to tell you your business, but they make me nervous. Reds, uppers, downers, Nembutals— now they've got these things they call Phase Fours. I won't get anything like that. Never have."

"No," Andy said. "I don't like the pills, either. Never have. But I'm not much of a one for cigarettes or booze, either. But I don't push the pills. I don't bring them in, and I don't sell them once they are in. Mostly it's the screws who do that."

"But—"

"Yeah, I know. There's a fine line there. What it comes down to, Red, is some people refuse to get their hands dirty at all. That's called sainthood, and the pigeons land on your shoulders and crap all over your shirt. The other extreme is to take a bath in the dirt and deal any goddamned thing that will turn a dollar—guns, switchblades, big H, what the hell. You ever have a con come up to you and offer you a contract?"

I nodded. It's happened a lot of times over the years. You are, after all, the man who can get it. And they figure if you can get them batteries for their transistor radios or cartons of Luckies or lids of reefer, you can put them in touch with a guy who'll use a knife.

"Sure you have," Andy agreed. "But you don't do it. Because guys like us, Red, we know there's a third choice. An alternative to staying simon-pure or bathing in the filth and the slime. It's the alternative that grown-ups all over the world pick. You balance off your walk through the hog-wallow against what it gains you. You choose the lesser of two evils and try to keep your good intentions in front of you. And I guess you judge how well you're doing by how well you sleep at night . . . and what your dreams are like."

"Good intentions," I said, and laughed. "I know all about that, Andy. A fellow can toddle right off to hell on that road."

"Don't you believe it," he said, growing somber. "This is hell right here. Right here in The Shank. They sell pills and I tell them what to do with the money. But I've also got the library, and I know of over two dozen guys who have used the books in there to help them pass their high school equivalency tests. Maybe when they get out of here they'll be able to crawl off the shitheap. When we needed that second room back in 1957, I got it. Because they want to keep me happy. I work cheap. That's the trade-off."

"And you've got your own private quarters."

"Sure. That's the way I like it."

The prison population had risen slowly all through the fifties, and it damn near exploded in the sixties, what with every college-age kid in America wanting to try dope and the perfectly ridiculous penalties for the use of a little reefer. But in all that time Andy never had a cellmate, except for a big, silent Indian named Normaden (like all Indians in The Shank, he was called Chief), and Normaden didn't last long. A lot of the other long-timers thought Andy was crazy, but Andy just smiled. He lived alone and he liked it that way . . . and as he'd said, they liked to keep him happy. He worked cheap.

Prison time is slow time, sometimes you'd swear it's stop-time, but it passes. It passes. George Dunahy departed the scene in a welter of newspaper headlines shouting SCANDAL and NEST-FEA-THERING. Stammas succeeded him, and for the next six years

Shawshank was a kind of living hell. During the reign of Greg Stammas, the beds in the infirmary and the cells in the Solitary Wing were always full.

One day in 1958 I looked at myself in a small shaving mirror I kept in my cell and saw a forty-year-old man looking back at me. A kid had come in back in 1938, a kid with a big mop of carroty red hair, half-crazy with remorse, thinking about suicide. That kid was gone. The red hair was going gray and starting to recede. There were crow's tracks around the eyes. On that day I could see an old man inside, waiting his time to come out. It scared me. Nobody wants to grow old in stir.

Stammas went early in 1959. There had been several investigative reporters sniffing around, and one of them even did four months under an assumed name, for a crime made up out of whole cloth. They were getting ready to drag out SCANDAL and NEST-FEATHERING again, but before they could bring the hammer down on him, Stammas ran. I can understand that; boy, can I ever. If he had been tried and convicted, he could have ended up right in here. If so, he might have lasted all of five hours. Byron Hadley had gone two years earlier. The sucker had a heart attack and took an early retirement.

Andy never got touched by the Stammas affair. In early 1959 a new warden was appointed, and a new assistant warden, and a new chief of guards. For the next eight months or so, Andy was just another con again. It was during that period that Normaden, the big half-breed Passamaquoddy, shared Andy's cell with him. Then everything just started up again. Normaden was moved out, and Andy was living in solitary splendor again. The names at the top change, but the rackets never do.

I talked to Normaden once about Andy. "Nice fella," Normaden said. It was hard to make out anything he said because he had a harelip and a cleft palate; his words all came out in a slush. "I liked it there. He never made fun. But he didn't want me there. I could tell." Big shrug. "I was glad to go, me. Bad draft in that cell. All the time cold. He don't let nobody touch his things. That's okay. Nice man, never made fun. But big draft."

* * *

Rita Hayworth hung in Andy's cell until 1955, if I remember right. Then it was Marilyn Monroe, that picture from *The Seven-Year Itch* where she's standing over a subway grating and the warm air is flipping her skirt up. Marilyn lasted until 1960, and she was considerably tattered about the edges when Andy replaced her with Jayne Mansfield. Jayne was, you should pardon the expression, a bust. After only a year or so she was replaced with an English actress—might have been Hazel Court, but I'm not sure. In 1966 that one came down and Raquel Welch went up for a record-breaking six-year engagement in Andy's cell. The last poster to hang there was a pretty country-rock singer whose name was Linda Ronstadt.

I asked him once what the posters meant to him, and he gave me a peculiar, surprised sort of look. "Why, they mean the same thing to me as they do to most cons, I guess," he said. "Freedom. You look at those pretty women and you feel like you could almost . . . not quite but *almost* . . . step right through and be beside them. Be free. I guess that's why I always liked Raquel Welch the best. It wasn't just her; it was that beach she was standing on. Looked like she was down in Mexico somewhere. Someplace quiet, where a man would be able to hear himself think. Didn't you ever feel that way about a picture, Red? That you could almost step right through it?"

I said I'd never really thought of it that way.

"Maybe someday you'll see what I mean," he said, and he was right. Years later I saw exactly what he meant . . . and when I did, the first thing I thought of was Normaden, and about how he'd said it was always cold in Andy's cell.

A terrible thing happened to Andy in late March or early April of 1963. I have told you that he had something that most of the other prisoners, myself included, seemed to lack. Call it a sense of equanimity, or a feeling of inner peace, maybe even a constant and unwavering faith that someday the long nightmare would end. Whatever you want to call it, Andy Dufresne always seemed to have his act together. There was none of that sullen desperation about him that seems to afflict most lifers after awhile; you could never smell hopelessness on him. Until that late winter of '63.

We had another warden by then, a man named Samuel Norton. The Mathers, Cotton and Increase, would have felt right at home with Sam Norton. So far as I know, no one had ever seen him so much as crack a smile. He had a thirty-year pin from the Baptist Advent Church of Eliot. His major innovation as the head of our happy family was to make sure that each incoming prisoner had a New Testament. He had a small plaque on his desk, gold letters inlaid in teakwood, which said CHRIST IS MY SAVIOR. A sampler on the wall, made by his wife, read: HIS JUDGMENT COMETH AND THAT RIGHT EARLY. This latter sentiment cut zero ice with most of us. We felt that the judgment had already occurred, and we would be willing to testify with the best of them that the rock would not hide us nor the dead tree give us shelter. He had a Bible quote for every occasion, did Mr. Sam Norton, and whenever you meet a man like that, my best advice to you would be to grin big and cover up your balls with both hands.

There were less infirmary cases than in the days of Greg Stammas, and so far as I know the moonlight burials ceased altogether, but this is not to say that Norton was not a believer in punishment. Solitary was always well populated. Men lost their teeth not from beatings but from bread and water diets. It began to be called grain and drain, as in "I'm on the Sam Norton grain and drain train, boys."

The man was the foulest hypocrite that I ever saw in a high position. The rackets I told you about earlier continued to flourish, but Sam Norton added his own new wrinkles. Andy knew about them all, and because we had gotten to be pretty good friends by that time, he let me in on some of them. When Andy talked about them, an expression of amused, disgusted wonder would come over his face, as if he were telling me about some ugly, predatory species of bug that was, by its very ugliness and greed, somehow more comic than terrible.

It was Warden Norton who instituted the "Inside-Out" program you may have read about some sixteen or seventeen years back; it was even written up in *Newsweek*. In the press it sounded like a real advance in practical corrections and rehabilitation. There were prisoners out cutting pulpwood, prisoners repairing bridges and causeways, prisoners constructing potato cellars. Norton called it "Inside-Out" and was invited to explain it to damn near every Rotary and Kiwanis club in New England, especially after he got his picture in *Newsweek*. The prisoners called it "road-ganging," but so far as I know, none of them were ever invited to express their views to the Kiwanians or the Loyal Order of Moose.

Norton was right in there on every operation, thirty-year church-pin and all; from cutting pulp to digging storm-drains to laying new culverts under state highways, there was Norton, skimming off the top. There were a hundred ways to do it—men, materials, you name it. But he had it coming another way, as well. The construction businesses in the area were deathly afraid of Norton's Inside-Out program, because prison labor is slave labor, and you can't compete with that. So Sam Norton, he of the Testaments and the thirty-year church-pin, was passed a good many thick envelopes under the table during his sixteen-year tenure as Shawshank's warden. And when an envelope was passed, he would either overbid the project, not bid at all, or claim that all his Inside-Outers were committed elsewhere. It has always been something of a wonder to me that Norton was never found in the trunk of a Thunderbird parked off a highway somewhere down in Massachusetts with his hands tied behind his back and half a dozen bullets in his head.

Anyway, as the old barrelhouse song says, My God, how the money rolled in. Norton must have subscribed to the old Puritan notion that the best way to figure out which folks God favors is by checking their bank accounts.

Andy Dufresne was his right hand in all of this, his silent partner. The prison library was Andy's hostage to fortune. Norton knew it, and Norton used it. Andy told me that one of Norton's favorite aphorisms was *One hand washes the other*. So Andy gave good advice and made useful suggestions. I can't say for sure that he hand-tooled Norton's Inside-Out program, but I'm damned sure he processed the money for the Jesus-shouting son of a whore. He gave good advice, made useful suggestions, the money got spread around, and . . . son of a bitch! The library would get a new set of automotive repair manuals, a fresh set of Grolier Encyclopedias, books on how to prepare for the Scholastic Achievement Tests. And, of course, more Erle Stanley Gardners and more Louis L'Amours.

And I'm convinced that what happened happened because Norton just didn't want to lose his good right hand. I'll go further: it happened because he was scared of what might happen—what Andy might say against him—if Andy ever got clear of Shawshank State Prison.

I got the story a chunk here and a chunk there over a space of seven years, some of it from Andy—but not all. He never wanted to talk about that part of his life, and I don't blame him. I got parts of it from maybe half a dozen different sources. I've said once that prisoners are nothing but slaves, but they have that slave habit of looking dumb and keeping their ears open. I got it backwards and forwards and in the middle, but I'll give it to you from point A to point Z, and maybe you'll understand why the man spent about ten months in a bleak, depressed daze. See, I don't think he knew the truth until 1963, fifteen years after he came into this sweet little hell-hole. Until he met Tommy Williams, I don't think he knew how bad it could get.

Tommy Williams joined our happy little Shawshank family in November of 1962. Tommy thought of himself as a native of Massachusetts, but he wasn't proud; in his twenty-seven years he'd done time all over New England. He was a professional thief, and as you may have guessed, my own feeling was that he should have picked another profession.

He was a married man, and his wife came to visit each and every week. She had an idea that things might go better with Tommy—and consequently better with their three-year-old son and herself—if he got his high school degree. She talked him into it, and so Tommy Williams started visiting the library on a regular basis.

For Andy, this was an old routine by then. He saw that Tommy got a series of high school equivalency tests. Tommy would brush up on the subjects he had passed in high school—there weren't many—and then take the test. Andy also saw that he was enrolled in a number of correspondence courses covering the subjects he had failed in school or just missed by dropping out.

He probably wasn't the best student Andy ever took over the jumps, and I don't know if he ever did get his high school diploma, but that forms no part of my story. The important thing was that he came to like Andy Dufresne very much, as most people did after awhile.

On a couple of occasions he asked Andy "what a smart guy like you is doing in the joint"—a question which is the rough equivalent of that one that goes "What's a nice girl like you doing in a place like this?" But Andy wasn't the type to tell him; he would only smile and turn the conversation into some other channel. Quite normally, Tommy asked someone else, and when he finally got the story, I guess he also got the shock of his young life.

The person he asked was his partner on the laundry's steam ironer and folder. The inmates call this device the mangler, because that's exactly what it will do to you if you aren't paying attention and get your bad self caught in it. His partner was Charlie Lathrop, who had been in for about twelve years on a murder charge. He was more than glad to reheat the details of the Dufresne murder trial for Tommy; it broke the monotony of pulling freshly pressed bedsheets out of the machine and tucking them into the basket. He was just getting to the jury waiting until after lunch to bring in their guilty verdict when the trouble whistle went off and the mangle grated to a stop. They had been feeding in freshly washed sheets from the Eliot Nursing Home at the far end; these were spat out dry and neatly pressed at Tommy's and Charlie's end at the rate of one every five seconds. Their job was to grab them, fold them, and slap them into the cart, which had already been lined with clean brown paper.

But Tommy Williams was just standing there, staring at Charlie Lathrop, his mouth unhinged all the way to his chest. He was standing in a drift of sheets that had come through clean and which were now sopping up all the wet muck on the floor—and in a laundry wetwash, there's plenty of muck.

So the head bull that day, Homer Jessup, comes rushing over, bellowing his head off and on the prod for trouble. Tommy took no notice of him. He spoke to Charlie as if old Homer, who had busted more heads than he could probably count, hadn't been there.

"What did you say that golf pro's name was?"

"Quentin," Charlie answered back, all confused and upset by now. He later said that the kid was as white as a truce flag. "Glenn Quentin, I think. Something like that, anyway—"

"Here now, here now," Homer Jessup roared, his neck as red as a rooster's comb. "Get them sheets in cold water! Get quick! Get quick, by Jesus, you—"

"Glenn Quentin, oh my God," Tommy Williams said, and that was all he got to say because Homer Jessup, that least peaceable of men, brought his billy down behind his ear. Tommy hit the floor so hard he broke off three of his front teeth. When he woke up he was in solitary, and confined to same for a week, riding a boxcar on Sam Norton's famous grain and drain train. Plus a black mark on his report card.

That was in early February of 1963, and Tommy Williams went around to six or seven other long-timers after he got out of solitary and got pretty much the same story. I know; I was one of them. But when I asked him why he wanted it, he just clammed up.

Then one day he went to the library and spilled one helluva big budget of information to Andy Dufresne. And for the first and last time, at least since he had approached me about the Rita Hayworth poster like a kid buying his first pack of Trojans, Andy lost his cool . . . only this time he blew it entirely.

I saw him later that day, and he looked like a man who has stepped on the business end of a rake and given himself a good one, whap between the eyes. His hands were trembling, and when I spoke to him, he didn't answer. Before that afternoon was out he had caught up with Billy Hanlon, who was the head screw, and set up an appointment with Warden Norton for the following day. He told me later that he didn't sleep a wink all that night; he just listened to a cold winter wind howling outside, watched the searchlights go around and around, putting long, moving shadows on the cement walls of the cage he had called home since Harry Truman was President, and tried to think it all out. He said it was as if Tommy had produced a key which fit a cage in the back of his mind, a cage like his own cell. Only instead of holding a man, that cage held a tiger, and that tiger's name was Hope. Williams had produced the key that unlocked the cage and the tiger was out, willy-nilly, to roam his brain.

Four years before, Tommy Williams had been arrested in Rhode Island, driving a stolen car that was full of stolen merchandise. Tommy turned in his accomplice, the DA played ball, and he got a lighter sentence . . . two to four, with time served. Eleven months after beginning his term, his old cellmate got a ticket out and Tommy got a new one, a man named Elwood Blatch. Blatch had been busted for burglary with a weapon and was serving six to twelve.

"I never seen such a high-strung guy," Tommy told me. "A man like that should never want to be a burglar, specially not with a gun. The slightest little noise, he'd go three feet into the air . . . and come down shooting, more likely than not. One night he almost strangled me because some guy down the hall was whopping on his cell bars with a tin cup.

"I did seven months with him, until they let me walk free. I got time served and time off, you understand. I can't say we talked because you didn't, you know, exactly hold a conversation with El Blatch. *He* held a conversation with *you*. He talked all the time. Never shut up. If you tried to get a word in, he'd shake his fist at you and roll his eyes. It gave me the cold chills whenever he done that. Big tall guy he was, mostly bald, with these green eyes set way down deep in the sockets. Jeez, I hope I never see him again.

"It was like a talkin jag every night. Where he grew up, the orphanages he run away from, the jobs he done, the women he fucked, the crap games he cleaned out. I just let him run on. My face ain't much, but I didn't want it, you know, rearranged for me.

"According to him, he'd burgled over two hundred joints. It was hard for me to believe, a guy like him who went off like a firecracker every time someone cut a loud fart, but he swore it was true. Now . . . listen to me, Red. I know guys sometimes make things up after they know a thing, but even before I knew about this golf pro guy, Quentin, I remember thinking that if El Blatch ever burgled *my* house, and I found out about it later, I'd have to count myself just about the luckiest motherfucker going still to be alive. Can you imagine him in some lady's bedroom, sifting through her jool'ry box, and she coughs in her sleep or turns over quick? It gives me the cold chills just to think of something like that, I swear on my mother's name it does.

"He said he'd killed people, too. People that gave him shit. At least that's what he said. And I believed him. He sure looked like a man that could do some killing. He was just so fucking high-strung! Like a pistol with a sawed-off firing pin. I knew a guy who had a Smith and Wesson Police Special with a sawed-off firing pin. It wasn't no good for nothing, except maybe for something to jaw about. The pull on that gun was so light that it would fire if this guy, Johnny Callahan, his name was, if he turned his record-player on full volume and put it on top of one of the speakers. That's how El Blatch was. I can't explain it any better. I just never doubted that he had greased some people.

"So one night, just for something to say, I go: 'Who'd you kill?' Like a joke, you know. So he laughs and says: 'There's one guy doing time up-Maine for these two people I killed. It was this guy and the wife of the slob who's doing the time. I was creeping their place and the guy started to give me some shit.'

"I can't remember if he ever told me the woman's name or not," Tommy went on. "Maybe he did. But in New England, Dufresne's like Smith or Jones in the rest of the country, because there's so many Frogs up here. Dufresne, Lavesque, Ouelette, Poulin, who can remember Frog names? But he told me the guy's name. He said the guy was Glenn Quentin and he was a prick, a big rich prick, a golf pro. El said he thought the guy might have cash in the house, maybe as much as five thousand dollars. That was a lot of money back then, he says to me. So I go: 'When was that?' And he goes: 'After the war. Just after the war.'

"So he went in and he did the joint and they woke up and the guy gave him some trouble. That's what *El* said. Maybe the guy just started to snore, that's what *I* say. Anyway, El said Quentin was in the sack with some hotshot lawyer's wife and they sent the lawyer up to Shawshank State Prison. Then he laughs this big laugh. Holy Christ, I was never so glad of anything as I was when I got my walking papers from that place."

* * *

I guess you can see why Andy went a little wonky when Tommy told him that story, and why he wanted to see the warden right away. Elwood Blatch had been serving a six-to-twelve rap when Tommy knew him four years before. By the time Andy heard all of this, in 1963, he might be on the verge of getting out . . . or already out. So those were the two prongs of the spit Andy was roasting on—the idea that Blatch might still be in on one hand, and the very real possibility that he might be gone like the wind on the other.

There were inconsistencies in Tommy's story, but aren't there always in real life? Blatch told Tommy the man who got sent up was a hotshot lawyer, and Andy was a banker, but those are two professions that people who aren't very educated could easily get mixed up. And don't forget that twelve years had gone by between the time Blatch was reading the clippings about the trial and the time he told the tale to Tommy Williams. He also told Tommy he got better than a thousand dollars from a footlocker Quentin had in his closet, but the police said at Andy's trial that there had been no sign of burglary. I have a few ideas about that. First, if you take the cash and the man it belonged to is dead, how are you going to know anything was stolen, unless someone else can tell you it was there to start with? Second, who's to say Blatch wasn't lying about that part of it? Maybe he didn't want to admit killing two people for nothing. Third, maybe there were signs of burglary and the cops either overlooked them—cops can be pretty dumb—or deliberately covered them up so they wouldn't screw the DA's case. The guy was running for public office, remember, and he needed a conviction to run on. An unsolved burglary-murder would have done him no good at all.

But of the three, I like the middle one best. I've known a few Elwood Blatches in my time at Shawshank—the trigger-pullers with the crazy eyes. Such fellows want you to think they got away with the equivalent of the Hope Diamond on every caper, even if they got caught with a two-dollar Timex and nine bucks on the one they're doing time for.

And there was one thing in Tommy's story that convinced Andy beyond a shadow of a doubt. Blatch hadn't hit Quentin at random.

He had called Quentin "a big rich prick," and he had *known* Quentin was a golf pro. Well, Andy and his wife had been going out to that country club for drinks and dinner once or twice a week for a couple of years, and Andy had done a considerable amount of drinking there once he found out about his wife's affair. There was a marina with the country club, and for awhile in 1947 there had been a part-time grease-and-gas jockey working there who matched Tommy's description of Elwood Blatch. A big tall man, mostly bald, with deep-set green eyes. A man who had an unpleasant way of looking at you, as though he was sizing you up. He wasn't there long, Andy said. Either he quit or Briggs, the fellow in charge of the marina, fired him. But he wasn't a man you forgot. He was too striking for that.

So Andy went to see Warden Norton on a rainy, windy day with big gray clouds scudding across the sky above the gray walls, a day when the last of the snow was starting to melt away and show lifeless patches of last year's grass in the fields beyond the prison.

The warden has a good-sized office in the Administration Wing, and behind the warden's desk there's a door which connects with the assistant warden's office. The assistant warden was out that day, but a trusty was there. He was a half-lame fellow whose real name I have forgotten; all the inmates, me included, called him Chester, after Marshal Dillon's sidekick. Chester was supposed to be watering the plants and waxing the floor. My guess is that the plants went thirsty that day and the only waxing that was done happened because of Chester's dirty ear polishing the keyhole plate of that connecting door.

He heard the warden's main door open and close and then Norton saying: "Good morning, Dufresne, how can I help you?"

"Warden," Andy began, and old Chester told us that he could hardly recognize Andy's voice it was so changed. "Warden . . . there's something . . . something's happened to me that's . . . that's so . . . so . . . I hardly know where to begin."

"Well, why don't you just begin at the beginning?" the warden said, probably in his sweetest let's-all-turn-to-the-Twenty-third-Psalm-and-read-in-unison voice. "That usually works the best."

And so Andy did. He began by refreshing Norton on the details of the crime he had been imprisoned for. Then he told the warden exactly what Tommy Williams had told him. He also gave out Tommy's name, which you may think wasn't so wise in light of later developments, but I'd just ask you what else he could have done, if his story was to have any credibility at all.

When he had finished, Norton was completely silent for some time. I can just see him, probably tipped back in his office chair under the picture of Governor Reed hanging on the wall, his fingers steepled, his liver lips pursed, his brow wrinkled into ladder rungs halfway to the crown of his head, his thirty-year pin gleaming mellowly.

"Yes," he said finally. "That's the damnedest story I ever heard. But I'll tell you what surprises me most about it, Dufresne."

"What's that, sir?"

"That you were taken in by it."

"Sir? I don't understand what you mean." And Chester said that Andy Dufresne, who had faced down Byron Hadley on the plate-shop roof thirteen years before, was almost floundering for words.

"Wellnow," Norton said. "It's pretty obvious to me that this young fellow Williams is impressed with you. Quite taken with you, as a matter of fact. He hears your tale of woe, and it's quite natural of him to want to . . . cheer you up, let's say. Quite natural. He's a young man, not terribly bright. Not surprising he didn't realize what a state it would put you into. Now what I suggest is—"

"Don't you think I thought of that?" Andy asked. "But I'd never told Tommy about the man working down at the marina. I never told *anyone* that—it never even crossed my mind! But Tommy's description of his cellmate and that man . . . they're *identical!*"

"Wellnow, you may be indulging in a little selective perception there," Norton said with a chuckle. Phrases like that, selective perception, are required learning for people in the penology and corrections business, and they use them all they can.

"That's not it at all. Sir."

"That's your slant on it," Norton said, "but mine differs. And let's remember that I have only your word that there *was* such a man working at the Falmouth Hills Country Club back then."

"No, sir," Andy broke in again. "No, that isn't true. Because—"

"Anyway," Norton overrode him, expansive and loud, "let's just look at it from the other end of the telescope, shall we? Suppose—just suppose, now—that there really *was* a fellow named Elwood Blotch."

"Blatch," Andy said tightly.

"Blatch, by all means. And let's say he *was* Thomas Williams's cellmate in Rhode Island. The chances are excellent that he has been released by now. *Excellent.* Why, we don't even know how much time he might have done there before he ended up with Williams, do we? Only that he was doing a six-to-twelve."

"No. We don't know how much time he'd done. But Tommy said he was a bad actor, a cut-up. I think there's a fair chance that he may still be in. Even if he's been released, the prison will have a record of his last known address, the names of his relatives—"

"And both would almost certainly be dead ends."

Andy was silent for a moment, and then he burst out: "Well, it's a *chance*, isn't it?"

"Yes, of course it is. So just for a moment, Dufresne, let's assume that Blatch exists and that he is still safely ensconced in the Rhode Island State Penitentiary. Now what is he going to say if we bring this kettle of fish to him in a bucket? Is he going to fall down on his knees, roll his eyes, and say: 'I did it! I did it! By all means add a life term onto my charge!'?"

"How can you be so obtuse?" Andy said, so low that Chester could barely hear. But he heard the warden just fine.

"What? What did you call me?"

"*Obtuse!*" Andy cried. "Is it deliberate?"

"Dufresne, you've taken five minutes of my time—no, seven—and I have a very busy schedule today. So I believe we'll just declare this little meeting closed and—"

"The country club will have all the old time-cards, don't you realize that?" Andy shouted. "They'll have tax-forms and W-twos and unemployment compensation forms, all with his name on them! There will be employees there now that were there then, maybe Briggs himself! It's been fifteen years, not forever! They'll remember him! *They will remember Blatch!* If I've got Tommy to testify to what Blatch told him, and Briggs to testify that Blatch was there, actually *working* at the country club, I can get a new trial! I can—"

"Guard! *Guard!* Take this man away!"

"What's the *matter* with you?" Andy said, and Chester told me he was very nearly screaming by then. "It's my life, my chance to get out, don't you see that? And you won't make a single long-distance call to at least verify Tommy's story? Listen, I'll pay for the call! I'll pay for—"

Then there was a sound of thrashing as the guards grabbed him and started to drag him out.

"Solitary," Warden Norton said dryly. He was probably fingering his thirty-year pin as he said it. "Bread and water."

And so they dragged Andy away, totally out of control now, still screaming at the warden; Chester said you could hear him even after the door was shut: *"It's my life! It's my life, don't you understand it's my life?"*

Twenty days on the grain and drain train for Andy down there in solitary. It was his second jolt in solitary, and his dust-up with Norton was his first real black mark since he had joined our happy little family.

I'll tell you a little bit about Shawshank's solitary while we're on the subject. It's something of a throwback to those hardy pioneer days of the early to mid-1700s in Maine. In those days no one wasted much time with such things as "penology" and "rehabilitation" and "selective perception." In those days, you were taken care of in terms of absolute black and white. You were either guilty or innocent. If you were guilty, you were either hung or put in gaol. And if you were sentenced to gaol, you did not go to an institution. No, you dug your own gaol with a spade provided by the Province of Maine. You dug it as wide and as deep as you could during the period between sunup and sundown. Then they gave you a couple of skins and a bucket, and down you went. Once down, the gaoler would bar the top of your hole, throw down some grain or maybe a piece of maggoty meat once or twice a week, and maybe there would be a dipperful of barley soup on Sunday night. You pissed in the bucket, and you held up the same bucket for water when the gaoler came around at six in the morning. When it rained, you used the bucket to bail out your gaol-cell . . . unless, that is, you wanted to drown like a rat in a rainbarrel.

No one spent a long time "in the hole," as it was called; thirty months was an unusually long term, and so far as I've been able to tell, the longest term ever spent from which an inmate actually emerged alive was served by the so-called "Durham Boy," a fourteen-year-old psychopath who castrated a schoolmate with a piece of rusty metal. He did seven years, but of course he went in young and strong.

You have to remember that for a crime that was more serious than petty theft or blasphemy or forgetting to put a snotrag in your pocket when out of doors on the Sabbath, you were hung. For low crimes such as those just mentioned and for others like them, you'd do your three or six or nine months in the hole and come out fishbelly white, cringing from the wide-open spaces, your eyes half-blind, your teeth more than likely rocking and rolling in their sockets from the scurvy, your feet crawling with fungus. Jolly old Province of Maine. Yo-ho-ho and a bottle of rum.

Shawshank's Solitary Wing was nowhere as bad as that . . . I guess. Things come in three major degrees in the human experience, I think. There's good, bad, and terrible. And as you go down into progressive darkness toward terrible, it gets harder and harder to make subdivisions.

To get to Solitary Wing you were led down twenty-three steps to a basement level where the only sound was the drip of water. The only light was supplied by a series of dangling sixty-watt bulbs. The cells were keg-shaped, like those wall-safes rich people sometimes hide behind a picture. Like a safe, the round doorways were hinged, and solid instead of barred. You got ventilation from above, but no light except for your own sixty-watt bulb, which was turned off from a master-switch promptly at 8:00 P.M., an hour before lights-out in the rest of the prison. The lightbulb wasn't in a wire

mesh cage or anything like that. The feeling was that if you wanted
to exist down there in the dark, you were welcome to it. Not many
did . . . but after eight, of course, you had no choice. You had a
bunk bolted to the wall and a can with no toilet seat. You had three
ways to spend your time: sitting, shitting, or sleeping. Big choice.
Twenty days could get to seem like a year. Thirty days could seem
like two, and forty days like ten. Sometimes you could hear rats in
the ventilation system. In a situation like that, subdivisions of
terrible tend to get lost.

If anything at all can be said in favor of solitary, it's just that you
get time to think. Andy had twenty days in which to think while he
enjoyed his grain and drain, and when he got out he requested
another meeting with the warden. Request denied. Such a meeting,
the warden told him, would be "counter-productive." That's
another of those phrases you have to master before you can go to
work in the prisons and corrections field.

Patiently, Andy renewed his request. And renewed it. And
renewed it. He had changed, had Andy Dufresne. Suddenly, as that
spring of 1963 bloomed around us, there were lines in his face and
sprigs of gray showing in his hair. He had lost that little trace of a
smile that always seemed to linger around his mouth. His eyes
stared out into space more often, and you get to know that when a
man stares that way, he is counting up the years served, the
months, the weeks, the days.

He renewed his request and renewed it. He was patient. He had
nothing but time. It got to be summer. In Washington, President
Kennedy was promising a fresh assault on poverty and on civil
rights inequalities, not knowing he had only half a year to live. In
Liverpool, a musical group called The Beatles was emerging as a
force to be reckoned with in British music, but I guess that no one
Stateside had yet heard of them. The Boston Red Sox, still four
years away from what New England folks call The Miracle of '67,
were languishing in the cellar of the American League. All of those
things were going on out in a larger world where people walked
free.

Norton saw him near the end of June, and this conversation I
heard about from Andy himself some seven years later.

"If it's the squeeze, you don't have to worry," Andy told Norton in a low voice. "Do you think I'd talk that up? I'd be cutting my own throat. I'd be just as indictable as—"

"That's enough," Norton interrupted. His face was as long and cold as a slate gravestone. He leaned back in his office chair until the back of his head almost touched the sampler reading HIS JUDGMENT COMETH AND THAT RIGHT EARLY.

"But—"

"Don't you ever mention money to me again," Norton said. "Not in this office, not anywhere. Not unless you want to see that library turned back into a storage room and paint-locker again. Do you understand?"

"I was trying to set your mind at ease, that's all."

"Wellnow, when I need a sorry son of a bitch like you to set my mind at ease, I'll retire. I agreed to this appointment because I got tired of being pestered, Dufresne. I want it to stop. If you want to buy this particular Brooklyn Bridge, that's your affair. Don't make it mine. I could hear crazy stories like yours twice a week if I wanted to lay myself open to them. Every sinner in this place would be using me for a crying towel. I had more respect for you. But this is the end. The end. Have we got an understanding?"

"Yes," Andy said. "But I'll be hiring a lawyer, you know."

"What in God's name for?"

"I think we can put it together," Andy said. "With Tommy Williams and with my testimony and corroborative testimony from records and employees at the country club, I think we can put it together."

"Tommy Williams is no longer an inmate of this facility."

"*What?*"

"He's been transferred."

"Transferred *where?*"

"Cashman."

At that, Andy fell silent. He was an intelligent man, but it would have taken an extraordinarily stupid man not to smell *deal* all over that. Cashman was a minimum-security prison far up north in Aroostook County. The inmates pick a lot of potatoes, and that's hard work, but they are paid a decent wage for their labor and they can attend classes at CVI, a pretty decent vocational-technical institute, if they so desire. More important to a fellow like Tommy, a fellow with a young wife and a child, Cashman had a furlough program . . . which meant a chance to live like a normal man, at least on the weekends. A chance to build a model plane with his kid, have sex with his wife, maybe go on a picnic.

Norton had almost surely dangled all of that under Tommy's nose with only one string attached: not one more word about Elwood Blatch, not now, not ever. Or you'll end up doing hard time in Thomaston down there on scenic Route 1 with the real hard guys, and instead of having sex with your wife you'll be having it with some old bull queer.

"But why?" Andy said. "Why would—"

"As a favor to you," Norton said calmly, "I checked with Rhode Island. They did have an inmate named Elwood Blatch. He was given what they call a PP—provisional parole, another one of these crazy liberal programs to put criminals out on the streets. He's since disappeared."

Andy said: "The warden down there . . . is he a friend of yours?"

Sam Norton gave Andy a smile as cold as a deacon's watchchain. "We are acquainted," he said.

"*Why?*" Andy repeated. "Can't you tell me why you did it? You knew I wasn't going to talk about . . . about anything you might have had going. You *knew* that. So *why?*"

"Because people like you make me sick," Norton said deliberately. "I like you right where you are, Mr. Dufresne, and as long as I am warden here at Shawshank, you are going to be right here. You see, you used to think that you were better than anyone else. I have gotten pretty good at seeing that on a man's face. I marked it on yours the first time I walked into the library. It might as well have been written on your forehead in capital letters. That look is gone now, and I like that just fine. It is not just that you are a useful vessel, never think that. It is simply that men like you need to learn humility. Why, you used to walk around that exercise yard as if it was a living room and you were at one of those cocktail parties where the hellbound walk around coveting each others' wives and husbands and getting swinishly drunk. But you don't walk around that way anymore. And I'll be watching to see if you should start to walk that way again. Over a period of years, I'll be watching you with great pleasure. Now get the hell out of here."

"Okay. But all the extracurricular activities stop now, Norton. The investment counseling, the scams, the free tax advice. It all stops. Get H and R Block to tell you how to declare your income."

Warden Norton's face first went brick-red . . . and then all the color fell out of it. "You're going back into solitary for that. Thirty days. Bread and water. Another black mark. And while you're in, think about this: if *anything* that's been going on should stop, the library goes. I will make it my personal business to see that it goes back to what it was before you came here. And I will make your life . . . very hard. Very difficult. You'll do the hardest time it's possible to do. You'll lose that one-bunk Hilton down in Cellblock Five, for starters, and you'll lose those rocks on the windowsill, and you'll lose any protection the guards have given you against the sodomites. You will . . . lose everything. Clear?"

I guess it was clear enough.

Time continued to pass—the oldest trick in the world, and maybe the only one that really is magic. But Andy Dufresne had changed. He had grown harder. That's the only way I can think of to put it. He went on doing Warden Norton's dirty work and he held onto the library, so outwardly things were about the same. He continued to have his birthday drinks and his year-end holiday drinks; he continued to share out the rest of each bottle. I got him fresh rock-polishing cloths from time to time, and in 1967 I got him a new rock-hammer—the one I'd gotten him nineteen years ago had, as I told you, plumb worn out. *Nineteen years!* When you say it sudden like that, those three syllables sound like the thud and double-locking of a tomb door. The rock-hammer, which had been a ten-dollar item back then, went for twenty-two by '67. He and I had a sad little grin over that.

Andy continued to shape and polish the rocks he found in the exercise yard, but the yard was smaller by then; half of what had been there in 1950 had been asphalted over in 1962. Nonetheless, he found enough to keep him occupied, I guess. When he had finished with each rock he would put it carefully on his window ledge, which faced east. He told me he liked to look at them in the sun, the pieces of the planet he had taken up from the dirt and shaped. Schists, quartzes, granites. Funny little mica-sculptures that were held together with airplane glue. Various sedimentary conglomerates that were polished and cut in such a way that you could see why Andy called them "millennium sandwiches"—the layers of different material that had built up over a period of decades and centuries.

Andy would give his stones and his rock-sculptures away from time to time in order to make room for new ones. He gave me the greatest number, I think—counting the stones that looked like matched cufflinks, I had five. There was one of the mica-sculptures I told you about, carefully crafted to look like a man throwing a javelin, and two of the sedimentary conglomerates, all the levels showing in smoothly polished cross-section. I've still got them, and I take them down every so often and think about what a man can do, if he has time enough and the will to use it, a drop at a time.

So, on the outside, at least, things were about the same. If Norton had wanted to break Andy as badly as he had said, he would have had to look below the surface to see the change. But if he *had* seen how different Andy had become, I think Norton would have been well-satisfied with the four years following his clash with Andy.

He had told Andy that Andy walked around the exercise yard as if he were at a cocktail party. That isn't the way I would have put it, but I know what he meant. It goes back to what I said about Andy wearing his freedom like an invisible coat, about how he never really developed a prison mentality. His eyes never got that dull look. He never developed the walk that men get when the day is over and they are going back to their cells for another endless night—that flat-footed, hump-shouldered walk. Andy walked with his shoulders squared, and his step was always light, as if he were heading home to a good home-cooked meal and a good woman instead of to a tasteless mess of soggy vegetables, lumpy mashed potato, and a slice or two of that fatty, gristly stuff most of the cons called mystery meat . . . that, and a picture of Raquel Welch on the wall.

But for those four years, although he never became *exactly* like the others, he did become silent, introspective, and brooding. Who could blame him? So maybe it was Warden Norton who was pleased . . . at least, for awhile.

His dark mood broke around the time of the 1967 World Series. That was the dream year, the year the Red Sox won the pennant instead of placing ninth, as the Las Vegas bookies had predicted. When it happened—when they won the American League pennant —a kind of ebullience engulfed the whole prison. There was a goofy sort of feeling that if the Dead Sox could come to life, then maybe *anybody* could do it. I can't explain that feeling now, any more than an ex-Beatlemaniac could explain *that* madness, I suppose. But it was real. Every radio in the place was tuned to the games as the Red Sox pounded down the stretch. There was gloom when the Sox dropped a pair in Cleveland near the end, and a nearly riotous joy when Rico Petrocelli put away the pop fly that clinched it. And then there was the gloom that came when Lonborg was beaten in the seventh game of the Series to end the dream just sort of complete fruition. It probably pleased Norton to no end, the son of a bitch. He liked his prison wearing sackcloth and ashes.

But for Andy, there was no tumble back down into gloom. He wasn't much of a baseball fan anyway, and maybe that was why. Nevertheless, he seemed to have caught the current of good feeling, and for him it didn't peter out again after the last game of the Series. He had taken that invisible coat out of the closet and put it on again.

I remember one bright-gold fall day in very late October, a couple of weeks after the World Series had ended. It must have been a Sunday, because the exercise yard was full of men "walking off the week"—tossing a Frisbee or two, passing around a football, bartering what they had to barter. Others would be at the long table in the Visitors' Hall, under the watchful eyes of the screws, talking with their relatives, smoking cigarettes, telling sincere lies, receiving their picked-over care-packages.

Andy was squatting Indian fashion against the wall, chunking two small rocks together in his hands, his face turned up into the sunlight. It was surprisingly warm, that sun, for a day so late in the year.

"Hello, Red," he called. "Come on and sit a spell."

I did.

"You want this?" he asked, and handed me one of the two carefully polished "millennium sandwiches" I just told you about.

"I sure do," I said. "It's very pretty. Thank you."

He shrugged and changed the subject. "Big anniversary coming up for you next year."

I nodded. Next year would make me a thirty-year man. Sixty per cent of my life spent in Shawshank State Prison.

"Think you'll ever get out?"

"Sure. When I have a long white beard and just about three marbles left rolling around upstairs."

He smiled a little and then turned his face up into the sun again, his eyes closed. "Feels good."

"I think it always does when you know the damn winter's almost right on top of you."

He nodded, and we were silent for awhile.

"When I get out of here," Andy said finally, "I'm going where it's warm all the time." He spoke with such calm assurance you would have thought he had only a month or so left to serve. "You know where I'm goin, Red?"

"Nope."

"Zihuatanejo," he said, rolling the word softly from his tongue like music. "Down in Mexico. It's a little place maybe twenty miles from Playa Azul and Mexico Highway Thirty-seven. It's a hundred miles northwest of Acapulco on the Pacific Ocean. You know what the Mexicans say about the Pacific?"

I told him I didn't.

"They say it has no memory. And that's where I want to finish out my life, Red. In a warm place that has no memory."

He had picked up a handful of pebbles as he spoke; now he tossed them, one by one, and watched them bounce and roll across the baseball diamond's dirt infield, which would be under a foot of snow before long.

"Zihuatanejo. I'm going to have a little hotel down there. Six cabanas along the beach, and six more set further back, for the highway trade. I'll have a guy who'll take my guests out charter-fishing. There'll be a trophy for the guy who catches the biggest marlin of the season, and I'll put his picture up in the lobby. It won't be a family place. It'll be a place for people on their honeymoons . . . first or second varieties."

"And where are you going to get the money to buy this fabulous place?" I asked. "Your stock account?"

He looked at me and smiled. "That's not so far wrong," he said. "Sometimes you startle me, Red."

"What are you talking about?"

"There are really only two types of men in the world when it comes to bad trouble," Andy said, cupping a match between his hands and lighting a cigarette. "Suppose there was a house full of rare paintings and sculptures and fine old antiques, Red? And suppose the guy who owned the house heard that there was a monster of a hurricane headed right at it? One of those two kinds of men just hopes for the best. The hurricane will change course, he says to himself. No right-thinking hurricane would ever dare wipe out all these Rembrandts, my two Degas horses, my Grant Woods, and my Bentons. Furthermore, God wouldn't allow it. And if worse comes to worst, they're insured. That's one sort of man. The other sort just assumes that hurricane is going to tear right through the middle of his house. If the weather bureau says the hurricane just changed course, this guy assumes it'll change back in order to put his house on ground-zero again. This second type of guy knows there's no harm in hoping for the best as long as you're prepared for the worst."

I lit a cigarette of my own. "Are you saying you prepared for the eventuality?"

"Yes. I prepared for the *hurricane*. I knew how bad it looked. I didn't have much time, but in the time I had, I operated. I had a friend—just about the only person who stood by me—who worked for an investment company in Portland. He died about six years ago."

"Sorry."

"Yeah." Andy tossed his butt away. "Linda and I had about

fourteen thousand dollars. Not a big bundle, but hell, we were young. We had our whole lives ahead of us." He grimaced a little, then laughed. "When the shit hit the fan, I started lugging my Rembrandts out of the path of the hurricane. I sold my stocks and paid the capital gains tax just like a good little boy. Declared everything. Didn't cut any corners."

"Didn't they freeze your estate?"

"I was charged with murder, Red, not dead! You can't freeze the assets of an innocent man—thank God. And it was awhile before they even got brave enough to charge me with the crime. Jim—my friend—and I, we had some time. I got hit pretty good, just dumping everything like that. Got my nose skinned. But at the time I had worse things to worry about than a small skinning on the stock market."

"Yeah, I'd say you did."

"But when I came to Shawshank it was all safe. It's still safe. Outside these walls, Red, there's a man that no living soul has ever seen face to face. He has a Social Security card and a Maine driver's license. He's got a birth certificate. Name of Peter Stevens. Nice, anonymous name, huh?"

"Who is he?" I asked. I thought I knew what he was going to say, but I couldn't believe it.

"Me."

"You're not going to tell me that you had time to set up a false identity while the bulls were sweating you," I said, "or that you finished the job while you were on trial for—"

"No, I'm not going to tell you that. My friend Jim was the one who set up the false identity. He started after my appeal was turned down, and the major pieces of identification were in his hands by the spring of 1950."

"He must have been a pretty close friend," I said. I was not sure how much of this I believed—a little, a lot, or none. But the day was warm and the sun was out, and it was one hell of a good story. "All of that's one hundred per cent illegal, setting up a false ID like that."

"He was a close friend," Andy said. "We were in the war together. France, Germany, the occupation. He was a good friend.

He knew it was illegal, but he also knew that setting up a false identity in this country is very easy and very safe. He took my money—my money with all the taxes on it paid so the IRS wouldn't get too interested—and invested it for Peter Stevens. He did that in 1950 and 1951. Today it amounts to three hundred and seventy thousand dollars, plus change."

I guess my jaw made a thump when it dropped against my chest, because he smiled.

"Think of all the things people wish they'd invested in since 1950 or so, and two or three of them will be things Peter Stevens was into. If I hadn't ended up in here, I'd probably be worth seven or eight million bucks by now. I'd have a Rolls . . . and probably an ulcer as big as a portable radio."

His hands went to the dirt and began sifting out more pebbles. They moved gracefully, restlessly.

"It was hoping for the best and expecting the worst—nothing but that. The false name was just to keep what little capital I had untainted. It was lugging the paintings out of the path of the hurricane. But I had no idea that the hurricane . . . that it could go on as long as it has."

I didn't say anything for awhile. I guess I was trying to absorb the idea that this small, spare man in prison gray next to me could be worth more money than Warden Norton would make in the rest of his miserable life, even with the scams thrown in.

"When you said you could get a lawyer, you sure weren't kidding," I said at last. "For that kind of dough you could have hired Clarence Darrow, or whoever's passing for him these days. Why didn't you, Andy? Christ! You could have been out of here like a rocket."

He smiled. It was the same smile that had been on his face when he'd told me he and his wife had had their whole lives ahead of them. "No," he said.

"A good lawyer would have sprung the Williams kid from Cashman whether he wanted to go or not," I said. I was getting carried away now. "You could have gotten your new trial, hired private detectives to look for that guy Blatch, and blown Norton out of the water to boot. Why not, Andy?"

"Because I outsmarted myself. If I ever try to put my hands on Peter Stevens's money from inside here, I'll lose every cent of it. My friend Jim could have arranged it, but Jim's dead. You see the problem?"

I saw it. For all the good that money could do Andy, it might as well have really belonged to another person. In a way, it did. And if the stuff it was invested in suddenly turned bad, all Andy could do would be to watch the plunge, to trace it day after day on the stocks-and-bonds page of the *Press-Herald*. It's a tough life if you don't weaken, I guess.

"I'll tell you how it is, Red. There's a big hayfield in the town of Buxton. You know where Buxton is at, don't you?"

I said I did. It lies right next door to Scarborough.

"That's right. And at the north end of this particular hayfield there's a rock wall, right out of a Robert Frost poem. And somewhere along the base of that wall is a rock that has no business in a Maine hayfield. It's a piece of volcanic glass, and until 1947 it was a paperweight on my office desk. My friend Jim put it in that wall. There's a key underneath it. The key opens a safe deposit box in the Portland branch of the Casco Bank."

"I guess you're in a peck of trouble," I said. "When your friend Jim died, the IRS must have opened all of his safe deposit boxes. Along with the executor of his will, of course."

Andy smiled and tapped the side of my head. "Not bad. There's more up there than marshmallows, I guess. But we took care of the possibility that Jim might die while I was in the slam. The box is in the Peter Stevens name, and once a year the firm of lawyers that served as Jim's executors sends a check to the Casco to cover the rental of the Stevens box.

"Peter Stevens is inside that box, just waiting to get out. His birth certificate, his Social Security card, and his driver's license. The license is six years out of date because Jim died six years ago, true, but it's still perfectly renewable for a five-dollar fee. His stock certificates are there, the tax-free municipals, and about eighteen bearer bonds in the amount of ten thousand dollars each."

I whistled.

"Peter Stevens is locked in a safe deposit box at the Casco Bank in Portland and Andy Dufresne is locked in a safe deposit box at

Shawshank," he said. "Tit for tat. And the key that unlocks the box and the money and the new life is under a hunk of black glass in a Buxton hayfield. Told you this much, so I'll tell you something else, Red—for the last twenty years, give or take, I have been watching the papers with a more than usual interest for news of any construction projects in Buxton. I keep thinking that someday soon I'm going to read that they're putting a highway through there, or erecting a new community hospital, or building a shopping center. Burying my new life under ten feet of concrete, or spitting it into a swamp somewhere with a big load of fill."

I blurted, "Jesus Christ, Andy, if all of this is true, how do you keep from going crazy?"

He smiled. "So far, all quiet on the Western front."

"But it could be years—"

"It will be. But maybe not as many as the State and Warden Norton think it's going to be. I just can't afford to wait that long. I keep thinking about Zihuatanejo and that small hotel. That's all I want from my life now, Red, and I don't think that's too much to want. I didn't kill Glenn Quentin and I didn't kill my wife, and that hotel . . . it's not too much to want. To swim and get a tan and sleep in a room with open windows and *space* . . . that's not too much to want."

He slung the stones away.

"You know, Red," he said in an offhand voice, "A place like that . . . I'd have to have a man who knows how to get things."

I thought about it for a long time. And the biggest drawback in my mind wasn't even that we were talking pipedreams in a shitty little prison exercise yard with armed guards looking down at us from their sentry posts. "I couldn't do it," I said. "I couldn't get along on the outside. I'm what they call an institutional man now. In here I'm the man who can get it for you, yeah. But out there, anyone can get it for you. Out there, if you want posters or rock-hammers or one particular record or a boat-in-a-bottle model kit, you can use the fucking Yellow Pages. In here, *I'm* the fucking Yellow Pages. I wouldn't know how to begin. Or where."

"You underestimate yourself," he said. "You're a self-educated man, a self-made man. A rather remarkable man, I think."

"Hell, I don't even have a high school diploma."

"I know that," he said. "But it isn't just a piece of paper that makes a man. And it isn't just prison that breaks one, either."

"I couldn't hack it outside, Andy. I know that."

He got up. "You think it over," he said casually, just as the inside whistle blew. And he strolled off, as if he were a free man who had just made another free man a proposition. And for awhile just that was enough to make me *feel* free. Andy could do that. He could make me forget for a time that we were both lifers, at the mercy of a hard-ass parole board and a psalm-singing warden who liked Andy Dufresne right where he was. After all, Andy was a lap-dog who could do tax-returns. What a wonderful animal!

But by that night in my cell I felt like a prisoner again. The whole idea seemed absurd, and that mental image of blue water and white beaches seemed more cruel than foolish—it dragged at my brain like a fishhook. I just couldn't wear that invisible coat the way Andy did. I fell asleep that night and dreamed of a great glassy black stone in the middle of a hayfield; a stone shaped like a giant blacksmith's anvil. I was trying to rock the stone up so I could get the key that was underneath. It wouldn't budge; it was just too damned big.

And in the background, but getting closer, I could hear the baying of bloodhounds.

Which leads us, I guess, to the subject of jailbreaks.

Sure, they happen from time to time in our happy little family. You don't go over the wall, though, not at Shawshank, not if you're smart. The searchlight beams go all night, probing long white fingers across the open fields that surround the prison on three sides and the stinking marshland on the fourth. Cons do go over the wall from time to time, and the searchlights almost always catch them. If not, they get picked up trying to thumb a ride on Highway 6 or Highway 99. If they try to cut across country, some farmer sees them and just phones the location in to the prison. Cons who go over the wall are stupid cons. Shawshank is no Canon City, but in a rural area a man humping his ass across country in a gray pajama suit sticks out like a cockroach on a wedding cake.

Over the years, the guys who have done the best—maybe oddly, maybe not so oddly—are the guys who did it on the spur of the moment. Some of them have gone out in the middle of a cartful of sheets; a convict sandwich on white, you could say. There was a lot of that when I first came in here, but over the years they have more or less closed that loophole.

Warden Norton's famous "Inside-Out" program produced its share of escapees, too. They were the guys who decided they liked what lay to the right of the hyphen better than what lay to the left. And again, in most cases it was a very casual kind of thing. Drop your blueberry rake and stroll into the bushes while one of the screws is having a glass of water at the truck or when a couple of them get too involved in arguing over yards passing or rushing on the old Boston Patriots.

In 1969, the Inside-Outers were picking potatoes in Sabbatus. It was the third of November and the work was almost done. There was a guard named Henry Pugh—and he is no longer a member of our happy little family, believe me—sitting on the back bumper of one of the potato trucks and having his lunch with his carbine across his knees when a beautiful (or so it was told to me, but sometimes these things get exaggerated) ten-point buck strolled out of the cold early afternoon mist. Pugh went after it with visions of just how that trophy would look mounted in his rec room, and while he was doing it, three of his charges just walked away. Two were recaptured in a Lisbon Falls pinball parlor. The third has not been found to this day.

I suppose the most famous case of all was that of Sid Nedeau. This goes back to 1958, and I guess it will never be topped. Sid was out lining the ballfield for a Saturday intramural baseball game when the three o'clock inside whistle blew, signalling the shift-change for the guards. The parking lot is just beyond the exercise yard, on the other side of the electrically operated main gate. At three the gate opens and the guards coming on duty and those going off mingle. There's a lot of back-slapping and bullyragging, comparison of league bowling scores and the usual number of tired old ethnic jokes.

Sid just trundled his lining machine right out through the gate, leaving a three-inch baseline all the way from home plate in the exercise yard to the ditch on the far side of Route 6, where they found the machine overturned in a pile of lime. Don't ask me how he did it. He was dressed in his prison uniform, he stood six-feet-two, and he was billowing clouds of lime-dust behind him. All I can figure is that, it being Friday afternoon and all, the guards going off were so happy to be going off, and the guards coming on were so downhearted to be coming on, that the members of the former group never got their heads out of the clouds and those in the latter never got their noses off their shoetops . . . and old Sid Nedeau just sort of slipped out between the two.

So far as I know, Sid is still at large. Over the years, Andy Dufresne and I had a good many laughs over Sid Nedeau's great escape, and when we heard about that airline hijacking for ransom, the one where the guy parachuted from the back door of the airplane, Andy swore up and down that D. B. Cooper's real name was Sid Nedeau.

"And he probably had a pocketful of baseline lime in his pocket for good luck," Andy said. "That lucky son of a bitch."

But you should understand that a case like Sid Nedeau, or the fellow who got away clean from the Sabbatus potato-field crew, guys like that are winning the prison version of the Irish Sweepstakes. Purely a case of six different kinds of luck somehow jelling together all at the same moment. A stiff like Andy could wait ninety years and not get a similar break.

Maybe you remember, a ways back, I mentioned a guy named Henley Backus, the washroom foreman in the laundry. He came to Shawshank in 1922 and died in the prison infirmary thirty-one years later. Escapes and escape attempts were a hobby of his, maybe because he never quite dared to take the plunge himself. He could tell you a hundred different schemes, all of them crackpot, and all of them had been tried in The Shank at one time or another. My favorite was the tale of Beaver Morrison, a b&e convict who tried to build a glider from scratch in the plate-factory basement. The plans he was working from were in a circa-1900 book called *The Modern Boy's Guide to Fun and Adventure*. Beaver got it built without being discovered, or so the story goes, only to discover there was no door from the basement big enough to get the damned thing out. When

Henley told that story, you could bust a gut laughing, and he knew a dozen—no, two dozen—almost as funny.

When it came to detailing Shawshank bust-outs, Henley had it down chapter and verse. He told me once that during his time there had been better than four hundred escape attempts *that he knew of.* Really think about that for a moment before you just nod your head and read on. Four *hundred* escape attempts! That comes out to 12.9 escape attempts for every year Henley Backus was in Shawshank and keeping track of them. The Escape-Attempt-of-the-Month Club. Of course most of them were pretty slipshod affairs, the sort of thing that ends up with a guard grabbing some poor, sidling slob's arm and growling, "Where do you think *you're* going, you happy asshole?"

Henley said he'd class maybe sixty of them as more serious attempts, and he included the "prison break" of 1937, the year before I arrived at The Shank. The new Administration Wing was under construction then and fourteen cons got out, using construction equipment in a poorly locked shed. The whole of southern Maine got into a panic over those fourteen "hardened criminals," most of whom were scared to death and had no more idea of where they should go than a jackrabbit does when it's headlight-pinned to the highway with a big truck bearing down on it. Not one of those fourteen got away. Two of them were shot dead—by civilians, not police officers or prison personnel—but none got away.

How many *had* gotten away between 1938, when I came here, and that day in October when Andy first mentioned Zihuatanejo to me? Putting my information and Henley's together, I'd say ten. Ten that got away clean. And although it isn't the kind of thing you can know for sure, I'd guess that at least half of those ten are doing time in other institutions of lower learning like The Shank. Because you *do* get institutionalized. When you take away a man's freedom and teach him to live in a cell, he seems to lose his ability to think in dimensions. He's like that jackrabbit I mentioned, frozen in the oncoming lights of the truck that is bound to kill it. More often than not a con who's just out will pull some dumb job that hasn't a chance in hell of succeeding . . . and why? Because it'll get him back inside. Back where he understands how things work.

Andy wasn't that way, but I was. The idea of seeing the Pacific *sounded* good, but I was afraid that actually being there would scare me to death—the bigness of it.

Anyhow, the day of that conversation about Mexico, and about Mr. Peter Stevens . . . that was the day I began to believe that Andy had some idea of doing a disappearing act. I hoped to God he would be careful if he did, and still, I wouldn't have bet money on his chances of succeeding. Warden Norton, you see, was watching Andy with a special close eye. Andy wasn't just another deadhead with a number to Norton; they had a working relationship, you might say. Also, Andy had brains and he had heart. Norton was determined to use the one and crush the other.

As there are honest politicians on the outside—ones who stay bought—there are honest prison guards, and if you are a good judge of character and if you have some loot to spread around, I suppose it's possible that you could buy enough look-the-other-way to make a break. I'm not the man to tell you such a thing has never been done, but Andy Dufresne wasn't the man who could do it. Because, as I've said, Norton was watching. Andy knew it, and the screws knew it, too.

Nobody was going to nominate Andy for the Inside-Out program, not as long as Warden Norton was evaluating the nominations. And Andy was not the kind of man to try a casual Sid Nedeau type of escape.

If I had been him, the thought of that key would have tormented me endlessly. I would have been lucky to get two hours' worth of honest shut-eye a night. Buxton was less than thirty miles from Shawshank. So near and yet so far.

I still thought his best chance was to engage a lawyer and try for the retrial. Anything to get out from under Norton's thumb. Maybe Tommy Williams could be shut up by nothing more than a cushy furlough program, but I wasn't entirely sure. Maybe a good old Mississippi hard-ass lawyer could crack him . . . and maybe that lawyer wouldn't even have to work that hard. Williams had honestly liked Andy. Every now and then I'd bring these points up to Andy, who would only smile, his eyes far away, and say he was thinking about it.

Apparently he'd been thinking about a lot of other things, as well.

*   *   *

In 1975, Andy Dufresne escaped from Shawshank. He hasn't been recaptured, and I don't think he ever will be. In fact, I don't think Andy Dufresne even exists anymore. But I think there's a man down in Zihuatanejo, Mexico, named Peter Stevens. Probably running a very new small hotel in this year of our Lord 1976.

I'll tell you what I know and what I think; that's about all I can do, isn't it?

On March 12th, 1975, the cell doors in Cellblock 5 opened at 6:30 A.M., as they do every morning around here except Sunday. And as they do every day except Sunday, the inmates of those cells stepped forward into the corridor and formed two lines as the cell doors slammed shut behind them. They walked up to the main cellblock gate, where they were counted off by two guards before being sent on down to the cafeteria for a breakfast of oatmeal, scrambled eggs, and fatty bacon.

All of this went according to routine until the count at the cellblock gate. There should have been twenty-seven. Instead, there were twenty-six. After a call to the Captain of the Guards, Cellblock 5 was allowed to go to breakfast.

The Captain of the Guards, a not half-bad fellow named Richard Gonyar, and his assistant, a jolly prick named Dave Burkes, came down to Cellblock 5 right away. Gonyar re-opened the cell doors and he and Burkes went down the corridor together, dragging their sticks over the bars, their guns out. In a case like that what you usually have is someone who has been taken sick in the night, so sick he can't even step out of his cell in the morning. More rarely, someone has died . . . or committed suicide.

But this time, they found a mystery instead of a sick man or a dead man. They found no man at all. There were fourteen cells in Cellblock 5, seven to a side, all fairly neat—restriction of visiting privileges is the penalty for a sloppy cell at Shawshank—and all very empty.

Gonyar's first assumption was that there had been a miscount or a practical joke. So instead of going off to work after breakfast, the inmates of Cellblock 5 were sent back to their cells, joking and happy. Any break in the routine was always welcome.

Cell doors opened; prisoners stepped in; cell doors closed. Some clown shouting, "I want my lawyer, I want my lawyer, you guys run this place just like a frigging prison."

Burkes: "Shut up in there, or I'll rank you."

The clown: "I ranked your wife, Burkie."

Gonyar: "Shut up, all of you, or you'll spend the day in there."

He and Burkes went up the line again, counting noses. They didn't have to go far.

"Who belongs in this cell?" Gonyar asked the rightside night guard.

"Andrew Dufresne," the rightside answered, and that was all it took. Everything stopped being routine right then. The balloon went up.

In all the prison movies I've seen, this wailing horn goes off when there's been a break. That never happens at Shawshank. The first thing Gonyar did was to get in touch with the warden. The second thing was to get a search of the prison going. The third was to alert the state police in Scarborough to the possibility of a breakout.

That was the routine. It didn't call for them to search the suspected escapee's cell, and so no one did. Not then. Why would they? It was a case of what you see is what you get. It was a small square room, bars on the window and bars on the sliding door. There was a toilet and an empty cot. Some pretty rocks on the windowsill.

And the poster, of course. It was Linda Ronstadt by then. The poster was right over his bunk. There had been a poster there, in that exact same place, for twenty-six years. And when someone—it was Warden Norton himself, as it turned out, poetic justice if there ever was any—looked behind it, they got one hell of a shock.

But that didn't happen until six-thirty that night, almost twelve hours after Andy had been reported missing, probably twenty hours after he had actually made his escape.

Norton hit the roof.

I have it on good authority—Chester, the trusty, who was waxing the hall floor in the Admin Wing that day. He didn't have to polish any keyplates with his ear that day; he said you could hear the warden clear down to Records & Files as he chewed on Rich Gonyar's ass.

"What do you mean, you're 'satisfied he's not on the prison grounds'? What does that mean? It means you didn't find him! You better find him! You better! Because I want him! Do you hear me? I want him!"

Gonyar said something.

"Didn't happen on your shift? That's what *you* say. So far as *I* can tell, no one knows *when* it happened. Or how. Or if it really did. Now, I want him in my office by three o'clock this afternoon, or some heads are going to roll. I can promise you that, and I *always* keep my promises."

Something else from Gonyar, something that seemed to provoke Norton to even greater rage.

"No? Then look at this! *Look at this!* You recognize it? Last night's tally for Cellblock Five. Every prisoner accounted for! Dufresne was locked up last night at nine and it is impossible for him to be gone now! *It is impossible! Now you find him!*"

But at three that afternoon Andy was still among the missing. Norton himself stormed down to Cellblock 5 a few hours later, where the rest of us had been locked up all of that day. Had we been questioned? We had spent most of that long day being questioned by harried screws who were feeling the breath of the dragon on the backs of their necks. We all said the same thing: we had seen nothing, heard nothing. And so far as I know, we were all telling the truth. I know that I was. All we could say was that Andy had indeed been in his cell at the time of the lock-in, and at lights-out an hour later.

One wit suggested that Andy had poured himself out through the keyhole. The suggestion earned the guy four days in solitary. They were uptight.

So Norton came down—stalked down—glaring at us with blue eyes nearly hot enough to strike sparks from the tempered steel bars of our cages. He looked at us as if he believed we were all in on it. Probably he did believe it.

He went into Andy's cell and looked around. It was just as Andy had left it, the sheets on his bunk turned back but without looking slept-in. Rocks on the windowsill . . . but not all of them. The ones he liked best he took with him.

"Rocks," Norton hissed, and swept them off the window ledge with a clatter. Gonyar, who was now on overtime, winced but said nothing.

Norton's eyes fell on the Linda Ronstadt poster. Linda was looking back over her shoulder, her hands tucked into the back pockets of a very tight pair of fawn-colored slacks. She was wearing a halter and she had a deep California tan. It must have offended the hell out of Norton's Baptist sensibilities, that poster. Watching him glare at it, I remembered what Andy had once said about feeling he could almost step through the picture and be with the girl.

In a very real way, that was exactly what he did—as Norton was only seconds from discovering.

"Wretched thing!" he grunted, and ripped the poster from the wall with a single swipe of his hand.

And revealed the gaping, crumbled hole in the concrete behind it.

Gonyar wouldn't go in.

Norton ordered him—God, they must have heard Norton ordering Rich Gonyar to go in there all over the prison—and Gonyar just refused him, point blank.

"I'll have your job for this!" Norton screamed. He was as hysterical as a woman having a hot-flash. He had utterly blown his cool. His neck had turned a rich, dark red, and two veins stood out, throbbing, on his forehead. "You can count on it, you . . . you Frenchman! I'll have your job and I'll see to it that you never get another one in any prison system in New England!"

Gonyar silently held out his service pistol to Norton, butt first. He'd had enough. He was then two hours overtime, going on three, and he'd just had enough. It was as if Andy's defection from our happy little family had driven Norton right over the edge of some private irrationality that had been there for a long time . . . certainly he was crazy that night.

I don't know what that private irrationality might have been, of course. But I do know that there were twenty-six cons listening to Norton's little dust-up with Rich Gonyar that evening as the last of the light faded from a dull late-winter sky, all of us hard-timers and long-line riders who had seen the administrators come and go, the hard-asses and the candy-asses alike, and we all knew that Warden Samuel Norton had just passed what the engineers like to call "the breaking strain."

And by God, it almost seemed to me that somewhere I could hear Andy Dufresne laughing.

Norton finally got a skinny drink of water on the night shift to go into the hole that had been behind Andy's poster of Linda Ronstadt. The skinny guard's name was Rory Tremont, and he was not exactly a ball of fire in the brains department. Maybe he thought he was going to win a Bronze Star or something. As it turned out, it was fortunate that Norton got someone of Andy's approximate height and build to go in there; if they had sent a big-assed fellow—as most prison guards seem to be—the guy would have stuck in there as sure as God made green grass . . . and he might be there still.

Tremont went in with a nylon filament rope, which someone had found in the trunk of his car, tied around his waist and a big six-battery flashlight in one hand. By then Gonyar, who had changed his mind about quitting and who seemed to be the only one there still able to think clearly, had dug out a set of blueprints. I knew well enough what they showed him—a wall which looked, in cross-section, like a sandwich. The entire wall was ten feet thick. The inner and outer sections were each about four feet thick. In the center was two feet of pipe-space, and you want to believe that was the meat of the thing . . . in more ways than one.

Tremont's voice came out of the hole, sounding hollow and dead. "Something smells awful in here, Warden."

"Never mind that! Keep going."

Tremont's lower legs disappeared into the hole. A moment later his feet were gone, too. His light flashed dimly back and forth.

"Warden, it smells pretty damn bad."

"Never *mind*, I said!" Norton cried.

Dolorously, Tremont's voice floated back: "Smells like shit. Oh God, that's what it is, it's *shit*, oh my God lemme outta here I'm gonna blow my groceries oh shit it's shit oh my *Gawwwwwd*—" And then came the unmistakable sound of Rory Tremont losing his last couple of meals.

Well, that was it for me. I couldn't help myself. The whole day—hell no, the last thirty *years*—all came up on me at once and I started laughing fit to split, a laugh such as I'd never had since I was a free man, the kind of laugh I never expected to have inside these gray walls. And oh dear *God* didn't it feel good!

"Get that man out of here!" Warden Norton was screaming, and I was laughing so hard I didn't know if he meant me or Tremont. I just went on laughing and kicking my feet and holding onto my belly. I couldn't have stopped if Norton had threatened to shoot me dead-bang on the spot. *"Get him OUT!"*

Well, friends and neighbors, I was the one who went. Straight down to solitary, and there I stayed for fifteen days. A long shot. But every now and then I'd think about poor old not-too-bright Rory Tremont bellowing *oh shit it's shit*, and then I'd think about Andy Dufresne heading south in his own car, dressed in a nice suit, and I'd just have to laugh. I did that fifteen days in solitary practically standing on my head. Maybe because half of me was with Andy Dufresne, Andy Dufresne who had waded in shit and came out clean on the other side, Andy Dufresne, headed for the Pacific.

I heard the rest of what went on that night from half a dozen sources. There wasn't all that much, anyway. I guess that Rory Tremont decided he didn't have much left to lose after he'd lost his lunch and dinner, because he did go on. There was no danger of falling down the pipe-shaft between the inner and outer segments of the cellblock wall; it was so narrow that Tremont actually had to wedge himself down. He said later that he could only take half-breaths and that he knew what it would be like to be buried alive.

What he found at the bottom of the shaft was a master sewer-pipe which served the fourteen toilets in Cellblock 5, a porcelain pipe that had been laid thirty-three years before. It had been broken into. Beside the jagged hole in the pipe, Tremont found Andy's rock-hammer.

Andy had gotten free, but it hadn't been easy.

The pipe was even narrower than the shaft Tremont had just descended. Rory Tremont didn't go in, and so far as I know, no one else did, either. It must have been damn near unspeakable. A rat jumped out of the pipe as Tremont was examining the hole and the rock-hammer, and he swore later that it was nearly as big as a cocker spaniel pup. He went back up the crawlspace to Andy's cell like a monkey on a stick.

Andy had gone into that pipe. Maybe he knew that it emptied into a stream five hundred yards beyond the prison on the marshy western side. I think he did. The prison blueprints were around, and Andy would have found a way to look at them. He was a methodical cuss. He would have known or found out that the sewer-pipe running out of Cellblock 5 was the last one in Shawshank not hooked into the new waste-treatment plant, and he would have known it was do it by mid-1975 or do it never, because in August they were going to switch us over to the new waste-treatment plant, too.

Five hundred yards. The length of five football fields. Just shy of half a mile. He crawled that distance, maybe with one of those small Penlites in his hand, maybe with nothing but a couple of books of matches. He crawled through foulness that I either can't imagine or don't want to imagine. Maybe the rats scattered in front of him, or maybe they went for him the way such animals sometimes will when they've had a chance to grow bold in the dark. He must have had just enough clearance at the shoulders to keep moving, and he probably had to shove himself through the places where the lengths of pipe were joined. If it had been me, the claustrophobia would have driven me mad a dozen times over. But he did it.

At the far end of the pipe they found a set of muddy footprints leading out of the sluggish, polluted creek the pipe fed into. Two miles from there a search party found his prison uniform—that was a day later.

The story broke big in the papers, as you might guess, but no

one within a fifteen-mile radius of the prison stepped forward to
report a stolen car, stolen clothes, or a naked man in the moonlight.
There was not so much as a barking dog in a farmyard. He came out
of the sewer-pipe and he disappeared like smoke.

But I am betting he disappeared in the direction of Buxton.

Three months after that memorable day, Warden Norton resigned. He was a broken man, it gives me great pleasure to report.
The spring was gone from his step. On his last day he shuffled out
with his head down like an old con shuffling down to the infirmary
for his codeine pills. It was Gonyar who took over, and to Norton
that must have seemed like the unkindest cut of all. For all I know,
Sam Norton is down there in Eliot now, attending services at the
Baptist church every Sunday, and wondering how the hell Andy
Dufresne ever could have gotten the better of him.

I could have told him; the answer to the question is simplicity
itself. Some have got it, Sam. And some don't, and never will.

That's what I know; now I'm going to tell you what I think. I
may have it wrong on some of the specifics, but I'd be willing to bet
my watch and chain that I've got the general outline down pretty
well. Because, with Andy being the sort of man that he was, there's
only one or two ways that it could have been. And every now and
then, when I think it out, I think of Normaden, that half-crazy
Indian. "Nice fella," Normaden had said after celling with Andy for
eight months. "I was glad to go, me. Bad draft in that cell. All the
time cold. He don't let nobody touch his things. That's okay. Nice
man, never made fun. But big draft." Poor crazy Normaden. He
knew more than all the rest of us, and he knew it sooner. And it was
eight long months before Andy could get him out of there and have
the cell to himself again. If it hadn't been for the eight months
Normaden had spent with him after Warden Norton first came in, I
do believe that Andy would have been free before Nixon resigned.

I believe now that it began in 1949, way back then—not with
the rock-hammer, but with the Rita Hayworth poster. I told you
how nervous he seemed when he asked for that, nervous and filled

with suppressed excitement. At the time I thought it was just embarrassment, that Andy was the sort of guy who'd never want someone else to know that he had feet of clay and wanted a woman . . . especially if it was a fantasy-woman. But I think now that I was wrong. I think now that Andy's excitement came from something else altogether.

What was responsible for the hole that Warden Norton eventually found behind the poster of a girl that hadn't even been born when that photo of Rita Hayworth was taken? Andy Dufresne's perseverance and hard work, yeah—I don't take any of that away from him. But there were two other elements in the equation: a lot of luck, and WPA concrete.

You don't need me to explain the luck, I guess. The WPA concrete I checked out for myself. I invested some time and a couple of stamps and wrote first to the University of Maine History Department and then to a fellow whose address they were able to give me. This fellow had been foreman of the WPA project that built the Shawshank Max Security Wing.

The wing, which contains Cellblocks 3, 4, and 5, was built in the years 1934–37. Now, most people don't think of cement and concrete as "technological developments," the way we think of cars and oil furnaces and rocket-ships, but they really are. There was no modern cement until 1870 or so, and no modern concrete until after the turn of the century. Mixing concrete is as delicate a business as making bread. You can get it too watery or not watery enough. You can get the sand-mix too thick or too thin, and the same is true of the gravel-mix. And back in 1934, the science of mixing the stuff was a lot less sophisticated than it is today.

The walls of Cellblock 5 were solid enough, but they weren't exactly dry and toasty. As a matter or fact, they were and are pretty damned dank. After a long wet spell they would sweat and sometimes even drip. Cracks had a way of appearing, some an inch deep. They were routinely mortared over.

Now here comes Andy Dufresne into Cellblock 5. He's a man who graduated from the University of Maine's school of business, but he's also a man who took two or three geology courses along the way. Geology had, in fact, become his chief hobby. I imagine it appealed to his patient, meticulous nature. A ten-thousand-year ice age here. A million years of mountain-building there. Plates of bedrock grinding against each other deep under the earth's skin over the millennia. *Pressure.* Andy told me once that all of geology is the study of pressure.

And time, of course.

He had time to study those walls. Plenty of time. When the cell door slams and the lights go out, there's nothing else to look at.

First-timers usually have a hard time adjusting to the confinement of prison life. They get screw-fever. Sometimes they have to be hauled down to the infirmary and sedated a couple of times before they get on the beam. It's not unusual to hear some new member of our happy little family banging on the bars of his cell and screaming to be let out . . . and before the cries have gone on for long, the chant starts up along the cellblock: "Fresh *fish*, hey little fishie, fresh *fish*, fresh *fish*, got fresh *fish* today!"

Andy didn't flip out like that when he came to The Shank in 1948, but that's not to say that he didn't feel many of the same things. He may have come close to madness; some do, and some go sailing right over the edge. Old life blown away in the wink of an eye, indeterminate nightmare stretching out ahead, a long season in hell.

So what did he do, I ask you? He searched almost desperately for something to divert his restless mind. Oh, there are all sorts of ways to divert yourself, even in prison; it seems like the human mind is full of an infinite number of possibilities when it comes to diversion. I told you about the sculptor and his *Three Ages of Jesus*. There were coin collectors who were always losing their collections to thieves, stamp collectors, one fellow who had postcards from thirty-five different countries—and let me tell you, he would have turned out your lights if he'd caught you diddling with his postcards.

Andy got interested in rocks. And the walls of his cell.

I think that his initial intention might have been to do no more than to carve his initials into the wall where the poster of Rita Hayworth would soon be hanging. His initials, or maybe a few lines from some poem. Instead, what he found was that interestingly weak concrete. Maybe he started to carve his initials and a big chunk of the wall just fell out. I can see him, lying there on his bunk, looking at that broken chunk of concrete, turning it over in his hands. Never mind the wreck of your whole life, never mind that you got railroaded into this place by a whole trainload of bad luck. Let's forget all that and look at this piece of concrete.

Some months further along he might have decided it would be fun to see how much of that wall he could take out. But you can't just start digging into your wall and then, when the weekly inspection (or one of the surprise inspections that are always turning up interesting caches of booze, drugs, dirty pictures, and weapons) comes around, say to the guard: "This? Just excavating a little hole in my cell wall. Not to worry, my good man."

No, he couldn't have that. So he came to me and asked if I could get him a Rita Hayworth poster. Not a little one but a big one.

And, of course, he had the rock-hammer. I remember thinking when I got him that gadget back in '48 that it would take a man six hundred years to burrow through the wall with it. True enough. But Andy only had to go through *half* the wall—and even with the soft concrete, it took him two rock-hammers and twenty-seven years to do it.

Of course he lost most of one of those years to Normaden, and he could only work at night, preferably late at night, when almost everybody is asleep—including the guards who work the night shift. But I suspect the thing which slowed him down the most was getting rid of the wall as he took it out. He could muffle the sound of his work by wrapping the head of his hammer in rock-polishing cloths, but what to do with the pulverized concrete and the occasional chunks that came out whole?

I think he must have broken up the chunks into pebbles and . . .

I remembered the Sunday after I had gotten him the rock-hammer. I remember watching him walk across the exercise yard, his face puffy from his latest go-round with the sisters. I saw him stoop, pick up a pebble . . . and it disappeared up his sleeve. That inside sleeve-pocket is an old prison trick. Up your sleeve or just inside the cuff of your pants. And I have another memory, very strong but unfocused, maybe something I saw more than once. This memory is of Andy Dufresne walking across the exercise yard on a hot summer day when the air was utterly still. Still, yeah . . . except for the little breeze that seemed to be blowing sand around Andy Dufresne's feet.

So maybe he had a couple of cheaters in his pants below the knees. You loaded the cheaters up with fill and then just strolled around, your hands in your pockets, and when you felt safe and unobserved, you gave the pockets a little twitch. The pockets, of course, are attached by string or strong thread to the cheaters. The fill goes cascading out of your pantslegs as you walk. The World War II POWs who were trying to tunnel out used the dodge.

The years went past and Andy brought his wall out to the exercise yard cupful by cupful. He played the game with administrator after administrator, and they thought it was because he wanted to keep the library growing. I have no doubt that was part of it, but the main thing Andy wanted was to keep Cell 14 in Cellblock 5 a single occupancy.

I doubt if he had any real plans or hopes of breaking out, at least not at first. He probably assumed the wall was ten feet of solid concrete, and that if he succeeded in boring all the way through it, he'd come out thirty feet over the exercise yard. But like I say, I don't think he was worried overmuch about breaking through. His assumption could have run this way: I'm only making a foot of progress every seven years or so; therefore, it would take me seventy years to break through; that would make me one hundred and one years old.

Here's a second assumption I would have made, had I been Andy: that eventually I would be caught and get a lot of solitary time, not to mention a very large black mark on my record. After all, there was the regular weekly inspection and a surprise toss—which usually came at night—every second week or so. He must have decided that things couldn't go on for long. Sooner or later, some screw was going to peek behind Rita Hayworth just to make sure Andy didn't have a sharpened spoon-handle or some marijuana reefers Scotch-taped to the wall.

And his response to that second assumption must have been *To hell with it*. Maybe he even made a game out of it. How far in can I get before they find out? Prison is a goddam boring place, and the chance of being surprised by an unscheduled inspection in the middle of the night while he had his poster unstuck probably added some spice to his life during the early years.

And I do believe it would have been impossible for him to get away with it just on dumb luck. Not for twenty-seven years. Nevertheless, I have to believe that for the first two years—until mid-May of 1950, when he helped Byron Hadley get around the tax on his windfall inheritance—that's exactly what he did get by on.

Or maybe he had something more than dumb luck going for him even back then. He had money, and he might have been slipping someone a little squeeze every week to take it easy on him. Most guards will go along with that if the price is right; it's money in their pockets and the prisoner gets to keep his whack-off pictures or his tailormade cigarettes. Also, Andy was a model prisoner—quiet, well-spoken, respectful, non-violent. It's the crazies and the stamp-eders that get their cells turned upside-down at least once every six months, their mattresses unzipped, their pillows taken away and cut open, the outflow pipe from their toilets carefully probed.

Then, in 1950, Andy became something more than a model prisoner. In 1950, he became a valuable commodity, a murderer who did tax-returns better than H & R Block. He gave gratis estate-planning advice, set up tax-shelters, filled out loan applications (sometimes creatively). I can remember him sitting behind his desk in the library, patiently going over a car-loan agreement paragraph by paragraph with a screwhead who wanted to buy a used DeSoto, telling the guy what was good about the agreement and what was bad about it, explaining to him that it was possible to shop for a loan and not get hit quite so bad, steering him away from the finance companies, which in those days were sometimes little better than legal loan-sharks. When he'd finished, the screwhead started to put out his hand . . . and then drew it back to himself quickly. He'd forgotten for a moment, you see, that he was dealing with a mascot, not a man.

Andy kept up on the tax laws and the changes in the stock market, and so his usefulness didn't end after he'd been in cold storage for awhile, as it might have done. He began to get his library money, his running war with the sisters had ended, and nobody tossed his cell very hard. He was a good nigger.

Then one day, very late in the going—perhaps around October of 1967—the long-time hobby suddenly turned into something else. One night while he was in the hole up to his waist with Raquel Welch hanging down over his ass, the pick end of his rock-hammer must have suddenly sunk into concrete past the hilt.

He would have dragged some chunks of concrete back, but maybe he heard others falling down into that shaft, bouncing back and forth, clinking off that standpipe. Did he know by then that he was going to come upon that shaft, or was he totally surprised? I don't know. He might have seen the prison blueprints by then or he might not have. If not, you can be damned sure he found a way to look at them not long after.

All at once he must have realized that, instead of just playing a game, he was playing for high stakes . . . in terms of his own life and his own future, the highest. Even then he couldn't have known for sure, but he must have had a pretty good idea because it was right around then that he talked to me about Zihuatanejo for the first time. All of a sudden, instead of just being a toy, that stupid hole in the wall became his master—if he knew about the sewer-pipe at the bottom, and that it led under the outer wall, it did, anyway.

He'd had the key under the rock in Buxton to worry about for years. Now he had to worry that some eager-beaver new guard would look behind his poster and expose the whole thing, or that he would get another cellmate, or that he would, after all those years, suddenly be transferred. He had all those things on his mind for the next eight years. All I can say is that he must have been one of the coolest men who ever lived. I would have gone completely nuts after awhile, living with all that uncertainty. But Andy just went on playing the game.

He had to carry the possibility of discovery for another eight years—the *probability* of it, you might say, because no matter how carefully he stacked the cards in his favor, as an inmate of a state prison, he just didn't have that many to stack . . . and the gods had been kind to him for a very long time; some nineteen years.

The most ghastly irony I can think of would have been if he had been offered a parole. Can you imagine it? Three days before the parolee is actually released, he is transferred into the light security wing to undergo a complete physical and a battery of vocational tests. While he's there, his old cell is completely cleaned out. Instead of getting his parole, Andy would have gotten a long turn downstairs in solitary, followed by some more time upstairs . . . but in a different cell.

If he broke into the shaft in 1967, how come he didn't escape until 1975?

I don't know for sure—but I can advance some pretty good guesses.

First, he would have become more careful than ever. He was too smart to just push ahead at flank speed and try to get out in eight months, or even in eighteen. He must have gone on widening the opening on the crawlspace a little at a time. A hole as big as a teacup by the time he took his New Year's Eve drink that year. A hole as big as a dinner-plate by the time he took his birthday drink in 1968. As big as a serving-tray by the time the 1969 baseball season opened.

For a time I thought it should have gone much faster than it apparently did—after he broke through, I mean. It seemed to me that, instead of having to pulverize the crap and take it out of his cell in the cheater gadgets I have described, he could simply let it drop down the shaft. The length of time he took makes me believe that he didn't dare do that. He might have decided that the noise would arouse someone's suspicions. Or, if he knew about the sewer-pipe, as I believe he must have, he would have been afraid that a falling chunk of concrete would break it before he was ready, screwing up the cellblock sewage system and leading to an investigation. And an investigation, needless to say, would lead to ruin.

Still and all, I'd guess that, by the time Nixon was sworn in for his second term, the hole would have been wide enough for him to wriggle through . . . and probably sooner than that. Andy was a small guy.

Why didn't he go then?

That's where my educated guesses run out, folks; from this point they become progressively wilder. One possibility is that the crawlspace itself was clogged with crap and he had to clear it out. But that wouldn't account for all the time. So what was it?

I think that maybe Andy got scared.

I've told you as well as I can how it is to be an institutional man. At first you can't stand those four walls, then you get so you can abide them, then you get so you accept them . . . and then, as your body and your mind and your spirit adjust to life on an HO scale, you get to love them. You are told when to eat, when you can write letters, when you can smoke. If you're at work in the laundry or the plate-shop, you're assigned five minutes of each hour when you can go to the bathroom. For thirty-five years, my time was twenty-five minutes after the hour, and after thirty-five years, that's the only time I ever felt the need to take a piss or have a crap: twenty-five minutes past the hour. And if for some reason I couldn't go, the need would pass at thirty after, and come back at twenty-five past the next hour.

I think Andy may have been wrestling with that tiger—that institutional syndrome—and also with the bulking fears that all of it might have been for nothing.

How many nights must he have lain awake under his poster, thinking about that sewer line, knowing that the one chance was all he'd ever get? The blueprints might have told him how big the pipe's bore was, but a blueprint couldn't tell him what it would be like inside that pipe—if he would be able to breathe without choking, if the rats were big enough and mean enough to fight instead of retreating . . . and a blueprint couldn't've told him what he'd find at the end of the pipe, when and if he got there. Here's a joke even funnier than the parole would have been: Andy breaks into the sewer line, crawls through five hundred yards of choking, shit-smelling darkness, and comes up against a heavy-gauge mesh screen at the end of it all. Ha, ha, very funny.

That would have been on his mind. And if the long shot actually came in and he was able to get out, would he be able to get some civilian clothes and get away from the vicinity of the prison undetected? Last of all, suppose he got out of the pipe, got away from Shawshank before the alarm was raised, got to Buxton, overturned the right rock . . . and found nothing beneath? Not necessarily something so dramatic as arriving at the right field and discovering that a highrise apartment building had been erected on the spot, or that it had been turned into a supermarket parking lot. It could have been that some little kid who liked rocks noticed that piece of volcanic glass, turned it over, saw the deposit-box key, and took both it and the rock back to his room as souvenirs. Maybe a November hunter kicked the rock, left the key exposed, and a squirrel or a crow with a liking for bright shiny things had taken it away. Maybe there had been spring floods one year, breaching the wall, washing the key away. Maybe anything.

So I think—wild guess or not—that Andy just froze in place for awhile. After all, you can't lose if you don't bet. What did he have to lose, you ask? His library, for one thing. The poison peace of institutional life, for another. Any future chance to grab his safe identity.

But he finally did it, just as I have told you. He tried . . . and, my! Didn't he succeed in spectacular fashion? You tell me!

But *did* he get away, you ask? What happened after? What happened when he got to that meadow and turned over that rock . . . always assuming the rock was still there?

I can't describe that scene for you, because this institutional man is still in this institution, and expects to be for years to come.

But I'll tell you this. Very late in the summer of 1975, on September 15th, to be exact, I got a postcard which had been mailed from the tiny town of McNary, Texas. That town is on the American side of the border, directly across from El Porvenir. The message side of the card was totally blank. But I know. I know it in my heart as surely as I know that we're all going to die someday.

McNary was where he crossed. McNary, Texas.

So that's my story, Jack. I never believed how long it would take to write it all down, or how many pages it would take. I started writing just after I got that postcard, and here I am finishing up on January 14th, 1976. I've used three pencils right down to knuckle-stubs, and a whole tablet of paper. I've kept the pages carefully hidden . . . not that many could read my hen-tracks, anyway.

It stirred up more memories than I ever would have believed. Writing about yourself seems to be a lot like sticking a branch into clear river-water and roiling up the muddy bottom.

Well, you weren't writing about yourself, I hear someone in the peanut-gallery saying. *You were writing about Andy Dufresne. You're nothing but a minor character in your own story.* But you know, that's just not so. It's *all* about me, every damned word of it. Andy was the part of me they could never lock up, the part of me that will rejoice when the gates finally open for me and I walk out in my cheap suit with my twenty dollars of mad-money in my pocket. That part of me will rejoice no matter how old and broken and scared the rest of me is. I guess it's just that Andy had more of that part than me, and used it better.

There are others here like me, others who remember Andy. We're glad he's gone, but a little sad, too. Some birds are not meant to be caged, that's all. Their feathers are too bright, their songs too sweet and wild. So you let them go, or when you open the cage to feed them they somehow fly out past you. And the part of you that knows it was wrong to imprison them in the first place rejoices, but still, the place where you live is that much more drab and empty for their departure.

That's the story and I'm glad I told it, even if it is a bit inconclusive and even though some of the memories the pencil prodded up (like that branch poking up the river-mud) made me feel a little sad and even older than I am. Thank you for listening. And Andy, if you're really down there, as I believe you are, look at the stars for me just after sunset, and touch the sand, and wade in the water, and feel free.

———

I never expected to take up this narrative again, but here I am with the dog-eared, folded pages open on the desk in front of me. Here I am adding another three or four pages, writing in a brand-new tablet. A tablet I bought in a store—I just walked into a store on Portland's Congress Street and bought it.

I thought I had put finish to my story in a Shawshank prison cell on a bleak January day in 1976. Now it's May of 1977 and I am sitting in a small, cheap room of the Brewster Hotel in Portland, adding to it.

The window is open, and the sound of the traffic floating in seems huge, exciting, and intimidating. I have to look constantly over at the window and reassure myself that there are no bars on it. I sleep poorly at night because the bed in this room, as cheap as the room is, seems much too big and luxurious. I snap awake every morning promptly at six-thirty, feeling disoriented and frightened. My dreams are bad. I have a crazy feeling of free fall. The sensation is as terrifying as it is exhilarating.

What has happened in my life? Can't you guess? I was paroled. After thirty-eight years of routine hearings and routine denials (in the course of those thirty-eight years, three lawyers died on me), my parole was granted. I suppose they decided that, at the age of fifty-eight, I was finally used up enough to be deemed safe.

I came very close to burning the document you have just read. They search outgoing parolees almost as carefully as they search incoming "new fish." And beyond containing enough dynamite to assure me of a quick turnaround and another six or eight years inside, my "memoirs" contained something else: the name of the town where I believe Andy Dufresne to be. Mexican police gladly cooperate with the American police, and I didn't want my freedom—or my unwillingness to give up the story I'd worked so long and hard to write—to cost Andy his.

Then I remembered how Andy had brought in his five hundred dollars back in 1948, and I took out my story of him the same way. Just to be on the safe side, I carefully rewrote each page which mentioned Zihuatanejo. If the papers had been found during my "outside search," as they call it at The Shank, I would have gone back in on turnaround . . . but the cops would have been looking for Andy in a Peruvian seacoast town named Las Intrudres.

The Parole Committee got me a job as a "stock-room assistant" at the big FoodWay Market at the Spruce Mall in South Portland—

which means I became just one more ageing bag-boy. There's only two kinds of bag-boys, you know; the old ones and the young ones. No one ever looks at either kind. If you shop at the Spruce Mall FoodWay, I may have even taken your groceries out to your car . . . but you'd have had to have shopped there between March and April of 1977, because that's as long as I worked there.

At first I didn't think I was going to be able to make it on the outside at all. I've described prison society as a scaled-down model of your outside world, but I had no idea of how *fast* things moved on the outside; the *raw speed* people move at. They even talk faster. And louder.

It was the toughest adjustment I've ever had to make, and I haven't finished making it yet . . . not by a long way. Women, for instance. After hardly knowing that they were half of the human race for forty years, I was suddenly working in a store filled with them. Old women, pregnant women wearing tee-shirts with arrows pointing downward and a printed motto reading BABY HERE, skinny women with their nipples poking out at their shirts—a woman wearing something like that when I went in would have gotten arrested and then had a sanity hearing—women of every shape and size. I found myself going around with a semi-hard almost all the time and cursing myself for being a dirty old man.

Going to the bathroom, that was another thing. When I had to go (and the urge always came on me at twenty-five past the hour), I had to fight the almost overwhelming need to check it with my boss. Knowing that was something I could just go and do in this too-bright outside world was one thing; adjusting my inner self to that knowledge after all those years of checking it with the nearest screwhead or facing two days in solitary for the oversight . . . that was something else.

My boss didn't like me. He was a young guy, twenty-six or -seven, and I could see that I sort of disgusted him, the way a cringing, servile old dog that crawls up to you on its belly to be petted will disgust a man. Christ, I disgusted myself. But . . . I couldn't make myself stop. I wanted to tell him: *That's what a whole life in prison does for you, young man. It turns everyone in a position of authority into a master, and you into every master's dog. Maybe you know you've become a dog, even in prison, but since everyone else in gray is a dog, too, it doesn't seem to matter so much. Outside, it does.* But I couldn't tell a young guy like him. He would never understand. Neither would my PO, a big, bluff ex-Navy man with a huge red beard and a large stock of Polish jokes. He saw me for about five minutes every week. "Are you staying out of the bars, Red?" he'd ask when he'd run out of Polish jokes. I'd say yeah, and that would be the end of it until next week.

Music on the radio. When I went in, the big bands were just getting up a good head of steam. Now every song sounds like it's about fucking. So many cars. At first I felt like I was taking my life into my hands every time I crossed the street.

There was more—*everything* was strange and frightening—but maybe you get the idea, or can at least grasp a corner of it. I began to think about doing something to get back in. When you're on parole, almost anything will serve. I'm ashamed to say it, but I began to think about stealing some money or shoplifting stuff from the FoodWay, anything, to get back in where it was quiet and you knew everything that was going to come up in the course of the day.

If I had never known Andy, I probably would have done that. But I kept thinking of him, spending all those years chipping patiently away at the cement with his rock-hammer so he could be free. I thought of that and it made me ashamed and I'd drop the idea again. Oh, you can say he had more reason to be free than I did—he had a new identity and a lot of money. But that's not really true, you know. Because he didn't know for sure that the new identity was still there, and without the new identity, the money would always be out of reach. No, what he needed was just to be free, and if I kicked away what I had, it would be like spitting in the face of everything he had worked so hard to win back.

So what I started to do on my time off was to hitchhike rides down to the little town of Buxton. This was in the early April of 1977, the snow just starting to melt off the fields, the air just beginning to be warm, the baseball teams coming north to start a new season playing the only game I'm sure God approves of. When I went on these trips, I carried a Silva compass in my pocket.

There's a big hayfield in Buxton, Andy had said, *and at the north end of that hayfield there's a rock wall, right out of a Robert Frost poem. And somewhere along the base of that wall is a rock that has no earthly business in a Maine hayfield.*

A fool's errand, you say. How many hayfields are there in a small rural town like Buxton? Fifty? A hundred? Speaking from personal experience, I'd put it at even higher than that, if you add in the fields now cultivated which might have been haygrass when Andy went in. And if I did find the right one, I might never know it. Because I might overlook that black piece of volcanic glass, or, much more likely, Andy put it into his pocket and took it with him.

So I'd agree with you. A fool's errand, no doubt about it. Worse, a dangerous one for a man on parole, because some of those fields were clearly marked with NO TRESPASSING signs. And, as I've said, they're more than happy to slam your ass back inside if you get out of line. A fool's errand . . . but so is chipping at a blank concrete wall for twenty-seven years. And when you're no longer the man who can get it for you and just an old bag-boy, it's nice to have a hobby to take your mind off your new life. My hobby was looking for Andy's rock.

So I'd hitchhike to Buxton and walk the roads. I'd listen to the birds, to the spring runoff in the culverts, examine the bottles the retreating snows had revealed—all useless non-returnables, I am sorry to say; the world seems to have gotten awfully spendthrift since I went into the slam—and looking for hayfields.

Most of them could be eliminated right off. No rock walls. Others had rock walls, but my compass told me they were facing the wrong direction. I walked these wrong ones anyway. It was a comfortable thing to be doing, and on those outings I really *felt* free, at peace. An old dog walked with me one Saturday. And one day I saw a winter-skinny deer.

Then came April 23rd, a day I'll not forget even if I live another fifty-eight years. It was a balmy Saturday afternoon, and I was walking up what a little boy fishing from a bridge told me was called The Old Smith Road. I had taken a lunch in a brown FoodWay bag, and had eaten it sitting on a rock by the road. When

I was done I carefully buried my leavings, as my dad taught me before he died, when I was a sprat no older than the fisherman who had named the road for me.

Around two o'clock I came to a big field on my left. There was a stone wall at the far end of it, running roughly northwest. I walked back to it, squelching over the wet ground, and began to walk the wall. A squirrel scolded me from an oak tree.

Three-quarters of the way to the end, I saw the rock. No mistake. Black glass and as smooth as silk. A rock with no earthly business in a Maine hayfield. For a long time I just looked at it, feeling that I might cry, for whatever reason. The squirrel had followed me, and it was still chattering away. My heart was beating madly.

When I felt I had myself under control, I went to the rock, squatted beside it—the joints in my knees went off like a double-barrelled shotgun—and let my hand touch it. It was real. I didn't pick it up because I thought there would be anything under it; I could just as easily have walked away without finding what was beneath. I certainly had no plans to take it away with me, because I didn't feel it was mine to take—I had a feeling that taking that rock from the field would have been the worst kind of theft. No, I only picked it up to feel it better, to get the heft of the thing, and, I suppose, to prove its reality by feeling its satiny texture against my skin.

I had to look at what was underneath for a long time. My eyes saw it, but it took awhile for my mind to catch up. It was an envelope, carefully wrapped in a plastic bag to keep away the damp. My name was written across the front in Andy's clear script.

I took the envelope and left the rock where Andy had left it, and Andy's friend before him.

Dear Red,

If you're reading this, then you're out. One way or another, you're out. And if you've followed along this far, you might be willing to come a little further. I think you remember the name of the town, don't you? I could use a good man to help me get my project on wheels.

Meantime, have a drink on me—and do think it over. I will be keeping an eye out for you. Remember that hope is a good thing, Red, maybe the best of things, and no good thing ever dies. I will be hoping that this letter finds you, and finds you well.

Your friend,
Peter Stevens

I didn't read that letter in the field. A kind of terror had come over me, a need to get away from there before I was seen. To make what may be an appropriate pun, I was in terror of being apprehended.

I went back to my room and read it there, with the smell of old men's dinners drifting up the stairwell to me—Beefaroni, Rice-a-Roni, Noodle Roni. You can bet that whatever the old folks of America, the ones on fixed incomes, are eating tonight, it almost certainly ends in *roni*.

I opened the envelope and read the letter and then I put my head in my arms and cried. With the letter there were twenty new fifty-dollar bills.

And here I am in the Brewster Hotel, technically a fugitive from justice again—parole violation is my crime. No one's going to throw up any roadblocks to catch a criminal wanted on that charge, I guess—wondering what I should do now.

I have this manuscript. I have a small piece of luggage about the size of a doctor's bag that holds everything I own. I have nineteen fifties, four tens, a five, three ones, and assorted change. I broke one of the fifties to buy this tablet of paper and a deck of smokes.

Wondering what I should do.

But there's really no question. It always comes down to just two choices. Get busy living or get busy dying.

First I'm going to put this manuscript back in my bag. Then I'm going to buckle it up, grab my coat, go downstairs, and check out of this fleabag. Then I'm going to walk uptown to a bar and put that five-dollar bill down in front of the bartender and ask him to bring me two straight shots of Jack Daniel's—one for me and one for Andy Dufresne. Other than a beer or two, they'll be the first drinks I've taken as a free man since 1938. Then I am going to tip the bartender a dollar and thank him kindly. I will leave the bar and walk up Spring Street to the Greyhound terminal there and buy a bus ticket to El Paso by way of New York City. When I get to El Paso, I'm going to buy a ticket to McNary. And when I get to McNary, I guess I'll have a chance to find out if an old crook like me can find a way to float across the border and into Mexico.

Sure I remember the name. Zihuatanejo. A name like that is just too pretty to forget.

I find I am excited, so excited I can hardly hold the pencil in my trembling hand. I think it is the excitement that only a free man can feel, a free man starting a long journey whose conclusion is uncertain.

I hope Andy is down there.

I hope I can make it across the border.

I hope to see my friend and shake his hand.

I hope the Pacific is as blue as it has been in my dreams.

I *hope*.

Summer of Corruption

For Elaine Koster and Herbert Schnall

Apt Pupil

1

He looked like the total all-American kid as he pedaled his twenty-six-inch Schwinn with the apehanger handlebars up the residential suburban street, and that's just what he was: Todd Bowden, thirteen years old, five-feet-eight and a healthy one hundred and forty pounds, hair the color of ripe corn, blue eyes, white even teeth, lightly tanned skin marred by not even the first shadow of adolescent acne.

He was smiling a summer vacation smile as he pedaled through the sun and shade not too far from his own house. He looked like the kind of kid who might have a paper route, and as a matter of fact, he did—he delivered the Santo Donato *Clarion*. He also looked like the kind of kid who might sell greeting cards for premiums, and he had done that, too. They were the kind that come with your name printed inside—JACK AND MARY BURKE, or DON AND SALLY, or THE MURCHISONS. He looked like the sort of boy who might whistle while he worked, and he often did so. He whistled quite prettily, in fact. His dad was an architectural engineer who made forty thousand dollars a year. His mom had majored in French in college and had met Todd's father when he desperately needed a tutor. She typed manuscripts in her spare time. She had kept all of Todd's old school report cards in a folder. Her favorite was his final fourth-grade card, on which Mrs. Upshaw had scratched: "Todd is an extremely apt pupil." He was, too. Straight A's and B's all the way up the line. If he'd done any better—straight A's, for example—his friends might have begun to think he was weird.

Now he brought his bike to a halt in front of 963 Claremont

Street and stepped off it. The house was a small bungalow set discreetly back on its lot. It was white with green shutters and green trim. A hedge ran around the front. The hedge was well-watered and well-clipped.

Todd brushed his blonde hair out of his eyes and walked the Schwinn up the cement path to the steps. He was still smiling, and his smile was open and expectant and beautiful. He pushed down the bike's kickstand with the toe of one Nike running-shoe and then picked the folded newspaper off the bottom step. It wasn't the *Clarion*; it was the L.A. *Times*. He put it under his arm and mounted the steps. At the top was a heavy wooden door with no window inside of a latched screen door. There was a doorbell on the right-hand doorframe, and below the bell were two small signs, each neatly screwed into the wood and covered with protective plastic so they wouldn't yellow or waterspot. German efficiency, Todd thought, and his smile widened a little. It was an adult thought, and he always mentally congratulated himself when he had one of those.

The top sign said ARTHUR DENKER.

The bottom one said NO SOLICITORS, NO PEDDLERS, NO SALES-MEN.

Smiling still, Todd rang the bell.

He could barely hear its muted burring, somewhere far off inside the small house. He took his finger off the bell and cocked his head a little, listening for footsteps. There were none. He looked at his Timex watch (one of the premiums he had gotten for selling personalized greeting cards) and saw that it was twelve past ten. The guy should be up by now. Todd himself was always up by seven-thirty at the latest, even during summer vacation. The early bird catches the worm.

He listened for another thirty seconds and when the house remained silent he leaned on the bell, watching the sweep second hand on his Timex as he did so. He had been pressing the doorbell for exactly seventy-one seconds when he finally heard shuffling footsteps. Slippers, he deduced from the soft *wish-wish* sound. Todd was into deductions. His current ambition was to become a private detective when he grew up.

"All right! All right!" the man who was pretending to be Arthur Denker called querulously. "I'm coming! Let it go! I'm coming!"

Todd stopped pushing the doorbell button.

A chain and bolt rattled on the far side of the windowless inner door. Then it was pulled open.

An old man, hunched inside a bathrobe, stood looking out through the screen. A cigarette smouldered between his fingers. Todd thought the man looked like a cross between Albert Einstein and Boris Karloff. His hair was long and white but beginning to yellow in an unpleasant way that was more nicotine than ivory. His face was wrinkled and pouched and puffy with sleep, and Todd saw with some distaste that he hadn't bothered shaving for the last couple of days. Todd's father was fond of saying, "A shave puts a shine on the morning." Todd's father shaved every day, whether he had to work or not.

The eyes looking out at Todd were watchful but deeply sunken, laced with snaps of red. Todd felt an instant of deep disappointment. The guy *did* look a little bit like Albert Einstein, and he *did* look a little bit like Boris Karloff, but what he looked like more than anything else was one of the seedy old winos that hung around down by the railroad yard.

But of course, Todd reminded himself, the man had just gotten up. Todd had seen Denker many times before today (although he had been very careful to make sure that Denker hadn't seen *him*, no *way*, José), and on his public occasions, Denker looked very natty, every inch an officer in retirement, you might say, even though he was seventy-six if the articles Todd had read at the library had his birth-date right. On the days when Todd had shadowed him to the Shoprite where Denker did his shopping or to one of the three movie theaters on the bus line—Denker had no car—he was always dressed in one of three neatly kept suits, no matter how warm the weather. If the weather looked threatening he carried a furled umbrella under one arm like a swagger stick. He sometimes wore a trilby hat. And on the occasions when Denker went out, he was always neatly shaved and his white moustache (worn to conceal an imperfectly corrected harelip) was carefully trimmed.

"A boy," he said now. His voice was thick and sleepy. Todd saw with new disappointment that his robe was faded and tacky. One rounded collar point stood up at a drunken angle to poke at his wattled neck. There was a splotch of something that might have been chili or possibly A-1 Steak Sauce on the left lapel, and he smelled of cigarettes and stale booze.

"A boy," he repeated. "I don't need anything, boy. Read the sign. You can read, can't you? Of course you can. All American boys can read. Don't be a nuisance, boy. Good day."

The door began to close.

He might have dropped it right there, Todd thought much later on one of the nights when sleep was hard to find. His disappointment at seeing the man for the first time at close range, seeing him with his street-face put away—hanging in the closet, you might say, along with his umbrella and his trilby—might have done it. It could have ended in that moment, the tiny, unimportant snicking sound of the latch cutting off everything that happened later as neatly as a pair of shears. But, as the man himself had observed, he was an American boy, and he had been taught that persistence is a virtue.

"Don't forget your paper, Mr. Dussander," Todd said, holding the *Times* out politely.

The door stopped dead in its swing, still inches from the jamb. A tight and watchful expression flitted across Kurt Dussander's face and was gone at once. There might have been fear in that expression. It was good, the way he had made that expression disappear, but Todd was disappointed for the third time. He hadn't expected Dussander to be good; he had expected Dussander to be *great*.

Boy, Todd thought with real disgust. *Boy oh boy.*

He pulled the door open again. One hand, bunched with arthritis, unlatched the screen door. The hand pushed the screen door open just enough to wriggle through like a spider and close over the edge of the paper Todd was holding out. The boy saw with distaste that the old man's fingernails were long and yellow and horny. It was a hand that had spent most of its waking hours holding one cigarette after another. Todd thought smoking was a filthy dangerous habit, one he himself would never take up. It really was a wonder that Dussander had lived as long as he had.

The old man tugged. "Give me my paper."

"Sure thing, Mr. Dussander." Todd released his hold on the paper. The spider-hand yanked it inside. The screen closed.

"My name is Denker," the old man said. "Not this Doo-Zander. Apparently you cannot read. What a pity. Good day."

The door started to close again. Todd spoke rapidly into the narrowing gap. "Bergen-Belsen, January 1943 to June 1943. Auschwitz, June 1943 to June of 1944, *Unterkommandant*. Patin—"

The door stopped again. The old man's pouched and pallid face hung in the gap like a wrinkled, half-deflated balloon. Todd smiled.

"You left Patin just ahead of the Russians. You got to Buenos Aires. Some people say you got rich there, investing the gold you took out of Germany in the drug trade. Whatever, you were in Mexico City from 1950 to 1952. Then—"

"Boy, you are crazy like a cuckoo bird." One of the arthritic fingers twirled circles around a misshapen ear. But the toothless mouth was quivering in an infirm, panicky way.

"From 1952 until 1958, I don't know," Todd said, smiling more widely still. "No one does, I guess, or at least they're not telling. But an Israeli agent spotted you in Cuba, working as the concierge in a big hotel just before Castro took over. They lost you when the rebels came into Havana. You popped up in West Berlin in 1965. They almost got you." He pronounced the last two words as one: *gotcha*. At the same time he squeezed all of his fingers together into one large, wriggling fist. Dussander's eyes dropped to those well-made and well-nourished American hands, hands that were made for building soapbox racers and Aurora models. Todd had done both. In fact, the year before, he and his dad had built a model of the *Titanic*. It had taken almost four months, and Todd's father kept it in his office.

"I don't know what you are talking about," Dussander said. Without his false teeth, his words had a mushy sound Todd didn't like. It didn't sound . . . well, authentic. Colonel Klink on *Hogan's Heroes* sounded more like a Nazi than Dussander did. But in his time he must have been a real whiz. In an article on the death-camps in *Men's Action*, the writer had called him The Blood-Fiend of Patin. "Get out of here, boy. Before I call the police."

"Gee, I guess you better call them, Mr. Dussander. Or Herr Dussander, if you like that better." He continued to smile, showing perfect teeth that had been fluoridated since the beginning of his life and bathed thrice a day in Crest toothpaste for almost as long. "After 1965, no one saw you again . . . until I did, two months ago, on the downtown bus."

"You're insane."

"So if you want to call the police," Todd said, smiling, "you go right ahead. I'll wait on the stoop. But if you don't want to call them right away, why don't I come in? We'll talk."

There was a long moment while the old man looked at the smiling boy. Birds twitted in the trees. On the next block a power mower was running, and far off, on busier streets, horns honked out their own rhythm of life and commerce.

In spite of everything, Todd felt the onset of doubt. He couldn't be wrong, could he? Was there some mistake on his part? He didn't think so, but this was no schoolroom exercise. It was real life. So he felt a surge of relief (*mild* relief, he assured himself later) when Dussander said: "You may come in for a moment, if you like. But only because I do not wish to make trouble for you, you understand?"

"Sure, Mr. Dussander," Todd said. He opened the screen and came into the hall. Dussander closed the door behind them, shutting off the morning.

The house smelled stale and slightly malty. It smelled the way Todd's own house smelled sometimes the morning after his folks had thrown a party and before his mother had had a chance to air it out. But this smell was worse. It was lived-in and ground-in. It was liquor, fried food, sweat, old clothes, and some stinky medicinal smell like Vick's or Mentholatum. It was dark in the hallway, and Dussander was standing too close, his head hunched into the collar of his robe like the head of a vulture waiting for some hurt animal to give up the ghost. In that instant, despite the stubble and the loosely hanging flesh, Todd could see the man who had stood inside the black SS uniform more clearly than he had ever seen him on the street. And he felt a sudden lancet of fear slide into his belly. *Mild* fear, he amended later.

"I should tell you that if anything happens to me—" he began, and then Dussander shuffled past him and into the living room, his slippers *wish-wishing* on the floor. He flapped a contemptuous hand at Todd, and Todd felt a flush of hot blood mount into his throat and cheeks.

Todd followed him, his smile wavering for the first time. He had not pictured it happening quite like this. But it would work out. Things would come into focus. Of course they would. Things always did. He began to smile again as he stepped into the living room.

It was another disappointment—and how!—but one he supposed he should have been prepared for. There was of course no oil portrait of Hitler with his forelock dangling and eyes that followed you. No medals in cases, no ceremonial sword mounted on the wall, no Luger or PPK Walther on the mantel (there was, in fact, no mantel). Of course, Todd told himself, the guy would have to be crazy to put any of those things out where people could see them. Still, it was hard to put everything you saw in the movies or on TV out of your head. It looked like the living room of any old man living alone on a slightly frayed pension. The fake fireplace was faced with fake bricks. A Westclox hung over it. There was a black and white Motorola TV on a stand; the tips of the rabbit ears had been wrapped in aluminum foil to improve reception. The floor was covered with a gray rug; its nap was balding. The magazine rack by the sofa held copies of *National Geographic, Reader's Digest*, and the L.A. *Times*. Instead of Hitler or a ceremonial sword hung on the wall, there was a framed certificate of citizenship and a picture of a woman in a funny hat. Dussander later told him that sort of hat was called a cloche, and they had been popular in the twenties and thirties.

"My wife," Dussander said sentimentally. "She died in 1955 of a lung disease. At that time I was working at the Menschler Motor Works in Essen. I was heartbroken."

Todd continued to smile. He crossed the room as if to get a better look at the woman in the picture. Instead of looking at the picture, he fingered the shade on a small table-lamp.

"*Stop that!*" Dussander barked harshly. Todd jumped back a little.

"That was good," he said sincerely. "Really commanding. It was Ilse Koch who had the lampshades made out of human skin, wasn't it? And she was the one who had the trick with the little glass tubes."

"I don't know what you're talking about," Dussander said. There was a package of Kools, the kind with no filter, on top of the TV. He offered them to Todd. "Cigarette?" he asked, and grinned. His grin was hideous.

"No. They give you lung cancer. My dad used to smoke, but he gave it up. He went to Smokenders."

"Did he." Dussander produced a wooden match from the pocket of his robe and scratched it indifferently on the plastic case of the Motorola. Puffing, he said: "Can you give me one reason why I shouldn't call the police and tell them of the monstrous accusations you've just made? One reason? Speak quickly, boy. The telephone is just down the hall. Your father would spank you, I think. You would sit for dinner on a cushion for a week or so, eh?"

"My parents don't believe in spanking. Corporal punishment causes more problems than it cures." Todd's eyes suddenly gleamed. "Did you spank any of them? The women? Did you take off their clothes and—"

With a muffled exclamation, Dussander started for the phone.

Todd said coldly: "You better not do that."

Dussander turned. In measured tones that were spoiled only slightly by the fact that his false teeth were not in, he said: "I tell you this once, boy, and once only. My name is Arthur Denker. It has never been anything else; it has not even been Americanized. I was in fact named Arthur by my father, who greatly admired the stories of Arthur Conan Doyle. It has never been Doo-Zander, or Himmler, or Father Christmas. I was a reserve lieutenant in the war. I never joined the Nazi party. In the battle of Berlin I fought for three weeks. I will admit that in the late thirties, when I was first married, I supported Hitler. He ended the depression and returned some of the pride we had lost in the aftermath of the sickening and unfair Treaty of Versailles. I suppose I supported him mostly because I got a job and there was tobacco again, and I didn't need to hunt through the gutters when I needed to smoke. I thought, in the late thirties, that he was a great man. In his own way, perhaps he was. But at the end he was mad, directing phantom armies at the whim of an astrologer. He even gave Blondi, his dog, a death-capsule. The act of a madman; by the end they were all madmen, singing the 'Horst Wessel Song' as they fed poison to their children. On May 2nd, 1945, my regiment gave up to the Americans. I remember that a private soldier named Hackermeyer gave me a chocolate bar. I wept. There was no reason to fight on; the war was over, and really had been since February. I was interned at Essen and was treated very well. We listened to the Nuremberg trials on the radio, and when Goering committed suicide, I traded fourteen American cigarettes for half a bottle of *Schnaps* and got drunk. When I was released, I put wheels on cars at the Essen Motor Works until 1963, when I retired. Later I emigrated to the United States. To come here was a lifelong ambition. In 1967 I became a citizen. I am an American. I vote. No Buenos Aires. No drug dealing. No Berlin. No Cuba." He pronounced it *Koo-ba*. "And now, unless you leave, I make my telephone call."

He watched Todd do nothing. Then he went down the hall and picked up the telephone. Still Todd stood in the living room, beside the table with the small lamp on it.

Dussander began to dial. Todd watched him, his heart speeding up until it was drumming in his chest. After the fourth number, Dussander turned and looked at him. His shoulders sagged. He put the phone down.

"A boy," he breathed. "A *boy*."

Todd smiled widely but rather modestly.

"How did you find out?"

"One piece of luck and a lot of hard work," Todd said. "There's this friend of mine, Harold Pegler his name is, only all the kids call him Foxy. He plays second base for our team. His dad's got all these magazines out in his garage. Great big stacks of them. War magazines. They're old. I looked for some new ones, but the guy who runs the newsstand across from the school says most of them went out of business. In most of them there's pictures of krauts— German soldiers, I mean—and Japs torturing these women. And articles about the concentration camps. I really groove on all that concentration camp stuff."

"You . . . groove on it." Dussander was staring at him, one hand rubbing up and down on his cheek, producing a very small sandpapery sound.

"Groove. You know. I get off on it. I'm interested."

He remembered that day in Foxy's garage as clearly as anything in his life—more clearly, he suspected. He remembered in the fifth grade, before Careers Day, how Mrs. Anderson (all the kids called her Bugs because of her big front teeth) had talked to them about what she called finding YOUR GREAT INTEREST.

"It comes all at once," Bugs Anderson had rhapsodized. "You see something for the first time, and right away you know you have found YOUR GREAT INTEREST. It's like a key turning in a lock. Or falling in love for the first time. That's why Careers Day is so important, children—it may be the day on which you find YOUR GREAT INTEREST." And she had gone on to tell them about her own GREAT INTEREST, which turned out not to be teaching the fifth grade but collecting nineteenth-century postcards.

Todd had thought Mrs. Anderson was full of bullspit at the time, but that day in Foxy's garage, he remembered what she had said and wondered if maybe she hadn't been right after all.

The Santa Anas had been blowing that day, and to the east there were brush-fires. He remembered the smell of burning, hot and greasy. He remembered Foxy's crewcut, and the flakes of Butch Wax clinging to the front of it. He remembered *everything*.

"I know there's comics here someplace," Foxy had said. His mother had a hangover and had kicked them out of the house for making too much noise. "Neat ones. They're Westerns, mostly, but there's some *Turok, Son of Stone* and—"

"What are those?" Todd asked, pointing at the bulging cardboard cartons under the stairs.

"Ah, they're no good," Foxy said. "True war stories, mostly. Boring."

"Can I look at some?"

"Sure. I'll find the comics."

But by the time fat Foxy Pegler found them, Todd no longer wanted to read comics. He was lost. Utterly lost.

It's like a key turning in a lock. Or falling in love for the first time.

It *had* been like that. He had known about the war, of course—not the stupid one going on now, where the Americans had gotten the shit kicked out of them by a bunch of gooks in black pajamas—but World War II. He knew that the Americans wore round helmets with net on them and the krauts wore sort of square ones. He knew that the Americans won most of the battles and that the Germans had invented rockets near the end and shot them from Germany onto London. He had even known something about the concentration camps.

The difference between all of that and what he found in the magazines under the stairs in Foxy's garage was like the difference between being *told* about germs and then actually *seeing* them in a microscope, squirming around and alive.

Here was Ilse Koch. Here were crematoriums with their doors standing open on their soot-clotted hinges. Here were officers in SS uniforms and prisoners in striped uniforms. The smell of the old pulp magazines was like the smell of the brush-fires burning out of control on the east of Santo Donato, and he could feel the old paper crumbling against the pads of his fingers, and he turned the pages, no longer in Foxy's garage but caught somewhere crosswise in time, trying to cope with the idea that *they had really done those things*, that *somebody had really done those things*, and that *somebody had let them do those things*, and his head began to ache with a mixture of revulsion and excitement, and his eyes were hot and strained, but he read on, and from a column of print beneath a picture of tangled bodies at a place called Dachau, this figure jumped out at him:

6,000,000.

And he thought: *Somebody goofed there, somebody added a zero or two, that's twice as many people as there are in L.A.!* But then, in another magazine (the cover of this one showed a woman chained to a wall while a guy in a Nazi uniform approached her with a poker in his hand and a grin on his face), he saw it again:

6,000,000.

His headache got worse. His mouth went dry. Dimly, from some distance, he heard Foxy saying he had to go in for supper. Todd asked Foxy if he could stay out here in the garage and read while Foxy ate. Foxy gave him a look of mild puzzlement, shrugged, and said sure. And Todd read, hunched over the boxes of the old true war magazines, until his mother called and asked if he was *ever* going to go home.

Like a key turning in a lock.

All the magazines said it was bad, what had happened. But all the stories were continued at the back of the book, and when you turned to those pages, the words saying it was bad were surrounded by ads, and these ads sold German knives and belts and helmets as well as Magic Trusses and Guaranteed Hair Restorer. These ads sold German flags emblazoned with swastikas and Nazi Lugers and a game called Panzer Attack as well as correspondence lessons and offers to make you rich selling elevator shoes to short men. They said it was bad, but it seemed like a lot of people must not mind.

Like falling in love.

Oh yes, he remembered that day very well. He remembered everything about it—a yellowing pin-up calendar for a defunct year on the back wall, the oil-stain on the cement floor, the way the magazines had been tied together with orange twine. He remembered how his headache had gotten a little worse each time he thought of that incredible number,

6,000,000.

He remembered thinking: *I want to know about everything that happened in those places. Everything. And I want to know which is more true—the words, or the ads they put beside the words.*

He remembered Bugs Anderson as he at last pushed the boxes back under the stairs and thought: *She was right. I've found my GREAT INTEREST.*

Dussander looked at Todd for a long time. Then he crossed the living room and sat down heavily in a rocking chair. He looked at Todd again, unable to analyze the slightly dreamy, slightly nostalgic expression on the boy's face.

"Yeah. It was the magazines that got me interested, but I figured a lot of what they said was just, you know, bullspit. So I went to the library and found out a lot more stuff. Some of it was even neater.

At first the crummy librarian didn't want me to look at any of it because it was in the adult section of the library, but I told her it was for school. If it's for school they have to let you have it. She called my dad, though." Todd's eyes turned up scornfully. "Like she thought Dad didn't know what I was doing, if you can dig that."

"He did know?"

"Sure. My dad thinks kids should find out about life as soon as they can—the bad as well as the good. Then they'll be ready for it. He says life is a tiger you have to grab by the tail, and if you don't know the nature of the beast it will eat you up."

"Mmmm," Dussander said.

"My mom thinks the same way."

"Mmmmm." Dussander looked dazed, not quite sure where he was.

"Anyhow," Todd said, "the library stuff was real good. They must have had a hundred books with stuff in them about the Nazi concentration camps, just here in the Santo Donato library. A *lot* of people must like to read about that stuff. There weren't as many pictures as in Foxy's dad's magazines, but the other stuff was real gooshy. Chairs with spikes sticking up through the seats. Pulling out gold teeth with pliers. Poison gas that came out of the showers." Todd shook his head. "You guys just went overboard, you know that? You really did."

"Gooshy," Dussander said heavily.

"I really *did* do a research paper, and you know what I got on it? An A-plus. Of course I had to be careful. You have to write that stuff in a certain way. You got to be careful."

"Do you?" Dussander asked. He took another cigarette with a hand that trembled.

"Oh yeah. All those library books, they read a certain way. Like the guys who wrote them got puking sick over what they were writing about." Todd was frowning, wrestling with the thought, trying to bring it out. The fact that *tone*, as that word is applied to writing, wasn't yet in his vocabulary, made it more difficult. "They all write like they lost a lot of sleep over it. How we've got to be careful so nothing like that ever happens again. I made my paper like that, and I guess the teacher gave me an A just cause I read the source material without losing my lunch." Once more, Todd smiled winningly.

Dussander dragged heavily on his unfiltered Kool. The tip trembled slightly. As he feathered smoke out of his nostrils, he coughed an old man's dank, hollow cough. "I can hardly believe this conversation is taking place," he said. He leaned forward and peered closely at Todd. "Boy, do you know the word 'existentialism'?"

Todd ignored the question. "Did you ever meet Ilse Koch?"

"Ilse Koch?" Almost inaudibly, Dussander said: "Yes. I met her."

"Was she beautiful?" Todd asked eagerly. "I mean . . ." His hands described an hourglass in the air.

"Surely you have seen her photograph?" Dussander asked. "An aficionado such as yourself?"

"What's an af . . . aff . . ."

"An aficionado," Dussander said, "is one who grooves. One who . . . gets off on something."

"Yeah? Cool." Todd's grin, puzzled and weak for a moment, shone out triumphantly again. "Sure, I've seen her picture. But you know how they are in those books." He spoke as if Dussander had them all. "Black and white, fuzzy . . . just snapshots. None of those guys knew they were taking pictures for, you know, *history*. Was she really stacked?"

"She was fat and dumpy and she had bad skin," Dussander said shortly. He crushed his cigarette out half-smoked in a Table Talk pie-dish filled with dead butts.

"Oh. Golly." Todd's face fell.

"Just luck," Dussander mused, looking at Todd. "You saw my picture in a war-adventures magazine and happened to ride next to me on the bus. *Tcha!*" He brought a fist down on the arm of his chair, but without much force.

"No sir, Mr. Dussander. There was more to it than that. A *lot*," Todd added earnestly, leaning forward.

"Oh? Really?" The bushy eyebrows rose, signalling polite disbelief.

"Sure. I mean, the pictures of you in my scrapbook were all thirty years old, at least. I mean, it *is* 1974."

"You keep a . . . a scrapbook?"

"Oh, yes, sir! It's a good one. Hundreds of pictures. I'll show it to you sometime. You'll go ape."

Dussander's face pulled into a revolted grimace, but he said nothing.

"The first couple of times I saw you, I wasn't sure at all. And then you got on the bus one day when it was raining, and you had this shiny black slicker on—"

"That," Dussander breathed.

"Sure. There was a picture of you in a coat like that in one of the magazines out in Foxy's garage. Also, a photo of you in your SS greatcoat in one of the library books. And when I saw you that day, I just said to myself, 'It's for sure. That's Kurt Dussander.' So I started to shadow you—"

"You did *what*?"

"Shadow you. Follow you. My ambition is to be a private detective like Sam Spade in the books, or Mannix on TV. Anyway, I was super careful. I didn't want you to get wise. Want to look at some pictures?"

Todd took a folded-over manila envelope from his back pocket. Sweat had stuck the flap down. He peeled it back carefully. His eyes were sparkling like a boy thinking about his birthday, or Christmas, or the firecrackers he will shoot off on the Fourth of July.

"You took pictures of me?"

"Oh, you bet. I got this little camera. A Kodak. It's thin and flat and fits right into your hand. Once you get the hang of it, you can take pictures of the subject just by holding the camera in your hand and spreading your fingers enough to let the lens peek through. Then you hit the button with your thumb." Todd laughed modestly. "I got the hang of it, but I took a lot of pictures of my fingers while I did. I hung right in there, though. I think a person can do anything if they try hard enough, you know it? It's corny but true."

Kurt Dussander had begun to look white and ill, shrunken inside his robe. "Did you have these pictures finished by a commercial developer, boy?"

"Huh?" Todd looked shocked and startled, then contemptuous.

"No! What do you think I am, stupid? My dad's got a darkroom. I've been developing my own pictures since I was nine."

Dussander said nothing, but he relaxed a little and some color came back into his face.

Todd handed him several glossy prints, the rough edges confirming that they had been home-developed. Dussander went through them, silently grim. Here he was sitting erect in a window seat of the downtown bus, with a copy of the latest James Michener, *Centennial*, in his hands. Here he was at the Devon Avenue bus stop, his umbrella under his arm and his head cocked back at an angle which suggested De Gaulle at his most imperial. Here he was standing on line just under the marquee of the Majestic Theater, erect and silent, conspicuous among the leaning teenagers and blank-faced housewives in curlers by his height and his bearing. Finally, here he was peering into his own mailbox.

"I was scared you might see me on that one," Todd said. "It was a calculated risk. I was right across the street. Boy oh boy, I wish I could afford a Minolta with a telephoto lens. Someday . . ." Todd looked wistful.

"No doubt you had a story ready, just in case."

"I was going to ask you if you'd seen my dog. Anyway, after I developed the pix, I compared them to these."

He handed Dussander three Xeroxed photographs. He had seen them all before, many times. The first showed him in his office at the Patin resettlement camp; it had been cropped so nothing showed but him and the Nazi flag on its stand by his desk. The second was a picture that had been taken on the day of his enlistment. The last showed him shaking hands with Heinrich Gluecks, who had been subordinate only to Himmler himself.

"I was pretty sure then, but I couldn't see if you had the harelip because of your goshdamn moustache. But I had to be sure, so I got this."

He handed over the last sheet from his envelope. It had been folded over many times. Dirt was grimed into the creases. The corners were lopped and milled—the way papers get when they spend a long time in the pockets of young boys who have no shortage of things to do and places to go. It was a copy of the Israeli want-sheet on Kurt Dussander. Holding it in his hands, Dussander reflected on corpses that were unquiet and refused to stay buried.

"I took your fingerprints," Todd said, smiling. "And then I did the compares to the one on the sheet."

Dussander gaped at him and then uttered the German word for shit. "You did not!"

"Sure I did. My mom and dad gave me a fingerprint set for Christmas last year. A real one, not just a toy. It had the powder and three brushes for three different surfaces and special paper for lifting them. My folks know I want to be a PI when I grow up. Of course, they think I'll grow out of it." He dismissed this idea with a disinterested lift and drop of his shoulders. "The book explained all about whorls and lands and points of similarity. They're called *compares*. You need eight compares for a fingerprint to get accepted in court.

"So anyway, one day when you were at the movies, I came here and dusted your mailbox and doorknob and lifted all the prints I could. Pretty smart, huh?"

Dussander said nothing. He was clutching the arms of his chair, and his toothless, deflated mouth was trembling. Todd didn't like that. It made him look like he was on the verge of tears. That, of course, was ridiculous. The Blood-Fiend of Patin in tears? You might as well expect Chevrolet to go bankrupt or McDonald's to give up burgers and start selling caviar and truffles.

"I got two sets of prints," Todd said. "One of them didn't look anything like the ones on the wanted poster. I figured those were the postman's. The rest were yours. I found more than eight compares. I found fourteen good ones." He grinned. "And that's how I did it."

"You are a little *bastard*," Dussander said, and for a moment his eyes shone dangerously. Todd felt a tingling little thrill, as he had in the hall. Then Dussander slumped back again.

"Whom have you told?"

"No one."

"Not even this friend? This Cony Pegler?"

"Foxy. Foxy Pegler. Nah, he's a blabbermouth. I haven't told anybody. There's nobody I trust that much."

"What do you want? Money? There is none, I'm afraid. In South America there was, although it was nothing as romantic or dangerous as the drug trade. There is—there *was*—a kind of 'old boy network' in Brazil and Paraguay and Santo Domingo. Fugitives from the war. I became part of their circle and did modestly well in minerals and ores—tin, copper, bauxite. Then the changes came. Nationalism, anti-Americanism. I might have ridden out the changes, but then Wiesenthal's men caught my scent. Bad luck follows bad luck, boy, like dogs after a bitch in heat. Twice they almost had me; once I heard the Jew-bastards in the next room.

"They hanged Eichmann," he whispered. One hand went to his neck, and his eyes had become as round as the eyes of a child listening to the darkest passage of a scary tale—"Hansel and Gretel," perhaps, or "Bluebeard." "He was an old man, of no danger to anyone. He was apolitical. Still, they hanged him."

Todd nodded.

"At last, I went to the only people who could help me. They had helped others, and I could run no more."

"You went to the Odessa?" Todd asked eagerly.

"To the Sicilians," Dussander said dryly, and Todd's face fell again. "It was arranged. False papers, false past. Would you care for a drink, boy?"

"Sure. You got a Coke?"

"No Coke." He pronounced it *Kök*.

"Milk?"

"Milk." Dussander went through the archway and into the kitchen. A fluorescent bar buzzed into life. "I live now on stock dividends," his voice came back. "Stocks I picked up after the war under yet another name. Through a bank in the State of Maine, if you please. The banker who bought them for me went to jail for murdering his wife a year after I bought them . . . life is sometimes strange, boy, *hein?*"

A refrigerator door opened and closed.

"The Sicilian jackals didn't know about those stocks," he said. "Today the Sicilians are everywhere, but in those days, Boston was as far north as they could be found. If they had known, they would have had those as well. They would have picked me clean and sent me to America to starve on welfare and food stamps."

Todd heard a cupboard door opened; he heard liquid poured into a glass.

"A little General Motors, a little American Telephone and Telegraph, a hundred and fifty shares of Revlon. All this banker's choices. Dufresne, his name was—I remember, because it sounds a little like mine. It seems he was not so smart at wife-killing as he was at picking growth stocks. The *crime passionel*, boy. It only proves that all men are donkeys who can read."

He came back into the room, slippers whispering. He held two green plastic glasses that looked like the premiums they sometimes gave out at gas station openings. When you filled your tank, you got a free glass. Dussander thrust a glass at Todd.

"I lived adequately on the stock portfolio this Dufresne had set up for me for the first five years I was here. But then I sold my Diamond Match stock in order to buy this house and a small cottage not far from Big Sur. Then, inflation. Recession. I sold the cottage and one by one I sold the stocks, many of them at fantastic profits. I wish to God I had bought more. But I thought I was well-protected in other directions; the stocks were, as you Americans say, a 'flier . . .' " He made a toothless hissing sound and snapped his fingers.

Todd was bored. He had not come here to listen to Dussander whine about his money or mutter about his stocks. The thought of blackmailing Dussander had never even crossed Todd's mind. Money? What would he do with it? He had his allowance; he had his paper route. If his monetary needs went higher than what these could provide during any given week, there was always someone who needed his lawn mowed.

Todd lifted his milk to his lips and then hesitated. His smile shone out again . . . an admiring smile. He extended the gas station premium glass to Dussander.

"*You* have some of it," he said slyly.

Dussander stared at him for a moment, uncomprehending, and then rolled his bloodshot eyes. "*Grüss Gott!*" He took the glass, swallowed twice, and handed it back. "No gasping for breath. No clawing at the t'roat. No smell of bitter almonds. It is milk, boy. *Milk*. From the Dairylea Farms. On the carton is a picture of a smiling cow."

Todd watched him warily for a moment, then took a small sip. Yes, it *tasted* like milk, sure did, but somehow he didn't feel very thirsty anymore. He put the glass down. Dussander shrugged, raised his own glass, and took a swallow. He smacked his lips over it.

"*Schnaps?*" Todd asked.

"Bourbon. Ancient Age. Very nice. And cheap."

Todd fiddled his fingers along the seams of his jeans.

"So," Dussander said, "if you have decided to have a 'flier' of your own, you should be aware that you have picked a worthless stock."

"Huh?"

"Blackmail," Dussander said. "Isn't that what they call it on *Mannix* and *Hawaii Five-O* and *Barnaby Jones?* Extortion. If that was what—"

But Todd was laughing—hearty, boyish laughter. He shook his head, tried to speak, could not, and went on laughing.

"No," Dussander said, and suddenly he looked gray and more frightened than he had since he and Todd had begun to speak. He took another large swallow of his drink, grimaced, and shuddered. "I see that is not it . . . at least, not the extortion of money. But, though you laugh, I smell extortion in it somewhere. What is it? Why do you come here and disturb an old man? Perhaps, as you say, I was once a Nazi. SS, even. Now I am only old, and to have a bowel movement I have to use a suppository. So what do you want?"

Todd had sobered again. He stared at Dussander with an open and appealing frankness. "Why . . . I want to hear about it. That's all. That's all I want. Really."

"*Hear* about it?" Dussander echoed. He looked utterly perplexed.

Todd leaned forward, tanned elbows on bluejeaned knees. "Sure. The firing squads. The gas chambers. The ovens. The guys who had to dig their own graves and then stand on the ends so they'd fall into them. The . . ." His tongue came out and wetted his lips. "The examinations. The experiments. Everything. All the gooshy stuff."

Dussander stared at him with a certain amazed detachment, the way a veterinarian might stare at a cat who was giving birth to a succession of two-headed kittens. "You are a monster," he said softly.

Todd sniffed. "According to the books I read for my report, *you're* the monster, Mr. Dussander. Not me. You sent them to the ovens, not me. Two thousand a day at Patin before you came, three thousand after, thirty-five hundred before the Russians came and made you stop. Himmler called you an efficiency expert and gave you a medal. So you call me a monster. Oh *boy*."

"All of that is a filthy American lie," Dussander said, stung. He set his glass down with a bang, slopping bourbon onto his hand and the table. "The problem was not of my making, nor was the solution. I was given orders and directives, which I followed."

Todd's smile widened; it was now almost a smirk.

"Oh, I know how the Americans have distorted that," Dussander muttered. "But your own politicians make our Dr. Goebbels look like a child playing with picture books in a kindergarten. They speak of morality while they douse screaming children and old women in burning napalm. Your draft-resisters are called cowards and 'peaceniks.' For refusing to follow orders they are either put in jails or scourged from the country. Those who demonstrate against this country's unfortunate Asian adventure are clubbed down in the streets. The GI soldiers who kill the innocent are decorated by Presidents, welcomed home from the bayoneting of children and the burning of hospitals with parades and bunting. They are given dinners, Keys to the City, free tickets to pro football games." He toasted his glass in Todd's direction. "Only those who lose are tried as war criminals for following orders and directives." He drank and then had a coughing fit that brought thin color to his cheeks.

Through most of this Todd fidgeted the way he did when his parents discussed whatever had been on the news that night—good old Walter Klondike, his dad called him. He didn't care about Dussander's politics any more than he cared about Dussander's stocks. His idea was that people made up politics so they could do things. Like when he wanted to feel around under Sharon Ackerman's dress last year. Sharon said it was bad for him to want to do that, even though he could tell from her tone of voice that the idea sort of excited her. So he told her he wanted to be a doctor when he grew up and then she let him. That was politics. He wanted to hear about German doctors trying to mate women with dogs, putting identical twins into refrigerators to see whether they would die at the same time or if one of them would last longer, and electroshock therapy, and operations without anesthetic, and German soldiers raping all the women they wanted. The rest was just so much tired bullspit to cover up the gooshy stuff after someone came along and put a stop to it.

"If I hadn't followed orders, I would have been dead." Dussander was breathing hard, his upper body rocking back and forth in the chair, making the springs squeak. A little cloud of liquor-smell hung around him. "There was always the Russian front, *nicht wahr?* Our leaders were madmen, granted, but does one argue with madmen . . . especially when the maddest of them all has the luck of Satan. He escaped a brilliant assassination attempt by inches. Those who conspired were strangled with piano-wire, strangled slowly. Their death-agonies were filmed for the edification of the elite—"

"Yeah! Neat!" Todd cried impulsively. "Did you see that movie?"

"Yes. I saw. We all saw what happened to those unwilling or unable to run before the wind and wait for the storm to end. What we did then was the right thing. For that time and that place, it was the right thing. I would do it again. But . . ."

His eyes dropped to his glass. It was empty.

". . . but I don't wish to speak of it, or even think of it. What we did was motivated only by survival, and nothing about survival is pretty. I had dreams . . ." He slowly took a cigarette from the box on the TV. "Yes. For years I had them. Blackness, and sounds in the blackness. Tractor engines. Bulldozer engines. Gunbutts thudding against what might have been frozen earth, or human skulls. Whistles, sirens, pistol-shots, screams. The doors of cattle-cars rumbling open on cold winter afternoons.

"Then, in my dreams, all sounds would stop—and eyes would open in the dark, gleaming like the eyes of animals in a rainforest. For many years I lived on the edge of the jungle, and I suppose that is why it is always the jungle I smelled and felt in those dreams. When I woke from them I would be drenched with sweat, my heart thundering in my chest, my hand stuffed into my mouth to stifle the screams. And I would think: *The dream is the truth.* Brazil,

Paraguay, Cuba . . . those places are the dream. In the reality I am
still at Patin. The Russians are closer today than yesterday. Some of
them are remembering that in 1943 they had to eat frozen German
corpses to stay alive. Now they long to drink hot German blood.
There were rumors, boy, that some of them did just that when they
crossed into Germany: cut the t'roats of some prisoners and drank
their blood out of a boot. I would wake up and think: *The work must
go on, if only so there is no evidence of what we did here, or so little that the
world, which doesn't want to believe it, won't have to.* I would think: *The
work must go on if we are to survive."*

Todd listened to this with close attention and great interest. This
was pretty good, but he was sure there would be better stuff in the
days ahead. All Dussander needed was a little prodding. Heck, he
was lucky. Lots of men his age were senile.

Dussander dragged deeply on his cigarette. "Later, after the
dreams went away, there were days when I would think I had seen
someone from Patin. Never guards or fellow officers, always
inmates. I remember one afternoon in West Germany, ten years
ago. There was an accident on the Autobahn. Traffic was frozen in
every lane. I sat in my Morris, listening to the radio, waiting for the
traffic to move. I looked to my right. There was a very old Simca in
the next lane, and the man behind the wheel was looking at me. He
was perhaps fifty, and he looked ill. There was a scar on his cheek.
His hair was white, short, cut badly. I looked away. The minutes
passed and still the traffic didn't move. I began snatching glances at
the man in the Simca. Every time I did, he was looking at me, his
face as still as death, his eyes sunken in their sockets. I became
convinced he had been at Patin. He had been there and he had
recognized me."

Dussander wiped a hand across his eyes.

"It was winter. The man was wearing an overcoat. But I was
convinced that if I got out of my car and went to him, made him
take off his coat and push up his shirtsleeves, I would see the
number on his arm.

"At last the traffic began to move again. I pulled away from the
Simca. If the jam had lasted another ten minutes, I believe I would
have gotten out of my car and pulled the old man out of his. I would

have beaten him, number or no number. I would have beaten him for looking at me that way.

"Shortly after that, I left Germany forever."

"Lucky for you," Todd said.

Dussander shrugged. "It was the same everywhere. Havana, Mexico City, Rome. I was in Rome for three years, you know. I would see a man looking at me over his *cappuccino* in a café . . . a woman in a hotel lobby who seemed more interested in me than in her magazine . . . a waiter in a restaurant who would keep glancing at me no matter whom he was serving. I would become convinced that these people were studying me, and that night the dream would come—the sounds, the jungle, the eyes.

"But when I came to America I put it out of my mind. I go to movies. I eat out once a week, always at one of those fast-food places that are so clean and so well-lighted by fluorescent bars. Here at my house I do jigsaw puzzles and I read novels—most of them bad ones —and watch TV. At night I drink until I'm sleepy. The dreams don't come anymore. When I see someone looking at me in the supermarket or the library or the tobacconist's, I think it must be because I look like their grandfather . . . or an old teacher . . . or a neighbor in a town they left some years ago." He shook his head at Todd. "Whatever happened at Patin, it happened to another man. Not to me."

"Great!" Todd said. "I want to hear all about it."

Dussander's eyes squeezed closed, and then opened slowly. "You don't understand. I do not wish to speak of it."

"You will, though. If you don't, I'll tell everyone who you are."

Dussander stared at him, gray-faced. "I knew," he said, "that I would find the extortion sooner or later."

"Today I want to hear about the gas ovens," Todd said. "How you baked them after they were dead." His smile beamed out, rich and radiant. "But put your teeth in before you start. You look better with your teeth in."

Dussander did as he was told. He talked to Todd about the gas ovens until Todd had to go home for lunch. Every time he tried to slip over into generalities, Todd would frown severely and ask him specific questions to get him back on the track. Dussander drank a great deal as he talked. He didn't smile. Todd smiled. Todd smiled enough for both of them.

2

August, 1974.

They sat on Dussander's back porch under a cloudless, smiling sky. Todd was wearing jeans, Keds, and his Little League shirt. Dussander was wearing a baggy gray shirt and shapeless khaki pants held up with suspenders—wino-pants, Todd thought with private contempt; they looked like they had come straight from a box in the back of the Salvation Army store downtown. He was really going to have to do something about the way Dussander dressed when he was at home. It spoiled some of the fun.

The two of them were eating Big Macs that Todd had brought in his bike-basket, pedaling fast so they wouldn't get cold. Todd was sipping a Coke through a plastic straw. Dussander had a glass of bourbon.

His old man's voice rose and fell, papery, hesitant, sometimes nearly inaudible. His faded blue eyes, threaded with the usual snaps of red, were never still. An observer might have thought them grandfather and grandson, the latter perhaps attending some rite of passage, a handing down.

"And that's all I remember," Dussander finished presently, and took a large bite of his sandwich. McDonald's Secret Sauce dribbled down his chin.

"You can do better than that," Todd said softly.

Dussander took a large swallow from his glass. "The uniforms were made of paper," he said finally, almost snarling. "When one inmate died, the uniform was passed on if it could still be worn. Sometimes one paper uniform could dress as many as forty inmates. I received high marks for my frugality."

"From Gluecks?"

"From Himmler."

"But there was a clothing factory in Patin. You told me that just last week. Why didn't you have the uniforms made there? The inmates themselves could have made them."

"The job of the factory in Patin was to make uniforms for German soldiers. And as for us . . ." Dussander's voice faltered for a moment, and then he forced himself to go on. "We were not in the business of rehabilitation," he finished.

Todd smiled his broad smile.

"Enough for today? Please? My throat is sore."

"You shouldn't smoke so much, then," Todd said, continuing to smile. "Tell me some more about the uniforms."

"Which? Inmate or SS?" Dussander's voice was resigned.

Smiling, Todd said: "Both."

3

September, 1974.

Todd was in the kitchen of his house, making himself a peanut butter and jelly sandwich. You got to the kitchen by going up half a dozen redwood steps to a raised area that gleamed with chrome and stainless steel. His mother's electric typewriter had been going steadily ever since Todd had gotten home from school. She was typing a master's thesis for a grad student. The grad student had short hair, wore thick glasses, and looked like a creature from outer space, in Todd's humble opinion. The thesis was on the effect of fruitflies in the Salinas Valley after World War II, or some good shit like that. Now her typewriter stopped and she came out of her office.

"Todd-baby," she greeted him.

"Monica-baby," he hailed back, amiably enough.

His mother wasn't a bad-looking chick for thirty-six, Todd thought; blonde hair that was streaked ash in a couple of places, tall, shapely, now dressed in dark red shorts and a sheer blouse of a warm whiskey color—the blouse was casually knotted below her breasts, putting her flat, unlined midriff on show. A typewriter eraser was tucked into her hair, which had been pinned carelessly back with a turquoise clip.

"So how's school?" she asked him, coming up the steps into the kitchen. She brushed his lips casually with hers and then slid onto one of the stools in front of the breakfast counter.

"School's cool."

"Going to be on the honor roll again?"

"Sure." Actually, he thought his grades might slip a notch this first quarter. He had been spending a lot of time with Dussander, and when he wasn't actually with the old kraut, he was thinking about the things Dussander had told him. Once or twice he had dreamed about the things Dussander had told him. But it was nothing he couldn't handle.

"Apt pupil," she said, ruffling his shaggy blonde hair. "How's that sandwich?"

"Good," he said.

"Would you make me one and bring it into my office?"

"Can't," he said, getting up. "I promised Mr. Denker I'd come over and read to him for an hour or so."

"Are you still on *Robinson Crusoe?*"

"Nope." He showed her the spine of a thick book he had bought in a junkshop for twenty cents. *"Tom Jones."*

"Ye gods and little fishes! It'll take you the whole school-year to get through that, Todd-baby. Couldn't you at least find an abridged edition, like with *Crusoe?*"

"Probably, but he wanted to hear all of this one. He said so."

"Oh." She looked at him for a moment, then hugged him. It was rare for her to be so demonstrative, and it made Todd a little uneasy. "You're a peach to be taking so much of your spare time to read to him. Your father and I think it's just . . . just exceptional."

Todd cast his eyes down modestly.

"And to not want to tell anybody," she said. "Hiding your light under a bushel."

"Oh, the kids I hang around with—they'd probably think I was some kind of weirdo," Todd said, smiling modestly down at the floor. "All that good shit."

"Don't say that," she admonished absently. Then: "Do you think Mr. Denker would like to come over and have dinner with us some night?"

"Maybe," Todd said vaguely. "Listen, I gotta put an egg in my shoe and beat it."

"Okay. Supper at six-thirty. Don't forget."

"I won't."

"Your father's got to work late so it'll just be me and thee again, okay?"

"Crazy, baby."

She watched him go with a fond smile, hoping there was nothing in *Tom Jones* he shouldn't be reading; he was only thirteen. She didn't suppose there was. He was growing up in a society where magazines like *Penthouse* were available to anyone with a dollar and a quarter, or to any kid who could reach up to the top shelf of the magazine rack and grab a quick peek before the clerk could shout for him to put that up and get lost. In a society that seemed to believe most of all in the creed of hump thy neighbor, she didn't think there could be much in a book two hundred years old to screw up Todd's head—although she supposed the old man might get off on it a little. And as Richard liked to say, for a kid the whole world's a laboratory. You have to let them poke around in it. And if the kid in question has a healthy home life and loving parents, he'll be all the stronger for having knocked around a few strange corners.

And there went the healthiest kid she knew, pedaling up the street on his Schwinn. *We did okay by the lad*, she thought, turning to make her sandwich. *Damned if we didn't do okay.*

4

October, 1974.

Dussander had lost weight. They sat in the kitchen, the shopworn copy of *Tom Jones* between them on the oilcloth-covered table (Todd, who tried never to miss a trick, had purchased the Cliff's Notes on the book with part of his allowance and had carefully read the entire summary against the possibility that his mother or father might ask him questions about the plot). Todd was eating a Ring Ding he had bought at the market. He had bought one for Dussander, but Dussander hadn't touched it. He only looked at it morosely from time to time as he drank his bourbon. Todd hated to see anything as tasty as Ring Dings go to waste. If he didn't eat it pretty quick, Todd was going to ask him if he could have it.

"So how did the stuff get to Patin?" he asked Dussander.

"In railroad cars," Dussander said. "In railroad cars labelled MEDICAL SUPPLIES. It came in long crates that looked like coffins. Fitting, I suppose. The inmates off-loaded the crates and stacked them in the infirmary. Later, our own men stacked them in the storage sheds. They did it at night. The storage sheds were behind the showers."

"Was it always Zyklon-B?"

"No, from time to time we would be sent something else. Experimental gases. The High Command was always interested in improving efficiency. Once they sent us a gas code-named PEGASUS. A nerve-gas. Thank God they never sent it again. It—" Dussander saw Todd lean forward, saw those eyes sharpen, and he suddenly stopped and gestured casually with his gas station premium glass. "It didn't work very well," he said. "It was . . . quite boring."

But Todd was not fooled, not in the least. "What did it do?"

"It killed them—what did you think it did, made them walk on water? It killed them, that's all."

"Tell me."

"No," Dussander said, now unable to hide the horror he felt. He hadn't thought of PEGASUS in . . . how long? Ten years? Twenty? "I won't tell you! I refuse!"

"Tell me," Todd repeated, licking chocolate icing from his fingers. "Tell me or you know what."

Yes, Dussander thought. *I know what. Indeed I do, you putrid little monster.*

"It made them dance," he said reluctantly.

"Dance?"

"Like the Zyklon-B, it came in through the shower-heads. And they . . . they began to leap about. Some were screaming. Most of them were laughing. They began to vomit, and to . . . to defecate helplessly."

"Wow," Todd said. "Shit themselves, huh?" He pointed at the Ring Ding on Dussander's plate. He had finished his own. "You going to eat that?"

Dussander didn't reply. His eyes were hazed with memory. His face was far away and cold, like the dark side of a planet which does not rotate. Inside his mind he felt the *queerest* combination of revulsion and—could it be?—*nostalgia*?

"They began to twitch all over and to make high, strange sounds in their throats. My men . . . they called PEGASUS the Yodeling

Gas. At last they all collapsed and just lay there on the floor in their own filth, they lay there, yes, they lay there on the concrete, screaming and yodeling, with bloody noses. But I lied, boy. The gas didn't kill them, either because it wasn't strong enough or because we couldn't bring ourselves to wait long enough. I suppose it was that. Men and women like that could not have lived long. Finally I sent in five men with rifles to end their agonies. It would have looked bad on my record if it had shown up, I've no doubt of that—it would have looked like a waste of cartridges at a time when the Fuehrer had declared every cartridge a national resource. But those five men I trusted. There were times, boy, when I thought I would never forget the sound they made. The yodeling sound. The laughing."

"Yeah, I bet," Todd said. He finished Dussander's Ring Ding in two bites. Waste not, want not, Todd's mother said on the rare occasions when Todd complained about left-overs. "That was a good story, Mr. Dussander. You always tell them good. Once I get you going."

Todd smiled at him. And incredibly—certainly not because he wanted to—Dussander found himself smiling back.

5

November, 1974.

Dick Bowden, Todd's father, looked remarkably like a movie and TV actor named Lloyd Bochner. He—Bowden, not Bochner—was thirty-eight. He was a thin, narrow man who liked to dress in Ivy League—style shirts and solid-color suits, usually dark. When he was on a construction site, he wore khakis and a hard-hat that was a souvenir of his Peace Corps days, when he had helped to design and build two dams in Africa. When he was working in his study at home, he wore half-glasses that had a way of slipping down to the end of his nose and making him look like a college dean. He was wearing these glasses now as he tapped his son's first-quarter report card against his desk's gleaming glass top.

"One B. Four C's. One D. A D, for Christ's sake! Todd, your mother's not showing it, but she's really upset."

Todd dropped his eyes. He didn't smile. When his dad swore, that wasn't exactly the best of news.

"My God, you've *never* gotten a report like this. A *D* in Beginning Algebra? What *is* this?"

"I don't know, Dad." He looked humbly at his knees.

"Your mother and I think that maybe you've been spending a little too much time with Mr. Denker. Not hitting the books enough. We think you ought to cut it down to weekends, slugger. At least until we see where you're going academically . . ."

Todd looked up, and for a single second Bowden thought he saw a wild, pallid anger in his son's eyes. His own eyes widened, his fingers clenched on Todd's buff-colored report card . . . and then it was just Todd, looking at him openly if rather unhappily. Had that anger really been there? Surely not. But the moment had unsettled him, made it hard for him to know exactly how to proceed. Todd hadn't been mad, and Dick Bowden didn't want to *make* him mad. He and his son were friends, always had been friends, and Dick wanted things to stay that way. They had no secrets from each other, none at all (except for the fact that Dick Bowden was sometimes unfaithful with his secretary, but that wasn't exactly the sort of thing you told your thirteen-year-old son, was it? . . . and besides, that had absolutely no bearing on his home life, his *family* life). That was the way it was supposed to be, the way it *had* to be in a cockamamie world where murderers went unpunished, high school kids skin-popped heroin, and junior high schoolers—kids Todd's age—turned up with VD.

"No, Dad, please don't do that. I mean, don't punish Mr. Denker for something that's my fault. I mean, he'd be lost without me. I'll do better. Really. That algebra . . . it just threw me to start with. But I went over to Ben Tremaine's, and after we studied together for a few days, I started to get it. I just . . . I dunno, I sorta choked at first."

"I think you're spending too much time with him," Bowden said, but he was weakening. It was hard to refuse Todd, hard to disappoint him, and what he said about punishing the old man for Todd's falling-off . . . goddammit, it made sense. The old man looked forward to his visits so much.

"That Mr. Storrman, the algebra teacher, is really hard," Todd said. "Lots of kids got D's. Three or four got F's."

Bowden nodded thoughtfully.

"I won't go Wednesdays anymore. Not until I bring my grades up." He had read his father's eyes. "And instead of going out for anything at school, I'll stay after every day and study. I promise."

"You really like the old guy that much?"

"He's really neat," Tod said sincerely.

"Well . . . okay. We'll try it your way, slugger. But I want to see a big improvement in your marks come January, you understand me? I'm thinking of your future. You may think junior high's too soon to start thinking about that, but it's not. Not by a long chalk." As his mother liked to say *Waste not, want not,* so Dick Bowden liked to say *Not by a long chalk.*

"I understand, Dad," Todd said gravely. Man-to-man stuff.

"Get out of here and give those books a workout then." He pushed his half-glasses up on his nose and clapped Todd on the shoulder.

Todd's smile, broad and bright, broke across his face. "Right on, Dad!"

Bowden watched Todd go with a prideful smile of his own. One in a million. And that hadn't been anger on Todd's face. For sure. Pique, maybe . . . but not that high-voltage emotion he had at first thought he'd seen there. If Todd was that mad, he would have known; he could read his son like a book. It had always been that way.

Whistling, his fatherly duty discharged, Dick Bowden unrolled a blueprint and bent over it.

6

December, 1974.

The face that came in answer to Todd's insistent finger on the bell was haggard and yellowed. The hair, which had been lush in July, had now begun to recede from the bony brow; it looked lusterless and brittle. Dussander's body, thin to begin with, was now gaunt . . . although, Todd thought, he was nowhere near as gaunt as the inmates who had once been delivered into his hands.

Todd's left hand had been behind his back when Dussander came to the door. Now he brought it out and handed a wrapped package to Dussander. "Merry Christmas!" he yelled.

Dussander had cringed from the box; now he took it with no expression of pleasure or surprise. He handled it gingerly, as if it might contain explosive. Beyond the porch, it was raining. It had been raining off and on for almost a week, and Todd had carried the box inside his coat. It was wrapped in gay foil and ribbon.

"What is it?" Dussander asked without enthusiasm as they went to the kitchen.

"Open it and see."

Todd took a can of Coke from his jacket pocket and put it on the red and white checked oilcloth that covered the kitchen table. "Better pull down the shades," he said confidentially.

Distrust immediately leaked onto Dussander's face. "Oh? Why?"

"Well . . . you can never tell who's lookin," Todd said, smiling. "Isn't that how you got along all those years? By seeing the people who might be lookin before they saw you?"

Dussander pulled down the kitchen shades. Then he poured himself a glass of bourbon. Then he pulled the bow off the package. Todd had wrapped it the way boys so often wrap Christmas packages—boys who have more important things on their minds, things like football and street hockey and the Friday Nite Creature Feature you'll watch with a friend who's sleeping over, the two of you wrapped in a blanket and crammed together on one end of the couch, laughing. There were a lot of ragged corners, a lot of uneven seams, a lot of Scotch tape. It spoke of impatience with such a womanly thing.

Dussander was a little touched in spite of himself. And later, when the horror had receded a little, he thought: *I should have known*.

It was a uniform. An SS uniform. Complete with jackboots.

He looked numbly from the contents of the box to its cardboard cover: PETER'S QUALITY COSTUME CLOTHIERS—AT THE SAME LOCATION SINCE 1951!

"No," he said softly. "I won't put it on. This is where it ends, boy. I'll die before I put it on."

"Remember what they did to Eichmann," Todd said solemnly.

"He was an old man and he had no politics. Isn't that what you said? Besides, I saved the whole fall for it. It cost over eighty bucks, with the boots thrown in. You didn't mind wearing it in 1944, either. Not at all."

"You little *bastard!*" Dussander raised one fist over his head. Todd didn't flinch at all. He stood his ground, eyes shining.

"Yeah," he said softly. "Go ahead and touch me. You just touch me *once.*"

Dussander lowered the hand. His lips were quivering. "You are a fiend from hell," he muttered.

"Put it on," Todd invited.

Dussander's hands went to the tie of his robe and paused there. His eyes, sheeplike and begging, looked into Todd's. "Please," he said. "I am an old man. No more."

Todd shook his head slowly but firmly. His eyes were still shining. He liked it when Dussander begged. The way they must have begged him once. The inmates at Patin.

Dussander let the robe fall to the floor and stood naked except for his slippers and his boxer shorts. His chest was sunken, his belly slightly bloated. His arms were scrawny old man's arms. But the uniform, Todd thought. The uniform will make a difference.

Slowly, Dussander took the tunic out of the box and began to put it on.

Ten minutes later he stood fully dressed in the SS uniform. The cap was slightly askew, the shoulders slumped, but still the death's-head insignia stood out clearly. Dussander had a dark dignity—at least in Todd's eyes—that he had not possessed earlier. In spite of his slump, in spite of the cockeyed angle of his feet, Todd was pleased. For the first time Dussander looked to Todd as Todd believed he should look. Older, yes. Defeated, certainly. But in uniform again. Not an old man spinning away his sunset years watching Lawrence Welk on a cruddy black and white TV with tinfoil on the rabbit ears, but Kurt Dussander, The Blood-Fiend of Patin.

As for Dussander, he felt disgust, discomfort . . . and a mild, sneaking sense of relief. He partly despised this latter emotion, recognizing it as the truest indicator yet of the psychological domination the boy had established over him. He was the boy's prisoner, and every time he found he could live through yet another indignity, every time he felt that mild relief, the boy's power grew. And yet he *was* relieved. It was only cloth and buttons and snaps . . . and it was a sham at that. The fly was a zipper; it should have been buttons. The marks of rank were wrong, the tailoring sloppy, the boots a cheap grade of imitation leather. It was only a trumpery uniform after all, and it wasn't exactly *killing* him, was it? No. It—

"Straighten your cap!" Todd said loudly.

Dussander blinked at him, startled.

"Straighten your cap, soldier!"

Dussander did so, unconsciously giving it that final small insolent twist that had been the trademark of his *Oberleutnants*—and, sadly wrong as it was, this was an *Oberleutnant's* uniform.

"Get those feet together!"

He did so, bringing the heels together with a smart rap, doing the correct thing with hardly a thought, doing it as if the intervening years had slipped off along with his bathrobe.

"Achtung!"

He snapped to attention, and for a moment Todd was scared—really scared. He felt like the sorcerer's apprentice, who had brought the brooms to life but who had not possessed enough wit to stop them once they got started. The old man living in genteel poverty was gone. Dussander was here.

Then his fear was replaced by a tingling sense of power.

"About face!"

Dussander pivoted neatly, the bourbon forgotten, the torment of the last four months forgotten. He heard his heels click together again as he faced the grease-splattered stove. Beyond it, he could see the dusty parade ground of the military academy where he had learned his soldier's trade.

"About face!"

He whirled again, this time not executing the order as well, losing his balance a little. Once it would have been ten demerits and the butt of a swagger stick in his belly, sending his breath out in a hot and agonized gust. Inwardly he smiled a little. The boy didn't know all the tricks. No indeed.

"Now *march!*" Todd cried. His eyes were hot, glowing.

The iron went out of Dussander's shoulders; he slumped forward again. "No," he said. "Please—"

"March! March! March, I said!"

With a strangled sound, Dussander began to goose-step across the faded linoleum of his kitchen floor. He right-faced to avoid the table; right-faced again as he approached the wall. His face was uptilted slightly, expressionless. His legs rammed out before him, then crashed down, making the cheap china rattle in the cabinet over the sink. His arms moved in short arcs.

The image of the walking brooms recurred to Todd, and his fright recurred with it. It suddenly struck him that he didn't want Dussander to be enjoying any part of this, and that perhaps—just perhaps—he had wanted to make Dussander appear ludicrous even more than he had wanted to make him appear authentic. But somehow, despite the man's age and the cheap dime-store furnishings of the kitchen, he didn't look ludicrous in the least. He looked frightening. For the first time the corpses in the ditches and the crematoriums seemed to take on their own reality for Todd. The photographs of the tangled arms and legs and torsos, fishbelly white in the cold spring rains of Germany, were not something staged like a scene in a horror film—a pile of bodies created from department-store dummies, say, to be picked up by the grips and propmen when the scene was done—but simply a real fact, stupendous and inexplicable and evil. For a moment it seemed to him that he could smell the bland and slightly smoky odor of decomposition.

Terror gathered him in.

"Stop!" he shouted.

Dussander continued to goose-step, his eyes blank and far away. His head had come up even more, pulling the scrawny chicken-tendons of his throat tight, tilting his chin at an arrogant angle. His nose, blade-thin, jutted obscenely.

Todd felt sweat in his armpits. *"Halt!"* he cried out.

Dussander halted, right foot forward, left coming up and then down beside the right with a single pistonlike stamp. For a moment

the cold lack of expression held on his face—robotic, mindless—
and then it was replaced by confusion. Confusion was followed by
defeat. He slumped.

Todd let out a silent breath of relief and for a moment he was
furious with himself. *Who's in charge here, anyway?* Then his
self-confidence flooded back in. *I am, that's who. And he better not
forget it.*

He began to smile again. "Pretty good. But with a little practice,
I think you'll be a lot better."

Dussander stood mute, panting, his head hanging.

"You can take it off now," Todd added generously . . . and
couldn't help wondering if he really wanted Dussander to put it on
again. For a few seconds there—

7

January, 1975.

Todd left school by himself after the last bell, got his bike, and
pedaled down to the park. He found a deserted bench, set his
Schwinn up on its kickstand, and took his report card out of his hip
pocket. He took a look around to see if there was anyone in the area
he knew, but the only other people in sight were two high school
kids making out by the pond and a pair of gross-looking winos
passing a paper bag back and forth. Dirty fucking winos, he
thought, but it wasn't the winos that had upset him. He opened his
card.

English: C. American History: C. Earth Science: D. Your
Community and You: B. Primary French: F. Beginning Algebra: F.

He stared at the grades, unbelieving. He had known it was going
to be bad, but this was disaster.

Maybe that's best, an inner voice spoke up suddenly. *Maybe you even
did it on purpose, because a part of you wants it to end. Needs for it to end.
Before something bad happens.*

He shoved the thought roughly aside. Nothing bad was going to
happen. Dussander was under his thumb. Totally under his thumb.
The old man thought one of Todd's friends had a letter, but he
didn't know which friend. If anything happened to Todd—*anything*

—that letter would go to the police. Once he supposed Dussander might have tried it anyway. Now he was too old to run, even with a head start.

"He's under control, dammit," Todd whispered, and then pounded his thigh hard enough to make the muscle knot. Talking to yourself was bad shit—crazy people talked to themselves. He had picked up the habit over the last six weeks or so, and didn't seem able to break it. He'd caught several people looking at him strangely because of it. A couple of them had been teachers. And that asshole Bernie Everson had come right out and asked him if he was going fruitcrackers. Todd had come very, very close to punching the little pansy in the mouth, and that sort of stuff— brawls, scuffles, punch-outs—was no good. That sort of stuff got you noticed in all the wrong ways. Talking to yourself was bad, right, okay, but—

"The dreams are bad, too," he whispered. He didn't catch himself that time.

Just lately the dreams had been very bad. In the dreams he was always in uniform, although the type varied. Sometimes it was a paper uniform and he was standing in line with hundreds of gaunt men; the smell of burning was in the air and he could hear the choppy roar of bulldozer engines. Then Dussander would come up the line, pointing out this one or that one. They were left. The others were marched away toward the crematoriums. Some of them kicked and struggled, but most were too undernourished, too exhausted. Then Dussander was standing in front of Todd. Their eyes met for a long, paralyzing moment, and then Dussander levelled a faded umbrella at Todd.

"Take this one to the laboratories," Dussander said in the dream. His lip curled back to reveal his false teeth. "Take this American boy."

In another dream he wore an SS uniform. His jackboots were shined to a mirrorlike reflecting surface. The death's-head insignia and the lightning-bolts glittered. But he was standing in the middle of Santo Donato Boulevard and everyone was looking at him. They began to point. Some of them began to laugh. Others looked shocked, angry, or revolted. In this dream an old car came to a squalling, creaky halt and Dussander peered out at him, a Dussander who looked two hundred years old and nearly mummified, his skin a yellowed scroll.

"I know you!" the dream-Dussander proclaimed shrilly. He looked around at the spectators and then back to Todd. "You were in charge at Patin! Look, everybody! This is The Blood-Fiend of Patin! Himmler's 'Efficiency Expert'! I denounce you, murderer! I denounce you, butcher! I denounce you, killer of infants! I denounce you!"

In yet another dream, he wore a striped convict's uniform and was being led down a stone-walled corridor by two guards who looked like his parents. Both wore conspicuous yellow armbands with the Star of David on them. Walking behind them was a minister, reading from the Book of Deuteronomy. Todd looked back over his shoulder and saw that the minister was Dussander, and he was wearing the black tunic of an SS officer.

At the end of the stone corridor, double doors opened on an octagonal room with glass walls. There was a scaffold in the center of it. Behind the glass walls stood ranks of emaciated men and women, all naked, all watching with the same dark, flat expression. On each arm was a blue number.

"It's all right," Todd whispered to himself. "It's okay, really, everything's under control."

The couple that had been making out glanced over at him. Todd stared at them fiercely, daring them to say anything. At last they looked back the other way. Had the boy been grinning?

Todd got up, jammed his report card into his hip pocket, and mounted his bike. He pedaled down to a drugstore two blocks away. There he bought a bottle of ink eradicator and a fine-point pen that dispensed blue ink. He went back to the park (the make-out couple was gone, but the winos were still there, stinking the place up) and changed his English grade to a B, American History to A, Earth Science to B, Primary French to C, and Beginning Algebra to B. Your Community and You he eradicated and then simply wrote in again, so the card would have a uniform look.

Uniforms, right.

"Never mind," he whispered to himself. "That'll hold them. That'll hold them, all right."

One night late in the month, sometime after two o'clock, Kurt Dussander awoke struggling with the bedclothes, gasping and moaning, into a darkness that seemed close and terrifying. He felt half-suffocated, paralyzed with fear. It was as if a heavy stone lay on his chest, and he wondered if he could be having a heart attack. He clawed in the darkness for the bedside lamp and almost knocked it off the nightstand turning it on.

I'm in my own room, he thought, my own bedroom, here in Santo Donato, here in California, here in America. See, the same brown drapes pulled across the same window, the same bookshelves filled with dime paperbacks from the bookshop on Soren Street, same gray rug, same blue wallpaper. No heart attack. No jungle. No eyes.

But the terror still clung to him like a stinking pelt, and his heart went on racing. The dream had come back. He had known that it would, sooner or later, if the boy kept on. The cursed boy. He thought the boy's letter of protection was only a bluff, and not a very good one at that; something he had picked up from the TV detective programs. What friend would the boy trust not to open such a momentous letter? No friend, that was who. Or so he thought. If he could be *sure*—

His hands closed with an arthritic, painful snap and then opened slowly.

He took the packet of cigarettes from the table and lit one, scratching the wooden match on the bedpost. The clock's hands stood at 2:41. There would be no more sleep for him this night. He inhaled smoke and then coughed it out in a series of racking spasms. No more sleep unless he wanted to go downstairs and have a drink or two. Or three. And there had been altogether too much drinking over the last six weeks or so. He was no longer a young man who could toss them off one after the other, the way he had when he had been an officer on leave in Berlin in '39, when the scent of victory had been in the air and everywhere you heard the Fuehrer's voice, saw his blazing, commanding eyes—

The boy . . . the cursed boy!

"Be honest," he said aloud, and the sound of his own voice in the quiet room made him jump a little. He was not in the habit of talking to himself, but neither was it the first time he had ever done so. He remembered doing it off and on during the last few weeks at Patin, when everything had come down around their ears and in the east the sound of Russian thunder grew louder first every day and then every hour. It had been natural enough to talk to himself then. He had been under stress, and people under stress often do strange things—cup their testicles through the pockets of their pants, click their teeth together . . . Wolff had been a great teeth-clicker. He grinned as he did it. Huffmann had been a finger-snapper and a thigh-patter, creating fast, intricate rhythms that he seemed utterly unaware of. He, Kurt Dussander, had sometimes talked to himself. But now—

"You are under stress again," he said aloud. He was aware that he had spoken in German this time. He hadn't spoken German in many years, but the language now seemed warm and comfortable. It lulled him, eased him. It was sweet and dark.

"Yes. You are under stress. Because of the boy. But be honest with yourself. It is too early in the morning to tell lies. You have not entirely regretted talking. At first you were terrified that the boy could not or would not keep his secret. He would have to tell a friend, who would tell another friend, and that friend would tell two. But if he has kept it this long, he will keep it longer. If I am taken away, he loses his . . . his talking book. Is that what I am to him? I think so."

He fell silent, but his thoughts went on. He had been lonely— no one would ever know just how lonely. There had been times when he thought almost seriously of suicide. He made a bad hermit. The voices he heard came from the radio. The only people who visited were on the other side of a dirty glass square. He was an old man, and although he was afraid of death, he was more afraid of being an old man who is alone.

His bladder sometimes tricked him. He would be halfway to the bathroom when a dark stain spread on his pants. In wet weather his joints would first throb and then begin to cry out, and there had been days when he had chewed an entire tin of Arthritis Pain Formula between sunrise and sunset . . . and still the aspirin only subdued the aches. Even such acts as taking a book from the shelf or switching the TV channel became an essay in pain. His eyes were bad; sometimes he knocked things over, barked his shins, bumped his head. He lived in fear of breaking a bone and not being able to get to the telephone, and he lived in fear of getting there and having some doctor uncover his real past as he became suspicious of Mr. Denker's nonexistent medical history.

The boy had alleviated some of those things. When the boy was here, he could call back the old days. His memory of those days was perversely clear; he spilled out a seemingly endless catalogue of names and events, even the weather of such and such a day. He remembered Private Henreid, who manned a machine-gun in the northeast tower and the wen private Henreid had had between his eyes. Some of the men called him Three-Eyes, or Old Cyclops. He remembered Kessel, who had a picture of his girlfriend naked, lying on a sofa with her hands behind her head. Kessel charged the men to look at it. He remembered the names of the doctors and their experiments—thresholds of pain, the brainwaves of dying men and women, physiological retardation, effects of different sorts of radiation, dozens more. *Hundreds* more.

He supposed he talked to the boy as all old men talk, but he guessed he was luckier than most old men, who had impatience, disinterest, or outright rudeness for an audience. *His* audience was endlessly fascinated.

Were a few bad dreams too high a price to pay?

He crushed out his cigarette, lay looking at the ceiling for a moment, and then swung his feet out onto the floor. He and the boy were loathsome, he supposed, feeding off each other . . . eating each other. If his own belly was sometimes sour with the dark but rich food they partook of in his afternoon kitchen, what was the boy's like? Did he sleep well? Perhaps not. Lately Dussander thought the boy looked rather pale, and thinner than when he had first come into Dussander's life.

He walked across the bedroom and opened the closet door. He brushed hangers to the right, reached into the shadows, and brought out the sham uniform. It hung from his hand like a vulture-skin. He touched it with his other hand. Touched it . . . and then stroked it.

After a very long time he took it down and put it on, dressing slowly, not looking into the mirror until the uniform was completely buttoned and belted (and the sham fly zipped).

He looked at himself in the mirror, then, and nodded.

He went back to bed, lay down, and smoked another cigarette. When it was finished, he felt sleepy again. He turned off the bedlamp, not believing it, that it could be this easy. But he was asleep five minutes later, and this time his sleep was dreamless.

8

February, 1975.

After dinner, Dick Bowden produced a cognac that Dussander privately thought dreadful. But of course he smiled broadly and complimented it extravagantly. Bowden's wife served the boy a chocolate malted. The boy had been unusually quiet all through the meal. Uneasy? Yes. For some reason the boy seemed very uneasy.

Dussander had charmed Dick and Monica Bowden from the moment he and the boy had arrived. The boy had told his parents that Mr. Denker's vision was much worse than it actually was (which made poor old Mr. Denker in need of a Seeing Eye dog, Dussander thought dryly), because that explained all the reading the boy had supposedly been doing. Dussander had been very careful about that, and he thought there had been no slips.

He was dressed in his best suit, and although the evening was damp, his arthritis had been remarkably mellow—nothing but an occasional twinge. For some absurd reason the boy had wanted him to leave his umbrella home, but Dussander had insisted. All in all, he had had a pleasant and rather exciting evening. Dreadful cognac or no, he had not been out to dinner in nine years.

During the meal he had discussed the Essen Motor Works, the rebuilding of postwar Germany—Bowden had asked several intelligent questions about that, and had seemed impressed by Dussander's answers—and German writers. Monica Bowden had asked him how he had happened to come to America so late in life and Dussander, adopting the proper expression of myopic sorrow, had explained about the death of his fictitious wife. Monica Bowden was meltingly sympathetic.

And now, over the absurd cognac, Dick Bowden said: "If this is too personal, Mr. Denker, please don't answer . . . but I couldn't help wondering what you did in the war."

The boy stiffened ever so slightly.

Dussander smiled and felt for his cigarettes. He could see them perfectly well, but it was important to make not the tiniest slip. Monica put them in his hand.

"Thank you, dear lady. The meal was superb. You are a fine cook. My own wife never did better."

Monica thanked him and looked flustered. Todd gave her an irritated look.

"Not personal at all," Dussander said, lighting his cigarette and turning to Bowden. "I was in the reserves from 1943 on, as were all able-bodied men too old to be in the active services. By then the handwriting was on the wall for the Third Reich, and for the madmen who created it. One madman in particular, of course."

He blew out his match and looked solemn.

"There was great relief when the tide turned against Hitler. Great relief. Of course," and here he looked at Bowden disarmingly, as man to man, "one was careful not to express such a sentiment. Not aloud."

"I suppose not," Dick Bowden said respectfully.

"No," Dussander said gravely. "Not aloud. I remember one evening when four or five of us, all friends, stopped at a local *Ratskeller* after work for a drink—by then there was not always *Schnaps*, or even beer, but it so happened that night there were both. We had all known each other for upwards of twenty years. One of our number, Hans Hassler, mentioned in passing that perhaps the Fuehrer had been ill-advised to open a second front against the Russians. I said, 'Hans, God in Heaven, watch what you say!' Poor Hans went pale and changed the subject entirely. Yet three days later he was gone. I never saw him again, nor, as far as I know, did anyone else who was sitting at our table that night."

"How awful!" Monica said breathlessly. "More cognac, Mr. Denker?"

"No thank you." He smiled at her. "My wife had a saying from her mother: 'One must never overdo the sublime.'"

Todd's small, troubled frown deepened slightly.

"Do you think he was sent to one of the camps?" Dick asked. "Your friend Hessler?"

"*Hassler*," Dussander corrected gently. He grew grave. "Many were. The camps . . . they will be the shame of the German people for a thousand years to come. They are Hitler's real legacy."

"Oh, I think that's too harsh," Bowden said, lighting his pipe and puffing out a choking cloud of Cherry Blend. "According to what I've read, the majority of the German people had no idea of what was going on. The locals around Auschwitz thought it was a sausage plant."

"Ugh, how *terrible*," Monica said, and pulled a grimacing that's-enough-of-that expression at her husband. Then she turned to Dussander and smiled. "I just love the smell of a pipe, Mr. Denker, don't you?"

"Indeed I do, madam," Dussander said. He had just gotten an almost insurmountable urge to sneeze under control.

Bowden suddenly reached across the table and clapped his son on the shoulder. Todd jumped. "You're awfully quiet tonight, son. Feeling all right?"

Todd offered a peculiar smile that seemed divided between his father and Dussander. "I feel okay. I've heard most of these stories before, remember."

"Todd!" Monica said. "That's hardly—"

"The boy is only being honest," Dussander said. "A privilege of boys which men often have to give up. Yes, Mr. Bowden?"

Dick laughed and nodded.

"Perhaps I could get Todd to walk back to mine house with me now," Dussander said. "I'm sure he has his studies."

"Todd is a very apt pupil," Monica said, but she spoke almost automatically, looking at Todd in a puzzled sort of way. "All A's and B's, usually. He got a C this last quarter, but he's promised to bring his French up to snuff on his March report. Right, Todd-baby?"

Todd offered the peculiar smile again and nodded.

"No need for you to walk," Dick said. "I'll be glad to run you back to your place."

"I walk for the air and the exercise," Dussander said. "Really, I must insist . . . unless Todd prefers not to."

"Oh, no, I'd like a walk," Todd said, and his mother and father beamed at him.

They were almost to Dussander's corner when Dussander broke the silence. It was drizzling, and he hoisted his umbrella over both of them. And yet still his arthritis lay quiet, dozing. It was amazing.

"You are like my arthritis," he said.

Todd's head came up. "Huh?"

"Neither of you have had much to say tonight. What's got your tongue, boy? Cat or cormorant?"

"Nothing," Todd muttered. They turned down Dussander's street.

"Perhaps I could guess," Dussander said, not without a touch of malice. "When you came to get me, you were afraid I might make a slip . . . 'let the cat out of the bag,' you say here. Yet you were determined to go through with the dinner because you had run out of excuses to put your parents off. Now you are disconcerted that all went well. Is that not the truth?"

"Who cares?" Todd said, and shrugged sullenly.

"Why shouldn't it go well?" Dussander demanded. "I was dissembling before you were born. You keep a secret well enough, I give you that. I give it to you most graciously. But did you see me tonight? I charmed them. *Charmed* them!"

Todd suddenly burst out: "You didn't have to do that!"

Dussander came to a complete stop, staring at Todd.

"Not do it? *Not?* I thought that was what you wanted, boy! Certainly they will offer no objections if you continue to come over and 'read' to me."

"You're sure taking a lot for granted!" Todd said hotly. "Maybe I've got all I want from you. Do you think there's anybody *forcing* me to come over to your scuzzy house and watch you slop up booze like those old wino pusbags that hang around the old trainyards? Is that what you think?" His voice had risen and taken on a thin, wavering, hysterical note. "Because there's nobody *forcing* me. If I want to come, I'll come, and if I don't, I won't."

"Lower your voice. People will hear."

"Who cares?" Todd said, but he began to walk again. This time he deliberately walked outside the umbrella's span.

"No, nobody forces you to come," Dussander said. And then he took a calculated shot in the dark: "In fact, you are welcome to stay away. Believe me, boy, I have no scruples about drinking alone. None at all."

Todd looked at him scornfully. "You'd like that, wouldn't you?"

Dussander only smiled noncommittally.

"Well, don't count on it." They had reached the concrete walk leading up to Dussander's stoop. Dussander fumbled in his pocket for his latchkey. The arthritis flared a dim red in the joints of his fingers and then subsided, waiting. Now Dussander thought he understood what it was waiting for: for him to be alone again. Then it could come out.

"I'll tell you something," Todd said. He sounded oddly breathless. "If they knew what you were, if I ever told them, they'd spit on you and then kick you out on your skinny old ass."

Dussander looked at Todd closely in the drizzling dark. The boy's face was turned defiantly up to his, but the skin was pallid, the sockets under the eyes dark and slightly hollowed—the skin-tones of someone who has brooded long while others are asleep.

"I am sure they would have nothing but revulsion for me," Dussander said, although he privately thought that the elder Bowden might stay his revulsion long enough to ask many of the questions his son had asked already. "Nothing but revulsion. But what would they feel for you, boy, when I told them you had known about me for eight months . . . and said nothing?"

Todd stared at him wordlessly in the dark.

"Come and see me if you please," Dussander said indifferently, "and stay home if you don't. Goodnight, boy."

He went up the walk to his front door, leaving Todd standing in the drizzle and looking after him with his mouth slightly ajar.

*   *   *

The next morning at breakfast, Monica said: "Your dad liked Mr. Denker a lot, Todd. He said he reminded him of your grandfather."

Todd muttered something unintelligible around his toast. Monica looked at her son and wondered if he had been sleeping well. He looked pale. And his grades had taken that inexplicable dip. Todd *never* got C's.

"You feeling okay these days, Todd?"

He looked at her blankly for a moment, and then that radiant smile spread over his face, charming her . . . comforting her. There was a dab of strawberry preserves on his chin. "Sure," he said. "Four-oh."

"Todd-baby," she said.

"Monica-baby," he responded, and they both started to laugh.

9

March, 1975.

"Kitty-kitty," Dussander said. "*Heeere*, kitty-kitty. Puss-puss? Puss-puss?"

He was sitting on his back stoop, a pink plastic bowl by his right foot. The bowl was full of milk. It was one-thirty in the afternoon; the day was hazy and hot. Brush-fires far to the west tinged the air with an autumnal smell that jagged oddly against the calendar. If the boy was coming, he would be here in another hour. But the boy didn't always come now. Instead of seven days a week he came sometimes only four times, or five. An intuition had grown in him, little by little, and his intuition told him that the boy was having troubles of his own.

"Kitty-kitty," Dussander coaxed. The stray cat was at the far end of the yard, sitting in the ragged verge of weeds by Dussander's fence. It was a tom, and every bit as ragged as the weeds it sat in. Every time he spoke, the cat's ears cocked forward. Its eyes never left the pink bowl filled with milk.

Perhaps, Dussander thought, the boy was having troubles with his studies. Or bad dreams. Or both.

That last made him smile.

"Kitty-kitty," he called softly. The cat's ears cocked forward again. It didn't move, not yet, but it continued to study the milk.

Dussander had certainly been afflicted with problems of his own. For three weeks or so he had worn the SS uniform to bed like grotesque pajamas, and the uniform had warded off the insomnia and the bad dreams. His sleep had been—at first—as sound as a lumberjack's. Then the dreams had returned, not little by little, but all at once, and worse than ever before. Dreams of running as well as the dreams of the eyes. Running through a wet, unseen jungle where heavy leaves and damp fronds struck his face, leaving trickles that felt like sap . . . or blood. Running and running, the luminous eyes always around him, peering soullessly at him, until he broke into a clearing. In the darkness he sensed rather than saw the steep rise that began on the clearing's far side. At the top of that rise was Patin, its low cement buildings and yards surrounded by barbed wire and electrified wire, its sentry towers standing like Martian dreadnoughts straight out of *War of the Worlds*. And in the middle, huge stacks billowed smoke against the sky, and below these brick columns were the furnaces, stoked and ready to go, glowing in the night like the eyes of fierce demons. They had told the inhabitants of the area that the Patin inmates made clothes and candles, and of course the locals had believed that no more than the locals around Auschwitz had believed that the camp was a sausage factory. It didn't matter.

Looking back over his shoulder in the dream, he would at last see *them* coming out of hiding, the restless dead, the *Juden*, shambling toward him with blue numbers glaring from the livid flesh of their outstretched arms, their hands hooked into talons, their faces no longer expressionless but animated with hate, lively with vengeance, vivacious with murder. Toddlers ran beside their mothers and grandfathers were borne up by their middle-aged children. And the dominant expression on all their faces was desperation.

Desperation? Yes. Because in the dreams he knew (and so did they) that if he could climb the hill, he would be safe. Down here in these wet and swampy lowlands, in this jungle where the night-flowering plants extruded blood instead of sap, he was a hunted animal . . . prey. But up there, he was in command. If this was a jungle, then the camp at the top of the hill was a zoo, all the wild animals safely in cages, he the head keeper whose job it was to decide which would be fed, which would live, which would be handed over to the vivisectionists, which would be taken to the knacker's in the remover's van.

He would begin to run up the hill, running in all the slowness of nightmare. He would feel the first skeletal hands close about his neck, feel their cold and stinking breath, smell their decay, hear their birdlike cries of triumph as they pulled him down with salvation not only in sight but almost at hand—

"Kitty-kitty," Dussander called. "Milk. Nice milk."

The cat came at last. It crossed half of the back yard and then sat again, but lightly, its tail twitching with worry. It didn't trust him; no. But Dussander knew the cat could smell the milk and so he was sanguine. Sooner or later it would come.

At Patin there had never been a contraband problem. Some of the prisoners came in with their valuables poked far up their asses in small chamois bags (and how often their valuables turned out not to be valuable at all—photographs, locks of hair, fake jewelry), often pushed up with sticks until they were past the point where even the long fingers of the trusty they had called Stinky-Thumbs could reach. One woman, he remembered, had had a small diamond, flawed, it turned out, really not valuable at all—but it had been in her family for six generations, passed from mother to eldest daughter (or so she said, but of course she was a Jew and all of them lied). She swallowed it before entering Patin. When it came out in her waste, she swallowed it again. She kept doing this, although eventually the diamond began to cut her insides and she bled.

There had been other ruses, although most only involved petty items such as a hoard of tobacco or a hair-ribbon or two. It didn't matter. In the room Dussander used for prisoner interrogations there was a hotplate and a homely kitchen table covered with a red checked cloth much like the one in his own kitchen. There was always a pot of lamb stew bubbling mellowly away on that hotplate. When contraband was suspected (and when was it not?) a member of the suspected clique would be brought to that room. Dussander would stand them by the hotplate, where the rich fumes from the stew wafted. Gently, he would ask them *Who*. Who is hiding gold?

Who is hiding jewelry? Who has tobacco? Who gave the Givenet woman the pill for her baby? Who? The stew was never specifically promised; but always the aroma eventually loosened their tongues. Of course, a truncheon would have done the same, or a gun-barrel jammed into their filthy crotches, but the stew was . . . was *elegant*. Yes.

"Kitty-kitty," Dussander called. The cat's ears cocked forward. It half-rose, then half-remembered some long-ago kick, or perhaps a match that had burned its whiskers, and it settled back on its haunches. But soon it would move.

He had found a way of propitiating his nightmare. It was, in a way, no more than wearing the SS uniform . . . but raised to a greater power. Dussander was pleased with himself, only sorry that he had never thought of it before. He supposed he had the boy to thank for this new method of quieting himself, for showing him that the key to the past's terrors was not in rejection but in contemplation and even something like a friend's embrace. It was true that before the boy's unexpected arrival last summer he hadn't had any bad dreams for a long time, but he believed now that he had come to a coward's terms with his past. He had been forced to give up a part of himself. Now he had reclaimed it.

"Kitty-kitty," called Dussander, and a smile broke on his face, a kindly smile, a reassuring smile, the smile of all old men who have somehow come through the cruel courses of life to a safe place, still relatively intact, and with at least some wisdom.

The tom rose from its haunches, hesitated only a moment longer, and then trotted across the remainder of the back yard with lithe grace. It mounted the steps, gave Dussander a final mistrustful look, laying back its chewed and scabby ears; then it began to drink the milk.

"*Nice* milk," Dussander said, pulling on the Playtex rubber gloves that had lain in his lap all the while. "*Nice* milk for a *nice* kitty." He had bought these gloves in the supermarket. He had stood in the express lane, and older women had looked at him approvingly, even speculatively. The gloves were advertised on TV. They had cuffs. They were so flexible you could pick up a dime while you were wearing them.

He stroked the cat's back with one green finger and talked to it soothingly. Its back began to arch with the rhythm of his strokes.

Just before the bowl was empty, he seized the cat.

It came electrically alive in his clenching hands, twisting and jerking, clawing at the rubber. Its body lashed limberly back and forth, and Dussander had no doubt that if its teeth or claws got into him, it would come off the winner. It was an old campaigner. It takes one to know one, Dussander thought, grinning.

Holding the cat prudently away from his body, the painful grin stamped on his face, Dussander pushed the back door open with his foot and went into the kitchen. The cat yowled and twisted and ripped at the rubber gloves. Its feral, triangular head flashed down and fastened on one green thumb.

"Nasty kitty," Dussander said reproachfully.

The oven door stood open. Dussander threw the cat inside. Its claws made a ripping, prickly sound as they disengaged from the gloves. Dussander slammed the oven door shut with one knee, provoking a painful twinge from his arthritis. Yet he continued to grin. Breathing hard, nearly panting, he propped himself against the stove for a moment, his head hanging down. It was a gas stove. He rarely used it for anything fancier than TV dinners and killing stray cats.

Faintly, rising up through the gas burners, he could hear the cat scratching and yowling to be let out.

Dussander twisted the oven dial over to 500°. There was an audible *pop!* as the oven pilot-light lit two double rows of hissing gas. The cat stopped yowling and began to scream. It sounded . . . yes . . . . almost like a young boy. A young boy in terrible pain. The thought made Dussander smile even more broadly. His heart thundered in his chest. The cat scratched and whirled madly in the oven, still screaming. Soon, a hot, furry, burning smell began to seep out of the oven and into the room.

He scraped the remains of the cat out of the oven half an hour later, using a barbecue fork he had acquired for two dollars and ninety-eight cents at the Grant's in the shopping center a mile away.

The cat's roasted carcass went into an empty flour sack. He took the sack down cellar. The cellar floor had never been cemented. Shortly, Dussander came back up. He sprayed the kitchen with Glade until it reeked of artificial pine scent. He opened all the windows. He washed the barbecue fork and hung it up on the pegboard. Then he sat down to wait and see if the boy would come. He smiled and smiled.

Todd did come, about five minutes after Dussander had given up on him for the afternoon. He was wearing a warmup jacket with his school colors on it; he was also wearing a San Diego Padres baseball cap. He carried his schoolbooks under his arm.

"Yucka-ducka," he said, coming into the kitchen and wrinkling his nose. "What's that smell? It's awful."

"I tried the oven," Dussander said, lighting a cigarette. "I'm afraid I burned my supper. I had to throw it out."

One day later that month the boy came much earlier than usual, long before school usually let out. Dussander was sitting in the kitchen, drinking Ancient Age bourbon from a chipped and discolored cup that had the words HERE'S YER CAWFEE MAW, HAW! HAW! HAW! written around the rim. He had his rocker out in the kitchen now and he was just drinking and rocking, rocking and drinking, bumping his slippers on the faded linoleum. He was pleasantly high. There had been no more bad dreams at all until just last night. Not since the tomcat with the chewed ears. Last night's had been particularly horrible, though. That could not be denied. *They* had dragged him down after he had gotten halfway up the hill, and *they* had begun to do unspeakable things to him before he was able to wake himself up. Yet, after his initial thrashing return to the world of real things, he had been confident. He could end the dreams whenever he wished. Perhaps a cat would not be enough this time. But there was always the dog pound. Yes. Always the pound.

Todd came abruptly into the kitchen, his face pale and shiny and strained. He had lost weight, all right, Dussander thought. And there was a queer white look in his eyes that Dussander did not like at all.

"You're going to help me," Todd said suddenly and defiantly.

"Really?" Dussander said mildly, but sudden apprehension leaped inside of him. He didn't let his face change as Todd slammed his books down on the table with a sudden, vicious overhand stroke. One of them spun-skated across the oilcloth and landed in a tent on the floor by Dussander's foot.

"Yes, you're fucking-A right!" Todd said shrilly. "You better believe it! Because this is your fault! All your fault!" Hectic spots of red mounted into his cheeks. "But you're going to have to help me get out of it, because I've got the goods on you! *I've got you right where I want you!*"

"I'll help you in any way I can," Dussander said quietly. He saw that he had folded his hands neatly in front of himself without even thinking about it—just as he had once done. He leaned forward in the rocker until his chin was directly over his folded hands—as he had once done. His face was calm and friendly and enquiring; none of his growing apprehension showed. Sitting just so, he could almost imagine a pot of lamb stew simmering on the stove behind him. "Tell me what the trouble is."

"This is the fucking *trouble*," Todd said viciously, and threw a folder at Dussander. It bounced off his chest and landed in his lap, and he was momentarily surprised by the heat of the anger which leaped up in him; the urge to rise and backhand the boy smartly. Instead, he kept the mild expression on his face. It was the boy's school-card, he saw, although the school seemed to be at ridiculous pains to hide the fact. Instead of a school-card, or a Grade Report, it was called a "Quarterly Progress Report." He grunted at that, and opened the card.

A typed half-sheet of paper fell out. Dussander put it aside for later examination and turned his attention to the boy's grades first.

"You seem to have fallen on the rocks, my boy," Dussander said, not without some pleasure. The boy had passed only English and American History. Every other grade was an F.

"It's not my fault," Todd hissed venomously. "It's *your* fault. All those *stories*. I have nightmares about them, do you know that? I sit down and open my books and I start thinking about whatever you told me that day and the next thing I know, my mother's telling me it's time to go to bed. Well, that's not my fault! *It isn't! You hear me? It isn't!*"

"I hear you very well," Dussander said, and read the typed note that had been tucked into Todd's card.

Dear Mr. and Mrs. Bowden,

This note is to suggest that we have a group conference concerning Todd's second- and third-quarter grades. In light of Todd's previous good work in this school, his current grades suggest a specific problem which may be affecting his academic performance in a deleterious way. Such a problem can often be solved by a frank and open discussion.

I should point out that although Todd has passed the half-year, his final grades may be failing in some cases unless his work improves radically in the fourth quarter. Failing grades would entail summer school to avoid being kept back and causing a major scheduling problem.

I must also note that Todd is in the college division, and that his work so far this year is far below college acceptance levels. It is also below the level of academic ability assumed by the SAT tests.

Please be assured that I am ready to work out a mutually convenient time for us to meet. In a case such as this, earlier is usually better.

Sincerely yours,
Edward French

"Who is this Edward French?" Dussander asked, slipping the note back inside the card (part of him still marvelled at the American love of jargon; such a rolling missive to inform the parents that their son was flunking out!) and then refolding his hands. His premonition of disaster was stronger than ever, but he refused to give in to it. A year before, he would have done; a year ago he had been ready for disaster. Now he was not, but it seemed that the cursed boy had brought it to him anyway. "Is he your headmaster?"

"Rubber Ed? Hell, no. He's the guidance counsellor."

"*Guidance* counsellor? What is that?"

"You can figure it out," Todd said. He was nearly hysterical. "You read the goddam note!" He walked rapidly around the room, shooting sharp, quick glances at Dussander. "Well, I'm not going to let any of this shit go down. I'm just not. I'm not going to any summer school. My dad and mom are going to Hawaii this summer and I'm going with them." He pointed at the card on the table. "Do you know what my dad will do if he sees that?"

Dussander shook his head.

"He'll get everything out of me. *Everything.* He'll know it was you. It couldn't be anything else, because nothing else has changed. He'll poke and pry and he'll get it all out of me. And then . . . then I'll . . . I'll be in dutch."

He stared at Dussander resentfully.

"They'll watch me. Hell, they might make me see a doctor, I don't know. How should *I* know? But I'm not getting in dutch. And I'm not going to any fucking summer school."

"Or to the reformatory," Dussander said. He said it very quietly.

Todd stopped circling the room. His face became very still. His cheeks and forehead, already pale, became even whiter. He stared at Dussander, and had to try twice before he could speak. "*What? What* did you just say?"

"My dear boy," Dussander said, assuming an air of great patience, "for the last five minutes I have listened to you pule and whine, and what all your puling and whining comes down to is this. *You* are in trouble. *You* might be found out. *You* might find yourself in adverse circumstances." Seeing that he had the boy's complete attention—at last—Dussander sipped reflectively from his cup.

"My boy," he went on, "that is a very dangerous attitude for you to have. And dangerous for me. The potential harm is much greater for me. You worry about your school-card. Pah! *This* for your school-card."

He flicked it off the table and onto the floor with one yellow finger.

"I am worried about my *life!*"

Todd did not reply; he simply went on looking at Dussander with that white-eyed, slightly crazed stare.

"The Israelis will not scruple at the fact that I am seventy-six. The death-penalty is still very much in favor over there, you know, especially when the man in the dock is a Nazi war criminal associated with the camps."

"You're a U.S. citizen," Todd said. "America wouldn't let them take you. I read up on that. I—"

"You read, but you don't *listen*! I am *not* a U.S. citizen! My papers came from *la cosa nostra*. I would be deported, and Mossad agents would be waiting for me wherever I deplaned."

"I wish they *would* hang you," Todd muttered, curling his hands into fists and staring down at them. "I was crazy to get mixed up with you in the first place."

"No doubt," Dussander said, and smiled thinly. "But you *are* mixed up with me. We must live in the present, boy, not in the past of 'I-should-have-nevers.' You must realize that your fate and my own are now inextricably entwined. If you 'blow the horn on me,' as your saying goes, do you think I will hesitate to blow the horn on you? Seven hundred thousand died at Patin. To the world at large I am a criminal, a monster, even the butcher your scandal-rags would have me. You are an accessory to all of that, my boy. You have criminal knowledge of an illegal alien, but you have not reported it. And if I am caught, I will tell the world all about you. When the reporters put their microphones in my face, it will be your name I'll repeat over and over again. 'Todd Bowden, yes, that is his name . . . how long? Almost a year. He wanted to know everything . . . all the gooshy parts. That's how he put it, yes: "All the gooshy parts." ' "

Todd's breath had stopped. His skin appeared transparent. Dussander smiled at him. He sipped bourbon.

"I think they will put you in jail. They may call it a reformatory, or a correctional facility—there may be a fancy name for it, like this 'Quarterly Progress Report' "—his lip curled—"but no matter what they call it, there will be bars on the windows."

Todd wet his lips. "I'd call you a liar. I'd tell them I just found out. They'd believe me, not you. You just better remember that."

Dussander's thin smile remained. "I thought you told me your father would get it all out of you."

Todd spoke slowly, as a person speaks when realization and

verbalization occur simultaneously. "Maybe not. Maybe not this time. This isn't just breaking a window with a rock."

Dussander winced inwardly. He suspected that the boy's judgment was right—with so much at stake, he might indeed be able to convince his father. After all, when faced with such an unpleasant truth, what parent would not want to be convinced?

"Perhaps. Perhaps not. But how are you going to explain all those books you had to read to me because poor Mr. Denker is half-blind? My eyes are not what they were, but I can still read fine print with my spectacles. I can prove it."

"I'd say you fooled me!"

"Will you? And what reason will you be able to give for my fooling?"

"For . . . for friendship. Because you were lonely."

That, Dussander reflected, was just close enough to the truth to be believable. And once, in the beginning, the boy might have been able to bring it off. But now he was ragged; now he was coming apart in strings like a coat that has reached the end of its useful service. If a child shot off his cap pistol across the street, this boy would jump into the air and scream like a girl.

"Your school-card will also support my side of it," Dussander said. "It was not *Robinson Crusoe* that caused your grades to fall down so badly, my boy, was it?"

"Shut up, why don't you? Just shut up about it!"

"No," Dussander said. "I won't shut up about it." He lit a cigarette, scratching the wooden match alight on the gas oven door. "Not until I make you see the simple truth. We are in this together, sink or swim." He looked at Todd through the raftering smoke, not smiling, his old, lined face reptilian. "I will drag you down, boy. I promise you that. If anything comes out, *everything* will come out. That is my promise to you."

Todd stared at him sullenly and didn't reply.

"Now," Dussander said briskly, with the air of a man who has put a necessary unpleasantness behind him, "the question is, what are we going to do about this situation? Have you any ideas?"

"This will fix the report card," Todd said, and took a new bottle of ink eradicator from his jacket pocket. "About that fucking letter, I don't know."

Dussander looked at the ink eradicator approvingly. He had falsified a few reports of his own in his time. When the quotas had gone up to the point of fantasy . . . and far, far beyond. And . . . more like the situation they were now in—there had been the matter of the invoices . . . those which enumerated the spoils of war. Each week he would check the boxes of valuables, all of them to be sent back to Berlin in special train-cars that were like big safes on wheels. On the side of each box was a manila envelope, and inside the envelope there had been a verified invoice of that box's contents. So many rings, necklaces, chokers, so many grams of gold. Dussander, however, had had his own box of valuables—not very valuable valuables, but not insignificant, either. Jades. Tour-malines. Opals. A few flawed pearls. Industrial diamonds. And when he saw an item invoiced for Berlin that caught his eye or seemed a good investment, he would remove it, replace it with an item from his own box, and use ink eradicator on the invoice, changing their item for his. He had developed into a fairly expert forger . . . a talent that had come in handy more than once after the war was over.

"Good," he told Todd. "As for this other matter . . ."

Dussander began to rock again, sipping from his cup. Todd pulled a chair up to the table and began to go to work on his report card, which he had picked up from the floor without a word. Dussander's outward calm had had its effect on him and now he worked silently, his head bent studiously over the card, like any American boy who has set out to do the best by God job he can, whether that job be planting corn, pitching a no-hitter in the Little League World Series, or forging grades on his report card.

Dussander looked at the nape of his neck, lightly tanned and cleanly exposed between the fall of his hair and the round neck of his tee-shirt. His eyes drifted from there to the top counter drawer where he kept the butcher knives. One quick thrust—he knew where to put it—and the boy's spinal cord would be severed. His lips would be sealed forever. Dussander smiled regret-fully. There would be questions asked if the boy disappeared. Too many of them. Some directed at him. Even if there was no letter with a friend, close scrutiny was something he could not afford. Too bad.

"This man French," he said, tapping the letter. "Does he know your parents in a social way?"

"Him?" Todd edged the word with contempt. "My mom and dad don't go anywhere that he could even get in."

"Has he ever met them in his professional capacity? Has he ever had conferences with them before?"

"No. I've always been near the top of my classes. Until now."

"So what does he know about them?" Dussander said, looking dreamily into his cup, which was now nearly empty. "Oh, he knows about *you*. He no doubt has all the records on you that he can use. Back to the fights you had in the kindergarten play yard. But what does he know about *them*?"

Todd put his pen and the small bottle of ink eradicator away. "Well, he knows their names. Of course. And their ages. He knows we're all Methodists. You don't have to fill that line out, but my folks always do. We don't go much, but he'd know that's what we are. He must know what my dad does for a living; that's on the forms, too. All that stuff they have to fill out every year. And I'm pretty sure that's all."

"Would he know if your parents were having troubles at home?"

"What's that supposed to mean?"

Dussander tossed off the last of the bourbon in his cup. "Squabbles. Fights. Your father sleeping on the couch. Your mother drinking too much." His eyes gleamed. "A divorce brewing."

Indignantly, Todd said: "There's nothing like that going on! No way!"

"I never said there was. But just think, boy. Suppose that things at your house were 'going to hell in a streetcar,' as the saying is."

Todd only looked at him, frowning.

"You would be worried about them," Dussander said. "Very worried. You would lose your appetite. You would sleep poorly. Saddest of all, your schoolwork would suffer. True? Very sad for the children, when there are troubles in the home."

Understanding dawned in the boy's eyes—understanding and something like dumb gratitude. Dussander was gratified.

"Yes, it is an unhappy situation when a family totters on the edge of destruction," Dussander said grandly, pouring more bourbon. He was getting quite drunk. "The daytime television dramas, they make this absolutely clear. There is acrimony. Backbiting and lies. Most of all, there is pain. Pain, my boy. You have no idea of the hell your parents are going through. They are so swallowed up by their own troubles that they have little time for the problems of their own son. His problems seem minor compared to theirs, *hein?* Someday, when the scars have begun to heal, they will no doubt take a fuller interest in him once again. But now the only concession they can make is to send the boy's kindly grandfather to Mr. French."

Todd's eyes had been gradually brightening to a glow that was nearly fervid. "Might work," he was muttering. "Might, yeah, might work, might—" He broke off suddenly. His eyes darkened again. "No, it won't. You don't look like me, not even a little bit. Rubber Ed will never believe it."

"*Himmel! Gott im Himmel!*" Dussander cried, getting to his feet, crossing the kitchen (a bit unsteadily), opening the cellar door, and pulling out a fresh bottle of Ancient Age. He spun off the cap and poured liberally. "For a smart boy, you are such a *Dummkopf*. When do grandfathers ever look like their grandsons? Huh? I got white hair. Do you have white hair?"

Approaching the table again, he reached out with surprising quickness, snatched an abundant handful of Todd's blonde hair, and pulled briskly.

"Cut it out!" Todd snapped, but he smiled a little.

"Besides," Dussander said, settling back into his rocker, "you have yellow hair and blue eyes. My eyes are blue, and before my hair turned white, it was yellow. You can tell me your whole family history. Your aunts and uncles. The people your father works with. Your mother's little hobbies. I will remember. I will study and remember. Two days later it will all be forgotten again—these days my memory is like a cloth bag filled with water—but I will remember for long enough." He smiled grimly. "In my time I have stayed ahead of Wiesenthal and pulled the wool over the eyes of Himmler himself. If I cannot fool one American public school teacher, I will pull my winding-shroud around me and crawl down into my grave."

"Maybe," Todd said slowly, and Dussander could see he had already accepted it. His eyes were luminous with relief.

"No—*surely!*" Dussander cried.

He began to cackle with laughter, the rocking chair squeaking back and forth. Todd looked at him, puzzled and a little frightened, but after a bit he began to laugh, too. In Dussander's kitchen they laughed and laughed, Dussander by the open window where the warm California breeze wafted in, and Todd rocked back on the rear legs of his kitchen chair, so that its back rested against the oven door, the white enamel of which was crisscrossed by the dark, charred-looking streaks made by Dussander's wooden matches as he struck them alight.

Rubber Ed French (his nickname, Todd had explained to Dussander, referred to the rubbers he always wore over his sneakers during wet weather) was a slight man who made an affectation of always wearing Keds to school. It was a touch of informality which he thought would endear him to the one hundred and six children between the ages of twelve and fourteen who made up his counselling load. He had five pairs of Keds, ranging in color from Fast Track Blue to Screaming Yellow Zonkers, totally unaware that behind his back he was known not only as Rubber Ed but as Sneaker Pete and The Ked Man, as in The Ked Man Cometh. He had been known as Pucker in college, and he would have been most humiliated of all to learn that even that shameful fact had somehow gotten out.

He rarely wore ties, preferring turtleneck sweaters. He had been wearing these ever since the mid-sixties, when David McCallum had popularized them in *The Man from U.N.C.L.E.* In his college days his classmates had been known to spy him crossing the quad and remark, "Here comes Pucker in his U.N.C.L.E. sweater." He had majored in Educational Psychology, and he privately considered himself to be the only good guidance counsellor he had ever met. He had real *rapport* with his kids. He could *get right down to it* with them; he could *rap* with them and be silently sympathetic if they had to do some shouting and *kick out the jams*. He could *get into their hangups* because he understood what a *bummer* it was to be thirteen when someone was *doing a number on your head* and you couldn't *get your shit together*.

The thing was, he had a damned hard time remembering what it had been like to be thirteen himself. He supposed that was the ultimate price you had to pay for growing up in the fifties. That, and travelling into the brave new world of the sixties nicknamed Pucker.

Now, as Todd Bowden's grandfather came into his office, closing the pebbled-glass door firmly behind him, Rubber Ed stood up respectfully but was careful not to come around his desk to greet the old man. He was aware of his sneakers. Sometimes the old-timers didn't understand that the sneakers were a psychological aid with kids who had teacher hangups—which was to say that some of the older folks couldn't *get behind* a guidance counsellor in Keds.

This is one fine-looking dude, Rubber Ed thought. His white hair was carefully brushed back. His three-piece suit was spotlessly clean. His dove-gray tie was impeccably knotted. In his left hand he held a furled black umbrella (outside, a light drizzle had been falling since the weekend) in a manner that was almost military. A few years ago Rubber Ed and his wife had gone on a Dorothy Sayers jag, reading everything by that estimable lady that they could lay their hands upon. It occurred to him now that this was her brainchild, Lord Peter Wimsey, to the life. It was Wimsey at seventy-five, years after both Bunter and Harriet Vane had passed on to their rewards. He made a mental note to tell Sondra about this when he got home.

"Mr. Bowden," he said respectfully, and offered his hand.

"A pleasure," Bowden said, and shook it. Rubber Ed was careful not to put on the firm and uncompromising pressure he applied to the hands of the fathers he saw; it was obvious from the gingerly way the old boy offered it that he had arthritis.

"A pleasure, Mr. French," Bowden repeated, and took a seat, carefully pulling up the knees of his trousers. He propped the umbrella between his feet and leaned on it, looking like an elderly, extremely urbane vulture that had come in to roost in Rubber Ed French's office. He had the slightest touch of an accent, Rubber Ed thought, but it wasn't the clipped intonation of the British upper class, as Wimsey's would have been; it was broader, more European. Anyway, the resemblance to Todd was quite striking. Especially through the nose and eyes.

"I'm glad you could come," Rubber Ed told him, resuming his

own seat, "although in these cases the student's mother or father—"

This was the opening gambit, of course. Almost ten years of experience in the counselling business had convinced him that when an aunt or an uncle or a grandparent showed up for a conference, it usually meant trouble at home—the sort of trouble that invariably turned out to be the root of the problem. To Rubber Ed, this came as a relief. Domestic problems were bad, but for a boy of Todd's intelligence, *a heavy drug trip* would have been much, much worse.

"Yes, of course," Bowden said, managing to look both sorrowful and angry at the same time. "My son and his wife asked me if I could come and talk this sorry business over with you, Mr. French. Todd is a good boy, believe me. This trouble with his school marks is only temporary."

"Well, we all hope so, don't we, Mr. Bowden? Smoke if you like. It's supposed to be off-limits on school property, but I'll never tell."

"Thank you."

Mr. Bowden took a half-crushed package of Camel cigarettes from his inner pocket, put one of the last two zig-zagging smokes in his mouth, found a Diamond Blue-Tip match, scratched it on the heel of one black shoe, and lit up. He coughed an old man's dank cough over the first drag, shook the match out, and put the blackened stump into the ashtray Rubber Ed had produced. Rubber Ed watched this ritual, which seemed almost as formal as the old man's shoes, with frank fascination.

"Where to begin," Bowden said, his distressed face looking at Rubber Ed through a swirling raft of cigarette smoke.

"Well," Rubber Ed said kindly, "the very fact that you're here instead of Todd's parents tells me something, you know."

"Yes, I suppose it does. Very well." He folded his hands. The Camel protruded from between the second and third fingers of his right. He straightened his back and lifted his chin. There was something almost Prussian in his mental coming to terms, Rubber Ed thought, something that made him think of all those war movies he'd seen as a kid.

"My son and my daughter-in-law are having troubles in their home," Bowden said, biting off each word precisely. "Rather bad troubles, I should think." His eyes, old but amazingly bright, watched as Rubber Ed opened the folder centered in front of him on the desk blotter. There were sheets of paper inside, but not many.

"And you feel that these troubles are affecting Todd's academic performance?"

Bowden leaned forward perhaps six inches. His blue eyes never left Rubber Ed's brown ones. There was a heavily charged pause, and then Bowden said: "The mother drinks."

He resumed his former ramrod-straight position.

"Oh," Rubber Ed said.

"Yes," Bowden replied, nodding grimly. "The boy has told me that he has come home on two occasions and has found her sprawled out on the kitchen table. He knows how my son feels about her drinking problem, and so the boy has put dinner in the oven himself on these occasions, and has gotten her to drink enough black coffee so she will at least be awake when Richard comes home."

"That's bad," Rubber Ed said, although he had heard worse —mothers with heroin habits, fathers who had abruptly taken it into their heads to start banging their daughters . . . or their sons. "Has Mrs. Bowden thought about getting professional help for her problem?"

"The boy has tried to persuade her that would be the best course. She is much ashamed, I think. If she was given a little time . . ." He made a gesture with his cigarette that left a dissolving smoke-ring in the air. "You understand?"

"Yes, of course." Rubber Ed nodded, privately admiring the gesture that had produced the smoke-ring. "Your son . . . Todd's father . . ."

"He is not without blame," Bowden said harshly. "The hours he works, the meals he has missed, the nights when he must leave suddenly . . . I tell you, Mr. French, he is more married to his job than he is to Monica. I was raised to believe that a man's family came before everything. Was it not the same for you?"

"It sure was," Rubber Ed responded heartily. His father had been a night watchman for a large Los Angeles department store and he had really only seen his pop on weekends and vacations.

"That is another side of the problem," Bowden said.

Rubber Ed nodded and thought for a moment. "What about your other son, Mr. Bowden? Uh . . ." He looked down at the folder. "Harold. Todd's uncle."

"Harry and Deborah are in Minnesota now," Bowden said, quite truthfully. "He has a position there at the University medical school. It would be quite difficult for him to leave, and very unfair to ask him." His face took on a righteous cast. "Harry and his wife are quite happily married."

"I see." Rubber Ed looked at the file again for a moment and then closed it. "Mr. Bowden, I appreciate your frankness. I'll be just as frank with you."

"Thank you," Bowden said stiffly.

"We can't do as much for our students in the counselling area as we would like. There are six counsellors here, and we're each carrying a load of over a hundred students. My newest colleague, Hepburn, has a hundred and fifteen. At this age, in our society, all children need help."

"Of course." Bowden mashed his cigarette brutally into the ashtray and folded his hands once more.

"Sometimes bad problems get by us. Home environment and drugs are the two most common. At least Todd isn't mixed up with speed or mescaline or PCP."

"God forbid."

"Sometimes," Rubber Ed went on, "there's simply nothing we can do. It's depressing, but it's a fact of life. Usually the ones that are first to get spit out of the machine we're running here are the class troublemakers, the sullen, uncommunicative kids, the ones who refuse to even try. They are simply warm bodies waiting for the system to buck them up through the grades or waiting to get old enough so they can quit without their parents' permission and join the Army or get a job at the Speedy-Boy Carwash or marry their boyfriends. You understand? I'm being blunt. Our system is, as they say, not all it's cracked up to be."

"I appreciate your frankness."

"But it hurts when you see the machine starting to mash up someone like Todd. He ran out a ninety-two average for last year's work, and that puts him in the ninety-fifth percentile. His English averages are even better. He shows a flair for writing, and that's something special in a generation of kids that think culture begins in front of the TV and ends in the neighborhood movie theater. I was talking to the woman who had Todd in Comp last year. She said Todd passed in the finest term-paper she'd seen in twenty years of teaching. It was on the German death-camps during World War Two. She gave him the only A-plus she's ever given a composition student."

"I have read it," Bowden said. "It is very fine."

"He has also demonstrated above-average ability in the life sciences and social sciences, and while he's not going to be one of the great math whizzes of the century, all the notes I have indicate that he's given it the good old college try . . . until this year. Until this year. That's the whole story, in a nutshell."

"Yes."

"I hate like *hell* to see Todd go down the tubes this way, Mr. Bowden. And summer school . . . well, I said I'd be frank. Summer school often does a boy like Todd more harm than good. Your usual junior high school summer session is a zoo. All the monkeys and the laughing hyenas are in attendance, plus a full complement of dodo birds. Bad company for a boy like Todd."

"Certainly."

"So let's get to the bottom line, shall we? I suggest a series of appointments for Mr. and Mrs. Bowden at the Counselling Center downtown. Everything in confidence, of course. The man in charge down there, Harry Ackerman, is a good friend of mine. And I don't think Todd should go to them with the idea; I think you should." Rubber Ed smiled widely. "Maybe we can get everybody back on track by June. It's not impossible."

But Bowden looked positively alarmed by this idea.

"I believe they might resent the boy if I took that proposal to them now," he said. "Things are very delicate. They could go either way. The boy has promised me he will work harder in his studies. He is very alarmed at this drop in his marks." He smiled thinly, a smile Ed French could not quite interpret. "More alarmed than you know."

"But—"

"And they would resent *me*," Bowden pressed on quickly. "God knows they would. Monica already regards me as something of a meddler. I try not to be, but you see the situation. I feel that things are best left alone . . . for now."

"I've had a great deal of experience in these matters," Rubber Ed told Bowden. He folded his hands on Todd's file and looked at the old man earnestly. "I really think counselling is in order here. You'll understand that my interest in the marital problems your son and daughter-in-law are having begins and ends with the effect they're having on Todd . . . and right now, they're having quite an effect."

"Let me make a counter-proposal," Bowden said. "You have, I believe, a system of warning parents of poor grades?"

"Yes," Rubber Ed agreed cautiously. "Interpretation of Progress cards—IOP cards. The kids, of course, call them Flunk Cards. They only get them if their grade in a given course falls below seventy-eight. In other words, we give out IOP cards to kids who are pulling a D or an F in a given course."

"Very good," Bowden said. "Then what I suggest is this: if the boy gets one of those cards . . . even *one*"—he held up one gnarled finger—"I will approach my son and his wife about your counselling. I will go further." He pronounced it *furdah*. "If the boy receives one of your Flunk Cards in April—"

"We give them out in May, actually."

"Yes? If he receives one then, I guarantee that they will accept the counselling proposal. They are worried about their son, Mr. French. But now they are so wrapped up in their own problem that . . ." He shrugged.

"I understand."

"So let us give them that long to solve their own problems. Pulling one's self up by one's own shoelaces . . . that is the American way, is it not?"

"Yes, I guess it is," Rubber Ed told him after a moment's thought . . . and after a quick glance at the clock, which told him he had another appointment in five minutes. "I'll accept that."

He stood, and Bowden stood with him. They shook hands again,

Rubber Ed being carefully mindful of the old party's arthritis.

"But in all fairness, I ought to tell you that very few students can pull out of an eighteen-week tailspin in just four weeks of classes. There's a huge amount of ground to be made up—a *huge* amount. I suspect you'll have to come through on your guarantee, Mr. Bowden."

Bowden offered his thin, disconcerting smile again. "Do you?" was all he said.

Something had troubled Rubber Ed through the entire interview, and he put his finger on it during lunch in the cafeteria, more than an hour after "Lord Peter" had left, umbrella once again neatly tucked under his arm.

He and Todd's grandfather had talked for fifteen minutes at least, probably closer to twenty, and Ed didn't think the old man had once referred to his grandson by name.

Todd pedaled breathlessly up Dussander's walk and parked his bike on its kickstand. School had let out only fifteen minutes before. He took the front steps at one jump, used his doorkey, and hurried down the hall to the sunlit kitchen. His face was a mixture of hopeful sunshine and gloomy clouds. He stood in the kitchen doorway for a moment, his stomach and his vocal cords knotted, watching Dussander as he rocked with his cupful of bourbon in his lap. He was still dressed in his best, although he had pulled his tie down two inches and loosened the top button of his shirt. He looked at Todd expressionlessly, his lizardlike eyes at half-mast.

"Well?" Todd finally managed.

Dussander left him hanging a moment longer, a moment that seemed at least ten years long to Todd. Then, deliberately, Dussander set his cup on the table next to his bottle of Ancient Age and said:

"The fool believed everything."

Todd let out his pentup breath in a whooping gust of relief.

Before he could draw another breath in, Dussander added: "He wanted your poor, troubled parents to attend counselling sessions downtown with a friend of his. He was really quite insistent."

"Jesus! Did you . . . what did you . . . how did you handle it?"

"I thought quickly," Dussander replied. "Like the little girl in the Saki story, invention on short notice is one of my strong points. I promised him your parents would go in for such counselling if you received even one Flunk Card when they are given in May."

The blood fell out of Todd's face.

"You did *what?*" he nearly screamed. "I've already flunked two algebra quizzes and a history test since the marking period started!" He advanced into the room, his pale face now growing shiny with breaking sweat. "There was a French quiz this afternoon and I flunked that, too . . . I know I did. All I could think about was that goddamned Rubber Ed and whether or not you were taking care of him. You took care of him, all right," he finished bitterly. "Not get one Flunk Card? I'll probably get five or six."

"It was the best I could do without arousing suspicions," Dussander said. "This French, fool that he is, is only doing his job. Now you will do yours."

"What's that supposed to mean?" Todd's face was ugly and thunderous, his voice truculent.

"You will work. In the next four weeks you will work harder than you have ever worked in your life. Furthermore, on Monday you will go to each of your instructors and apologize to them for your poor showing thus far. You will—"

"It's impossible," Todd said. "You don't get it, man. It's *impossible.* I'm at least five weeks behind in science and history. In algebra it's more like ten."

"Nevertheless," Dussander said. He poured more bourbon.

"You think you're pretty smart, don't you?" Todd shouted at him. "Well, I don't take orders from you. The days when you gave orders are long over. *Do you get it?*" He lowered his voice abruptly. "The most lethal thing you've got around the house these days is a Shell No-Pest Strip. You're nothing but a broken-down old man who farts rotten eggs if he eats a taco. I bet you even pee in your bed."

"Listen to me, snotnose," Dussander said quietly.

Todd's head jerked angrily around at that.

"Before today," Dussander said carefully, "it was possible, *just barely* possible, that you could have denounced me and come out clean yourself. I don't believe you would have been up to the job with your nerves in their present state, but never mind that. It would have been technically possible. But now things have changed. Today I impersonated your grandfather, one Victor Bowden. No one can have the slightest doubt that I did it with . . . how is the word? . . . your connivance. If it comes out now, boy, you will look blacker than ever. And you will have no defense. I took care of that today."

"I wish—"

"You *wish*! You *wish*!" Dussander roared. "Never mind your wishes, your wishes make me *sick*, your wishes are no more than little piles of dogshit in the gutter! *All I want from you is to know if you understand the situation we are in!*"

"I understand it," Todd muttered. His fists had been tightly clenched while Dussander shouted at him—he was not used to being shouted at. Now he opened his hands and dully observed that he had dug bleeding half-moons into his palms. The cuts would have been worse, he supposed, but in the last four months or so he had taken up biting his nails.

"Good. Then you will make your sweet apologies, and you will study. In your free time at school you will study. During your lunch hours you will study. After school you will come here and study, and on your weekends you will come here and do more of the same."

"Not here," Todd said quickly. "At home."

"No. At home you will dawdle and daydream as you have all along. If you are here I can stand over you if I have to and watch you. I can protect my own interests in this matter. I can quiz you. I can listen to your lessons."

"If I don't want to come here, you can't make me."

Dussander drank. "That is true. Things will then go on as they have. You will fail. This guidance person, French, will expect me to make good on my promise. When I don't, he will call your parents. They will find out that kindly Mr. Denker impersonated your grandfather at your request. They will find out about the altered grades. They—"

"Oh, shut up. I'll come."

"You're already here. Begin with algebra."

"No *way*! It's Friday afternoon!"

"You study *every* afternoon now," Dussander said softly. "Begin with algebra."

Todd stared at him—only for a moment before dropping his eyes and fumbling his algebra text out of his bookbag—and Dussander saw murder in the boy's eyes. Not figurative murder; literal murder. It had been years since he had seen that dark, burning, speculative glance, but one never forgot it. He supposed he would have seen it in his own eyes if there had been a mirror at hand on the day he had looked at the white and defenseless nape of the boy's neck.

I must protect myself, he thought with some amazement. *One underestimates at one's own risk.*

He drank his bourbon and rocked and watched the boy study.

It was nearly five o'clock when Todd biked home. He felt washed out, hot-eyed, drained, impotently angry. Every time his eyes had wandered from the printed page—from the maddening, incomprehensible, fucking *stupid* world of sets, subsets, ordered pairs, and Cartesian co-ordinates—Dussander's sharp old man's voice had spoken. Otherwise he had remained completely silent . . . except for the maddening bump of his slippers on the floor and the squeak of the rocker. He sat there like a vulture waiting for its prey to expire. Why had he ever gotten into this? *How* had he gotten into it? This was a mess, a terrible mess. He had picked up some ground this afternoon—some of the set theory that had stumped him so badly just before the Christmas break had fallen into place with an almost audible click—but it was impossible to think he could pick up enough to scrape through next week's algebra test with even a D.

It was four weeks until the end of the world.

On the corner he saw a bluejay lying on the sidewalk, its beak slowly opening and closing. It was trying vainly to get onto its birdy-feet and hop away. One of its wings had been crushed, and Todd supposed a passing car had hit it and flipped it up onto the sidewalk like a tiddlywink. One of its beady eyes stared up at him.

Todd looked at it for a long time, holding the grips of his bike's apehanger handlebars lightly. Some of the warmth had gone out of the day and the air felt almost chilly. He supposed his friends had spent the afternoon goofing off down at the Babe Ruth diamond on Walnut Street, maybe playing a little scrub, more likely playing pepper or three-flies-six-grounders or rolly-bat. It was the time of year when you started working your way up to baseball. There was some talk about getting up their own sandlot team this year to compete in the informal city league; there were dads enough willing to shlepp them around to games. Todd, of course, would pitch. He had been a Little League pitching star until he had grown out of the Senior Little League division last year. *Would have pitched.*

So what? He'd just have to tell them no. He'd just have to tell them: *Guys, I got mixed up with this war criminal. I got him right by the balls, and then—ha-ha, this'll killya, guys—then I found out he was holding my balls as tight as I was holding his. I started having funny dreams and the cold sweats. My grades went to hell and I changed them on my report card so my folks wouldn't find out and now I've got to hit the books really hard for the first time in my life. I'm not afraid of getting grounded, though. I'm afraid of going to the reformatory. And that's why I can't play any sandlot with you guys this year. You see how it is, guys.*

A thin smile, much like Dussander's and not at all like his former broad grin, touched his lips. There was no sunshine in it; it was a shady smile. There was no fun in it; no confidence. It merely said: *You see how it is, guys.*

He rolled his bike forward over the jay with exquisite slowness, hearing the newspaper crackle of its feathers and the crunch of its small hollow bones as they fractured inside it. He reversed, rolling over it again. It was still twitching. He rolled over it again, a single bloody feather stuck to his front tire, revolving up and down, up and down. By then the bird had stopped moving, the bird had kicked the bucket, the bird had punched out, the bird had gone to that great aviary in the sky, but Todd kept going forwards and backwards across its mashed body just the same. He did it for almost five minutes, and that thin smile never left his face. You see how it is, guys.

10

April, 1975.

The old man stood halfway down the compound's aisle, smiling broadly, as Dave Klingerman walked up to meet him. The frenzied barking that filled the air didn't seem to bother him in the slightest, or the smells of fur and urine, or the hundred different strays yapping and howling in their cages, dashing back and forth, leaping against the mesh. Klingerman pegged the old guy as a dog-lover right off the bat. His smile was sweet and pleasant. He offered Dave a swollen, arthritis-bunched hand carefully, and Klingerman shook it in the same spirit.

"Hello, sir!" he said, speaking up. "Noisy as hell, isn't it?"

"I don't mind," the old man said. "Not at all. My name is Arthur Denker."

"Klingerman. Dave Klingerman."

"I am pleased to meet you, sir. I read in the paper—I could not believe it—that you *give* dogs away here. Perhaps I misunderstood. In fact I think I must have misunderstood."

"No, we give em away, all right," Dave said. "If we can't, we have to destroy em. Sixty days, that's what the State gives us. Shame. Come on in the office here. Quieter. Smells better, too."

In the office, Dave heard a story that was familiar (but nonetheless affecting): Arthur Denker was in his seventies. He had come to California when his wife died. He was not rich, but he tended what he did have with great care. He was lonely. His only friend was the boy who sometimes came to his house and read to him. In Germany he had owned a beautiful Saint Bernard. Now, in Santo Donató, he had a house with a good-sized back yard. The yard was fenced. And he had read in the paper . . . would it be possible that he could . . .

"Well, we don't have any Bernards," Dave said. "They go fast because they're so good with kids—"

"Oh, I understand. I didn't mean that—"

"—but I do have a half-grown shepherd pup. How would that be?"

Mr. Denker's eyes grew bright, as if he might be on the verge of tears. "Perfect," he said. "That would be perfect."

"The dog itself is free, but there are a few other charges. Distemper and rabies shots. A city dog licence. All of it goes about twenty-five bucks for most people, but the State pays half if you're over sixty-five—part of the California Golden Ager program."

"Golden Ager . . . is that what I am?" Mr. Denker said, and laughed. For just a moment—it was silly—Dave felt a kind of chill.

"Uh . . . I guess so, sir."

"It is very reasonable."

"Sure, we think so. The same dog would cost you a hundred and twenty-five dollars in a pet shop. But people go to those places instead of here. They are paying for a set of papers, of course, not the dog." Dave shook his head. "If they only understood how many fine animals are abandoned every year."

"And if you can't find a suitable home for them within sixty days, they are destroyed?"

"We put them to sleep, yes."

"Put them to . . . ? I'm sorry, my English—"

"It's a city ordinance," Dave said. "Can't have dog-packs running the streets."

"You shoot them."

"No, we give them gas. It's very humane. They don't feel a thing."

"No," Mr. Denker said. "I am sure they don't."

Todd's seat in Beginning Algebra was four desks down in the second row. He sat there, trying to keep his face expressionless, as Mr. Storrman passed back the exams. But his ragged fingernails were digging into his palms again, and his entire body seemed to be running with a slow and caustic sweat.

Don't get your hopes up. Don't be such a goddam chump. There's no way you could have passed. You know *you didn't pass.*

Nevertheless, he could not completely squash the foolish hope. It had been the first algebra exam in weeks that looked as if it had been written in something other than Greek. He was sure that in his nervousness (nervousness? no, call it what it had really been: outright terror) he had not done that well, but maybe . . . well, if it had been anyone else but Storrman, who had a Yale padlock for a heart . . .

STOP IT! he commanded himself, and for a moment, a coldly horrible moment, he was positive he had screamed those two words aloud in the classroom. *You flunked, you know you did, not a thing in the world is going to change it.*

Storrman handed him his paper expressionlessly and moved on. Todd laid it face down on his initial-scarred desk. For a moment he didn't think he possessed sufficient will to even turn it over and know. At last he flipped it with such convulsive suddenness that the exam sheet tore. His tongue stuck to the roof of his mouth as he stared at it. His heart seemed to stop for a moment.

The number 83 was written in a circle at the top of the sheet. Below it was a letter-grade: C+. Below the letter-grade was a brief notation: *Good improvement! I think I'm twice as relieved as you should be. Check errors carefully. At least three of them are arithmetical rather than conceptual.*

His heartbeat began again, at triple-time. Relief washed over him, but it was not cool—it was hot and complicated and strange. He closed his eyes, not hearing the class as it buzzed over the exam and began the pre-ordained fight for an extra point here or there. Todd saw redness behind his eyes. It pulsed like flowing blood with the rhythm of his heartbeat. In that instant he hated Dussander more than he ever had before. His hands snapped shut into fists and he only wished, wished, wished, that Dussander's scrawny chicken neck could have been between them.

Dick and Monica Bowden had twin beds, separated by a nightstand with a pretty imitation Tiffany lamp standing on it. Their room was done in genuine redwood, and the walls were comfortably lined with books. Across the room, nestled between two ivory bookends (bull elephants on their hind legs) was a round Sony TV. Dick was watching Johnny Carson with the earplug in while Monica read the new Michael Crichton that had come from the book club that day.

"Dick?" She put a bookmark (THIS IS WHERE I FELL ASLEEP, it said) into the Crichton and closed it.

On the TV, Buddy Hackett had just broken everyone up. Dick smiled.

"Dick?" she said more loudly.

He pulled the earplug out. "What?"

"Do you think Todd's all right?"

He looked at her for a moment, frowning, then shook his head a little. *"Je ne comprends pas, chérie."* His limping French was a joke between them. His father had sent him an extra two hundred dollars to hire a tutor when he was flunking French. He had gotten Monica Darrow, picking her name at random from the cards tacked up on the Union bulletin board. By Christmas she had been wearing his pin . . . and he had managed a C in French.

"Well . . . he's lost weight."

"He looks a little scrawny, sure," Dick said. He put the TV earplug in his lap, where it emitted tiny squawking sounds. "He's growing up, Monica."

"So soon?" she asked uneasily.

He laughed. "So soon. I shot up seven inches as a teenager —from a five-foot-six shrimp at twelve to the beautiful six-foot-one mass of muscle you see before you today. My mother said that when I was fourteen you could hear me growing in the night."

"Good thing not all of you grew that much."

"It's all in how you use it."

"Want to use it tonight?"

"The wench grows bold," Dick Bowden said, and threw the earplug across the room.

After, as he was drifting off to sleep:

"Dick, he's having bad dreams, too."

"Nightmares?" he muttered.

"Nightmares. I've heard him moaning in his sleep two or three times when I've gone down to use the bathroom in the night. I didn't want to wake him up. It's silly, but my grandmother used to say you could drive a person insane if you woke them up in the middle of a bad dream."

"She was the Polack, wasn't she?"

"The Polack, yeah, the Polack. Nice talk!"

"You know what I mean. Why don't you just use the upstairs john?" He had put it in himself two years ago.

"You know the flush always wakes you up," she said.

"So don't flush it."

"Dick, that's nasty."

He sighed.

"Sometimes when I go in, he's sweating. And the sheets are damp."

He grinned in the dark. "I bet."

"What's *that* . . . oh." She slapped him lightly. "That's nasty, too. Besides, he's only thirteen."

"Fourteen next month. He's not too young. A little precocious, maybe, but not too young."

"How old were you?"

"Fourteen or fifteen. I don't remember exactly. But I remember I woke up thinking I'd died and gone to heaven."

"But you were older than Todd is now."

"All that stuff's happening younger. It must be the milk . . . or the fluoride. Do you know they have sanitary napkin dispensers in all the girls' rooms of the school we built in Jackson Park last year? And that's a *grammar school.* Now your average sixth-grader is only eleven. How old were you when you started?"

"I don't remember," she said. "All I know is Todd's dreams don't sound like . . . like he died and went to heaven."

"Have you asked him about them?"

"Once. About six weeks ago. You were off playing golf with that horrible Ernie Jacobs."

"That horrible Ernie Jacobs is going to make me a full partner by 1977, if he doesn't screw himself to death with that high-yellow secretary of his before then. Besides, he always pays the greens fees. What did Todd say?"

"That he didn't remember. But a sort of . . . shadow crossed his face. I think he *did* remember."

"Monica, I don't remember everything from my dear dead youth, but one thing I do remember is that wet dreams are not always pleasant. In fact, they can be downright unpleasant."

"How can that be?"

"Guilt. All kinds of guilt. Some of it maybe all the way from babyhood, when it was made very clear to him that wetting the bed was wrong. Then there's the sex thing. Who knows what brings a wet dream on? Copping a feel on the bus? Looking up a girl's skirt in study hall? I don't know. The only one I can really remember was going off the high board at the YMCA pool on co-ed day and losing my trunks when I hit the water."

"You got off on that?" she asked, giggling a little.

"Yeah. So if the kid doesn't want to talk to you about his John Thomas problems, don't force him."

"We did our damn best to raise him without all those needless guilts."

"You can't escape them. He brings them home from school like the colds he used to pick up in the first grade. From his friends, or the way his teachers mince around certain subjects. He probably got it from my dad, too. 'Don't touch it in the night, Todd, or your hands'll grow hair and you'll go blind and you'll start to lose your memory, and after awhile your thing will turn black and rot off. So be careful, Todd.' "

"Dick Bowden! Your dad would never—"

"He wouldn't? Hell, he *did*. Just like your Polack grandmother told you that waking somebody up in the middle of a nightmare might drive them nuts. He also told me to always wipe off the ring of a public toilet before I sat on it so I wouldn't get 'other people's germs.' I guess that was his way of saying syphilis. I bet your grandmother laid that one on you, too."

"No, my mother," she said absently. "And she told me to always flush. Which is why I go downstairs."

"It still wakes me up," Dick mumbled.

"What?"

"Nothing."

This time he had actually drifted halfway over the threshold of sleep when she spoke his name again.

"What?" he asked, a little impatiently.

"You don't suppose . . . oh, never mind. Go back to sleep."

"No, go on, finish. I'm awake again. I don't suppose what?"

"That old man. Mr. Denker. You don't think Todd's seeing too much of him, do you? Maybe he's . . . oh, I don't know . . . filling Todd up with a lot of stories."

"The real heavy horrors," Dick said. "The day the Essen Motor Works dropped below quota." He snickered.

"It was just an idea," she said, a little stiffly. The covers rustled as she turned over on her side. "Sorry I bothered you."

He put a hand on her bare shoulder. "I'll tell you something, babe," he said, and stopped for a moment, thinking carefully, choosing his words. "I've been worried about Todd, too, some- times. Not the same things you've been worried about, but worried is worried, right?"

She turned back to him. "About what?"

"Well, I grew up a lot different than he's growing up. My dad had the store. Vic the Grocer, everyone called him. He had a book where he kept the names of the people who owed him, and how much they owed. You know what he called it?"

"No." Dick rarely talked about his boyhood; she had always thought it was because he hadn't enjoyed it. She listened carefully now.

"He called it the Left Hand Book. He said the right hand was business, but the right hand should never know what the left hand was doing. He said if the right hand *did* know, it would probably grab a meat-cleaver and chop the left hand right off."

"You never told me that."

"Well, I didn't like the old man very much when we first got married, and the truth is I still spend a lot of time not liking him. I couldn't understand why I had to wear pants from the Goodwill box while Mrs. Mazursky could get a ham on credit with that same old story about how her husband was going back to work next week. The only work that fucking wino Bill Mazursky ever had was holding onto a twelve-cent bottle of musky so it wouldn't fly away.

"All I ever wanted in those days was to get out of the neighborhood and away from my old man's life. So I made grades and played sports I didn't really like and got a scholarship at UCLA. And I made damn sure I stayed in the top ten per cent of my classes because the only Left Hand Book the colleges kept in those days was for the GIs that fought the war. My dad sent me money for my textbooks, but the only other money I ever took from him was the time I wrote home in a panic because I was flunking funnybook French. I met you. And I found out later from Mr. Halleck down the block that my dad put a lien on his car to scare up that two hundred bucks.

"And now I've got you, and we've got Todd. I've always thought he was a damned fine boy, and I've tried to make sure he's always had everything he ever needed . . . anything that would help him grow into a fine man. I used to laugh at that old wheeze about a man wanting his son to be better than he was, but as I get older it seems less funny and more true. I never want Todd to have to wear pants from a Goodwill box because some wino's wife got a ham on credit. You understand?"

"Yes, of course I do," she said quietly.

"Then, about ten years ago, just before my old man finally got tired of fighting off the urban renewal guys and retired, he had a minor stroke. He was in the hospital for ten days. And the people from the neighborhood, the guineas and the krauts, even some of the jigs that started to move in around 1955 or so . . . they paid his bill. Every fucking cent. I couldn't believe it. They kept the store open, too. Fiona Castellano got four or five of her friends who were out of work to come in on shifts. When my old man got back, the books balanced out to the cent."

"Wow," she said, very softly.

"You know what he said to me? My old man? That he'd always been afraid of getting old—of being scared and hurting and all by himself. Of having to go into the hospital and not being able to make ends meet anymore. Of dying. He said that after the stroke he wasn't scared anymore. He said he thought he could die well. 'You mean die happy, Pap?' I asked him. 'No,' he said. 'I don't think anyone dies happy, Dickie.' He always called me Dickie, still does, and that's another thing I guess I'll never be able to like. He said he didn't think anyone died happy, but you could die well. That impressed me."

He was silent for a long, thoughtful time.

"The last five or six years I've been able to get some perspective on my old man. Maybe because he's down there in San Remo and out of my hair. I started thinking that maybe the Left Hand Book wasn't such a bad idea. That was when I started to worry about Todd. I kept wanting to tell him about how there was maybe something more to life than me being able to take all of you to Hawaii for a month or being able to buy Todd pants that don't smell like the mothballs they used to put in the Goodwill box. I could never figure out how to tell him those things. But I think maybe he knows. And it takes a load off my mind."

"Reading to Mr. Denker, you mean?"

"Yes. He's not getting anything for that. Denker can't pay him. Here's this old guy, thousands of miles from any friends or relatives that might still be living, here's this guy that's everything my father was afraid of. And there's Todd."

"I never thought of it just like that."

"Have you noticed the way Todd gets when you talk to him about that old man?"

"He gets very quiet."

"Sure. He gets tongue-tied and embarrassed, like he was doing something nasty. Just like my pop used to when someone tried to thank him for laying some credit on them. We're Todd's right hand, that's all. You and me and all the rest—the house, the ski-trips to Tahoe, the Thunderbird in the garage, his color TV. All his right hand. And he doesn't want us to see what his left hand is up to.

"You don't think he's seeing too much of Denker, then?"

"Honey, look at his grades! If *they* were falling off, I'd be the first one to say Hey, enough is enough, already, don't go overboard. His grades are the first place trouble would show up. And how have they been?"

"As good as ever, after that first slip."

"So what are we talking about? Listen, I've got a conference at nine, babe. If I don't get some sleep, I'm going to be sloppy."

"Sure, go to sleep," she said indulgently, and as he turned over, she kissed him lightly on one shoulderblade. "I love you."

"Love you too," he said comfortably, and closed his eyes. "Everything's fine, Monica. You worry too much."

"I know I do. Goodnight."

They slept.

* * *

"Stop looking out the window," Dussander said. "There is nothing out there to interest you."

Todd looked at him sullenly. His history text was open on the table, showing a color plate of Teddy Roosevelt cresting San Juan Hill. Helpless Cubans were falling away from the hooves of Teddy's horse. Teddy was grinning a wide American grin, the grin of a man who knew that God was in His heaven and everything was bully. Todd Bowden was not grinning.

"You like being a slave-driver, don't you?" he asked.

"I like being a free man," Dussander said. "Study."

"Suck my cock."

"As a boy," Dussander said, "I would have had my mouth washed out with lye soap for saying such a thing."

"Times change."

"Do they?" Dussander sipped his bourbon. "Study."

Todd stared at Dussander. "You're nothing but a goddamned rummy. You know that?"

"Study."

"*Shut up!*" Todd slammed his book shut. It made a riflecrack sound in Dussander's kitchen. "I can never catch up, anyway. Not in time for the test. There's fifty pages of this shit left, all the way up to World War One. I'll make a crib in Study Hall Two tomorrow."

Harshly, Dussander said: "You will do no such thing!"

"Why not? Who's going to stop me? You?"

"Boy, you are still having a hard time comprehending the stakes we play for. Do you think I enjoy keeping your snivelling brat nose in your books?" His voice rose, whipsawing, demanding, commanding. "Do you think I enjoy listening to your tantrums, your kindergarten swears? 'Suck my cock,' " Dussander mimicked savagely in a high, falsetto voice that made Todd flush darkly. " 'Suck my cock, so what, who cares, I'll do it tomorrow, suck my cock'!"

"Well, you *like* it!" Todd shouted back. "Yeah, you *like* it! The only time you don't feel like a zombie is when you're on my back! So give me a fucking break!"

"If you are caught with one of these cribbing papers, what do you think will happen? Who will be told first?"

Todd looked at his hands with their ragged, bitten fingernails and said nothing.

"Who?"

"Jesus, you know. Rubber Ed. Then my folks, I guess."

Dussander nodded. "Me, I guess that too. Study. Put your cribbing paper in your head, where it belongs."

"I hate you," Todd said dully. "I really do." But he opened his book again and Teddy Roosevelt grinned up at him, Teddy galloping into the twentieth century with his saber in his hand, Cubans falling back in disarray before him—possibly before the force of his fierce American grin.

Dussander began to rock again. He held his teacup of bourbon in his hands. "That's a good boy," he said, almost tenderly.

Todd had his first wet dream on the last night of April, and he awoke to the sound of rain whispering secretly through the leaves and branches of the tree outside his window.

In the dream, he had been in one of the Patin laboratories. He was standing at the end of a long, low table. A lush young girl of amazing beauty had been secured to this table with clamps. Dussander was assisting him. Dussander wore a white butcher's apron and nothing else. When he pivoted to turn on the monitoring equipment, Todd could see Dussander's scrawny buttocks grinding at each other like misshapen white stones.

He handed something to Todd, something he recognized immediately, although he had never actually seen one. It was a dildo. The tip of it was polished metal, winking in the light of the overhead fluorescents like heartless chrome. The dildo was hollow. Snaking out of it was a black electrical cord that ended in a red rubber bulb.

"Go ahead," Dussander said. "The Fuehrer says it's all right. He says it's your reward for studying."

Todd looked down at himself and saw that he was naked. His small penis was fully erect, jutting plumply up at an angle from the thin peachdown of his public hair. He slipped the dildo on. The fit was tight but there was some sort of lubricant in there. The friction was pleasant. No; it was more than pleasant. It was delightful.

He looked down at the girl and felt a strange shift in his thoughts . . . as if they had slipped into a perfect groove. Suddenly all things seemed right. Doors had been opened. He would go through them. He took the red rubber bulb in his left hand, put his knees on the table, and paused for just a moment, gauging the angle while his Norseman's prick made its own angle up and out from his slight boy's body.

Dimly, far off, he could hear Dussander reciting: "Test run eighty-four. Electricity, sexual stimulus, metabolism. Based on the Thyssen theories of negative reinforcement. Subject is a young Jewish girl, approximately sixteen years of age, no scars, no identifying marks, no known disabilities—"

She cried out when the tip of the dildo touched her. Todd found the cry pleasant, as he did her fruitless struggles to free herself, or, lacking that, to at least bring her legs together.

This is what they can't show in those magazines about the war, he thought, *but it's there, just the same.*

He thrust forward suddenly, parting her with no grace. She shrieked like a firebell.

After her initial thrashings and efforts to expel him, she lay perfectly still, enduring. The lubricated interior of the dildo pulled and slid against Todd's engorgement. Delightful. Heavenly. His fingers toyed with the rubber bulb in his left hand.

Far away, Dussander recited pulse, blood pressure, respiration, alpha waves, beta waves, stroke count.

As the climax began to build inside him, Todd became perfectly still and squeezed the bulb. Her eyes, which had been closed, flew open, bulging. Her tongue fluttered in the pink cavity of her mouth. Her arms and legs thrummed. But the real action was in her torso, rising and falling, vibrating, every muscle

(oh every muscle every muscle moves tightens closes every)

every muscle and the sensation at climax was

(ecstasy)

oh it was, it was

(the end of the world thundering outside)

He woke to that sound and the sound of rain. He was huddled on his side in a dark ball, his heart beating at a sprinter's pace. His lower belly was covered with a warm, sticky liquid. There was an instant of panicky horror when he feared he might be bleeding to death . . . and then he realized what it *really* was, and he felt a fainting, nauseated revulsion. Semen. Come. Jizz. Jungle-juice. Words from fences and locker rooms and the walls of gas station bathrooms. There was nothing here he wanted.

His hands balled helplessly into fists. His dream-climax recurred to him, pallid now, senseless, frightening. But nerve-endings still tingled, retreating slowly from their spike-point. That final scene, fading now, was disgusting and yet somehow compulsive, like an unsuspecting bite into a piece of tropical fruit which, you realized (a second too late), had only tasted so amazingly sweet because it was rotten.

It came to him then. What he would have to do.

There was only one way he could get himself back again. He would have to kill Dussander. It was the only way. Games were done; storytime was over. This was survival.

"Kill him and it's all over," he whispered in the darkness, with the rain in the tree outside and semen drying on his belly. Whispering it made it seem real.

Dussander always kept three or four fifths of Ancient Age on a shelf over the steep cellar stairs. He would go to the door, open it (half-crocked already, more often than not), and go down two steps. Then he would lean out, put one hand on the shelf, and grip the fresh bottle by the neck with his other hand. The cellar floor was not paved, but the dirt was hard-packed and Dussander, with a machinelike efficiency that Todd now thought of as Prussian rather than German, oiled it once every two months to keep bugs from breeding in the dirt. Cement or no cement, old bones break easily. And old men have accidents. The post-mortem would show that "Mr. Denker" had had a skinful of booze when he "fell."

What happened, Todd?

He didn't answer the door so I used the key he gave me. Sometimes he falls asleep. I went into the kitchen and saw the cellar door was open. I went down the stairs and he . . . he . . .

Then, of course, tears.

It would work.

He would have himself back again.

For a long time Todd lay awake in the dark, listening to the thunder retreat westward, out over the Pacific, listening to the secret sound of the rain. He thought he would stay awake the rest of the night, going over it and over it. But he fell asleep only moments later and slept dreamlessly with one fist curled under his chin. He woke on the first of May fully rested for the first time in months.

11

May, 1975.

For Todd, that Friday was the longest of his life. He sat in class after class, hearing nothing, waiting only for the last five minutes, when the instructor would take out his or her small pile of Flunk Cards and distribute them. Each time an instructor approached Todd's desk with that pile of cards, he grew cold. Each time he or she passed him without stopping, he felt waves of dizziness and semi-hysteria.

Algebra was the worst. Storrman approached . . . hesitated . . . and just as Todd became convinced he was going to pass on, he laid a Flunk Card face down on Todd's desk. Todd looked at it coldly, with no feelings at all. Now that it had happened, he was only cold. *Well, that's it,* he thought. *Point, game, set, and match. Unless Dussander can think of something else. And I have my doubts.*

Without much interest, he turned the Flunk Card over to see by how much he had missed his C. It must have been close, but trust old Stony Storrman not to give anyone a break. He saw that the grade-spaces were utterly blank—both the letter-grade space and the numerical-grade space. Written in the COMMENTS section was this message: *I'm sure glad I don't have to give you one of these for* REAL! *Chas. Storrman.*

The dizziness came again, more savagely this time, roaring through his head, making it feel like a balloon filled with helium. He gripped the sides of his desk as hard as he could, holding one thought with total obsessive tightness: *You will not faint, not faint, not faint.* Little by little the waves of dizziness passed, and then he had to control an urge to run up the aisle after Storrman, turn him around, and poke his eyes out with the freshly sharpened pencil he held in his hand. And through it all his face remained carefully blank. The only sign that anything at all was going on inside was a mild tic in one eyelid.

School let out for the week fifteen minutes later. Todd walked slowly around the building to the bike-racks, his head down, his hands shoved into his pockets, his books tucked into the crook of his right arm, oblivious of the running, shouting students. He tossed the books into his bike-basket, unlocked the Schwinn, and pedaled away. Toward Dussander's house.

Today, he thought. *Today is your day, old man.*

"And so," Dussander said, pouring bourbon into his cup as Todd entered the kitchen, "the accused returns from the dock. How said they, prisoner?" He was wearing his bathrobe and a pair of hairy wool socks that climbed halfway up his shins. Socks like that, Todd thought, would be easy to slip in. He glanced at the bottle of Ancient Age Dussander was currently working. It was down to the last three fingers.

"No D's, no F's, no Flunk Cards," Todd said. "I'll still have to change some of my grades in June, but maybe just the averages. I'll be getting all A's and B's this quarter if I keep up my work."

"Oh, you'll keep it up, all right," Dussander said. "We will see to it." He drank and then tipped more bourbon into his cup. "This calls for a celebration." His speech was slightly blurred—hardly enough to be noticeable, but Todd knew the old fuck was as drunk as he ever got. Yes, today. It would have to be today.

But he was cool.

"Celebrate pigshit," he told Dussander.

"I'm afraid the delivery boy hasn't arrived with the beluga and the truffles yet," Dussander said, ignoring him. "Help is so unreliable these days. What about a few Ritz crackers and some Velveeta while we wait?"

"Okay," Todd said. "What the hell."

Dussander stood up (one knee banged the table, making him wince) and crossed to the refrigerator. He got out the cheese, took a knife from the drawer and a plate from the cupboard, and a box of Ritz crackers from the breadbox.

"All carefully injected with prussic acid," he told Todd as he set the cheese and crackers down on the table. He grinned, and Todd saw that he had left out his false teeth again today. Nevertheless, Todd smiled back.

"So quiet today!" Dussander exclaimed. "I would have expected you to turn handsprings all the way up the hall." He emptied the last of the bourbon into his cup, sipped, smacked his lips.

"I guess I'm still numb," Todd said. He bit into a cracker. He had stopped refusing Dussander's food a long time ago. Dussander thought there was a letter with one of Todd's friends—there was not, of course; he had friends, but none he trusted *that* much. He supposed Dussander had guessed that long ago, but he knew Dussander didn't quite dare put his guess to such an extreme test as murder.

"What shall we talk about today?" Dussander enquired, tossing off the last shot. "I give you the day off from studying, how's that? Uh? Uh?" When he drank, his accent became thicker. It was an accent Todd had come to hate. Now he felt okay about the accent; he felt okay about everything. He felt very cool all over. He looked at his hands, the hands which would give the push, and they looked just as they always did. They were not trembling; they were cool.

"I don't care," he said. "Anything you want."

"Shall I tell you about the special soap we made? Our experiments with enforced homosexuality? Or perhaps you would like to hear how I escaped Berlin after I had been foolish enough to go back. That was a close one, I can tell you." He pantomimed shaving one stubbly cheek and laughed.

"Anything," Todd said. "Really." He watched Dussander examine the empty bottle and then get up with it in one hand. Dussander took it to the wastebasket and dropped it in.

"No, none of those, I think," Dussander said. "You don't seem to be in the mood." He stood reflectively by the wastebasket for a moment and then crossed the kitchen to the cellar door. His wool socks whispered on the hilly linoleum. "I think today I will instead tell you the story of an old man who was afraid."

Dussander opened the cellar door. His back was now to the table. Todd stood up quietly.

"He was afraid," Dussander went on, "of a certain young boy who was, in a queer way, his friend. A smart boy. His mother called this boy 'apt pupil,' and the old man had already discovered he *was* an apt pupil . . . although perhaps not in the way his mother thought."

Dussander fumbled with the old-fashioned electrical switch on the wall, trying to turn it with his bunched and clumsy fingers. Todd walked—almost glided—across the linoleum, not stepping on any of the places where it squeaked or creaked. He knew this kitchen as well as his own, now. Maybe better.

"At first, the boy was not the old man's friend," Dussander said. He managed to turn the switch at last. He descended the first step with a veteran drunk's care. "At first the old man disliked the boy a great deal. Then he grew to . . . to enjoy his company, although there was still a strong element of dislike there." He was looking at the shelf now but still holding the railing. Todd, cool—no, now he was *cold*—stepped behind him and calculated the chances of one strong push dislodging Dussander's hold on the railing. He decided to wait until Dussander leaned forward.

"Part of the old man's enjoyment came from a feeling of equality," Dussander went on thoughtfully. "You see, the boy and the old man had each other in mutual deathgrips. Each knew something the other wanted kept secret. And then . . . ah, then it became apparent to the old man that things were changing. Yes. He was losing his hold—some of it or all of it, depending on how desperate the boy might be, and how clever. It occurred to this old man on one long and sleepless night that it might be well for him to acquire a new hold on the boy. For his own safety."

Now Dussander let go of the railing and leaned out over the steep cellar stairs, but Todd remained perfectly still. The bone-deep cold was melting out of him, being replaced by a rosy flush of anger and confusion. As Dussander grasped his fresh bottle, Todd thought viciously that the old man had the stinkiest cellar in town, oil or no oil. It smelled as if something had died down there.

"So the old man got out of his bed right then. What is sleep to an old man? Very little. And he sat at his small desk, thinking about how cleverly he had enmeshed the boy in the very crimes the boy was holding over his own head. He sat thinking about how hard the boy had worked, how very hard, to bring his school marks back up. And how, when they *were* back up, he would have no further need for the old man alive. And if the old man were dead, the boy could be free."

He turned around now, holding the fresh bottle of Ancient Age by the neck.

"I heard you, you know," he said, almost gently. "From the moment you pushed your chair back and stood up. You are not as quiet as you imagine, boy. At least not yet."

Todd said nothing.

"So!" Dussander exclaimed, stepping back into the kitchen and closing the cellar door firmly behind him. "The old man wrote everything down, *nicht wahr?* From first word to last he wrote it down. When he was finally finished it was almost dawn and his hand was singing from the arthritis—the *verdammt* arthritis—but he felt good for the first times in weeks. He felt *safe*. He got back into his bed and slept until mid-afternoon. In fact, if he had slept any longer, he would have missed his favorite—*General Hospital*."

He had regained his rocker now. He sat down, produced a worn jackknife with a yellow ivory handle, and began to cut painstakingly around the seal covering the top of the bourbon bottle.

"On the following day the old man dressed in his best suit and went down to the bank where he kept his little checking and savings accounts. He spoke to one of the bank officers, who was able to answer all the old man's questions most satisfactorily. He rented a safety deposit box. The bank officer explained to the old man that he would have a key and the bank would have a key. To open the box, both keys would be needed. No one but the old man could use the old man's key without a signed, notarized letter of permission from the old man himself. With one exception."

Dussander smiled toothlessly into Todd Bowden's white, set face.

"That exception is made in the event of the box-holder's death," he said. Still looking at Todd, still smiling, Dussander put his jackknife back into the pocket of his robe, unscrewed the cap of the bourbon bottle, and poured a fresh jolt into his cup.

"What happens then?" Todd asked hoarsely.

"Then the box is opened in the presence of a bank official and a representative of the Internal Revenue Service. The contents of the box are inventoried. In this case they will find only a twelve-page document. Non-taxable . . . but highly interesting."

The fingers of Todd's hands crept toward each other and locked tightly. "You can't do that," he said in a stunned and unbelieving voice. It was the voice of a person who observes another person walking on the ceiling. "You can't . . . can't do that."

"My boy," Dussander said kindly, "I have."

"But . . . I . . . you . . ." His voice suddenly rose to an agonized howl. "You're *old*! Don't you know that you're *old*? You could die! *You could die anytime!*"

Dussander got up. He went to one of the kitchen cabinets and took down a small glass. This glass had once held jelly. Cartoon characters danced around the rim. Todd recognized them all—Fred and Wilma Flintstone, Barney and Betty Rubble, Pebbles and Bamm-Bamm. He had grown up with them. He watched as Dussander wiped this jelly-glass almost ceremonially with a dishtowel. He watched as Dussander set it in front of him. He watched as Dussander poured a finger of bourbon into it.

"What's that for?" Todd muttered. "I don't drink. Drinking's for cheap stewbums like you."

"Lift your glass, boy. It is a special occasion. Today you drink."

Todd looked at him for a long moment, then picked up the glass. Dussander clicked his cheap ceramic cup smartly against it.

"I make a toast, boy—long life! Long life to both of us! *Prosit!*" He tossed his bourbon off at a gulp and then began to laugh. He rocked back and forth, stockinged feet hitting the linoleum, laughing, and Todd thought he had never looked so much like a vulture, a vulture in a bathrobe, a noisome beast of carrion.

"I hate you," he whispered, and then Dussander began to choke on his own laughter. His face turned a dull brick color; it sounded as if he were coughing, laughing, and strangling, all at the same time. Todd, scared, got up quickly and clapped him on the back until the coughing fit had passed.

"*Danke schön,*" he said. "Drink your drink. It will do you good."

Todd drank it. It tasted like very bad cold-medicine and lit a fire in his gut.

"I can't believe you drink this shit all day," he said, putting the glass back on the table and shuddering. "You ought to quit it. Quit drinking *and* smoking."

"Your concern for my health is touching," Dussander said. He produced a crumpled pack of cigarettes from the same bathrobe pocket into which the jackknife had disappeared. "And I am equally solicitous of your own welfare, boy. Almost every day I read in the paper where a cyclist has been killed at a busy intersection. You should give it up. You should walk. Or ride the bus, like me."

"Why don't you go fuck yourself?" Todd burst out.

"My boy," Dussander said, pouring more bourbon and beginning to laugh again, "we are fucking each other—didn't you know that?"

One day about a week later, Todd was sitting on a disused mail platform down in the old trainyard. He chucked cinders out across the rusty, weed-infested tracks one at a time.

Why shouldn't I kill him anyway?

Because he was a logical boy, the logical answer came first. No reason at all. Sooner or later Dussander was going to die, and given Dussander's habits, it would probably be sooner. Whether he killed the old man or whether Dussander died of a heart attack in his bathtub, it was all going to come out. At least he could have the pleasure of wringing the old vulture's neck.

Sooner or later—that phrase defied logic.

Maybe it'll be later, Todd thought. *Cigarettes or not, booze or not, he's a tough old bastard. He's lasted this long, so . . . so maybe it'll be later.*

From beneath him came a fuzzy snort.

Todd jumped to his feet, dropping a handful of cinders he had been holding. That snorting sound came again.

He paused, on the verge of running, but the snort didn't recur. Nine hundred yards away, an eight-lane freeway swept across the horizon above this weed- and junk-strewn cul-de-sac with its deserted buildings, rusty Cyclone fences, and splintery, warped platforms. The cars up on the freeway glistened in the sun like exotic hard-shelled beetles. Eight lanes of traffic up there, nothing down here but Todd, a few birds . . . and whatever had snorted.

Cautiously, he bent down with his hands on his knees and peered under the mail platform. There was a wino lying up in there among the yellow weeds and empty cans and dusty old bottles. It was impossible to tell his age; Todd put him at somewhere between thirty and four hundred. He was wearing a strappy tee-shirt that was caked with dried vomit, green pants that were far too big for him, and gray leather workshoes cracked in a hundred places. The cracks gaped like agonized mouths. Todd thought he smelled like Dussander's cellar.

The wino's red-laced eyes opened slowly and stared at Todd with a bleary lack of wonder. As they did, Todd thought of the Swiss Army knife in his pocket, the Angler model. He had purchased it at a sporting goods store in Redondo Beach almost a year ago. He could hear the clerk that had waited on him in his mind: *You couldn't pick a better knife that that one, son—a knife like that could save your life someday. We sell fifteen hundred Swiss knives every damn year.*

Fifteen hundred a year.

He put his hand in his pocket and gripped the knife. In his mind's eye he saw Dussander's jackknife working slowly around the neck of the bourbon bottle, slitting the seal. A moment later he became aware that he had an erection.

Cold terror stole into him.

The wino swiped a hand over his cracked lips and then licked them with a tongue which nicotine had turned a permanent dismal yellow. "Got a dime, kid?"

Todd looked at him expressionlessly.

"Gotta get to L.A. Need another dime for the bus. I got a pointment, me. Got a job offertunity. Nice kid like you must have a dime. Maybe you got a quarter."

Yessir, you could clean out a damn bluegill with a knife like that . . . hell, you could clean out a damn marlin with it if you had to. We sell fifteen hundred of those a year. Every sporting goods store and Army-Navy Surplus in America sells them, and if you decided to use this one to clean out some dirty, shitty old wino, nobody *could trace it back to you, absolutely NOBODY.*

The wino's voice dropped; it became a confidential, tenebrous whisper. "For a buck I'd do you a blowjob, you never had a better. You'd come your brains out, kid, you'd—"

Todd pulled his hand out of his pocket. He wasn't sure what was in it until he opened it. Two quarters. Two nickles. A dime. Some pennies. He threw them at the wino and fled.

12

June, 1975.

Todd Bowden, now fourteen, came biking up Dussander's walk and parked his bike on the kickstand. The L.A. *Times* was on the bottom step; he picked it up. He looked at the bell, below which the neat legends ARTHUR DENKER and NO SOLICITORS, NO PED-DLERS, NO SALESMEN still kept their places. He didn't bother with the bell now, of course; he had his key.

Somewhere close by was the popping, burping sound of a Lawn-Boy. He looked at Dussander's grass and saw it could use a cutting; he would have to tell the old man to find a boy with a mower. Dussander forgot little things like that more often now. Maybe it was senility; maybe it was just the pickling influence of Ancient Age on his brains. That was an adult thought for a boy of fourteen to have, but such thoughts no longer struck Todd as singular. He had many adult thoughts these days. Most of them were not so great.

He let himself in.

He had his usual instant of cold terror as he entered the kitchen and saw Dussander slumped slightly sideways in his rocker, the cup on the table, a half-empty bottle of bourbon beside it. A cigarette had burned its entire length down to lacy gray ash in a mayonnaise cover where several other butts had been mashed out. Dussander's mouth hung open. His face was yellow. His big hands dangled limply over the rocker's arms. He didn't seem to be breathing.

"Dussander," he said, a little too harshly. "Rise and shine, Dussander."

He felt a wave of relief as the old man twitched, blinked, and finally sat up.

"Is it you? And so early?"

"They let us out early on the last day of school," Todd said. He pointed to the remains of the cigarette in the mayonnaise cover. "Someday you'll burn down the house doing that."

"Maybe," Dussander said indifferently. He fumbled out his cigarettes, shot one from the pack (it almost rolled off the edge of the table before Dussander was able to catch it), and at last got it going. A protracted fit of coughing followed, and Todd winced in disgust. When the old man really got going, Todd half-expected him to start spitting out grayish-black chunks of lung-tissue onto the table . . . and he'd probably grin as he did it.

At last the coughing eased enough for Dussander to say, "What have you got there?"

"Report card."

Dussander took it, opened it, and held it away from him at arm's length so he could read it. "English . . . A. American History . . . A. Earth Science . . . B-plus. Your Community and You . . . A. Primary French . . . B-minus. Beginning Algebra . . . B." He put it down. "Very good. What is the slang? We have saved your bacon, boy. Will you have to change any of these averages in the last column?"

"French and algebra, but no more than eight or nine points in all. I don't think any of this is ever going to come out. And I guess I owe that to you. I'm not proud of it, but it's the truth. So, thanks."

"What a touching speech," Dussander said, and began to cough again.

"I guess I won't be seeing you around too much from now on," Todd said, and Dussander abruptly stopped coughing.

"No?" he said, politely enough.

"No," Todd said. "We're going to Hawaii for a month starting on June twenty-fifth. In September I'll be going to school across town. It's this bussing thing."

"Oh yes, the *Schwarzen*," Dussander said, idly watching a fly as it trundled across the red and white check of the oilcloth. "For twenty years this country has worried and whined about the *Schwarzen*. But we know the solution . . . don't we, boy?" He smiled toothlessly at Todd and Todd looked down, feeling the old sickening lift and drop in his stomach. Terror, hate, and a desire to do something so awful it could only be fully contemplated in his dreams.

"Look, I plan to go to college, in case you didn't know," Todd said. "I know that's a long time off, but I think about it. I even know what I want to major in. History."

"Admirable. He who will not learn from the past is—"

"Oh, shut up," Todd said.

Dussander did so, amiably enough. He knew the boy wasn't done . . . not yet. He sat with his hands folded, watching him.

"I could get my letter back from my friend," Todd suddenly blurted. "You know that? I could let you read it, and then you could watch me burn it. If—"

"—if I would remove a certain document from my safety deposit box."

"Well . . . yeah."

Dussander uttered a long, windy, rueful sigh. "My boy," he said. "Still you do not understand the situation. You never have, right from the beginning. Partly because you are only a boy, but not entirely . . . even in the beginning, you were a very *old* boy. No, the real villain was and is your absurd American self-confidence that never allowed you to consider the possible consequences of what you were doing . . . which does not allow it even now."

Todd began to speak and Dussander raised his hand adamantly, suddenly the world's oldest traffic cop.

"No, don't contradict me. It's true. Go on if you like. Leave the house, get out of here, never come back. Can I stop you? No. Of course I can't. Enjoy yourself in Hawaii while I sit in this hot, grease-smelling kitchen and wait to see if the *Schwarzen* in Watts will decide to start killing policemen and burning their shitty tenements again this year. I can't stop you any more than I can stop getting older a day at a time."

He looked at Todd fixedly, so fixedly that Todd looked away.

"Down deep inside, I don't like you. Nothing could make me like you. You forced yourself on me. You are an unbidden guest in my house. You have made me open crypts perhaps better left shut, because I have discovered that some of the corpses were buried alive, and that a few of those *still* have some wind left in them.

"You yourself have become enmeshed, but do I pity you because of that? *Gott im Himmel!* You have made your bed; should I pity you if you sleep badly in it? No . . . I don't pity you, and I don't like you, but I have come to respect you a little bit. So don't try my patience by asking me to explain this twice. We could obtain our documents and destroy them here in my kitchen. And still it would not be over. We would, in fact, be no better off than we are at this minute."

"I don't understand you."

"No, because you have never studied the consequences of what you have set in motion. But attend me, boy. If we burned our letters here, in this jar cover, how would I know you hadn't made a copy? Or two? Or three? Down at the library they have a Xerox machine, for a nickle anyone can make a photocopy. For a dollar, you could post a copy of my death-warrant on every streetcorner for twenty blocks. Two *miles* of death-warrants, boy! Think of it! Can you tell me how I would know you hadn't done such a thing?"

"I . . . well, I . . . I . . ." Todd realized he was floundering and forced himself to shut his mouth. All of a sudden his skin felt too warm, and for no reason at all he found himself remembering something that had happened when he was seven or eight. He and a friend of his had been crawling through a culvert which ran beneath the old Freight Bypass Road just out of town. The friend, skinnier than Todd, had had no problem . . . but Todd had gotten stuck. He had become suddenly aware of the feet of rock and earth over his head, all that dark *weight*, and when an L.A.-bound semi passed above, shaking the earth and making the corrugated pipe vibrate with a low tuneless, and somehow sinister note, he had begun to cry and to struggle witlessly, throwing himself forward, pistoning with his legs, yelling for help. At last he had gotten moving again, and when he finally struggled out of the pipe, he had fainted.

Dussander had just outlined a piece of duplicity so fundamental that it had never even crossed his mind. He could feel his skin getting hotter, and he thought: *I won't cry.*

"And how would you know I hadn't made *two* copies for my safety deposit box . . . that I had burned one and left the other there?"

Trapped. I'm trapped just like in the pipe that time and who are you going to yell for now?

His heart speeded up in his chest. He felt sweat break on the backs of his hands and the nape of his neck. He remembered how it had been in that pipe, the smell of old water, the feel of the cool, ribbed metal, the way everything shook when the truck passed overhead. He remembered how hot and desperate the tears had been.

"Even if there were some impartial third party we could go to, always there would be doubts. The problem is insoluble, boy. Believe it."

Trapped. Trapped in the pipe. No way out of this one.

He felt the world go gray. *Won't cry. Won't faint.* He forced himself to come back.

Dussander took a deep drink from his cup and looked at Todd over the rim.

"Now I tell you two more things. First, that if your part in this matter came out, your punishment would be quite small. It is even possible—no, more than that, *likely*—that it would never come out in the papers at all. I frightened you with reform school once, when I was badly afraid you might crack and tell everything. But do I believe that? No—I used it the way a father will use the 'boogerman' to frighten a child into coming home before dark. I don't believe that they would send you there, not in this country where they spank killers on the wrist and send them out onto the streets to kill again after two years of watching color TV in a penitentiary.

"But it might well ruin your life all the same. There are records . . . and people talk. Always, they talk. Such a juicy scandal is not allowed to wither; it is bottled, like wine. And, of course, as the years pass, your culpability will grow with you. Your silence will grow more damning. If the truth came out today, people would say, 'But he is just a child!' . . . not knowing, as I do, what an *old* child you are. But what would they say, boy, if the truth about me, coupled with the fact that you knew about me as early as 1974 *but kept silent*, came out while you are in high school? That would be bad. For it to come out while you are in college would be disaster. As a young man just starting out in business . . . Armageddon. You understand this first thing?"

Todd was silent, but Dussander seemed satisfied. He nodded.

Still nodding, he said: "Second, I don't believe you *have* a letter."

Todd strove to keep a poker face, but he was terribly afraid his eyes had widened in shock. Dussander was studying him avidly, and Todd was suddenly, nakedly aware that this old man had interrogated hundreds, perhaps *thousands* of people. He was an expert. Todd felt that his skull had turned to window-glass and all things were flashing inside in large letters.

"I asked myself whom you would trust so much. Who are your friends . . . whom do you run with? Whom does this boy, this self-sufficient, coldly controlled little *boy*, go to with his loyalty? The answer is, nobody."

Dussander's eyes gleamed yellowly.

"Many times I have studied you and calculated the odds. I know you, and I know much of your character—no, not all, because one human being can never know everything that is in another human being's heart—but I know so little about what you do and whom you see outside of this house. So I think, 'Dussander, there is a chance that you are wrong. After all these years, do you want to be captured and maybe killed because you misjudged a boy?' Maybe when I was younger I would have taken the chance—the odds are good odds, and the chance is a small chance. It is very strange to me, you know—the older one becomes, the less one has to lose in matters of life and death . . . and yet, one becomes more and more conservative."

He looked hard into Todd's face.

"I have one more thing to say, and then you can go when you want. What I have to say is that, while I doubt the existence of your letter, never doubt the existence of mine. *The document I have described to you exists.* If I die today . . . tomorrow . . . everything will come out. *Everything.*"

"Then there's nothing for me," Todd said. He uttered a dazed little laugh. "Don't you see that?"

"But there is. Years will go by. As they pass, your hold on me will become worth less and less, because no matter how important my life and liberty remain to me, the Americans and—yes, even the Israelis—will have less and less interest in taking them away."

"Yeah? Then why don't they let that guy Hess go?"

"If the Americans had sole custody of him—the Americans who let killers out with a spank on the wrist—they *would* have let him go," Dussander said. "Are the Americans going to allow the Israelis to extradite a eighty-year-old man so they can hang him as they hanged Eichmann? I think not. Not in a country where they put photographs of firemen rescuing kittens from trees on the front pages of city newspapers.

"No, your hold over me will weaken even as mine over you grows stronger. No situation is static. And there will come a time—if I live long enough—when I will decide what you know no longer matters. Then I will destroy the document."

"But so many things could happen to you in between! Accidents, sickness, disease—"

Dussander shrugged. " 'There will be water if God wills it, and we will find it if God wills it, and we will drink it if God wills it.' What happens is not up to us."

Todd looked at the old man for a long time—for a very long time. There were flaws in Dussander's arguments—there had to be. A way out, an escape hatch either for both of them or for Todd alone. A way to cry it off—times, guys, I hurt my foot, allee-allee-in-free. A black knowledge of the years ahead trembled somewhere behind his eyes; he could feel it there, waiting to be born as conscious thought. Everywhere he went, everything he did—

He thought of a cartoon character with an anvil suspended over its head. By the time he graduated from high school, Dussander would be eighty-one, and that would not be the end; by the time he collected his B.A., Dussander would be eighty-five and he would still feel that he wasn't old enough, he would finish his master's thesis and graduate school the year Dussander turned eighty-seven . . . and Dussander still might not feel safe.

"No," Todd said thickly. "What you're saying . . . I can't face that."

"My boy," Dussander said gently, and Todd heard for the first time and with dawning horror the slight accent the old man had put on the first word. "My boy . . . you must."

Todd stared at him, his tongue swelling and thickening in his mouth until it seemed it must fill his throat and choke him. Then he wheeled and blundered out of the house.

Dussander watched all of this with no expression at all, and when the door had slammed shut and the boy's running footsteps stopped, meaning that he had mounted his bike, he lit a cigarette. There was, of course, no safe deposit box, no document. But the boy believed those things existed; he had believed utterly. He was safe. It was ended.

But it was not ended.

That night they both dreamed of murder, and both of them awoke in mingled terror and exhilaration.

Todd awoke with the now familiar stickiness of his lower belly. Dussander, too old for such things, put on the SS uniform and then lay down again, waiting for his racing heart to slow. The uniform was cheaply made and already beginning to fray.

In Dussander's dream he had finally reached the camp at the top of the hill. The wide gate slid open for him and then rumbled shut on its steel track once he was inside. Both the gate and the fence surrounding the camp were electrified. His scrawny, naked pursuers threw themselves against the fence in wave after wave; Dussander had laughed at them and he had strutted back and forth, his chest thrown out, his cap cocked at exactly the right angle. The high, winey smell of burning flesh filled the black air, and he had awakened in southern California thinking of jack-o'-lanterns and the night when vampires seek the blue flame.

Two days before the Bowdens were scheduled to fly to Hawaii, Todd went back to the abandoned trainyard where folks had once boarded trains for San Francisco, Seattle, and Las Vegas; where other, older folks had once boarded the trolley for Los Angeles.

It was nearly dusk when he got there. On the curve of freeway nine hundred yards away, most of the cars were now showing their parking lights. Although it was warm, Todd was wearing a light jacket. Tucked into his belt under it was a butcher knife wrapped in an old hand-towel. He had purchased the knife in a discount department store, one of the big ones surrounded by acres of parking lot.

He looked under the platform where the wino had been the

month before. His mind turned and turned, but it turned on nothing; everything inside him at that moment was shades of black on black.

What he found was the same wino or possibly another; they all looked pretty much the same.

"Hey!" Todd said. "Hey! You want some money?"

The wino turned over, blinking. He saw Todd's wide, sunny grin and began to grin back. A moment later the butcher knife descended, all whicker-snicker and chrome-white, slicker-slicing through the stubbly right cheek. Blood sprayed. Todd could see the blade in the wino's opening mouth . . . and then its tip caught for a moment in the left corner of the wino's lips, pulling his mouth into an insanely cockeyed grin. Then it was the knife that was making the grin; he was carving the wino like a Halloween pumpkin.

He stabbed the wino thirty-seven times. He kept count. Thirty-seven, counting the first strike, which went through the wino's cheek and then turned his tentative smile into a great grisly grin. The wino stopped trying to scream after the fourth stroke. He stopped trying to scramble away from Todd after the sixth. Todd then crawled all the way under the platform and finished the job.

On his way home he threw the knife into the river. His pants were bloodstained. He tossed them into the washing machine and set it to wash cold. There were still faint stains on the pants when they came out, but they didn't concern Todd. They would fade in time. He found the next day that he could barely lift his right arm to the level of his shoulder. He told his father he must have strained it throwing pepper with some of the guys in the park.

"It'll get better in Hawaii," Dick Bowden said, ruffling Todd's hair, and it did; by the time they came home, it was as good as new.

13

It was July again.

Dussander, carefully dressed in one of his three suits (not his best), was standing at the bus stop and waiting for the last local of the day to take him home. It was 10:45 P.M. He had been to a film, a light and frothy comedy that he had enjoyed a great deal. He had been in a fine mood ever since the morning mail. There had been a postcard from the boy, a glossy color photo of Waikiki Beach with bone-white highrise hotels standing in the background. There was a brief message on the reverse.

Dear Mr. Denker,

Boy this sure is some place. I've been swimming every day. My dad caught a big fish and my mom is catching up on her reading (joke). Tomorrow we're going to a volcano. I'll try not to fall in! Hope you're okay.

Stay healthy,
Todd

He was still smiling faintly at the significance of that last when a hand touched his elbow.

"Mister?"

"Yes?"

He turned, on his guard—even in Santo Donato, muggers were not unknown—and then winced at the aroma. It seemed to be a combination of beer, halitosis, dried sweat, and possibly Musterole. It was a bum in baggy pants. He—it—wore a flannel shirt and very old loafers that were currently being held together with dirty bands of adhesive tape. The face looming above this motley costume looked like the death of God.

"You got an extra dime, mister? I gotta get to L.A., me. Got a job offertunity. I need just a dime more for the express bus. I wudn't ask if it wadn't a big chance for me."

Dussander had begun to frown, but now his smile reasserted itself.

"Is it really a bus ride you wish?"

The wino smiled sickly, not understanding.

"Suppose you ride the bus home with me," Dussander proposed. "I can offer you a drink, a meal, a bath, and a bed. All I ask in return is a little conversation. I am an old man. I live alone. Company is sometimes very welcome."

The drunk's smile abruptly grew more healthy as the situation clarified itself. Here was a well-to-do old faggot with a taste for slumming.

"All by yourself! Bitch, innit?"

Dussander answered the broad, insinuating grin with a polite smile. "I only ask that you sit away from me on the bus. You smell rather strongly."

"Maybe you don't want me stinking up your place, then," the drunk said with sudden, tipsy dignity.

"Come, the bus will be here in a minute. Get off one stop after I do and then walk back two blocks. I'll wait for you on the corner. In the morning I will see what I can spare. Perhaps two dollars."

"Maybe even five," the drunk said brightly. His dignity, tipsy or otherwise, had been forgotten.

"Perhaps, perhaps," Dussander said impatiently. He could now hear the low diesel drone of the approaching bus. He pressed a quarter, the correct bus fare, into the bum's grimy hand and strolled a few paces away without looking back.

The bum stood undecided as the headlights of the local swept over the rise. He was still standing and frowning down at the quarter when the old faggot got on the bus without looking back. The bum began to walk away and then—at the last second—he reversed direction and boarded the bus just before the doors folded closed. He put the quarter into the fare-box with the expression of a man putting a hundred dollars down on a long shot. He passed Dussander without doing more than glancing at him and sat at the back of the bus. He dozed off a little, and when he woke up, the rich old faggot was gone. He got off at the next stop, not knowing if it was the right one or not, and not really caring.

He walked back two blocks and saw a dim shape under the streetlight. It was the old faggot, all right. The faggot was watching him approach, and he was standing as if at attention.

For just a moment the bum felt a chill of apprehension, an urge to just turn away and forget the whole thing.

Then the old man was gripping him by the arm . . . and his grip was surprisingly firm.

"Good," the old man said. "I'm very glad you came. My house is down here. It's not far."

"Maybe even ten," the bum said, allowing himself to be led.

"Maybe even ten," the old faggot agreed, and then laughed. "Who knows?"

14

The Bi-Centennial year arrived.

Todd came by to see Dussander half a dozen times between his return from Hawaii in the summer of 1975 and the trip he and his parents took to Rome just as all the drum-thumping, flag-waving, and Tall Ships—watching was approaching its climax.

These visits to Dussander were low-key and in no way unpleasant; the two of them found they could pass the time civilly enough. They spoke more in silences than they did in words, and their actual conversations would have put an FBI agent to sleep. Todd told the old man that he had been seeing a girl named Angela Farrow off and on. He wasn't nuts about her, but she was the daughter of one of his mother's friends. The old man told Todd he had taken up braiding rugs because he had read such an activity was good for arthritis. He showed Todd several samples of his work, and Todd dutifully admired them.

The boy had grown quite a bit, had he not? (Well, two inches.) Had Dussander given up smoking? (No, but he had been forced to cut down; they made him cough too much now.) How had his schoolwork been? (Challenging but exciting; he had made all A's and B's, had gone to the state finals with his Science Fair project on solar power, and was now thinking of majoring in anthropology instead of history when he got to college.) Who was mowing Dussander's lawn this year? (Randy Chambers from just down the street—a good boy, but rather fat and slow.)

During that year Dussander had put an end to three winos in his kitchen. He had been approached at the downtown bus stop some twenty times, had made the drink-dinner-bath-and-bed offer seven times. He had been turned down twice, and on two other occasions the winos had simply walked off with the quarters Dussander gave them for the fare-box. After some thought, he had worked out a way around this; he simply bought a book of coupons. They were two dollars and fifty cents, good for fifteen rides, and non-negotiable at the local liquor stores.

On very warm days just lately, Dussander had noticed an unpleasant smell drifting up from his cellar. He kept his doors and windows firmly shut on these days.

Todd Bowden had found a wino sleeping it off in an abandoned drainage culvert behind a vacant lot on Cienaga Way—this had been in December, during the Christmas vacation. He had stood there for some time, hands stuffed into his pockets, looking at the wino and trembling. He had returned to the lot six times over a period of five weeks, always wearing his light jacket, zipped halfway up to conceal the Craftsman hammer tucked into his belt. At last he had come upon the wino again—that one or some other, and who really gave a fuck—on the first day of March. He had begun with the hammer end of the tool, and then at some point (he didn't really remember when; everything had been swimming in a red haze) he had switched to the claw end, obliterating the wino's face.

For Kurt Dussander, the winos were a half-cynical propitiation of gods he had finally recognized . . . or re-recognized. And the winos were fun. They made him feel alive. He was beginning to feel that the years he had spent in Santo Donato—the years before the boy had turned up on his doorstep with his big blue eyes and his wide American grin—had been years spent being old before his time. He had been just past his mid-sixties when he came here. And he felt much younger than that now.

The idea of propitiating gods would have startled Todd at first—but it might have gained eventual acceptance. After stabbing the wino under the train platform, he had expected his nightmares to intensify—to perhaps even drive him crazy. He had expected waves of paralyzing guilt that might well end with a blurted confession or the taking of his own life.

Instead of any of those things, he had gone to Hawaii with his parents and enjoyed the best vacation of his life.

He had begun high school last September feeling oddly new and refreshed, as if a different person had jumped into his Todd Bowden skin. Things that had made no particular impression on him since earliest childhood—the sunlight just after dawn, the look of the ocean off the Fish Pier, the sight of people hurrying on a downtown street at just that moment of dusk when the streetlights come on—these things now imprinted themselves on his mind again in a series of bright cameos, in images so clear they seemed electroplated. He tasted life on his tongue like a draught of wine straight from the bottle.

After he had seen the stewbum in the culvert, but before he killed him, the nightmares had begun again.

The most common one involved the wino he had stabbed to death in the abandoned trainyard. Home from school, he burst into the house, a cheery *Hi, Monica-baby!* on his lips. It died there as he saw the dead wino in the raised breakfast nook. He was sitting slumped over their butcher-block table in his puke-smelling shirt and pants. Blood had streaked across the bright tiled floor; it was drying on the stainless steel counters. There were bloody handprints on the natural pine cupboards.

Clipped to the note-board by the fridge was a message from his mother: *Todd—Gone to the store. Back by 3:30.* The hands of the stylish sunburst clock over the Jenn-Air range stood at 3:20 and the drunk was sprawled dead up there in the nook like some horrid oozing relic from the subcellar of a junkshop and there was blood everywhere, and Todd began trying to clean it up, wiping every exposed surface, all the time screaming at the dead wino that he had to *go*, had to leave him *alone*, and the wino just lolled there and stayed dead, grinning up at the ceiling, and freshets of blood kept pouring from the stab-wounds in his dirty skin. Todd grabbed the O Cedar mop from the closet and began to slide it madly back and forth across the floor, aware that he was not really getting the blood up, only diluting it, spreading it around, but unable to stop. And just as he heard his mother's Town and Country wagon turn into the driveway, he realized the wino was Dussander. He woke from these dreams sweating and gasping, clutching double handfuls of the bedclothes.

But after he finally found the wino in the culvert again—that wino or some other—and used the hammer on him, these dreams went away. He supposed he might have to kill again, and maybe more than once. It was too bad, but of course their time of usefulness as human creatures was over. Except their usefulness to Todd, of course. And Todd, like everyone else he knew, was only tailoring his lifestyle to fit his own particular needs as he grew older. Really, he was no different than anybody. You had to make your own way in the world; if you were going to get along, you had to do it by yourself.

15

In the fall of his junior year, Todd played varsity tailback for the Santo Donato Cougars and was named All-Conference. And in the second quarter of that year, the quarter which ended in late January of 1977, he won the American Legion Patriotic Essay Contest. This contest was open to all city high school students who were taking American history courses. Todd's piece was called "An American's Responsibility." During the baseball season that year he was the school's star pitcher, winning four and losing none. His batting average was .361. At the awards assembly in June he was named Athlete of the Year and given a plaque by Coach Haines (Coach Haines, who had once taken him aside and told him to keep practicing his curve "because none of these niggers can hit a curve-ball, Bowden, not one of them"). Monica Bowden burst into tears when Todd called her from school and told her he was going to get the award. Dick Bowden strutted around his office for two weeks following the ceremony, trying not to boast. That summer they rented a cabin in Big Sur and stayed there for two weeks and Todd snorkled his brains out. During that same year Todd killed four derelicts. He stabbed two of them and bludgeoned two of them. He had taken to wearing two pairs of pants on what he now acknowledged to be hunting expeditions. Sometimes he rode the city busses, looking for likely spots. The best two, he found, were the Santo Donato Mission for the Indigent on Douglas Street, and around the corner from the Salvation Army on Euclid. He would walk slowly through both of these neighborhoods, waiting to be panhandled. When a wino approached him, Todd would tell him that he, Todd, wanted a bottle of whiskey, and if the wino would buy it, Todd would share the bottle. He knew a place, he said, where they could go. It was a different place every time, of course. He resisted a strong urge to go back either to the trainyard or to the culvert behind the vacant lot on Cienaga Way. Revisiting the scene of a previous crime would have been unwise.

During the same year Dussander smoked sparingly, drank Ancient Age bourbon, and watched TV. Todd came by once in awhile, but their conversations became increasingly arid. They were growing apart. Dussander celebrated his seventy-ninth birthday that year, which was also the year Todd turned sixteen. Dussander remarked that sixteen was the best year of a young man's life, forty-one the best year of a middle-aged man's, and seventy-nine the best of an old man's. Todd nodded politely. Dussander had been quite drunk, and cackled in a way that made Todd distinctly uneasy.

Dussander had dispatched two winos during Todd's academic year of 1976–77. The second had been livelier than he looked; even after Dussander had gotten the man soddenly drunk he had tottered around the kitchen with the haft of a steak-knife jutting from the base of his neck, gushing blood down the front of his shirt and onto the floor. The wino had re-discovered the front hall after two staggering circuits of the kitchen and had almost escaped the house.

Dussander had stood in the kitchen, eyes wide with shocked unbelief, watching the wino grunt and puff his way toward the door, rebounding from one side of the hall to the other and knocking cheap Currier & Ives reproductions to the floor. His paralysis had not broken until the wino was actually groping for the doorknob. Then Dussander had bolted across the room, jerked open the utility drawer, and pulled out his meat-fork. He ran down the hall with the meat-fork held out in front of him and drove it into the wino's back.

Dussander had stood over him, panting, his old heart racing in a frightening way . . . racing like that of a heart-attack victim on that Saturday night TV program he enjoyed, *Emergency!* But at last it had slowed back into a normal rhythm and he knew he was going to be all right.

There had been a great deal of blood to clean up.

That had been four months ago, and since then he had not made his offer at the downtown bus stop. He was frightened of the way he had almost bungled the last one . . . but when he remembered the way he had handled things at the last moment, pride rose in his heart. In the end the wino had never made it out the door, and that was the important thing.

16

In the fall of 1977, during the first quarter of his senior year, Todd joined the Rifle Club. By June of 1978 he had qualified as a marksman. He made All-Conference in football again, won five and lost one during the baseball season (the loss coming as the result of two errors and one unearned run), and made the third highest Merit Scholarship score in the school's history. He applied to Berkeley and was promptly accepted. By April he knew he would either be valedictorian or salutatorian on graduation night. He very badly wanted to be valedictorian.

During the latter half of his senior year, an odd impulse came on him—one which was as frightening to Todd as it was irrational. He seemed to be clearly and firmly in control of it, and *that* at least was comforting, but that such a thought should have occurred at all was scary. He had made an arrangement with life. He had worked things out. His life was much like his mother's bright and sunshiny kitchen, where all the surfaces were dressed in chrome, Formica, or stainless steel—a place where everything worked when you pressed the buttons. There were deep and dark cupboards in this kitchen, of course, but many things could be stored in them and their doors still be closed.

This new impulse reminded him of the dream in which he had come home to discover the dead and bleeding wino in his mother's clean, well-lighted place. It was as if, in the bright and careful arrangement he had made, in that a-place-for-everything-and-everything-in-its-place kitchen of his mind, a dark and bloody intruder now lurched and shambled, looking for a place to die conspicuously . . .

A quarter of a mile from the Bowden house was the freeway,

running eight lanes wide. A steep and brushy bank led down to it. There was plenty of good cover on the bank. His father had given him a Winchester .30-.30 for Christmas, and it had a removable telescopic sight. During rush hour, when all eight lanes were jammed, he could pick a spot on that bank and . . . why, he could easily . . .

Do what?

Commit suicide?

Destroy everything he had worked for these last four years?

Say *what*?

No *sir*, no *ma'am*, no *way*.

It is, as they say, to laugh.

Sure it was . . . but the impulse remained.

One Saturday a few weeks before his high school graduation, Todd cased the .30-.30 after carefully emptying the magazine. He put the rifle in the back seat of his father's new toy—a used Porsche. He drove to the spot where the brushy slope dropped steeply down to the freeway. His mother and father had taken the station wagon and had driven to L.A. for the weekend. Dick, now a full partner, would be holding discussions with the Hyatt people about a new Reno hotel.

Todd's heart bumped in his chest and his mouth was full of sour, electric spit as he worked his way down the grade with the cased rifle in his arms. He came to a fallen tree and sat cross-legged behind it. He uncased the rifle and laid it on the dead tree's smooth trunk. A branch jutting off at an angle made a nice rest for the barrel. He snugged the buttplate into the hollow of his right shoulder and peered into the telescopic sight.

Stupid! his mind screamed at him. *Boy, this is really stupid! If someone sees you, it's not going to matter if the gun's loaded or not! You'll get in plenty of trouble, maybe even end up with some Chippie shooting at you!*

It was mid-morning and the Saturday traffic was light. He settled the crosshairs on a woman behind the wheel of a blue Toyota. The woman's window was half-open and the round collar of her sleeveless blouse was fluttering. Todd centered the crosshairs on her temple and dry-fired. It was bad for the firing-pin, but what the fuck.

"Pow," he whispered as the Toyota disappeared beneath the underpass half a mile up from the slope where Todd sat. He swallowed around a lump that tasted like a stuck-together mass of pennies.

Here came a man behind the wheel of a Subaru Brat pickup truck. This man had a scuzzy-looking gray beard and was wearing a San Diego Padres baseball hat.

"You're . . . you're the dirty rat . . . the dirty rat that shot my brudduh," Todd whispered, giggling a little, and dry-fired the .30-.30 again.

He shot at five others, the impotent snap of the hammer spoiling the illusion at the end of each "kill." Then he cased the rifle again. He carried it back up the slope, bending low to keep from being seen. He put it into the back of the Porsche. There was a dry hot pounding in his temples. He drove home. Went up to his room. Masturbated.

17

The stewbum was wearing a ragged, unravelling reindeer sweater that looked so startling it almost seemed surreal here in southern California. He also wore seaman's issue bluejeans which were out at the knees, showing white, hairy flesh and a number of peeling scabs. He raised the jelly-glass—Fred and Wilma, Barney and Betty dancing around the rim in what might have been some grotesque fertility rite—and tossed off the knock of Ancient Age at a gulp. He smacked his lips for the last time in this world.

"Mister, that hits the old spot. I don't mind saying so."

"I always enjoy a drink in the evening," Dussander agreed from behind him, and then rammed the butcher knife into the stewbum's neck. There was the sound of ripping gristle, a sound like a drumstick being torn enthusiastically from a freshly roasted chicken. The jelly-glass fell from the stewbum's hand and onto the table. It rolled toward the edge, its movement enhancing the illusion that the cartoon characters on it were dancing.

The stewbum threw his head back and tried to scream. Nothing came out but a hideous whistling sound. His eyes widened, widened . . . and then his head thumped soggily onto the red and white oilcloth check that covered Dussander's kitchen table. The stewbum's upper plate slithered halfway out of his mouth like a semi-detachable grin.

Dussander yanked the knife free—he had to use both hands to do it—and crossed to the kitchen sink. It was filled with hot water, Lemon Fresh Joy, and dirty supper dishes. The knife disappeared into a billow of citrus-smelling suds like a very small fighter plane diving into a cloud.

He crossed to the table again and paused there, resting one hand on the dead stewbum's shoulder while a spasm of coughing rattled through him. He took his handkerchief from his back pocket and spat yellowish-brown phlegm into it. He had been smoking too much lately. He always did when he was making up his mind to do another one. But this one had gone smoothly; really very smoothly. He had been afraid after the mess he had made with the last one that he might be tempting fate sorely to try it again.

Now, if he hurried, he would still be able to watch the second half of *Lawrence Welk.*

He bustled across the kitchen, opened the cellar door, and turned on the light switch. He went back to the sink and got the package of green plastic garbage bags from the cupboard beneath. He shook one out as he walked back to the slumped wino. Blood had run across the oilcloth in all directions. It had puddled in the wino's lap and on the hilly, faded linoleum. It would be on the chair, too, but all of those things would clean up.

Dussander grabbed the stewbum by the hair and yanked his head up. It came with boneless ease, and a moment later the wino was lolling backwards, like a man about to get a pre-haircut shampoo. Dussander pulled the garbage bag down over the wino's head, over his shoulders, and down his arms to the elbows. That was as far as it would go. He unbuckled his late guest's belt and pulled it free of the fraying belt-loops. He wrapped the belt around the garbage bag two or three inches above the elbows and buckled it tight. Plastic rustled. Dussander began to hum under his breath.

The wino's feet were clad in scuffed and dirty Hush Puppies. They made a limp V on the floor as Dussander seized the belt and dragged the corpse toward the cellar door. Something white tumbled out of the plastic bag and clicked on the floor. It was the stewbum's upper plate, Dussander saw. He picked it up and stuffed it into one of the wino's front pockets.

He laid the wino down in the cellar doorway with his head now lolling backwards onto the second stair-level. Dussander climbed around the body and gave it three healthy kicks. The body moved slightly on the first two, and the third sent it slithering bonelessly down the stairs. Halfway down, the feet flew up over the head and the body executed an acrobatic roll. It belly-whopped onto the packed dirt of the cellar floor with a solid thud. One Hush Puppy flew off, and Dussander made a mental note to pick it up.

He went down the stairs, skirted the body, and approached his toolbench. To the left of the bench a spade, a rake, and a hoe leaned against the wall in a neat rank. Dussander selected the spade. A little exercise was good for an old man. A little exercise could make you feel young.

The smell down here was not good, but it didn't bother him much. He limed the place once a month (once every three days after he had "done" one of his winos) and he had gotten a fan which he ran upstairs to keep the smell from permeating the house on very warm still days. Josef Kramer, he remembered, had been fond of saying that the dead speak, but we hear them with our noses.

Dussander picked a spot in the cellar's north corner and went to work. The dimensions of the grave were two and a half feet by six feet. He had gotten to a depth of two feet, half deep enough, when the first paralyzing pain struck him in the chest like a shotgun blast. He straightened up, eyes flaring wide. Then the pain rolled down his arm . . . unbelievable pain, as if an invisible hand had siezed all the blood-vessels in there and was now pulling them. He watched the spade tumble sideways and felt his knees buckle. For one horrible moment he felt sure that he was going to fall into the grave himself.

Somehow he staggered backwards three paces and sat down on his workbench with a plop. There was an expression of stupid surprise on his face—he could feel it—and he thought he must look like one of those silent movie comedians after he's been hit by the swinging door or stepped in the cow patty. He put his head down between his knees and gasped.

Fifteen minutes crawled by. The pain had begun to abate somewhat, but he did not believe he would be able to stand. For the first time he understood all the truths of old age which he had been spared until now. He was terrified almost to the point of whimpering. Death had brushed by him in this dank, smelly cellar; it had touched Dussander with the hem of its robe. It might be back for him yet. But he would not die down here; not if he could help it.

He got up, hands still crossed on his chest, as if to hold the fragile machinery together. He staggered across the open space between the workbench and the stairs. His left foot tripped over the dead wino's outstretched leg and he went to his knees with a small cry. There was a sullen flare of pain in his chest. He looked up the stairs—the steep, steep stairs. Twelve of them. The square of light at the top was mockingly distant.

"Ein," Kurt Dussander said, and pulled himself grimly up onto the first stair-level. *"Zwei, Drei, Vier."*

It took him twenty minutes to reach the linoleum floor of the kitchen. Twice, on the stairs, the pain had threatened to come back, and both times Dussander had waited with his eyes closed to see what would happen, perfectly aware that if it came back as strongly as it had come upon him down there, he would probably die. Both times the pain had faded away again.

He crawled across the kitchen floor to the table, avoiding the pools and streaks of blood, which were now congealing. He got the bottle of Ancient Age, took a swallow, and closed his eyes. Something that had been cinched tight in his chest seemed to loosen a little. The pain faded a bit more. After another five minutes he began to work his way slowly down the hall. His telephone sat on a small table halfway down.

It was quarter past nine when the phone rang in the Bowden house. Todd was sitting cross-legged on the couch, going over his notes for the trig final. Trig was a bitch for him, as all maths were and probably always would be. His father was seated across the room, going through the checkbook stubs with a portable calculator on his lap and a mildly disbelieving expression on his face. Monica, closest to the phone, was watching the James Bond movie Todd had taped off HBO two evenings before.

"Hello?" She listened. A faint frown touched her face and she held the handset out to Todd. "It's Mr. Denker. He sounds excited about something. Or upset."

Todd's heart leaped into his throat, but his expression hardly changed. "Really?" He went to the phone and took it from her. "Hi, Mr. Denker."

Dussander's voice was hoarse and short. "Come over right away, boy. I've had a heart attack. Quite a bad one, I think."

"Gee," Todd said, trying to collect his flying thoughts, to see around the fear that now bulked huge in his own mind. "That's interesting, all right, but it's pretty late and I was studying—"

"I understand that you cannot talk," Dussander said in that harsh, almost barking voice. "But you can listen. I cannot call an ambulance or dial two-two-two, boy . . . at least not yet. There is a mess here. I need help . . . and that means *you* need help."

"Well . . . if you put it that way . . . " Todd's heartbeat had reached a hundred and twenty beats a minute, but his face was calm, almost serene. Hadn't he known all along that a night like this would come? Yes, of course he had.

"Tell your parents I've had a letter," Dussander said. "An important letter. You understand?"

"Yeah, okay," Todd said.

"Now we see, boy. We see what you are made of."

"Sure," Todd said. He suddenly became aware that his mother was watching him instead of the movie, and he forced a stiff grin onto his face. "Bye."

Dussander was saying something else now, but Todd hung up on it.

"I'm going over to Mr. Denker's for awhile," he said, speaking to both of them but looking at his mother—that faint expression of concern was still on her face. "Can I pick up anything for either of you at the store?"

"Pipe cleaners for me and a small package of fiscal responsibility for your mother," Dick said.

"Very funny," Monica said. "Todd, is Mr. Denker—"

"What in the name of *God* did you get at Fielding's?" Dick interrupted.

"That knick-knack shelf in the closet. I told you that. There's nothing wrong with Mr. Denker, is there, Todd? He sounded a little strange."

"There really *are* such things as knick-knack shelves? I thought those crazy women who write British mysteries made them up so there would always be a place where the killer could find a blunt instrument."

"Dick, can I get a word in edgeways?"

"Sure. Be my guest. But for the *closet?*"

"He's okay, I guess," Todd said. He put on his letter jacket and zipped it up. "But he *was* excited. He got a letter from a nephew of his in Hamburg or Düsseldorf or someplace. He hasn't heard from any of his people in years, and now he's got this letter and his eyes aren't good enough for him to read it."

"Well isn't that a *bitch*," Dick said. "Go on, Todd. Get over there and ease the man's mind."

"I thought he had someone to read to him," Monica said. "A new boy."

"He does," Todd said, suddenly hating his mother, hating the half-formed intuition he saw swimming in her eyes. "Maybe he wasn't home, or maybe he couldn't come over this late."

"Oh. Well . . . go on, then. But be careful."

"I will. You don't need anything at the store?"

"No. How's your studying for that calculus final going?"

"It's trig," Todd said. "Okay, I guess. I was just getting ready to call it a night." This was a rather large lie.

"You want to take the Porsche?" Dick asked.

"No, I'll ride my bike." He wanted the extra five minutes to collect his thoughts and get his emotions under control—to try, at least. And in his present state, he would probably drive the Porsche into a telephone pole.

"Strap your reflector-patch on your knee," Monica said, "and tell Mr. Denker hello for us."

"Okay."

That doubt was still in his mother's eyes but it was less evident now. He blew her a kiss and then went out to the garage where his bike—a racing-style Italian bike rather than a Schwinn now—was parked. His heart was still racing in his chest, and he felt a mad urge to take the .30-.30 back into the house and shoot both of his parents and then go down to the slope overlooking the freeway. No more worrying about Dussander. No more bad dreams, no more winos. He would shoot and shoot and shoot, only saving one bullet back for the end.

Then reason came back to him and he rode away toward Dussander's, his reflector-patch revolving up and down just above his knee, his long blonde hair streaming back from his brow.

"Holy *Christ*!" Todd nearly screamed.

He was standing in the kitchen door. Dussander was slumped on his elbows, his china cup between them. Large drops of sweat stood out on his forehead. But it was not Dussander Todd was looking at. It was the blood. There seemed to be blood everywhere—it was puddled on the table, on the empty kitchen chair, on the floor.

"Where are you bleeding?" Todd shouted, at last getting his frozen feet to move again—it seemed to him that he had been standing in the doorway for at least a thousand years. *This is the end,* he was thinking, *this is the absolute end of everything. The balloon is going up high, baby, all the way to the sky, baby, and it's toot-toot-tootsie, goodbye.* All the same, he was careful not to step in any of the blood. "I thought you said you had a fucking heart attack!"

"It's not my blood," Dussander muttered.

"What?" Todd stopped. "What did you say?"

"Go downstairs. You will see what has to be done."

"What the hell *is* this?" Todd asked. A sudden terrible idea had come into his head.

"Don't waste our time, boy. I think you will not be too surprised at what you find downstairs. I think you have had experience in such matters as the one in my cellar. First-hand experience."

Todd looked at him, unbelieving, for another moment, and then he plunged down the cellar stairs two by two. His first look in the feeble yellow glow of the basement's only light made him think that Dussander had pushed a bag of garbage down here. Then he saw the protruding legs, and the dirty hands held down at the sides by the cinched belt.

"Holy Christ," he repeated, but this time the words had no force at all—they emerged in a slight, skeletal whisper.

He pressed the back of his right hand against lips that were as dry as sandpaper. He closed his eyes for a moment . . . and when he opened them again, he felt in control of himself at last.

Todd started moving.

He saw the spade-handle protruding from a shallow hole in the far corner and understood at once what Dussander had been doing when his ticker had seized up. A moment later he became fully aware of the cellar's fetid aroma—a smell like rotting tomatoes. He had smelled it before, but upstairs it was much fainter—and, of course, he hadn't been here very often over the last couple of years. Now he understood *exactly* what that smell meant and for several moments he had to struggle with his gorge. A series of choked gagging sounds, muffled by the hand he had clapped over his mouth and nose, came from him.

Little by little he got control of himself again.

He seized the wino's legs and dragged him across to the edge of the hole. He dropped them, skidded sweat from his forehead with the heel of his left hand, and stood absolutely still for a moment, thinking harder than he ever had in his life.

Then he seized the spade and began to deepen the hole. When it was five feet deep, he got out and shoved the derelict's body in with his foot. Todd stood at the edge of the grave, looking down. Tattered bluejeans. Filthy, scab-encrusted hands. It was a stewbum, all right. The irony was almost funny. So funny a person could scream with laughter.

He ran back upstairs.

"How are you?" he asked Dussander.

"I'll be all right. Have you taken care of it?"

"I'm doing it, okay?"

"Be quick. There's still up here."

"I'd like to find some pigs and feed you to them," Todd said, and went back down cellar before Dussander could reply.

He had almost completely covered the wino when he began to

think there was something wrong. He stared into the grave, grasping the spade's handle with one hand. The wino's legs stuck partway out of the mound of dirt, as did the tips of his feet—one old shoe, possibly a Hush Puppy, and one filthy athletic sock that might actually have been white around the time that Taft was President.

One Hush Puppy? *One?*

Todd half-ran back around the furnace to the foot of the stairs. He glanced around wildly. A headache was beginning to thud against his temples, dull drillbits trying to work their way out. He spotted the old shoe five feet away, overturned in the shadow of some abandoned shelving. Todd grabbed it, ran back to the grave with it, and threw it in. Then he started to shovel again. He covered the shoe, the legs, everything.

When all the dirt was back in the hole, he slammed the spade down repeatedly to tamp it. Then he grabbed the rake and ran it back and forth, trying to disguise the fact the earth here had been recently turned. Not much use; without good camouflage, a hole that has been recently dug and then filled in always looks like a hole that has been recently dug and then filled in. Still, no one would have any occasion to come down here, would they? He and Dussander would damn well have to hope not.

Todd ran back upstairs. He was starting to pant.

Dussander's elbows had spread wide and his head had sagged down to the table. His eyes were closed, the lids a shiny purple—the color of asters.

"Dussander!" Todd shouted. There was a hot, juicy taste in his mouth—the taste of fear mixed with adrenaline and pulsing hot blood. "Don't you *dare* die on me, you old fuck!"

"Keep your voice down," Dussander said without opening his eyes. "You'll have everyone on the block over here."

"Where's your cleaner? Lestoil . . . Top Job . . . something like that. And rags. I need rags."

"All that is under the sink."

A lot of the blood had now dried on. Dussander raised his head and watched as Todd crawled across the floor, scrubbing first at the puddle on the linoleum and then at the drips that had straggled down the legs of the chair the wino had been sitting in. The boy was biting compulsively at his lips, champing at them, almost, like a horse at a bit. At last the job was finished. The astringent smell of cleaner filled the room.

"There is a box of old rags under the stairs," Dussander said. "Put those bloody ones on the bottom. Don't forget to wash your hands."

"I don't need your advice. You got me into this."

"Did I? I must say you took hold well." For a moment the old mockery was in Dussander's voice, and then a bitter grimace pulled his face into a new shape. "Hurry."

Todd took care of the rags, then hurried up the cellar stairs for the last time. He looked nervously down the stairs for a moment, then snapped off the light and closed the door. He went to the sink, rolled up his sleeves, and washed in the hottest water he could stand. He plunged his hands into the suds . . . and came up holding the butcher knife Dussander had used.

"I'd like to cut your throat with this," Todd said grimly.

"Yes, and then feed me to the pigs. I have no doubt of it."

Todd rinsed the knife, dried it, and put it away. He did the rest of the dishes quickly, let the water out, and rinsed the sink. He looked at the clock as he dried his hands and saw it was twenty minutes after ten.

He went to the phone in the hallway, picked up the receiver, and looked at it thoughtfully. The idea that he had forgotten something —something as potentially damning as the wino's shoe—nagged unpleasantly at his mind. What? He didn't know. If not for the headache, he might be able to get it. The triple-damned headache. It wasn't like him to forget things, and it was scary.

He dialed 222 and after a single ring, a voice answered: "This is Santo Donato MED-Q. Do you have a medical problem?"

"My name is Todd Bowden. I'm at 963 Claremont Street. I need an ambulance."

"What's the problem, son?"

"It's my friend, Mr. D—" He bit down on his lip so hard that it squirted blood, and for a moment he was lost, drowning in the pulses of pain from his head. *Dussander.* He had almost given this anonymous MED-Q voice Dussander's real name.

"Calm down, son," the voice said. "Take it slow and you'll be fine."

"My friend Mr. Denker," Todd said. "I think he's had a heart attack."

"His symptoms?"

Todd began to give them, but the voice had heard enough as soon as Todd described the chest pain that had migrated to the left arm. He told Todd the ambulance would arrive in ten to twenty minutes, depending on the traffic. Todd hung up and pressed the heels of his hands against his eyes.

"Did you get it?" Dussander called weakly.

"Yes!" Todd screamed. *"Yes, I got it! Yes goddammit yes! Yes yes yes! Just shut up!"*

He pressed his hands even harder against his eyes, creating first senseless starflashes of light and then a bright field of red. *Get hold of yourself, Todd-baby. Get down, get funky, get cool. Dig it.*

He opened his eyes and picked up the telephone again. Now the hard part. Now it was time to call home.

"Hello?" Monica's soft, cultured voice in his ear. For a moment —just a moment—he saw himself slamming the muzzle of the .30-.30 into her nose and pulling the trigger into the first flow of blood.

"It's Todd, Mommy. Let me talk to Dad, quick."

He didn't call her mommy anymore. He knew she would get that signal quicker than anything else, and she did. "What's the matter? Is something wrong, Todd?"

"Just let me talk to him!"

"But what—"

The phone rattled and clunked. He heard his mother saying something to his father. Todd got ready.

"Todd? What's the problem?"

"It's Mr. Denker, Daddy. He . . . it's a heart attack, I think. I'm pretty sure it is."

"Jesus!" His father's voice lagged away for a moment and Todd heard him repeating the information to his wife. Then he was back. "He's still alive? As far as you can tell?"

"He's alive. Conscious."

"All right, thank God for that. Call an ambulance."

"I just did."

"Two-two-two?"

"Yes."

"Good boy. How bad is he, can you tell?"

"I don't know, Dad. They said the ambulance would be here soon, but . . . I'm sorta scared. Can you come over and wait with me?"

"You bet. Give me four minutes."

Todd could hear his mother saying something else as his father hung up, breaking the connection. Todd replaced the receiver on his end.

Four minutes.

Four minutes to do anything that had been left undone. Four minutes to remember whatever it was that had been forgotten. Or *had* he forgotten anything? Maybe it was just nerves. God, he wished he hadn't had to call his father. But it was the natural thing to do, wasn't it? Sure. Was there some natural thing that he *hadn't* done? Something—?

"Oh, you shit-for-brains!" he suddenly moaned, and bolted back into the kitchen. Dussander's head lay on the table, his eyes half-open, sluggish.

"Dussander!" Todd cried. He shook Dussander roughly, and the old man groaned. "Wake up! Wake up, you stinking old bastard!"

"What? Is it the ambulance?"

"The letter! My father is coming over, he'll be here in no time. *Where's the fucking letter?*"

"What . . . what letter?"

"You told me to tell them you got an important letter. I said . . ." His heart sank. "I said it came from overseas . . . from Germany. Christ!" Todd ran his hands through his hair.

"A letter." Dussander raised his head with slow difficulty. His seamed cheeks were an unhealthy yellowish-white, his lips blue. "From Willi, I think. Willi Frankel. Dear . . . dear Willi."

Todd looked at his watch and saw that already two minutes had passed since he had hung up the phone. His father would not, *could* not make it from their house to Dussander's in four minutes, but he could do it damn fast in the Porsche. Fast, that was it. Everything was moving too fast. And there was still something wrong here; he *felt* it. But there was no time to stop and hunt around for the loophole.

"Yes, okay, I was reading it to you, and you got excited and had this heart attack. Good. Where is it?"

Dussander looked at him blankly.

"The letter! Where is it?"

"What letter?" Dussander asked vacantly, and Todd's hands itched to throttle the drunken old monster.

"The one I was reading to you! The one from Willi What's-his-face! Where is it?"

They both looked at the table, as if expecting to see the letter materialize there.

"Upstairs," Dussander said finally. "Look in my dresser. The third drawer. There is a small wooden box in the bottom of that drawer. You will have to break it open. I lost the key a long time ago. There are some very old letters from a friend of mine. None signed. None dated. All in German. A page or two will serve for window-fittings, as you would say. If you hurry—"

"Are you *crazy*?" Todd raged. "I don't understand German! How could I read you a letter written in German, you numb fuck?"

"Why would Willi write me in English?" Dussander countered wearily. "If you read me the letter in German, *I* would understand it even if *you* did not. Of course your pronunciation would be butchery, but still, I could—"

Dussander was right—right again, and Todd didn't wait to hear more. Even after a heart attack the old man was a step ahead. Todd raced down the hall to the stairs, pausing just long enough by the front door to make sure his father's Porsche wasn't pulling up even now. It wasn't, but Todd's watch told him just how tight things were getting; it had been five minutes now.

He took the stairs two at a time and burst into Dussander's bedroom. He had never been up here before, hadn't even been curious, and for a moment he only looked wildly around at the unfamiliar territory. Then he saw the dresser, a cheap item done in the style his father called Discount Store Modern. He fell on his knees in front of it and yanked at the third drawer. It came halfway out, then jigged sideways in its slot and stuck firmly.

"Goddam you," he whispered at it. His face was dead pale except for the spots of dark, bloody color flaring in each cheek and his blue eyes, which looked as dark as Atlantic storm-clouds. "Goddam you fucking thing come *out!*"

He yanked so hard that the entire dresser tottered forward and almost fell on him before deciding to settle back. The drawer shot all the way out and landed in Todd's lap. Dussander's socks and underwear and handkerchiefs spilled out all around him. He pawed through the stuff that was still in the drawer and came up with a wooden box about nine inches long and three inches deep. He tried to pull up the lid. Nothing happened. It was locked, just as Dussander had said. Nothing was free tonight.

He stuffed the spilled clothes back into the drawer and then rammed the drawer back into its oblong slot. It stuck again. Todd worked to free it, wiggling it back and forth, sweat running freely down his face. At last he was able to slam it shut. He got up with the box. How much time had passed now?

Dussander's bed was the type with posts at the foot and Todd brought the lock side of the box down on one of these posts as hard as he could, grinning at the shock of pain that vibrated in his hands and travelled all the way up to his elbows. He looked at the lock. The lock looked a bit dented, but it was intact. He brought it down on the post again, even harder this time, heedless of the pain. This time a chunk of wood flew off the bedpost, but the lock still didn't give. Todd uttered a little shriek of laughter and took the box to the other end of the bed. He raised it high over his head this time and brought it down with all his strength. This time the lock splintered.

As he flipped the lid up, headlights splashed across Dussander's window.

He pawed wildly through the box. Postcards. A locket. A much-folded picture of a woman wearing frilly black garters and nothing else. An old billfold. Several sets of ID. An empty leather passport folder. At the bottom, letters.

The lights grew brighter, and now he heard the distinctive beat of the Porsche's engine. It grew louder . . . and then cut off.

Todd grabbed three sheets of airmail-type stationery, closely written in German on both sides of each sheet, and ran out of the room again. He had almost gotten to the stairs when he realized he had left the forced box lying on Dussander's bed. He ran back, grabbed it, and opened the third dresser drawer.

It stuck again, this time with a firm shriek of wood against wood.

Out front, he heard the ratchet of the Porsche's emergency brake, the opening of the driver's side door, the slam shut.

Faintly, Todd could hear himself moaning. He put the box in the askew drawer, stood up, and lashed out at it with his foot. The drawer closed neatly. He stood blinking at it for a moment and then fled back down the hall. He raced down the stairs. Halfway down them, he heard the rapid rattle of his father's shoes on Dussander's walk. Todd vaulted over the bannister, landed lightly, and ran into the kitchen, the airmail pages fluttering from his hand.

A hammering on the door. "Todd? Todd, it's me!"

And he could hear an ambulance siren in the distance as well. Dussander had drifted away into semi-consciousness again.

"Coming, Dad!" Todd shouted.

He put the airmail pages on the table, fanning them a little as if they had been dropped in a hurry, and then he went back down the hall and let his father in.

"Where is he?" Dick Bowden asked, shouldering past Todd.

"In the kitchen."

"You did everything just right, Todd," his father said, and hugged him in a rough, embarrassed way.

"I just hope I remembered everything," Todd said modestly, and then followed his father down the hall and into the kitchen.

In the rush to get Dussander out of the house, the letter was almost completely ignored. Todd's father picked it up briefly, then put it down when the medics came in with the stretcher. Todd and his father followed the ambulance, and his explanation of what had happened was accepted without question by the doctor attending Dussander's case. "Mr. Denker" was, after all, eighty years old, and his habits were not the best. The doctor also offered Todd a brusque commendation for his quick thinking and action. Todd thanked him wanly and then asked his father if they could go home.

As they rode back, Dick told him again how proud of him he was. Todd barely heard him. He was thinking about his .30-.30 again.

18

That was the same day Morris Heisel broke his back.

Morris had never *intended* to break his back; all he had *intended* to do was nail up the corner of the rain-gutter on the west side of his house. Breaking his back was the furthest thing from his mind, he had had enough grief in his life without that, thank you very much. His first wife had died at the age of twenty-five, and both of their daughters were also dead. His brother was dead, killed in a tragic car accident not far from Disneyland in 1971. Morris himself was nearing sixty, and had a case of arthritis that was worsening early and fast. He also had warts on both hands, warts that seemed to grow back as fast as the doctor could burn them off. He was *also* prone to migraine headaches, and in the last couple of years, that *potzer* Rogan next door had taken to calling him "Morris the Cat." Morris had wondered aloud to Lydia, his second wife, how Rogan would like it if Morris took up calling him "Rogan the hemorrhoid."

"Quit it, Morris," Lydia said on these occasions. "You can't take a joke, you never *could* take a joke, sometimes I wonder how I could marry a man with absolutely *no* sense of humor. We go to Las Vegas," Lydia had said, addressing the empty kitchen as if an invisible horde of spectators which only she could see were standing there, "we see Buddy Hackett, and Morris doesn't laugh *once*."

Besides arthritis, warts, and migraines, Morris also had Lydia, who, God love her, had developed into something of a nag over the last five years or so . . . ever since her hysterectomy. So he had plenty of sorrows and plenty of problems without adding a broken back.

"*Morris!*" Lydia cried, coming to the back door and wiping suds from her hands with a dishtowel. "Morris, you come down off that ladder right now!"

"What?" He twisted his head so he could see her. He was almost at the top of his aluminum stepladder. There was a bright yellow sticker on this step which said: DANGER! BALANCE MAY SHIFT WITHOUT WARNING ABOVE THIS STEP! Morris was wearing his carpenter's apron with the wide pockets, one of the pockets filled with nails and the other filled with heavy-duty staples. The ground under the stepladder's feet was slightly uneven and the ladder rocked a little when he moved. His neck ached with the unlovely prelude to one of his migraines. He was out of temper. "*What?*"

"Come down from there, I said, before you break your back."

"I'm almost finished."

"You're rocking on that ladder like you were on a boat, Morris. Come down."

"I'll come down when I'm done!" he said angrily. "Leave me alone!"

"You'll break your back," she reiterated dolefully, and went into the house again.

Ten minutes later, as he was hammering the last nail into the rain-gutter, tipped back nearly to the point of overbalancing, he heard a feline yowl followed by fierce barking.

"What in God's name—?"

He looked around and the stepladder rocked alarmingly. At that same moment, their cat—it was named Lover Boy, *not* Morris—tore around the corner of the garage, its fur bushed out into hackles and its green eyes flaring. The Rogans' collie pup was in hot pursuit, its tongue hanging out and its leash dragging behind it.

Lover Boy, apparently not superstitious, ran under the stepladder. The collie pup followed.

"Look out, look out, you dumb mutt!" Morris shouted.

The ladder rocked. The pup bunted it with the side of its body. The ladder tipped over and Morris tipped with it, uttering a howl of dismay. Nails and staples flew out of his carpenter's apron. He landed half on and half off the concrete driveway, and a gigantic agony flared in his back. He did not so much hear his spine snap as feel it happen. Then the world grayed out for awhile.

When things swam back into focus, he was still lying half on and half off the driveway in a litter of nails and staples. Lydia was kneeling over him, weeping. Rogan from next door was there, too, his face as white as a shroud.

"I told you!" Lydia babbled. "I told you to come down off that ladder! Now look! Now look at this!"

Morris found he had absolutely no desire to look. A suffocating, throbbing band of pain had cinched itself around his middle like a belt, and that was bad, but there was something much worse: he could feel nothing below that belt of pain—nothing at all.

"Wail later," he said huskily. "Call the doctor now."

"I'll do it," Rogan said, and ran back to his own house.

"Lydia," Morris said. He wet his lips.

"What? What, Morris?" She bent over him and a tear splashed on his cheek. It was touching, he supposed, but it had made him flinch, and the flinch had made the pain worse.

"Lydia, I also have one of my migraines."

"Oh, poor darling! Poor Morris! But I *told* you—"

"I've got the headache because that *potzer* Rogan's dog barked all night and kept me awake. Today the dog chases my cat and knocks over my ladder and I think my back is broken."

Lydia shrieked. The sound made Morris's head vibrate.

"Lydia," he said, and wet his lips again.

"What, darling?"

"I have suspected something for many years. Now I am sure."

"My poor Morris! What?"

"There is no God," Morris said, and fainted.

They took him to Santo Donato and his doctor told him, at about the same time that he would have ordinarily been sitting down to one of Lydia's wretched suppers, that he would never walk again. By then they had put him in a body-cast. Blood and urine samples had been taken. Dr. Kemmelman had peered into his eyes and tapped his knees with a little rubber hammer—but no reflexive twitch of the leg answered the taps. And at every turn there was Lydia, the tears streaming from her eyes, as she used up one handkerchief after another. Lydia, a woman who would have been at home married to Job, went everywhere well-supplied with little lace snotrags, just in case reason for an extended crying spell should occur. She had called her mother, and her mother would be here soon ("That's nice, Lydia"—although if there was anyone on earth Morris honestly loathed, it was Lydia's mother). She had called the rabbi, he would be here soon, too ("That's nice, Lydia"—although he hadn't set foot inside the synagogue in five years and wasn't sure what the rabbi's name was). She had called his boss, and while he wouldn't be here soon, he sent his greatest sympathies and condolences ("That's nice, Lydia"—although if there was anyone in a class with Lydia's mother, it was that cigar-chewing *putz* Frank Haskell). At last they gave Morris a Valium and took Lydia away. Shortly afterward, Morris just drifted away—no worries, no migraine, no nothing. If they kept giving him little blue pills like that, went his last thought, he would go on up that stepladder and break his back again.

When he woke up—or regained consciousness, that was more like it—dawn was just breaking and the hospital was as quiet as Morris supposed it ever got. He felt very calm . . . almost serene. He had no pain; his body felt swaddled and weightless. His bed had been surrounded by some sort of contraption like a squirrel cage—a thing of stainless steel bars, guy wires, and pulleys. His legs were being held up by cables attached to this gadget. His back seemed to be bowed by something beneath, but it was hard to tell—he had only the angle of his vision to judge by.

Others have it worse, he thought. *All over the world, others have it worse. In Israel, the Palestinians kill busloads of farmers who were committing the political crime of going into town to see a movie. The Israelis cope with this injustice by dropping bombs on the Palestinians and killing children along with whatever terrorists may be there. Others have it worse than me . . . which is not to say this is* good, *don't get that idea, but others have it worse.*

He lifted one hand with some effort—there was pain somewhere in his body, but it was very faint—and made a weak fist in front of his eyes. There. Nothing wrong with his hands. Nothing wrong with his arms, either. So he couldn't feel anything below the waist, so what? There were people all over the world paralyzed from the *neck* down. There were people with leprosy. There were people dying of syphilis. Somewhere in the world right now, there might be people walking down the jetway and onto a plane that was going to crash. No, this wasn't good, but there were worse things in the world.

And there had been, once upon a time, *much* worse things in the world.

He raised his left arm. It seemed to float, disembodied, before his eyes—a scrawny old man's arm with the muscles deteriorating. He was in a hospital johnny but it had short sleeves and he could still read the number on the forearm, tattooed there in faded blue ink. P499965214. Worse things, yes, worse things than falling off a suburban stepladder and breaking your back and being taken to a clean and sterile metropolitan hospital and being given a Valium that was guaranteed to bubble your troubles away.

There were the showers, they were worse. His first wife, Ruth, had died in one of their filthy showers. There were the trenches that became graves—he could close his eyes and still see the men lined up along the open maw of the trenches, could still hear the volley of rifle-fire, could still remember the way they flopped backwards into the earth like badly made puppets. There were the crematoriums, they were worse, too, the crematoriums that filled the air with the steady sweet smell of Jews burning like torches no one could see. The horror-struck faces of old friends and relatives . . . faces that melted away like guttering candles, faces that seemed to melt away *before your very eyes*—thin, thinner, thinnest. Then one day they were gone. Where? Where does a torch-flame go when the cold wind has blown it out? Heaven. Hell? Lights in the darkness, candles in the wind. When Job finally broke down and questioned, God asked him: *Where were you when I made the world?* If Morris Heisel had been Job, he would have responded: *Where were You when my Ruth was dying, You* potzer, *You? Watching the Yankees and the Senators? If You can't pay attention to Your business better than this, get out of my face.*

Yes, there were worse things than breaking your back, he had no doubt of it. But what sort of God would have allowed him to break his back and become paralyzed for life after watching his wife die, and his daughters, and his friends?

No God at all, that was Who.

A tear trickled from the corner of his eye and ran slowly down the side of his head to his ear. Outside the hospital room, a bell rang softly. A nurse squeaked by on white crepe-soled shoes. His door was ajar, and on the far wall of the corridor outside he could read the letters NSIVE CA and guessed that the whole sign must read INTENSIVE CARE.

There was movement in the room—a rustle of bedclothes.

Moving very carefully, Morris turned his head to the right, away from the door. He saw a night-table next to him with a pitcher of water on it. There were two call-buttons on the table. Beyond it was another bed, and in the bed was a man who looked even older and sicker than Morris felt. He was not hooked into a giant exercise-wheel for gerbils like Morris was, but an IV feed stood beside his bed and some sort of monitoring console stood at its foot. The man's skin was sunken and yellow. Lines around his mouth and eyes had driven deep. His hair was yellowish-white, dry and lifeless. His thin eyelids had a bruised and shiny look, and in his big nose Morris saw the burst capillaries of the life-long drinker.

Morris looked away . . . and then looked back. As the dawnlight grew stronger and the hospital began to wake up, he began to have the strangest feeling that he knew his roommate. Could that be? The man looked to be somewhere between seventy-five and eighty, and Morris didn't believe he knew anyone quite that old—except for Lydia's mother, a horror Morris sometimes believed to be older than the Sphinx, whom the woman closely resembled.

Maybe the guy was someone he had known in the past, maybe even before he, Morris, came to America. Maybe. Maybe not. And why all of a sudden did it seem to matter? For that matter, why had all his memories of the camp, of Patin, come flooding back tonight, when he always tried to—and most times succeeded in—keeping those things buried?

He broke out in a sudden rash of gooseflesh, as if he had stepped into some mental haunted house where old bodies were unquiet and old ghosts walked. Could that be, even here and now in this clean hospital, thirty years after those dark times had ended?

He looked away from the old man in the other bed, and soon he had begun to feel sleepy again.

It's a trick of your mind that this other man seems familiar. Only your mind, amusing you in the best way it can, amusing you the way it used to try to amuse you in—

But he would not think of that. He would not *allow* himself to think of that.

Drifting into sleep, he thought of a boast he had made to Ruth (but never to Lydia; it didn't pay to boast to Lydia; she was not like Ruth, who would always smile sweetly at his harmless puffing and crowing): *I never forget a face.* Here was his chance to find out if that was still so. If he had really known the man in the other bed at some time or other, perhaps he could remember when . . . and where.

Very close to sleep, drifting back and forth across its threshold, Morris thought: *Perhaps I knew him in the camp.*

That would be ironic indeed—what they called a "jest of God."

What God? Morris Heisel asked himself again, and slept.

19

Todd graduated salutatorian of his class, just possibly because of his poor grade on the trig final he had been studying for the night Dussander had his heart attack. It dragged his final grade in the course down to 89, one point below an A-minus average.

A week after graduation, the Bowdens went to visit Mr. Denker at Santo Donato General. Todd fidgeted through fifteen minutes of banalities and thank-yous and how-do-you-feels and was grateful for the break when the man in the other bed asked him if he could come over for a minute.

"You'll pardon me," the other man said apologetically. He was in a huge body-cast and was for some reason attached to an overhead system of pulleys and wires. "My name is Morris Heisel. I broke my back."

"That's too bad," Todd said gravely.

"*Oy*, too bad, he says! This boy has the gift of understatement!"

Todd started to apologize, but Heisel raised his hand, smiling a little. His face was pale and tired, the face of any old man in the hospital facing a life full of sweeping changes just ahead—and surely few of them for the better. In that way, Todd thought, he and Dussander were alike.

"No need," Morris said. "No need to answer a rude comment. You are a stranger. Does a stranger need to be inflicted with my problems?"

" 'No man is an island, entire of itself—' " Todd began, and Morris laughed.

"Donne, he quotes at me! A smart kid! Your friend there, is he very bad off?"

"Well, the doctors say he's doing fine, considering his age. He's eighty."

"That old!" Morris exclaimed. "He doesn't talk to me much, you know. But from what he does say, I'd guess he's naturalized. Like me. I'm Polish, you know. Originally, I mean. From Radom."

"Oh?" Todd said politely.

"Yes. You know what they call an orange manhole cover in Radom?"

"No," Todd said, smiling.

"Howard Johnson's," Morris said, and laughed. Todd laughed, too. Dussander glanced over at them, startled by the sound and frowning a little. Then Monica said something and he looked back at her again.

"*Is* your friend naturalized?"

"Oh, yes," Todd said. "He's from Germany. Essen. Do you know that town?"

"No," Morris said, "but I was only in Germany once. I wonder if he was in the war."

"I really couldn't say." Todd's eyes had gone distant.

"No? Well, it doesn't matter. That was a long time ago, the war. In another three years there will be people in this country constitutionally eligible to become President—President!—who weren't even born until after the war was over. To them it must seem there is no difference between the Miracle of Dunkirk and Hannibal taking his elephants over the Alps."

"Were you in the war?" Todd asked.

"I suppose I was, in a manner of speaking. You're a good boy to visit such an old man . . . two old men, counting me."

Todd smiled modestly.

"I'm tired now," Morris said. "Perhaps I'll sleep."

"I hope you'll feel better very soon," Todd said.

Morris nodded, smiled, and closed his eyes. Todd went back to Dussander's bed, where his parents were just getting ready to leave—his dad kept glancing at his watch and exclaiming with bluff heartiness at how late it was getting.

Two days later, Todd came back to the hospital alone. This time, Morris Heisel, immured in his body-cast, was deeply asleep in the other bed.

"You did well," Dussander said quietly. "Did you go back to the house later?"

"Yes. I burned the damned letter. I don't think anyone was too interested in that letter, and I was afraid . . . I don't know." He shrugged, unable to tell Dussander he'd been almost superstitiously afraid about the letter—afraid that maybe someone would wander into the house who could read German, someone who would notice references in the letter that were ten, perhaps twenty years out of date.

"Next time you come, smuggle me in something to drink," Dussander said. "I find I don't miss the cigarettes, but—"

"I won't be back again," Todd said flatly. "Not ever. It's the end. We're quits."

"Quits." Dussander folded his hands on his chest and smiled. It was not a gentle smile . . . but it was perhaps as close as Dussander could come to such a thing. "I thought that was in the cards. They are going to let me out of this graveyard next week . . . or so they promise. The doctor says I may have a few years left in my skin yet. I ask him how many, and he just laughs. I suspect that means no more than three, and probably no more than two. Still, I may give him a surprise."

Todd said nothing.

"But between you and me, boy, I have almost given up my hopes of seeing the century turn."

"I want to ask you about something," Todd said, looking at

Dussander steadily. "That's why I came in today. I want to ask you about something you said once."

Todd glanced over his shoulder at the man in the other bed and then drew his chair closer to Dussander's bed. He could smell Dussander's smell, as dry as the Egyptian room in the museum.

"So ask."

"That wino. You said something about me having experience. First-hand experience. What was that supposed to mean?"

Dussander's smile widened a bit. "I read the newspapers, boy. Old men always read the newspapers, but not in the same way younger people do. Buzzards are known to gather at the ends of certain airport runways in South America when the crosswinds are treacherous, did you know that? That is how an old man reads the newspaper. A month ago there was a story in the Sunday paper. Not a front-page story, no one cares enough about bums and alcoholics to put them on the front page, but it was the lead story in the feature section. IS SOMEONE STALKING SANTO DONATO'S DOWN-AND-OUT?—that's what it was called. Crude. Yellow journalism. You Americans are famous for it."

Todd's hands were clenched into fists, hiding the butchered nails. He never read the Sunday papers, he had better things to do with his time. He had of course checked the papers every day for at least a week following each of his little adventures, and none of his stew-bums had ever gotten beyond page three. The idea that someone had been making connections behind his back infuriated him.

"The story mentioned several murders, extremely brutal murders. Stabbings, bludgeonings. 'Subhuman brutality' was how the writer put it, but you know reporters. The writer of this lamentable piece admitted that there is a high death-rate among these unfortunates, and that Santo Donato has had more than its share of the indigent over the years. In any given year, not all of these men die naturally, or of their own bad habits. There are frequent murders. But in most cases the murderer is usually one of the deceased degenerate's compatriots, the motive no more than an argument over a penny-ante card-game or a bottle of muscatel. The killer is usually happy to confess. He is filled with remorse.

"But these recent killings have not been solved. Even more

ominous, to this yellow journalist's mind—or whatever passes for his mind—is the high disappearance rate over the last few years. Of course, he admits again, these men are not much more than modern-day hoboes. They come and go. But some of these left without picking up welfare checks or day-labor checks from Spell O' Work, which only pays on Fridays. Could some of these have been victims of this yellow journalist's Wino Killer, he asks? Victims who haven't been found? *Pah!*"

Dussander waved his hand in the air as if to dismiss such arrant irresponsibility.

"Only titillation, of course. Give people a comfortable little scare on Sunday morning. He calls up old bogies, threadbare but still useful—the Cleveland Torso Murderer, Zodiac, the mysterious Mr. X who killed the Black Dahlia, Springheel Jack. Such drivel. But it makes me think. What does an old man have to do but think when old friends don't come to visit anymore?"

Todd shrugged.

"I thought: 'If I wished to help this odious yellow-dog journalist, which I certainly do not, I could explain some of the disappearances. Not the corpses found stabbed or bludgeoned, not *them*, God rest their besotted souls, but some of the disappearances. Because at least some of the bums who disappeared are in my cellar.'"

"How many down there?" Todd asked in a low voice.

"Six," Dussander said calmly. "Counting the one you helped me dispose of, six."

"You're really nutso," Todd said. The skin below his eyes had gone white and shiny. "At some point you just blew all your fucking wheels."

" 'Blew my wheels.' What a charming idiom! Perhaps you're right! But then I said to myself: 'This newspaper jackal would love to pin the murders and the disappearances on the same somebody— his hypothetical Wino Killer. But I think maybe that's not what happened at all.'

"Then I say to myself: 'Do I know anybody who might be doing such things? Somebody who has been under as much strain as I have during the last few years? Someone who has also been listening to old ghosts rattle their chains?' And the answer is yes. I know *you*, boy."

"I've never killed anyone."

The image that came was not of the winos; they weren't people, not really people at all. The image that came was of himself crouched behind the dead tree, peering through the telescopic sight of his .30-.30, the crosshairs fixed on the temple of the man with the scuzzy beard, the man driving the Brat pickup.

"Perhaps not," Dussander agreed, amicably enough. "Yet you took hold so well that night. Your surprise was mostly anger at having been put in such a dangerous position by an old man's infirmity, I think. Am I wrong?"

"No, you're not wrong," Todd said. "I was pissed off at you, and I still am. I covered it up for you because you've got something in a safety deposit box that could destroy my life."

"No. I do not."

"What? What are you talking about?"

"It was as much a bluff as your 'letter left with a friend.' You never wrote such a letter, there never was such a friend, and I have never written a single word about our . . . association. shall I call it? Now I lay my cards on the table. You saved my life. Never mind that you acted only to protect yourself; that does not change how speedily and efficiently you acted. I cannot hurt you, boy. I tell you that freely. I have looked death in the face and it frightens me, but not as badly as I thought it would. There is no document. It is as you say: we are quits."

Todd smiled: a weird upward corkscrewing of the lips. A strange, sardonic light danced and fluttered in his eyes.

"Herr Dussander," he said, "if only I could believe that."

In the evening Todd walked down to the slope overlooking the freeway, climbed down to the dead tree, and sat on it. It was just past twilight. The evening was warm. Car headlights cut through the dusk in long yellow daisy chains.

There is no document.

He hadn't realized how completely irretrievable the entire situation was until the discussion that had followed. Dussander suggested Todd search the house for a safety deposit key, and when he didn't find one, that would prove there was no safety deposit box and hence no document. But a key could be hidden anywhere—it could be put in a Crisco can and then buried, it could be put in a Sucrets tin and slid behind a board that had been loosened and then replaced; he might even have ridden the bus to San Diego and put it behind one of the rocks in the decorative stone wall which surrounded the bears' environmental area. For that matter, Todd went on, Dussander could even have thrown the key away. Why not? He had only needed it once, to put his written document in. If he died, someone else would take it out.

Dussander nodded reluctantly at this, but after a moment's thought he made another suggestion. When he got well enough to go home, he would have the boy call every single bank in Santo Donato. He would tell each bank official he was calling for his grandfather. Poor grandfather, he would say, had grown lamentably senile over the last two years, and now he had misplaced the key to his safety deposit box. Even worse, he could no longer remember which bank the box was in. Could they just check their files for an Arthur Denker, no middle initial? And when Todd drew a blank at every bank in town—

Todd was already shaking his head again. First, a story like that was almost guaranteed to raise suspicions. It was too pat. They would probably suspect a con-game and get in touch with the police. Even if every one of them bought the story, it would do no good. If none of the almost nine dozen banks in Santo Donato had a box in the Denker name, it didn't mean that Dussander hadn't rented one in San Diego, L.A., or any town in between.

At last Dussander gave up.

"You have all the answers, boy. All, at least, but one. What would I stand to gain by lying to you? I invented this story to protect myself from you—that is a motive. Now I am trying to uninvent it. What possible gain do you see in that?"

Dussander got laboriously up on one elbow.

"For that matter, why would I need a document at all, at this point? I could destroy your life from this hospital bed, if that was what I wanted. I could open my mouth to the first passing doctor, they are all Jews, they would all know who I am, or at least who I was. But why would I do this? You are a fine student. You have a fine career ahead of you . . . unless you get careless with those winos of yours."

Todd's face froze. "I told you—"

"I know. You never heard of them, you never touched so much as a hair on their scaly, tick-ridden heads, all right, good, fine. I say no more about it. Only tell me, boy: why should I lie about this? We are quits, you say. But I tell you we can only be quits if we can trust each other."

Now, sitting behind the dead tree on the slope which ran down to the freeway, looking at all the anonymous headlights disappearing endlessly like slow tracer bullets, he knew well enough what he was afraid of.

Dussander talking about trust. That made him afraid.

The idea that Dussander might be tending a small but perfect flame of hatred deep in his heart, that made him afraid, too.

A hatred of Todd Bowden, who was young, clean-featured, unwrinkled; Todd Bowden, who was an apt pupil with a whole bright life stretching ahead of him.

But what he feared most was Dussander's refusal to use his name. *Todd.* What was so hard about that, even for an old kraut whose teeth were mostly false? *Todd.* One syllable. Easy to say. Put your tongue against the roof of your mouth, drop your teeth a little, replace your tongue, and it was out. Yet Dussander had always called him "boy." Only that. Contemptuous. *Anonymous.* Yes, that was it, anonymous. As anonymous as a concentration camp serial number.

Perhaps Dussander *was* telling the truth. No, not just perhaps; *probably.* But there were those fears . . . the worst of them being Dussander's refusal to use his name.

And at the root of it all was his own inability to make a hard and final decision. At the root of it all was a rueful truth: even after four years of visiting Dussander, he still didn't know what went on in the old man's head. Perhaps he wasn't such an apt pupil after all.

Cars and cars and cars. His fingers itched to hold his rifle. How many could he get? Three? Six? An even baker's dozen? And how many miles to Babylon?

He stirred restlessly, uneasily.

Only Dussander's death would tell the final truth, he supposed. Sometime during the next five years, maybe even sooner. Three to five . . . it sounded like a prison sentence. *Todd Bowden, this court hereby sentences you to three to five for associating with a known war criminal. Three to five at bad dreams and cold sweats.*

Sooner or later Dussander would simply drop dead. Then the waiting would begin. The knot in the stomach every time the phone or the doorbell rang.

He wasn't sure he could stand that.

His fingers itched to hold the gun and Todd curled them into fists and drove both fists into his crotch. Sick pain swallowed his belly and he lay for some time afterwards in a writhing ball on the ground, his lips pulled back in a silent shriek. The pain was dreadful, but it blotted out the endless parade of thoughts.

At least for a while.

20

For Morris Heisel, that Sunday was a day of miracles.

The Atlanta Braves, his favorite baseball team, swept a double-header from the high and mighty Cincinnati Reds by scores of 7–1 and 8–0. Lydia, who boasted smugly of always taking care of herself and whose favorite saying was "An ounce of prevention is worth a pound of cure," slipped on her friend Janet's wet kitchen floor and sprained her hip. She was at home in bed. It wasn't serious, not at all, and thank God (what God) for that, but it meant she wouldn't be able to visit him for at least two days, maybe as long as four.

Four days without Lydia! Four days that he wouldn't have to hear about how she had warned him that the stepladder was wobbly and how he was up too high on it in the bargain. Four days when he wouldn't have to listen to her tell him how she'd always said the Rogans' pup was going to cause them grief, always chasing Lover Boy that way. Four days without Lydia asking him if he wasn't glad now that she had kept after him about sending in that insurance application, for if she had not, they would surely be on their way to the poorhouse now. Four days without having Lydia tell him that

many people lived perfectly normal lives—almost, anyway—
paralyzed from the waist down; why, every museum and gallery in
the city had wheelchair ramps as well as stairs, and there were even
special busses. After the observation, Lydia would smile bravely and
then inevitably burst into tears.

Morris drifted off into a contented late afternoon nap.

When he woke up it was half-past five in the afternoon. His
roommate was asleep. He still hadn't placed Denker, but all the
same he felt sure that he had known the man at some time or other.
He had begun to ask Denker about himself once or twice, but then
something kept him from making more than the most banal
conversation with the man—the weather, the last earthquake, the
next earthquake, and yeah, the *Guide* says Myron Floren is going to
come back for a special guest appearance this weekend on the Welk
show.

Morris told himself he was holding back because it gave him a
mental game to play, and when you were in a body-cast from your
shoulders to your hips, mental games can come in handy. If you had
a little mental contest going on, you didn't have to spend quite so
much time wondering how it was going to be, pissing through a
catheter for the rest of your life.

If he came right out and asked Denker, the mental game would
probably come to a swift and unsatisfying conclusion. They would
narrow their pasts down to some common experience—a train trip,
a boat ride, possibly even the camp. Denker might have been in
Patin; there had been plenty of German Jews there.

On the other hand, one of the nurses had told him Denker would
probably be going home in a week or two. If Morris couldn't figure
it out by then, he would mentally declare the game lost and ask the
man straight out: *Say, I've had the feeling I know you—*

But there was more to it than just that, he admitted to himself.
There was something in his feelings, a nasty sort of undertow, that
made him think of that story "The Monkey's Paw," where every
wish had been granted as the result of some evil turn of fate. The old
couple who came into possession of the paw wished for a hundred
dollars and received it as a gift of condolence when their only son
was killed in a nasty mill accident. Then the mother had wished for

the son to return to them. They had heard footsteps dragging up their walk shortly afterwards; then pounding on the door. The mother, mad with joy, had gone rushing down the stairs to let in her only child. The father, mad with fear, scrabbled through the darkness for the dried paw, found it at last, and wished his son dead again. The mother threw the door open a moment later and found nothing on the stoop but an eddy of night wind.

In some way Morris felt that perhaps he *did* know where he and Denker had been acquainted, but that his knowledge was like the son of the old couple in the story—returned from the grave, but not as he was in his mother's memory; returned, instead, horribly crushed and mangled from his fall into the gnashing, whirling machinery. He felt that his knowledge of Denker might be a subconscious thing, pounding on the door between that area of his mind and that of rational understanding and recognition, demanding admittance . . . and that another part of him was searching frantically for the monkey's paw, or its psychological equivalent; for the talisman that would wish away the knowledge forever.

Now he looked at Denker, frowning.

Denker, Denker, Where have I known you, Denker? Was it Patin? Is that why I don't want to know? But surely, two survivors of a common horror do not have to be afraid of each other. Unless, of course . . .

He frowned. He felt very close to it, suddenly, but his feet were tingling, breaking his concentration, annoying him. They were tingling in just the way a limb tingles when you've slept on it and it's returning to normal circulation. If it wasn't for the damned body-cast, he could sit up and rub his feet until that tingle went away. He could—

Morris's eyes widened.

For a long time he lay perfectly still, Lydia forgotten, Denker forgotten, Patin forgotten, *everything* forgotten except that tingly feeling in his feet. Yes, *both* feet, but it was stronger in the right one. When you felt that tingle, you said *My foot went to sleep.*

But what you really meant, of course, was *My foot is waking up.*

Morris fumbled for a the call-button. He pressed it again and again until the nurse came.

*   *   *

The nurse tried to dismiss it—she had had hopeful patients before. His doctor wasn't in the building, and the nurse didn't want to call him at home. Dr. Kemmelman had a vast reputation for evil temper . . . especially when he was called at home. Morris wouldn't let her dismiss it. He was a mild man, but now he was prepared to make more than a fuss; he was prepared to make an uproar if that's what it took. The Braves had taken two. Lydia had sprained her hip. But good things came in threes, everyone knew that.

At last the nurse came back with an intern, a young man named Dr. Timpnell whose hair looked as if it had last been cut by a Lawn Boy with very dull blades. Dr. Timpnell pulled a Swiss Army knife from the pocket of his white pants, folded out the Phillips screwdriver attachment, and ran it from the toes of Morris's right foot down to the heel. The foot did not curl, but his toes twitched—it was an obvious twitch, too definite to miss. Morris burst into tears.

Timpnell, looking rather dazed, sat beside him on the bed and patted his hand.

"This sort of thing happens from time to time," he said (possibly from his wealth of practical experience, which stretched back perhaps as far as six months). "No doctor predicts it, but it *does* happen. And apparently it's happened to you."

Morris nodded through his tears.

"Obviously, you're not totally paralyzed." Timpnell was still patting his hand. "But I wouldn't try to predict if your recovery will be slight, partial, or total. I doubt if Dr. Kemmelman will, either. I suspect you'll have to undergo a lot of physical therapy, and not all of it will be pleasant. But it will be more pleasant than . . . you know."

"Yes," Morris said through his tears. "I know. Thank God!" He remembered telling Lydia there was no God and felt his face fill up with hot blood.

"I'll see that Dr. Kemmelman is informed," Timpnell said, giving Morris's hand a final pat and rising.

"Could you call my wife?" Morris asked. Because, doom-crying and hand-wringing aside, he felt *something* for her. Maybe it was even love, an emotion which seemed to have little to do with sometimes feeling like you could wring a person's neck.

"Yes, I'll see that it's done. Nurse, would you—?"

"Of course, doctor," the nurse said, and Timpnell could barely stifle his grin.

"Thank you," Morris said, wiping his eyes with a Kleenex from the box on the nightstand. "Thank you very much."

Timpnell went out. At some point during the discussion, Mr. Denker had awakened. Morris considered apologizing for all the noise, or perhaps for his tears, and then decided no apology was necessary.

"You are to be congratulated, I take it," Mr. Denker said.

"We'll see," Morris said, but like Timpnell, he was barely able to stifle his grin. "We'll see."

"Things have a way of working out," Denker replied vaguely, and then turned on the TV with the remote control device. It was now quarter to six, and they watched the last of *Hee Haw*. It was followed by the evening news. Unemployment was worse. Inflation was not so bad. Billy Carter was thinking about going into the beer business. A new Gallup poll showed that, if the election were to be held right then, there were four Republican candidates who could beat Billy's brother Jimmy. And there had been racial incidents following the murder of a black child in Miami. "A night of violence," the newscaster called it. Closer to home, an unidentified man had been found in an orchard near Highway 46, stabbed and bludgeoned.

Lydia called just before six-thirty. Dr. Kemmelman had called her and, based on the young intern's report, he had been cautiously optimistic. Lydia was cautiously joyous. She vowed to come in the following day even if it killed her. Morris told her he loved her. Tonight he loved everyone—Lydia, Dr. Timpnell with his Lawn Boy haircut, Mr. Denker, even the young girl who brought in the supper trays as Morris hung up.

Supper was hamburgers, mashed potatoes, a carrots-and-peas combination, and small dishes of ice cream for dessert. The candy striper who served it was Felice, a shy blonde girl of perhaps twenty. She had her own good news—her boyfriend had landed a job as a computer programmer with IBM and had formally asked her to marry him.

Mr. Denker, who exuded a certain courtly charm that all the young ladies responded to, expressed great pleasure. "Really, how wonderful. You must sit down and tell us all about it. Tell us everything. Omit nothing."

Felice blushed and smiled and said she couldn't do that. "We've still got the rest of the B Wing to do and C Wing after that. And look, here it is six-thirty!"

"Then tomorrow night, for sure. We insist . . . don't we, Mr. Heisel?"

"Yes, indeed," Morris murmured, but his mind was a million miles away.

(*you must sit down and tell us all about it*)

Words spoken in that exact-same bantering tone. He had heard them before; of that there could be no doubt. But had Denker been the one to speak them? *Had* he?

(*tell us everything*)

The voice of an urbane man. A cultured man. But there was a threat in the voice. A steel hand in a velvet glove. Yes.

Where?

(*tell us everything. omit nothing.*)

(*? PATIN ?*)

Morris Heisel looked at his supper. Mr. Denker had already fallen to with a will. The encounter with Felice had left him in the best of spirits—the way he had been after the young boy with the blonde hair came to visit him.

"A nice girl," Denker said, his words muffled by a mouthful of carrots and peas.

"Oh yes—

(*you must sit down*)

"—Felice, you mean. She's

(*and tell us all about it.*)

"very sweet."

(*tell us everything. omit nothing.*)

He looked down at his own supper, suddenly remembering how it got to be in the camps after awhile. At first you would have killed for a scrap of meat, no matter how maggoty or green with decay. But after awhile, that crazy hunger went away and your belly lay inside your middle like a small gray rock. You felt you would never be hungry again.

Until someone showed you food.

(*"tell us everything, my friend. omit nothing. you must sit down and tell us AAALLLLL about it."*)

The main course on Morris's plastic hospital tray was hamburger. Why should it suddenly make him think of lamb? Not mutton, not chops—mutton was often stringy, chops often tough, and a person whose teeth had rotted out like old stumps would perhaps not be overly tempted by mutton or a chop. No, what he thought of now was a savory lamb stew, gravy-rich and full of vegetables. Soft, tasty vegetables. Why think of lamb stew? Why, unless—

The door banged open. It was Lydia, her face rosy with smiles. An aluminum crutch was propped in her armpit and she was walking like Marshal Dillon's friend Chester. *"Morris!"* she trilled. Trailing her and looking just as tremulously happy was Emma Rogan from next door.

Mr. Denker, startled, dropped his fork. He cursed softly under his breath and picked it up off the floor with a wince.

"It's so *WONDERFUL!*" Lydia was almost baying with excitement. "I called Emma and asked her if we could come tonight instead of tomorrow, I had the crutch already, and I said, 'Em,' I said, 'if I can't bear this agony for Morris, what kind of wife am I to him?' Those were my very words, weren't they, Emma?"

Emma Rogan, perhaps remembering that her collie pup had caused at least some of the problem, nodded eagerly.

"So I called the hospital," Lydia said, shrugging her coat off and settling in for a good long visit, "and *they* said it was past visiting hours but in my case they would make an exception, except we couldn't stay too long because we might bother Mr. Denker. We aren't bothering you, are we, Mr. Denker?"

"No, dear lady," Mr. Denker said resignedly.

"Sit down, Emma, take Mr. Denker's chair, he's not using it. Here, Morris, stop with the ice cream, you're slobbering it all over yourself, just like a baby. Never mind, we'll have you up and around in no time. I'll feed it to you. Goo-goo, ga-ga. Open wide . . . over the teeth, over the gums . . . look out, stomach, here it comes! . . . No, don't say a word, Mommy knows best. Would you look at him, Emma, he hardly has any hair left and I don't wonder, thinking he might never walk again. It's God's mercy. I told him that stepladder was wobbly. I said, 'Morris,' I said, 'come down off there before—' "

She fed him ice cream and chattered for the next hour and by the time she left, hobbling ostentatiously on the crutch while Emma held her other arm, thoughts of lamb stew and voices echoing up through the years were the last things in Morris Heisel's mind. He was exhausted. To say it had been a busy day was putting it mildly. Morris fell deeply asleep.

He awoke sometime between 3:00 and 4:00 A.M. with a scream locked behind his lips.

Now he knew. He knew exactly where and exactly when he had been acquainted with the man in the other bed. Except his name had not been Denker *then*. Oh no, not at all.

He had awakened from the most terrible nightmare of his whole life. Someone had given him and Lydia a monkey's paw, and they had wished for money. Then, somehow, a Western Union boy in a Hitler Youth uniform had been in the room with them. He handed Morris a telegram which read: REGRET TO INFORM YOU BOTH DAUGHTERS DEAD STOP PATIN CONCENTRATION CAMP STOP GREATEST REGRETS AT THIS FINAL SOLUTION STOP COMMANDANT'S LETTER FOLLOWS STOP WILL TELL YOU EVERYTHING AND OMIT NOTHING STOP PLEASE ACCEPT OUR CHECK FOR 100 REICHMARKS ON DEPOSIT YOUR BANK TOMORROW STOP SIGNED ADOLF HITLER CHANCELLOR.

A great wail from Lydia, and although she had never even seen Morris's daughters, she held the monkey's paw high and wished for them to be returned to life. The room went dark. And suddenly, from outside, came the sound of dragging, lurching footfalls.

Morris was down on his hands and knees in a darkness that suddenly stank of smoke and gas and death. He was searching for the paw. One wish left. If he could find the paw he could wish this dreadful dream away. He would spare himself the sight of his daughters, thin as scarecrows, their eyes deep wounded holes, their numbers burning on the scant flesh of their arms.

Hammering on the door.

In the nightmare, his search for the paw became ever more frenzied, but it bore no fruit. It seemed to go on for years. And then, behind him, the door crashed open. *No,* he thought. *I won't look. I'll close my eyes. Rip them from my head if I have to, but I won't look.*

But he did look. He had to look. In the dream if was as if huge hands has grasped his head and wrenched it around.

It was not his daughters standing in the doorway; it was Denker. A much younger Denker, a Denker who wore a Nazi SS uniform, the cap with its death's-head insignia cocked rakishly to one side. His buttons gleamed heartlessly, his boots were polished to a killing gloss.

Clasped in his arms was a huge and slowly bubbling pot of lamb stew.

And the dream-Denker, smiling his dark, suave smile, said: *You must sit down and tell us all about it—as one friend to another, hein? We have heard that gold has been hidden. That tobacco has been hoarded. That it was not food-poisoning with Schneibel at all but powdered glass in his supper two nights ago. You must not insult our intelligence by pretending you know nothing. You knew EVERYTHING. So tell it all. Omit nothing.*

And in the dark, smelling the maddening aroma of the stew, he told them everything. His stomach, which had been a small gray rock, was now a ravening tiger. Words spilled helplessly from his lips. They spewed from him in the senseless sermon of a lunatic, truth and falsehood all mixed up together.

Brodin has his mother's wedding ring taped below his scrotum!

("you must sit down")

Laslo and Herman Dorksy have talked about rushing guard tower number three!

("and tell us everything!")

Rachel Tannenbaum's husband has tobacco, he gave the guard who comes on after Zeickert, the one they call Booger-Eater because he is always picking his nose and then putting his fingers in his mouth, Tannenbaum, some of it to Booger-Eater so he wouldn't take his wife's pearl earrings!

("oh that makes no sense no sense at all you've mixed up two different stories I think but that's all right quite all right we'd rather have you mix up two stories than omit one completely you must omit NOTHING!")

There is a man who has been calling out his dead son's name in order to get double rations!

("tell us his name")

I don't know it but I can point him out to you please yes I can show him to you I will I will I will I

("tell us everything you know")

will I will I will I will I will I will I will I

Until he swam up into consciousness with a scream in his throat like fire.

Trembling uncontrollably, he looked at the sleeping form in the other bed. He found himself staring particularly at the wrinkled, caved-in mouth. Old tiger with no teeth. Ancient and vicious rogue elephant with one tusk gone and the other rotted loose in its socket. Senile monster.

"Oh my *God*," Morris Heisel whispered. His voice was high and faint, inaudible to anyone but himself. Tears trickled down his cheeks toward his ears. "Oh dear *God*, the man who murdered my wife and my daughters is sleeping in the same room with me, my *God*, oh dear dear *God*, he is here with me now in this room."

The tears began to flow faster now—tears of rage and horror, hot, scalding.

He trembled and waited for morning, and morning did not come for an age.

21

The next day, Monday, Todd was up at six o'clock in the morning and poking listlessly at a scrambled egg he had fixed for himself when his father came down still dressed in his monogrammed bathrobe and slippers.

"Mumph," he said to Todd, going past him to the refrigerator for orange juice.

Todd grunted back without looking up from his book, one of the 87th Squad mysteries. He had been lucky enough to land a summer job with a landscaping outfit that operated out of Pasadena. That would have been much too far to commute ordinarily, even if one of his parents had been willing to loan him a car for the summer (neither was), but his father was working on-site not far from there, and he was able to drop Todd off at a bus stop on his way and pick him up at the same place on his way back. Todd was less than wild about the arrangement; he didn't like riding home from work with his father and absolutely detested riding to work with him in the morning. It was in the mornings that he felt the most naked, when the wall between what he was and what he might be seemed the thinnest. It was worse after a night of bad dreams, but even if no dreams had come in the night, it was bad. One morning he realized with a fright so sudden it was almost terror that he had been seriously considering reaching across his father's briefcase, grabbing the wheel of the Porsche, and sending them corkscrewing into the two express lanes, cutting a swath of destruction through the morning commuters.

"You want another egg, Todd-O?"

"No thanks, Dad." Dick Bowden ate them fried. How could anyone stand to eat a fried egg? On the grill of the Jenn-Air for two minutes, then over easy. What you got on your plate at the end looked like a giant dead eye with a cataract over it, an eye that would bleed orange when you poked it with your fork.

He pushed his scrambled egg away. He had barely touched it.

Outside, the morning paper slapped the step.

His father finished cooking, turned off the grill, and came to the table. "Not hungry this morning, Todd-O?"

You call me that one more time and I'm going to stick my knife right up your fucking nose . . . Dad-O.

"Not much appetite, I guess."

Dick grinned affectionately at his son; there was still a tiny dab of shaving cream on the boy's right ear. "Betty Trask stole your appetite. That's my guess."

"Yeah, maybe that's it." He offered a wan smile that vanished as soon as his father went down the stairs from the breakfast nook to get the paper. *Would it wake you up if I told you what a cunt she is, Dad-O? How about if I said, "Oh, by the way, did you know your good*

*friend Ray Trask's daughter is one of the biggest sluts in Santo Donato?
She'd kiss her own twat if she was double-jointed, Dad-O. That's how
much she thinks of it. Just a stinking little slut. Two lines of coke and she's
yours for the night. And if you don't happen to have any coke, she's still
yours for the night. She'd fuck a dog if she couldn't get a man." Think
that'd wake you up, Dad-O? Get you a flying start on the day?*

He pushed the thoughts away viciously, knowing they wouldn't
stay gone.

His father came back with the paper. Todd glimpsed the
headline: SPACE SHUTTLE WON'T FLY, EXPERT SAYS.

Dick sat down. "Betty's a fine-looking girl," he said. "She
reminds me of your mother when I first met her."

"Is that so?"

"Pretty . . . young . . . fresh . . . " Dick Bowden's eyes had
gone vague. Now they came back, focusing almost anxiously on his
son. "Not that your mother isn't still a fine-looking woman. But at
that age a girl has a certain . . . glow, I guess you'd say. It's there
for awhile, and then it's gone." He shrugged and opened the paper.
"C'est la vie, I guess."

She's a bitch in heat. Maybe that's what makes her glow.

"You're treating her right, aren't you, Todd-O?" His father was
making his usual rapid trip through the paper toward the sports
pages. "Not getting too fresh?"

"Everything's cool, Dad."

*(if he doesn't stop pretty soon I'll I'll do something. scream. throw his
coffee in his face. something.)*

"Ray thinks you're a fine boy," Dick said absently. He had at last
reached the sports. He became absorbed. There was blessed silence
at the breakfast table.

Betty Trask had been all over him the very first time they went
out. He had taken her to the local lovers' lane after the movie
because he knew it would be expected of him; they could swap spits
for half an hour or so and have all the right things to tell their
respective friends the next day. She could roll her eyes and tell how
she had fought off his advances—boys were so tiresome, really, and
she never fucked on the first date, she wasn't that kind of girl. Her
friends would agree and then all of them would troop into the girls'

room and do whatever it was they did in there—put on fresh makeup, smoke Tampax, whatever.

And for a guy . . . well, you had to make out. You had to get at least to second base and try for third. Because there were reputations and reputations. Todd couldn't have cared less about having a stud reputation; he only wanted a reputation for being normal. And if you didn't at least *try*, word got around. People started to wonder if you were all right.

So he took them up on Jane's Hill, kissed them, felt their tits, went a little further than that if they would allow it. And that was it. The girl would stop him, he would put up a little goodnatured argument, and then take her home. No worries about what might be said in the girls' room the next day. No worries that anyone was going to think Todd Bowden was anything but normal. Except—

Except Betty Trask *was* the kind of girl who fucked on the first date. On every date. And in between dates.

The first time had been a month or so before the goddam Nazi's heart attack, and Todd thought he had done pretty well for a virgin . . . perhaps for the same reason a young pitcher will do well if he's tapped to throw the biggest game of the year with no forewarning. There had been no time to worry, to get all strung up about it.

Always before, Todd had been able to sense when a girl had made up her mind that on the next date she would just allow herself to be carried away. He was aware that he was personable and that both his looks and his prospects were good. The kind of boy their cunty mothers regarded as "a good catch." And when he sensed that physical capitulation about to happen, he would start dating some other girl. And whatever it said about his personality, Todd was able to admit to himself that if he ever started dating a truly frigid girl, he would probably be happy to date her for years to come. Maybe even marry her.

But the first time with Betty had gone fairly well—*she* was no virgin, even if he was. She had to help him get his cock into her, but she seemed to take that as a matter of course. And halfway through the act itself she had gurgled up from the blanket they were lying on: "I just *love* to fuck!" It was the tone of voice another girl might have used to express her love for strawberry whirl ice cream.

Later encounters—there had been five of them (five and a half, he supposed, if you wanted to count last night)—hadn't been so good. They had, in fact, gotten worse at what seemed an exponential rate . . . although he didn't believe even now that Betty had been aware of that (at least not until last night). In fact, quite the opposite. Betty apparently believed she had found the battering-ram of her dreams.

Todd hadn't felt any of the things he was supposed to feel at a time like that. Kissing her lips was like kissing warm but uncooked liver. Having her tongue in his mouth only made him wonder what kind of germs she was carrying, and sometimes he thought he could smell her fillings—an unpleasant metallic odor, like chrome. Her breasts were bags of meat. No more.

Todd had done it twice more with her before Dussander's heart attack. Each time he had more trouble getting erect. In both cases he had finally succeeded by using a fantasy. She was stripped naked in front of all their friends. Crying. Todd was forcing her to walk up and down before them while he cried out: *Show your tits! Let them see your snatch, you cheap slut! Spread your cheeks! That's right, bend over and SPREAD them!*

Betty's appreciation was not at all surprising. He was a good lover, not in spite of his problems but because of them. Getting hard was only the first step. Once you achieved erection, you had to have an orgasm. The fourth time they had done it—this was three days after Dussander's heart attack—he had pounded away at her for over ten minutes. Betty Trask thought she had died and gone to heaven; she had three orgasms and was trying for a fourth when Todd recalled an old fantasy . . . what was, in fact, the First Fantasy. The girl on the table, clamped and helpless. The huge dildo. The rubber squeeze-bulb. Only now, desperate and sweaty and almost insane with his desire to come and get this horror over with, the face of the girl on the table became Betty's face. That brought on a joyless, rubbery spasm that he supposed was, technically, at least, an orgasm. A moment later Betty was whispering in his ear, her breath warm and redolent of Juicy Fruit gum: "Lover, you do me any old time. Just call me."

Todd had nearly groaned aloud.

The nub of his dilemma was this: Wouldn't his reputation suffer if he broke off with a girl who so obviously wanted to put out for him? Wouldn't people wonder why? Part of him said they would not. He remembered walking down the hall behind two senior boys during his freshman year and hearing one of them tell the other he had broken off with his girlfriend. The other wanted to know why. "Fucked 'er out," the first said, and both of them bellowed goatish laughter.

If someone asks me why I dropped her, I'll just say I fucked her out. But what if she says we only did it five times? Is that enough? What? . . . How much? . . . How many? . . . Who'll talk? . . . What'll they say?

So his mind ran on, as restless as a hungry rat in an insoluble maze. He was vaguely aware that he was turning a minor problem into a big problem, and that his very inability to solve the problem had something to say about how shaky he had gotten. But knowing it brought him no fresh ability to change his behavior, and he sank into a black depression.

College. College was the answer. College offered an excuse to break with Betty that no one could question. But September seemed so far away.

The fifth time it had taken him almost twenty minutes to get hard, but Betty had proclaimed the experience well worth the wait. And then, last night, he hadn't been able to perform at all.

"What are you, anyway?" Betty had asked petulantly. After twenty minutes of manipulating his lax penis, she was dishevelled and out of patience. "Are you one of those AC/DC guys?"

He very nearly strangled her on the spot. And if he'd had his .30-.30—

"Well, I'll be a son of a *gun!* Congratulations, son!"

"Huh?" He looked up and out of his black study.

"You made the Southern Cal High School All-Stars!" His father was grinning with pride and pleasure.

"Is that so?" For a moment he hardly knew what his father was talking about; he had to grope for the meaning of the words. "Say, yeah, Coach Haines mentioned something to me about that at the end of the year. Said he was putting me and Billy DeLyons up. I never expected anything to happen."

"Well Jesus, you don't seem very excited about it!"

"I'm still trying

(who gives a ripe fuck?)

to get used to the idea." With a huge effort, he managed a grin. "Can I see the article?"

His father handed the paper across the table to Todd and got to his feet. "I'm going to wake Monica up. She's got to see this before we leave."

No, God—I can't face both of them this morning.

"Aw, don't do that. You know she won't be able to get back to sleep if you wake her up. We'll leave it for her on the table."

"Yes, I suppose we could do that. You're a damned thoughtful boy, Todd." He clapped Todd on the back, and Todd squeezed his eyes closed. At the same time he shrugged his shoulders in an aw-shucks gesture that made his father laugh. Todd opened his eyes again and looked at the paper.

4 BOYS NAMED TO SOUTHERN CAL ALL-STARS, the headline read. Beneath were pictures of them in their uniforms—the catcher and left-fielder from Fairview High, the harp southpaw from Mountford, and Todd to the far right, grinning openly out at the world from beneath the bill of his baseball cap. He read the story and saw that Billy DeLyons had made the second squad. That, at least, was something to feel happy about. DeLyons could claim he was a Methodist until his tongue fell out, if it made him feel good, but he wasn't fooling Todd. He knew perfectly well what Billy DeLyons was. Maybe he ought to introduce him to Betty Trask, she was another sheeny. He had wondered about that for a long time, and last night he had decided for sure. The Trasks were passing for white. One look at her nose and that olive complexion—her old man's was even worse—and you knew. That was probably why he hadn't been able to get it up. It was simple: his cock had known the difference before his brain. Who did they think they were kidding, calling themselves Trask?

"Congratulations again, son."

He looked up and first saw his father's hand stuck out, then his father's foolishly grinning face.

Your buddy Trask is a yid! he heard himself yelling into his father's face. *That's why I was impotent with his slut of a daughter last night!*

That's the reason! Then, on the heels of that, the cold voice that sometimes came at moments like this rose up from deep inside him, shutting off the rising flood of irrationality, as if

(GET HOLD OF YOURSELF RIGHT NOW)

behind steel gates.

He took his father's hand and shook it. Smiled guilelessly into his father's proud face. Said: "Jeez, thanks, Dad."

They left that page of the newspaper folded back and a note for Monica, which Dick insisted Todd write and sign: *Your All-Star Son, Todd.*

22

Ed French, aka "Pucker" French, aka Sneaker Pete and The Ked Man, *also* aka Rubber Ed French, was in the small and lovely seaside town of San Remo for a guidance counsellors' convention. It was a waste of time if ever there had been one—all guidance counsellors could ever agree on was not to agree on anything—and he grew bored with the papers, seminars, and discussion periods after a single day. Halfway through the second day, he discovered he was also bored with San Remo, and that of the adjectives small, lovely, and seaside, the *key* adjective was probably *small*. Gorgeous views and redwood trees aside, San Remo didn't have a movie theater or a bowling alley, and Ed hadn't wanted to go in the place's only bar—it had a dirt parking lot filled with pickup trucks, and most of the pickups had Reagan stickers on their rusty bumpers and tailgates. He wasn't afraid of being picked on, but he hadn't wanted to spend an evening looking at men in cowboy hats and listening to Loretta Lynn on the jukebox.

So here he was on the third day of a convention which stretched out over an incredible four days; here he was in room 217 of the Holiday Inn, his wife and daughter at home, the TV broken, an unpleasant smell hanging around in the bathroom. There was a swimming pool, but his eczema was so bad this summer that he wouldn't have been caught dead in a bathing suit. From the shins down he looked like a leper. He had an hour before the next workshop (Helping the Vocally Challenged Child—what they meant was doing something for kids who stuttered or who had cleft palates, but we wouldn't want to come right out and *say* that, Christ no, someone might lower our salaries), he had eaten lunch at San Remo's only restaurant, he didn't feel like a nap, and the TV's one station was showing a re-run of *Bewitched*.

So he sat down with the telephone book and began to flip through it aimlessly, hardly aware of what he was doing, wondering distantly if he knew anyone crazy enough about either small, lovely, or seaside to live in San Remo. He supposed this was what all the bored people in all the Holiday Inns all over the world ended up doing—looking for a forgotten friend or relative to call up on the phone. It was that, *Bewitched*, or the Gideon Bible. And if you did happen to get hold of somebody, what the hell did you say? "Frank! How the hell are you? And by the way, which was it—small, lovely, or seaside?" Sure. Right. Give that man a cigar and set him on fire.

Yet, as he lay on the bed flipping through the thin San Remo white pages and half-scanning the columns, it seemed to him that he *did* know somebody in San Remo. A book salesman? One of Sondra's nieces or nephews, of which there were marching battalions? A poker buddy from college? The relative of a student? That seemed to ring a bell, but he couldn't fine it down any more tightly.

He kept thumbing, and found he was sleepy after all. He had almost dozed off when it came to him and he sat up, wide-awake again.

Lord Peter!

They were re-running those Wimsey stories on PBS just lately—*Clouds of Witness, Murder Must Advertise, The Nine Tailors*. He and Sondra were hooked. A man named Ian Carmichael played Wimsey, and Sondra was nuts for him. So nuts, in fact, that Ed, who didn't think Carmichael looked like Lord Peter at all, actually became quite irritated.

"Sandy, the shape of his face is all wrong. And he's wearing false teeth, for heaven's sake!"

"Poo," Sondra had replied airily from the couch where she was curled up. "You're just jealous. He's so *handsome*."

"Daddy's jealous, Daddy's jealous," little Norma sang, prancing around the living room in her duck pajamas.

"You should have been in bed an hour ago," Ed told her, gazing at his daughter with a jaundiced eye. "And if I keep noticing you're *here*, I'll probably remember that you aren't *there*."

Little Norma was momentarily abashed. Ed turned back to Sondra.

"I remember back three or four years ago. I had a kid named Todd Bowden, and his grandfather came in for a conference. Now *that* guy looked like Wimsey. A very *old* Wimsey, but the shape of his face was right, and—"

"Wim-zee, Wim-zee, *Dim*-zee, *Jim*-zee," little Norma sang. "*Wim*-zee, *Bim*-zee, doodle-oodle-ooo-doo—"

"Shh, both of you," Sondra said. "I think he's the most *beautiful* man." Irritating woman!

But hadn't Todd Bowden's grandfather retired to San Remo? Sure. It had been on the forms. Todd had been one of the brightest boys in that year's class. Then, all at once, his grades had gone to hell. The old man had come in, told a familiar tale of marital difficulties, and had persuaded Ed to let the situation alone for awhile and see if things didn't straighten themselves out. Ed's view was that the old *laissez-faire* bit didn't work—if you told a teenage kid to root, hog, or die, he or she usually died. But the old man had been almost eerily persuasive (it was the resemblance to Wimsey, perhaps), and Ed had agreed to give Todd to the end of the next Flunk Card period. And damned if Todd hadn't pulled through. The old man must have gone right through the whole family and really kicked some ass, Ed thought. He looked like the type who not only could do it, but who might derive a certain dour pleasure from it. Then, just two days ago, he had seen Todd's picture in the paper—he had made the Southern Cal All-Stars in baseball. No mean feat when you considered that about five hundred boys were nominated each spring. He supposed he might never have come up with the grandfather's name if he hadn't seen the picture.

He flicked through the white pages more purposefully now, ran his finger down a column of fine type, and there it was. BOWDEN,

VICTOR S. 403 Ridge Lane. Ed dialed the number and it rang several times at the other end. He was just about to hang up when an old man answered. "Hello?"

"Hello, Mr. Bowden. Ed French. From Santo Donato Junior High."

"Yes?" Politeness, but no more. Certainly no recognition. Well, the old guy was three years further along (weren't they all!) and things undoubtedly slipped his mind from time to time.

"Do you remember me, sir?"

"Should I?" Bowden's voice was cautious, and Ed smiled. The old man forgot things, but he didn't want anybody to know if he could help it. His own old man had been that way when his hearing started to go.

"I was your grandson Todd's guidance counsellor at S.D.J.H.S. I called to congratulate you. He sure tore up the pea-patch when he got to high school, didn't he? And now he's All-Conference to top it off. Wow!"

"*Todd!*" the old man said, his voice brightening immediately. "Yes, he certainly did a fine job, didn't he? Second in his class! And the girl who was ahead of him took the business courses." A sniff of disdain in the old man's voice. "My son called and offered to take me to Todd's commencement, but I'm in a wheelchair now. I broke my hip last January. I didn't want to go in a wheelchair. But I have his graduation picture right in the hall, you bet! Todd's made his parents very proud. And me, of course."

"Yes, I guess we got him over the hump," Ed said. He was smiling as he said it, but his smile was a trifle puzzled—somehow Todd's grandfather didn't sound the same. But it had been a long time ago, of course.

"Hump? What hump?"

"That little talk we had. When Todd was having problems with his course-work. Back in ninth."

"I'm not following you," the old man said slowly. "I would never presume to speak for Richard's son. It would cause trouble . . . ho-ho, you don't *know* how much trouble it would cause. You've made a mistake, young fellow."

"But—"

"Some sort of mistake. Got me confused with another student and another grandfather, I imagine."

Ed was moderately thunderstruck. For one of the few times in his life, he could not think of a single thing to say. If there was confusion, it sure wasn't on *his* part.

"Well," Bowden said doubtfully, "it was nice of you to call, Mr. —"

Ed found his tongue. "I'm right here in town, Mr. Bowden. It's a convention. Guidance counsellors. I'll be done around ten tomorrow morning, after the final paper is read. Could I come around to . . . " He consulted the phone book again. ". . . to Ridge Lane and see you for a few minutes?"

"What in the world for?"

"Just curiosity, I guess. It's all water over the dam now. But about three years ago, Todd got himself into a real crack with his grades. They were so bad I had to send a letter home with his report card requesting a conference with a parent, or, ideally, with both of his parents. What I got was his grandfather, a very pleasant man named Victor Bowden."

"But I've already told you—"

"Yes. I know. Just the same, I talked to *somebody* claiming to be Todd's grandfather. It doesn't matter much now, I suppose, but seeing is believing. I'd only take a few minutes of your time. It's all I *can* take, because I'm expected home by suppertime."

"Time is all I have," Bowden said, a bit ruefully. "I'll be here all day. You're welcome to stop in."

Ed thanked him, said goodbye, and hung up. He sat on the end of the bed, staring thoughtfully at the telephone. After awhile he got up and took a pack of Phillies Cheroots from the sport coat hanging on the back of the desk chair. He ought to go; there was a workshop, and if he wasn't there, he would be missed. He lit his Cheroot with a Holiday Inn match and dropped the burnt stub into a Holiday Inn ashtray. He went to the Holiday Inn window and looked blankly out into the Holiday Inn courtyard.

It doesn't matter much now, he had told Bowden, but it mattered to him. He wasn't used to being sold a bill of goods by one of his kids, and this unexpected news upset him. Technically he supposed it could still turn out to be a case of an old man's senility, but Victor Bowden hadn't sounded as if he was drooling in his beard yet. And, damn it, he didn't sound the *same*.

Had Todd Bowden jobbed him?

He decided it could have been done. Theoretically, at least. Especially by a bright boy like Todd. He could have jobbed *everyone*, not just Ed French. He could have forged his mother or father's name to the Flunk Cards he had been issued during his bad patch. Lots of kids discovered a latent forging ability when they got Flunk Cards. He could have used ink eradicator on his second- and third-quarter reports, changing the grades up for his parents and then back down again so that his home-room teacher wouldn't notice anything weird if he or she glanced at his card. The double application of eradicator would be visible to someone who was really looking, but home-room teachers carried an average of sixty students each. They were lucky if they could get the entire roll called before the first bell, let alone spot-checking returned cards for tampering.

As for Todd's final class standing, it would have dipped perhaps no more than three points overall—two bad marking periods out of a total of twelve. His other grades had been lopsidedly good enough to make up most of the difference. And how many parents drop by the school to look at the student records kept by the California Department of Education? Especially the parents of a bright student like Todd Bowden?

Frown lines appeared on Ed French's normally smooth forehead.

It doesn't matter much now. That was nothing but the truth. Todd's high school work had been exemplary; there was no way in the world you could fake a 94 average. The boy was going on to Berkeley, the newspaper article had said, and Ed supposed his folks were damned proud—as they had every right to be. More and more it seemed to Ed that there was a vicious downside of American life, a greased skid of opportunism, cut corners, easy drugs, easy sex, a morality that grew cloudier each year. When your kid got through in standout style, parents had a right to be proud.

It doesn't matter much now—but who was his frigging grandfather?

That kept sticking into him. Who, indeed? Had Todd Bowden gone to the local branch office of the Screen Actors' Guild and hung a notice on the bulletin board? YOUNG MAN IN GRADES TROUBLE

NEEDS OLDER MAN, PREF. 70–80 YRS., TO GIVE BOFFO PERFORM-
ANCE AS GRANDFATHER, WILL PAY UNION SCALE? Uh-uh. No way,
José. And just what sort of adult would have fallen in with such a
crazy conspiracy, and for what reason?

Ed French, aka Pucker, aka Rubber Ed, just didn't know. And
because it didn't really matter, he stubbed out his Cheroot and went
to his workshop. But his attention kept wandering.

The next day he drove out to Ridge Lane and had a long talk with
Victor Bowden. They discussed grapes; they discussed the retail
grocery business and how the big chain stores were pushing the
little guys out; they discussed the political climate in southern
California. Mr Bowden offered Ed a glass of wine. Ed accepted with
pleasure. He felt that he needed a glass of wine, even if it was only
ten-forty in the morning. Victor Bowden looked as much like Peter
Wimsey as a machine-gun looks like a shillelagh. Victor Bowden
had no trace of the faint accent Ed remembered, and he was quite
fat. The man who had purported to be Todd's grandfather had been
whip-thin.

Before leaving, Ed told him: "I'd appreciate it if you wouldn't
mention any of this to Mr. or Mrs. Bowden. There may be a
perfectly reasonable explanation for all of it . . . and even if there
isn't, it's all in the past."

"Sometimes," Bowden said, holding his glass of wine up to the
sun and admiring its rich dark color, "the past don't rest so easy.
Why else do people study history?"

Ed smiled uneasily and said nothing.

"But don't you worry. I never meddle in Richard's affairs. And
Todd is a good boy. Salutatorian of his class . . . he must be a good
boy. Am I right?"

"As rain," Ed French said heartily, and then asked for another
glass of wine.

23

Dussander's sleep was uneasy; he lay in a trench of bad dreams.
They were breaking down the fence. Thousands, perhaps millions of

them. They ran out of the jungle and threw themselves against the electrified barbed wire and now it was beginning to lean ominously inward. Some of the strands had given way and now coiled uneasily on the packed earth of the parade ground, squirting blue sparks. And still there was no end to them, no end. The Fuehrer was as mad as Rommel had claimed if he thought now—if he had ever thought—there could be a final solution to this problem. There were billions of them; they filled the universe; and they were all after him.

"Old man. Wake up, old man. Dussander. Wake up, old man, wake up."

At first he thought this was the voice of the dream.

Spoken in German; it had to be part of the dream. That was why the voice was so terrifying, of course. If he awoke he would escape it, so he swam upward . . .

The man was sitting by his bed on a chair that had been turned around backwards—a real man. "Wake up, old man," this visitor was saying. He was young—no more than thirty. His eyes were dark and studious behind plain steel-framed glasses. His brown hair was longish, collar-length, and for a confused moment Dussander thought it was the boy in a disguise. But this was not the boy, wearing a rather old-fashioned blue suit much too hot for the California climate. There was a small silver pin on one lapel of the suit. Silver, the metal you used to kill vampires and werewolves. It was a Jewish star.

"Are you speaking to me?" Dussander asked in German.

"Who else? Your roommate is gone."

"Heisel? Yes. He went home yesterday."

"Are you awake now?"

"Of course. But you've apparently mistaken me for someone else. My name is Arthur Denker. Perhaps you have the wrong room."

"My name is Weiskopf. And yours is Kurt Dussander."

Dussander wanted to lick his lips but didn't. Just possibly this was still all part of the dream—a new phase, no more. *Bring me a wino and a steak-knife, Mr. Jewish Star in the Lapel, and I'll blow you away like smoke.*

"I know no Dussander," he told the young man. "I don't understand you. Shall I ring for the nurse?"

"You understand," Weiskopf said. He shifted position slightly and brushed a lock of hair from his forehead. The prosiness of this gesture dispelled Dussander's last hope.

"Heisel," Weiskopf said, and pointed at the empty bed.

"Heisel, Dussander, Weiskopf—none of these names mean anything to me."

"Heisel fell off a ladder while he was nailing a new gutter onto the side of his house," Weiskopf said. "He broke his back. He may never walk again. Unfortunate. But that was not the only tragedy of his life. He was an inmate of Patin, where he lost his wife and daughters. Patin, which you commanded."

"I think you are insane," Dussander said. "My name is Arthur Denker. I came to this country when my wife died. Before that I was—"

"Spare me your tale," Weiskopf said, raising a hand. "He had not forgotten your face. This face."

Weiskopf flicked a photograph into Dussander's face like a magician doing a trick. It was one of those the boy had shown him years ago. A young Dussander in a jauntily cocked SS cap, seated behind his desk.

Dussander spoke slowly, in English now, enunciating carefully.

"During the war I was a factory machinist. My job was to oversee the manufacture of drive-columns and power-trains for armored cars and trucks. Later I helped to build Tiger tanks. My reserve unit was called up during the battle of Berlin and I fought honorably, if briefly. After the war I worked in Essen, at the Menschler Motor Works until—"

"—until it became necessary for you to run away to South America. With your gold that had been melted down from Jewish teeth and your silver melted down from Jewish jewelry and your numbered Swiss bank account. Mr. Heisel went home a happy man, you know. Oh, he had a bad moment when he woke up in the dark and realized with whom he was sharing a room. But he feels better now. He feels that God allowed him the sublime privilege of breaking his back so that he could be instrumental in the capture of one of the greatest butchers of human beings ever to live."

Dussander spoke slowly, enunciating carefully.

"During the war I was a factory machinist—"

"Oh, why not drop it? Your papers will not stand up to a serious examination. I know it and you know it. You are found out."

"My job was to oversee the manufacture of—"

"Of corpses! One way or another, you will be in Tel Aviv before the new year. The authorities are cooperating with us this time, Dussander. The Americans want to make us happy, and you are one of the things that will make us happy."

"—the manufacture of drive-columns and power-trains for armored cars and trucks. Later I helped to build Tiger tanks."

"Why be tiresome? Why drag it out?"

"My reserve unit was called up—"

"Very well then. You'll see me again. Soon."

Weiskopf rose. He left the room. For a moment his shadow bobbed on the wall and then that was gone, too. Dussander closed his eyes. He wondered if Weiskopf could be telling the truth about American cooperation. Three years ago, when oil was tight in America, he wouldn't have believed it. But the current upheaval in Iran might well harden American support for Israel. It was possible. And what did it matter? One way or the other, legal or illegal, Weiskopf and his colleagues would have him. On the subject of Nazis they were intransigent, and on the subject of the camps they were lunatics.

He was trembling all over. But he knew what he must do now.

24

The school records for the pupils who had passed through Santo Donato Junior High were kept in an old, rambling warehouse on the north side. It was not far from the abandoned trainyard. It was dark and echoing and it smelled of wax and polish and 999 Industrial Cleaner—it was also the school department's custodial warehouse.

Ed French got there around four in the afternoon with Norma in tow. A janitor let them in, told Ed what he wanted was on the fourth floor, and showed them to a creeping, clanking elevator that frightened Norma into an uncharacteristic silence.

She regained herself on the fourth floor, prancing and capering up and down the dim aisles of stacked boxes and files while Ed searched for and eventually found the files containing report cards from 1975. He pulled the second box and began to leaf through the B's. BORK. BOSTWICK. BOSWELL. BOWDEN, TODD. He pulled the card, shook his head impatiently over it in the dim light, and took it across to one of the high, dusty windows.

"Don't run around in here, honey," he called over his shoulder.

"Why, Daddy?"

"Because the trolls will get you," he said, and held Todd's card up to the light.

He saw it at once. This report card, in those files for three years now, had been carefully, almost professionally, doctored.

"Jesus Chirst," Ed French muttered.

"Trolls, trolls, trolls!" Norma sang gleefully, as she continued to dance up and down the aisles.

25

Dussander walked carefully down the hospital corridor. He was still a bit unsteady on his legs. He was wearing his blue bathrobe over his white hospital johnny. It was night now, just after eight o'clock, and the nurses were changing shifts. The next half hour would be confused—he had observed that all the shift changes were confused. It was a time for exchanging notes, gossip, and drinking coffee at the nurses' station, which was just around the corner from the drinking fountain.

What he wanted was just across from the drinking fountain.

He was not noticed in the wide hallway, which at this hour reminded him of a long and echoing train station minutes before a passenger train departs. The walking wounded paraded slowly up and down, some dressed in robes as he was, others holding the backs of their johnnies together. Disconnected music came from half a dozen different transistor radios in half a dozen different rooms. Visitors came and went. A man laughed in one room and another man seemed to be weeping across the hall. A doctor walked by with his nose in a paperback novel.

Dussander went to the fountain, got a drink, wiped his mouth with his cupped hand, and looked at the closed door across the hall. This door was always locked—at least, that was the theory. In practice he had observed that it was sometimes both unlocked and unattended. Most often during the chaotic half hour when the shifts were changing and the nurses were gathered around the corner. Dussander had observed all of this with the trained and wary eye of a man who has been on the jump for a long, long time. He only wished he could observe the unmarked door for another week or so, looking for dangerous breaks in the pattern—he would only have the one chance. But he didn't have another week. His status as Werewolf in Residence might not become known for another two or three days, but it might happen tomorrow. He did not dare wait. When it came out, he would be watched constantly.

He took another small drink, wiped his mouth again, and looked both ways. Then, casually, with no effort at concealment, he stepped across the hall, turned the knob, and walked into the drug closet. If the woman in charge had happened to already be behind her desk, he was only nearsighted Mr. Denker. So sorry, dear lady, I thought it was the W.C. Stupid of me.

But the drug closet was empty.

He ran his eye over the top shelf at his left. Nothing but eyedrops and eardrops. Second shelf: laxatives, suppositories. On the third shelf he saw both Seconal and Veronal. He slipped a bottle of Seconals into the pocket of his robe. Then he went back to the door and stepped out without looking around, a puzzled smile on his face—that certainly wasn't the W.C., was it? *There* it was, right next to the drinking fountain. Stupid me!

He crossed to the door labelled MEN, went inside, and washed his hands. Then he went back down the hall to the semi-private room that was now completely private since the departure of the illustrious Mr. Heisel. On the table between the beds was a glass and a plastic pitcher filled with water. Pity there was no bourbon; really, it was a shame. But the pills would float him off just as nicely no matter how they were washed down.

"Morris Heisel, *salud*," he said with a faint smile, and poured himself a glass of water. After all those years of jumping at shadows, of seeing faces that looked familiar on park benches or in restaurants or bus terminals, he had finally been recognized and turned in by a man he wouldn't have known from Adam. It was almost funny. He had barely spared Heisel two glances, Heisel and his broken back from God. On second thought, it wasn't *almost* funny; it was *very* funny.

He put three pills in his mouth, swallowed them with water, took three more, then three more. In the room across the hall he could see two old men hunched over a night-table, playing a grumpy game of cribbage. One of them had a hernia, Dussander knew. What was the other? Gallstones? Kidney stones? Tumor? Prostate? The horrors of old age. They were legion.

He refilled his water glass but didn't take any more pills right away. Too many could defeat his purpose. He might throw them up and they would pump the residue out of his stomach, saving him for whatever indignities the Americans and the Israelis could devise. He had no intention of trying to take his life stupidly, like a *Hausfrau* on a crying jag. When he began to get drowsy, he would take a few more. That would be fine.

The quavering voice of one of the cribbage players came to him, thin and triumphant: "A double run of three for eight . . . fifteens for twelve . . . and the right jack for thirteen. How do you like *those* apples?"

"Don't worry," the old man with the hernia said confidently. "I got first count. I'll peg out."

Peg out, Dussander thought, sleepy now. An apt enough phrase— but the Americans had a turn for idiom. *I don't give a tin shit, get hip or get out, stick it where the sun don't shine, money talks, nobody walks.* Wonderful idiom.

They thought they had him, but he was going to peg out before their very eyes.

He found himself wishing, of all absurd things, that he could leave a note for the boy. Wishing he could tell him to be very careful. To listen to an old man who had finally overstepped himself. He wished he could tell the boy that in the end he, Dussander, had come to respect him, even if he could never like him, and that talking to him had been better than listening to the run of his own thoughts. But any note, no matter how innocent, might cast suspicion on the boy, and Dussander did not want that. Oh, he would have a bad month or two, waiting for some government agent to show up and question him about a certain document that had been found in a safety deposit box rented to

Kurt Dussander, aka Arthur Denker . . . but after a time, the boy would come to believe he had been telling the truth. There was no need for the boy to be touched by any of this, as long as he kept his head.

Dussander reached out with a hand that seemed to stretch for miles, got the glass of water, and took another three pills. He put the glass back, closed his eyes, and settled deeper into his soft, soft pillow. He had never felt so much like sleeping, and his sleep would be long. It would be restful.

Unless there were dreams.

The thought shocked him. *Dreams? Please God, no. Not those dreams. Not for eternity, not with all possibility of awakening gone. Not—*

In sudden terror, he tried to struggle awake. It seemed that hands were reaching eagerly up out of the bed to grab him, hands with hungry fingers.

(! NO !)

His thoughts broke up in a steepening spiral of darkness, and he rode down that spiral as if down a greased slide, down and down, to whatever dreams there are.

His overdose was discovered at 1:35 A.M., and he was pronounced dead fifteen minutes later. The nurse on duty was young and had been susceptible to elderly Mr. Denker's slightly ironic courtliness. She burst into tears. She was a Catholic, and she could not understand why such a sweet old man, who had been getting better, would want to do such a thing and damn his immortal soul to hell.

26

On Saturday morning in the Bowden household, nobody got up until at least nine. This morning at nine-thirty Todd and his father were reading at the table and Monica, who was a slow waker, served them scrambled eggs, juice, and coffee without speaking, still half in her dreams.

Todd was reading a paperback science fiction novel and Dick was absorbed in *Architectural Digest* when the paper slapped against the door.

"Want me to get it, Dad?"

"I will."

Dick brought it in, started to sip his coffee, and then choked on it as he got a look at the front page.

"Dick, what's wrong?" Monica asked, hurrying toward him.

Dick coughed out coffee that had gone down the wrong pipe, and while Todd looked at him over the top of his paperback in mild wonder, Monica started to pound him on the back. On the third stroke, her eyes fell to the paper's headline and she stopped in mid-stroke, as if playing statues. Her eyes widened until it seemed they might actually fall out onto the table.

"Holy God up in heaven!" Dick Bowden managed in a choked voice.

"Isn't that . . . I can't believe . . ." Monica began, and then stopped. She looked at Todd. "Oh, honey—"

His father was looking at him, too.

Alarmed now, Todd came around the table. "What's the matter?"

"Mr. Denker," Dick said—it was all he could manage.

Todd read the headline and understood everything. In dark letters it read: FUGITIVE NAZI COMMITS SUICIDE IN SANTO DONATO HOSPITAL. Below were two photos, side by side. Todd had seen both of them before. One showed Arthur Denker, six years younger and spryer. Todd knew it had been taken by a hippie street photographer, and that the old man had bought it only to make sure it didn't fall into the wrong hands by chance. The other photo showed an SS officer named Kurt Dussander behind his desk at Patin, his cap cocked to one side.

If they had the photograph the hippie had taken, they had been in his house.

Todd skimmed the article, his mind whizzing frantically. No mention of the winos. But the bodies would be found, and when they were, it would be a worldwide story. PATIN COMMANDANT NEVER LOST HIS TOUCH. HORROR IN NAZI'S BASEMENT. HE NEVER STOPPED KILLING.

Todd Bowden swayed on his feet.

Far away, echoing, he heard his mother cry sharply: "Catch him, Dick! He's fainting!"

The word
(faintingfaintingfainting)
repeated itself over and over. He dimly felt his father's arms grab him, and then for a little while Todd felt nothing, heard nothing at all.

27

Ed French was eating a danish when he unfolded the paper. He coughed, made a strange gagging sound, and spat dismembered pastry all over the table.

"Eddie!" Sondra French said with some alarm. "Are you okay?"

"Daddy's chokun, Daddy's chokun," little Norma proclaimed with nervous good humor, and then happily joined her mother in slamming Ed on the back. Ed barely felt the blows. He was still goggling down at the newspaper.

"What's wrong, Eddie?" Sondra asked again.

"Him! Him!" Ed shouted, stabbing his finger down at the paper so hard that his fingernail tore all the way through the A section. "That man! Lord Peter!"

"What in God's name are you t—"

"That's Todd Bowden's grandfather!"

"What? That war criminal? Eddie, that's *crazy!*"

"But it's *him*," Ed almost moaned. "Jesus Christ *Almighty*, that's *him!*"

Sondra French looked at the picture long and fixedly.

"He doesn't look like Peter Wimsey at all," she said finally.

28

Todd, pale as window-glass, sat on a couch between his mother and father.

Opposite them was a graying, polite police detective named Richler. Todd's father had offered to call the police, but Todd had done it himself, his voice cracking through the registers as it had done when he was fourteen.

He finished his recital. It hadn't taken long. He spoke with a mechanical colorlessness that scared the hell out of Monica. He was seventeen, true enough, but he was still a boy in so many ways. This was going to scar him forever.

"I read him . . . oh, I don't know. *Tom Jones. The Mill on the Floss.* That was a boring one. I didn't think we'd ever get through it. Some stories by Hawthorne—I remember he especially liked 'The Great Stone Face' and 'Young Goodman Brown.' We started *The Pickwick Papers,* but he didn't like it. He said Dickens could only be funny when he was being serious, and *Pickwick* was only kittenish. That was his word, kittenish. We got along the best with *Tom Jones.* We both liked that one."

"And that was three years ago," Richler said.

"Yes. I kept stopping in to see him when I got the chance, but in high school we were bussed across town . . . and some of the kids got up a scratch ballteam . . . there was more homework . . . you know . . . things just came up."

"You had less time."

"Less time, that's right. The work in high school was a lot harder . . . making the grades to get into college."

"But Todd is a very apt pupil," Monica said almost automatically. "He graduated salutatorian. We were so proud."

"I'll bet you were," Richler said with a warm smile. "I've got two boys in Fairview, down in the Valley, and they're just about able to keep their sports eligibility." He turned back to Todd. "You didn't read him any more books after you started high school?"

"No. Once in awhile I'd read him the paper. I'd come over and he'd ask me what the headlines were. He was interested in Watergate when that was going on. And he always wanted to know about the stock market, and the print on that page used to drive him batshit—sorry, Mom."

She patted his hand.

"I don't know why he was interested in the stocks, but he was."

"He had a few stocks," Richler said. "That's how he was getting by. He also had five different sets of ID salted around that house. He was a cagey one, all right."

"I suppose he kept the stocks in a safe deposit box somewhere," Todd remarked.

"Pardon me?" Richler raised his eyebrows.

"His stocks," Todd said. His father, who had also looked puzzled, now nodded at Richler.

"His stock certificates, the few that were left, were in a footlocker under his bed," Richler said, "along with that photo of him as Denker. Did he have a safety deposit box, son? Did he ever say he did?"

Todd thought, and then shook his head. "I just thought that was where you kept your stocks. I don't know. This . . . this whole thing has just . . . you know . . . it blows my wheels." He shook his head in a dazed way that was perfectly real. He really *was* dazed. Yet, little by little, he felt his instinct of self-preservation surfacing. He felt a growing alertness, and the first stirrings of confidence. If Dussander had really taken a safety deposit box in which to store his insurance document, wouldn't he have transferred his remaining stock certificates there? And that photograph?

"We're working with the Israelis on this," Richler said. "In a very unofficial way. I'd be grateful if you didn't mention that if you decide to see any press people. They're real professionals. There's a man named Weiskopf who'd like to talk to you tomorrow, Todd. If that's okay by you and your folks."

"I guess so," Todd said, but he felt a touch of atavistic dread at the thought of being sniffed over by the same hounds that had chased Dussander for the last half of his life. Dussander had had a healthy respect for them, and Todd knew he would do well to keep that in mind.

"Mr. and Mrs. Bowden? Do you have any objections to Todd seeing Mr. Weiskopf?"

"Not if Todd doesn't," Dick Bowden said. "I'd like to be present, though. I've read about these Mossad characters—"

"Weiskopf isn't Mossad. He's what the Israelis call a special operative. In fact, he teaches Yiddish literature and English grammar. Also, he's written two novels." Richler smiled.

Dick raised a hand, dismissing it. "Whatever he is, I'm not going to let him badger Todd. From what I've read, these fellows can be a little *too* professional. Maybe he's okay. But I want you and this Weiskopf to remember that Todd tried to help that old man. He was flying under false colors, but Todd didn't know that."

"That's okay, Dad," Todd said with a wan smile.

"I just want you to help us all that you can," Richler said. "I appreciate your concern, Mr. Bowden. I think you're going to find that Weiskopf is a pleasant, low-pressure kind of guy. I've finished my own questions, but I'll break a little ground by telling you what the Israelis are most interested in. Todd was with Dussander when he had the heart attack that landed him in the hospital—"

"He asked me to come over and read him a letter," Todd said.

"We know." Richler leaned forward, elbows on his knees, tie swinging out to form a plumb-line to the floor. "The Israelis want to know about that letter. Dussander was a big fish, but he wasn't the last one in the lake—or so Sam Weiskopf says, and I believe him. They think Dussander might have known about a lot of the other fish. Most of those still alive are probably in South America, but there may be others in a dozen countries . . . including the United States. Did you know they collared a man who had been an *Unterkommandant* at Buchenwald in the lobby of a Tel Aviv hotel?"

"Really!" Monica said, her eyes widening.

"Really," Richler nodded. "Two years ago. The point is just that the Israelis think the letter Dussander wanted Todd to read might have been from one of those other fish. Maybe they're right, maybe they're wrong. Either way, they want to know."

Todd, who had gone back to Dussander's house and burned the letter, said: "I'd help you—or this Weiskopf—if I could, Lieutenant Richler, but the letter was in German. It was really tough to read. I felt like a fool. Mr. Denker . . . Dussander . . . kept getting more excited and asking me to spell the words he couldn't understand because of my, you know, pronunciation. But I guess he was following all right. I remember once he laughed and said, 'Yes, yes, that is what you'd do, isn't it?' Then he said something in German. This was about two or three minutes before he had the heart attack. Something about *Dummkopf*. That means stupid in German, I think."

He was looking at Richler uncertainly, inwardly quite pleased with this lie.

Richler was nodding. "Yes, we understand that the letter was in German. The admitting doctor heard the story from you and

corroborated it. But the letter *itself*, Todd . . . do you remember
what happened to it?"

Here it is, Todd thought. *The crunch.*

"I guess it was still on the table when the ambulance came.
When we all left. I couldn't testify to it in court, but—"

"I think there was a letter on the table," Dick said. "I picked
something up and glanced at it. Airmail stationery, I think, but I
didn't notice it was written in German."

"Then it should still be there," Richler said. "That's what we
can't figure out."

"It's not?" Dick said. "I mean, it wasn't?"

"It wasn't, and it isn't."

"Maybe somebody broke in," Monica suggested.

"There would have been no need to *break* in," Richler said. "In
the confusion of getting him out, the house was never locked.
Dussander himself never thought to ask someone to lock up,
apparently. His latchkey was still in the pocket of his pants when he
died. His house was unlocked from the time the MED-Q attendants
wheeled him out until we sealed it this morning at two-thirty
A.M."

"Well, there you are," Dick said.

"No," Todd said. "I see what's bugging Lieutenant Richler." Oh
yes, he saw it very well. You'd have to be blind to miss it. "Why
would a burglar steal nothing but a letter? Especially one written in
German? It doesn't listen. Mr. Denker didn't have much to steal,
but a guy who broke in could find something better than that."

"You've got it, all right," Richler said. "Not bad."

"Todd used to want to be a detective when he grew up," Monica
said, and ruffled Todd's hair a bit. Since he had gotten big he
seemed to object to that, but right now he didn't seem to mind.
God, she hated to see him looking so pale. "I guess he's changed his
mind to history these days."

"History is a good field," Richler said. "You can be an
investigative historian. Have you ever read Josephine Tey?"

"No, sir."

"Doesn't matter. I just wish my boys had some ambition greater
than seeing the Angels win the pennant this year."

Todd offered a wan smile and said nothing.

Richler turned serious again. "Anyway, I'll tell you the theory we're going on. We figure that someone, probably right here in Santo Donato, knew who and what Dussander was."

"Really?" Dick said.

"Oh yes. Someone who knew the truth. Maybe another fugitive Nazi. I know that sounds like Robert Ludlum stuff, but who would have thought there was even *one* fugitive Nazi in a quiet little suburb like this? And when Dussander was taken to the hospital, we think that Mr. X scooted over to the house and got that incriminating letter. And that by now it's so many decomposing ashes floating around in the sewer system."

"That doesn't make much sense either," Todd said.

"Why not, Todd?"

"Well, if Mr. Denk . . . if *Dussander* had an old buddy from the camps, or just an old Nazi buddy, why did he bother to have me come over and read him that letter? I mean, if you could have heard him correcting me, and stuff . . . at least this old Nazi buddy you're talking about would know how to speak German."

"A good point. Except maybe this other fellow is in a wheelchair, or blind. For all we know, it might be Bormann himself and he doesn't even dare go out and show his face."

"Guys that are blind or in wheelchairs aren't that good at scooting out to get letters," Todd said.

Richler looked admiring again. "True. But a blind man could steal a letter even if he couldn't read it, though. Or hire it done."

Todd thought this over, and nodded—but he shrugged at the same time to show how farfetched he thought the idea. Richler had progressed far beyond Robert Ludlum and into the land of Sax Rohmer. But how farfetched the idea was or wasn't didn't matter one fucking little bit, did it? No. What mattered was that Richler was still sniffing around . . . and that sheeny, Weiskopf, was also sniffing around. The letter, the goddam letter! Dussander's stupid goddam idea! And suddenly he was thinking of his .30-.30, cased and resting on its shelf in the cool, dark garage. He pulled his mind away from it quickly. The palms of his hands had gone damp.

"*Did* Dussander have any friends that you knew of?" Richler was asking.

"Friends? No. There used to be a cleaning lady, but she moved away and he didn't bother to get another one. In the summer he hired a kid to mow his lawn, but I don't think he'd gotten one this year. The grass is pretty long, isn't it?"

"Yes. We've knocked on a lot of doors, and it doesn't seem as if he'd hired anyone. Did he get phone calls?"

"Sure," Todd said off-handedly . . . here was a gleam of light, a possible escape-hatch that was relatively safe. Dussander's phone had actually rung only half a dozen times or so in all the time Todd had known him—salesmen, a polling organization asking about breakfast foods, the rest wrong numbers. He only had the phone in case he got sick . . . as he finally had, might his soul rot in hell. "He used to get a call or two every week."

"Did he speak German on those occasions?" Richler asked quickly. He seemed excited.

"No," Todd said, suddenly cautious. He didn't like Richler's excitement—there was something wrong about it, something dangerous. He felt sure of it, and suddenly Todd had to work furiously to keep himself from breaking a sweat. "He didn't talk much at all. I remember that a couple of times he said things like, 'The boy who reads to me is here right now. I'll call you back.' "

"I'll bet that's it!" Richler said, whacking his palms on his thighs. "I'd bet two weeks' pay that was the guy!" He closed his notebook with a snap (so far as Todd could see he had done nothing but doodle in it) and stood up. "I want to thank all three of you for your time. You in particular, Todd. I know all of this has been a hell of a shock to you, but it will be over soon. We're going to turn the house upside down this afternoon—cellar to attic and then back down to the cellar again. We're bringing in all the special teams. We may find some trace of Dussander's phonemate yet."

"I hope so," Todd said.

Richler shook hands all around and left. Dick asked Todd if he felt like going out back and hitting the badminton birdie around until lunch. Todd said he didn't feel much like badminton *or* lunch, and went upstairs with his head down and his shoulders slumped. His parents exchanged sympathetic, troubled glances. Todd lay down on his bed, stared at the ceiling, and thought about his .30-.30. He could see it very clearly in his mind's eye. He thought about shoving the blued steel barrel right up Betty Trask's slimy Jewish cooze—just what she needed, a prick that never went soft. *How do you like it, Betty?* he heard himself asking her. *You just tell me if you get enough, okay?* He imagined her screams. And at last a terrible flat smile came to his face. *Sure, just tell me, you bitch . . . okay? Okay? Okay? . . .*

"So what do you think?" Weiskopf asked Richler when Richler picked him up at a luncheonette three blocks from the Bowden home.

"Oh, I think the kid was in on it somehow," Richler said. "Somehow, some way, to some degree. But is he cool? If you poured hot water into his mouth I think he'd spit out ice-cubes. I tripped him up a couple of times, but I've got nothing I could use in court. And if I'd gone much further, some smart lawyer might be able to get him off on entrapment a year or two down the road even if something *does* pull together. I mean, the courts are still going to look at him as a juvenile—the kid's only seventeen. In some ways, I'd guess he hasn't *really* been a juvenile since he was maybe eight. He's creepy, man." Richler stuck a cigarette in his mouth and laughed—the laugh had a shaky sound. "I mean, really fuckin creepy."

"What slips did he make?"

"The phone calls. That's the main thing. When I slipped him the idea, I could see his eyes light up like a pinball machine." Richler turned left and wheeled the nondescript Chevy Nova down the freeway entrance ramp. Two hundred yards to their right was the slope and the dead tree where Todd had dry-fired his rifle at the freeway traffic one Saturday morning not long ago.

"He's saying to himself, 'This cop is off the wall if he thinks Dussander had a Nazi friend here in town, but if he *does* think that, it takes me off ground-zero.' So he says yeah, Dussander got one or two calls a week. Very mysterious. 'I can't talk now, Z-five, call later'—that type of thing. But Dussander's been getting a special 'quiet phone' rate for the last seven years. Almost no activity at all, and *no* long distance. He wasn't getting a call or two a week."

"What else?"

"He immediately jumped to the conclusion that the letter was gone and nothing else. He knew that was the only thing missing because he was the one who went back and took it."

Richler jammed his cigarette out in the ashtray.

"We *think* the letter was just a prop. We *think* that Dussander had the heart attack while he was trying to bury that body . . . the freshest body. There was dirt on his shoes and his cuffs, and so that's a pretty fair assumption. That means he called the kid *after* he had the heart attack, not before. He crawls upstairs and phones the kid. The kid flips out—as much as he ever flips out, anyway—and cooks up the letter story on the spur of the moment. It's not great, but not that bad, either . . . considering the circumstances. He goes over there and cleans up Dussander's mess for him. Now the kid is in fucking overdrive. MED-Q's coming, his father is coming, and he needs that letter for stage-dressing. He goes upstairs and breaks open that box—"

"You've got confirmation on that?" Weiskopf asked, lighting a cigarette of his own. It was an unfiltered Player, and to Richler it smelled like horseshit. No wonder the British Empire fell, he thought, if they started smoking cigarettes like that.

"Yes, we've got confirmation right up the ying-yang," Richler said. "There are fingerprints on the box which match those in his school records. But his fingerprints are on almost *everything* in the goddam house!"

"Still, if you confront him with all of that, you can rattle him," Weiskopf said.

"Oh, listen, hey, you don't know this kid. When I said he was cool, I meant it. He'd say Dussander asked him to fetch the box once or twice so he could put something in it or take something out of it."

"His fingerprints are on the shovel."

"He'd say he used it to plant a rose-bush in the back yard." Richler took out his cigarettes but the pack was empty. Weiskopf offered him a Player. Richler took one puff and began coughing. "They taste as bad as they smell," he choked.

"Like those hamburgers we had for lunch yesterday," Weiskopf said, smiling. "Those Mac-Burgers."

"Big Macs," Richler said, and laughed. "Okay. So cross-cultural pollination doesn't always work." His smile faded. "He looks so clean-cut, you know?"

"Yes."

"This is no j.d. from Vasco with hair down to his asshole and chains on his motorcycle boots."

"No." Weiskopf stared at the traffic all around them and was very glad he wasn't driving. "He's just a boy. A white boy from a good home. And I find it difficult to believe that—"

"I thought you had them ready to handle rifles and grenades by the time they were eighteen. In Israel."

"Yes. But he was *fourteen* when all of this started. Why would a fourteen-year-old boy mix himself up with such a man as Dussander? I have tried and tried to understand that and still I can't."

"I'd settle for how," Richler said, and flicked the cigarette out the window. It was giving him a headache.

"Perhaps, if it did happen, it was just luck. A coincidence. Serendipity. I think there is black serendipity as well as white."

"I don't know what you're talking about," Richler said gloomily. "All I know is the kid is creepier than a bug under a rock."

"What I'm saying is simple. Any other boy would have been more than happy to tell his parents, or the police. To say, 'I have recognized a wanted man. He is living at this address. Yes, I am sure.' And then let the authorities take over. Or do you feel I am wrong?"

"No, I wouldn't say so. The kid would be in the limelight for a few days. Most kids would dig that. Picture in the paper, an interview on the evening news, probably a school assembly award for good citizenship." Richler laughed. "Hell, the kid would probably get a shot on *Real People*."

"What't that?"

"Never mind," Richler said. He had to raise his voice slightly because ten-wheelers were passing the Nova on either side. Weiskopf looked nervously from one to the other. "You don't want to know. But you're right about most kids. *Most* kids."

"But not *this* kid," Weiskopf said. "This boy, probably by dumb luck alone, penetrates Dussander's cover. Yet instead of going to his parents or the authorities . . . he goes to Dussander. Why? You say you don't care, but I think you do. I think it haunts you just as it does me."

"Not blackmail," Richler said. "That's for sure. That kid's got everything a kid could want. There was a dune-buggy in the garage, not to mention an elephant gun on the wall. And even if he wanted to squeeze Dussander just for the thrill of it, Dussander was practically unsqueezable. Except for those few stocks, he didn't have a pot to piss in."

"How sure are you that the boy doesn't know you've found the bodies?"

"I'm sure. Maybe I'll go back this afternoon and hit him with that. Right now it looks like our best shot." Richler struck the steering wheel lightly. "If all of this had come out even one day sooner, I think I would have tried for a search warrant."

"The clothes the boy was wearing that night?"

"Yeah. If we could have found soil samples on his clothes that matched the dirt in Dussander's cellar, I almost think we could break him. But the clothes he was wearing that night have probably been washed six times since then."

"What about the other dead winos? The ones your police department has been finding around the city?"

"Those belong to Dan Bozeman. I don't think there's any connection anyhow. Dussander just wasn't that strong . . . and more to the point, he had such a neat little racket already worked out. Promise them a drink and a meal, take them home on the city bus—the fucking city bus!—and waste them right in his kitchen."

Weiskopf said quietly: "It wasn't *Dussander* I was thinking of."

"What do you mean by th—" Richler began, and then his mouth snapped suddenly closed. There was a long, unbelieving moment of silence, broken only by the drone of the traffic all around them. Then Richler said softly: "Hey. Hey, come on now. Give me a fucking br—"

"As an agent of my government, I am only interested in Bowden because of what, if anything, he may know about Dussander's remaining contacts with the Nazi underground. But as a human being, I am becoming more and more interested in the boy himself. I'd like to know what makes him tick. I want to know *why*. And as I try to answer that question to my own satisfaction, I find that more and more I am asking myself *What else*."

"But—"

"Do you suppose, I ask myself, that the very atrocities in which Dussander took part formed the basis of some attraction between them? That's an unholy idea, I tell myself. The things that happened in those camps still have power enough to make the stomach flutter with nausea. I feel that way myself, although the only close relative I ever had in the camps was my grandfather, and he died when I was three. But maybe there is something about what the Germans did that exercises a deadly fascination over us—something that opens the catacombs of the imagination. Maybe part of our dread and horror comes from a secret knowledge that under the right—or wrong—set of circumstances, we ourselves would be willing to build such places and staff them. Black serendipity. Maybe we know that under the right set of circumstances the things that live in the catacombs would be glad to crawl out. And what do you think they would look like? Like mad Fuehrers with forelocks and shoe-polish moustaches, *heil*-ing all over the place? Like red devils, or demons, or the dragon that floats on its stinking reptile wings?"

"I don't know," Richler said.

"I think most of them would look like ordinary accountants," Weiskopf said. "Little mind-men with graphs and flow-charts and electronic calculators, all ready to start maximizing the kill ratios so that *next* time they could perhaps kill twenty or thirty millions instead of only six. And some of them might look like Todd Bowden."

"You're damn near as creepy as he is," Richler said.

Weiskopf nodded. "It's a creepy subject. Finding those dead men and animals in Dussander's cellar . . . *that* was creepy, *nu?* Have you ever thought that maybe this boy began with a simple interest in the camps? An interest not much different from the interests of boys who collect coins or stamps or who like to read about Wild West desperados? And that he went to Dussander to get his information straight from the horse's head?"

"Mouth," Richler said automatically. "Man, at this point I could believe anything."

"Maybe," Weiskopf muttered. It was almost lost in the roar of another ten-wheeler passing them. BUDWEISER was printed on the side in letters six feet tall. *What an amazing country,* Weiskopf thought, and lit a fresh cigarette. *They don't understand how we can live surrounded by half-mad Arabs, but if I lived here for two years I would have a nervous breakdown.* "Maybe. And maybe it isn't possible to stand close to murder piled on murder and not be touched by it."

29

The short guy who entered the squadroom brought stench after him like a wake. He smelled like rotten bananas and Wildroot Cream Oil and cockroach shit and the inside of a city garbage truck at the end of a busy morning. He was dressed in a pair of ageing herringbone pants, a ripped gray institutional shirt, and a faded blue warmup jacket from which most of the zipper hung loose like a string of pygmy teeth. The uppers of his shoes were bound to the lowers with Krazy Glue. A pestiferous hat sat on his head.

"Oh Christ, get out of here!" The duty sergeant cried. "You're not under arrest, Hap! I swear to God! I swear it on my mother's name! Get out of here! I want to breathe again."

"I want to talk to Lieutenant Bozeman."

"He died, Hap. It happened yesterday. We're all really fucked up over it. So get out and let us mourn in peace."

"I want to talk to Lieutenant Bozeman!" Hap said more loudly. His breath drifted fragrantly from his mouth: a juicy, fermenting mixture of pizza, Hall's Mentho-lyptus lozenges, and sweet red wine.

"He had to go to Siam on a case, Hap. So why don't you just get out of here? Go someplace and eat a lightbulb."

"I want to talk to Lieutenant Bozeman and I ain't leaving until I do!"

The duty sergeant fled the room. He returned about five minutes later with Bozeman, a thin, slightly stooped man of fifty.

"Take him into your office, okay, Dan?" the duty sergeant begged. "Won't that be all right?"

"Come on, Hap," Bozeman said, and a minute later they were in the three-sided stall that was Bozeman's office. Bozeman prudently opened his only window and turned on his fan before sitting down. "Do something for you, Hap?"

"You still on those murders, Lieutenant Bozeman?"

"The derelicts? Yeah, I guess that's still mine."

"Well, I know who greased 'em."

"Is that so, Hap?" Bozeman asked. He was busy lighting his pipe. He rarely smoked the pipe, but neither the fan nor the open window was quite enough to overwhelm Hap's smell. Soon, Bozeman thought, the paint would begin to blister and peel. He sighed.

"You member I tole you Poley was talkin to a guy just a day before they found him all cut up in that pipe? You member me tellin you that, Lieutenant Bozeman?"

"I remember." Several of the winos who hung around the Salvation Army and the soup kitchen a few blocks away had told a similar story about two of the murdered derelicts, Charles "Sonny" Brackett and Peter "Poley" Smith. They had seen a guy hanging around, a young guy, talking to Sonny and Poley. Nobody knew for sure if Sonny had gone off with the guy, but Hap and two others claimed to have seen Poley Smith walk off with him. They had the idea that the "guy" was underage and willing to spring for a bottle of musky in exchange for some juice. Several other winos claimed to have seen a "guy" like that around. The description of this "guy" was superb, bound to stand up in court, coming as it did from such unimpeachable sources. Young, blonde, and white. What else did you need to make a bust?

"Well, last night I was in the park," Hap said, "and I just happened to have this old bunch of newspapers—"

"There's a law against vagrancy in this city, Hap."

"I was just collectin em up," Hap said righteously. "It's so awful the way people litter. I was doon a public surface, Lieutenant. A friggin public surface. Some of those papers was a week old."

"Yes, Hap," Bozeman said. He remembered—vaguely—being quite hungry and looking forward keenly to his lunch. That time seemed long ago now.

"Well, when I woke up, one of those papers had blew onto my face and I was lookin right *at* the guy. Gave me a hell of a jump, I can tell you. Look. This is the guy. This guy right here."

Hap pulled a crumpled, yellowed, water-spotted sheet of newspaper from his warmup jacket and unfolded it. Bozeman leaned forward, now moderately interested. Hap put the paper on his desk so he could read the headline: 4 BOYS NAMED TO SOUTHERN CAL ALL-STARS. Below the head were four photos.

"Which one, Hap?"

Hap put a grimy finger on the picture to the far right. "Him. It says his name is Todd Bowden."

Bozeman looked from the picture to Hap, wondering how many of Hap's brain-cells were still unfried and in some kind of working order after twenty years of being sautéed in a bubbling sauce of cheap wine seasoned with an occasional shot of sterno.

"How can you be sure, Hap? He's wearing a baseball cap in the picture. I can't tell if he's got blonde hair or not."

"The grin," Hap said. "It's the way he's grinnin. He was grinnin at Poley in just that same ain't-life-grand way when they walked off together. I couldn't mistake that grin in a million years. That's him, that's the guy."

Bozeman barely heard this last; he was thinking, and thinking hard. *Todd Bowden*. There was something very familiar about that name. Something that bothered him even worse than the thought that a local high school hero might be going around and offing winos. He thought he had heard that name just this morning in conversation. He frowned, trying to remember where.

Hap was gone and Dan Bozeman was still trying to figure it out when Richler and Weiskopf came in . . . and it was the sound of their voices as they got coffee in the squadroom that finally brought it home to him.

"Holy God," said Lieutenant Bozeman, and got up in a hurry.

30

Both of his parents had offered to cancel their afternoon plans—Monica at the market and Dick golfing with some business people—and stay home with him, but Todd told them he would rather be alone. He thought he would clean his rifle and just sort of think the whole thing over. Try to get it straight in his mind.

"Todd," Dick said, and suddenly found he had nothing much to say. He supposed if he had been his own father, he would have at this point advised prayer. But the generations had turned, and the Bowdens weren't much into that these days. "Sometimes these things happen," he finished lamely, because Todd was still looking at him. "Try not to brood about it."

"I'll be all right," Todd said.

After they were gone, he took some rags and a bottle of Alpaca gun oil out onto the bench beside the roses. He went back into the garage and got the .30-.30. He took it to the bench and broke it down, the dusty-sweet smell of the flowers lingering pleasantly in his nose. He cleaned the gun thoroughly, humming a tune as he did it, sometimes whistling a snatch between his teeth. Then he put the gun together again. He could have done it just as easily in the dark. His mind wandered free. When it came back some five minutes later, he observed that he had loaded the gun. The idea of target-shooting didn't much appeal, not today, but he had still loaded it. He told himself he didn't know why.

Sure you do, Todd-baby. The time, so to speak, has come.

And that was when the shiny yellow Saab turned into the driveway. The man who got out was vaguely familiar to Todd, but it wasn't until he slammed the car door and started to walk toward him that Todd saw the sneakers—low-topped Keds, light blue. Talk about Blasts from the Past; here, walking up the Bowden driveway, was Rubber Ed French, The Ked Man.

"Hi, Todd. Long time no see."

Todd leaned the rifle against the side of the bench and offered his wide and winsome grin. "Hi, Mr. French. What are you doing out here on the wild side of town?"

"Are your folks home?"

"Gee, no. Did you want them for something?"

"No," Ed French said after a long, thoughtful pause. "No, I guess not. I guess maybe it would be better if just you and I talked. For starters, anyway. You may be able to offer a perfectly reasonable explanation for all this. Although God knows I doubt it."

He reached into his hip pocket and brought out a newsclipping. Todd knew what it was even before Rubber Ed passed it to him, and for the second time that day he was looking at the side-by-side pictures of Dussander. The one the street photographer had taken had been circled in black ink. The meaning was clear enough to Todd; French had recognized Todd's "grandfather." And now he wanted to tell everyone in the world all about it. He wanted to midwife the good news. Good old Rubber Ed, with his jive talk and his motherfucking sneakers.

The police would be very interested—but, of course, they already were. He knew that now. The sinking feeling had begun about thirty minutes after Richler left. It was as if he had been riding high in a balloon filled with happy-gas. Then a cold steel arrow had ripped through the balloon's fabric, and now it was sinking steadily.

The phone calls, that was the biggie. Richler had trotted that out just as slick as warm owlshit. *Sure,* he had said, practically breaking his neck to rush into the trap. *He gets one or two calls a week.* Let them go ranting all over southern California looking for geriatric ex-Nazis. Fine. Except maybe they had gotten a different story from Ma Bell. Todd didn't know if the phone company could tell how much your phone got used . . . but there had been a look in Richler's eyes . . .

Then there was the letter. He had inadvertently told Richler that the house hadn't been burgled, and Richler had no doubt gone away thinking that the only way Todd could have known that was if he had been back . . . as he had been, not just once but three times, first to get the letter and twice more looking for anything incriminating. There had been nothing; even the SS uniform was gone, disposed of by Dussander sometime during the last four years.

And then there were the bodies. Richler had never mentioned the bodies.

At first Todd had thought that was good. Let them hunt a little longer while he got his own head—not to mention his story—straight. No fear about the dirt that had gotten on his clothes burying the body; they had all been cleaned later that same night. He ran them through the washer-dryer himself, perfectly aware that Dussander might die and then everything might come out. You can't be too careful, boy, as Dussander himself would have said.

Then, little by little, he had realized it was *not* good. The weather had been warm, and the warm weather always made the cellar smell worse; on his last trip to Dussander's house it had been a rank presence. Surely the police would have been interested in that smell, and would have tracked it to its source. So why had Richler withheld the information? Was he saving it for later? Saving it for a nasty little surprise? And if Richler was into planning nasty little surprises, it could only mean that he suspected.

Todd looked up from the clipping and saw that Rubber Ed had half-turned away from him. He was looking into the street, although not much was happening out there. Richler could suspect, but suspicion was the best he could do.

Unless there was some sort of concrete evidence binding Todd to the old man.

Exactly the sort of evidence Rubber Ed French could give.

Ridiculous man in a pair of ridiculous sneakers. Such a ridiculous man hardly deserved to live. Todd touched the barrel of the .30-.30.

Yes, Rubber Ed was a link they didn't have. They could *never* prove that Todd had been an accessory to one of Dussander's murders. But with Rubber Ed's testimony they could prove conspiracy. And would even *that* end it? Oh, no. They would get his high school graduation picture next and start showing it to the stewbums down in the Mission district. A long shot, but one Richler could ill afford not to play. If we can't pin one bunch of winos on him, maybe we can get him for the other bunch.

What next? Court next.

His father would get him a wonderful bunch of lawyers, of course. And the lawyers would get him off, of course. Too much circumstantial evidence. He would make too favorable an impression on the jury. But by then his life would be ruined anyway, just as Dussander had said it would be. It would all be dragged through the newspapers, dug up and brought into the light like the half-decayed bodies in Dussander's cellar.

"The man in that picture is the man who came to my office when you were in the ninth grade." Ed told him abruptly, turning to Todd again. "He purported to be your grandfather. Now it turns out he was a wanted war criminal."

"Yes," Todd said. His face had gone oddly blank. It was the face of a department-store dummy. All the healthiness, life, and vivacity had drained from it. What was left was frightening in its vacuous emptiness.

"How did it happen?" Ed asked, and perhaps he intended his question as a thundering accusation, but it came out sounding plaintive and lost and somehow cheated. "How did this happen, Todd?"

"Oh, one thing just followed another," Todd said, and picked up the .30-.30. "That's really how it happened. One thing just . . . followed another." He pushed the safety catch to the off position with his thumb and pointed the rifle at Rubber Ed. "As stupid as it sounds, that's just what happened. That's all there was to it."

"Todd," Ed said, his eyes widening. He took a step backwards. "Todd, you don't want to . . . please, Todd. We can talk this over. We can disc—"

"You and the fucking kraut can discuss it down in hell," Todd said, and pulled the trigger.

The sound of the shot rolled away in the hot and windless quiet of the afternoon. Ed French was flung back against his Saab. His hand groped behind him and tore off a windshield wiper. He stared at it foolishly as blood spread on his blue turtleneck, and then he dropped it and looked at Todd.

"Norma," he whispered.

"Okay," Todd said. "Whatever you say, champ." He shot Rubber Ed again and roughly half of his head disappeared in a spray of blood and bone.

Ed turned drunkenly and began to grope toward the driver's-side door, speaking his daughter's name over and over again in a choked and failing voice. Todd shot him again, aiming for the base of the spine, and Ed fell down. His feet drummed briefly on the gravel and then were still.

Sure did die hard for a guidance counsellor, Todd thought, and brief laughter escaped him. At the same moment a burst of pain as sharp as an icepick drove into his brain and he closed his eyes.

When he opened them again, he felt better than he had in months—maybe better than he had felt in years. Everything was fine. Everything was together. The blankness left his face and a kind of wild beauty filled it.

He went back into the garage and got all the shells he had, better than four hundred rounds. He put them in his old knapsack and shouldered it. When he came back out into the sunshine he was smiling excitedly, his eyes dancing—it was the way boys smile on their birthdays, on Christmas, on the Fourth of July. It was a smile that betokened skyrockets, treehouses, secret signs and secret meeting-places, the aftermath of the triumphal big game when the players are carried out of the stadium and into town on the shoulders of the exultant fans. The ecstatic smile of tow-headed boys going off to war in coal-scuttle helmets.

"I'm king of the world!" he shouted mightily at the high blue sky, and raised the rifle two-handed over his head for a moment. Then, switching it to his right hand, he started toward that place above the freeway where the land fell away and where the dead tree would give him shelter.

It was five hours later and almost dark before they took him down.

Fall from Innocence

For George McLeod

The Body

1

The most important things are the hardest things to say. They are the things you get ashamed of, because words diminish them— words shrink things that seemed limitless when they were in your head to no more than living size when they're brought out. But it's more than that, isn't it? The most important things lie too close to wherever your secret heart is buried, like landmarks to a treasure your enemies would love to steal away. And you may make revelations that cost you dearly only to have people look at you in a funny way, not understanding what you've said at all, or why you thought it was so important that you almost cried while you were saying it. That's the worst, I think. When the secret stays locked within not for want of a teller but for want of an understanding ear.

I was twelve going on thirteen when I first saw a dead human being. It happened in 1960, a long time ago . . . although sometimes it doesn't seem that long to me. Especially on the nights I wake up from dreams where the hail falls into his open eyes.

2

We had a treehouse in a big elm which overhung a vacant lot in Castle Rock. There's a moving company on that lot today, and the elm is gone. Progress. It was a sort of social club, although it had no name. There were five, maybe six steady guys and some other wet ends who just hung around. We'd let them come up when there was a card game and we needed some fresh blood. The game was usually blackjack and we played for pennies, nickle limit. But you got double money on blackjack and five-card-under . . . *triple* money

301

on six-card-under, although Teddy was the only guy crazy enough to go for that.

The sides of the treehouse were planks scavenged from the shitpile behind Mackey Lumber & Building Supply on Carbine Road—they were splintery and full of knotholes we plugged with either toilet paper or paper towels. The roof was a corrugated tin sheet we hawked from the dump, looking over our shoulders all the time we were hustling it out of there, because the dump custodian's dog was supposed to be a real kid-eating monster. We found a screen door out there on the same day. It was flyproof but really rusty—I mean, that rust was *extreme*. No matter what time of day you looked out that screen door, it looked like sunset.

Besides playing cards, the club was a good place to go and smoke cigarettes and look at girly books. There were half a dozen battered tin ashtrays that said CAMELS on the bottom, a lot of centerfolds tacked to the splintery walls, twenty or thirty dog-eared packs of Bike cards (Teddy got them from his uncle, who ran the Castle Rock Stationery Shoppe—when Teddy's unc asked him one day what kind of cards we played, Teddy said we had cribbage tournaments and Teddy's unc thought that was just fine), a set of plastic poker chips, and a pile of ancient *Master Detective* murder magazines to leaf through if there was nothing else shaking. We also built a 12" x 10" secret compartment under the floor to hide most of this stuff in on the rare occasions when some kid's father decided it was time to do the we're-really-good-pals routine. When it rained, being in the club was like being inside a Jamaican steel drum . . . but that summer there had been no rain.

It had been the driest and hottest since 1907—or so the newspapers said, and on that Friday preceding the Labor Day weekend and the start of another school year, even the goldenrod in the fields and the ditches beside the backroads looked parched and poorly. Nobody's garden had done doodly-squat that year, and the big displays of canning stuff in the Castle Rock Red & White were still there, gathering dust. No one had anything to put up that summer, except maybe dandelion wine.

Teddy and Chris and I were up in the club on that Friday morning, glooming to each other about school being so near and playing cards and swapping the same old travelling salesman jokes and frenchman jokes. How do you know when a frenchman's been in your back yard? Well, your garbage cans are empty and your dog is pregnant. Teddy would try to look offended, but he was the first one to bring in a joke as soon as he heard it, only switching frenchman to polack.

The elm gave good shade, but we already had our shirts off so we wouldn't sweat them up too bad. We were playing three-penny-scat, the dullest card-game ever invented, but it was too hot to think about anything more complicated. We'd had a pretty fair scratch ballteam until the middle of August and then a lot of kids just drifted away. Too hot.

I was down to my ride and building spades. I'd started with thirteen, gotten an eight to make twenty-one, and nothing had happened since then. Chris knocked. I took my last draw and got nothing helpful.

"Twenty-nine," Chris said, laying down diamonds.

"Twenty-two," Teddy said, looking disgusted.

"Piss up a rope," I said, and tossed my cards onto the table face down.

"Gordie's out, ole Gordie just bit the bag and stepped out the door," Teddy bugled, and then gave out with his patented Teddy Duchamp laugh—*Eeee-eee-eee*, like a rusty nail being slowly hauled out of a rotten board. Well, he was weird; we all knew it. He was close to being thirteen like the rest of us, but the thick glasses and the hearing aid he wore sometimes made him look like an old man. Kids were always trying to cadge smokes off him on the street, but the bulge in his shirt was just his hearing-aid battery.

In spite of the glasses and the flesh-colored button always screwed into his ear, Teddy couldn't see very well and often misunderstood the things people said to him. In baseball you had to have him play the fences, way beyond Chris in left field and Billy Greer in right. You just hoped no one would hit one that far because Teddy would go grimly after it, see it or not. Every now and then he got bonked a good one, and once he went out cold when he ran full-tilt-boogie into the fence by the treehouse. He lay there on his back with his eyes showing whites for almost five minutes, and I got scared. Then he woke up and walked around with a bloody nose and a huge purple lump rising on his forehead, trying to claim that the ball was foul.

His eyesight was just naturally bad, but there was nothing natural about what had happened to his ears. Back in those days, when it was cool to get your hair cut so that your ears stuck out like a couple of jug-handles, Teddy had Castle Rock's first Beatle haircut—four years before anyone in America had ever heard of the Beatles. He kept his ears covered because they looked like two lumps of warm wax.

One day when he was eight, Teddy's father got pissed at him for breaking a plate. His mother was working at the shoe factory in South Paris when it happened and by the time she found out about it, it was all over.

Teddy's dad took Teddy over to the big woodstove at the back of the kitchen and shoved the side of Teddy's head down against one of the cast-iron burner plates. He held it down there for about ten seconds. Then he yanked Teddy up by the hair of the head and did the other side. Then he called the Central Main General Emergency unit and told them to come get his boy. Then he hung up the phone, went into the closet, got his .410, and sat down to watch the daytime stories on TV with the shotgun laid across his knees. When Mrs. Burroughs from next door came over to ask if Teddy was all right—she'd heard the screaming—Teddy's dad pointed the shotgun at her. Mrs. Burroughs went out of the Duchamp house at roughly the speed of light, locked herself into her own house, and called the police. When the ambulance came, Mr. Duchamp let the orderlies in and then went out on the back porch to stand guard while they wheeled Teddy to the old portholed Buick ambulance on a stretcher.

Teddy's dad explained to the orderlies that while the fucking brass hats said the area was clear, there were still kraut snipers everywhere. One of the orderlies asked Teddy's dad if he thought he could hold on. Teddy's dad smiled tightly and told the orderly he'd hold until hell was a Frigidaire dealership, if that's what it took. The orderly saluted, and Teddy's dad snapped it right back at him. A few minutes after the ambulance left, the state police arrived and relieved Norman Duchamp of duty.

He'd been doing odd things like shooting cats and lighting fires in mailboxes for over a year, and after the atrocity he had visited upon his son, they had a quick hearing and sent him to Togus, which is a VA hospital. Togus is where you have to go if you're a section eight. Teddy's dad had stormed the beach at Normandy, and that's just the way Teddy always put it. Teddy was proud of his old man in spite of what his old man had done to him, and Teddy went with his mom to visit him every week.

He was the dumbest guy we hung around with, I guess, and he was crazy. He'd take the craziest chances you can imagine, and get away with them. His big thing was what he called "truck-dodging." He'd run out in front of them on 196 and sometimes they'd miss him by bare inches. God knew how many heart attacks he'd caused, and he'd be laughing while the windblast from the passing truck rippled his clothes. It scared us because his vision was so lousy, Coke-bottle glasses or not. It seemed like only a matter of time before he misjudged one of those trucks. And you had to be careful what you dared him, because Teddy would do anything on a dare.

"Gordie's out, eeeeee-eee-eee!"

"Screw," I said, and picked up a *Master Detective* to read while they played it out. I turned to "He Stomped the Pretty Co-Ed to Death in a Stalled Elevator" and got right into it.

Teddy picked up his cards, gave them one brief look, and said: "I knock."

"You four-eyed pile of shit!" Chris cried.

"The pile of shit has a thousand eyes," Teddy said gravely, and both Chris and I cracked up. Teddy stared at us with a slight frown, as if wondering what had gotten us laughing. That was another thing about the cat—he was always coming out with weird stuff like "The pile of shit has a thousand eyes," and you could never be sure if he *meant* it to be funny or if it just happened that way. He'd look at the people who were laughing with that slight frown on his face, as if to say: *O Lord what is it this time?*

Teddy had a natural thirty—jack, queen, and king of clubs. Chris had only sixteen and went down to his ride.

Teddy was shuffling the cards in his clumsy way and I was just getting to the gooshy part of the murder story, where this deranged sailor from New Orleans was doing the Bristol Stomp all over this college girl from Bryn Mawr because he couldn't stand being in closed-in places, when we heard someone coming fast up the ladder nailed to the side of the elm. A fist rapped on the underside of the trapdoor.

"Who goes?" Chris yelled.

"Vern!" He sounded excited and out of breath.

I went to the trapdoor and pulled the bolt. The trapdoor banged up and Vern Tessio, one of the other regulars, pulled himself into the clubhouse. He was sweating buckets and his hair, which he usually kept combed in a perfect imitation of his rock and roll idol, Bobby Rydell, was plastered to his bullet head in chunks and strings.

"Wow, man," he panted. "Wait'll you hear this."

"Hear what?" I asked.

"Lemme get my breath. I ran all the way from my house."

"*I ran all the way home,*" Teddy wavered in a dreadful Little Anthony falsetto, "*just to say I'm soh-ree—*"

"Fuck your hand, man," Vern said.

"Drop dead in a shed, Fred," Teddy returned smartly.

"You ran all the way from your place?" Chris asked unbelievingly. "Man, you're crazy." Vern's house was two miles down Grand Street. "It must be ninety out there."

"This is worth it," Vern said. "Holy Jeezum. You won't believe this. Sincerely." He slapped his sweaty forehead to show us how sincere he was.

"Okay, what?" Chris asked.

"Can you guys camp out tonight?" Vern was looking at us earnestly, excitedly. His eyes looked like raisins pushed into dark circles of sweat. "I mean, if you tell your folks we're gonna tent out in my back field?"

"Yeah, I guess so," Chris said, picking up his new hand and looking at it. "But my dad's on a mean streak. Drinkin, y'know."

"You got to, man," Vern said. "Sincerely. You won't *believe* this. Can you, Gordie?"

"Probably."

I was able to do most stuff like that—in fact, I'd been like the Invisible Boy that whole summer. In April my older brother,

Dennis, had been killed in a Jeep accident. That was at Fort Benning, Georgia, where he was in Basic. He and another guy were on their way to the PX and an Army truck hit them broadside. Dennis was killed instantly and his passenger had been in a coma ever since. Dennis would have been twenty-two later that week. I'd already picked out a birthday card for him at Dahlie's over in Castle Green.

I cried when I heard, and I cried more at the funeral, and I couldn't believe that Dennis was gone, that anyone that used to knuckle my head or scare me with a rubber spider until I cried or give me a kiss when I fell down and scraped both knees bloody and whisper in my ear, "Now stop cryin, ya baby!"—that a person who had *touched* me could be dead. It hurt me and it scared me that he could be dead . . . but it seemed to have taken all the heart out of my parents. For me, Dennis was hardly more than an acquaintance. He was ten years older than me if you can dig it, and he had his own friends and classmates. We ate at the same table for a lot of years, and sometimes he was my friend and sometimes my tormentor, but mostly he was, you know, just a guy. When he died he'd been gone for a year except for a couple of furloughs. We didn't even look alike. It took me a long time after that summer to realize that most of the tears I cried were for my mom and dad. Fat lot of good it did them, or me.

"So what are you pissing and moaning about, Vern-O?" Teddy asked.

"I knock," Chris said.

"*What?*" Teddy screamed, immediately forgetting all about Vern. "You friggin liar! You ain't got no pat hand. I didn't deal you no pat hand."

Chris smirked. "Make your draw, shitheap."

Teddy reached for the top card on the pile of Bikes. Chris reached for the Winstons on the ledge behind him. I bent over to pick up my detective magazine.

Vern Tessio said: "You guys want to go see a dead body?"

Everybody stopped.

3

We'd all heard about it on the radio, of course. The radio, a Philco with a cracked case which had also been scavenged from the dump, played all the time. We kept it tuned to WLAM in Lewiston, which churned out the super-hits and the boss oldies: "What in the World's Come Over You" by Jack Scott and "This Time" by Troy Shondell and "King Creole" by Elvis and "Only the Lonely" by Roy Orbison. When the news came on we usually switched some mental dial over to Mute. The news was a lot of happy horseshit about Kennedy and Nixon and Quemoy and Matsu and the missile gap and what a shit that Castro was turning out to be after all. But we had all listened to the Ray Brower story a little more closely, because he was a kid our age.

He was from Chamberlain, a town forty miles or so east of Castle Rock. Three days before Vern came busting into the clubhouse after a two-mile run up Grand Street, Ray Brower had gone out with one of his mother's pots to pick blueberries. When dark came and he still wasn't back, the Browers called the county sheriff and a search started—first just around the kid's house and then spreading to the surrounding towns of Motton and Durham and Pownal. Everybody got into the act—cops, deputies, game wardens, volunteers. But three days later the kid was still missing. You could tell, hearing about it on the radio, that they were never going to find that poor sucker alive; eventually the search would just peter away into nothing. He might have gotten smothered in a gravel pit slide or drowned in a brook, and ten years from now some hunter would find his bones. They were already dragging the ponds in Chamberlain, and the Motton Reservoir.

Nothing like that could happen in southwestern Maine today; most of the area has become suburbanized, and the bedroom communities surrounding Portland and Lewiston have spread out like the tentacles of a giant squid. The woods are still there, and they get heavier as you work your way west toward the White Mountains, but these days if you can keep your head long enough to walk five miles in one consistent direction, you're certain to cross two-lane blacktop. But in 1960 the whole area between Chamberlain and Castle Rock was undeveloped, and there were places that hadn't even been logged since before World War II. In those days it was still possible to walk into the woods and lose your direction there and die there.

4

Vern Tessio had been under his porch that morning, digging.

We all understood that right away, but maybe I should take just a minute to explain it to you. Teddy Duchamp was only about half-bright, but Vern Tessio would never be spending any of his spare time on *College Bowl* either. Still, his brother Billy was even dumber, as you will see. But first I have to tell you why Vern was digging under the porch.

Four years ago, when he was eight, Vern buried a quart jar of pennies under the long Tessio front porch. Vern called the dark space under the porch his "cave." He was playing a pirate sort of game, and the pennies were buried treasure—only if you were playing pirate with Vern, you couldn't call it buried treasure, you had to call it "booty." So he buried the jar of pennies deep, filled in the hole, and covered the fresh dirt with some of the old leaves that had drifted under there over the years. He drew a treasure map which he put up in his room with the rest of his junk. He forgot all about it for a month or so. Then, being low on cash for a movie or something, he remembered the pennies and went to get his map. But his mom had been in to clean two or three times since then, and had collected all the old homework papers and candy wrappers and comic magazines and joke books. She burned them in the stove to start the cook-fire one morning, and Vern's treasure map went right up the kitchen chimney.

Or so he figured it.

He tried to find the spot from memory and dug there. No luck. To the right and the left of that spot. Still no luck. He gave up for the day but had tried off and on ever since. Four years, man. Four *years*. Isn't that a pisser? You didn't know whether to laugh or cry.

It had gotten to be sort of an obsession with him. The Tessio front porch ran the length of the house, probably forty feet long and seven feet wide. He had dug through damn near every inch of that area two, maybe three times and no pennies. The *number* of pennies began to grow in his mind. When it first happened he told Chris and me that there had been maybe three dollars' worth. A year later he was up to five and just lately it was running around ten, more or less, depending on how broke he was.

Every so often we tried to tell him what was so clear to us—that Billy had known about the jar and dug it up himself. Vern refused to believe it, although he hated Billy like the Arabs hate the Jews and probably would have cheerfully voted the death-penalty on his brother for shoplifting, if the opportunity had ever presented itself. He also refused to ask Billy point blank. Probably he was afraid Billy would laugh and say *Course I got them; you stupid pussy, and there was twenty bucks' worth of pennies in that jar and I spent every fuckin cent of it.* Instead, Vern went out and dug for the pennies whenever the spirit moved him (and whenever Billy wasn't around). He always crawled out from under the porch with his jeans dirty and his hair leafy and his hands empty. We ragged him about it something wicked, and his nickname was Penny—Penny Tessio. I think he came up to the club with his news as quick as he did not just to get it out but to show us that some good had finally come of his penny-hunt.

He had been up that morning before anybody, ate his cornflakes, and was out in the driveway shooting baskets through the old hoop nailed up on the garage, nothing much to do, no one to play Ghost with or anything, and he decided to have another dig for his pennies. He was under the porch when the screen door slammed up above. He froze, not making a sound. If it was his dad, he would crawl out; if it was Billy, he'd stay put until Billy and his j.d. friend Charlie Hogan had taken off.

Two pair of footsteps crossed the porch, and then Charlie Hogan himself said in a trembling, crybaby voice: "Jesus Christ, Billy, what are we gonna do?"

Vern said that just hearing Charlie Hogan talk like that —Charlie, who was one of the toughest kids in town—made him prick up his ears. Charlie, after all, hung out with Ace Merrill and Eyeball Chambers, and if you hung out with cats like that, you had to be tough.

"Nuthin," Billy said. "That's all we're gonna do. Nuthin."

"We gotta do *somethin*," Charlie said, and they sat down on the porch close to where Vern was hunkered down. "Didn't you *see* him?"

Vern took a chance and crept a little closer to the steps, practically slavering. At that point he thought that maybe Billy and Charlie had been really drunked up and had run somebody down. Vern was careful not to crackle any of the old leaves as he moved. If the two of them found out he was under the porch and had overheard them, you could have put what was left of him in a Ken-L Ration dogfood can.

"It's nuthin to us," Billy Tessio said. "The kid's dead so it's nuthin to him, neither. Who gives a fuck if they ever find him? I don't."

"It was that kid they been talkin about on the radio," Charlie said. "It was, sure as shit. Brocker, Brower, Flowers, whatever his name is. Fuckin train must have hit him."

"Yeah," Billy said. Sound of a scratched match. Vern saw it flicked into the gravel driveway and then smelled cigarette smoke. "I sure did. And you puked."

No words, but Vern sensed emotional waves of shame radiating off Charlie Hogan.

"Well, the girls didn't see it," Billy said after awhile. "Lucky break." From the sound, he clapped Charlie on the back to buck him up. "They'd blab it from here to Portland. We tore out of there fast, though. You think they knew there was something wrong?"

"No," Charlie said. "Marie don't like to go down that Back Harlow Road past the cemetery, anyway. She's afraid of ghosts." Then again in that scared crybaby voice: "Jesus, I wish we'd never boosted no car last night! Just gone to the show like we was gonna!"

Charlie and Billy went with a couple of scags named Marie Dougherty and Beverly Thomas; you never saw such gross-looking broads outside of a carnival show—pimples, moustaches, the whole works. Sometimes the four of them—or maybe six or eight if Fuzzy Bracowicz or Ace Merrill were along with their girls—would boost a car from a Lewiston parking lot and go joyriding out into the country with two or three bottles of Wild Irish Rose wine and a six-pack of ginger ale. They'd take the girls parking somewhere in Castle View or Harlow or Shiloh, drink Purple Jesuses, and make out. Then they'd dump the car somewhere near home. Cheap thrills in the monkey-house, as Chris sometimes said. They'd never been caught at it, but Vern kept hoping. He really dug the idea of visiting Billy on Sundays at the reformatory.

"If we told the cops, they'd want to know how we got way the hell out in Harlow," Billy said. "We ain't got no car, neither of us. It's better if we just keep our mouths shut. Then they can't touch us."

"We could make a nonnamus call," Charlie said.

"They trace those fuckin calls," Billy said ominously. "I seen it on *Highway Patrol*. And *Dragnet*."

"Yeah, right," Charlie said miserably. "Jesus. I wish Ace'd been with us. We could have told the cops we was in his car."

"Well, he wasn't."

"Yeah," Charlie said. He sighed. "I guess you're right." A cigarette butt flicked into the driveway. "We hadda walk up and take a piss by the tracks, didn't we? Couldn't walk the other way, could we? And I got puke on my new P.F. Fliers." His voice sank a little. "Fuckin kid was laid right out, you know it? Didja see that sonofawhore, Billy?"

"I seen him," Billy said, and a second cigarette butt joined the first in the driveway. "Let's go see if Ace is up. I want some juice."

"We gonna tell him?"

"Charlie, we ain't gonna tell *nobody. Nobody never.* You dig me?"

"I dig you," Charlie said. "Christ Jesus, I wish we never boosted that fuckin Dodge."

"Aw, shut the fuck up and come on."

Two pairs of legs clad in tight, wash-faded pegged jeans, two pairs of feet in black engineer boots with side-buckles, came down the steps. Vern froze on his hands and knees ("My balls crawled up so high I thought they was trine to get back home," he told us), sure his brother would sense him beneath the porch and drag him out and kill him—he and Charlie Hogan would kick the few brains the good Lord had seen fit to give him right out his jug ears and then stomp him with their engineer boots. But they just kept going and when Vern was sure they were really gone, he had crawled out from under the porch and run here.

5

"You're really lucky," I said. "They *would* have killed you."

Teddy said, "I know the Back Harlow Road. It comes to a dead end by the river. We used to fish for cossies out there."

Chris nodded. "There used to be a bridge, but there was a flood. A long time ago. Now there's just the train-tracks."

"Could a kid really have gotten all the way from Chamberlain to Harlow?" I asked Chris. "That's twenty or thirty miles."

"I think so. He probably happened on the train-tracks and followed them the whole way. Maybe he thought they'd take him out, or maybe he thought he could flag down a train if he had to. But that's just a freight run now—GS&WM up to Derry and Brownsville—and not many of those anymore. He'd had to've walked all the way to Castle Rock to get out. After dark a train must have finally come along . . . and el smacko."

Chris drove his right fist down against his left palm, making a flat noise. Teddy, a veteran of many close calls dodging the pulp-trucks on 196, looked vaguely pleased. I felt a little sick, imagining that kid so far away from home, scared to death but doggedly following the GS&WM tracks, probably walking on the ties because of the night-noises from the overhanging trees and bushes . . . maybe even from the culverts underneath the railroad bed. And here comes the train, and maybe the big headlight on the front hypnotized him until it was too late to jump. Or maybe he was just lying there on the tracks in a hunger-faint when the train came along. Either way, any way, Chris had the straight of it: el smacko had been the final result. The kid was dead.

"So anyway, you want to go see it?" Vern asked. He was squirming around like he had to go to the bathroom he was so excited.

We all looked at him for a long second, no one saying anything. Then Chris tossed his cards down and said: "Sure! And I bet you anything we get our pictures in the paper!"

"Huh?" Vern said.

"Yeah?" Teddy said, and grinned his crazy truck-dodging grin.

"Look," Chris said, leaning across the ratty card-table. "We can find the body and report it! We'll be on the news!"

"I dunno," Vern said, obviously taken aback. "Billy will know where I found out. He'll beat the living shit outta me."

"No he won't," I said, "because it'll be *us* guys that find that kid, not Billy and Charlie Hogan in a boosted car. Then they won't have to worry about it anymore. They'll probably pin a medal on you, Penny."

"Yeah?" Vern grinned, showing his bad teeth. It was a dazed sort of grin, as if the thought of Billy being pleased with anything he did had acted on him like a hard shot to the chin. "Yeah, you think so?"

Teddy was grinning, too. Then he frowned and said: "Oh-oh."

"What?" Vern asked. He was squirming again, afraid that some really basic objection to the idea had just cropped up in Teddy's mind . . . or what passed for Teddy's mind.

"Our folks," Teddy said. "If we find that kid's body over in South Harlow tomorrow, they're gonna know we didn't spend the night campin out in Vern's back field."

"Yeah," Chris said. "They'll know we went lookin for that kid."

"No they won't," I said. I felt funny—both excited and scared because I knew we could do it and get away with it. The mixture of emotions made me feel heatsick and headachey. I picked up the Bikes to have something to do with my hands and started box-shuffling them. That and how to play cribbage was about all I got for older brother stuff from Dennis. The other kids envied that shuffle, and I guess everyone I knew had asked me to show them how it went . . . everyone except Chris. I guess only Chris knew that showing someone would be like giving away a piece of Dennis, and I just didn't have so much of him that I could afford to pass pieces around.

I said: "We'll just tell em we got bored tenting in Vern's field because we've done it so many times before. So we decided to hike up the tracks and have a campout in the woods. I bet we don't even get hided for it because everybody'll be so excited about what we found."

"My dad'll hide me anyway," Chris said. "He's on a really mean streak this time." He shook his head sullenly. "To hell, it's worth a hiding."

"Okay," Teddy said, getting up. He was still grinning like crazy, ready to break into his high-pitched, cackling laugh at any second. "Let's all get together at Vern's house after lunch. What can we tell em about supper?"

Chris said, "You and me and Gordie can say we're eating at Vern's."

"And I'll tell my mom I'm eating over at Chris's," Vern said.

That would work unless there was some emergency we couldn't control or unless any of the parents got together. And neither Vern's folks or Chris's had a phone. Back then there were a lot of families which still considered a telephone a luxury, especially families of the shirttail variety. And none of us came from the upper crust.

My dad was retired. Vern's dad worked in the mill and was still driving a 1952 DeSoto. Teddy's mom had a house on Danberry Street and she took in a border whenever she could get one. She didn't have one that summer; the FURNISHED ROOM TO LET sign had been up in the parlor window since June. And Chris's dad was always on a "mean streak," more or less; he was a drunk who got welfare off and on—mostly on—and spent most of his time hanging out in Sukey's Tavern with Junior Merrill, Ace Merrill's old man, and a couple of other local rumpots.

Chris didn't talk much about his dad, but we all knew he hated him like poison. Chris was marked up every two weeks or so, bruises on his cheeks and neck or one eye swelled up and as colorful as a sunset, and once he came into school with a big clumsy bandage on the back of his head. Other times he never got to school at all. His mom would call him in sick because he was too lamed up to come in. Chris was smart, really smart, but he played truant a lot, and Mr. Halliburton, the town truant officer, was always showing up at Chris's house, driving his old black Chevrolet with the NO RIDERS sticker in the corner of the windshield. If Chris was being truant and Bertie (as we called him—always behind his back, of course) caught him, he would haul him back to school and see that Chris got detention for a week. But if Bertie found out that Chris was home because his father had beaten the shit out of him, Bertie just went away and didn't say boo to a cuckoo-bird. It never occurred to me to question this set of priorities until about twenty years later.

The year before, Chris had been suspended from school for three days. A bunch of milk-money disappeared when it was Chris's turn to be room-monitor and collect it, and because he was a Chambers from those no-account Chamberses, he had to take a hike even though he always swore he never hawked that money. That was the time Mr. Chambers put Chris in the hospital for an overnight stay; when his dad heard Chris was suspended, he broke Chris's nose and his right wrist. Chris came from a bad family, all right, and everybody thought he would turn out bad . . . including Chris. His brothers had lived up to the town's expectations admirably. Frank, the eldest, ran away from home when he was seventeen, joined the Navy, and ended up doing a long stretch in Portsmouth for rape and criminal assault. The next-eldest, Richard (his right eye was all funny and jittery, which was why everybody called him Eyeball), had dropped out of high school in the tenth grade, and chummed around with Charlie and Billy Tessio and their j.d. buddies.

"I think all that'll work," I told Chris. "What about John and Marty?" John and Marty DeSpain were two other members of our regular gang.

"They're still away," Chris said. "They won't be back until Monday."

"Oh. That's too bad."

"So are we set?" Vern asked, still squirming. He didn't want the conversation sidetracked even for a minute.

"I guess we are," Chris said. "Who wants to play some more scat?"

No one did. We were too excited to play cards. We climbed down from the treehouse, climbed the fence into the vacant lot, and played three-flies-six-grounders for awhile with Vern's old friction-taped baseball, but that was no fun, either. All we could think about was that kid Brower, hit by a train, and how we were going to see him, or what was left of him. Around ten o'clock we all drifted away home to fix it with our parents.

6

I got to my house at quarter of eleven, after stopping at the drugstore to check out the paperbacks. I did that every couple of days to see if there were any new John D. MacDonalds. I had a quarter and I figured if there was, I'd take it along. But there were only the old ones, and I'd read most of those half a dozen times.

When I got home the car was gone and I remembered that my mom and some of her hen-party friends had gone to Boston to see a concert. A great old concert-goer, my mother. And why not? Her only kid was dead and she had to do something to take her mind off it. I guess that sounds pretty bitter. And I guess if you'd been there, you'd understand why I felt that way.

Dad was out back, passing a fine spray from the hose over his ruined garden. If you couldn't tell it was a lost cause from his glum face, you sure could by looking at the garden itself. The soil was a light, powdery gray. Everything in it was dead except for the corn, which had never grown so much as a single edible ear. Dad said he'd never known how to water a garden; it had to be mother nature or nobody. He'd water too long in one spot and drown the plants. In the next row, plants were dying of thirst. He could never hit a happy medium. But he didn't talk about it often. He'd lost a son in April and a garden in August. And if he didn't want to talk about either one, I guess that was his privilege. It just bugged me that he'd given up talking about everything else, too. That was taking democracy too fucking far.

"Hi, Daddy," I said, standing beside him. I offered him the Rollos I'd bought at the drugstore. "Want one?"

"Hello, Gordon. No thanks." He kept on flicking the fine spray over the hopeless gray earth.

"Be okay if I camp out in Vern Tessio's back field tonight with some of the guys?"

"What guys?"

"Vern. Teddy Duchamp. Maybe Chris."

I expected him to start right in on Chris—how Chris was bad company, a rotten apple from the bottom of the barrel, a thief, and an apprentice juvenile delinquent.

But he just sighed and said, "I suppose it's okay."

"Great! Thanks!"

I turned to go into the house and check out what was on the boob tube when he stopped me with: "Those are the only people you want to be with, aren't they, Gordon?"

I looked back at him, braced for an argument, but there was no argument in him that morning. It would have been better if there had been, I think. His shoulders were slumped. His face, pointed toward the dead garden and not toward me, sagged. There was a certain unnatural sparkle in his eyes that might have been tears.

"Aw, Dad, they're okay—"

"Of course they are. A thief and two feebs. Fine company for my son."

"Vern Tessio isn't feeble," I said. Teddy was a harder case to argue.

"Twelve years old and still in the fifth grade," my dad said. "And that time he slept over. When the Sunday paper came the next morning, he took an hour and a half to read the funnypages."

That made me mad, because I didn't think he was being fair. He was judging Vern the way he judged all my friends, from having seen them off and on, mostly going in and out of the house. He was wrong about them. And when he called Chris a thief I always saw red, because he didn't know *anything* about Chris. I wanted to tell him that, but if I pissed him off he'd keep me home. And he wasn't really mad anyway, not like he got at the supper-table sometimes, ranting so loud that nobody wanted to eat. Now he just looked sad and tired and used. He was sixty-three years old, old enough to be my grandfather.

My mom was fifty-five—no spring chicken, either. When she and dad got married they tried to start a family right away and my mom got pregnant and had a miscarriage. She miscarried two more and the doctor told her she'd never be able to carry a baby to term. I got all of this stuff, chapter and verse, whenever one of them was lecturing me, you understand. They wanted me to think I was a special delivery from God and I wasn't appreciating my great good fortune in being conceived when my mother was forty-two and starting to gray. I wasn't appreciating my great good fortune and I wasn't appreciating her tremendous pain and sacrifices, either.

Five years after the doctor said Mom would never have a baby she got pregnant with Dennis. She carried him for eight months and then he just sort of fell out, all eight pounds of him—my father used to say that if she had carried Dennis to term, the kid would have weighed fifteen pounds. The doctor said: Well, sometimes nature fools us, but he'll be the only one you'll ever have. Thank God for him and be content. Ten years later she got pregnant with me. She not only carried me to term, the doctor had to use forceps to yank me out. Did you ever hear of such a fucked-up family? I came into the world the child of two Geritol-chuggers, not to go on and on about it, and my only brother was playing league baseball in the big kids' park before I even got out of diapers.

In the case of my mom and dad, one gift from God had been enough. I won't say they treated me badly, and they sure never beat me, but I was a hell of a big surprise and I guess when you get into your forties you're not as partial to surprises as you were in your twenties. After I was born, Mom got that operation her hen-party friends referred to as "The Band-Aid." I guess she wanted to make a hundred per cent sure that there wouldn't be any more gifts from God. When I got to college I found out I'd beaten long odds just by not being born retarded . . . although I think my dad had his doubts when he saw my friend Vern taking ten minutes to puzzle out the dialogue in Beetle Baily.

This business about being ignored: I could never really pin it down until I did a book report in high school on this novel called *The Invisible Man.* When I agreed to do the book for Miss Hardy I thought it was going to be the science fiction story about the guy in bandages and Foster Grants—Claude Rains played him in the movies. When I found out this was a different story I tried to give the book back but Miss Hardy wouldn't let me off the hook. I ended up being real glad. This *Invisible Man* is about a Negro. Nobody ever notices him at all unless he fucks up. People look right through him. When he talks, nobody answers. He's like a black ghost. Once I got into it, I ate that book up like it was a John D. MacDonald, because that cat Ralph Ellison was writing about *me.* At the supper-table it was Denny how many did you strike out and Denny who asked you to the Sadie Hopkins dance and Denny I want to talk to you man to man about that car we were looking at. I'd say: "Pass the butter," and Dad would say: Denny, are you sure the Army is what you want? I'd say: "Pass the butter someone, okay?" and Mom would ask Denny if he wanted her to pick him up one of the Pendleton shirts on sale downtown, and I'd end up getting the butter myself. One night when I was nine, just to see what would happen: I said, "Please pass those goddam spuds." And my mom said: Denny, Auntie Grace called today and she asked after you and Gordon.

The night Dennis graduated with honors from Castle Rock High School I played sick and stayed home. I got Stevie Darabont's oldest brother Royce to buy me a bottle of Wild Irish Rose and I drank half of it and puked in my bed in the middle of the night.

In a family situation like that, you're supposed to either hate the older brother or idolize him hopelessly—at least that's what they teach you in college psychology. Bullshit, right? But so far as I can tell, I didn't feel either way about Dennis. We rarely argued and never had a fist-fight. That would have been ridiculous. Can you see a fourteen-year-old boy finding something to beat up his four-year-old brother about? And our folks were always a little too impressed with him to burden him with the care of his kid brother, so he never resented me the way some older kids come to resent their sibs. When Denny took me with him somewhere, it was of his own free will, and those were some of the happiest times I can remember.

"Hey Lachance, who the fuck is that?"

"My kid brother and you better watch your mouth, Davis. He'll beat the crap out of you. Gordie's tough."

They gather around me for a moment, huge, impossibly tall, just a moment of interest like a patch of sun. They are so big, they are so old.

"Hey kid! This wet end really your big brother?"

I nod shyly.

"He's a real asshole, ain't he, kid?"

I nod again and everybody, Dennis included, roars with laughter. Then Dennis claps his hands together twice, briskly, and says: "Come on, we gonna have a practice or stand around here like a bunch of pussies?"

They run to their positions, already peppering the ball around the infield.

"Go sit over there on the bench, Gordie. Be quiet. Don't bother anybody."

I go sit over there on the bench. I am good. I feel impossibly small under the sweet summer clouds. I watch my brother pitch. I don't bother anybody.

But there weren't many times like that.

Sometimes he read me bedtime stories that were better than Mom's; Mom's stories were about The Gingerbread Man and The Three Little Pigs, okay stuff, but Dennis's were about stuff like Bluebeard and Jack the Ripper. He also had a version of Billy Goat's Gruff where the troll under the bridge ended up the winner. And, as I have already said, he taught me the game of cribbage and how to do a box-shuffle. Not that much, but hey! in this world you take what you can get, am I right?

As I grew older, my feelings of love for Dennis were replaced with an almost clinical awe, the kind of awe so-so Christians feel for God, I guess. And when he died, I was mildly shocked and mildly sad, the way I imagine those same so-so Christians must have felt when *Time* magazine said God was dead. Let me put it this way: I was as sad for Denny's dying as I was when I heard on the radio that Dan Blocker had died. I'd seen them both about as frequently, and Denny never even got any re-runs.

He was buried in a closed coffin with the American flag on top (they took the flag off the box before they finally stuck it in the ground and folded it—the flag, not the box—into a cocked hat and gave it to my mom). My parents just fell to pieces. Four months hadn't been long enough to put them back together again; I didn't know if they'd *ever* be whole again. Mr. and Mrs. Dumpty. Denny's room was in suspended animation just one door down from my room, suspended animation or maybe in a time-warp. The Ivy League college pennants were still on the walls, and the senior pictures of the girls he had dated were still tucked into the mirror where he had stood for what seemed like hours at a stretch, combing his hair back into a ducktail like Elvis's. The stack of *True*s and *Sports Illustrated*s remained on his desk, their dates looking more and more antique as time passed. It's the kind of thing you see in sticky-sentimental movies. But it wasn't sentimental to me; it was terrible. I didn't go into Dennis's room unless I had to because I kept expecting that he would be behind the door, or under the bed, or in the closet. Mostly it was the closet that preyed on my mind, and if my mother sent me in to get Denny's postcard album or his shoebox of photographs so she could look at them, I would imagine that door swinging slowly open while I stood rooted to the spot with horror. I would imagine him pallid and bloody in the darkness, the side of his head walloped in, a gray-veined cake of blood and brains drying on his shirt. I would imagine his arms coming up, his bloody hands hooking into claws, and he would be croaking: *It should have been you, Gordon. It should have been you.*

7

Stud City, by Gordon Lachance. Originally published in *Greenspun Quarterly,* issue 45, Fall, 1970. Used by permission.

March.

Chico stands at the window, arms crossed, elbows on the ledge that divides upper and lower panes, naked, looking out, breath fogging the glass. A draft against his belly. Bottom right pane is gone. Blocked by a piece of cardboard.

"Chico."

He doesn't turn. She doesn't speak again. He can see a ghost of

her in the glass, in his bed, sitting, blankets pulled up in apparent
defiance of gravity. Her eye makeup has smeared into deep
hollows under her eyes.

Chico shifts his gaze beyond her ghost, out beyond the house.
Raining. Patches of snow sloughed away to reveal the bald ground
underneath. He sees last year's dead grass, a plastic toy—Billy's—
a rusty rake. His brother Johnny's Dodge is up on blocks, the
detired wheels sticking out like stumps. He remembers times he
and Johnny worked on it, listening to the super-hits and boss
oldies from WLAM in Lewiston pour out of Johnny's old transistor
radio—a couple of times Johnny would give him a beer. *She
gonna run fast, Chico,* Johnny would say. *She gonna eat up
everything on this road from Gates Falls to Castle Rock. Wait till we
get that Hearst shifter in her!*

But that had been then, and this was now.

Beyond Johnny's Dodge was the highway. Route 14, goes to
Portland and New Hampshire south, all the way to Canada north, if
you turned left on U.S. 1 at Thomaston.

"Stud City," Chico says to the glass. He smokes his cigarette.

"What?"

"Nothing, babe."

"Chico?" Her voice is puzzled. He will have to change the sheets
before Dad gets back. She bled.

"What?"

"I love you, Chico."

"That's right."

Dirty March. *You're some old whore,* Chico thinks. *Dirty, staggering old baggy-tits March with rain in her face.*

"This room used to be Johnny's," he says suddenly.

"Who?"

"My brother."

"Oh. Where is he?"

"In the Army," Chico says, but Johnny isn't in the Army. He had
been working the summer before at Oxford Plains Speedway and a
car went out of control and skidded across the infield toward the
pit area, where Johnny had been changing the back tires on a
Chevy Charger-class stocker. Some guys shouted at him to look
out, but Johnny never heard them. One of the guys who shouted
was Johnny's brother Chico.

"Aren't you cold?" she asks.

"No. Well, my feet. A little."

And he thinks suddenly: *Well, my God. Nothing happened to Johnny that isn't going to happen to you, too, sooner or later.* He sees it again, though: the skidding, skating Ford Mustang, the knobs of his brother's spine picked out in a series of dimpled shadows against the white of his Hanes tee-shirt; he had been hunkered down, pulling one of the Chevy's back tires. There had been time to see rubber flaying off the tires of the runaway Mustang, to see its hanging muffler scraping up sparks from the infield. It had struck Johnny even as Johnny tried to get to his feet. Then the yellow shout of flame.

Well, Chico thinks, *it could have been slow,* and he thinks of his grandfather. Hospital smells. Pretty young nurses bearing bedpans. A last papery breath. Were there any good ways?

He shivers and wonders about God. He touches the small silver St. Christopher's medal that hangs on a chain around his neck. He is not a Catholic and he's surely not a Mexican: his real name is Edward May and his friends all call him Chico because his hair is black and he greases it back with Brylcreem and he wears boots with pointed toes and Cuban heels. Not Catholic, but he wears this medallion. Maybe if Johnny had been wearing one, the runaway Mustang would have missed him. You never knew.

He smokes and stares out the window and behind him the girl gets out of bed and comes to him quickly, almost mincing, maybe afraid he will turn around and look at her. She puts a warm hand on his back. Her breasts push against his side. Her belly touches his buttock.

"Oh. It *is* cold."

"It's this place."

"Do you love me, Chico?"

"You bet!" he says off-handedly, and then, more seriously: "You were cherry."

"What does that—"

"You were a virgin."

The hand reaches higher. One finger traces the skin on the nape of his neck. "I said, didn't I?"

"Was it hard? Did it hurt?"

She laughs. "No. But I was scared."

They watch the rain. A new Oldsmobile goes by on 14, spraying up water.

"Stud City," Chico says.

"What?"

"That guy. He's going Stud City. In his new stud car."

She kisses the place her finger has been touching gently and he brushes at her as if she were a fly.

"What's the matter?"

He turns to her. Her eyes flick down to his penis and then up again hastily. Her arms twitch to cover herself, and then she remembers that they never do stuff like that in the movies and she drops them to her sides again. Her hair is black and her skin is winter white, the color of cream. Her breasts are firm, her belly perhaps a little too soft. One flaw to remind, Chico thinks, that this isn't the movies.

"Jane?"

"What?" He can feel himself getting ready. Not beginning, but getting ready.

"It's all right," he said. "We're friends." He eyes her deliberately, letting himself reach at her in all sorts of ways. When he looks at her face again, it is flushed. "Do you mind me looking at you?"

"I . . . no. No, Chico."

She steps back, closes her eyes, sits on the bed, and leans back, legs spread. He sees all of her. The muscles, the little muscles on the insides of her thighs . . . they're jumping, uncontrolled, and this suddenly excites him more than the taut cones of her breasts or the mild pink pearl of her cunt. Excitement trembles in him, some stupid Bozo on a spring. Love may be as divine as the poets say, he things, but sex is Bozo the Clown bouncing around on a spring. How could a woman look at an erect penis without going off into mad gales of laughter?

The rain beats against the roof, against the window, against the sodden cardboard patch blocking the glassless lower pane. He presses his hand against his chest, looking for a moment like a stage Roman about to orate. His hand is cold. He drops it to his side.

"Open your eyes. We're friends, I said."

Obediently, she opens them. She looks at him. Her eyes appear violet now. The rainwater running down the window makes rippling patterns on her face, her neck, her breasts. Stretched across the bed, her belly has been pulled tight. She is perfect in her moment.

"Oh," she says. "Oh Chico, it feels so *funny.*" A shiver goes through her. She has curled her toes involuntarily. He can see the insteps of her feet. Her insteps are pink. "Chico. Chico."

He steps toward her. His body is shivering and her eyes widen. She says something, one word, but he can't tell what it is. This isn't the time to ask. He half-kneels before her for just a second, looking at the floor with frowning concentration, touching her legs just above the knees. He measures the tide within himself. Its pull is thoughtless, fantastic. He pauses a little longer.

The only sound is the tinny tick of the alarm clock on the bedtable, standing brassy-legged atop a pile of Spiderman comic books. Her breathing flutters faster and faster. His muscles slide smoothly as he dives upward and forward. They begin. It's better this time. Outside, the rain goes on washing away the snow.

A half-hour later Chico shakes her out of a light doze. "We gotta move," he says. "Dad and Virginia will be home pretty quick."

She looks at her wristwatch and sits up. This time she makes no attempt to shield herself. Her whole tone—her body English—has changed. She has not matured (although she probably believes she has) or learned anything more complex than tying a shoe, but her tone has changed just the same. He nods and she smiles tentatively at him. He reaches for the cigarettes on the bedtable. As she draws on her panties, he thinks of a line from an old novelty song: *Keep playin till I shoot through, Blue . . . play your digeree, do.* "Tie Me Kangaroo Down," by Rolf Harris. He grins. That was a song Johnny used to sing. It ended: *So we tanned his hide when he died, Clyde, and that's it hanging on the shed.*

She hooks her bra and begins buttoning her blouse. "What are you smiling about, Chico?"

"Nothing," he says.

"Zip me up?"

He goes to her, still naked, and zips her up. He kisses her cheek. "Go on in the bathroom and do your face if you want," he says. "Just don't take too long, okay?"

She goes up the hall gracefully, and Chico watches her, smoking. She is a tall girl—taller than he—and she has to duck her head a little going through the bathroom door. Chico finds his underpants under the bed. He puts them in the dirty clothes bag hanging just inside the closet door, and gets another pair from the bureau. He puts them on, and then, while walking back to the bed, he slips and almost falls in a patch of wetness the square of cardboard has let in.

"Goddam," he whispers resentfully.

He looks around at the room, which had been Johnny's until Johnny died *(why did I tell her he was in the* Army, *for Christ's sake?* he wonders . . . a little uneasily). Fiberboard walls, so thin he can hear Dad and Virginia going at it at night, that don't quite make it all the way to the ceiling. The floor has a slightly crazy hipshot angle so that the room's door will only stay open if you block it open—if you forget, it swings stealthily closed as soon as your back is turned. On the far wall is a movie poster from *Easy Rider—Two Men Went Looking for America and Couldn't Find It Anywhere.* The room had more life when Johnny lived here. Chico doesn't know how or why; only that it's true. And he knows something else, as well. He knows that sometimes the room spooks him at night. Sometimes he thinks that the closet door will swing open and Johnny will be standing there, his body charred and twisted and blackened, his teeth yellow dentures poking out of wax that has partially melted and re-hardened; and Johnny will be whispering: *Get out of my room, Chico. And if you lay a hand on my Dodge, I'll fuckin kill you. Got it?*

Got it, bro, Chico thinks.

For a moment he stands still, looking at the rumpled sheet spotted with the girl's blood, and then he spreads the blankets up in one quick gesture. Here. Right here. How do you like that, Virginia? How does that grab your snatch? He puts on his pants, his engineer boots, finds a sweater.

He's dry-combing his hair in front of the mirror when she comes out of the john. She looks classy. Her too-soft stomach doesn't show in the jumper. She looks at the bed, does a couple of things to it, and it comes out looking made instead of just spread up.

"Good," Chico says.

She laughs a little self-consciously and pushes a lock of hair behind her ear. It is an evocative, poignant gesture.

"Let's go," he says.

They go out through the hall and the living room. Jane pauses in front of the tinted studio photograph on top of the TV. It shows his father and Virginia, a high-school-age Johnny, a grammar-school-age Chico, and an infant Billy—in the picture, Johnny is holding Billy. All of them have fixed, stone grins . . . all except Virginia, whose face is its sleepy, indecipherable self. That picture, Chico remembers, was taken less than a month after his dad married the bitch.

"That your mother and father?"

"It's my father," Chico said. "She's my stepmother, Virginia. Come on."

"Is she still that pretty?" Jane asks, picking up her coat and handing Chico his windbreaker.

"I guess my old man thinks so," Chico says.

They step out into the shed. It's a damp and drafty place—the wind hoots through the cracks in its slapstick walls. There is a pile of old bald tires, Johnny's old bike that Chico inherited when he was ten and which he promptly wrecked, a pile of detective magazines, returnable Pepsi bottles, a greasy monolithic engine block, an orange crate full of paperback books, an old paint-by-numbers of a horse standing on dusty green grass.

Chico helps her pick her way outside. The rain is falling with disheartening steadiness. Chico's old sedan stands in a driveway puddle, looking downhearted. Even up on blocks and with a piece of plastic covering the place where the windshield should go, Johnny's Dodge has more class. Chico's car is a Buick. The paint is dull and flowered with spots of rust. The front seat upholstery has been covered with a brown Army blanket. A large button pinned to the sun visor on the passenger side says: I WANT IT EVERY DAY. There is a rusty starter assembly on the back seat; if it ever stops raining he will clean it, he thinks, and maybe put it into the Dodge. Or maybe not.

The Buick smells musty and his own starter grinds a long time before the Buick starts up.

"Is it your battery?" she asks.

"Just the goddam rain, I guess." He backs out onto the road, flicking on the windshield wipers and pausing for a moment to look at the house. It is a completely unappetizing aqua color. The shed sticks off from it at a ragtag, double-jointed angle, tarpaper and peeled-looking shingles.

The radio comes on with a blare and Chico shuts it off at once. There is the beginning of a Sunday afternoon headache behind his forehead. They ride past the Grange hall and the Volunteer Fire Department and Brownie's Store. Sally Morrison's T-Bird is parked by Brownie's hi-test pump, and Chico raises a hand to her as he turns off onto the old Lewiston road.

"Who's that?"

"Sally Morrison."

"Pretty lady." Very neutral.

He feels for his cigarettes. "She's been married twice and divorced twice. Now she's the town pump, if you believe half the talk that goes on in this shitass little town."

"She looks young."

"She is."

"Have you ever—"

He slides his hand up her leg and smiles. "No," he says. "My brother, maybe, but not me. I like Sally, though. She's got her alimony and her big white Bird, she doesn't care what people say about her."

It starts to seem like a long drive. The Androscoggin, off to the right, is slaty and sullen. The ice is all out of it now. Jane has grown quiet and thoughtful. The only sound is the steady snap of the windshield wipers. When the car rolls through the dips in the road there is groundfog, waiting for evening when it will creep out of these pockets and take over the whole River Road.

They cross into Auburn and Chico drives the cutoff and swings onto Minot Avenue. The four lanes are nearly deserted, and all the suburban homes look packaged. They see one little boy in a yellow plastic raincoat walking up the sidewalk, carefully stepping in all the puddles.

"Go, man," Chico says softly.

"What?" Jane asks.

"Nothing, babe. Go back to sleep."

She laughs a little doubtfully.

Chico turns up Keston Street and into the driveway of one of the packaged houses. He doesn't turn off the ignition.

"Come in and I'll give you cookies," she says.

He shakes his head. "I have to get back."

"I know." She puts her arms around him and kisses him. "Thank you for the most wonderful time of my life."

He smiles suddenly. His face shines. It is nearly magical. "I'll see you Monday, Janey-Jane. Still friends, right?"

"You know we are," she says, and kisses him again . . . but when he cups a breast through her jumper, she pulls away. "Don't. My father might see."

He lets her go, only a little of the smile left. She gets out of the car quickly and runs through the rain to the back door. A second later she's gone. Chico pauses for a moment to light a cigarette and then he backs out of the driveway. The Buick stalls and the starter seems to grind forever before the engine manages to catch. It is a long ride home.

When he gets there, Dad's station wagon is parked in the driveway. He pulls in beside it and lets the engine die. For a moment he sits inside silently, listening to the rain. It is like being inside a steel drum.

Inside, Billy is watching Carl Stormer and His Country Buckaroos on the TV set. When Chico comes in, Billy jumps up, excited. "Eddie, hey Eddie, you know what Uncle Pete said? He said him and a whole mess of other guys sank a kraut sub in the war! Will you take me to the show next Saturday?"

"I don't know," Chico says, grinning. "Maybe if you kiss my shoes every night before supper all week." He pulls Billy's hair. Billy hollers and laughs and kicks him in the shins.

"Cut it out, now," Sam May says, coming into the room. "Cut it out, you two. You know how your mother feels about the rough-housing." He has pulled his tie down and unbuttoned the top button of his shirt. He's got a couple-three red hotdogs on a plate. The hotdogs are wrapped in white bread, and Sam May has put the old mustard right to them. "Where you been, Eddie?"

"At Jane's."

The toilet flushes in the bathroom. Virginia. Chico wonders briefly if Jane has left any hairs in the sink, or a lipstick, or a bobby pin.

"You should have come with us to see your Uncle Pete and Aunt Ann," his father says. He eats a frank in three quick bites. "You're getting to be like a stranger around here, Eddie. I don't like that. Not while we provide the bed and board."

"Some bed," Chico says. "Some board."

Sam looks up quickly, hurt at first, then angry. When he speaks, Chico sees that his teeth are yellow with French's mustard. He feels vaguely nauseated. "Your lip. Your goddam lip. You aren't too big yet, snotnose."

Chico shrugs, peels a slice of Wonder Bread off the loaf standing on the TV tray by his father's chair, and spreads it with ketchup. "In three months I'm going to be gone anyway."

"What the hell are you talking about?"

"I'm gonna fix up Johnny's car and go out to California. Look for work."

"Oh yeah. Right." He is a big man, big in a shambling way, but Chico thinks now that he got smaller after he married Virginia, and smaller again after Johnny died. And in his mind he hears himself saying to Jane: *My brother, maybe, but not me.* And on the heels of that: *Play your digeree, do, Blue.* "You ain't never going to get that car as far as Castle Rock, let alone California."

"You don't think so? Just watch my fucking dust."

For a moment his father only looks at him and then he throws the frank he has been holding. It hits Chico in the chest, spraying mustard on his sweater and on the chair.

"Say that word again and I'll break your nose for you, smartass."

Chico picks up the frank and looks at it. Cheap red frank, smeared with French's mustard. Spread a little sunshine. He throws it back at his father. Sam gets up, his face the color of an old brick, the vein in the middle of his forehead pulsing. His thigh connects with the TV tray and it overturns. Billy stands in the kitchen doorway watching them. He's gotten himself a plate of franks and beans and the plate has tipped and beanjuice runs onto the floor. Billy's eyes are wide, his mouth trembling. On the TV, Carl Stormer and the Country Buckaroos are tearing through "Long Black Veil" at a breakneck pace.

"You raise them up best you can and they spit on you," his father says thickly. "Ayuh. That's how it goes." He gropes blindly on the seat of his chair and comes up with the half-eaten hotdog. He holds it in his fist like a severed phallus. Incredibly, he begins to eat it . . . at the same time, Chico sees that he has begun to cry. "Ayuh, they spit on you, that's just how it goes."

"Well, why in the hell did you have to marry *her*?" he bursts out, and then has to bite down on the rest of it: *If you hadn't married her, Johnny would still be alive.*

"That's none of your goddam business!" Sam May roars through his tears. "That's my business!"

"Oh?" Chico shouts back. "Is that so? I only have to live with her! Me and Billy, we have to live with her! Watch her grind you down! And you don't even know—"

"What?" his father says, and his voice is suddenly low and ominous. The chunk of hotdog left in his closed fist is like a bloody chunk of bone. "What don't I know?"

"You don't know shit fron Shinola," he says, appalled at what has almost come out of his mouth.

"You want to stop it now," his father says. "Or I'll beat the hell out of you, Chico." He only calls him this when he is very angry indeed.

Chico turns and sees that Virginia is standing at the other side of the room, adjusting her skirt minutely, looking at him with her large, calm, brown eyes. Her eyes are beautiful; the rest of her is not so beautiful, so self-renewing, but those eyes will carry her for years yet, Chico thinks, and he feels the sick hate come back—*So we tanned his hide when he died, Clyde, and that's it hanging on the shed.*

"She's got you pussywhipped and you don't have the guts to do anything about it!"

All of this shouting has finally become too much for Billy—he gives a great wail of terror, drops his plate of franks and beans, and covers his face with his hands. Beanjuice splatters his Sunday shoes and sprays across the rug.

Sam takes a single step forward and then stops when Chico makes a curt beckoning gesture, as if to say: *Yeah, come on, let's get down to it, what took you so fuckin long?* They stand like statues until Virginia speaks—her voice is low, as calm as her brown eyes.

"Have you had a girl in your room, Ed? You know how your father and I feel about that." Almost as an afterthought: "She left a handkerchief."

He stares at her, savagely unable to express the way he feels, the way she is dirty, the way she shoots unerringly at the back, the way she clips in behind you and cuts at your hamstrings.

You could hurt me if you wanted to, the calm brown eyes say. *I know you know what was going on before he died. But that's the only way you can hurt me, isn't it, Chico? And only then if your father believed you. And if he believed you, it would kill him.*

His father lunges at the new gambit like a bear. "Have you been screwing in my house, you little bastard?"

"Watch your language, please, Sam," Virginia says calmly.

"Is that why you didn't want to come with us? So you could scr—so you could—"

"Say it!" Chico weeps. "Don't let her do it to you! Say it! Say what you mean!"

"Get out," he says dully. "Don't you come back until you can apologize to your mother and me."

"Don't you dare!" he cries. "Don't you dare call that bitch my mother! I'll kill you!"

"Stop it, Eddie!" Billy screams. The words are muffled, blurred through his hands, which still cover his face. "Stop yelling at Daddy! Stop it, *please!*"

Virginia doesn't move from the doorway. Her calm eyes remain on Chico.

Sam blunders back a step and the backs of his knees strike the edge of his easy chair. He sits down in it heavily and averts his face against a hairy forearm. "I can't even look at you when you got words like that in your mouth, Eddie. You are making me feel so bad."

"*She* makes you feel bad! Why won't you admit it?"

He does not reply. Still not looking at Chico, he fumbles another frank wrapped in bread from the plate on the TV tray. He fumbles for the mustard. Billy goes on crying. Carl Stormer and His Country Buckaroos are singing a truck-driving song. "My rig is old, but that don't mean she's slow," Carl tells all his western Maine viewers.

"The boy doesn't know what he's saying, Sam," Virginia says gently. "It's hard, at his age. It's hard to grow up."

She's whipped him. That's the end, all right.

He turns and heads for the door which leads first into the shed and then outdoors. As he opens it he looks back at Virginia, and she gazes at him tranquilly when he speaks her name.

"What is it, Ed?"

"The sheets are bloody." He pauses. "I broke her in."

He thinks something has stirred in her eyes, but that is probably only his wish. "Please go now, Ed. You're scaring Billy."

He leaves. The Buick doesn't want to start and he has almost resigned himself to walking in the rain when the engine finally catches. He lights a cigarette and backs out onto 14, slamming the clutch back in and racing the mill when it starts to jerk and splutter. The generator light blinks balefully at him twice, and then the car settles into a ragged idle. At last he is on his way, creeping up the road toward Gates Falls.

He spares Johnny's Dodge one last look.

Johnny could have had steady work at Gates Mills & Weaving, but only on the night shift. Nightwork didn't bother him, he had told Chico, and the pay was better than at the Plains, but their father worked days, and working nights at the mill would have meant Johnny would have been home with her, home alone or with Chico in the next room . . . and the walls were thin. *I can't stop and she won't let me try,* Johnny said. *Yeah, I know what it would do to him. But she's . . . she just won't stop and it's like I can't stop . . . she's always at me, you know what I mean, you've seen her, Billy's too young to understand, but you've seen her . . .*

Yes, He had seen her. And Johnny had gone to work at the Plains, telling their father it was because he could get parts for the Dodge on the cheap. And that's how it happened that he had been changing a tire when the Mustang came skidding and skating across the infield with its muffler dragging up sparks; that was how his stepmother had killed his brother, so just keep playing until I shoot through, Blue, cause we goin Stud City right here in this shitheap Buick, and he remembers how the rubber smelled, and how the knobs of Johnny's spine cast small crescent shadows on the bright white of his tee-shirt, he remembers seeing Johnny get halfway up from the squat he had been working in when the Mustang hit him, squashing him between it and the Chevy, and there had been a hollow bang as the Chevy came down off its jacks, and then the bright yellow flare of flame, the rich smell of gasoline—

Chico strikes the brakes with both feet, bringing the sedan to a crunching, juddering halt on the sodden shoulder. He leans wildly across the seat, throws open the passenger door, and sprays yellow puke onto the mud and snow. The sight of it makes him puke again, and the thought of it makes him dry-heave one more time. The car almost stalls, but he catches it in time. The generator light winks out reluctantly when he guns the engine. He sits, letting the shakes work their way out of him. A car goes by him fast, a new Ford, white, throwing up great dirty fans of water and slush.

"Stud City," Chico says. "In his new stud car. Funky."

He tastes puke on his lips and in his throat and coating his sinuses. He doesn't want a cigarette. Danny Carter will let him sleep over. Tomorrow will be time enough for further decisions. He pulls back onto Route 14 and gets rolling.

8

Pretty fucking melodramatic, right?

The world has seen one or two better stories, I know that—one

or two hundred thousand better ones, more like it. It ought to have
THIS IS A PRODUCT OF AN UNDERGRADUATE CREATIVE WRITING
WORKSHOP stamped on every page . . . because that's just what it
was, at least up to a certain point. It seems both painfully derivative
and painfully sophomoric to me now; style by Hemingway (except
we've got the whole thing in the present tense for some reason—
how too fucking trendy), theme by Faulkner. Could anything be
more *serious*? More *lit'ry*?

But even its pretensions can't hide the fact that it's an extremely
sexual story written by an extremely inexperienced young man (at
the time I wrote "Stud City," I had been to bed with two girls and
had ejaculated prematurely all over one of them—not much like
Chico in the foregoing tale, I guess). Its attitude toward women
goes beyond hostility and to a point which verges on actual
ugliness—two of the women in "Stud City" are sluts, and the third
is a simple receptacle who says things like "I love you, Chico" and
"Come in, I'll give you cookies." Chico, on the other hand, is
a macho cigarette-smoking working-class hero who could have
stepped whole and breathing from the grooves of a Bruce
Springsteen record—although Springsteen was yet to be heard from
when I published the story in the college literary magazine (where it
ran between a poem called "Images of Me" and an essay on student
parietals written entirely in lower case). It is the work of a young
man every bit as insecure as he was inexperienced.

And yet it was the first story I ever wrote that felt like *my*
story—the first one that really felt *whole*, after five years of trying.
The first one that might still be able to stand up, even with its
props taken away. Ugly but alive. Even now when I read it, stifling
a smile at its pseudo-toughness and its pretensions, I can see the
true face of Gordon Lachance lurking just behind the lines of print,
a Gordon Lachance younger than the one living and writing now,
one certainly more idealistic than the best-selling novelist who is
more apt to have his paperback contracts reviewed than his books,
but not so young as the one who went with his friends that day to
see the body of a dead kid named Ray Brower. A Gordon Lachance
halfway along in the process of losing the shine.

No, it's not a very good story—its author was too busy listening to other voices to listen as closely as he should have to the one coming from inside. But it was the first time I had ever really used the places I knew and the things I felt in a piece of fiction, and there was a kind of dreadful exhilaration in seeing things that had troubled me for years come out in a new form, *a form over which I had imposed control.* It had been years since that childhood idea of Denny being in the closet of his spookily preserved room had occurred to me; I would have honestly believed I had forgotten it. Yet there it is in "Stud City," only slightly changed . . . but *controlled.*

I've resisted the urge to change it a lot more, to rewrite it, to juice it up—and that urge was fairly strong, because I find the story quite embarrassing now. But there are still things in it I like, things that would be cheapened by changes made by this later Lachance, who has the first threads of gray in his hair. Things, like that image of the shadows on Johnny's white tee-shirt or that of the rain-ripples on Jane's naked body, that seem better than they have any right to be.

Also, it was the first story I never showed to my mother and father. There was too much Denny in it. Too much Castle Rock. And most of all, too much 1960. You always know the truth, because when you cut yourself or someone else with it, there's always a bloody show.

9

My room was on the second floor, and it must have been at least ninety degrees up there. It would be a hundred and ten by afternoon, even with all the windows open. I was really glad I wasn't sleeping there that night, and the thought of where we were going made me excited all over again. I made two blankets into a bedroll and tied it with my old belt. I collected all my money, which was sixty-eight cents. Then I was ready to go.

I went down the back stairs to avoid meeting my dad in front of the house, but I hadn't needed to worry; he was still out in the garden with the hose, making useless rainbows in the air and looking through them.

I walked down Summer Street and cut through a vacant lot to

Carbine—where the offices of the Castle Rock *Call* stand today. I was headed up Carbine toward the clubhouse when a car pulled over to the curb and Chris got out. He had his old Boy Scout pack in one hand and two blankets rolled up and tied with clothesrope in the other.

"Thanks, mister," he said, and trotted over to join me as the car pulled away. His Boy Scout canteen was slung around his neck and under one arm so that it finally ended up banging on his hip. His eyes were sparkling.

"Gordie! You wanna see something?"

"Sure, I guess so. What?"

"Come on down here first." He pointed at the narrow space between the Blue Point Diner and the Castle Rock Drugstore.

"What is it, Chris?"

"Come on, I said!"

He ran down the alley and after a brief moment (that's all it took me to cast aside my better judgment) I ran after him. The two buildings were set slightly toward each other rather than running parallel, and so the alley narrowed as it went back. We waded through trashy drifts of old newspapers and stepped over cruel, sparkly nests of broken beer and soda bottles. Chris cut behind the Blue Point and put his bedroll down. There were eight or nine garbage cans lined up here and the stench was incredible.

"Phew! Chris! Come on, gimme a break!"

"Gimme your arm," Chris said, by rote.

"No, sincerely, I'm gonna throw u—"

The words broke off in my mouth and I forgot all about the smelly garbage cans. Chris had unslung his pack and opened it and reached inside. Now he was holding out a huge pistol with dark wood grips.

"You wanna be the Lone Ranger or the Cisco Kid?" Chris asked, grinning.

"Walking, talking Jesus! Where'd you get that?"

"Hawked it out of my dad's bureau. It's a forty-five."

"Yeah, I can see that," I said, although it could have been a .38 or a .357 for all I knew—in spite of all the John D. MacDonalds and Ed McBains I'd read, the only pistol I'd ever seen up close was the one Constable Bannerman carried . . . and although all the kids asked him to take it out of its holster, Bannerman never would. "Man, your dad's gonna hide you when he finds out. You said he was on a mean streak *anyway*."

His eyes just went on dancing. "That's *it*, man. He ain't gonna find out *nothing*. Him and these other rummies are all laid up down in Harrison with six or eight bottles of wine. They won't be back for a week. Fucking rummies." His lip curled. He was the only guy in our gang who would never take a drink, even to show he had, you know, big balls. He said he wasn't going to grow up to be a fucking tosspot like his old man. And he told me once privately—this was after the DeSpain twins showed up with a six-pack they'd hawked from their old man and everybody teased Chris because he wouldn't take a beer or even a swallow—that he was *scared* to drink. He said his father never got his nose all the way out of the bottle anymore, that his older brother had been drunk out of his tits when he raped that girl, and that Eyeball was always guzzling Purple Jesuses with Ace Merrill and Charlie Hogan and Billy Tessio. What, he asked me, did I think his chances of letting go of the bottle would be once he picked it up? Maybe you think that's funny, a twelve-year-old worrying that he might be an incipient alcoholic, but it wasn't funny to Chris. Not at all. He'd thought about the possibility a lot. He'd had occasion to.

"You got shells for it?"

"Nine of them—all that was left in the box. He'll think he used em himself, shooting at cans while he was drunk."

"Is it loaded?"

"*No!* Chrissake, what do you think I *am*?"

I finally took the gun. I liked the heavy way it sat there in my hand. I could see myself as Steve Carella of the 87th Squad, going after that guy The Heckler or maybe covering Meyer Meyer or Kling while they broke into a desperate junkie's sleazy apartment. I sighted on one of the smelly trashcans and squeezed the trigger.

KA-BLAM!

The gun bucked in my hand. Fire licked from the end. It felt as if my wrist had just been broken. My heart vaulted nimbly into the back of my mouth and crouched there, trembling. A big hole appeared in the corrugated metal surface of the trashcan—it was the work of an evil conjuror.

"Jesus!" I screamed.

Chris was cackling wildly—in real amusement or hysterical terror I couldn't tell. "You did it, you did it! *Gordie did it!*" he bugled. *"Hey, Gordon Lachance is shooting up Castle Rock!"*

"Shut up! Let's get out of here!" I screamed, and grabbed him by the shirt.

As we ran, the back door of the Blue Point jerked open and Francine Tupper stepped out in her white rayon waitress's uniform. "Who did that? Who's letting off cherry-bombs back here?"

We ran like hell, cutting behind the drugstore and the hardware store and the Emporium Galorium, which sold antiques and junk and dime books. We climbed a fence, spiking our palms with splinters, and finally came out on Curran Street. I threw the .45 at Chris as we ran; he was killing himself laughing but caught it and somehow managed to stuff it back into his knapsack and close one of the snaps. Once around the corner of Curran and back on Carbine Street, we slowed to a walk so we wouldn't look suspicious, running in the heat. Chris was still giggling.

"Man, you shoulda seen your face, Oh man, that was priceless. That was really fine. My fucking-A." He shook his head and slapped his leg and howled.

"You knew it was loaded, didn't you? You wet! I'm gonna be in trouble. That Tupper babe saw me."

"Shit, she thought it was a firecracker. Besides, ole Thunderjugs Tupper can't see past the end of her own nose, you know that. Thinks wearing glasses would spoil her *pret*-ty *face*." He put one palm against the small of his back and bumped his hips and got laughing again.

"Well, I don't care. That was a mean trick, Chris. Really."

"Come on, Gordie." He put a hand on my shoulder. "I didn't know it was loaded, honest to God, I swear on my mother's name. I just took it out of my dad's bureau. He always unloads it. He must have been really drunk when he put it away the last time."

"You really didn't load it?"

"No sir."

"You swear it on your mother's name even if she goes to hell for you telling a lie?"

"I swear." He crossed himself and spit, his face as open and repentant as any choirboy's. But when we turned into the vacant lot where our treehouse was and saw Vern and Teddy sitting on their bedrolls waiting for us, he started to laugh again. He told them the whole story, and after everybody had had their yucks, Teddy asked him what Chris thought they needed a pistol for.

"Nothin," Chris said. "Except we might see a bear. Something like that. Besides, it's spooky sleeping out at night in the woods."

Everybody nodded at that. Chris was the biggest, toughest guy in our gang, and he could always get away with saying things like that. Teddy, on the other hand, would have gotten his ass ragged off if he even hinted he was afraid of the dark.

"Did you set your tent up in the field?" Teddy asked Vern.

"Yeah. And I put two turned-on flashlights in it so it'll look like we're there after dark."

"Hot shit!" I said, and clapped Vern on the back. For him, that was real thinking. He grinned and blushed.

"So let's *go*," Teddy said. "Come on, it's almost twelve already!"

Chris got up and we gathered around him.

"We'll walk across Beeman's field and behind that furniture place by Sonny's Texaco," he said. "Then we'll get on the railroad tracks down by the dump and just walk across the trestle into Harlow."

"How far do you think it's gonna be?" Teddy asked.

Chris shrugged. "Harlow's big. We're gonna be walking at least twenty miles. That sound right to you, Gordie?"

"Yeah. It might even be thirty."

"Even if it's thirty we ought to be there by tomorrow afternoon, if no one goes pussy."

"No pussies here," Teddy said at once.

We all looked at each other for a second.

"Miaoww," Vern said, and we all laughed.

"Come on, you guys," Chris said, and shouldered his pack.

We walked out of the vacant lot together, Chris slightly in the lead.

10

By the time we got across Beeman's field and had struggled up the cindery embankment to the Great Southern and Western Maine tracks, we had all taken our shirts off and tied them around our waists. We were sweating like pigs. At the top of the embankment we looked down the tracks, toward where we'd have to go.

I'll never forget that moment, no matter how old I get. I was the only one with a watch—a cheap Timex I'd gotten as a premium for selling Cloverine Brand Salve the year before. Its hands stood at straight up noon, and the sun beat down on the dry, shadeless vista before us with savage heat. You could feel it working to get in under your skull and fry your brains.

Behind us was Castle Rock, spread out on the long hill that was known as Castle View, surrounding its green and shady common. Further down Castle River you could see the stacks of the woollen mill spewing smoke into a sky the color of gunmetal and spewing waste into the water. The Jolly Furniture Barn was on our left. And straight ahead of us the railroad tracks, bright and heliographing in the sun. They paralleled the Castle River, which was on our left. To our right was a lot of overgrown scrubland (there's a motorcycle track there today—they have scrambles every Sunday afternoon at 2:00 P.M.). An old abandoned water tower stood on the horizon, rusty and somehow scary.

We stood there for that one noontime moment and then Chris said impatiently, "Come on, let's get going."

We walked beside the tracks in the cinders, kicking up little puffs of blackish dust at every step. Our socks and sneakers were soon gritty with it. Vern started singing "Roll Me Over in the Clover" but soon quit it, which was a break for our ears. Only Teddy and Chris had brought canteens, and we were all hitting them pretty hard.

"We could fill the canteens again at the dump faucet," I said. "My dad told me that's a safe well. It's a hundred and ninety feet deep."

"Okay," Chris said, being the tough platoon leader. "That'll be a good place to take five, anyway."

"What about food?" Teddy asked suddenly. "I bet nobody thought to bring something to eat. I know I didn't."

Chris stopped. "Shit! I didn't, either. Gordie?"

I shook my head, wondering how I could have been so dumb. "Vern?"

"Zip," Vern said. "Sorry."

"Well, let's see how much money we got," I said. I untied my shirt, spread it on the cinders, and dropped my own sixty-eight cents onto it. The coins glittered feverishly in the sunlight. Chris had a tattered dollar and two pennies. Teddy had two quarters and two nickles. Vern had exactly seven cents.

"Two-thirty-seven," I said. "Not bad. There's a store at the end of that little road that goes to the dump. Somebody'll have to walk down there and get some hamburger and some tonics while the others rest."

"Who?" Vern asked.

"We'll match for it when we get to the dump. Come on."

I slid all the money into my pants pocket and was just tying my shirt around my waist again when Chris hollered: *"Train!"*

I put my hand out on one of the rails to feel it, even though I could already hear it. The rail was thrumming crazily; for a moment it was like holding the train in my hand.

"Paratroops over the side!" Vern bawled, and leaped halfway down the embankment in one crazy, clownish stride. Vern was nuts for playing paratroops anyplace the ground was soft—a gravel pit, a haymow, an embankment like this one. Chris jumped after him. The train was really loud now, probably headed straight up our side of the river toward Lewiston. Instead of jumping, Teddy turned in the direction from which it was coming. His thick glasses glittered in the sun. His long hair flopped untidily over his brow in sweat-soaked stringers.

"Go on, Teddy," I said.

"No, huh-uh, I'm gonna dodge it." He looked at me, his magnified eyes frantic with excitement. "A train-dodge, dig it? What's trucks after a fuckin train-dodge?"

"You're crazy, man. You want to get killed?"

"Just like the beach at Normandy!" Teddy yelled, and strode out into the middle of the tracks. He stood on one of the crossties, lightly balanced.

I stood stunned for a moment, unable to believe stupidity of such width and breadth. Then I grabbed him, dragged him fighting and protesting to the embankment, and pushed him over. I jumped after him and Teddy caught me a good one in the guts while I was still in the air. The wind whooshed out of me, but I was still able to hit him in the sternum with my knee and knock him flat on his back before he could get all the way up. I landed, gasping and sprawling, and Teddy grabbed me around the neck. We went rolling all the way to the bottom of the embankment, hitting and clawing at each other while Chris and Vern stared at us, stupidly surprised.

"You little son of a bitch!" Teddy was screaming at me. "You fucker! Don't you throw your weight around on me! I'll kill you, you dipshit!"

I was getting my breath back now, and I made it to my feet. I backed away as Teddy advanced, holding my open hands up to slap away his punches, half-laughing and half-scared. Teddy was no one to fool around with when he went into one of his screaming fits. He'd take on a big kid in that state, and after the big kid broke both of his arms, he'd bite.

"Teddy, you can dodge anything you want after we see what we're going to see but

whack on the shoulder as one wildly swinging fist got past me

"until then no one's supposed to *see* us, you

whack on the side of the face, and then we might have had a real fight if Chris and Vern

"stupid wet end!"

hadn't grabbed us and kept us apart. Above us, the train roared by in a thunder of diesel exhaust and the great heavy clacking of boxcar wheels. A few cinders bounced down the embankment and the argument was over . . . at least until we could hear ourselves talk again.

It was only a short freight, and when the caboose had trailed by, Teddy said: "I'm gonna kill him. At least give him a fat lip." He struggled against Chris, but Chris only grabbed him tighter.

"Calm down, Teddy," Chris said quietly, and he kept saying it until Teddy stopped struggling and just stood there, his glasses hanging askew and his hearing-aid cord dangling limply against his chest on its way down to the battery, which he had shoved into the pocket of his jeans.

When he was completely still, Chris turned to me and said: "What the hell are you fighting with him about, Gordon?"

"He wanted to dodge the train. I figured the engineer would see him and report it. They might send a cop out."

"Ahhh, he'd be too busy makin chocolate in his drawers," Teddy said, but he didn't seem angry anymore. The storm had passed.

"Gordie was just tryin to do the right thing," Vern said. "Come on, peace."

"Peace, you guys," Chris agreed.

"Yeah, okay," I said, and held out my hand, palm up. "Peace, Teddy?"

"I coulda dodged it," he said to me. "You know that, Gordie?"

"Yeah," I said, although the thought turned me cold inside. "I know it."

"Okay. Peace, then."

"Skin it, man," Chris ordered, and let go of Teddy.

Teddy slapped his hand down on mine hard enough to sting and then turned it over. I slapped his.

"Fuckin pussy Lachance," Teddy said.

"*Meeiowww,*" I said.

"Come on, you guys," Vern said. "Let's go, okay?"

"Go anywhere you want, but don't go here," Chris said solemnly, and Vern drew back as if to hit him.

11

We got to the dump around one-thirty, and Vern led the way down the embankment with a *Paratroops over the side!* We went to the bottom in big jumps and leaped over the brackish trickle of water oozing listlessly out of the culvert which poked out of the cinders. Beyond this small boggy area was the sandy, trash-littered verge of the dump.

There was a six-foot security fence surrounding it. Every twenty feet weather-faded signs were posted. They said:

CASTLE ROCK DUMP
HOURS 4–8 P.M.
CLOSED MONDAYS
TRESPASSING STRICTLY FORBIDDEN

We climbed to the top of the fence, swung over, and jumped down. Teddy and Vern led the way toward the well, which you tapped with an old-fashioned pump—the kind from which you had to call the water with elbow-grease. There was a Crisco can filled with water next to the pump handle, and the great sin was to forget to leave it filled for the next guy to come along. The iron handle stuck off at an angle, looking a one-winged bird that was trying to fly. It had once been green, but almost all of the paint had been rubbed off by the thousands of hands that had worked that handle since 1940.

The dump is one of my strongest memories of Castle Rock. It always reminds me of the surrealist painters when I think of it—those fellows who were always painting pictures of clockfaces lying limply in the crotches of trees or Victorian living rooms standing in the middle of the Sahara or steam engines coming out of fireplaces. To my child's eye, *nothing* in the Castle Rock Dump looked as if it really belonged there.

We had entered from the back. If you came from the front, a wide dirt road came in through the gate, broadened out into a semicircular area that had been bulldozed as flat as a dirt landing-strip, and then ended abruptly at the edge of the dumping-pit. The pump (Teddy and Vern were currently standing there and squabbling about who was going to prime it) was at the back of this great pit. It was maybe eighty feet deep and filled with all the American things that get empty, wear out, or just don't work anymore. There was so much stuff that my eyes hurt just looking at it—or maybe it was your brain that actually hurt, because it could never quite decide what your eye should stop on. Then your eye *would* stop, or be stopped, by something that seemed as out of place as those limp clockfaces or the living room in the desert. A brass bedstead leaning drunkenly in the sun. A little girl's dolly looking amazedly between her thighs as she gave birth to stuffing. An overturned Studebaker automobile with its chrome bullet nose glittering in the sun like some Buck Rogers missile. One of those giant water bottles they have in office buildings, transformed by the summer sun into a hot, blazing sapphire.

There was plenty of wildlife there, too, although it wasn't the kind you see in the Walt Disney nature films or at those tame zoos where you can pet the animals. Plump rats, woodchucks grown sleek and lumbering on such rich chow as rotting hamburger and maggoty vegetables, seagulls by the thousands, and stalking among the gulls like thoughtful, introspective ministers, an occasional huge crow. It was also the place where the town's stray dogs came for a meal when they couldn't find any trashcans to knock over or any deer to run. They were a miserable, ugly-tempered, mongrel lot; slat-sided and grinning bitterly, they would attack each other over a flyblown piece of bologna or a pile of chicken guts fuming in the sun.

But these dogs never attacked Milo Pressman, the dump-keeper, because Milo was never without Chopper at his heel. Chopper was—at least until Joe Camber's dog Cujo went rabid twenty years later—the most feared and least seen dog in Castle Rock. He was the meanest dog for forty miles around (or so we heard), and ugly enough to stop a striking clock. The kids whispered legends about Chopper's meanness. Some said he was half German shepherd, some said he was mostly boxer, and a kid from Castle View with the unfortunate name of Harry Horr claimed that Chopper was a Doberman pinscher whose vocal cords had been surgically removed so you couldn't hear him when he was on the attack. There were other kids who claimed Chopper was a maniacal Irish wolfhound and Milo Pressman fed him a special mixture of Gaines Meal and chicken blood. These same kids claimed that Milo didn't dare take Chopper out of his shack unless the dog was hooded like a hunting falcon.

The most common story was that Pressman had trained Chopper not just to sic but to sic specific *parts* of the human anatomy. Thus an unfortunate kid who had illegally scaled the dump fence to pick for illicit treasures might hear Milo Pressman cry: "Chopper! Sic! Hand!" And Chopper would grab that hand and hold on, ripping skin and tendons, powdering bones between his slavering jaws, until Milo told him to quit. It was rumored that Chopper could take an ear, an eye, a foot, or a leg . . . and that a second offender who was surprised by Milo and the ever-loyal Chopper would hear the dread cry: "Chopper! Sic! Balls!" And that kid would be a soprano for the rest of his life. Milo himself was more commonly seen and thus more commonly regarded. He was just a half-bright working joe who supplemented his small town salary by fixing things people threw away and selling them around town.

There was no sign of either Milo or Chopper today.

Chris and I watched Vern prime the pump while Teddy worked the handle frantically. At last he was rewarded with a flood of clear water. A moment later both of them had their heads under the trough, Teddy still pumping away a mile a minute.

"Teddy's crazy," I said softly.

"Oh yeah," Chris said matter-of-factly. "He won't live to be twice the age he is now, I bet. His dad burnin his ears like that. That's what did it. He's crazy to dodge trucks the way he does. He can't see worth a shit, glasses or no glasses."

"You remember that time in the tree?"

"Yeah."

The year before, Teddy and Chris had been climbing the big pine tree behind my house. They were almost to the top and Chris said they couldn't go any further because all of the branches up there were rotten. Teddy got that crazy, stubborn look on his face and said fuck that, he had pine tar all over his hands and he was gonna go up until he could touch the top. Nothing Chris said could talk him out of it. So up he went, and he actually made it—he only weighed seventy-five pounds or so, remember. He stood there, clutching the top of the pine in one tar-gummy hand, shouting that he was king of the world or some stupid thing like that, and then there was a sickening, rotted crack as the branch he was standing on gave way and he plummeted. What happened next was one of those things that make you sure there must be a God. Chris reached out, purely on reflex, and what he caught was a fistful of Teddy Duchamp's hair. And although his wrist swelled up fat and he was unable to use his right hand very well for almost two weeks, Chris held him until Teddy, screaming and cursing, got his foot on a live branch thick enough to support his weight. Except for Chris's blind grab, he would have turned and crashed and smashed all the way to the foot of the tree, a hundred and twenty feet below. When they got down, Chris was gray-faced and almost puking with the fear reaction. And Teddy wanted to fight him for pulling his hair. They would have gone at it, too, if I hadn't been there to make peace.

"I dream about that every now and then," Chris said, and looked at me with strangely defenseless eyes. "Except in this dream I have, I always miss him. I just get a couple of hairs and Teddy screams and down he goes. Weird, huh?"

"Weird," I agreed, and for just one moment we looked in each other's eyes and saw some of the true things that made us friends. Then we looked away again and watched Teddy and Vern throwing water at each other, screaming and laughing and calling each other pussies.

"Yeah, but you didn't miss him," I said. "Chris Chambers never misses, am I right?"

"Not even when the ladies leave the seat down," he said. He winked at me, formed an O with his thumb and forefinger, and spat a neat white bullet through it.

"Eat me raw, Chambers," I said.

"Through a Flavor Straw," he said, and we grinned at each other.

Vern yelled: *"Come on and get your water before it runs back down the pipe!"*

"Race you," Chris said.

"In this heat? You're off your gourd."

"Come on," he said, still grinning. "On my go."

"Okay."

"Go!"

We raced, our sneakers digging up the hard, sunbaked dirt, our torsos leaning out ahead of our flying bluejeaned legs, our fists doubled. It was a dead heat, with both Vern on Chris's side and

Teddy on mine holding up their middle fingers at the same moment. We collapsed laughing in the still, smoky odor of the place, and Chris tossed Vern his canteen. When it was full, Chris and I went to the pump and first Chris pumped for me and then I pumped for him, the shockingly cold water sluicing off the soot and the heat all in a flash, sending our suddenly freezing scalps four months ahead into January. Then I re-filled the lard can and we all walked over to sit down in the shade of the dump's only tree, a stunted ash forty feet from Milo Pressman's tarpaper shack. The tree was hunched slightly to the west, as if what it really wanted to do was pick up its roots the way an old lady would pick up her skirts and just get the hell out of the dump.

"The most!" Chris said, laughing, tossing his tangled hair back from his brow.

"A blast," I said, nodding, still laughing myself.

"This is really a good time," Vern said simply, and he didn't just mean being off-limits inside the dump, or fudging our folks, or going on a hike up the railroad tracks into Harlow; he meant those things but it seems to me now that there was more, and that we all knew it. Everything was there and around us. We knew exactly who we were and exactly where we were going. It was grand.

We sat under the tree for awhile, shooting the shit like we always did—who had the best ballteam (still the Yankees with Mantle and Maris, of course), what was the best car ('55 Thunderbird, with Teddy holding out stubbornly for the '58 Corvette), who was the toughest guy in Castle Rock who wasn't in our gang (we all agreed it was Jamie Gallant, who gave Mrs. Ewing the finger and then sauntered out of her class with his hands in his pockets while she shouted at him), the best TV show (either *The Untouchables* or *Peter Gunn*—both Robert Stack as Eliot Ness and Craig Stevens as Gunn were cool), all that stuff.

It was Teddy who first noticed that the shade of the ash tree was getting longer and asked me what time it was. I looked at my watch and was surprised to see it was quarter after two.

"Hey man," Vern said. "Somebody's got to go for provisions. Dump opens at four. I don't want to still be here when Milo and Chopper make the scene."

Even Teddy agreed. He wasn't afraid of Milo, who had a pot belly and was at least forty, but every kid in Castle Rock squeezed his balls between his legs when Chopper's name was mentioned.

"Okay," I said. "Odd man goes?"

"That's you, Gordie," Chris said, smiling. "Odd as a cod."

"So's your mother," I said, and gave them each a coin. "Flip."

Four coins glittered up into the sun. Four hands snatched them from the air. Four flat smacks on four grimy wrists. We uncovered. Two heads and two tails. We flipped again and this time all four of us had tails.

"Oh Jesus, that's a goocher," Vern said, not telling us anything we didn't know. Four heads, or a moon, was supposed to be extraordinarily good luck. Four tails was a goocher, and that meant very bad luck.

"Fuck that shit," Chris said. "It doesn't mean anything. Go again."

"No, man," Vern said earnestly. "A goocher, that's really bad. You remember when Clint Bracken and those guys got wiped out on Sirois Hill in Durham? Billy tole me they was flippin for beers and they came up a goocher just before they got into the car. And bang! they all get fuckin totalled. I don't like that. Sincerely."

"Nobody believes that crap about moons and goochers," Teddy said impatiently. "It's baby stuff, Vern. You gonna flip or not?"

Vern flipped, but with obvious reluctance. This time he, Chris, and Teddy all had tails. I was showing Thomas Jefferson on a nickle. And I was suddenly scared. It was as if a shadow had crossed some inner sun. They still had a goocher, the three of them, as if dumb fate had pointed at them a second time. Abruptly I thought of Chris saying: *I just get a couple of hairs and Teddy screams and down he goes. Weird, huh?*

Three tails, one head.

Then Teddy was laughing his crazy, cackling laugh and pointing at me and the feeling was gone.

"I heard that only fairies laugh like that," I said, and gave him the finger.

"Eeee-eeee-eeee, Gordie," Teddy laughed. "Go get the provisions, you fuckin morphadite."

I wasn't really sorry to be going. I was rested up and didn't mind going down the road to the Florida Market.

"Don't call me any of your mother's pet names," I said to Teddy.

"Eeee-eee-eeee, what a fuckin wet you are, Lachance."

"Go on, Gordie," Chris said. "We'll wait over by the tracks."

"You guys better not go without me," I said.

Vern laughed. "Goin without you'd be like goin with Slitz instead of Budweiser's, Gordie."

"Ah, shut up."

They chanted together: "I don't shut up, I *grow* up. And when I look at you I *throw* up."

"Then your mother goes around the corner and licks it up," I said, and hauled ass out of there, giving them the finger over my shoulder as I went. I never had any friends later on like the ones I had when I was twelve. Jesus, did you?

12

Different strokes for different folks, they say now, and that's cool. So if I say *summer* to you, you get one set of private, personal images that are all the way different from mine. That's cool. But for me, *summer* is always going to mean running down the road to the Florida Market with change jingling in my pockets, the temperature in the gay nineties, my feet dressed in Keds. The word conjures an image of the GS&WM railroad tracks running into a perspective-point in the distance, burnished so white under the sun that when you closed your eyes you could still see them there in the dark, only blue instead of white.

But there was more to that summer than our trip across the river to look for Ray Brower, although that looms the largest. Sounds of The Fleetwoods singing "Come Softly to Me" and Robin Luke singing "Susie Darlin" and Little Anthony popping the vocal on "I Ran All the Way Home." Were they all hits in that summer of 1960? Yes and no. Mostly yes. In the long purple evenings when rock and roll from WLAM blurred into night baseball from WCOU, time shifted. I think it was all 1960 and that the summer went on for a space of years, held magically intact in a web of sounds: the sweet hum of crickets, the machine-gun roar of playing-cards riffling against the spokes of some kid's bicycle as he pedaled home for a late supper of cold cuts and iced tea, the flat Texas voice of Buddy Knox singing "Come along and be my party doll, and I'll make love to you, to you," and the baseball announcer's voice mingling with the song and with the smell of freshly cut grass: "Count's three and two now. Whitey Ford leans over . . . shakes off the sign . . . now he's got it . . . Ford pauses . . . pitches . . . *and there it goes! Williams got all of that one! Kiss it goodbye! RED SOX LEAD, THREE TO ONE!*" Was Ted Williams still playing for the Red Sox in 1960? You bet your ass he was—.316 for my man Ted. I remember that very clearly. Baseball had become important to me in the last couple of years, ever since I'd had to face the knowledge that baseball players were as much flesh and blood as I was. That knowledge came when Roy Campanella's car overturned and the papers screamed mortal news from the front pages: his career was done, he was going to sit in a wheelchair for the rest of his life. How that came back to me, with that same sickening mortal thud, when I sat down to this typewriter one morning two years ago, turned on the radio, and heard that Thurman Munson had died while trying to land his airplane.

There were movies to go see at the Gem, which has long since been torn down; science fiction movies like *Gog* with Richard Egan and westerns with Audie Murphy (Teddy saw every movie Audie Murphy made at least three times; he believed Murphy was almost a god) and war movies with John Wayne. There were games and endless bolted meals, lawns to mow, places to run to, walls to pitch pennies against, people to clap you on the back. And now I sit here trying to look through an IBM keyboard and see that time, trying to recall the best and worst of that green and brown summer, and I can almost feel the skinny, scabbed boy still buried in this advancing body and hear those sounds. But the apotheosis of the memory and the time is Gordon Lachance running down the road to the Florida Market with change in his pockets and sweat running down his back.

I asked for three pounds of hamburger and got some hamburger rolls, four bottles of Coke and a two-cent churchkey to open them with. The owner, a man named George Dusset, got the meat and then leaned by his cash register, one hammy hand planted on the counter by the big bottle of hardcooked eggs, a toothpick in his mouth, his huge beer belly rounding his white tee-shirt like a sail filled with a good wind. He stood right there as I shopped, making sure I didn't try to hawk anything. He didn't say a word until he was weighing up the hamburger.

"I know you. You're Denny Lachance's brother. Ain't you?" The toothpick journeyed from one corner of his mouth to the other, as if on ball bearings. He reached behind the cash register, picked up a bottle of S'OK cream soda, and chugged it.

"Yes, sir. But Denny, he—"

"Yeah, I know. That's a sad thing, kid. The Bible says: 'In the midst of life, we are in death.' Did you know that? Yuh. I lost a brother in Korea. You look just like Denny, people ever tell you that? Yuh. Spitting image."

"Yes, sir, sometimes," I said glumly.

"I remember the year he was All-Conference. Halfback, he played. Yuh. Could he run? Father God and Sonny Jesus! You're probably too young to remember." He was looking over my head, out through the screen door and into the blasting heat, as if he were having a beautiful vision of my brother.

"I remember. Uh, Mr. Dusset?"

"What, kid?" His eyes were still misty with memory; the toothpick trembled a little between his lips.

"Your thumb is on that scales."

"*What?*" He looked down, astounded, to where the ball of his thumb was pressed firmly on the white enamel. If I hadn't moved away from him a little bit when he started talking about Dennis, the ground meat would have hidden it. "Why, so it is. Yuh. I guess I just got thinkin about your brother, God love him." George Dusset signed a cross on himself. When he took his thumb off the scales, the needle sprang back six ounces. He patted a little more meat on top and then did the package up with white butcher's paper.

"Okay," he said past the toothpick. "Let's see what we got here. Three pounds of hamburg, that's a dollar forty-four. Hamburg rolls, that's twenty-seven. Four sodas, forty cents. One churchkey, two pence. Comes to . . . " He added it up on the bag he was going to put the stuff in. "Two-twenty-nine."

"Thirteen," I said.

He looked up at me very slowly, frowning. "Huh?"

"Two-thirteen. You added it wrong."

"Kid, are you—"

"You added it wrong," I said. "First you put your thumb on the scales and then you overcharged on the groceries, Mr. Dusset. I was gonna throw some Hostess Twinkies on top of that order but now I guess I won't." I spanged two dollars and thirteen cents down on the Schlitz placemat in front of him.

He looked at the money, then at me. The frown was now tremendous, the lines on his face as deep as fissures. "What are you, kid?" he said in a low voice that was ominously confidential. "Are you some kind of smartass?"

'No, sir," I said. "But you ain't gonna jap me and get away with it. What would your mother say if she knew you was japping little kids?"

He thrust our stuff into the paper bag with quick stiff movements, making the Coke bottles clink together. He thrust the bag at me roughly, not caring if I dropped it and broke the sodas or not. His swarthy face was flushed and dull, the frown now frozen in place. "Okay, kid. Here you go. Now what you do is you get the Christ out of my store. I see you in here again and I going to throw you out, me. Yuh. Smartass little sonofawhore."

"I won't come in again," I said, walking over to the screen door and pushing it open. The hot afternoon buzzed somnolently along its appointed course outside, sounding green and brown and full of silent light. "Neither will none of my friends. I guess I got fifty or so."

"Your brother wasn't no smartass!" George Dusset yelled.

"*Fuck you!*" I yelled, and ran like hell down the road.

I heard the screen door bang open like a gunshot and his bull roar came after me: "*If you ever come in here again I'll fat your lip for you, you little punk!*"

I ran until I was over the first hill, scared and laughing to myself, my heart beating out a triphammer pulse in my chest. Then I slowed to a fast walk, looking back over my shoulder every now and then to make sure he wasn't going to take after me in his car, or anything.

He didn't, and pretty soon I got to the dump gate. I put the bag inside my shirt, climbed the gate, and monkeyed down the other side. I was halfway across the dump area when I saw something I didn't like—Milo Pressman's portholed '56 Buick was parked behind his tarpaper shack. If Milo saw me, I was going to be in a world of hurt. As yet there was no sign of either him or the infamous Chopper, but all at once the chain-link fence at the back of the dump seemed very far away. I found myself wishing I'd gone around the outside, but I was now too far into the dump to want to turn around and go back. If Milo saw me climbing the dump fence, I'd probably be in dutch when I got home, but that didn't scare me as much as Milo yelling for Chopper to sic would.

Scary violin music started to play in my head. I kept putting one foot in front of the other, trying to look casual, trying to look as if I belonged here with a paper grocery sack poking out of my shirt, heading for the fence between the dump and the railroad tracks.

I was about fifty feet from the fence and just beginning to think that everything was going to be all right after all when I heard Milo shout: "Hey! Hey, you! Kid! Get away f'n that fence! Get outta here!"

The smart thing to have done would have been to just agree with the guy and go around, but by then I was so keyed that instead of doing the smart thing I just broke for the fence with a wild yell, my sneakers kicking up dust. Vern, Teddy, and Chris came out of the underbrush on the other side of the fence and stared anxiously through the chain-link.

"You come back here!" Milo bawled. *"Come back here or I'll sic my dawg on you, goddammit!"*

I did not exactly find that to be the voice of sanity and conciliation, and I ran even faster for the fence, my arms pumping, the brown grocery bag crackling against my skin. Teddy started to laugh his idiotic chortling laugh, *eee-eee-eeee* into the air like some reed instrument being played by a lunatic.

"Go, Gordie! Go!" Vern screamed.

And Milo yelled: "Sic 'im, Chopper! Go get 'im, boy!"

I threw the bag over the fence and Vern elbowed Teddy out of the way to catch it. Behind me I could hear Chopper coming, shaking the earth, blurting fire out of one distended nostril and ice out of the other, dripping sulphur from his champing jaws. I threw myself halfway up the fence with one leap, screaming. I made it to the top in no more than three seconds and simply leaped—I never thought about it, never even looked down to see what I might land on. What I *almost* landed on was Teddy, who was doubled over and laughing like crazy. His glasses had fallen off and tears were streaming out of his eyes. I missed him by inches and hit the clay-gravel embankment just to his left. At the same instant, Chopper hit the chain-link fence behind me and let out a howl of mingled pain and disappointment. I turned around, holding one skinned knee, and got my first look at the famous Chopper—and my first lesson in the vast difference between myth and reality.

Instead of some huge hellhound with red, savage eyes and teeth jutting out of his mouth like straight-pipes from a hotrod, I was looking at a medium-sized mongrel dog that was a perfectly common black and white. He was yapping and jumping fruitlessly, going up on his back legs to paw the fence.

Teddy was now strutting up and down in front of the fence, twiddling his glasses in one hand, and inciting Chopper to ever greater rage.

"Kiss my ass, Choppie!" Teddy invited, spittle flying from his lips. "Kiss my ass! Bite shit!"

He bumped his fanny against the chain-link fence and Chopper did his level best to take Teddy up on his invitation. He got nothing for his pains but a good healthy nose-bump. He began to bark crazily, foam flying from his snout. Teddy kept bumping his rump against the fence and Chopper kept lunging at it, always missing, doing nothing but racking out his nose, which was now bleeding. Teddy kept exhorting him, calling him by the somehow grisly diminutive "Choppie," and Chris and Vern were lying weakly on the embankment, laughing so hard that they could now do little more than wheeze.

And here came Milo Pressman, dressed in sweat-stained fatigues and a New York Giants baseball cap, his mouth drawn down in distracted anger.

"Here, here!" he was yelling. "You boys stop a-teasing that dawg! You hear me? *Stop it right now!*"

"Bite it, Choppie!" Teddy yelled, strutting up and down on our side of the fence like a mad Prussian reviewing his troops. "Come on and sic me! Sic me!"

Chopper went nuts. I mean it sincerely. He ran around in a big circle, yelping and barking and foaming, rear feet spewing up tough little dry clods. He went around about three times, getting his courage up, I guess, and then he launched himself straight at the security fence. He must have been going thirty miles an hour when he hit it, I kid you not—his doggy lips were stretched back from his teeth and his ears were flying in the slipstream. The whole fence made a low, musical sound as the chain-link was not just driven back against the posts but sort of *stretched* back. It was like a zither note—*yimmmmmmmm*. A strangled yawp came out of Chopper's mouth, both eyes came up blank, and he did a totally amazing reverse snap-roll, landing on his back with a solid thump that sent dust puffing up around him. He just lay there for a moment and then he crawled off with his tongue hanging crookedly from the left side of his mouth.

At this, Milo himself went almost berserk with rage. His complexion darkened to a scary plum color—even his scalp was purple under the short hedgehog bristles of his flattop haircut. Sitting stunned in the dirt, both knees of my jeans torn out, my heart still thudding from the nearness of my escape, I thought that Milo looked like a human version of Chopper.

"I know you!" Milo raved. "You're Teddy Duchamp! I know *all* of you! Sonny, I'll beat your ass, teasing my dawg like that!"

"Like to see you try!" Teddy raved right back. "Let's see you climb over this fence and get me, fatass!"

"*WHAT? WHAT DID YOU CALL ME?*"

"*FATASS!*" Teddy screamed happily. "*LARD-BUCKET! TUBBAGUTS! COME ON! COME ON!*" He was jumping up and down, fists clenched, sweat flying from his hair. "*TEACH YOU TO*

*SIC YOUR STUPID DOG ON PEOPLE! COME ON! LIKE TO SEE
YOU TRY!"*

"You little tin-weasel peckerwood loony's son! I'll see your
mother gets an invitation to go down and talk to the judge in court
about what you done to my dawg!"

"What did you call me?" Teddy asked hoarsely. He had stopped
jumping up and down. His eyes had gone huge and glassy, and his
skin was the color of lead.

Milo had called Teddy a lot of things, but he was able to go back
and get the one that had struck home with no trouble at all—since
then I have noticed again and again what a genius people have for
that . . . for finding the LOONY button down inside and not just
pressing it but hammering on the fucker.

"Your dad was a loony," he said, grinning. "Loony up in Togus,
that's what. Crazier'n a shithouse rat. Crazier'n a buck with
tickwood fever. Nuttier'n a long-tailed cat in a room fulla rockin
chairs. Loony. No wonder you're actin the way you are, with a loony
for a f—"

"YOUR MOTHER BLOWS DEAD RATS!" Teddy screamed.
*"AND IF YOU CALL MY DAD A LOONY AGAIN, I'LL
FUCKING KILL YOU, YOU COCKSUCKER!"*

"Loony," Milo said smugly. He'd found the button, all right.
"Loony's kid, loony's kid, your father's got toys in the attic, kid,
tough break."

Vern and Chris had been getting over their laughing fit, perhaps
getting ready to appreciate the seriousness of the situation and call
Teddy off, but when Teddy told Milo that his mother blew dead
rats, they went back into hysterics again, lying there on the bank,
rolling from side to side, their feet kicking, holding their bellies.

"No more," Chris said weakly. "No more, please, no more, I swear
to God I'm gonna *bust!*"

Chopper was walking around in a large, dazed figure-eight
behind Milo. He looked like the losing fighter about ten seconds
after the ref has ended the match and awarded the winner a TKO.
Meanwhile, Teddy and Milo continued their discussion of Teddy's
father, standing nose to nose, with the wire fence Milo was too old
and too fat to climb between them.

"Don't you say nothing else about my dad! My dad stormed the beach at Normandy, you fucking wet end!"

"Yeah, well, where is he now, you ugly little four-eyed turd? He's up to Togus, ain't he? He's up to Togus because *HE WENT FUCKING SECTION EIGHT!*"

"Okay, that's it," Teddy said. "That's it, that's the end, I'm gonna kill you." He threw himself at the fence and started up.

"You come on and try it, you slimy little bastard." Milo stood back, grinning and waiting.

"No!" I shouted. I got to my feet, grabbed Teddy by the loose seat of his jeans, and pulled him off the fence. We both staggered back and fell over, him on top. He squashed my balls pretty good and I groaned. Nothing hurts like having your balls squashed, you know it? But I kept my arms locked around Teddy's middle.

"Lemme up!" Teddy sobbed, writhing in my arms. "Lemme up, Gordie! Nobody ranks out my old man. *LEMME UP GODDAM-MIT LEMME UP!*"

"That's just what he wants!" I shouted in his ear. "He wants to get you over there and beat the piss out of you and then take you to the cops!"

"Huh?" Teddy craned around to look at me, his face dazed.

"Never mind your smartmouth, kid," Milo said, advancing to the fence again with his hands curled into ham-sized fists. "Let' im fight his own battles."

"Sure," I said. "You only outweigh him by five hundred pounds."

"I know you, too," Milo said ominously. "Your name's Lachance." He pointed to where Vern and Chris were finally picking themselves up, still breathing fast from laughing so hard. "And those guys are Chris Chambers and one of those stupid Tessio kids. All your fathers are going to get calls from me, except for the loony up to Togus. You'll go to the 'formatory, every one of you. Juvenile delinquents!"

He stood flat on his feet, big freckled hands held out like a guy who wanted to play One Potato Two Potato, breathing hard, eyes narrow, waiting for us to cry or say we were sorry or maybe give him Teddy so he could feed Teddy to Chopper.

Chris made an O out of his thumb and index finger and spat neatly through it.

Vern hummed and looked at the sky.

Teddy said: "Come on, Gordie. Let's get away from this asshole before I puke."

"Oh, you're gonna get it, you foulmouthed little whoremaster. Wait'll I get you to the Constable."

"We heard what you said about his father," I told him. "We're all witnesses. And you sicced that dog on me. That's against the law."

Milo looked a trifle uneasy. "You was trespassin."

"The hell I was. The dump's public property."

"You climbed the fence."

"Sure I did, after you sicced your dog on me," I said, hoping that Milo wouldn't recall that I'd also climbed the gate to get in. "What'd you think I was gonna do? Stand there and let 'im rip me to pieces? Come on, you guys. Let's go. It stinks around here."

" 'Formatory," Milo promised hoarsely, his voice shaking. " 'Formatory for you wiseguys."

"Can't wait to tell the cops how you called a war vet a fuckin loony," Chris called back over his shoulder as we moved away. "What did *you* do in the war, Mr. Pressman?"

"NONE OF YOUR DAMN BUSINESS!" Milo shrieked. *"YOU HURT MY DAWG!"*

"Put it on your t.s. slip and send it to the chaplain," Vern muttered, and then we were climbing the railroad embankment again.

"Come back here!" Milo shouted, but his voice was fainter now and he seemed to be losing interest.

Teddy shot him the finger as we walked away. I looked back over my shoulder when we got to the top of the embankment. Milo was standing there behind the security fence, a big man in a baseball cap with his dog sitting beside him. His fingers were hooked through the small chain-link diamonds as he shouted at us, and all at once I felt very sorry for him—he looked like the biggest third-grader in the world, locked inside the playground by mistake, yelling for someone to come and let him out. He kept on yelling for awhile and then he either gave up or we got out of range. No more was seen or heard of Milo Pressman and Chopper that day.

13

There was some discussion—in righteous tones that were actually kind of forced-sounding—about how we had shown that creepy Milo Pressman we weren't just another bunch of pussies. I told how the guy at the Florida Market had tried to jap us, and then we fell into a gloomy silence, thinking it over.

For my part, I was thinking that maybe there was something to that stupid goocher business after all. Things couldn't have turned out much worse—in fact, I thought, it might be better to just keep going and spare my folks the pain of having one son in the Castle View Cemetery and one in South Windham Boys' Correctional. I had no doubt that Milo would go to the cops as soon as the importance of the dump having been closed at the time of the incident filtered into his thick skull. When that happened, he would realize that I really *had* been trespassing, public property or not. Probably that gave him every right in the world to sic his stupid dog on me. And while Chopper wasn't the hellhound he was cracked up to be, he sure would have ripped the sitdown out of my jeans if I hadn't won the race to the fence. All of it put a big dark crimp in the day. And there was another gloomy idea rolling around inside my head—the idea that this was no lark after all, and maybe we deserved our bad luck. Maybe it was even God warning us to go home. What were we doing, anyway, going to look at some kid that had gotten himself all mashed up by a freight train?

But we were doing it, and none of us wanted to stop.

We had almost reached the trestle which carried the tracks across the river when Teddy burst into tears. It was as if a great inner tidal wave had broken through a carefully constructed set of mental dykes. No bullshit—it was that sudden and that fierce. The sobs doubled him over like punches and he sort of collapsed into a heap, his hands going from his stomach to the mutilated gobs of flesh that were the remains of his ears. He went on crying in hard, violent bursts.

None of us knew what the fuck to do. It wasn't crying like when you got hit by a line drive while you were playing shortstop or smashed on the head playing tackle football on the common or when you fell off your bike. There was nothing physically wrong

with him. We walked away a little and watched him, our hands in
our pockets.

"Hey, man . . ." Vern said in a very thin voice. Chris and I
looked at Vern hopefully. "Hey, man" was always a good start. But
Vern couldn't follow it up.

Teddy leaned forward onto the crossties and put a hand over his
eyes. Now he looked like he was doing the Allah bit—"Salami,
salami, baloney," as Popeye says. Except it wasn't funny.

At last, when the force of his crying had trailed off a little, it was
Chris who went to him. He was the toughest guy in our gang
(maybe even tougher than Jamie Gallant, I thought privately), but
he was also the guy who made the best peace. He had a way about
it. I'd seen him sit down on the curb next to a little kid with a
scraped knee, a kid he didn't even fucking *know,* and get him
talking about something—the Shrine Circus that was coming to
town or Huckleberry Hound on TV—until the kid forgot he was
supposed to be hurt. Chris was good at it. He was tough enough to
be good at it.

"Lissen, Teddy, what do you care what a fat old pile of shit like
him said about your father? Huh? I mean, sincerely! That don't
change nothing, does it? What a fat old pile of shit like him says?
Huh? Huh? Does it?"

Teddy shook his head violently. It changed nothing. But to hear
it spoken of in bright daylight, something he must have gone over
and over in his mind while he was lying awake in bed and looking at
the moon off-center in one windowpane, something he must have
thought about in his slow and broken way until it seemed almost
holy, trying to make sense out of it, and then to have it brought
home to him that everybody else had merely dismissed his dad as a
loony . . . that had rocked him. But it changed nothing. Nothing.

"He still stormed the beach at Normandy, right?" Chris said. He
picked up one of Teddy's sweaty, grimy hands and patted it.

Teddy nodded fiercely, crying. Snot was running out of his nose.

"Do you think that pile of shit was at Normandy?"

Teddy shook his head violently. *"Nuh-Nuh-No!"*

"Do you think that guy knows you?"

"Nuh-No! No, b-b-but—"

"Or your father? He one of your father's buddies?"

"*NO!*" Angry, horrified. The thought. Teddy's chest heaved and more sobs came out of it. He had pushed his hair away from his ears and I could see the round brown plastic button of the hearing aid set in the middle of the right one. The shape of the hearing aid made more sense than the shape of his ear, if you get what I mean.

Chris said calmly: "Talk is cheap."

Teddy nodded, still not looking up.

"And whatever's between you and your old man, talk can't change that."

Teddy's head shook without definition, unsure if this was true. Someone had redefined his pain, and redefined it in shockingly common terms. That would

(*loony*)

have to be examined

(*fucking section eight*)

later. In depth. On long sleepless nights.

Chris rocked him. "He was rankin you, man," he said in soothing cadences that were almost a lullaby. "He was tryin to rank you over that friggin fence, you know it? No strain, man. No fuckin strain. He don't know nothin about your old man. He don't know nothin but stuff he heard from those rumdums down at The Mellow Tiger. He's just dogshit, man. Right, Teddy? Huh? Right?"

Teddy's crying was down to sniffles. He wiped his eyes, leaving two sooty rings around them, and sat up.

"I'm okay," he said, and the sound of his own voice seemed to convince him. "Yeah, I'm okay." He stood up and put his glasses back on—dressing his naked face, it seemed to me. He laughed thinly and swiped his bare arm across the snot on his upper lip. "Fuckin crybaby, right?"

"No, man," Vern said uncomfortably. "If anyone was rankin out my dad—"

"Then you got to kill em!" Teddy said briskly, almost arrogantly. "Kill their asses. Right, Chris?"

"Right," Chris said amiably, and clapped Teddy on the back. "Right, Gordie?"

"Absolutely," I said, wondering how Teddy could care so much for his dad when his dad had practically killed him, and how I couldn't seem to give much of a shit one way or the other about my own dad, when so far as I could remember, he had never laid a hand on me since I was three and got some bleach from under the sink and started to eat it.

We walked another two hundred yards down the tracks and Teddy said in a quieter voice: "Hey, if I spoiled your good time, I'm sorry. I guess that was pretty stupid shit back there at that fence."

"I ain't sure I want it to be no good time," Vern said suddenly.

Chris looked at him. "You sayin you want to go back, man?"

"No, huh-uh!" Vern's face knotted in thought. "But goin to see a dead kid—it shouldn't be a party, maybe. I mean, if you can dig it. I mean . . ." He looked at us rather wildly. "I mean, I could be a little scared. If you get me."

Nobody said anything and Vern plunged on:

"I mean, sometimes I get nightmares. Like . . . aw, you guys remember the time Danny Naughton left that pile of old funnybooks, the ones with the vampires and people gettin cut up and all that shit? Jeezum-crow, I'd wake up in the middle of the night dreamin about some guy hangin in a house with his face all green or somethin, you know, like that, and it seems like there's somethin under the bed and if I dangled a hand over the side, that thing might, you know, grab me . . ."

We all began to nod. We knew about the night shift. I would have laughed then, though, if you had told me that one day not too many years from then I'd parlay all those childhood fears and night-sweats into about a million dollars.

"And I don't dare say anything because my friggin *brother* . . . well, you know Billy . . . he'd broadcast it . . ." He shrugged miserably. "So I'm ascared to look at that kid cause if he's, you know, if he's really *bad* . . ."

I swallowed and glanced at Chris. He was looking gravely at Vern and nodding for him to go on.

"If he's really *bad*," Vern resumed, "I'll have nightmares about *him* and wake up thinkin it's *him* under my bed, all cut up in a pool of blood like he just came out of one of those Saladmaster gadgets they show on TV, just eyeballs and hair, but *movin* somehow, if you can dig that, *mooovin* somehow, you know, and gettin ready to *grab*—"

"Jesus Christ," Teddy said thickly. "What a fuckin bedtime story."

"Well I can't *help* it," Vern said, his voice defensive. "But I feel like we *hafta* see him, even if there are bad dreams. You know? Like we *hafta*. But . . . but maybe it shouldn't be no good time."

"Yeah," Chris said softly. "Maybe it shouldn't."

Vern said pleadingly: "You won't tell none of the other guys, will you? I don't mean about the nightmares, everybody has those—I mean about wakin up and thinkin there might be somethin under the bed. I'm too fuckin old for the boogeyman."

We all said we wouldn't tell, and a glum silence fell over us again. It was only quarter to three, but it felt much later. It was too hot and too much had happened. We weren't even over into Harlow yet. We were going to have to pick them up and lay them down if we were going to make some real miles before dark.

We passed the railroad junction and a signal on a tall, rusty pole and all of us paused to chuck cinders at the steel flag on top, but nobody hit it. And around three-thirty we came to the Castle River and the GS&WM trestle which crossed it.

14

The river was better than a hundred yards across at that point in 1960; I've been back to look at it since then, and found it had narrowed up quite a bit during the years between. They're always fooling with the river, trying to make it work better for the mills, and they've put in so many dams that it's pretty well tamed. But in those days there were only three dams on the whole length of the river as it ran across New Hampshire and half of Maine. The Castle was still almost free back then, and every third spring it would overflow its banks and cover Route 136 in either Harlow or Danvers Junction or both.

Now, at the end of the driest summer western Maine had seen since the depression, it was still broad. From where we stood on the

Castle Rock side, the bulking forest on the Harlow side looked like a different country altogether. The pines and spruces over there were bluish in the heat-haze of the afternoon. The rails went across the water fifty feet up, supported by an underpinning of tarred wooden support posts and crisscrossing beams. The water was so shallow you could look down and see the tops of the cement plugs which had been planted ten feet deep in the riverbed to hold up the trestle.

The trestle itself was pretty chintzy—the rails ran over a long, narrow wooden platform of six-by-fours. There was a four-inch gap between each pair of these beams where you could look all the way down into the water. On the sides, there was no more than eighteen inches between the rail and the edge of the trestle. If a train came, it was maybe enough room to avoid getting plastered . . . but the wind generated by a highballing freight would surely sweep you off to fall to a certain death against the rocks just below the surface of the shallow running water.

Looking at the trestle, we all felt fear start to crawl around in our bellies . . . and mixing uneasily with the fear was the excitement of a boss dare, a really big one, something you could brag on for weeks after you got home . . . *if* you got home. That queer light was creeping back into Teddy's eyes and I thought he wasn't seeing the GS&WM train trestle at all but a long sandy beach, a thousand LSTs aground in the foaming waves, ten thousand GIs charging up the sand, combat boots digging. They were leaping rolls of barbed wire! Tossing grenades at pillboxes! Overrunning machine-gun nests!

We were standing beside the tracks where the cinders sloped away toward the river's cut—the place where the embankment stopped and the trestle began. Looking down, I could see where the slope started to get steep. The cinders gave way to scraggly, tough-looking bushes and slabs of gray rock. Further down there were a few stunted firs with exposed roots writhing their way out of fissures in the plates of rock; they seemed to be looking down at their own miserable reflections in the running water.

At this point, the Castle River actually looked fairly clean; at Castle Rock it was just entering Maine's textile-mill belt. But there

were no fish jumping out there, although the river was clear enough
to see bottom—you had to go another ten miles upstream and
toward New Hampshire before you could see any fish in the Castle.
There were no fish, and along the edges of the river you could see
dirty collars of foam around some of the rocks—the foam was the
color of old ivory. The river's smell was not particularly pleasant,
either; it smelled like a laundry hamper full of mildewy towels.
Dragonflies stitched at the surface of the water and laid their eggs
with impunity. There were no trout to eat them. Hell, there
weren't even any shiners.

"Man," Chris said softly.

"Come on," Teddy said in that brisk, arrogant way. "Let's go."
He was already edging his way out, walking on the six-by-fours
between the shining rails.

"Say," Vern said uneasily, "any of you guys know when the next
train's due?"

We all shrugged.

I said: "There's the Route 136 bridge . . ."

"Hey, come on, gimme a break!" Teddy cried. "That means
walkin five miles down the river on this side and then five miles
back up on the other side . . . it'll take us until dark! If we use the
trestle, we can get to the same place in *ten minutes*!"

"But if a train comes, there's nowheres to go," Vern said. He
wasn't looking at Teddy. He was looking down at the fast, bland
river.

"Fuck there isn't!" Teddy said indignantly. He swung over the
edge and held one of the wooden supports between the rails. He
hadn't gone out very far—his sneakers were almost touching the
ground—but the thought of doing that same thing above the
middle of the river with a fifty-foot drop beneath and a train
bellowing by just over my head, a train that would probably be
dropping some nice hot sparks into my hair and down the back of
my neck . . . none of that actually made me feel like Queen for a
Day.

"See how easy it is?" Teddy said. He dropped to the embankment, dusted his hands, and climbed back up beside us.

"You tellin me you're gonna hang on that way if it's a

two-hundred-car freight?" Chris asked. "Just sorta hang there by your hands for five or ten minutes?"

"You chicken?" Teddy shouted.

"No, just askin what you'd do," Chris said, grinning. "Peace, man."

"Go around if you want to!" Teddy brayed. "Who gives a fuck? I'll wait for you! I'll take a *nap!*"

"One train already went by," I said reluctantly. "And there probably isn't any more than one, two trains a day that go through Harlow. Look at this." I kicked the weeds growing up through the railroad ties with one sneaker. There were no weeds growing between the tracks which ran between Castle Rock and Lewiston.

"There. See?" Teddy triumphant.

"But still, there's a *chance*," I added.

"Yeah," Chris said. He was looking only at me, his eyes sparkling. "Dare you, Lachance."

"Dares go first."

"Okay," Chris said. He widened his gaze to take in Teddy and Vern. "Any pussies here?'

"*NO!*" Teddy shouted.

Vern cleared his throat, croaked, cleared it again, and said "No" in a very small voice. He smiled a weak, sick smile.

"Okay," Chris said . . . but we hesitated for a moment, even Teddy, looking warily up and down the tracks. I knelt down and took one of the steel rails firmly in my hand, never minding that it was almost hot enough to blister the skin. The rail was mute.

"Okay," I said, and as I said it some guy pole-vaulted in my stomach. He dug his pole all the way into my balls, it felt like, and ended up sitting astride my heart.

We went out onto the trestle single file: Chris first, then Teddy, then Vern, and me playing tail-end Charlie because I was the one who said dares go first. We walked on the platform crossties between the rails, and you had to look at your feet whether you were scared of heights or not. A misstep and you would go down to your crotch, probably with a broken ankle to pay.

The embankment dropped away beneath me, and every step further out seemed to seal our decision more firmly . . . and to make it feel more suicidally stupid. I stopped to look up when I saw the rocks giving way to water far beneath me. Chris and Teddy were a long way ahead, almost out over the middle, and Vern was tottering slowly along behind them, peering studiously down at his feet. He looked like an old lady trying out stilts with his head poked downward, his back hunched, his arms held out for balance. I looked back over my shoulder. Too far, man. I had to keep going now, and not only because a train might come. If I went back, I'd be a pussy for life.

So I got walking again. After looking down at that endless series of crossties for awhile, with a glimpse of running water between each pair, I started to feel dizzy and disoriented. Each time I brought my foot down, part of my brain assured me it was going to plunge through into space, even though I could see it was not.

I became acutely aware of all the noises inside me and outside me, like some crazy orchestra tuning up to play. The steady thump of my heart, the bloodbeat in my ears like a drum being played with brushes, the creak of sinews like the strings of a violin that has been tuned radically upward, the steady hiss of the river, the hot hum of a locust digging into tight bark, the monotonous cry of a chickadee, and somewhere, far away, a barking dog. Chopper, maybe. The mildewy smell of the Castle River was strong in my nose. The long muscles in my thighs were trembling. I kept thinking how much safer it would be (probably faster, as well) if I just got down on my hands and knees and scuttered along that way. But I wouldn't do that—none of us would. If the Saturday matinee movies down to the Gem had taught us anything, it was that Only Losers Crawl. It was one of the central tenets of the Gospel According to Hollywood. Good guys walk firmly upright, and if your sinews are creaking like overtuned violin strings because of the adrenaline rush going on in your body, and if the long muscles in your thighs are trembling for the same reason, why, so be it.

I had to stop in the middle of the trestle and look up at the sky for awhile. That dizzy feeling had been getting worse. I saw phantom crossties—they seemed to float right in front of my nose. Then they faded out and I began to feel okay again. I looked ahead and saw I had almost caught up with Vern, who was slowpoking along worse than ever. Chris and Teddy were almost all the way across.

And although I've since written seven books about people who can do such exotic things as read minds and precognit the future, that was when I had my first and last psychic flash. I'm sure that's what it was; how else to explain it? I squatted and made a fist around the rail on my left. It thrummed in my hand. It was thrumming so hard that it was like gripping a bundle of deadly metallic snakes.

You've heard it said "His bowels turned to water"? I know what that phrase means—*exactly* what it means. It may be the most accurate cliché ever coined. I've been scared since, badly scared, but I've never been as scared as I was in that moment, holding that hot live rail. It seemed that for a moment all my works below throat level just went limp and lay there in an internal faint. A thin stream of urine ran listlessly down the inside of one thigh. My mouth opened. I didn't open it, it opened by itself, the jaw dropping like a trapdoor from which the hingepins had suddenly been removed. My tongue was plastered suffocatingly against the roof of my mouth. All my muscles were locked. That was the worst. My works went limp but my muscles were in a kind of dreadful lockbolt and I couldn't move at all. It was only for a moment, but in the subjective timestream, it seemed forever.

All sensory input became intensified, as if some power-surge had occurred in the electrical flow of my brain, cranking everything up from a hundred and ten volts to two-twenty. I could hear a plane passing in the sky somewhere near and had time to wish I was on it, just sitting in a window seat with a Coke in my hand and gazing idly down at the shining line of a river whose name I did not know. I could see every little splinter and gouge in the tarred crosstie I was squatting on. And out of the corner of my eye I could see the rail itself with my hand still clutched around it, glittering insanely. The vibration from that rail sank so deeply into my hand that when I took it away it still vibrated, the nerve-endings kicking each other over again and again, tingling the way a hand or foot tingles when it has been asleep and is starting to wake up. I could taste my saliva, suddenly all electric and sour and thickened to curds along my gums. And worst, somehow most horrible of all, I couldn't *hear* the train yet, could not know if it was rushing at me from ahead or behind, or how close it was. It was invisible. It was unannounced, except for that shaking rail. There was only that to advertise its imminent arrival. An image of Ray Brower, dreadfully mangled and thrown into a ditch somewhere like a ripped-open laundry bag, reeled before my eyes. We would join him, or at least Vern and I would, or at least I would. We had invited ourselves to our own funerals.

The last thought broke the paralysis and I shot to my feet. I probably would have looked like a jack-in-the-box to anyone watching, but to myself I felt like a boy in underwater slow motion, shooting up not through five feet of air but rather up through five hundred feet of water, moving slowly, moving with a dreadful languidness as the water parted grudgingly.

But at last I did break the surface.

I screamed: *"TRAIN!"*

The last of the paralysis fell from me and I began to run.

Vern's head jerked back over his shoulder. The surprise that distorted his face was almost comically exaggerated, written as large as the letters in a Dick and Jane primer. He saw me break into my clumsy, shambling run, dancing from one horribly high crosstie to the next, and knew I wasn't joking. He began to run himself.

Far ahead, I could see Chris stepping off the ties and onto the solid safe embankment and I hated him with a sudden bright green hate as juicy and as bitter as the sap in an April leaf. He was safe. *That* fucker was *safe.* I watched him drop to his knees and grab a rail.

My left foot almost slipped into the yaw beneath me. I flailed with my arms, my eyes as hot as ball bearings in some runaway piece of machinery, got my balance, and ran on. Now I was right behind Vern. We were past the halfway point and for the first time I heard the train. It was coming from behind us, coming from the Castle Rock side of the river. It was a low rumbling noise that began to rise slightly and sort itself into the diesel thrum of the engine and the higher, more sinister sound of big grooved wheels turning heavily on the rails.

"Awwwwwww, shit!" Vern screamed.

"Run, you pussy!" I yelled, and thumped him on the back.

"I can't! I'll fall!"

"Run faster!"

"AWWWWWWWWWWW-SHIT!"

But he ran faster, a shambling scarecrow with a bare, sunburnt back, the collar of his shirt swinging and dangling below his butt. I could see the sweat standing out on his peeling shoulderblades, standing out in perfect little beads. I could see the fine down on the nape of his neck. His muscles clenched and loosened, clenched and loosened, clenched and loosened. His spine stood out in a series of knobs, each knob casting its own crescent-shaped shadow—I could see that these knobs grew closer together as they approached his neck. He was still holding his bedroll and I was still holding mine. Vern's feet thudded on the crossties. He almost missed one, lunged forward with his arms out, and I whacked him on the back again to keep him going.

"Gordeeee I can't AWWWWWWWWWWW-SHEEEEEYIT—"

"RUN FASTER, DICKFACE!" I bellowed and was I *enjoying* this?

Yeah—in some peculiar, self-destructive way that I have experienced since only when completely and utterly drunk, I was. I was driving Vern Tessio like a drover getting a particularly fine cow to market. And maybe he was enjoying his own fear in that same way, bawling like that self-same cow, hollering and sweating, his ribcage rising and falling like the bellows of a blacksmith on a speed-trip, clumsily keeping his footing, lurching ahead.

The train was very loud now, its engine deepening to a steady rumble. Its whistle sounded as it crossed the junction point where we had paused to chuck cinders at the rail-flag. I had finally gotten my hellhound, like it or not. I kept waiting for the trestle to start shaking under my feet. When that happened, it would be right behind us.

"GO FASTER, VERN! FAAASTER!"

"Oh Gawd Gordie oh Gawd Gordie oh Gawd *AWWWWWWW-SHEEEEEEEYIT!"*

The freight's electric horn suddenly spanked the air into a hundred pieces with one long loud blast, making everything you ever saw in a movie or a comic book or one of your own daydreams fly apart, letting you know what both the heroes and the cowards really heard when death flew at them:

WHHHHHHHHONNNNNNK! WHHHHHHHHHHONNNNNN-NNK!

And then Chris was below us and to the right, and Teddy was behind him, his glasses flashing back arcs of sunlight, and they were both mouthing a single word and the word was *jump!* but the train had sucked all the blood out of the word, leaving only its shape in their mouths. The trestle began to shake as the train charged across it. We jumped.

Vern landed full-length in the dust and the cinders and I landed right beside him, almost on top of him. I never did see that train, nor do I know if its engineer saw us—when I mentioned the possibility that he hadn't seen us to Chris a couple of years later, he said: "They don't blow the horn like that just for chucks, Gordie." But he *could* have; he could have been blowing it just for the hell of it, I suppose. Right then, such fine points didn't much matter. I clapped my hands over my ears and dug my face into the hot dirt as the freight went by, metal squalling against metal, the air buffeting us. I had no urge to look at it. It was a long freight but I never looked at all. Before it had passed completely, I felt a warm hand on my neck and knew it was Chris's.

When it was gone—when I was *sure* it was gone—I raised my head like a soldier coming out of his foxhole at the end of a day-long artillery barrage. Vern was still plastered into the dirt, shivering. Chris was sitting cross-legged between us, one hand on Vern's sweaty neck, the other still on mine.

When Vern finally sat up, shaking all over and licking his lips compulsively, Chris said: "What you guys think if we drink those Cokes? Could anybody use one besides me?"

We all thought we could use one.

15

About a quarter of a mile along on the Harlow side, the GS&WM tracks plunged directly into the woods. The heavily wooded land sloped down to a marshy area. It was full of mosquitoes almost as big as fighter-planes, but it was cool . . . blessedly cool.

We sat down in the shade to drink our Cokes. Vern and I threw our shirts over our shoulders to keep the bugs off, but Chris and Teddy just sat naked to the waist, looking as cool and collected as two Eskimos in an icehouse. We hadn't been there five minutes when Vern had to go off into the bushes and take a squat, which led to a good deal of joking and elbowing when he got back.

"Train scare you much, Vern?"

"No," Vern said. "I was gonna squat when we got acrosst, anyway, I *hadda* take a squat, you know?"

"*Verrrrrrrn?*" Chris and Teddy chorused.

"Come on, you guys, I *did*. Sincerely."

"Then you won't mind if we examine the seat of your Jockeys for Hershey-squirts, willya?" Teddy asked, and Vern laughed, finally understanding that he was getting ribbed.

"Go screw."

Chris turned to me. "That train scare you, Gordie?"

"Nope," I said, and sipped my Coke.

"Not much, you sucker." He punched my arm.

"Sincerely! I wasn't scared at all."

"Yeah? You wasn't scared?" Teddy was looking me over carefully.

"No. I was fuckin *petrified*."

This slew all of them, even Vern, and we laughed long and hard. Then we just lay back, not goofing anymore, just drinking our Cokes and being quiet. My body felt warm, exercised, at peace with itself. Nothing in it was working crossgrain to anything else. I was alive and glad to be. Everything seemed to stand out with a special dearness, and although I never could have said that out loud I didn't think it mattered—maybe that sense of dearness was something I wanted just for myself.

I think I began to understand a little bit that day what makes men become daredevils. I paid twenty dollars to watch Evel Kneivel attempt his jump over the Snake River Canyon a couple of years ago and my wife was horrified. She told me that if I'd been born a Roman I would have been right there in the Colosseum, munching grapes and watching as the lions disemboweled the Christians. She was wrong, although it was hard for me to explain why (and, really, I think *she* thought I was just jiving her). I didn't cough up that twenty to watch the man die on coast-to-coast closed-circuit TV, although I was quite sure that was exactly what was going to happen. I went because of the shadows that are always somewhere behind our eyes, because of what Bruce Springsteen calls the darkness on the edge of town in one of his songs, and at one time or another I think everyone wants to dare that darkness in spite of the jalopy bodies that some joker of a God gave us human beings. No . . . not in *spite* of our jalopy bodies but *because* of them.

"Hey, tell that story," Chris said suddenly, sitting up.

"What story?" I asked, although I guess I knew.

I always felt uncomfortable when the talk turned to my stories, although all of them seemed to like them—wanting to tell stories, even wanting to write them down . . . that was just peculiar enough to be sort of cool, like wanting to grow up to be a sewer inspector or a Grand Prix mechanic. Richie Jenner, a kid who hung around with us until his family moved to Nebraska in 1959, was the first one to find out that I wanted to be a writer when I grew up, that I wanted to do that for my full-time job. We were up in my room, just fooling around, and he found a bunch of handwritten pages under the comic books in a carton in my closet. What's *this*? Richie asks. Nothin, I say, and try to grab them back. Richie held the pages up out of reach . . . and I must admit that I didn't try very *hard* to get them back. I wanted him to read them and at the same time I didn't—an uneasy mix of pride and shyness that has never changed in me very much when someone asks to look. The act of writing itself is done in secret, like masturbation—oh, I have one friend who has done things like write stories in the display windows of bookshops and department stores, but this is a man who is nearly crazy with courage, the kind of man you'd like to have with you if you just happened to fall down with a heart attack in a city where no one knew you. For me, it always wants to be sex and always falls short—it's always that adolescent handjob in the bathroom with the door locked.

Richie sat right there on the end of my bed for most of the afternoon reading his way through the stuff I had been doing, most of it influenced by the same sort of comic books as the ones that had given Vern nightmares. And when he was done, Richie looked at me in a strange new way that made me feel very peculiar, as if he had been forced to re-appraise my whole personality. He said; You're pretty good at this. Why don't you show these to Chris? I said no, I wanted it to be a secret, and Richie said: Why? It ain't pussy. You ain't no queer. I mean, it ain't *poetry*.

Still, I made him promise not to tell anybody about my stories and of course he did and it turned out most of them liked to read the stuff I wrote, which was mostly about getting buried alive or some crook coming back from the dead and slaughtering the jury that had condemned him in Twelve Interesting Ways or a maniac that went crazy and chopped a lot of people into veal cutlets before the hero, Curt Cannon, "cut the subhuman, screeching madman to pieces with round after round from his smoking .45 automatic."

In my stories, there were always rounds. *Never* bullets.

For a change of pace, there were the Le Dio stories. Le Dio was a town in France, and during 1942, a grim squad of tired American dogfaces were trying to retake it from the Nazis (this was two years before I discovered that the Allies didn't land in France until 1944). They went on trying to re-take it, fighting their way from street to street, through about forty stories which I wrote between the ages of nine and fourteen. Teddy was absolutely mad for the Le Dio stories, and I think I wrote the last dozen or so just for him—by then I was heartily sick of Le Dio and writing things like *Mon Dieu* and *Cherchez le Boche!* and *Feremez le porte!* In Le Dio, French peasants were always hissing to GI dogfaces to *Feremez le porte!* But Teddy would hunch over the pages, his eyes big, his brow beaded with sweat, his face twisting. There were times when I could almost hear air-cooled Brownings and whistling 88s going off in his skull. The way he clamored for more Le Dio stories was both pleasing and frightening.

Nowadays writing is my work and the pleasure has diminished a little, and more and more often that guilty, masturbatory pleasure has become associated in my head with the coldly clinical images of artificial insemination: I come according to the rules and regs laid down in my publishing contract. And although no one is ever going

to call me the Thomas Wolfe of my generation, I rarely feel like a
cheat: I get it off as hard as I can every fucking time. Doing less
would, in an odd way, be like going faggot—or what that meant to
us back then. What scares me is how often it hurts these days. Back
then I was sometimes disgusted by how damned *good* it felt to write.
These days I sometimes look at this typewriter and wonder when it's
going to run out of good words. I don't want that to happen. I
guess I can stay cool as long as I don't run out of good words, you
know?

"What's this story?" Vern asked uneasily. "It ain't a horror story,
is it, Gordie? I don't think I want to hear no horror stories. I'm not
up for that, man."

"No, it ain't a horror," Chris said. "It's really funny. Gross, but
funny. Go on, Gordie. Hammer that fucker to us."

"Is it about Le Dio?" Teddy asked.

"No, it ain't about Le Dio, you psycho," Chris said, and
rabbit-punched him. "It's about this pie-eatin contest."

"Hey, I didn't even write it down yet," I said.

"Yeah, but tell it."

"You guys want to hear it?"

"Sure," Teddy said. "Boss."

"Well, it's about this made-up town. Gretna, I call it. Gretna,
Maine."

"*Gretna?*" Vern said, grinning. "What kind of name is that?
There ain't no *Gretna* in Maine."

"Shut up, fool," Chris said. "He just toldja it was made-up,
didn't he?"

"Yeah, but *Gretna,* that sounds pretty stupid—"

"Lots of *real* towns sound stupid," Chris said. "I mean, what
about *Alfred,* Maine? Or *Saco,* Maine? Or Jerusalem's Lot? Or
Castle-fuckin-Rock? There ain't no castle here. *Most* town names are
stupid. You just don't think so because you're used to em. Right,
Gordie?"

"Sure," I said, but privately I thought Vern was right—Gretna
was a pretty stupid name for a town. I just hadn't been able to think
of another one. "So anyway, they're having their annual Pioneer
Days, just like in Castle Rock—"

"Yeah, Pioneer Days, that's a fuckin *blast,*" Vern said earnestly.

"I put my whole family in that jail on wheels they have, even fuckin Billy. It was only for half an hour and it cost me my whole allowance but it was worth it just to know where that sonofawhore was—"

"Will you shut up and let him tell it?" Teddy hollered.

Vern blinked. "Sure. Yeah. Okay."

"Go on, Gordie," Chris said.

"It's not really much—"

"Naw, we don't expect much from a wet end like you," Teddy said, "but tell it anyway."

I cleared my throat. "So anyway. It's Pioneer Days, and on the last night they have these three big events. There's an egg-roll for the little kids and a sack-race for kids that are like eight or nine, and then there's the pie-eating contest. And the main guy of the story is this fat kid nobody likes named Davie Hogan."

"Like Charlie Hogan's brother if he had one," Vern said, and then shrank back as Chris rabbit-punched him again.

"This kid, he's our age, but he's fat. He weighs like one-eighty and he's always gettin beat up and ranked out. And all the kids, instead of callin him Davie, they call him Lard Ass Hogan and rank him out whenever they get the chance."

They nodded respectfully, showing the proper sympathy for Lard Ass, although if such a guy ever showed up in Castle Rock, we all would have been out teasing him and ranking him to the dogs and back.

"So he decides to take revenge because he's, like, fed up, you know? He's only in the pie-eating contest, but that's like the final event during Pioneer Days and everyone really digs it. The prize is five bucks—"

"So he wins it and gives the finger to everybody!" Teddy said. "Boss!"

"No, it's better than that," Chris said. "Just shut up and listen."

"Lard Ass figures to himself, five bucks, what's that? If anybody remembers anything at all in two weeks, it'll just be that fuckin pig Hogan out-ate everybody, well, it figures, let's go over his house and rank the shit out of him, only now we'll call him Pie Ass instead of Lard Ass."

They nodded some more, agreeing that Davie Hogan was a thinking cat. I began to warm to my own story.

"But everybody expects him to enter the contest, you know. Even his mom and dad. Hey, they practically got that five bucks spent for him already."

"Yeah, right," Chris said.

"So he's thinkin about it and hating the whole thing, because being fat isn't really his fault. See, he's got these weird fuckin glands, somethin, and—"

"My cousin's like that!" Vern said excitedly. "Sincerely! She weighs close to three hundred pounds! Supposed to be Hyboid Gland or somethin like that. I dunno about her Hyboid Gland, but what a fuckin blimp, no shit, she looks like a fuckin Thanksgiving turkey, and this one time—"

"Will you shut the fuck *up,* Vern?" Chris cried violently. "For the last time! Honest to God!" He had finished his Coke and now he turned the hourglass-shaped green bottle upside down and brandished it over Vern's head.

"Yeah, right, I'm sorry. Go on, Gordie. It's a swell story."

I smiled. I didn't really mind Vern's interruptions, but of course I couldn't tell Chris that; he was the self-appointed Guardian of Art.

"So he's turnin it over in his mind, you know, the whole week before the contest. At school, kids keep comin up to him and sayin: Hey Lard Ass, how many pies ya gonna eat? Ya gonna eat ten? Twenty? Fuckin *eighty*? And Lard Ass, *he* says: How should I know. I don't even know what *kind* they are. And see, there's quite a bit of interest in the contest because the champ is this grownup whose name is, uh, Bill Traynor, I guess. And this guy Traynor, he ain't even fat. In fact, he's a real stringbean. But he can eat pies like a whiz, and the year before he ate six pies in five minutes."

"*Whole* pies?" Teddy asked, awe-struck.

"Right you are. And Lard Ass, he's the youngest guy to ever be in the contest."

"Go, Lard Ass!" Teddy cried excitedly. "Scoff up those fuckin pies!"

"Tell em about the other guys in it," Chris said.

"Okay. Besides Lard Ass Hogan and Bill Traynor, there was Calvin Spier, the fattest guy in town—he ran the jewelry store—"

"Gretna Jewels," Vern said, and snickered. Chris gave him a black look.

"And then there's this guy who's a disc jockey at a radio station up in Lewiston, he ain't exactly fat but he's sorta chubby, you know. And the last guy was Hubert Gretna the Third, who was the principal of Lard Ass Hogan's school."

"He was eatin against his own *principal?*" Teddy asked.

Chris clutched his knees and rocked back and forth joyfully. "Ain't that *great?* Go on, Gordie!"

I had them now. They were all leaning forward. I felt an intoxicating sense of power. I tossed my empty Coke bottle into the woods and scrunched around a little bit to get comfortable. I remember hearing the chickadee again, off in the woods, farther away now, lifting its monotonous, endless call into the sky: *dee-dee-dee-dee* . . .

"So he gets this idea," I said. "The greatest revenge idea a kid ever had. The big night comes—the end of Pioneer Days. The pie-eating contest comes just before the fireworks. The Main Street of Gretna has been closed off so people can walk around in it, and there's this big platform set up right in the street. There's bunting hanging down and a big crowd in front. There's also a photographer from the paper, to get a picture of the winner with blueberries all over his face, because it turned out to be blueberry pies that year. Also, I almost forgot to tell you this, they had to eat the pies with their hands tied behind their backs. So, dig it, they come up onto the platform . . ."

16

From *The Revenge of Lard Ass Hogan,* by Gordon Lachance. Originally published in *Cavalier* magazine, March, 1975. Used by permission.

They came up onto the platform one by one and stood behind a long trestle table covered with a linen cloth. The table was stacked high with pies and stood at the edge of the platform. Above it were looped necklaces of bare 100-watt bulbs, moths and night-fliers banging softly against them and haloing them. Above the platform, bathed in spotlights, was a long sign which read: THE GREAT

GRETNA PIE-EAT OF 1960! To either side of this sign hung battered loudspeakers, supplied by Chuck Day of the Great Day Appliance Shop. Bill Travis, the reigning champion, was Chuck's cousin.

As each contestant came up, his hands bound behind him and his shirtfront open, like Sydney Carton on his way to the guillotine, Mayor Charbonneau would announce his name over Chuck's PA system and tie a large white bib around his neck. Calvin Spier received token applause only; in spite of his belly, which was the size of a twenty-gallon waterbarrel, he was considered an underdog second only to the Hogan kid (most considered Lard Ass a comer, but too young and inexperienced to do much this year).

After Spier, Bob Cormier was introduced. Cormier was a disc jockey who did a popular afternoon program at WLAM in Lewiston. He got a bigger hand, accompanied by a few screams from the teenaged girls in the audience. The girls thought he was "cute." John Wiggins, principal of Gretna Elementary School, followed Cormier. He received a hearty cheer from the older section of the audience—and a few scattered boos from fractious members of his student body. Wiggins managed to beam paternally and frown sternly down on the audience at the same time.

Next, Mayor Charbonneau introduced Lard Ass.

"A new participant in the annual Great Gretna Pie-Eat, but one we expect great things from in the future . . . *young Master David Hogan!*" Lard Ass got a big round of applause as Mayor Charbonneau tied on his bib, and as it was dying away, a rehearsed Greek chorus just beyond the reach of the 100-watt bulbs cried out in wicked unison: *"Go-get-'em-Lard-Ass!"*

There were muffled shrieks of laughter, running footsteps, a few shadows that no one could (or would) identify, some nervous laughter, some judicial frowns (the largest from Hizzoner Charbonneau, the most visible figure of authority). Lard Ass himself appeared to not even notice. The small smile greasing his thick lips and creasing his thick chops did not change as the Mayor, still frowning largely, tied his bib around his neck and told him not to pay any attention to fools in the audience (as if the Mayor had even the faintest inkling of what monstrous fools Lard Ass Hogan had suffered and would continue to suffer as he rumbled through life like a Nazi Tiger tank). The Mayor's breath was warm and smelled of beer.

The last contestant to mount the bunting-decorated stage drew the loudest and most sustained applause; this was the legendary Bill Travis, six feet five inches tall, gangling, voracious. Travis was a mechanic at the local Amoco station down by the railyard, a likeable fellow if there ever was one.

It was common knowledge around town that there was more involved in the Great Gretna Pie-Eat than a mere five dollars—at least, for Bill Travis there was. There were two reasons for this. First, people always came by the station to congratulate Bill after he won the contest, and most everyone who came to congratulate stayed to get his gas-tank filled. And the two garage-bays were sometimes booked up for a solid month after the contest. Folks would come in to get a muffler replaced or their wheel-bearings greased, and would sit in the theater chairs ranged along one wall (Jerry Maling, who owned the Amoco, had salvaged them from the old Gem Theater when it was torn down in 1957), drinking Cokes and Moxies from out of the machine and gassing with Bill about the contest as he changed sparkplugs or rolled around on a crawlie-wheelie under someone's International Harvester pickup, looking for holes in the exhaust system. Bill always seemed willing to talk, which was one of the reasons he was so well-liked in Gretna.

There was some dispute around town as to whether Jerry Maling gave Bill a flat bonus for the extra business his yearly feat (or yearly eat, if you prefer) brought in, or if he got an out-and-out raise. Whatever way it was, there could be no doubt that Travis did much better than most small-town wrench jockeys. He had a nice-looking two-storey ranch out on the Sabbatus Road, and certain snide people referred to it as "the house that pies built." That was probably an exaggeration, but Bill had it coming another way—which brings us to the second reason there was more in it for Travis than just five dollars.

The Pie-Eat was a hot wagering event in Gretna. Perhaps most people only came to laugh, but a goodly minority also came to lay their money down. Contestants were observed and discussed by these bettors as ardently as thoroughbreds are observed and discussed by racing touts. The wagerers accosted contestants' friends, relatives, even mere acquaintances. They pried out any and all details concerning the contestants' eating habits. There was always a lot of discussion about that year's official pie—apple was considered a "heavy" pie, apricot a "light" one (although a

contestant had to resign himself to a day or two of the trots after
downing three or four apricot pies). That year's official pie, blueberry, was considered a happy medium. Bettors, of course, were
particularly interested in their man's stomach for blueberry dishes.
How did he do on blueberry buckle? Did he favor blueberry jam
over strawberry preserves? Had he been known to sprinkle blueberries on his breakfast cereal, or was he strictly a bananas-and-
cream sort of fellow?

There were other questions of some moment. Was he a fast
eater who slowed down or a slow eater who started to speed up as
things got serious or just a good steady all-around trencherman?
How many hotdogs could he put away while watching a Babe Ruth
League game down at the St. Dom's baseball field? Was he much
of a beer-drinker, and, if so, how many bottles did he usually put
away in the course of an evening? Was he a belcher? It was
believed that a good belcher was a bit tougher to beat over the
long haul.

All of this and other information was sifted, the odds laid, the
bets made. How much money actually changed hands during the
week or so following pie-night I have no way of knowing, but if you
held a gun to my head and forced me to guess, I'd put it at close to
a thousand dollars—that probably sounds like a pretty paltry
figure, but it was a lot of money to be passing around in such a small
town fifteen years ago.

And because the contest was honest and a strict time-limit of ten
minutes was observed, no one objected to a competitor betting on
himself, and Bill Travis did so every year. Talk was, as he nodded,
smiling, to his audience on that summer night in 1960, that he had
bet a substantial amount on himself again, and that the best he
had been able to do this year was one-for-five odds. If you're not
the betting type, let me explain it this way: he'd have to put two
hundred and fifty dollars at risk to win fifty. Not a good deal at all,
but it was the price of success—and as he stood there, soaking up
the applause and smiling easy, he didn't look too worried about it.

"And the defending champ*een,*" Mayor Charbonneau trumpet-
ed, "Gretna's own *Bill Travis*!"

"Hoo, Bill!"

"How many you goin through tonight, Bill?"

"You goin for ten, Billy-boy?"

"I got a two-spot on you, Bill! Don't let me down, boy!"

"Save me one of those pies, Trav!"

Nodding and smiling with all proper modesty, Bill Travis allowed the mayor to tie his bib around his neck. Then he sat down at the far right end of the table, near the place where Mayor Charbonneau would stand during the contest. From right to left, then, the eaters were Bill Travis, David "Lard Ass" Hogan, Bob Cormier, principal John Wiggins, and Calvin Spier holding down the stool on the far left.

Mayor Charbonneau introduced Sylvia Dodge, who was even more of a contest figure than Bill Travis himself. She had been President of the Gretna Ladies' Auxiliary for years beyond telling (since the First Manassas, according to some town wits), and it was she who oversaw the baking of each year's pies, strictly subjecting each to her own rigorous quality control, which included a weigh-in ceremony on Mr. Bancichek's butcher's scales down at the Freedom Market—this to make sure that each pie weighed within an ounce of the others.

Sylvia smiled regally down at the crowd, her blue hair twinkling under the hot glow of the lightbulbs. She made a short speech about how glad she was that so much of the town had turned out to celebrate their hardy pioneer forebears, the people who made this country great, for it *was* great, not only on the grassroots level where Mayor Charbonneau would be leading the local Republicans to the hallowed seats of town government again in November, but on the national level where the team of Nixon and Lodge would take the torch of freedom from Our Great and Beloved General and hold it high for—

Calvin Spier's belly rumbled noisily—*goinnngg!* There was and even some applause. Sylvia Dodge, who knew perfectly well that Calvin was both a Democrat and a Catholic (either would have been forgivable alone, but the two combined, never), managed to blush, smile, and look furious all at the same time. She cleared her throat and wound up with a ringing exhortation to every boy and girl in the audience, telling them to always hold the red, white, and blue high, both in their hands and in their hearts, and to remember that smoking was a dirty, evil habit which made you cough. The boys and girls in the audience, most of whom would be wearing peace medallions and smoking not Camels but marijuana in another eight years, shuffled their feet and waited for the action to begin.

"Less talk, more eatin!" someone in the back row called, and there was another burst of applause—it was heartier this time.

Mayor Charbonneau handed Sylvia a stopwatch and a silver police whistle, which she would blow at the end of the ten minutes of all-out pie-eating. Mayor Charbonneau would then step forward and hold up the hand of the winner.

"Are you *ready*??" Hizzoner's voice rolled triumphantly through the Great Day PA and off down Main Street.

The five pie-eaters declared they were ready.

"Are you *SET*??" Hizzoner enquired further.

The eaters growled that they were indeed set. Downstreet, a boy set off a rattling skein of firecrackers.

Mayor Charbonneau raised one pudgy hand and then dropped it. *"GO!!!"*

Five heads dropped into five pie-plates. The sound was like five large feet stamping firmly into mud. Wet chomping noises rose on the mild night air and then were blotted out as the bettors and partisans in the crowd began to cheer on their favorites. And no more than the first pie had been demolished before most people realized that a possible upset was in the making.

Lard Ass Hogan, a seven-to-one underdog because of his age and inexperience, was eating like a boy possessed. His jaws machine-gunned up crust (the contest rules required that only the top crust of the pie be eaten, not the bottom), and when that had disappeared, a huge sucking sound issued from between his lips. It was like the sound of an industrial vacuum cleaner going to work. Then his whole head disappeared into the pie-plate. He raised it fifteen seconds later to indicate he was done. His cheeks and forehead were smeared with blueberry juice, and he looked like an extra in a minstrel show. He was done—done before the legendary Bill Travis had finished *half* of *his* first pie.

Startled applause went up as the Mayor examined Lard Ass's pie-plate and pronounced it clean enough. He whipped a second pie into place before the pace-maker. Lard Ass had gobbled a regulation-size pie in just forty-two seconds. It was a contest record.

He went at the second pie even more furiously yet, his head bobbing and smooching in the soft blueberry filling, and Bill Travis threw him a worried glance as he called for his second blueberry pie. As he told friends later, he felt he was in a real contest for the first time since 1957, when George Gamache gobbled three pies in four minutes and then fainted dead away. He had to wonder, he said, if he was up against a boy or a demon. He thought of the money he had riding on this and redoubled his efforts.

But if Travis had redoubled, Lard Ass had trebled. Blueberries flew from his second pie-dish, staining the tablecloth around him like a Jackson Pollock painting. There were blueberries in his hair, blueberries on his bib, blueberries standing out on his forehead as if, in an agony of concentration, he had actually begun to *sweat* blueberries.

"Done!" he cried, lifting his head from his second pie-dish before Bill Travis had even consumed the crust on his new pie.

"Better slow down, boy," Hizzoner murmured. Charbonneau himself had ten dollars riding on Bill Travis. "You got to pace yourself if you want to hold out."

It was as if Lard Ass hadn't heard. He tore into his third pie with lunatic speed, jaws moving with lightning rapidity. And then—

But I must interrupt for a moment to tell you that there was an empty bottle in the medicine cabinet at Lard Ass Hogan's house. Earlier, that bottle had been three-quarters full of pearl-yellow castor oil, perhaps the most noxious fluid that the good Lord, in His infinite wisdom, ever allowed upon or beneath the face of the earth. Lard Ass had emptied that bottle himself, drinking every last drop and then licking the rim, his mouth twisting, his belly gagging sourly, his brain filled with thoughts of sweet revenge.

And as he rapidly worked his way through his third pie (Calvin Spier, dead last as predicted, had not yet finished his first), Lard Ass began to deliberately torture himself with grisly fantasies. He was not eating pies at all; he was eating cowflops. He was eating great big gobs of greasy grimy gopher-guts. He was eating diced-up woodchuck intestines with blueberry sauce poured over them. *Rancid* blueberry sauce.

He finished his third pie and called for his fourth, now one full pie ahead of the legendary Bill Travis. The fickle crowd, sensing a new and unexpected champ in the making, began to cheer him on lustily.

But Lard Ass had no hope or intention of winning. He could not have continued at the pace he was currently setting if his own mother's life had been the prize. And besides, winning for him was losing; revenge was the only blue ribbon he sought. His belly groaning with castor oil, his throat opening and closing sickly, he finished his fourth pie and called for his fifth, the Ultimate Pie—Blueberries Become Electra, so to speak. He dropped his head into the dish, breaking the crust, and snuffled blueberries up his nose. Blueberries went down his shirt. The contents of his stomach seemed to suddenly gain weight. He chewed up pasty pastry crust and swallowed it. He inhaled blueberries.

And suddenly the moment of revenge was at hand. His stomach, loaded beyond endurance, revolted. It clenched like a strong hand encased in a slick rubber glove. His throat opened.

Lard Ass raised his head.

He grinned at Bill Travis with blue teeth.

Puke rumbled up his throat like a six-ton Peterbilt shooting through a tunnel.

It roared out of his mouth in a huge blue-and-yellow glurt, warm and gaily steaming. It covered Bill Travis, who only had time to utter one nonsense syllable—*"Goog!"* was what it sounded like. Women in the audience screamed. Calvin Spier, who had watched this unannounced event with a numb and surprised expression on his face, leaned conversationally over the table as if to explain to the gaping audience just what was happening, and puked on the head of Marguerite Charbonneau, the Mayor's wife. She screamed and backed away, pawing futilely at her hair, which was now covered with a mixture of crushed berries, baked beans, and partially digested frankfurters (the latter two had been Cal Spier's dinner). She turned to her good friend Maria Lavin and threw up on the front of Maria's buckskin jacket.

In rapid succession, like a replay of the firecrackers:

Bill Travis blew a great—and seemingly supercharged—jet of vomit out over the first two rows of spectators, his stunned face proclaiming to one and all, *Man, I just can't believe I'm doing this;*

Chuck Day, who had received a generous portion of Bill Travis's surprise gift, threw up on his Hush Puppies and then blinked at them wonderingly, knowing full well that stuff would *never* come off suede;

John Wiggins, principal of Gretna Elementary, opened his blue-lined mouth and said reprovingly: "Really, this has . . . *YURRK!"* As befitted a man of his breeding and position, he did it in his own pie-plate;

Hizzoner Charbonneau, who found himself suddenly presiding

over what must have seemed more like a stomach-flu hospital ward than a pie-eating contest, opened his mouth to call the whole thing off and upchucked all over the microphone.

"Jesus save us!" moaned Sylvia Dodge, and then her outraged supper—fried clams, cole slaw, butter-and-sugar corn (two ears' worth), and a generous helping of Muriel Harrington's Bosco chocolate cake—bolted out the emergency exit and landed with a large wet splash on the back of the Mayor's Robert Hall suitcoat.

Lard Ass Hogan, now at the absolute apogee of his young life, beamed happily out over the audience. Puke was everywhere. People staggered around in drunken circles, holding their throats and making weak cawing noises. Somebody's pet Pekingese ran past the stage, yapping crazily, and a man wearing jeans and a Western-style silk shirt threw up on it, nearly drowning it. Mrs. Brockway, the Methodist minister's wife, made a long, basso belching noise which was followed by a gusher of degenerated roast beef and mashed potatoes and apple cobbler. The cobbler looked as if it might have been quite good when it first went down. Jerry Maling, who had come to see his pet mechanic walk away with all the marbles again, decided to get the righteous fuck out of this madhouse. He got about fifteen yards before tripping over a kid's little red wagon and realizing he had landed in a puddle of warm bile. Jerry tossed his cookies in his own lap and told folks later he only thanked Providence he had been wearing his coveralls. And Miss Norman, who taught Latin and English Fundamentals at the Gretna Consolidated High School, vomited into her own purse in an agony of propriety.

Lard Ass Hogan watched it all, his large face calm and beaming, his stomach suddenly sweet and steady with a warm balm it might never know again—that balm was a feeling of utter and complete satisfaction. He stood up, took the slightly tacky microphone from the trembling hand of Mayor Charbonneau, and said . . .

17

" 'I declare this contest a draw.' Then he puts the mike down, walks off the back of the platform, and goes straight home. His mother's there, on account of she couldn't get a baby-sitter for Lard Ass's little sister, who was only two. And as soon as he comes in, all covered with puke and pie-drool, still wearin his bib, she says, 'Davie, did you win?' But he doesn't say a fuckin word, you know. Just goes upstairs to his room, locks the door, and lays down on his bed."

I downed the last swallow in Chris's Coke and tossed it into the woods.

"Yeah, that's cool, then what happened?" Teddy asked eagerly.

"I don't know."

"What do you mean, you don't *know*?" Teddy asked.

"It means it's the end. When you don't know what happens next, that's the end."

"*Whaaaat?*" Vern cried. There was an upset, suspicious look on his face, like he thought maybe he'd just gotten rooked playing penny-up Bingo at the Topsham Fair. "What's all this happy crappy? How'd it come *out?*"

"You have to use your imagination," Chris said patiently.

"No, I ain't!" Vern said angrily. "*He's* supposed to use *his* imagination! He made up the fuckin story!"

"Yeah, what happened to the cat?" Teddy persisted. "Come on, Gordie, tell us."

"I think his dad was at the Pie-Eat and when he came home he beat the living crap out of Lard Ass."

"Yeah, right," Chris said. "I bet that's just what happened."

"And," I said, "the kids went right on calling him Lard Ass. Except that maybe some of them started calling him Puke-Yer-Guts, too."

"That ending sucks," Teddy said sadly.

"That's why I didn't want to tell it."

"You could have made it so he shot his father and ran away and joined the Texas Rangers," Teddy said. "How about that?"

Chris and I exchanged a glance. Chris raised one shoulder in a barely perceptible shrug.

"I guess so," I said.

"Hey, you got any new Le Dio stories, Gordie?'

"Not just now. Maybe I'll think of some." I didn't want to upset Teddy, but I wasn't very interested in checking out what was happening in Le Dio, either. "Sorry you didn't go for this one better."

"Nah, it was good," Teddy said. "Right up to the end, it was good. All that pukin was really cool."

"Yeah, that was cool, really gross," Vern agreed. "But Teddy's right about the ending. It was sort of a gyp."

"Yeah," I said, and sighed.

Chris stood up. "Let's do some walking," he said. It was still bright daylight, the sky a hot, steely blue, but our shadows had begun to trail out long. I remember that as a kid, September days always seemed to end much too soon, catching me by surprise—it was as if something inside my heart expected it to always be June, with daylight lingering in the sky until almost nine-thirty. "What time is it, Gordie?'

I looked at my watch and was astonished to see it was after five.

"Yeah, let's go," Teddy said. "But let's make camp before dark so we can see to get wood and stuff. I'm gettin hungry, too."

"Six-thirty," Chris promised. "Okay with you guys?"

It was. We started to walk again, using the cinders beside the tracks now. Soon the river was so far behind us we couldn't even hear its sound. Mosquitoes hummed and I slapped one off my neck. Vern and Teddy were walking up ahead, working out some sort of complicated comic-book trade. Chris was beside me, hands in his pockets, shirt slapping against his knees and thighs like an apron.

"I got some Winstons," he said. "Hawked em off my old man's dresser. One apiece. For after supper."

"Yeah? That's boss."

"That's when a cigarette tastes best," Chris said. "After supper."

"Right."

We walked in silence for awhile.

"That's a really fine story," Chris said suddenly. "They're just a little too dumb to understand."

"No, it's not that hot. It's a mumbler."

"That's what you always say. Don't give me that bullshit you don't believe. Are you gonna write it down? The story?"

"Probably. But not for awhile. I can't write em down right after I tell em. It'll keep."

"What Vern said? About the ending being a gyp?'

"Yeah?"

Chris laughed. *"Life's* a gyp, you know it? I mean, look at us."

"Nah, we have a great time."

"Sure," Chris said. "All the fuckin time, you wet."

I laughed. Chris did, too.

"They come outta you just like bubbles out of soda-pop," he said after awhile.

"What does?" But I thought I knew what he meant.

"The stories. That really bugs me, man. It's like you could tell a million stories and still only get the ones on top. You'll be a great writer someday, Gordie."

"No, I don't think so."

"Yeah, you will. Maybe you'll even write about us guys if you ever get hard up for material."

"Have to be pretty fuckin hard up." I gave him the elbow.

There was another period of silence and then he asked suddenly: "You ready for school?"

I shrugged. Who ever was? You got a little excited thinking about going back, seeing your friends; you were curious about your new teachers and what they would be like—pretty young things just out of teachers' college that you could rag or some old topkick that had been there since the Alamo. In a funny way you could even get excited about the long droning classes, because as the summer vacation neared its end you sometimes got bored enough to believe you could learn something. But summer boredom was nothing like the school boredom that always set in by the end of the second week, and by the beginning of the third week you got down to the *real* business: Could you hit Stinky Fiske in the back of the head with your Art-Gum while the teacher was putting The Principal Exports of South America on the board? How many good loud squeaks could you get off on the varnished surface of your desk if your hands were real sweaty? Who could cut the loudest farts in the locker room while changing up for phys ed? How many girls could you get to play Who Goosed the Moose during lunch hour? Higher learning, baby.

"Junior High," Chris said. "And you know what, Gordie? By next June, we'll all be quits."

"What are you talking about? Why would *that* happen?"

"It's not gonna be like grammar school, that's why. You'll be in the college courses. Me and Teddy and Vern, we'll all be in the shop courses, playing pocket-pool with the rest of the retards, making ashtrays and birdhouses. Vern might even have to go into Remedial. You'll meet a lot of new guys. Smart guys. That's just the way it works, Gordie. That's how they got it set up."

"Meet a lot of pussies is what you mean," I said.

He gripped my arm. "No, man. Don't say that. Don't even *think* that. They'll get your stories. Not like Vern and Teddy."

"Fuck the stories. I'm not going in with a lot of pussies. No sir."

"If you don't, then you're an asshole."

"What's asshole about wanting to be with your friends?"

He looked at me thoughtfully, as if deciding whether or not to tell me something. We had slowed down; Vern and Teddy had pulled almost half a mile ahead. The sun, lower now, came at us through the overlacing trees in broken, dusty shafts, turning everything gold—but it was a tawdry gold, dime-store gold, if you can dig that. The tracks stretched ahead of us in the gloom that was just starting to gather—they seemed almost to twinkle. Star-pricks of light stood out on them here and there, as if some nutty rich guy masquerading as a common laborer had decided to embed a diamond in the steel every sixty yards or so. It was still hot. The sweat rolled off us, slicking our bodies.

"It's asshole if your friends can drag you down," Chris said finally. "I know about you and your folks. They don't give a shit about you. Your big brother was the one they cared about. Like my dad, when Frank got thrown into the stockade in Portsmouth. That was when he started always bein mad at us other kids and hitting us all the time. Your dad doesn't beat on you, but maybe that's even worse. He's got you asleep. You could tell him you were enrolling in the fuckin shop division and you know what he'd do? He'd turn to the next page in his paper and say: Well, that's nice, Gordon, go ask your mother what's for dinner. And don't try to tell me different. I've met him."

I didn't try to tell him different. It's scary to find out that someone else, even a friend, knows just how things are with you.

"You're just a kid, Gordie—"

"Gee, thanks, Dad."

"I wish to fuck I *was* your father!" he said angrily. "You wouldn't go around talking about taking those stupid shop courses if I was! It's like God gave you something, all those stories you can make up, and He said: This is what we got for you, kid. Try not to lose it. But kids lose *everything* unless somebody looks out for them and if your folks are too fucked up to do it then maybe I ought to."

His face looked like he was expecting me to take a swing at him; it was set and unhappy in the green-gold late afternoon light. He had broken the cardinal rule for kids in those days. You could say anything about another kid, you could rank him to the dogs and back, but you didn't say a bad word *ever* about his mom and dad. That was the Fabled Automatic, the same way not inviting your Catholic friends home to dinner on Friday unless you'd checked first to make sure you weren't having meat was the Fabled Automatic. If a kid ranked out your mom and dad, you had to feed him some knuckles.

"Those stories you tell, they're no good to anybody but you, Gordie. If you go along with us just because you don't want the gang to break up, you'll wind up just another grunt, makin C's to get on the teams. You'll get to High and take the same fuckin shop courses and throw erasers and pull your meat along with the rest of the grunts. Get detentions. Fuckin *suspensions.* And after awhile all you'll care about is gettin a car so you can take some skag to the hops or down to the fuckin Twin Bridges Tavern. Then you'll knock her up and spend the rest of your life in the mill or some fuckin shoeshop in Auburn or maybe even up to Hillcrest pluckin chickens. And that pie story will never get written down. *Nothin'*ll get written down. Cause you'll just be another wiseguy with shit for brains."

Chris Chambers was twelve when he said all that to me. But while he was saying it his face crumpled and folded into something older, oldest, ageless. He spoke tonelessly, colorlessly, but nevertheless, what he said struck terror into my bowels. It was as if he had lived that whole life already, that life where they tell you to step right up and spin the Wheel of Fortune, and it spins so pretty and the guy steps on a pedal and it comes up double zeros, house number, everybody loses. They give you a free pass and then they turn on the rain machine, pretty funny, huh, a joke even Vern Tessio could appreciate.

He grabbed my naked arm and his fingers closed tight. They dug grooves in my flesh. They ground at the bones. His eyes were hooded and dead—so dead, man, that he might have just fallen out of his own coffin.

"I know what people think of my family in this town. I know what they think of me and what they expect. Nobody even *asked* me if I took the milk-money that time. I just got a three-day vacation."

"*Did* you take it?" I asked. I had never asked him before, and if you had told me I ever would, I would have called you crazy. The words came out in a little dry bullet.

"Yeah," he said. "Yeah, I took it." He was silent for a moment, looking ahead at Teddy and Vern. "You knew I took it, Teddy knew, *Everybody* knew. Even Vern knew, I think."

I started to deny it, and then closed my mouth. He was right. No matter what I might have said to my mother and father about how a person was supposed to be innocent until proved guilty, I had known.

"Then maybe I was sorry and tried to give it back," Chris said.

I stared at him, my eyes widening. "You tried to give it *back*?"

"*Maybe*, I said. Just *maybe*. And maybe I took it to old lady Simons and told her, and maybe the money was all there but I got a three-day vacation *anyway*, because the money never showed up. And maybe the next week old lady Simons had this brand-new skirt on when she came to school."

I stared at Chris, speechless with horror. He smiled at me, but it was a crimped, terrible smile that never touched his eyes.

"Just *maybe*," he said, but I remembered the new skirt—a light brown paisley, sort of full. I remembered thinking that it made old lady Simons look younger, almost pretty.

"Chris, how much was that milk-money?"

"Almost seven bucks."

"Christ," I whispered.

"So just say that *I* stole the milk-money but then old lady Simons stole it from *me*. Just suppose I told that story. Me, Chris Chambers. Kid brother of Frank Chambers and Eyeball Chambers. You think anybody would have believed it?"

"No way," I whispered. "Jesus Christ!"

He smiled his wintry, awful smile. "And do you think that bitch would have dared try something like that if it had been one of those dootchbags from up on The View that had taken the money?"

"No," I said.

"Yeah. If it had been one of them, Simons would have said: 'Kay, 'kay, we'll forget it this time, but we're gonna spank your wrist real hard and if you ever do it again we'll have to spank *both* wrists. But *me* . . . well, maybe she had her eye on that skirt for a long time. Anyway, she saw her chance and she took it. I was the stupid one for even trying to give that money back. But I never thought . . . I never thought that a *teacher* . . . oh, who gives a fuck, anyway? Why am I even talkin about it?"

He swiped an arm angrily across his eyes and I realized he was almost crying.

"Chris," I said, "why don't you go into the college courses? You're smart enough."

"They decide all of that in the office. And in their smart little conferences. The teachers, they sit around in this big circle-jerk and all they say is Yeah, Yeah, Right, Right. All they give a fuck about is whether you behaved yourself in grammar school and what the town thinks of your family. All they're deciding is whether or not you'll contaminate all those precious college-course dootchbags. But maybe I'll try to work myself up. I don't know if I could do it, but I might try. Because I want to get out of Castle Rock and go to college and never see my old man or any of my brothers again. I want to go someplace where nobody knows me and I don't have any black marks against me before I start. But I don't know if I can do it."

"Why not?"

"People. People drag you down."

"Who?" I asked, thinking he must mean the teachers, or adult monsters like Miss Simons, who had wanted a new skirt, or maybe his brother Eyeball who hung around with Ace and Billy and Charlie and the rest, or maybe his own mom and dad.

But he said: "Your friends drag you down, Gordie. Don't you know that?" He pointed at Vern and Teddy, who were standing and waiting for us to catch up. They were laughing about something; in fact, Vern was just about busting a gut. "Your friends do. They're like drowning guys that are holding onto your legs. You can't save them. You can only drown with them."

"Come on, you fuckin slowpokes!" Vern shouted, still laughing.

"Yeah, comin!" Chris called, and before I could say anything else, he began to run. I ran, too, but he caught up to them before I could catch up to him.

18

We went another mile and then decided to camp for the night. There was still some daylight left, but nobody really wanted to use it. We were pooped from the scene at the dump and from our scare on the train trestle, but it was more than that. We were in Harlow now, in the woods. Somewhere up ahead was a dead kid, probably mangled and covered with flies. Maggots, too, by this time. Nobody wanted to get too close to him with the night coming on. I had read somewhere—in an Algernon Blackwood story, I think— that a guy's ghost hangs out around his dead body until that body is given a decent Christian burial, and there was no way I wanted to wake up in the night and confront the glowing, disembodied ghost of Ray Brower, moaning and gibbering and floating among the dark and rustling pines. By stopping here we figured there had to be at least ten miles between us and him, and of course all four of us knew there were no such things as ghosts, but ten miles seemed just about far enough in case what everybody knew was wrong.

Vern, Chris, and Teddy gathered wood and got a modest little campfire going on a bed of cinders. Chris scraped a bare patch all around the fire—the woods were powder-dry, and he didn't want to take any chances. While they were doing that I sharpened some sticks and made what my brother Denny used to call "Pioneer Drumsticks"—lumps of hamburger pushed onto the ends of green branches. The three of them laughed and bickered over their woodcraft (which was almost nil; there was a Castle Rock Boy Scout troop, but most of the kids who hung around our vacant lot considered it to be an organization made up mostly of pussies), arguing about whether it was better to cook over flames or over coals (a moot point; we were too hungry to wait for coals), whether dried moss would work as kindling, what they would do if they used up all the matches before they got the fire to stay lit. Teddy claimed he could make a fire by rubbing two sticks together. Chris claimed he was so full of shit he squeaked. They didn't have to try; Vern got the small pile of twigs and dry moss to catch from the second match. The day was perfectly still and there was no wind to puff out the light. We all took turns feeding the thin flames until they began to grow stouter on wrist-chunks of wood fetched from an old deadfall some thirty yards into the forest.

When the flames began to die back a little bit, I stuck the sticks holding the Pioneer Drumsticks firmly into the ground at an angle over the fire. We sat around watching them as they shimmered and dripped and finally began to brown. Our stomachs made pre-dinner conversation.

Unable to wait until they were really cooked, we each took one of them, stuck it in a roll, and yanked the hot stick out of the center. They were charred outside, raw inside, and totally delicious. We wolfed them down and wiped the grease from our mouths with our bare arms. Chris opened his pack and took out a tin Band-Aids box (the pistol was way at the bottom of his pack, and because he hadn't told Vern and Teddy, I guessed it was to be our secret). He opened it and gave each of us a battered Winston. We lit them with flaming twigs from the fire and then leaned back, men of the world, watching the cigarette smoke drift away into the soft twilight. None of us inhaled because we might cough and that would mean a day or two of ragging from the others. And it was pleasant enough just to drag and blow, hawking into the fire to hear the sizzle (that was the summer I learned how you can pick out someone who is just learning to smoke: if you're new at it you spit a lot). We were feeling good. We smoked the Winstons down to the filters, then tossed them into the fire.

"Nothin like a smoke after a meal," Teddy said.

"Fucking-A," Vern agreed.

Crickets had started to hum in the green gloom. I looked up at the lane of sky visible through the railroad cut and saw that the blue was now bruising toward purple. Seeing that outrider of twilight made me feel sad and calm at the same time, brave but not really brave, comfortably lonely.

We tromped down a flat place in the underbrush beside the embankment and laid out our bedrolls. Then, for an hour or so, we fed the fire and talked, the kind of talk you can never quite remember once you get past fifteen and discover girls. We talked about who was the best dragger in Castle Rock, if Boston could maybe stay out of the cellar this year, and about the summer just past. Teddy told about the time he had been at White's Beach in Brunswick and some kid had hit his head while diving off the float and almost drowned. We discussed at some length the relative merits of the teachers we had had. We agreed that Mr. Brooks was the biggest pussy in Castle Rock Elementary—he would just about cry if you sassed him back. On the other hand, there was Mrs. Cote (pronounced Cody)—she was just about the meanest bitch God had ever set down on the earth. Vern said he'd heard she hit a kid so hard two years ago that the kid almost went blind. I looked at Chris, wondering if he would say anything about Miss Simons, but he didn't say anything at all, and he didn't see me looking at him—he was looking at Vern and nodding soberly at Vern's story.

We didn't talk about Ray Brower as the dark drew down, but I was thinking about him. There's something horrible and fascinating about the way dark comes to the woods, its coming unsoftened by headlights or streetlights or houselights or neon. It comes with no mothers' voices, calling for their kids to leave off and come on in now, to herald it. If you're used to the town, the coming of the dark in the woods seems more like a natural disaster than a natural phenomenon; it rises like the Castle River rises in the spring.

And as I thought about the body of Ray Brower in this light—or lack of it—what I felt was not queasiness or fear that he would suddenly appear before us, a green and gibbering banshee whose purpose was to drive us back the way we had come before we could disturb his—its—peace, but a sudden and unexpected wash of pity that he should be so alone and so defenseless in the dark that was now coming over our side of the earth. If something wanted to eat on him, it would. His mother wasn't here to stop that from happening, and neither was his father, nor Jesus Christ in the company of all the saints. He was dead and he was all alone, flung off the railroad tracks and into the ditch, and I realized that if I didn't stop thinking about it I was going to cry.

So I told a Le Dio story, made up on the spot and not very good, and when it ended as most of my Le Dio stories did, with one lone American dogface coughing out a dying declaration of patriotism and love for the girl back home into the sad and wise face of the platoon sergeant, it was not the white, scared face of some pfc from Castle Rock or White River Junction I saw in my mind's eye but the face of a much younger boy, already dead, his eyes closed, his features troubled, a rill of blood running from the left corner of his mouth to his jawline. And in back of him, instead of the shattered shops and churches of my Le Dio dreamscape, I saw only dark forest and the cindered railway bed bulking against the starry sky like a prehistoric burial mound.

19

I came awake in the middle of the night, disoriented, wondering why it was so chilly in my bedroom and who had left the windows open. Denny, maybe. I had been dreaming of Denny, something about body-surfing at Harrison State Park. But it had been four years ago that we had done that.

This wasn't my room; this was someplace else. Somebody was holding me in a mighty bearhug, somebody else was pressed against my back, and a shadowy third was crouched beside me, head cocked in a listening attitude.

"What the fuck?" I asked in honest puzzlement.

A long-drawn-out groan in answer. It sounded like Vern.

That brought things into focus, and I remembered where I was . . . but what was everybody doing awake in the middle of the night? Or had I only been asleep for seconds? No, that couldn't be, because a thin sliver of moon was floating dead center in an inky sky.

"Don't let it get me!" Vern gibbered. "I swear I'll be a good boy, I won't do nothin bad, I'll put the ring up before I take a piss, I'll . . . I'll . . ." With some astonishment I realized that I was listening to a prayer—or at least the Vern Tessio equivalent of a prayer.

I sat bolt upright, scared. "Chris?"

"Shut up, Vern," Chris said. He was the one crouching and listening. "It's nothing."

"Oh, yes it is," Teddy said ominously. "It's something."

"*What* is?" I asked. I was still sleepy and disoriented, unstrung from my place in space and time. It scared me that I had come in late on whatever had developed—too late to defend myself properly, maybe.

Then, as if to answer my question, a long and hollow scream rose languidly from the woods—it was the sort of scream you might expect from a woman dying in extreme agony and extreme fear.

"Oh-dear-to-Jesus!" Vern whimpered, his voice high and filled with tears. He re-applied the bearhug that had awakened me, making it hard for me to breathe and adding to my own terror. I threw him loose with an effort but he scrambled right back beside me like a puppy which can't think of anyplace else to go.

"It's that Brower kid," Teddy whispered hoarsely. "His ghost's out walkin in the woods."

"Oh God!" Vern screamed, apparently not crazy about that idea at all. "I promise I won't hawk no more dirty books out of Dahlie's Market! I promise I won't give my carrots to the dog no more! I . . . I . . . I . . . ." He floundered there, wanting to bribe God with everything but unable to think of anything really good in the extremity of his fear. *"I won't smoke no more unfiltered cigarettes! I won't say no bad swears! I won't put my Bazooka in the offerin plate! I won't—"*

"Shut up, Vern," Chris said, and beneath his usual authoritative toughness I could hear the hollow boom of awe. I wondered if his arms and back and belly were as stiff with gooseflesh as my own were, and if the hair on the nape of his neck was trying to stand up in hackles, as mine was.

Vern's voice dropped to a whisper as he continued to expand the reforms he planned to institute if God would only let him live through this night.

"It's a bird, isn't it?" I asked Chris.

"No. At least, I don't think so. I think it's a wildcat. My dad says they scream bloody murder when they're getting ready to mate. Sounds like a woman, doesn't it?"

"Yeah," I said. My voice hitched in the middle of the word and two ice-cubes broke off in the gap.

"But no woman could scream that loud," Chris said . . . and then added helplessly: "Could she, Gordie?"

"It's his ghost," Teddy whispered again. His eyeglasses reflected the moonlight in weak, somehow dreamy smears. "I'm gonna go look for it."

I don't think he was serious, but we took no chances. When he started to get up, Chris and I hauled him back down. Perhaps we were too rough with him, but our muscles had been turned to cables with fear.

"Let me up, fuckheads!" Teddy hissed, struggling. "If I say I wanna go look for it, then I'm gonna go look for it! I wanna see it! I wanna see the ghost! I wanna see if—"

The wild, sobbing cry rose into the night again, cutting the air like a knife with a crystal blade, freezing us with our hands on Teddy—if he'd been a flag, we would have looked like that picture of the Marines claiming Iwo Jima. The scream climbed with a crazy ease through octave after octave, finally reaching a glassy, freezing edge. It hung there for a moment and then whirled back down again, disappearing into an impossible bass register that buzzed like a monstrous honeybee. This was followed by a burst of what sounded like mad laughter . . . and then there was silence again.

"Jesus H Baldheaded Christ," Teddy whispered, and he talked no more of going into the woods to see what was making that screaming noise. All four of us huddled up together and I thought of running. I doubt if I was the only one. If we had been tenting in Vern's field—where our folks *thought* we were—we probably *would* have run. But Castle Rock was too far, and the thought of trying to run across that trestle in the dark made my blood freeze. Running deeper into Harlow and closer to the corpse of Ray Brower was equally unthinkable. We were stuck. If there was a ha'ant out there in the woods—what my dad called a Goosalum—and it wanted us, it would probably get us.

Chris proposed we keep a guard and everyone was agreeable to that. We flipped for watches and Vern got the first one. I got the last. Vern sat up cross-legged by the husk of the campfire while the rest of us lay down again. We huddled together like sheep.

I was positive that sleep would be impossible, but I did sleep—a light, uneasy sleep that skimmed through unconsciousness like a sub with its periscope up. My half-sleeping dreams were populated with wild cries that might have been real or might have only been products of my imagination. I saw—or thought I saw—something white and shapeless steal through the trees like a grotesquely ambulatory bedsheet.

At last I slipped into something I knew was a dream. Chris and I were swimming at White's Beach, a gravel-pit in Brunswick that had been turned into a miniature lake when the gravel-diggers struck water. It was where Teddy had seen the kid hit his head and almost drown.

In my dream we were out over our heads, stroking lazily along, with a hot July sun blazing down. From behind us, on the float, came cries and shouts and yells of laughter as kids climbed and dived or climbed and were pushed. I could hear the empty kerosene drums that held the float up clanging and booming together—a sound not unlike that of churchbells, which are so solemn and emptily profound. On the sand-and-gravel beach, oiled bodies lay face down on blankets, little kids with buckets squatted on the verge of the water or sat happily flipping muck into their hair with plastic shovels, and teenagers clustered in grinning groups, watching the young girls promenade endlessly back and forth in pairs and trios, never alone, the secret places of their bodies wrapped in Jantzen tank suits. People walked up the hot sand on the balls of their feet, wincing, to the snackbar. They came back with chips, Devil Dogs, Red Ball Popsicles.

Mrs. Cote drifted past us on an inflatable rubber raft. She was lying on her back, dressed in her typical September-to-June school uniform: a gray two-piece suit with a thick sweater instead of a blouse under the jacket, a flower pinned over one almost nonexistent breast, thick support hose the color of Canada Mints on her legs. Her black old lady's high-heeled shoes were trailing in the water, making small V's. Her hair was blue-rinsed, like my mother's, and done up in those tight, medicinal-smelling clockspring curls. Her glasses flashed brutally in the sun.

"Watch your steps, boys," she said. "Watch your steps or I'll hit you hard enough to strike you blind. I can do that; I have been given that power by the school board. Now, Mr. Chambers, 'Mending Wall,' if you please. By rote."

"I tried to give the money back," Chris said. "Old lady Simons said okay, but she *took* it! Do you hear me? She *took* it! Now what are you going to do about it? Are you going to whack *her* blind?"

" 'Mending Wall,' Mr. Chambers, if you please. By *rote*."

Chris threw me a despairing glance, as if to say *Didn't I tell you it would be this way?*, and then began to tread water. He began: " 'Something there is that doesn't love a wall, that sends the frozen-ground-swell under it—' " And then his head went under, his reciting mouth filling with water.

He popped back up, crying: "Help me, Gordie! Help me!"

Then he was dragged under again. Looking into the clear water I could see two bloated, naked corpses holding his ankles. One was Vern and the other was Teddy, and their open eyes were as blank and pupilless as the eyes of Greek statues. Their small pre-pubescent penises floated limply up from their distended bellies like albino strands of kelp. Chris's head broke water again. He held one hand up limply to me and voiced a screaming, womanish cry that rose and rose, ululating in the hot sunny summer air. I looked wildly toward the beach but nobody had heard. The lifeguard, his bronzed, athletic body lolling attractively on the seat at the top of his whitewashed cruciform wooden tower, just went on smiling down at a girl in a red bathing suit. Chris's scream turned into a bubbling water-choked gurgle as the corpses pulled him under again. And as they dragged him down to black water I could see his rippling, distorted eyes turned up to me in a pleading agony; I could see his white starfish hands held helplessly up to the sun-burnished roof of the water. But instead of diving down and trying to save him, I stroked madly for the shore, or at least to a place where the water would not be over my head. Before I could get there—before I could even get close—I felt a soft, rotted, implacable hand wrap itself around my calf and begin to pull. A scream built up in my chest . . . but before I could utter it, the dream washed away into a grainy facsimile of reality. It was Teddy with his hand on my leg. He was shaking me awake. It was my watch.

Still half in the dream, almost talking in my sleep, I asked him thickly: "You alive, Teddy?"

"No. I'm dead and you're a black nigger," he said crossly. It dispelled the last of the dream. I sat up by the campfire and Teddy lay down.

20

The others slept heavily through the rest of the night. I was in and out, dozing, waking, dozing again. The night was far from silent; I heard the triumphant screech-squawk of a pouncing owl, the tiny cry of some small animal perhaps about to be eaten, a larger something blundering wildly through the undergrowth. Under all of this, a steady tone, were the crickets. There were no more screams. I dozed and woke, woke and dozed, and I suppose if I had been discovered standing such a slipshod watch in Le Dio, I probably would have been courtmartialed and shot.

I snapped more solidly out of my last doze and became aware that something was different. It took a moment or two to figure it out: although the moon was down, I could see my hands resting on my jeans. My watch said quarter to five. It was dawn.

I stood, hearing my spine crackle, walked two dozen feet away from the lumped-together bodies of my friends, and pissed into a clump of sumac. I was starting to shake the night-willies; I could feel them sliding away. It was a fine feeling.

I scrambled up the cinders to the railroad tracks and sat on one of the rails, idly chucking cinders between my feet, in no hurry to wake the others. At that precise moment the new day felt too good to share.

Morning came on apace. The noise of the crickets began to drop, and the shadows under the trees and bushes evaporated like puddles after a shower. The air had that peculiar lack of taste that presages the latest hot day in a famous series of hot days. Birds that had maybe cowered all night just as we had done now began to twitter self-importantly. A wren landed on top of the deadfall from which we had taken our firewood, preened itself, and then flew off.

I don't know how long I sat there on that rail, watching the purple steal out of the sky as noiselessly as it had stolen in the evening before. Long enough for my butt to start complaining anyway. I was about to get up when I looked to my right and saw a deer standing in the railroad bed not ten yards from me.

My heart went up into my throat so high that I think I could have put my hand in my mouth and touched it. My stomach and genitals filled with a hot dry excitement. I didn't move. I couldn't have moved if I had wanted to. Her eyes weren't brown but a dark, dusty black—the kind of velvet you see backgrounding jewelry displays. Her small ears were scuffed suede. She looked serenely at me, head slightly lowered in what I took for curiosity, seeing a kid with his hair in a sleep-scarecrow of whirls and many-tined cowlicks, wearing jeans with cuffs and a brown khaki shirt with the elbows mended and the collar turned up in the hoody tradition of the day. What I was seeing was some sort of gift, something given with a carelessness that was appalling.

We looked at each other for a long time . . . I *think* it was a long time. Then she turned and walked off to the other side of the tracks, white bobtail flipping insouciantly. She found grass and began to crop. I couldn't believe it. She had begun to *crop.* She didn't look back at me and didn't need to; I was frozen solid.

Then the rail started to thrum under my ass and bare seconds later the doe's head came up, cocked back toward Castle Rock. She stood there, her branch-black nose working on the air, coaxing it a little. Then she was gone in three gangling leaps, vanishing into the woods with no sound but one rotted branch, which broke with a sound like a track ref's starter-gun.

I sat there, looking mesmerized at the spot where she had been, until the actual sound of the freight came up through the stillness. Then I skidded back down the bank to where the others were sleeping.

The freight's slow, loud passage woke them up, yawning and

scratching. There was some funny, nervous talk about "the case of the screaming ghost," as Chris called it, but not as much as you might imagine. In daylight it seemed more foolish than interesting —almost embarrassing. Best forgotten.

It was on the tip of my tongue to tell them about the deer, but I ended up not doing it. That was one thing I kept to myself. I've never spoken or written of it until just now, today. And I have to tell you that it seems a lesser thing written down, damn near inconsequential. But for me it was the best part of that trip, the cleanest part, and it was a moment I found myself returning to, almost helplessly, when there was trouble in my life—my first day in the bush in Vietnam, and this fellow walked into the clearing where we were with his hand over his nose and when he took his hand away there was no nose there because it had been shot off; the time the doctor told us our youngest son might be hydrocephalic (he turned out just to have an oversized head, thank God); the long, crazy weeks before my mother died. I would find my thoughts turning back to that morning, the scuffed suede of her ears, the white flash of her tail. But eight hundred million Red Chinese don't give a shit, right? The most important things are the hardest to say, because words diminish them. It's hard to make strangers care about the good things in your life.

21

The tracks now bent southwest and ran through tangles of second-growth fir and heavy underbrush. We got a breakfast of late blackberries from some of these bushes, but berries never fill you up; your stomach just gives them a thirty-minute option and then begins growling again. We went back to the tracks—it was about eight o'clock by then—and took five. Our mouths were a dark purple and our naked torsos were scratched from the blackberry brambles. Vern wished glumly aloud for a couple of fried eggs with bacon on the side.

That was the last day of the heat, and I think it was the worst of all. The early scud of clouds melted away and by nine o'clock the sky was a pale steel color that made you feel hotter just looking at it.

The sweat rolled and ran from our chests and backs, leaving clean streaks through the accumulated soot and grime. Mosquitoes and blackflies whirled and dipped around our heads in aggravating clouds. Knowing that we had long miles to go didn't make us feel any better. Yet the fascination of the thing drew us on and kept us walking faster than we had any business doing, in that heat. We were all crazy to see that kid's body—I can't put it any more simply or honestly than that. Whether it was harmless or whether it turned out to have the power to murder sleep with a hundred mangled dreams, we wanted to see it. I think that we had come to believe we *deserved* to see it.

It was about nine-thirty when Teddy and Chris spotted water up ahead—they shouted to Vern and me. We ran over to where they were standing. Chris was laughing, delighted. "Look there! Beavers did that!" He pointed.

It was the work of beavers, all right. A large-bore culvert ran under the railroad embankment a little way ahead, and the beavers had sealed the right end with one of their neat and industrious little dams—sticks and branches cemented together with leaves, twigs, and dried mud. Beavers are busy little fuckers, all right. Behind the dam was a clear and shining pool of water, brilliantly mirroring the sunlight. Beaver houses humped up and out of the water in several places—they looked like wooden igloos. A small creek trickled into the far end of the pool, and the trees which bordered it were gnawed a clean bone-white to a height of almost three feet in places.

"Railroad'll clean this shit out pretty soon," Chris said.

"Why?" Vern asked.

"They can't have a pool here," Chris said. "It'd undercut their precious railroad line. That's why they put that culvert in there to start with. They'll shoot them some beavers and scare off the rest and then knock out their dam. Then this'll go back to being a bog, like it probably was before."

"I think that eats the meat," Teddy said.

Chris shrugged. "Who cares about beavers? Not the Great Southern and Western Maine, that's for sure."

"You think it's deep enough to swim in?" Vern asked, looking hungrily at the water.

"One way to find out," Teddy said.

"Who goes first?" I asked.

"Me!" Chris said. He went running down the bank, kicking off his sneakers and untying his shirt from around his waist with a jerk. He pushed his pants and undershorts down with a single shove of his thumbs. He balanced, first on one leg and then on the other, to get his socks. Then he made a shallow dive. He came up shaking his head to get his wet hair out of his eyes. "It's fuckin *great!*" he shouted.

"How deep?" Teddy called back. He had never learned to swim.

Chris stood up in the water and his shoulders broke the surface. I saw something on one of them—a blackish-grayish something. I decided it was a piece of mud and dismissed it. If I had looked more closely I could have saved myself a lot of nightmares later on. "Come on in, you chickens!"

He turned and thrashed off across the pool in a clumsy breast-stroke, turned over, and thrashed back. By then we were all getting undressed. Vern was in next, then me.

Hitting the water was fantastic—clean and cool. I swam across to Chris, loving the silky feel of having nothing on but water. I stood up and we grinned into each others' faces.

"Boss!" We said it at exactly the same instant.

"Fuckin jerkoff," he said, splashed water in my face, and swam off the other way.

We goofed off in the water for almost half an hour before we realized that the pond was full of bloodsuckers. We dived, swam under water, ducked each other. We never knew a thing. Then Vern swam into the shallower part, went under, and stood on his hands. When his legs broke water in a shaky but triumphant V, I saw that they were covered with blackish-gray lumps, just like the one I had seen on Chris's shoulder. They were slugs—big ones.

Chris's mouth dropped open, and I felt all the blood in my body go as cold as dry ice. Teddy screamed, his face going pale. Then all three of us were thrashing for the bank, going just as fast as we could. I know more about freshwater slugs now than I did then, but the fact that they are mostly harmless has done nothing to allay the almost insane horror of them I've had ever since that day in the beaver-pool. They carry a local anesthetic and an anti-coagulant in their alien saliva, which means that the host never feels a thing when they attach themselves. If you don't happen to see them they'll go on feeding until their swelled, loathsome bodies fall off you, sated, or until they actually burst.

We pulled ourselves up on the bank and Teddy went into a hysterical paroxysm as he looked down at himself. He was screaming as he picked the leeches off his naked body.

Vern broke the water and looked at us, puzzled. "What the hell's wrong with h—"

"*Leeches!*" Teddy screamed, pulling two of them off his trembling thighs and throwing them just as far as he could. "Dirty mother-fuckin *bloodsuckers!*" His voice broke shrilly on the last word.

"*OhGodOhGodOhGod!*" Vern cried. He paddled across the pool and stumbled out.

I was still cold; the heat of the day had been suspended. I kept telling myself to catch hold. Not to get screaming. Not to be a pussy. I picked half a dozen off my arms and several more off my chest.

Chris turned his back to me. "Gordie? Are there any more? Take em off if there are, please, Gordie!" There *were* more, five or six, running down his back like grotesque black buttons. I pulled their soft, boneless bodies off him.

I brushed even more off my legs, then got Chris to do my back.

I was starting to relax a little—and that was when I looked down at myself and saw the granddaddy of them all clinging to my testicles, its body swelled to four times its normal size. Its blackish-gray skin had gone a bruised purplish-red. That was when I began to lose control. Not outside, at least not in any big way, but inside, where it counts.

I brushed its slick, glutinous body with the back of my hand. It held on. I tried to do it again and couldn't bring myself to actually touch it. I turned to Chris, tried to speak, couldn't. I pointed instead. His cheeks, already ashy, went whiter still.

"I can't get it off," I said through numb lips. "You . . . can you . . ."

But he backed away, shaking his head, his mouth twisted. "I

can't, Gordie," he said, unable to take his eyes away. "I'm sorry but I can't. No. Oh. No." He turned away, bowed with one hand pressed to his midsection like the butler in a musical comedy, and was sick in a stand of juniper bushes.

You got to hold onto yourself, I thought, looking at the leech that hung off me like a crazy beard. Its body was still visibly swelling. *You got to hold onto yourself and get him. Be tough. It's the last one. The. Last. One.*

I reached down again and picked it off and it burst between my fingers. My own blood ran across my palm and inner wrist in a warm flood. I began to cry.

Still crying, I walked back to my clothes and put them on. I wanted to stop crying, but I just didn't seem able to turn off the waterworks. Then the shakes set in, making it worse. Vern ran up to me, still naked.

"They off, Gordie? They off me? They off me?"

He twirled in front of me like an insane dancer on a carnival stage.

"They off? Huh? Huh? They off me, Gordie?"

His eyes kept going past me, as wide and white as the eyes of a plaster horse on a merry-go-round.

I nodded that they were and just kept on crying. It seemed that crying was going to be my new career. I tucked my shirt in and then buttoned it all the way to the neck. I put on my socks and my sneakers. Little by little the tears began to slow down. Finally there was nothing left but a few hitches and moans, and then they stopped, too.

Chris walked over to me, wiping his mouth with a handful of elm leaves. His eyes were wide and mute and apologetic.

When we were all dressed we just stood there looking at each other for a moment, and then we began to climb the railroad embankment. I looked back once at the burst leech lying on top of the tromped-down bushes where we had danced and screamed and groaned them off. It looked deflated . . . but still ominous.

Fourteen years later I sold my first novel and made my first trip to New York. "It's going to be a three-day celebration," my new editor told me over the phone. "People slinging bullshit will be summarily shot." But of course it was three days of unmitigated bullshit.

While I was there I wanted to do all the standard out-of-towner things—see a stage show at the Radio City Music Hall, go to the top of the Empire State Building (fuck the World Trade Center; the building King Kong climbed in 1933 is always gonna be the tallest one in the world for me), visit Times Square by night. Keith, my editor, seemed more than pleased to show his city off. The last touristy thing we did was to take a ride on the Staten Island Ferry, and while leaning on the rail I happened to look down and see scores of used condoms floating on the mild swells. And I had a moment of almost total recall—or perhaps it was an actual incidence of time-travel. Either way, for one second I was literally *in* the past, pausing halfway up that embankment and looking back at the burst leech: dead, deflated . . . but still ominous.

Keith must have seen something in my face because he said: "Not very pretty, are they?"

I only shook my head, wanting to tell him not to apologize, wanting to tell him that you didn't have to come to the Apple and ride the ferry to see used rubbers, wanting to say: *The only reason anyone writes stories is so they can understand the past and get ready for some future mortality; that's why all the verbs in stories have -ed endings, Keith my good man, even the ones that sell millions of paperbacks. The only two useful artforms are religion and stories.*

I was pretty drunk that night, as you may have guessed.

What I did tell him was: "I was thinking of something else, that's all." The most important things are the hardest things to say.

22

We walked further down the tracks—I don't know just how far—and I was starting to think: *Well, okay, I'm going to be able to handle it, it's all over anyway, just a bunch of leeches, what the fuck;* I was still thinking it when waves of whiteness suddenly began to come over my sight and I fell down.

I must have fallen hard, but landing on the crossties was like plunging into a warm and puffy feather bed. Someone turned me over. The touch of hands was faint and unimportant. Their faces were disembodied balloons looking down at me from miles up. They looked the way the ref's face must look to a fighter who has been punched silly and is currently taking a ten-second rest on the canvas. Their words came in gentle oscillations, fading in and out.

". . . him?"

". . . be all . . ."

". . . if you think the sun . . ."

"Gordie, are you . . ."

Then I must have said something that didn't make much sense because they began to look *really* worried.

"We better take him back, man," Teddy said, and then the whiteness came over everything again.

When it cleared, I seemed to be all right. Chris was squatting next to me, saying: "Can you hear me, Gordie? You there, man?"

"Yes," I said, and sat up. A swarm of black dots exploded in front of my eyes, and then went away. I waited to see if they'd come back, and when they didn't, I stood up.

"You scared the cheesly old shit outta me, Gordie," he said. "You want a drink of water?"

"Yeah."

He gave me his canteen, half-full of water, and I let three warm gulps roll down my throat.

"Why'd you faint, Gordie?" Vern asked anxiously.

"Made a bad mistake and looked at your face," I said.

"Eeee-eee-eeeee!" Teddy cackled. "Fuckin Gordie! You wet!"

"You really okay?" Vern persisted.

"Yeah. Sure. It was . . . bad there for a minute. Thinking about those suckers."

They nodded soberly. We took five in the shade and then went on walking, me and Vern on one side of the tracks again, Chris and Teddy on the other. We figured we must be getting close.

23

We weren't as close as we thought, and if we'd had the brains to spend two minutes looking at a roadmap, we would have seen why. We knew that Ray Brower's corpse had to be near the Back Harlow

Road, which dead-ends on the bank of the Royal River. Another trestle carries the GS&WM tracks across the Royal. So this is the way we figured: Once we got close to the Royal, we'd be getting close to the Back Harlow Road, where Billy and Charlie had been parked when they saw the boy. And since the Royal was only ten miles from the Castle River, we figured we had it made in the shade.

But that was ten miles as the crow flies, and the tracks didn't move on a straight line between the Castle and the Royal. Instead, they made a very shallow loop to avoid a hilly, crumbling region called The Bluffs. Anyway, we could have seen that loop quite clearly if we had looked on a map, and figured out that, instead of ten miles, we had about sixteen to walk.

Chris began to suspect the truth when noon had come and gone and the Royal still wasn't in sight. We stopped while he climbed a high pine tree and took a look around. He came down and gave us a simple enough report: it was going to be at least four in the afternoon before we got to the Royal, and we would only make it by then if we humped right along.

"Ah, *shit*!" Teddy cried. "So what're we gonna do now?"

We looked into each others' tired, sweaty faces. We were hungry and out of temper. The big adventure had turned into a long slog—dirty and sometimes scary. We would have been missed back home by now, too, and if Milo Pressman hadn't already called the cops on us, the engineer of the train crossing the trestle might have done it. We had been planning to hitchhike back to Castle Rock, but four o'clock was just three hours from dark, and *nobody* gives four kids on a back country road a lift after dark.

I tried to summon up the cool image of my deer, cropping at green morning grass, but even that seemed dusty and no good, no better than a stuffed trophy over the mantel in some guy's hunting lodge, the eyes sprayed to give them that phony lifelike shine.

Finally Chris said: "It's still closer out going ahead. Let's go."

He turned and started to walk along the tracks in his dusty sneakers, head down, his shadow only a puddle at his feet. After a minute or so the rest of us followed him, strung out in Indian file.

24

In the years between then and the writing of this memoir, I've thought remarkably little about those two days in September, at least consciously. The associations the memories bring to the surface are as unpleasant as week-old rivercorpses brought to the surface by cannonfire. As a result, I never really questioned our decision to walk down the tracks. Put another way, I've wondered sometimes about *what* we had decided to do but never how we did it.

But now a much simpler scenario comes to mind. I'm confident that if the idea *had* come up it would have been shot down—walking down the tracks would have seemed neater, *bosser*, as we said then. But if the idea had come up and *hadn't* been shot down in flames, none of the things which occurred later would have happened. Maybe Chris and Teddy and Vern would even be alive today. No, they didn't die in the woods or on the railroad tracks; nobody dies in this story except some bloodsuckers and Ray Brower, and if you want to be completely fair about it, he was dead before it even started. But it *is* true that, of the four of us who flipped coins to see who would go down to the Florida Market to get supplies, only the one who actually went is still alive. The Ancient Mariner at thirty-four, with you, Gentle Reader, in the role of Wedding Guest (at this point shouldn't you flip to the jacket photo to see if my eye holdeth you in its spell?). If you sense a certain flipness on my part, you're right—but maybe I have cause. At an age when all four of us would be considered too young and immature to be President, three of us are dead. And if small events really do echo up larger and larger through time, yes, maybe if we had done the simple thing and simply hitched into Harlow, they would still be alive today.

We could have hooked a ride all the way up Route 7 to the Shiloh Church, which stood at the intersection of the highway and the Back Harlow Road (at least until 1967, when it was levelled by a fire attributed to a tramp's smouldering cigarette butt). With reasonable luck we could have gotten to where the body was by sundown of the previous day.

But the idea wouldn't have lived. It wouldn't have been shot down with tightly buttressed arguments and debating society rhetoric, but with grunts and scowls and farts and raised middle fingers. The verbal part of the discussion would have been carried forward with such trenchant and sparkling contributions as "Fuck no," "That sucks," and that old reliable standby, "Did your mother ever have any kids that lived?"

Unspoken—maybe it was too fundamental to be spoken—was the idea that this was a *big* thing. It wasn't screwing around with firecrackers or trying to look through the knothole in the back of the girls' privy at Harrison State Park. This was something on a par with getting laid for the first time, or going into the Army, or buying your first bottle of legal liquor—just bopping into that state store, if you can dig it, selecting a bottle of good Scotch, showing the clerk your draft-card and driver's licence, then walking out with a grin on your face and that brown bag in your hand, member of a club with just a few more rights and privileges than our old treehouse with the tin roof.

There's a high ritual to all fundamental events, the rites of passage, the magic corridor where the change happens. Buying the condoms. Standing before the minister. Raising your hand and taking the oath. Or, if you please, walking down the railroad tracks to meet a fellow your own age halfway, the same as I'd walk halfway over to Pine Street to meet Chris if he was coming over to my house, or the way Teddy would walk halfway down Gates Street to meet me if I was going to his. It seemed right to do it this way, because the rite of passage *is* a magic corridor and so we always provide an aisle—it's what you walk down when you get married, what they carry you down when you get buried. Our corridor was those twin rails, and we walked between them, just bopping along toward whatever this was supposed to mean. You don't hitchhike your way to a thing like that, maybe. And maybe we thought it was also right that it should have turned out to be harder than we had expected. Events surrounding our hike had turned it into what we had suspected it was all along: serious business.

What we *didn't* know as we walked around The Bluffs was that Billy Tessio, Charlie Hogan, Jack Mudgett, Norman "Fuzzy" Bracowicz, Vince Desjardins, Chris's older brother Eyeball, and Ace

Merrill himself were all on their way to take a look at the body themselves—in a weird kind of way, Ray Brower had become famous, and our secret had turned into a regular roadshow. They were piling into Ace's chopped and channelled '52 Ford and Vince's pink '54 Studebaker even as we started on the last leg of our trip.

Billy and Charlie had managed to keep their enormous secret for just about thirty-six hours. Then Charlie spilled it to Ace while they were shooting pool, and Billy had spilled it to Jack Mudgett while they were fishing for steelies from the Boom Road Bridge. Both Ace and Jack had sworn solemnly on their mothers' names to keep the secret, and that was how everybody in their gang knew about it by noon. Guess you could tell what those assholes thought about their mothers.

They all congregated down at the pool hall, and Fuzzy Bracowicz advanced a theory (which you have heard before, Gentle Reader) that they could all become heroes—not to mention instant radio and TV personalities—by "discovering" the body. All they had to do, Fuzzy maintained, was to take two cars with a lot of fishing gear in the trunks. After they found the body, their story would be a hundred per cent. We was just plannin to take a few pickerel out of the Royal River, officer. Heh-heh-heh. Look what we found.

They were burning up the road from Castle Rock to the Back Harlow area just as we started to finally get close.

25

Clouds began to build in the sky around two o'clock, but at first none of us took them seriously. It hadn't rained since the early days of July, so why should it rain now? But they kept building to the south of us, up and up and up, thunderheads in great pillars as purple as bruises, and they began to move slowly our way. I looked at them closely, checking for that membrane beneath that means it's already raining twenty miles away, or fifty. But there was no rain yet. The clouds were still just building.

Vern got a blister on his heel and we stopped and rested while he packed the back of his left sneaker with moss stripped from the bark of an old oak tree.

"Is it gonna rain, Gordie?" Teddy asked.

"I think so."

"Pisser!" he said, and sighed. "The pisser good end to a pisser good day."

I laughed and he tipped me a wink.

We started to walk again, a little more slowly now out of respect for Vern's hurt foot. And in the hour between two and three, the quality of the day's light began to change, and we knew for sure that rain was coming. It was just as hot as ever, and even more humid, but we knew. And the birds did. They seemed to appear from nowhere and swoop across the sky, chattering and crying shrilly to each other. And the light. From a steady, beating brightness it seemed to evolve into something filtered, almost pearly. Our shadows, which had begun to grow long again, also grew fuzzy and ill-defined. The sun had begun to sail in and out through the thickening decks of clouds, and the southern sky had gone a coppery shade. We watched the thunderheads lumber closer, fascinated by their size and their mute threat. Every now and then it seemed that a giant flashbulb had gone off inside one of them, turning their purplish, bruised color momentarily to a light gray. I saw a jagged fork of lightning lick down from the underside of the closest. It was bright enough to print a blue tattoo on my retinas. It was followed by a long, shaking blast of thunder.

We did a little bitching about how we were going to get caught out in the rain, but only because it was the expected thing—of course we were all looking forward to it. It would be cold and refreshing . . . and leech-free.

At a little past three-thirty, we saw running water through a break in the trees.

"That's it!" Chris yelled jubilantly. "That's the Royal!"

We began to walk faster, taking our second wind. The storm was getting close now. The air began to stir, and it seemed that the temperature dropped ten degrees in a space of seconds. I looked down and saw that my shadow had disappeared entirely.

We were walking in pairs again, each two watching a side of the railroad embankment. My mouth was dry, throbbing with a sickish tension. The sun sailed behind another cloudbank and this time it didn't come back out. For a moment the bank's edges were embroidered with gold, like a cloud in an Old Testament Bible illustration, and then the wine-colored, dragging belly of the thunderhead blotted out all traces of the sun. The day became gloomy—the clouds were rapidly eating up the last of the blue. We could smell the river so clearly that we might have been horses—or perhaps it was the smell of rain impending in the air as well. There was an ocean above us, held in by a thin sac that might rupture and let down a flood at any second.

I kept trying to look into the underbrush, but my eyes were continually drawn back to that turbulent, racing sky; in its deepening colors you could read whatever doom you liked: water, fire, wind, hail. The cool breeze became more insistent, hissing in the firs. A sudden impossible bolt of lightning flashed down, seemingly from directly overhead, making me cry out and clap my hands to my eyes. God had taken my picture, a little kid with his shirt tied around his waist, duckbumps on his bare chest and cinders on his cheeks. I heard the rending fall of some big tree not sixty yards away. The crack of thunder which followed made me cringe. I wanted to be at home reading a good book in a safe place . . . like down in the potato cellar.

"Jeezis!" Vern screamed in a high, fainting voice. "Oh my Jeezis Chrise, lookit *that!*"

I looked in the direction Vern was pointing and saw a blue-white fireball bowling its way up the lefthand rail of the GS&WM tracks, crackling and hissing for all the world like a scalded cat. It hurried past us as we turned to watch it go, dumbfounded, aware for the first time that such things could exist. Twenty feet beyond us it made a sudden —*pop!!*— and just disappeared, leaving a greasy smell of ozone behind.

"What am I *doin* here, anyway?" Teddy muttered.

"What a pisser!" Chris exclaimed happily, his face upturned. "This is gonna be a pisser like you wouldn't *believe!*" But I was with Teddy. Looking up at that sky gave me a dismaying sense of vertigo. It was more like looking into some deeply mysterious marbled gorge. Another lightning-bolt crashed down, making us duck. This time the ozone smell was hotter, more urgent. The following clap of thunder came with no perceptible pause at all.

My ears were still ringing from it when Vern began to screech triumphantly: *"THERE! THERE HE IS! RIGHT THERE! I SEE HIM!"*

I can see Vern right this minute, if I want to—all I have to do is sit back for a minute and close my eyes. He's standing there on the lefthand rail like an explorer on the prow of his ship, one hand shielding his eyes from the silver stroke of lightning that has just come down, the other extended and pointing.

We ran up beside him and looked. I was thinking to myself: *Vern's imagination just ran away with him, that's all. The suckers, the heat, now this storm . . . his eyes are dealing wild cards, that's all.* But that wasn't what it was, although there was a split second when I wanted it to be. In that split second I knew I never wanted to see a corpse, not even a runover woodchuck.

In the place where we were standing, early spring rains had washed part of the embankment away, leaving a gravelly, uncertain four-foot drop-off. The railroad maintenance crews had either not yet gotten around to it in their yellow diesel-operated repair carts, or it had happened so recently it hadn't yet been reported. At the bottom of this washout was a marshy, mucky tangle of undergrowth that smelled bad. And sticking out of a wild clockspring of blackberry brambles was a single pale white hand.

Did any of us breathe? I didn't.

The breeze was now a wind—harsh and jerky, coming at us from no particular direction, jumping and whirling, slapping at our sweaty skins and open pores. I hardly noticed. I think part of my mind was waiting for Teddy to cry out *Paratroops over the side!*, and I thought if he did that I might just go crazy. It would have been better to see the whole body, all at once, but instead there was only that limp outstretched hand, horribly white, the fingers limply splayed, like the hand of a drowned boy. It told us the truth of the whole matter. It explained every graveyard in the world. The image of that hand came back to me every time I heard or read of an atrocity. Somewhere, attached to that hand, was the rest of Ray Brower.

Lightning flickered and stroked. Thunder ripped in behind each stroke as if a drag race had started over our heads.

"Sheeeee . . ." Chris said, the sound not quite a cuss word, not quite the country version of *shit* as it is pronounced around a slender stem of timothy grass when the baler breaks down—instead it was a long, tuneless syllable without meaning; a sigh that had just happened to pass through the vocal cords.

Vern was licking his lips in a compulsive sort of way, as if he had tasted some obscure new delicacy, a Howard Johnson's 29th flavor, Tibetan Sausage Rolls, Interstellar Escargot, something so weird that it excited and revolted him at the same time.

Teddy only stood and looked. The wind whipped his greasy, clotted hair first away from his ears and then back over them. His face was a total blank. I could tell you I saw something there, and perhaps I did, in hindsight . . . but not then.

There were black ants trundling back and forth across the hand.

A great whispering noise began to rise in the woods on either side of the tracks, as if the forest had just noticed we were there and was commenting on it. The rain had started.

Dime-sized drops fell on my head and arms. They struck the embankment, turning the fill dark for a moment—and then the color changed back again as the greedy dry ground sucked the moisture up.

Those big drops fell for maybe five seconds and then they stopped. I looked at Chris and he blinked back at me.

Then the storm came all at once, as if a shower chain had been pulled in the sky. The whispering sound changed to loud contention. It was as if we were being rebuked for our discovery, and it was frightening. Nobody tells you about the pathetic fallacy until you're in college . . . and even then I noticed that nobody but the total dorks completely believed it *was* a fallacy.

Chris jumped over the side of the washout, his hair already soaked and clinging to his head. I followed. Vern and Teddy came close behind, but Chris and I were first to reach the body of Ray Brower. He was face down. Chris looked into my eyes, his face set and stern—an adult's face. I nodded slightly, as if he had spoken aloud.

I think he was down here and relatively intact instead of up there between the rails and completely mangled because he was trying to get out of the way when the train hit him, knocking him head over heels. He had landed with his head pointed toward the tracks, arms over his head like a diver about to execute. He had landed in this boggy cup of land that was becoming a small swamp. His hair was a dark reddish color. The moisture in the air had made it curl slightly at the ends. There was blood in it, but not a great deal, not a gross-out amount. The ants were grosser. He was wearing a solid color dark green tee-shirt and bluejeans. His feet were bare, and a few feet behind him, caught in tall blackberry brambles, I saw a pair of filthy low-topped Keds. For a moment I was puzzled—why was he here and his tennies there? Then I realized, and the realization was like a dirty punch below the belt. My wife, my kids, my friends—they all think that having an imagination like mine must be quite nice; aside from making all this dough, I can have a little mind-movie whenever things get dull. Mostly they're right. But every now and then it turns around and bites the shit out of you with these long teeth, teeth that have been filed to points like the teeth of a cannibal. You see things you'd just as soon not see, things that keep you awake until first light. I saw one of those things now, saw it with absolute clarity and certainty. He had been knocked spang out of his Keds. The train had knocked him out of his Keds just as it had knocked the life out of his body.

That finally rammed it all the way home for me. The kid was dead. The kid wasn't sick, the kid wasn't sleeping. The kid wasn't going to get up in the morning anymore or get the runs from eating too many apples or catch poison ivy or wear out the eraser on the end of his Ticonderoga No. 2 during a hard math test. The kid was dead; stone dead. The kid was never going to go out bottling with his friends in the spring, gunnysack over his shoulder to pick up the returnables the retreating snow uncovered. The kid wasn't going to wake up at two o'clock A.M. on the morning of November 1st this year, run to the bathroom, and vomit up a big glurt of cheap Halloween candy. The kid wasn't going to pull a single girl's braid in home room. The kid wasn't going to give a bloody nose, or get one. The kid was *can't, don't, won't, never, shouldn't, wouldn't, couldn't.* He was the side of the battery where the terminal says NEG. The fuse you have to put a penny in. The wastebasket by the teacher's desk, which always smells of wood-shavings from the sharpener and dead orange peels from lunch. The haunted house outside of town where the windows are crashed out, the NO TRESPASSING signs whipped away across the fields, the attic full of bats, the cellar full of rats. The kid was dead, mister, ma'am, young sir, little miss. I could go on all day and never get it right about the distance between his bare feet on the ground and his dirty Keds hanging in the bushes. It was thirty-plus inches, it was a googol of light-years. The kid was disconnected from his Keds beyond all hope of reconciliation. He was dead.

We turned him face up into the pouring rain, the lightning, the steady crack of thunder.

There were ants and bugs all over his face and neck. They ran briskly in and out of the round collar of his tee-shirt. His eyes were open, but terrifyingly out of sync—one was rolled back so far that we could see only a tiny arc of iris; the other stared straight up into the storm. There was a dried froth of blood above his mouth and on his chin—from a bloody nose, I thought—and the right side of his face was lacerated and darkly bruised. Still, I thought, he didn't really look bad. I had once walked into a door my brother Dennis was shoving open, came off with bruises even worse than this kid's, *plus* the bloody nose, and still had two helpings of everything for supper after it happened.

Teddy and Vern stood behind us, and if there had been any sight at all left in that one upward-staring eye, I suppose we would have looked to Ray Brower like pallbearers in a horror movie.

A beetle came out of his mouth, trekked across his fuzzless cheek, stepped onto a nettle, and was gone.

"D'joo see that?" Teddy asked in a high, strange, fainting voice. "I bet he's fuckin *fulla* bugs! I bet his *brains'* re—"

"Shut up, Teddy," Chris said, and Teddy did, looking relieved.

Lightning forked blue across the sky, making the boy's single eye light up. You could almost believe he was glad to be found, and found by boys his own age. His torso had swelled up and there was a faint gassy odor about him, like the smell of old farts.

I turned away, sure I was going to be sick, but my stomach was dry, hard, steady. I suddenly rammed two fingers down my throat, trying to *make* myself heave, needing to do it, as if I could sick it up and get rid of it. But my stomach only hitched a little and then was steady again.

The roaring downpour and the accompanying thunder had completely covered the sound of cars approaching along the Back Harlow Road, which lay bare yards beyond this boggy tangle. It likewise covered the crackle-crunch of the underbrush as they blundered through it from the dead end where they had parked.

And the first we knew of them was Ace Merrill's voice raised above the tumult of the storm, saying: "Well what the fuck do you know about this?"

26

We all jumped like we had been goosed and Vern cried out—he admitted later that he thought, for just a second, that the voice had come from the dead boy.

On the far side of the boggy patch, where the woods took up again, masking the butt end of the road, Ace Merrill and Eyeball Chambers stood together, half-obscured by a pouring gray curtain of rain. They were both wearing red nylon high school jackets, the kind you can buy in the office if you're a regular student, the same kind they give away free to varsity sports players. Their d.a. haircuts had been plastered back against their skulls and a mixture of rainwater and Vitalis ran down their cheeks like ersatz tears.

"Sumbitch!" Eyeball said. "That's my little brother!"

Chris was staring at Eyeball with his mouth open. His shirt, wet, limp, and dark, was still tied around his skinny middle. His pack, stained a darker green by the rain, was hanging against his naked shoulderblades.

"You get away, Rich," he said in a trembling voice. "We found him. We got dibs."

"Fuck your dibs. We're gonna report 'im."

"No you're not," I said. I was suddenly furious with them, turning up this way at the last minute. If we'd thought about it, we'd have known something like this was going to happen . . . but this was one time, somehow, that the older, bigger kids weren't going to steal it—to take something they wanted as if by divine

right, as if their easy way was the right way, the only way. They had
come in *cars*—I think that was what made me angriest. They had
come in *cars*. "There's four of us, Eyeball. You just try."

"Oh, we'll *try,* don't worry," Eyeball said, and the trees shook
behind him and Ace. Charlie Hogan and Vern's brother Billy
stepped through them, cursing and wiping water out of their eyes. I
felt a lead ball drop into my belly. It grew bigger as Jack Mudgett,
Fuzzy Bracowicz and Vince Desjardins stepped out behind Charlie
and Billy.

"Here we all are," Ace said, grinning. "So you just—"

"*VERN!!*" Billy Tessio cried in a terrible, accusing, my-
judgment-cometh-and-that-right-early voice. He made a pair of
dripping fists. "You little sonofawhore! You was under the porch!
Cock-*knocker*!"

Vern flinched.

Charlie Hogan waxed positively lyrical: "You little keyhole-
peeping cunt-licking *bungwipe*! I ought to beat the living shit out of
you!"

"Yeah? Well, try it!" Teddy brayed suddenly. His eyes were
crazily alight behind his rainspotted glasses. "Come on, fightcha for
'im! Come on! Come on, big men!"

Billy and Charlie didn't need a second invitation. They started
forward together and Vern flinched again—no doubt visualizing the
ghosts of Beatings Past and Beatings Yet to Come. He flinched . . .
but hung tough. He was with his friends, and we had been through
a lot, and we hadn't got here in a couple of *cars*.

But Ace held Billy and Charlie back, simply by touching each of
them on the shoulder.

"Now listen, you guys," Ace said. He spoke patiently, just as if
we weren't all standing in a roaring rainstorm. "There's more of us
than there are of you. We're bigger. We'll give you one chance to
just blow away. I don't give a fuck where. Just make like a tree and
leave."

Chris's brother giggled and Fuzzy clapped Ace on the back in
appreciation of his great wit. The Sid Caesar of the j.d. set.

"Cause *we're* takin him." Ace smiled gently, and you could
imagine him smiling that same gentle smile just before breaking his

cue over the head of some uneducated punk who had made the terrible mistake of lipping off while Ace was lining up a shot. "If you go, we'll take him. If you stay, we'll beat the piss outta you and still take him. Besides," he added, trying to gild the thuggery with a little righteousness, "Charlie and Billy found him, so it's their dibs anyway."

"They was chicken!" Teddy shot back. "Vern told us about it! They was fuckin chicken right outta their fuckin minds!" He screwed his face up into a terrified, snivelling parody of Charlie Hogan. " 'I wish we never boosted that car! I wish we never went out on no Back Harlow Road to whack off a piece! Oh, Billee, what are we gonna do? Oh Billee, I think I just turned my Fruit of the Looms into a fudge factory! Oh Billee—"

"That's it," Charlie said, starting forward again. His face was knotted with rage and sullen embarrassment, "Kid, whatever your name is, get ready to reach down your fuckin throat the next time you need to pick your nose."

I looked wildly down at Ray Brower. He stared calmly up into the rain with his one eye, below us but above it all. The thunder was still booming steadily, but the rain had begun to slack off.

"What do you say, Gordie?" Ace asked. He was holding Charlie lightly by the arm, the way an accomplished trainer would restrain a vicious dog. "You must have at least some of your brother's sense. Tell these guys to back off. I'll let Charlie beat up the foureyes el punko a little bit and then we all go about our business. What do you say?"

He was wrong to mention Denny. I had wanted to reason with him, to point out what Ace knew perfectly well, that we had every right to take Billy and Charlie's dibs since Vern had heard them giving said dibs away. I wanted to tell him how Vern and I had almost gotten run down by a freight train on the trestle which spans the Castle River. About Milo Pressman and his fearless—if stupid—sidekick, Chopper the Wonder-Dog. About the blood-suckers, too. I guess all I really wanted to tell him was Come on, Ace, fair is fair. You know that. But he had to bring Denny into it, and what I heard coming out of my mouth instead of sweet reason was my own death-warrant: "Suck my fat one, you cheap dime-store hood."

Ace's mouth formed a perfect O of surprise—the expression was so unexpectedly prissy that under other circumstances it would have been a laff riot, so to speak. All of the others—on both sides of the bog—stared at me, dumbfounded.

Then Teddy screamed gleefully: "That's telling 'im, Gordie! Oh boy! Too cool!"

I stood numbly, unable to believe it. It was like some crazed understudy had shot onstage at the critical moment and declaimed lines that weren't even in the play. Telling a guy to suck was as bad as you could get without resorting to his mother. Out of the corner of my eye I saw that Chris had unshouldered his knapsack and was digging into it frantically, but I didn't get it—not then, anyway.

"Okay," Ace said softly. "Let's take em. Don't hurt nobody but the Lachance kid. I'm gonna break both his fuckin arms."

I went dead cold. I didn't piss myself the way I had on the railroad trestle, but it must have been because I had nothing inside to let out. He meant it, you see; the years between then and now have changed my mind about a lot of things, but not about that. When Ace said he was going to break both of my arms, he absolutely meant it.

They started to walk toward us through the slackening rain. Jackie Mudgett took a switchknife out of his pocket and hit the chrome. Six inches of steel flicked out, dove-gray in the afternoon half-light. Vern and Teddy dropped suddenly into fighting crouches on either side of me. Teddy did so eagerly, Vern with a desperate, cornered grimace on his face.

The big kids advanced in a line, their feet splashing through the bog, which was now one big sludgy puddle because of the storm. The body of Ray Brower lay at our feet like a waterlogged barrel. I got ready to fight . . . and that was when Chris fired the pistol he had hawked out of his old man's dresser.

KA-BLAM!

God, what a wonderful sound that was! Charlie Hogan jumped

right up into the air. Ace Merrill, who had been staring straight at me, now jerked around and looked at Chris. His mouth made that O again. Eyeball looked absolutely astounded.

"Hey, Chris, that's Daddy's," he said. "You're gonna get the tar whaled out of you—"

"That's nothing to what you'll get," Chris said. His face was horribly pale, and all the life in him seemed to have been sucked upward, into his eyes. They blazed out of his face.

"Gordie was right, you're nothing but a bunch of cheap hoods. Charlie and Billy didn't want their fuckin dibs and you all know it. We wouldn't have walked way to fuck out here if they said they did. They just went someplace and puked the story up and let Ace Merrill do their thinkin for them." His voice rose to a scream. "*But you ain't gonna get him, do you hear me?*"

"Now listen," Ace said. "You better put that down before you take your foot off with it. You ain't got the sack to shoot a woodchuck." He began to walk forward again, smiling his gentle smile as he came. "You're just a sawed-off pint-sized pissy-assed little runt and I'm gonna make you *eat* that fuckin gun."

"Ace, if you don't stand still I'm going to shoot you. I swear to God."

"You'll go to *jayyy-ail*," Ace crooned, not even hesitating. He was still smiling. The others watched him with horrified fascination . . . much the same way as Teddy and Vern and I were looking at Chris. Ace Merrill was the hardest case for miles around and I didn't think Chris could bluff him down. And what did that leave? Ace didn't think a twelve-year-old punk would actually shoot him. I thought he was wrong; I thought Chris would shoot Ace before he let Ace take his father's pistol away from him. In those few seconds I was sure there was going to be bad trouble, the worst I'd ever known. Killing trouble, maybe. And all of it over who got dibs on a dead body.

Chris said softly, with great regret: "Where do you want it, Ace? Arm or leg? I can't pick. You pick for me."

And Ace stopped.

27

His face sagged, and I saw sudden terror on it. It was Chris's tone rather than his actual words, I think; the real regret that things were going to go from bad to worse. If it was a bluff, it's still the best I've ever seen. The other big kids were totally convinced; their faces were squinched up as if someone had just touched a match to a cherry-bomb with a short fuse.

Ace slowly got control of himself. The muscles in his face tightened again, his lips pressed together, and he looked at Chris the way you'd look at a man who has made a serious business proposition—to merge with your company, or handle your line of credit, or shoot your balls off. It was a waiting, almost curious expression, one that made you know that the terror was either gone or tightly lidded. Ace had re-computed the odds on not getting shot and had decided that they weren't as much in his favor as he had thought. But he was still dangerous—maybe more than before. Since then I've thought it was the rawest piece of brinkmanship I've ever seen. Neither of them was bluffing, they both meant business.

"All right," Ace said softly, speaking to Chris. "But I know how you're going to come out of this, motherfuck."

"No you don't," Chris said.

"You little prick!" Eyeball said loudly. "You're gonna wind up in traction for this!"

"Bite my bag," Chris told him.

With an inarticulate sound of rage Eyeball started forward and Chris put a bullet into the water about ten feet in front of him. It kicked up a splash. Eyeball jumped back, cursing.

"Okay, now what?" Ace asked.

"Now you guys get into your cars and bomb on back to Castle Rock. After that I don't care. But you ain't getting him." He touched Ray Brower lightly, almost reverently, with the toe of one sopping sneaker. "You dig me?"

"But we'll get *you*," Ace said. He was starting to smile again. "Don't you know that?"

"You might. You might not."

"We'll get you hard," Ace said, smiling. "We'll hurt you. I can't believe you don't *know* that. We'll put you all in the fuckin hospital with fuckin ruptures. Sincerely."

"Oh, why don't you go home and fuck your mother some more? I hear she loves the way you do it."

Ace's smile froze. "I'll kill you for that. Nobody ranks my mother."

"I heard your mother fucks for bucks," Chris informed him, and as Ace began to pale, as his complexion began to approach Chris's own ghastly whiteness, he added: "In fact, I heard she throws blowjobs for jukebox nickles. I heard—"

Then the storm came back, viciously, all at once. Only this time it was hail instead of rain. Instead of whispering or talking, the woods now seemed alive with hokey B-movie jungle drums—it was the sound of big icy hailstones bonking off treetrunks. Stinging pebbles began to hit my shoulders—it felt as if some sentient, malevolent force were throwing them. Worse than that, they began to strike Ray Brower's upturned face with an awful splatting sound that reminded us of him again, of his terrible and unending patience.

Vern caved in first, with a wailing scream. He fled up the embankment in huge, gangling strides. Teddy held out a minute longer, then ran after Vern, his hands held up over his head. On their side, Vince Desjardins floundered back under some nearby trees and Fuzzy Bracowicz joined him. But the others stood pat, and Ace began to grin again.

"Stick with me, Gordie," Chris said in a low, shaky voice. "Stick with me, man."

"I'm right here."

"Go on, now," Chris said to Ace, and he was able, by some magic, to get the shakiness out of his voice. He sounded as if he were instructing a stupid infant.

"We'll get you," Ace said. "We're not going to forget it, if that's what you're thinking. This is big time, baby."

"That's fine. You just go on and do your getting another day."

"We'll fuckin ambush you, Chambers. We'll—"

"*Get out!*" Chris screamed, and levelled the gun. Ace stepped back.

He looked at Chris a moment longer, nodded, then turned around. "Come on," he said to the others. He looked back over his shoulder at Chris and me once more. "Be seeing you."

They went back into the screen of trees between the bog and the road. Chris and I stood perfectly still in spite of the hail that was welting us, reddening our skins, and piling up all around us like summer snow. We stood and listened and above the crazy calypso sound of the hail hitting the treetrunks we heard two cars start up.

"Stay right here," Chris told me, and he started across the bog.

"Chris!" I said, panicky.

"I got to. Stay here."

It seemed he was gone a very long time. I became convinced that either Ace or Eyeball had lurked behind and grabbed him. I stood my ground with nobody but Ray Brower for company and waited for somebody—anybody—to come back. After a while, Chris did.

"We did it," he said. "They're gone."

"You sure?"

"Yeah. Both cars." He held his hands up over his head, locked together with the gun between them, and shook the double fist in a wry championship gesture. Then he dropped them and smiled at me. I think it was the saddest scaredest smile I ever saw. " 'Suck my fat one'—whoever told you you had a fat one, Lachance?"

"Biggest one in four counties," I said. I was shaking all over.

We looked at each other warmly for a second, and then, maybe embarrassed by what we were seeing, looked down together. A nasty thrill of fear shot through me, and the sudden *splash/splash* as Chris shifted his feet let me know that he had seen, too. Ray Brower's eyes had gone wide and white, starey and pupilless, like the eyes that look out at you from Grecian statuary. It only took a second to understand what had happened, but understanding didn't lessen the horror. His eyes had filled up with round white hailstones. Now they were melting and the water ran down his cheeks as if he were weeping for his own grotesque position—a tatty prize to be fought over by two bunches of stupid hick kids. His clothes were also white with hail. He seemed to be lying in his own shroud.

"Oh, Gordie, hey," Chris said shakily. "Say-hey, man. What a creepshow for him."

"I don't think he knows—"

"Maybe that *was* his ghost we heard. Maybe he knew this was gonna happen. What a fuckin creepshow, I'm sincere."

Branches crackled behind us. I whirled, sure they had flanked us, but Chris went back to contemplating the body after one short, almost casual glance. It was Vern and Teddy, their jeans soaked black and plastered to their legs, both of them grinning like dogs that have been sucking eggs.

"What are we gonna do, man?" Chris asked, and I felt a weird chill steal through me. Maybe he was talking to me, maybe he was . . . but he was still looking down at the body.

"We're gonna take him back, ain't we?" Teddy asked, puzzled. "We're gonna be heroes. Ain't that right?" He looked from Chris to me and back to Chris again.

Chris looked up as if startled out of a dream. His lip curled. He took big steps toward Teddy, planted both hands on Teddy's chest, and pushed him roughly backwards. Teddy stumbled, pinwheeled his arms for balance, then sat down with a soggy splash. He blinked up at Chris like a surprised muskrat. Vern was looking warily at Chris, as if he feared madness. Perhaps that wasn't far from the mark.

"You keep your trap shut," Chris said to Teddy. "Paratroops over the side my ass. You lousy rubber chicken."

"It was the *hail*!" Teddy cried out, angry and ashamed. "It wasn't those guys, Chris! I'm ascared of *storms*! I can't help it! I would have taken all of em on at once, I swear on my mother's name! But I'm ascared of *storms*! Shit! I can't help it!" He began to cry again, sitting there in the water.

"What about you?" Chris asked, turning to Vern. "Are you ascared of storms, too?"

Vern shook his head vacuously, still astounded by Chris's rage. "Hey, man, I thought we was all runnin."

"You must be a mind-reader then, because you ran first."

Vern swallowed twice and said nothing.

Chris stared at him, his eyes sullen and wild. Then he turned to me. "Going to build him a litter, Gordie."

"If you say so, Chris."

"Sure! Like in Scouts." His voice had begun to climb into

strange, reedy levels. "Just like in the fuckin Scouts. A litter—poles and shirts. Like in the handbook. Right, Gordie?"

"Yeah. If you want. But what if those guys—"

"Fuck those guys!" he screamed. *"You're all a bunch of chickens! Fuck off, creeps!"*

"Chris, they could call the Constable. To get back at us."

"He's ours and we're gonna take him OUT!"

"Those guys would say anything to get us in dutch," I told him. My words sounded thin, stupid, sick with the flu. "Say anything and then lie each other up. You know how people can get other people in trouble telling lies, man. Like with the milk-mo—"

"I DON'T CARE!" he screamed, and lunged at me with his fists up. But one of his feet struck Ray Brower's ribcage with a soggy thump, making the body rock. He tripped and fell full-length and I waited for him to get up and maybe punch me in the mouth but instead he lay where he had fallen, head pointing toward the embankment, arms stretched out over his head like a diver about to execute, in the exact posture Ray Brower had been in when we found him. I looked wildly at Chris's feet to make sure his sneakers were still on. Then he began to cry and scream, his body bucking in the muddy water, splashing it around, fists drumming up and down in it, head twisting from side to side. Teddy and Vern were staring at him, agog, because nobody had ever seen Chris Chambers cry. After a moment or two I walked back to the embankment, climbed it, and sat down on one of the rails. Teddy and Vern followed me. And we sat there in the rain, not talking, looking like those three Monkeys of Virtue they sell in dime-stores and those sleazy gift-shops that always look like they are tottering on the edge of bankruptcy.

28

It was twenty minutes before Chris climbed the embankment to sit down beside us. The clouds had begun to break. Spears of sun came down through the rips. The bushes seemed to have gone three shades darker green in the last forty-five minutes. He was mud all the way up one side and down the other. His hair was standing up in muddy spikes. The only clean parts of him were the whitewashed circles around his eyes.

"You're right, Gordie," he said. "Nobody gets last dibs. Goocher all around, huh?"

I nodded. Five minutes passed. No one said anything. And I happened to have a thought—just in case they *did* call Bannerman. I went back down the embankment and over to where Chris had been standing. I got down on my knees and began to comb carefully through the water and marshgrass with my fingers.

"What you doing?" Teddy asked, joining me.

"It's to your left, I think," Chris said, and pointed.

I looked there and after a minute or two I found both shell casings. They winked in the fresh sunlight. I gave them to Chris. He nodded and stuffed them into a pocket of his jeans.

"Now we go," Chris said.

"Hey, come *on!*" Teddy yelled, in real agony. "I wanna *take* 'im!"

"Listen, dummy," Chris said, "if we take him back we could all wind up in the reformatory. It's like Gordie says. Those guys could make up any story they wanted to. What if they said *we* killed him, huh? How would you like that?"

"I don't give a damn," Teddy said sulkily. Then he looked at us with absurd hope. "Besides, we might only get a couple of months or so. As excessories. I mean, we're only twelve fuckin years old, they ain't gonna put us in Shawshank."

Chris said softly: "You can't get in the Army if you got a record, Teddy."

I was pretty sure that was nothing but a bald-faced lie—but somehow this didn't seem the time to say so. Teddy just looked at Chris for a long time, his mouth trembling. Finally he managed to squeak out: "No shit?"

"Ask Gordie."

He looked at me hopefully.

"He's right," I said, feeling like a great big turd. "He's right, Teddy. First thing they do when you volunteer is to check your name through R&I."

"Holy *God!*"

"We're gonna shag ass back to the trestle," Chris said. "Then we'll get off the tracks and come into Castle Rock from the other direction. If people ask where we were, we'll say we went campin up on Brickyard Hill and got lost."

"Milo Pressman knows better," I said. "That creep at the Florida Market does, too."

"Well, we'll say Milo scared us and that's when we decided to go up on the Brickyard."

I nodded. That might work. If Vern and Teddy could remember to stick to it.

"What about if our folks get together?" Vern asked.

"You worry about it if you want," Chris said. "My dad'll still be juiced up."

"Come on, then," Vern said, eyeing the screen of trees between us and the Back Harlow Road. He looked like he expected Bannerman, along with a brace of bloodhounds, to come crashing through at any moment. "Let's get while the gettin's good."

We were all on our feet now, ready to go. The birds were singing like crazy, pleased with the rain and the shine and the worms and just about everything in the world, I guess. We all turned around, as if pulled on strings, and looked back at Ray Brower.

He was lying there, alone again. His arms had flopped out when we turned him over and now he was sort of spreadeagled, as if to welcome the sunshine. For a moment it seemed all right, a more natural deathscene than any ever constructed for a viewing-room audience by a mortician. Then you saw the bruise, the caked blood on the chin and under the nose, and the way the corpse was beginning to bloat. You saw that the bluebottles had come out with the sun and that they were circling the body, buzzing indolently. You remembered that gassy smell, sickish but dry, like farts in a closed room. He was a boy our age, he was dead, and I rejected the idea that anything about it could be natural; I pushed it away with horror.

"Okay," Chris said, and he meant to be brisk but his voice came out of his throat like a handful of dry bristles from an old whiskbroom. "Double-time."

We started to almost-trot back the way we had come. We didn't talk. I don't know about the others, but I was too busy thinking to talk. There were things that bothered me about the body of Ray Brower—they bothered me then and they bother me now.

A bad bruise on the side of his face, a scalp laceration, a bloody nose. No more—at least, no more visible. People walk away from bar-fights in worse condition and go right on drinking. Yet the train *must* have hit him; why else would his sneakers be off his feet that way? And how come the engineer hadn't seen him? Could it be that the train had hit him hard enough to toss him but not to kill him? I thought that, under just the right combination of circumstances, that could have happened. Had the train hit him a hefty, teeth-rattling sideswipe as he tried to get out of the way? Hit him and knocked him in a flying, backwards somersault over that caved-in banking? Had he perhaps lain awake and trembling in the dark for hours, not just lost now but disoriented as well, cut off from the world? Maybe he had died of fear. A bird with crushed tailfeathers once died in my cupped hands in just that way. Its body trembled and vibrated lightly, its beak opened and closed, its dark, bright eyes stared up at me. Then the vibration quit, the beak froze half-open, and the black eyes became lackluster and uncaring. It could have been that way with Ray Brower. He could have died because he was simply too frightened to go on living.

But there was another thing, and that bothered me most of all, I think. He had started off to go berrying. I seemed to remember the news reports saying he'd been carrying a pot to put his berries in. When we got back I went to the library and looked it up in the newspapers just to be sure, and I was right. He'd been berrying, and he'd had a pail, or a pot—something like that. But we hadn't found it. We found him, and we found his sneakers. He must have thrown it away somewhere between Chamberlain and the boggy patch of ground in Harlow where he died. He perhaps clutched it even tighter at first, as though it linked him to home and safety. But as his fear grew, and with it that sense of being utterly alone, with no chance of rescue except for whatever he could do by himself, as the real cold terror set in, he maybe threw it away into the woods on one side of the tracks or the other, hardly even noticing it was gone.

I've thought of going back and looking for it—how does that

strike you for morbid? I've thought of driving to the end of the Back Harlow Road in my almost new Ford van and getting out of it some bright summer morning, all by myself, my wife and children far off in another world where, if you turn a switch, lights come on in the dark. I've thought about how it would be. Pulling my pack out of the back and resting it on the customized van's rear bumper while I carefully remove my shirt and tie it around my waist. Rubbing my chest and shoulders with Muskol insect repellent and then crashing through the woods to where that boggy place was, the place where we found him. Would the grass grow up yellow there, in the shape of his body? Of course not, there would be no sign, but still you wonder, and you realize what a thin film there is between your rational man costume—the writer with leather elbow-patches on his corduroy jacket—and the capering, Gorgon myths of child-hood. Then climbing the embankment, now overgrown with weeds, and walking slowly beside the rusted tracks and rotted ties toward Chamberlain.

Stupid fantasy. An expedition looking for a twenty-year-old blueberry bucket, which was probably cast deep into the woods or plowed under by a bulldozer readying a half-acre plot for a tract house or so deeply overgrown by weeds and brambles it had become invisible. But I feel sure it is still there, somewhere along the old discontinued GS&WM line, and at times the urge to go and look is almost a frenzy. It usually comes early in the morning, when my wife is showering and the kids are watching *Batman* and *Scooby-Doo* on channel 38 out of Boston, and I am feeling the most like the pre-adolescent Gordon Lachance that once strode the earth, walking and talking and occasionally crawling on his belly like a reptile. That boy was *me*, I think. And the thought which follows, chilling me like a dash of cold water, is: *Which boy do you mean?*

Sipping a cup of tea, looking at sun slanting through the kitchen windows, hearing the TV from one end of the house and the shower from the other, feeling the pulse behind my eyes that means I got through one beer too many the night before, I feel sure I could find it. I would see clear metal winking through rust, the bright summer sun reflecting it back to my eyes. I would go down the side of the embankment, push aside the grasses that had grown up and twined toughly around its handle, and then I would . . . what? Why, simply pull it out of time. I would turn it over and over in my hands, wondering at the feel of it, marvelling at the knowledge that the last person to touch it had been long years in his grave. Suppose there was a note in it? *Help me, I'm lost.* Of course there wouldn't be—boys don't go out to pick blueberries with paper and pencil—but just suppose. I imagine the awe I'd feel would be as dark as an eclipse. Still, it's mostly just the idea of holding that pail in my two hands, I guess—as much a symbol of my living as his dying, proof that I really do know which boy it was—which boy of the five of us. Holding it. Reading every year in its cake of rust and the fading of its bright shine. Feeling it, trying to understand the suns that shone on it, the rains that fell on it, and the snows that covered it. And to wonder where I was when each thing happened to it in its lonely place, where I was, what I was doing, who I was loving, how I was getting along, where I was. I'd hold it, read it, feel it . . . and look at my own face in whatever reflection might be left. Can you dig it?

29

We got back to Castle Rock a little past five o'clock on Sunday morning, the day before Labor Day. We had walked all night. Nobody complained, although we all had blisters and were all ravenously hungry. My head was throbbing with a killer headache, and my legs felt twisted and burning with fatigue. Twice we had to scramble down the embankment to get out of the way of freights. One of them was going our way, but moving far too fast to hop. It was seeping daylight when we got to the trestle spanning the Castle again. Chris looked at it, looked at the river, looked back at us.

"Fuck it. I'm walkin across. If I get hit by a train I won't have to watch out for fuckin Ace Merrill."

We all walked across it—plodded might be the better verb. No train came. When we got to the dump we climbed the fence (no Milo and no Chopper, not this early, and not on a Sunday morning) and went directly to the pump. Vern primed it and we all took turns sticking our heads under the icy flow, slapping the water over our bodies, drinking until we could hold no more. Then we had to put our shirts on again because the morning seemed chilly. We walked—limped—back into town and stood for a moment on the sidewalk in front of the vacant lot. We looked at our treehouse so we wouldn't have to look at each other.

"Well," Teddy said at last, "seeya in school on Wednesday. I think I'm gonna sleep until then."

"Me too," Vern said. "I'm too pooped to pop."

Chris whistled tunelessly through his teeth and said nothing.

"Hey, man," Teddy said awkwardly. "No hard feelins, okay?"

"No," Chris said, and suddenly his somber, tired face broke into a sweet and sunny grin. "We did it, didn't we? We did the bastard."

"Yeah," Vern said. "You're fuckin-A. Now Billy's gonna do *me*."

"So what?" Chris said. "Richie's gonna tool up on me and Ace is probably gonna tool up on Gordie and somebody else'll tool up on Teddy. But we *did* it."

"That's right," Vern said. But he still sounded unhappy.

Chris looked at me. "We did it, didn't we?" he asked softly. "It was worth it, wasn't it?"

"Sure it was," I said.

"Fuck this," Teddy said in his dry I'm-losing-interest way. "You guys sound like fuckin *Meet the Press*. Gimme some skin, man. I'm gonna toot home and see if Mom's got me on the Ten Most Wanted List."

We all laughed, Teddy gave us his surprised Oh-Lord-what-now look, and we gave him skin. Then he and Vern started off in their direction and I should have gone in mine . . . but I hesitated for a second.

"Walk with you," Chris offered.

"Sure, okay."

We walked a block or so without talking. Castle Rock was awesomely quiet in the day's first light, and I felt an almost holy tiredness-is-slipping-away sort of feeling. We were awake and the whole world was asleep and I almost expected to turn the corner and see my deer standing at the far end of Carbine Street, where the GS&WM tracks pass through the mill's loading yard.

Finally Chris spoke. "They'll tell," he said.

"You bet they will. But not today or tomorrow, if that's what you're worried about. It'll be a long time before they tell, I think. Years, maybe."

He looked at me, surprised.

"They're scared, Chris. Teddy especially, that they won't take him in the Army. But Vern's scared, too. They'll lose some sleep over it, and there's gonna be times this fall when it's right on the tips of their tongues to tell somebody, but I don't think they will. And then . . . you know what? It sounds fucking crazy, but . . . I think they'll almost forget it ever happened."

He was nodding slowly. "I didn't think of it just like that. You see through people, Gordie."

"Man, I wish I did."

"You do, though."

We walked another block in silence.

"I'm never gonna get out of this town," Chris said, and sighed. "When you come back from college on summer vacation, you'll be able to look me and Vern and Teddy up down at Sukey's after the seven-to-three shift's over. If you want to. Except you'll probably never want to." He laughed a creepy laugh.

"Quit jerking yourself off," I said, trying to sound tougher than I felt—I was thinking about being out there in the woods, about Chris saying: *And maybe I took it to old lady Simons and told her, and maybe the money was all there and I got a three-day vacation anyway, because the money never showed up. And maybe the next week old lady Simons had this brand-new skirt on when she came to school . . .* The look. The look in his eyes.

"No jerkoff, daddy-O," Chris said.

I rubbed my first finger against my thumb. "This is the world's smallest violin playing 'My Heart Pumps Purple Piss for You.' "

"He was *ours*," Chris said, his eyes dark in the morning light.

We had reached the corner of my street and we stopped there. It was quarter past six. Back toward town we could see the Sunday *Telegram* truck pulling up in front of Teddy's uncle's stationery shop. A man in bluejeans and a tee-shirt threw off a bundle of papers. They bounced upside down on the sidewalk, showing the color funnies (always Dick Tracy and Blondie on the first page). Then the truck drove on, its driver intent on delivering the outside world to the rest of the whistlestops up the line—Otisfield, Norway–South Paris, Waterford, Stoneham. I wanted to say something more to Chris and didn't know how to.

"Gimme some skin, man," he said, sounding tired.

"Chris—"

"Skin."

I gave him some skin. "I'll see you."

He grinned—that same sweet, sunny grin. "Not if I see you first, fuckface."

He walked off, still laughing, moving easily and gracefully, as though he didn't hurt like me and have blisters like me and like he wasn't lumped and bumped with mosquito and chigger and black fly bites like me. As if he didn't have a care in the world, as if he was going to some real boss place instead of just home to a three-room house (shack would have been closer to the truth) with no indoor plumbing and broken windows covered with plastic and a brother who was probably laying for him in the front yard. Even if I'd known the right thing to say, I probably couldn't have said it. Speech destroys the functions of love, I think—that's a hell of a thing for a writer to say, I guess, but I believe it to be true. If you speak to tell a deer you mean it no harm, it glides away with a single flip of its tail. The word is the harm. Love isn't what these asshole poets like McKuen want you to think it is. Love has teeth; they bite; the wounds never close. No word, no combination of words, can close those lovebites. It's the other way around, that's the joke. If those wounds dry up, the words die with them. Take it from me. I've made my life from the words, and I know that is so.

30

The back door was locked so I fished the spare key out from under the mat and let myself in. The kitchen was empty, silent, suicidally clean. I could hear the hum the fluorescent bars over the sink made when I turned on the switch. It had been literally years since I had been up before my mother; I couldn't even remember the last time such a thing had happened.

I took off my shirt and put it in the plastic clothesbasket behind the washing machine. I got a clean rag from under the sink and sponged off with it—face, neck, pits, belly. Then I unzipped my pants and scrubbed my crotch—my testicles in particular—until my skin began to hurt. It seemed I couldn't get clean enough down there, although the red weal left by the bloodsucker was rapidly fading. I still have a tiny crescent-shaped scar there. My wife once asked about it and I told her a lie before I was even aware I meant to do so.

When I was done with the rag, I threw it away. It was filthy.

I got out a dozen eggs and scrambled six of them together. When they were semi-solid in the pan, I added a side dish of crushed pineapple and half a quart of milk. I was just sitting down to eat when my mother came in, her gray hair tied in a knot behind her head. She was wearing a faded pink bathrobe and smoking a Camel.

"Gordon, where have you been?"

"Camping," I said, and began to eat. "We started off in Vern's field and then went up the Brickyard Hill. Vern's mom said she would call you. Didn't she?"

"She probably talked to your father," she said, and glided past me to the sink. She looked like a pink ghost. The fluorescent bars were less than kind to her face; they made her complexion look almost yellow. She sighed . . . almost sobbed. "I miss Dennis most in the mornings," she said. "I always look in his room and it's always empty, Gordon. Always."

"Yeah, that's a bitch," I said.

"He always slept with his window open and the blankets . . . Gordon? Did you say something?"

"Nothing important, Mom."

". . . and the blankets pulled up to his chin," she finished. Then she just stared out the window, her back to me. I went on eating. I was trembling all over.

31

The story never did get out.

Oh, I don't mean that Ray Brower's body was never found; it was. But neither our gang nor their gang got the credit. In the end,

Ace must have decided that an anonymous phonecall was the safest course, because that's how the location of the corpse was reported. What I meant was that none of our parents ever found out what we'd been up to that Labor Day weekend.

Chris's dad was still drinking, just as Chris had said he would be. His mom had gone off to Lewiston to stay with her sister, the way she almost always did when Mr. Chambers was on a bender. She went and left Eyeball in charge of the younger kids. Eyeball had fulfilled his responsibility by going off with Ace and his j.d. buddies, leaving nine-year-old Sheldon, five-year-old Emery, and two-year-old Deborah to sink or swim on their own.

Teddy's mom got worried the second night and called Vern's mom. Vern's mom, who was also never going to do the game-show circuit, said we were still out in Vern's tent. She knew because she had seen a light on in there the night before. Teddy's mom said she sure hoped no one was smoking cigarettes in there and Vern's mom said it looked like a flashlight to her, and besides, she was sure that none of Vern's or Billy's friends smoked.

My dad asked me some vague questions, looking mildly troubled at my evasive answers, said we'd go fishing together sometime, and that was the end of it. If the parents had gotten together in the week or two afterwards, everything would have fallen down . . . but they never did.

Milo Pressman never spoke up, either. My guess is that he thought twice about it being our word against his, and how we would all swear that he sicced Chopper on me.

So the story never came out—but that wasn't the end of it.

32

One day near the end of the month, while I was walking home from school, a black 1952 Ford cut into the curb in front of me. There was no mistaking that car. Gangster whitewalls and spinner hubcaps, highrise chrome bumpers and Lucite death-knob with a rose embedded in it clamped to the steering wheel. Painted on the back deck was a deuce and a one-eyed jack. Beneath them, in Roman Gothic script, were the words WILD CARD.

The doors flew open; Ace Merrill and Fuzzy Bracowicz stepped out.

"Cheap hood, right?" Ace said, smiling his gentle smile. "My mother loves the way I do it to her, right?"

"We're gonna rack you, baby," Fuzzy said.

I dropped my schoolbooks on the sidewalk and ran. I was busting my buns but they caught me before I even made the end of the block. Ace hit me with a flying tackle and I went full-length on the paving. My chin hit the cement and I didn't just see stars; I saw whole constellations, whole nebulae. I was already crying when they picked me up, not so much from my elbows and knees, both pairs scraped and bleeding, or even from fear—it was vast, impotent rage that made me cry. Chris was right. He had been ours.

I twisted and turned and almost squiggled free. Then Fuzzy hoicked his knee into my crotch. The pain was amazing, incredible, nonpareil; it widened the horizons of pain from plain old wide screen to VistaVision. I began to scream. Screaming seemed to be my best chance.

Ace punched me twice in the face, long and looping haymaker blows. The first one closed my left eye; it would be four days before I was really able to see out of that eye again. The second broke my nose with a crunch that sounded the way crispy cereal sounds inside your head when you chew. Then old Mrs. Chalmers came out on her porch with her cane clutched in one arthritis-twisted hand and a Herbert Tareyton jutting from one corner of her mouth. She began to bellow at them:

"Hi! Hi there, you boys! You stop that! Police! Poleeeece!"

"Don't let me see you around, dipshit," Ace said, smiling, and they let go of me and backed off. I sat up and then leaned over, cupping my wounded balls, sickly sure I was going to throw up and then die. I was still crying, too. But when Fuzzy started to walk around me, the sight of his pegged jeans-leg snugged down over the top of his motorcycle boot brought all the fury back. I grabbed him and bit his calf through his jeans. I bit him just as hard as I could. Fuzzy began to do a little screaming of his own. He also began hopping around on one leg, and, incredibly, he was calling me a dirty-fighter. I was watching him hop around and that was when

Ace stamped down on my left hand, breaking the first two fingers. I heard them break. They didn't sound like crispy cereal. They sounded like pretzels. Then Ace and Fuzzy were going back to Ace's '52, Ace sauntering with his hands in his back pockets, Fuzzy hopping on one leg and throwing curses back over his shoulder at me. I curled up on the sidewalk, crying. Aunt Evvie Chalmers came down her walk, thudding her cane angrily as she came. She asked me if I needed the doctor. I sat up and managed to stop most of the crying. I told her I didn't.

"Bullshit," she bellowed—Aunt Evvie was deaf and bellowed everything. "I saw where that bully got you. Boy, your sweetmeats are going to swell up to the size of Mason jars."

She took me into her house, gave me a wet rag for my nose—it had begun to resemble a summer squash by then—and gave me a big cup of medicinal-tasting coffee that was somehow calming. She kept bellowing at me that she should call the doctor and I kept telling her not to. Finally she gave up and I walked home. Very slowly, I walked home. My balls weren't the size of Mason jars yet, but they were on their way.

My mom and dad got a look at me and wigged right out—I was sort of surprised that they noticed anything at all, to tell the truth. Who were the boys? Could I pick them out of a line-up? That from my father, who never missed *Naked City* and *The Untouchables*. I said I didn't think I could pick the boys out of a line-up. I said I was tired. Actually I think I was in shock—in shock and more than a little drunk from Aunt Evvie's coffee, which must have been at least sixty per cent VSOP brandy. I said I thought they were from some other town, or from "up the city"—a phrase everyone understood to mean Lewiston-Auburn.

They took me to Dr. Clarkson in the station wagon—Dr. Clarkson, who is still alive today, was even then old enough to have quite possibly been on armchair-to-armchair terms with God. He set my nose and my fingers and gave my mother a prescription for painkiller. Then he got them out of the examining room on some pretext or other and came over to me, shuffling, head forward, like Boris Karloff approaching Igor.

"Who did it, Gordon?"

"I don't know, Dr. Cla—"

"You're lying."

"No, sir. Huh-uh."

His sallow cheeks began to flow with color. "Why should you protect the cretins who did this? Do you think they will respect you? They will laugh and call you stupid-fool! 'Oh,' they'll say, 'there goes the stupid-fool we beat up for kicks the other day. Ha-ha! Hoo-hoo! Har-de-har-har-har!' "

"I didn't know them. Really."

I could see his hands itching to shake me, but of course he couldn't do that. So he sent me out to my parents, shaking his white head and muttering about juvenile delinquents. He would no doubt tell his old friend God all about it that night over their cigars and sherry.

I didn't care if Ace and Fuzzy and the rest of those assholes respected me or thought I was stupid or never thought about me at all. But there was Chris to think of. His brother Eyeball had broken his arm in two places and had left his face looking like a Canadian sunrise. They had to set the elbow-break with a steel pin. Mrs. McGinn from down the road saw Chris staggering along the soft shoulder, bleeding from both ears and reading a Richie Rich comic book. She took him to the CMG Emergency Room where Chris told the doctor he had fallen down the cellar stairs in the dark.

"Right," the doctor said, every bit as disgusted with Chris as Dr. Clarkson had been with me, and then he went to call Constable Bannerman.

While he did that from his office, Chris went slowly down the hall, holding the temporary sling against his chest so the arm wouldn't swing and grate the broken bones together, and used a nickle in the pay phone to call Mrs. McGinn—he told me later it was the first collect call he had ever made and he was scared to death that she wouldn't accept the charges—but she did.

"Chris, are you all right?" she asked.

"Yes, thank you," Chris said.

"I'm sorry I couldn't stay with you, Chris, but I had pies in the—"

"That's all right, Missus McGinn," Chris said. "Can you see the

Buick in our dooryard?" The Buick was the car Chris's mother drove. It was ten years old and when the engine got hot it smelled like frying Hush Puppies.

"It's there," she said cautiously. Best not to mix in too much with the Chamberses. Poor white trash; shanty Irish.

"Would you go over and tell Mamma to go downstairs and take the lightbulb out of the socket in the cellar?"

"Chris, I really, my pies—"

"Tell her," Chris said implacably, "to do it right away. Unless she maybe wants my brother to go to jail."

There was a long, long pause and then Mrs. McGinn agreed. She asked no questions and Chris told her no lies. Constable Bannerman did indeed come out to the Chambers house, but Richie Chambers didn't go to jail.

Vern and Teddy took their lumps, too, although not as bad as either Chris or I. Billy was laying for Vern when Vern got home. He took after him with a stovelength and hit him hard enough to knock him unconscious after only four or five good licks. Vern was no more than stunned, but Billy got scared he might have killed him and stopped. Three of them caught Teddy walking home from the vacant lot one afternoon. They punched him out and broke his glasses. He fought them, but they wouldn't fight him when they realized he was groping after them like a blindman in the dark.

We hung out together at school looking like the remains of a Korean assault force. Nobody knew exactly what had happened, but everybody understood that we'd had a pretty serious run-in with the big kids and comported ourselves like men. A few stories went around. All of them were wildly wrong.

When the casts came off and the bruises healed, Vern and Teddy just drifted away. They had discovered a whole new group of contemporaries that they could lord it over. Most of them were real wets—scabby, scrubby little fifth-grade assholes—but Vern and Teddy kept bringing them to the treehouse, ordering them around, strutting like Nazi generals.

Chris and I began to drop by there less and less frequently, and after awhile the place was theirs by default. I remember going up one time in the spring of 1961 and noticing that the place smelled like a shootoff in a haymow. I never went there again that I can recall. Teddy and Vern slowly became just two more faces in the halls or in three-thirty detention. We nodded and said hi. That was all. It happens. Friends come in and out of your life like busboys in a restaurant, did you ever notice that? But when I think of that dream, the corpses under the water pulling implacably at my legs, it seems right that it should be that way. Some people drown, that's all. It's not fair, but it happens. Some people drown.

33

Vern Tessio was killed in a housefire that swept a Lewiston apartment building in 1966—in Brooklyn and the Bronx, they call that sort of apartment building a slum tenement, I believe. The Fire Department said it started around two in the morning, and the entire building was nothing but cinders in the cellarhole by dawn. There had been a large drunken party; Vern was there. Someone fell asleep in one of the bedrooms with a live cigarette going. Vern himself, maybe, drifting off, dreaming of his pennies. They identified him and the four others who died by their teeth.

Teddy went in a squalid car crash. That was 1971, I think, or maybe it was early 1972. There used to be a saying when I was growing up: "If you go out alone you're a hero. Take somebody else with you and you're dogpiss." Teddy, who had wanted nothing but the service since the time he was old enough to want anything, was turned down by the Air Force and classified 4-F by the draft. Anyone who had seen his glasses and his hearing aid knew it was going to happen—anyone but Teddy. In his junior year at high school he got a three-day vacation from school for calling the guidance counsellor a lying sack of shit. The g.o. had observed Teddy coming in every so often—like every day—and checking over his career-board for new service literature. He told Teddy that maybe he should think about another career, and that was when Teddy blew his stack.

He was held back a year for repeated absences, tardies, and the attendant flunked courses . . . but he *did* graduate. He had an ancient Chevrolet Bel Air, and he used to hang around the places where Ace and Fuzzy and the rest had hung around before him: the pool hall, the dance hall, Sukey's Tavern, which is closed now, and The Mellow Tiger, which isn't. He eventually got a job with the Castle Rock Public Works Department, filling up holes with hotpatch.

The crash happened over in Harlow. Teddy's Bel Air was full of his friends (two of them had been part of that group he and Vern took to bossing around way back in 1960), and they were all passing around a couple of joints and a couple of bottles of Popov. They hit a utility pole and sheared it off and the Chevrolet rolled six times. One girl came out technically still alive. She lay for six months in what the nurses and orderlies at Central Maine General call the C&T Ward—Cabbages and Turnips. Then some merciful phantom pulled the plug on her respirator. Teddy Duchamp was posthumously awarded the Dogpiss of the Year Award.

Chris enrolled in the college courses in his second year of junior high—he and I both knew that if he waited any longer it would be too late; he would never catch up. Everyone jawed at him about it: his parents, who thought he was putting on airs, his friends, most of whom dismissed him as a pussy, the guidance counsellor, who didn't believe he could do the work, and most of all the teachers, who didn't approve of this duck-tailed, leather-jacketed, engineer-booted apparition who had materialized without warning in their classrooms. You could see that the sight of those boots and that many-zippered jacket offended them in connection with such high-minded subjects as algebra, Latin, and earth science; such attire was meant for the shop courses only. Chris sat among the well-dressed, vivacious boys and girls from the middle-class families in Castle View and Brickyard Hill like some silent, brooding Grendel that might turn on them at any moment, produce a horrible roaring like the sound of dual glasspack mufflers, and gobble them up, penny loafers, Peter Pan collars, button-down paisley shirts, and all.

He almost quit a dozen times that year. His father in particular hounded him, accusing Chris of thinking he was better than his old man, accusing Chris of wanting "to go up there to the college so you can turn me into a bankrupt." He once broke a Rhinegold bottle over the back of Chris's head and Chris wound up in the CMG Emergency Room again, where it took four stitches to close his scalp. His old friends, most of whom were now majoring in Smoking Area, catcalled him on the streets. The guidance counsellor huckstered him to take at least *some* shop courses so he wouldn't flunk the whole slate. Worst of all, of course, was just this: he'd been fucking off for the entire first seven years of his public education, and now the bill had come due with a vengeance.

We studied together almost every night, sometimes for as long as six hours at a stretch. I always came away from those sessions exhausted, and sometimes I came away frightened as well—frightened by his incredulous rage at just how murderously high that bill was. Before he could even begin to understand introductory algebra, he had to re-learn the fractions that he and Teddy and Vern had played pocket-pool through in the fifth grade. Before he could even begin to understand *Pater noster qui est in caelis,* he had to be told what nouns and prepositions and objects were. On the inside of his English grammar, neatly lettered, were the words FUCK GERUNDS. His compositional ideas were good and not badly organized, but his grammar was bad and he approached the whole business of punctuation as if with a shotgun. He wore out his copy of Warriner's and bought another in a Portland bookstore—it was the first hardcover book he actually owned, and it became a queer sort of Bible to him.

But by our junior year in high school, he had been accepted. Neither of us made top honors, but I came out seventh and Chris stood nineteenth. We were both accepted at the University of Maine, but I went to the Orono campus while Chris enrolled at the Portland campus. Pre-law, can you believe that? More Latin.

We both dated through high school, but no girl ever came between us. Does that sound like we went faggot? It would have to most of our old friends, Vern and Teddy included. But it was only survival. We were clinging to each other in deep water. I've explained about Chris, I think; my reasons for clinging to him were less definable. His desire to get away from Castle Rock and out of the mill's shadow seemed to me to be my best part, and I could not just leave him to sink or swim on his own. If he had drowned, that part of me would have drowned with him, I think.

Near the end of 1971, Chris went into a Chicken Delight in Portland to get a three-piece Snack Bucket. Just ahead of him, two men started arguing about which one had been first in line. One of them pulled a knife. Chris, who had always been the best of us at making peace, stepped between them and was stabbed in the throat. The man with the knife had spent time in four different institutions; he had been released from Shawshank State Prison only the week before. Chris died almost instantly.

I read about it in the paper—Chris had been finishing his second year of graduate studies. Me, I had been married a year and a half and was teaching high school English. My wife was pregnant and I was trying to write a book. When I read the news item—STUDENT FATALLY STABBED IN PORTLAND RESTAURANT—I told my wife I was going out for a milkshake. I drove out of town, parked, and cried for him. Cried for damn near half an hour, I guess. I couldn't have done that in front of my wife, much as I love her. It would have been pussy.

34

Me?

I'm a writer now, like I said. A lot of critics think what I write is shit. A lot of the time I think they are right . . . but it still freaks me out to put those words, "Freelance Writer," down in the *Occupation* blank of the forms you have to fill out at credit desks and in doctors' offices. My story sounds so much like a fairytale that it's fucking absurd.

I sold the book and it was made into a movie and the movie got good reviews and it was a smash hit besides. This all had happened by the time I was twenty-six. The second book was made into a movie as well, as was the third. I told you—it's fucking absurd. Meantime, my wife doesn't seem to mind having me around the house and we have three kids now. They all seem perfect to me, and most of the time I'm happy.

But like I said, the writing isn't so easy or as much fun as it used to be. The phone rings a lot. Sometimes I get headaches, bad ones, and then I have to go into a dim room and lie down until they go away. The doctors says they aren't true migraines; he called them "stressaches" and told me to slow down. I worry about myself sometimes. What a stupid habit that is . . . and yet I can't quite seem to stop it. And I wonder if there is really any point to what I'm doing, or what I'm supposed to make of a world where a man can get rich playing "let's pretend."

But it's funny how I saw Ace Merrill again. My friends are dead but Ace is alive. I saw him pulling out of the mill parking lot just after the three o'clock whistle the last time I took my kids down home to see my dad.

The '52 Ford had become a '77 Ford station wagon. A faded bumper-sticker said REAGAN/BUSH 1980. His hair was mowed into a crewcut and he'd gotten fat. The sharp, handsome features I remembered were buried in an avalanche of flesh. I had left the kids with Dad long enough to go downtown and get the paper. I was standing on the corner of Main and Carbine and he glanced at me as I waited to cross. There was no sign of recognition on the face of this thirty-two-year-old man who had broken my nose in another dimension of time.

I watched him wheel the Ford wagon into the dirt parking lot beside The Mellow Tiger, get out, hitch at his pants, and walk inside. I could imagine the brief wedge of country-western as he opened the door, the brief sour whiff of Knick and Gansett on draft, the welcoming shouts of the other regulars as he closed the door and placed his large ass on the same stool which had probably held him up for at least three hours every day of his life—except Sundays—since he was twenty-one.

I thought: So *that's what Ace is now.*

I looked to the left, and beyond the mill I could see the Castle River not so wide now but a little cleaner, still flowing under the bridge between Castle Rock and Harlow. The trestle upstream is gone, but the river is still around. So am I.

A Winter's Tale

For Peter and Susan Straub

The Breathing Method

I.
The Club

I dressed a bit more speedily than normal on that snowy, windy, bitter night—I admit. It was December 23rd, 197-, and I suspect that there were other members of the club who did the same. Taxis are notoriously hard to come by in New York on stormy nights, so I called for a radio-cab. I did this at five-thirty for an eight o'clock pickup—my wife raised an eyebrow but said nothing. I was under the canopy of the apartment building on East Fifty-eighth Street, where Ellen and I had lived since 1946, by quarter to eight, and when the taxi was five minutes late, I found myself pacing up and down impatiently.

The taxi arrived at eight-ten and I got in, too glad to be out of the wind to be as angry with the driver as he probably deserved. That wind, part of a cold front that had swept down from Canada the day before, meant business. It whistled and whined around the cab's window, occasionally drowning out the salsa on the driver's radio and rocking the big Checker on its springs. Many of the stores were open but the sidewalks were nearly bare of last-minute shoppers. Those that were abroad looked uncomfortable or actually pained.

It had been flurrying off and on all day, and now the snow began again, coming first in thin membranes, then twisting into cyclone shapes ahead of us in the street. Coming home that night, I would think of the combination of snow, a taxi, and New York City with considerably greater unease . . . but I did not of course know that then.

455

At the corner of Second and Fortieth, a large tinsel Christmas bell went floating through the intersection like a spirit.

"Bad night," the cabbie said. "They'll have an extra two dozen in the morgue tomorrow. Wino Popsicles. Plus a few bag-lady Popsicles."

"I suppose."

The cabbie ruminated. "Well, good riddance," he said finally. "Less welfare, right?"

"Your Christmas spirit," I said, "is stunning in its width and depth."

The cabbie ruminated. "You one of those bleeding-heart liberals?" he asked finally.

"I refuse to answer on the grounds that my answer might tend to incriminate me," I said. The cabbie gave a why-do-I-always-get-the-wisenheimers snort . . . but he shut up.

He let me out at Second and Thirty-fifth, and I walked halfway down the block to the club, bent over against the whistling wind, holding my hat on my head with one gloved hand. In almost no time at all the life-force seemed to have been driven deep into my body, a flickering blue flame about the size of the pilot-light in a gas oven. At seventy-three a man feels the cold quicker and deeper. That man should be home in front of a fireplace . . . or at least in front of an electric heater. At seventy-three hot blood isn't even really a memory; it's more of an academic report.

The latest flurry was letting up, but snow as dry as sand still beat into my face. I was glad to see that the steps leading up to the door of 249B had been sanded—that was Stevens's work, of course—Stevens knew the base alchemy of old age well enough: not lead into gold but bones into glass. When I think about such things, I believe that God probably thinks a great deal like Groucho Marx.

Then Stevens was there, holding the door open, and a moment later I was inside. Down the mahogany-panelled hallway, through double doors standing three-quarters of the way open on their recessed tracks, into the library *cum* reading-room *cum* bar. It was a dark room in which occasional pools of light gleamed—reading-lamps. A richer, more textured light glowed across the oak parquet floor, and I could hear the steady snap of birch logs in the huge fireplace. The heat radiated all the way across the room—surely there is no welcome for a man or a woman that can equal a fire on the hearth. A paper rustled—dry, slightly impatient. That would be Johanssen, with his *Wall Street Journal*. After ten years, it was possible to recognize his presence simply by the way he read his stocks. Amusing . . . and in a quiet way, amazing.

Stevens helped me off with my overcoat, murmuring that it was a dirty night; WCBS was now forecasting heavy snow before morning.

I agreed that it was indeed a dirty night and looked back into that big, high-ceilinged room again. A dirty night, a roaring fire . . . and a ghost story. Did I say that at seventy-three hot blood is a thing of the past? Perhaps so. But I felt something warm in my chest at the thought . . . something that hadn't been caused by the fire or Stevens's reliable, dignified welcome.

I think it was because it was McCarron's turn to tell the tale.

I had been coming to the brownstone which stands at 249B East Thirty-fifth Street for ten years—coming at intervals that were almost—but not quite—regular. In my own mind I think of it as a "gentlemen's club," that amusing pre–Gloria Steinem antiquity. But even now I am not sure that's what it really is, or how it came to be in the first place.

On the night Emlyn McCarron told his story—the story of the Breathing Method—there were perhaps thirteen clubmembers in all, although only six of us had come out on that howling, bitter night. I can remember years when there might have been as few as eight full-time members, and others when there were at least twenty, and perhaps more.

I suppose Stevens might know how it all came to be—one thing I *am* sure of is that Stevens has been there from the first, no matter how long that may be . . . and I believe Stevens to be older than he looks. Much, *much* older. He has a faint Brooklyn accent, but in spite of that he is as brutally correct and as cuttingly punctilious as a third-generation English butler. His reserve is part of his often maddening charm, and Stevens's small smile is a locked and latched door. I have never seen any club records—if he keeps them. I have never gotten a receipt of dues—there are no dues. I have never been called by the club secretary—there is no secretary, and at 249B East

Thirty-fifth, there are no phones. There is no box of white marbles and black balls. And the club—if it *is* a club—has never had a name.

I first came to the club (as I must continue to call it) as the guest of George Waterhouse. Waterhouse headed the law firm for which I had worked since 1951. My progress upward in the firm—one of New York's three biggest—had been steady but extremely slow; I was a slogger, a mule for work, something of a centerpuncher . . . but I had no real flair or genius. I had seen men who had begun at the same time I had promoted in giant steps while I only continued to pace—and I saw it with no real surprise.

Waterhouse and I had exchanged pleasantries, attended the obligatory dinner put on by the firm each October, and had little more congress until the fall of 196-, when he dropped by my office one day in early November.

This in itself was unusual enough, and it had me thinking black thoughts (dismissal) that were counterbalanced by giddy ones (an unexpected promotion). It was a puzzling visit. Waterhouse leaned in the doorway, his Phi Beta Kappa key gleaming mellowly on his vest, and talked in amiable generalities—none of what he said seemed to have any real substance or importance. I kept expecting him to finish the pleasantries and get down to cases: "Now about this Casey brief" or "We've been asked to research the Mayor's appointment of Salkowitz to—" But it seemed there *were* no cases. He glanced at his watch, said he had enjoyed our talk and that he had to be going.

I was still blinking, bewildered, when he turned back and said casually: "There's a place where I go most Thursday nights—a sort of club. Old duffers, mostly, but some of them are good company. They keep a really excellent cellar, if you've a palate. Every now and then someone tells a good story as well. Why not come down some night, David? As my guest."

I stammered some reply—even now I'm not sure what it was. I was bewildered by the offer. It had a spur-of-the-moment sound, but there was nothing spur-of-the-moment about his eyes, blue Anglo-Saxon ice under the bushy white whorls of his eyebrows. And if I don't remember exactly how I replied, it was because I felt suddenly sure that this offer—vague and puzzling as it was—had been exactly the specific I had kept expecting him to get down to.

Ellen's reaction that evening was one of amused exasperation. I had been with Waterhouse, Carden, Lawton, Frasier, and Effingham for something like fifteen years, and it was clear enough that I could not expect to rise much above the mid-level position I now held; it was her idea that this was the firm's cost-efficient substitute for a gold watch.

"Old men telling war stories and playing poker," she said. "A night of that and you're supposed to be happy in the Reading Library until they pension you off, I suppose . . . oh, I put two Beck's on ice for you." And she kissed me warmly. I suppose she had seen something on my face—God knows she's good at reading me after all the years we've spent together.

Nothing happened over a course of weeks. When my mind turned to Waterhouse's odd offer—certainly odd coming from a man with whom I met less than a dozen times a year, and whom I only saw socially at perhaps three parties a year, including the company party in October—I supposed that I had been mistaken about the expression in his eyes, that he really had made the offer casually, and had forgotten it. Or regretted it—ouch! And then he approached me one late afternoon, a man of nearly seventy who was still broad-shouldered and athletic-looking. I was shrugging on my topcoat with my briefcase between my feet. He said: "If you'd still like to have a drink at the club, why not come tonight?"

"Well . . . I . . ."

"Good." He slapped a slip of paper into my hand. "Here's the address."

He was waiting for me at the foot of the steps that evening, and Stevens held the door for us. The wine was as excellent as Waterhouse had promised. He made no attempt whatsoever to "introduce me around"—I took that for snobbery but later recanted the idea—but two or three of them introduced themselves to me. One of those who did so was Emlyn McCarron, even then in his late sixties. He held out his hand and I clasped it briefly. His skin was dry, leathery, tough; almost turtlelike. He asked me if I played bridge. I said I did not.

"Goddamned good thing," he said. "That goddamned game has

done more in this century to kill intelligent after-dinner conversation than anything else I can think of." And with that pronouncement he walked away into the murk of the library, where shelves of books went up apparently to infinity.

I looked around for Waterhouse, but he had disappeared. Feeling a little uncomfortable and a lot out of place, I wandered over to the fireplace. It was, as I believe I have already mentioned, a huge thing—it seemed particularly huge in New York, where apartment-dwellers such as myself have trouble imagining such a benevolence big enough to do anything more than pop corn or toast bread. The fireplace at 249B East Thirty-fifth was big enough to broil an ox whole. There was no mantel; instead a brawny stone arch curved over it. This arch was broken in the center by a keystone which jutted out slightly. It was just on the level of my eyes, and although the light was dim, I could read the legend engraved on that stone with no trouble: *IT IS THE TALE, NOT HE WHO TELLS IT.*

"Here you go, David," Waterhouse said from my elbow, and I jumped. He hadn't deserted me after all; had only trudged off into some uncharted locale to bring back drinks. "Scotch and soda's yours, isn't it?"

"Yes. Thank you. Mr. Waterhouse—"

"George," he said. "Here it's just George."

"George, then," I said, although it seemed slightly mad to be using his first name. "What is all of—"

"Cheers," he said.

We drank.

"Stevens tends the bar. He makes fine drinks. He likes to say it's a small but vital skill."

The scotch took the edge off my feelings of disorientation and awkwardness (the edge, but the feelings themselves remained—I had spent nearly half an hour gazing into my closet and wondering what to wear; I had finally settled on dark brown slacks and a rough tweed jacket that almost matched them, hoping I would not be wandering into a group of men either turned out in tuxedos or wearing bluejeans and L. L. Bean's lumberjack shirts . . . it seemed that I hadn't gone too far wrong on the matter of dress, anyway). A new place and a new situation make one crucially aware of every social act, no matter how small, and at that moment, drink in hand and the obligatory small toast made, I wanted very much to be sure that I hadn't overlooked any of the amenities.

"Is there a guest book I ought to sign?" I asked. "Something like that?"

He looked mildly surprised. "We don't have anything like that," he said. "At least, I don't *think* we do." He glanced around the dim, quiet room. Johanssen rattled his *Wall Street Journal*. I saw Stevens pass in a doorway at the far end of the room, ghostly in his white messjacket. George put his drink on an endtable and tossed a fresh log onto the fire. Sparks corkscrewed up the black throat of the chimney.

"What does that mean?" I asked, pointing to the inscription on the keystone. "Any idea?"

Waterhouse read it carefully, as if for the first time. IT IS THE TALE, NOT HE WHO TELLS IT.

"I suppose I have an idea," he said. "You may, too, if you should come back. Yes, I should say you may have an idea or two. In time. Enjoy yourself, David."

He walked away. And, although it may seem odd, having been left to sink or swim in such an unfamiliar situation, I *did* enjoy myself. For one thing, I have always loved books, and there was a trove of interesting ones to examine here. I walked slowly along the shelves, examining the spines as best I could in the faint light, pulling one out now and then, and pausing once to look out a narrow window at the Second Avenue intersection up the street. I stood there and watched through the frost-rimed glass as the traffic light at the intersection cycled from red to green to amber and back to red again, and quite suddenly I felt the queerest—and yet very welcome—sense of peace come to me. It did not flood in; instead it seemed to almost steal in. *Oh yes,* I can hear you saying, *that makes great sense; watching a stop-and-go light gives* everyone *a sense of peace.*

All right; it made *no* sense. I grant you that. But the feeling was there, just the same. It made me think for the first time in years of the winter nights in the Wisconsin farmhouse where I grew up: lying in bed in a drafty upstairs room and marking the contrast between the whistle of the January wind outside, drifting snow as dry as sand along miles of snow-fence, and the warmth my body created under the two quilts.

There were some law books, but they were pretty damn strange: *Twenty Cases of Dismemberment and Their Outcomes Under British Law* is one title I remember. *Pet Cases* was another. I opened that one and, sure enough, it was a scholarly legal tome dealing with the law's treatment (American law, this time) of cases which bore in some important respect upon pets—everything from housecats that had inherited great sums of money to an ocelot that had broken its chain and seriously injured a postman.

There was a set of Dickens, a set of Defoe, a nearly endless set of Trollope; and there was also a set of novels—eleven of them—by a man named Edward Gray Seville. They were bound in handsome green leather, and the name of the firm gold-stamped on the spine was Stedham & Son. I had never heard of Seville or of his publishers. The copyright date of the first Seville—*These Were Our Brothers*—was 1911. The date of the last, *Breakers*, was 1935.

Two shelves down from the set of Seville novels was a large folio volume which contained careful step-by-step plans for Erector Set enthusiasts. Next to it was another folio volume which featured famous scenes from famous movies. Each of these pictures filled one whole page, and opposite each, filling the facing pages, were free-verse poems either about the scenes with which they were paired or inspired by them. Not a very remarkable concept, but the poets who were represented *were* remarkable—Robert Frost, Marianne Moore, William Carlos Williams, Wallace Stevens, Louis Zukofsky, and Erica Jong, to mention just a few. Halfway through the book I found a poem by Algernon Williams set next to that famous photograph of Marilyn Monroe standing on the subway grating and trying to hold her skirt down. The poem was titled "The Toll" and it began:

> The shape of the skirt is
> —we would say—
> the shape of a bell
> The legs are the clapper—

And some such more. Not a terrible poem, but certainly not Williams's best or anywhere near the top drawer. I felt I could hold such an opinion because I had read a good deal of Algernon Williams over the years. I could not, however, recall this poem about Marilyn Monroe (which it is; the poem announces it even when divorced from the picture—at the end Williams writes: *My legs clap my name:* / *Marilyn*, ma belle). I have looked for it since then and haven't been able to find it . . . which means nothing, of course. Poems are not like novels or legal opinions; they are more like blown leaves, and any omnibus volume titled The Complete So-and-So must certainly be a lie. Poems have a way of getting lost under sofas—it is one of their charms, and one of the reasons they endure. But—

At some point Stevens came by with a second scotch (by then I had settled into a chair of my own with a volume of Ezra Pound). It was as fine as the first. As I sipped it I saw two of those present, George Gregson and Harry Stein (Harry was six years dead on the night Emlyn McCarron told us the story of the Breathing Method), leave the room by a peculiar door that could not have been more than forty-two inches high. It was an Alice Down the Rabbit-Hole door if ever there was one. They left it open, and shortly after their odd exit from the library I heard the muted click of billiard balls.

Stevens passed by and asked if I would like another scotch. I declined with real regret. He nodded. "Very good, sir." His face never changed, and yet I had an obscure feeling that I had somehow pleased him.

Laughter startled me from my book sometime later. Someone had thrown a packet of chemical powder into the fire and turned the flames momentarily parti-colored. I thought of my boyhood again . . . but not in any wistful, sloppily romantic-nostalgic way. I feel a great need to emphasize that, God knows why. I thought of times when I had done just such a thing as a kid, but the memory was a strong one, pleasant, untinged with regret.

I saw that most of the others had drawn chairs up around the hearth in a semi-circle. Stevens had produced a heaping, smoking platter of marvellous hot sausages. Harry Stein returned through the down-the-rabbit-hole door, introducing himself hurriedly but pleasantly to me. Gregson remained in the billiard room—practicing shots, by the sound.

After a moment's hesitation I joined the others. A story was told—not a pleasant one. It was Norman Stett who told it, and while it is not my purpose to recount it here, perhaps you'll understand what I mean about its quality if I tell you that it was about a man who drowned in a telephone booth.

When Stett—who is also dead now—finished, someone said, "You should have saved it for Christmas, Norman." There was laughter, which I of course did not understand. At least, not then.

Waterhouse himself spoke up then, and such a Waterhouse I never would have dreamed of in a thousand years of dreaming. A graduate of Yale, Phi Beta Kappa, silver-haired, three-piece-suited, head of a law firm so large it was more enterprise than company—*this* Waterhouse told a story that had to do with a teacher who had gotten stuck in a privy. The privy stood behind the one-room schoolhouse in which she had taught, and the day she got her caboose jammed into one of the privy's two holes also happened to be the day the privy was scheduled to be taken away as Anniston County's contribution to the Life As It Was in New England exhibition being held at the Prudential Center in Boston. The teacher hadn't made a sound during all the time it took to load the privy onto the back of a flatbed truck and to spike it down; she was struck dumb with embarrassment and horror, Waterhouse said. And when the privy door blew off into the passing lane on Route 128 in Somerville during rush hour—

But draw a curtain over that, and over any other stories which might have followed it; they are not my stories tonight. At some point Stevens produced a bottle of brandy that was more than just good; it was damned near exquisite. It was passed around and Johanssen raised a toast—*the* toast, one might almost say: The tale, not he who tells it.

We drank to that.

Not long after, men began slipping away. It wasn't late; not yet midnight, anyway; but I've noticed that when your fifties give way to your sixties, late begins coming earlier and earlier. I saw Waterhouse slipping his arms into the overcoat Stevens was holding open for him, and decided that must be my cue. I thought it strange that Waterhouse would slip away without so much as a word to me (which certainly seemed to be what he was doing; if I had come back from shelving the Pound book forty seconds later, he would have been gone), but no stranger than most of the other things that had gone on that evening.

I stepped out just behind him, and Waterhouse glanced around, as if surprised to see me—and almost as if he had been startled out of a light doze. "Share a taxi?" he asked, as though we had just met by chance on this deserted, windy street.

"Thank you," I said. I meant thanks for a great deal more than his offer to share a cab, and I believe that was unmistakable in my tone, but he nodded as if that were all I had meant. A taxi with its for-hire light lit was cruising slowly down the street—fellows like George Waterhouse seem to luck onto cabs even on those miserably cold or snowy New York nights when you would swear there isn't a cab to be had on the entire island of Manhattan—and he flagged it.

Inside, safely warm, the taxi-meter charting our journey in measured clicks, I told him how much I had enjoyed his story. I couldn't remember laughing so hard or so spontaneously since I was eighteen, I told him, which was not flattery but only the simple truth.

"Oh? How kind of you to say." His voice was chillingly polite. I subsided, feeling a dull flush in my cheeks. One does not always need to hear a slam to know that the door has been closed.

When the taxi drew up to the curb in front of my building, I thanked him again, and this time he showed a trifle more warmth. "It was good of you to come on such short notice," he said. "Come again, if you like. Don't wait for an invitation; we don't stand much on ceremony at two-four-nine-B. Thursdays are best for stories, but the club is there every night."

Am I then to assume membership?

The question was on my lips. I meant to ask it; it seemed *necessary* to ask it. I was only mulling it over, listening to it in my head (in my tiresome lawyer's way) to hear if I had got the phrasing right—perhaps that was a little too blunt—when Waterhouse told the cabbie to drive on. The next moment the taxi was rolling on toward Park. I stood there on the sidewalk for a moment, the hem of my topcoat whipping around my shins, thinking: *He knew I was going to ask that question—he knew it, and he purposely had the driver go on before I could.* Then I told myself that was utterly absurd—paranoid, even. And it was. But it was also true. I could scoff all I liked; none of the scoffing changed that essential certainty.

I walked slowly to the door of my building and went inside.

Ellen was sixty per cent asleep when I sat down on the bed to take off my shoes. She rolled over and made a fuzzy interrogative sound deep in her throat. I told her to go back to sleep.

She made the muzzy sound again. This time it approximated English: "Howwuzzit?"

For a moment I hesitated, my shirt half-unbuttoned. And I thought with one moment's utter clarity: *If I tell her, I will never see the other side of that door again.*

"It was all right," I said. "Old men telling war stories."

"I told you so."

"But it wasn't bad. I might go back again. It might do me some good with the firm."

" 'The firm,' " she mocked lightly. "What an old buzzard you are, my love."

"It takes one to know one," I said, but she had already fallen asleep again. I undressed, showered, towelled, put on my pajamas . . . and then, instead of going to bed as I should have done (it was edging past one by that time), I put on my robe and had another bottle of Beck's. I sat at the kitchen table, drinking it slowly, looking out the window and up the cold canyon of Madison Avenue, thinking. My head was a trifle buzzy from my evening's intake of alcohol—for me an unexpectedly large intake. But the feeling was not at all unpleasant, and I had no sense of an impending hangover.

The thought which had come to me when Ellen asked me about my evening was as ridiculous as the one I'd entertained about George Waterhouse as the cab drew away from me—what in God's name could be wrong with telling my wife about a perfectly harmless evening at my boss's stuffy men's club . . . and even if something *were* wrong with telling her, who would know that I had? No, it was every bit as ridiculous and paranoid as those earlier musings . . . and, my heart told me, every bit as true.

see, no knocker, no closed-circuit TV camera mounted unobtrusively in the shadow of a deep eave, and, of course, no Waterhouse
waiting to take me in. I stopped at the foot of the steps and looked
around. East Thirty-fifth Street suddenly seemed darker, colder,
more threatening. The brownstones all looked somehow secret, as if
hiding mysteries best not investigated. Their windows looked like
eyes.

*Somewhere, behind one of those windows, there may be a man or woman
contemplating murder,* I thought. A shudder worked up my spine.
Contemplating it . . . or doing it.

Then, suddenly, the door was open and Stevens was there.

I felt an intense surge of relief. I am not an overly imaginative
man, I think—at least not under ordinary circumstances—but this
last thought had had all the eerie clarity of prophecy. I might have
babbled aloud if I hadn't glanced at Stevens's eyes first. His eyes did
not know me. His eyes did not know me at all.

Then there was another instance of that eerie, prophetic clarity; I
saw the rest of my evening in perfect detail. Three hours in a quiet
bar. Three scotches (perhaps four) to dull the embarrassment of
having been fool enough to go where I wasn't wanted. The
humiliation my mother's advice had been intended to avoid—that
which comes with knowing one has overstepped.

I saw myself going home a little tipsy, but not in a good way. I
saw myself merely sitting through the cab ride rather than
experiencing it through that childlike lens of excitement and
anticipation. I heard myself saying to Ellen, *It wears thin after
awhile . . . Waterhouse told the same story about winning a consignment of
T-bone steaks for the Third Battalion in a poker game . . . and they play
Hearts for a dollar a point, can you believe it? . . . Go back? . . . I
suppose I might, but I doubt it.* And that would be the end of it.
Except, I suppose, for my own humiliation.

I saw all of this in the nothing of Stevens's eyes. Then the eyes
warmed. He smiled slightly and said: "Mr. Adley! Come in. I'll
take your coat."

I mounted the steps and Stevens closed the door firmly behind
me. How different a door can feel when you are on the warm side of
it! He took my coat and was gone with it. I stood in the hall for a

moment, looking at my own reflection in the pier glass, a man of sixty-three whose face was rapidly becoming too gaunt to look middle-aged. And yet the reflection pleased me.

I slipped into the library.

Johanssen was there, reading his *Wall Street Journal*. In another island of light, Emlyn McCarron sat over a chessboard opposite Peter Andrews. McCarron was and is a cadaverous man, possessed of a narrow, bladelike nose; Andrews was huge, slope-shouldered, and choleric. A vast ginger-colored beard sprayed over his vest. Face to face over the inlaid board with its carved pieces of ivory and ebony, they looked like Indian totems: eagle and bear.

Waterhouse was there, frowning over that day's *Times*. He glanced up, nodded at me without surprise, and disappeared into the paper again.

Stevens brought me a scotch, unasked.

I took it into the stacks and found that puzzling, enticing set of green volumes again. I began reading the works of Edward Gray Seville that night. I started at the beginning, with *These Were Our Brothers*. Since then I have read them all, and believe them to be eleven of the finest novels of our century.

Near the end of the evening there was a story—just one—and Stevens brought brandy around. When the tale was told, people began to rise, preparing to leave. Stevens spoke from the double doorway which communicated with the hallway. His voice was low and pleasant, but carrying:

"Who will bring us a tale for Christmas, then?"

People stopped what they were doing and glanced around. There was some low, goodnatured talk and a burst of laughter.

Stevens, smiling but serious, clapped his hands together twice, like a grammar-school teacher calling an unruly class to order. "Come, gentlemen—who'll bring the tale?"

Peter Andrews, he of the sloped shoulders and gingery beard, cleared his throat. "I have something I've been thinking about. I don't know if it's quite right; that is, if it's—"

"That will be fine," Stevens interrupted, and there was more laughter. Andrews had his back slapped goodnaturedly. Cold drafts swirled up the hallway as men slipped out.

Then Stevens was there, as if by benign magic, holding my coat for me. "Good evening, Mr. Adley. Always a pleasure."

"Do you really meet on Christmas night?" I asked, buttoning my coat. I was a little disappointed that I was going to miss Andrews's story, but we had made firm plans to drive to Schenectady and keep the holiday with Ellen's sister.

Stevens managed to look both shocked and amused at the same time. "In no case," he said. "Christmas is a night a man should spend with his family. That night, if no other. Don't you agree, sir?"

"I certainly do."

"We always meet on the Thursday before Christmas. In fact, that is the one night of the year when we almost always have a large turnout."

He hadn't used the word *members*, I noticed—just happenstance? or neat avoidance?

"Many tales have been spun out in the main room, Mr. Adley, tales of every sort, from the comic to the tragic to the ironic to the sentimental. But on the Thursday before Christmas, it's always a tale of the uncanny. It's always been that way, at least as far back as I can remember."

That at least explained the comment I had heard on my first visit, the one to the effect that Norman Stett should have saved his story for Christmas. Other questions hovered on my lips, but I saw a reflected caution in Stevens's eyes. It was not a warning that he would not answer my questions; it was, rather, a warning that I should not even ask them.

"Was there something else, Mr. Adley?"

We were alone in the hall now. All the others had left. And suddenly the hallway seemed darker, Stevens's long face paler, his lips redder. A knot exploded in the fireplace and a red glow washed momentarily across the polished parquet floor. I thought I heard, from somewhere in those as-yet-unexplored rooms beyond, a kind of slithery bump. I did not like the sound. Not at all.

"No," I said in a voice that was not quite steady. "I think not."

"Goodnight, then," Stevens said, and I crossed the threshold. I heard the heavy door close behind me. I heard the lock turn. And then I was walking toward the lights of Third Avenue, not looking back over my shoulder, somehow afraid to look back, as if I might see some frightful fiend matching me stride for stride, or glimpse some secret better kept than known. I reached the corner, saw an empty cab, and flagged it.

"More war stories?" Ellen asked me that night. She was in bed with Philip Marlowe, the only lover she has ever taken.

"There was a war story or two," I said, hanging up my overcoat. "Mostly I sat and read a book."

"When you weren't oinking."

"Yes, that's right. When I wasn't oinking."

"Listen to this: *'The first time I laid eyes on Terry Lennox he was drunk in a Rolls-Royce Silver Wraith outside the terrace of The Dancers,'*" Ellen read. " *'He had a young-looking face but his hair was bone white. You could tell by his eyes that he was plastered to the hairline, but otherwise he looked like any other nice young guy in a dinner jacket who had been spending too much money in a joint that exists for that purpose and for no other.'* Nice, huh? It's—"

"*The Long Goodbye,*" I said, taking off my shoes. "You read me that same passage once every three years. It's part of your life-cycle."

She wrinkled her nose at me. "Oink-oink."

"Thank you," I said.

She went back to her book. I went out into the kitchen to get a bottle of Beck's. When I came back, she had laid *The Long Goodbye* open on the counterpane and was looking at me closely. "David, are you going to join this club?"

"I suppose I might . . . if I'm asked." I felt uncomfortable. I had perhaps told her another lie. If there was such a thing as membership at 249B East Thirty-fifth, I already was a member.

"I'm glad," she said. "You've needed something for a long time now. I don't think you even know it, but you have. I've got the Relief Committee and the Commission on Women's Rights and the Theater Society. But you've needed something. Some people to grow old with, I think."

I went to the bed and sat beside her and picked up *The Long Goodbye.* It was a bright, new-minted paperback. I could remember buying the original hardback edition as a birthday present for Ellen. In 1953. "Are we old?" I asked her.

"I suspect we are," she said, and smiled brilliantly at me.

I put the book down and touched her breast. "Too old for this?"

She turned the covers back with ladylike decorum . . . and then, giggling, kicked them onto the floor with her feet. "Beat me, daddy," Ellen said, "eight to the bar."

"Oink, oink," I said, and then we were both laughing.

The Thursday before Christmas came. That evening was much the same as the others, with two notable exceptions. There were more people there, perhaps as many as eighteen. And there was a sharp, indefinable sense of excitement in the air. Johanssen took only a cursory glance at his *Journal* and then joined McCarron, Hugh Beagleman, and myself. We sat near the windows, talking of this and that, and finally fell into a passionate—and often hilarious—discussion of pre-war automobiles.

There was, now that I think of it, a third difference as well—Stevens had concocted a delicious eggnog punch. It was smooth, but it was also hot with rum and spices. It was served from an incredible Waterford bowl that looked like an ice-sculpture, and the animated hum of the conversation grew ever higher as the level of the punch grew lower.

I looked over in the corner by the tiny door leading to the billiard room and was astounded to see Waterhouse and Norman Stett flipping baseball cards into what looked like a genuine beaver tophat. They were laughing uproariously.

Groups formed and re-formed. The hour grew late . . . and then, at the time when people usually began slipping out through the front door, I saw Peter Andrews seated in front of the fire with an unmarked packet, about the size of a seed envelope, in one hand. He tossed it into the flames without opening it, and a moment later the fire began to dance with every color of the spectrum—and some, I would have sworn, from outside it—before turning yellow again. Chairs were dragged around. Over Andrews's shoulder I could see the keystone with its etched homily: IT IS THE TALE, NOT HE WHO TELLS IT.

Stevens passed unobtrusively among us, taking punch glasses and replacing them with snifters of brandy. There were murmurs of "Merry Christmas" and "Top of the season, Stevens," and for the first time I saw money change hands—a ten-dollar bill was unobtrusively tendered here, a bill that looked like a fifty there, one which I clearly saw was a hundred from another chair.

"Thank you, Mr. McCarron . . . Mr. Johanssen . . . Mr. Beagleman . . ." A quiet, well-bred murmur.

I have lived in New York long enough to know that the Christmas season is a carnival of tips; something for the butcher, the baker, the candlestick-maker—not to mention the doorman, the super, and the cleaning lady who comes in Tuesdays and Fridays. I've never met anyone of my own class who regarded this as anything but a necessary nuisance . . . but I felt none of that grudging spirit on that night. The money was given willingly, even eagerly . . . and suddenly, for no reason (it was the way thoughts often seemed to come when one was at 249B), I thought of the boy calling up to Scrooge on the still, cold air of a London Christmas morning: "Wot? The goose that's as big as me?" And Scrooge, nearly crazed with joy, giggling: "A *good* boy! An *excellent* boy!"

I found my own wallet. In the back of this, behind the pictures of Ellen I keep, there has always been a fifty-dollar bill which I keep for emergencies. When Stevens gave me my brandy, I slipped it into his hand with never a qualm . . . although I was not a rich man.

"Happy Christmas, Stevens," I said.

"Thank you, sir. And the same to you."

He finished passing out the brandies and collecting his honorariums and retired. I glanced around once, at the midpoint of Peter Andrews's story, and saw him standing by the double doors, a dim manlike shadow, stiff and silent.

"I'm a lawyer now, as most of you know," Andrews said after sipping at his glass, clearing his throat, and then sipping again. "I've had offices on Park Avenue for the last twenty-two years. But before that, I was a legal assistant in a firm of lawyers which did business in Washington, D.C. One night in July I was required to stay late in order to finish indexing case citations in a brief which hasn't anything at all to do with this story. But then a man came in—a man who was at that time one of the most widely known Senators on the Hill, a man who later almost became President. His shirt was matted with blood and his eyes were bulging from their sockets.

" 'I've got to talk to Joe,' he said. Joe, you understand, was Joseph Woods, the head of my firm, one of the most influential private-sector lawyers in Washington, and this Senator's close personal friend.

" 'He went home hours ago,' I said. I was terribly frightened, I can tell you—he looked like a man who had just walked away from a dreadful car accident, or perhaps from a knife-fight. And somehow seeing his face—which I had seen in newspaper photos and on *Meet the Press*—seeing it streaked with gore, one cheek twitching spasmodically below one wild eye . . . all of that made my fright worse. 'I can call him if you—' I was already fumbling with the phone, mad with eagerness to turn this unexpected responsibility over to someone else. Looking behind him, I could see the caked and bloody footprints he had left on the carpet.

" 'I've got to talk to Joe right now,' he reiterated as if he hadn't heard me. 'There's something in the trunk of my car . . . something I found out at the Virginia place. I've shot it and stabbed it and I can't kill it. It's not human, and I can't kill it.'

"He began to giggle . . . and then to laugh . . . and finally to scream. And he was still screaming when I finally got Mr. Woods on the phone and told him to come, for God's sake, to come as fast as he could . . ."

It is not my purpose to tell Peter Andrews's story, either. As a matter of fact, I am not sure I would dare to tell it. Suffice it to say that it was a tale so gruesome that I dreamed of it for weeks afterwards, and Ellen once looked at me over the breakfast table and asked me why I had suddenly cried out "His head! His head is still speaking in the earth!" in the middle of the night.

"I suppose it was a dream," I said. "One of those you can't remember afterwards."

But my eyes dropped immediately to my coffee cup, and I think that Ellen knew the lie that time.

*   *   *

One day in August of the following year, I was buzzed as I worked in the Reading Library. It was George Waterhouse. He asked me if I could step up to his office. When I got there I saw that Robert Carden was also there, and Henry Effingham. For one moment I was positive I was about to be accused of some really dreadful act of stupidity or ineptitude.

Then Carden stepped around to me and said: "George believes the time has come to make you a junior partner, David. The rest of us agree."

"It's going to be a little bit like being the world's oldest JayCee," Effingham said with a grin, "but it's the channel you have to go through, David. With any luck, we can make you a full partner by Christmas."

There were no bad dreams that night. Ellen and I went out to dinner, drank too much, went on to a jazz place where we hadn't been in nearly six years, and listened to that amazing blue-eyed black man, Dexter Gordon, blow his horn until almost two in the morning. We woke up the next morning with fluttery stomachs and achey heads, both of us still unable to completely believe what had happened. One of them was that my salary had just climbed by eight thousand dollars a year long after our expectations of such a staggering income jump had fallen by the wayside.

The firm sent me to Copenhagen for six weeks that fall, and I returned to discover that John Hanrahan, one of the regular attendees at 249B, had died of cancer. A collection was taken up for his wife, who had been left in unpleasant circumstances. I was pressed into service to total the amount—which was given entirely in cash—and convert it to a cashier's check. It came to more than ten thousand dollars. I turned the check over to Stevens and I suppose he mailed it.

It just so happened that Arlene Hanrahan was a member of Ellen's Theater Society, and Ellen told me sometime later that Arlene had received an anonymous check for ten thousand four hundred dollars. Written on the check stub was the brief and unilluminating message: *Friends of your late husband John.*

"Isn't that the most amazing thing you ever heard in your *life?*" Ellen asked me.

"No," I said, "but it's right up there in the top ten. Are there any more strawberries, Ellen?"

The years went by. I discovered a warren of rooms upstairs at 249B—a writing room, a bedroom where guests sometimes stayed overnight (although, after that slithery bump I had heard—or imagined I had heard—I believe I personally would rather have registered at a good hotel), a small but well-equipped gymnasium, and a sauna bath. There was also a long, narrow room which ran the length of the building and contained two bowling alleys.

In those same years I re-read the novels of Edward Gray Seville, and discovered an absolutely stunning poet—the equal of Ezra Pound and Wallace Stevens, perhaps—named Norbert Rosen. According to the back flap on one of the three volumes of his work in the stacks, he had been born in 1924 and killed at Anzio. All three volumes of his work had been published by Stedham & Son, New York and Boston.

I remember going back to the New York Public Library on a bright spring afternoon during one of those years (of which year I am no longer sure) and requesting twenty years' worth of *Literary Market Place*. The *LMP* is an annual publication the size of a large city's Yellow Pages, and the reference room librarian was quite put out with me, I'm afraid. But I persisted, and went through each volume carefully. And although *LMP* is supposed to list every publisher, great and small, in the United States (in addition to agents, editors, and book club staffs), I found no listing for Stedham & Son. A year later—or perhaps it was two years later—I fell into conversation with an antiquarian book-dealer and asked him about the imprint. He said he had never heard of it.

I thought of asking Stevens—saw that warning light in his eyes—and dropped the question unasked.

And, over those years, there were stories.

Tales, to use Stevens's word. Funny tales, tales of love found and love lost, tales of unease. Yes, and even a few war stories, although none of the sort Ellen had likely been thinking of when she made the suggestion.

I remember Gerard Tozeman's story the most clearly—the tale of an American base of operations which took a direct hit from German artillery four months before the end of World War I, killing everyone present except for Tozeman himself.

Lathrop Carruthers, the American general who everyone had by then decided must be utterly insane (he had been responsible for better than eighteen *thousand* casualties by then—lives and limbs spent as casually as you or I might spend a quarter in a jukebox), was standing at a map of the front lines when the shell struck. He had been explaining yet another mad flanking operation at the moment—an operation which would have succeeded only on the level of all the others Carruthers had hatched: it would be wonderfully successful at making new widows.

And when the dust cleared, Gerard Tozeman, dazed and deaf, bleeding from his nose, his ears, and the corners of both eyes, his testicles already swelling from the force of the concussion, had come upon Carruthers's body while looking for a way out of the abbatoir that had been the staff HQ only minutes before. He looked at the general's body . . . and then began to scream and laugh. The sounds went unheard by his own shellshocked ears, but they served to notify the medicos that someone was still alive in that strew of matchwood.

Carruthers had not been mutilated by the blast . . . at least, Tozeman said, it hadn't been what the soldiers of that long-ago war had come to think of as mutilation—men whose arms had been blown off, men with no feet, no eyes; men whose lungs had been shrivelled by gas. No, he said, it was nothing like that. The man's mother would have known him at once. But the map . . .

. . . the map before which Carruthers had been standing with his butcher's pointer when the shell struck . . .

It had somehow *been driven into his face*. Tozeman had found himself staring into a hideous, tattooed deathmask. Here was the stony shore of Brittany on the bony ridge of Lathrop Carruthers's brow. Here was the Rhine flowing like a blue scar down his left cheek. Here were some of the finest wine-growing provinces in the world bumped and ridged over his chin. Here was the Saar drawn around his throat like a hangman's noose . . . and printed across one bulging eyeball was the word VERSAILLES.

That was our Christmas story in the year 197-.

I remember many others, but they do not belong here. Properly speaking, Tozeman's doesn't, either . . . but it was the first "Christmas tale" I heard at 249B, and I could not resist telling it. And then, on the Thursday after Thanksgiving of this year, when Stevens clapped his hands together for attention and asked who would favor us with a Christmas tale, Emlyn McCarron growled: "I suppose I've got something that bears telling. Tell it now or tell it never; God'll shut me up for good soon enough."

In the years I had been coming to 249B, I had never heard McCarron tell a story. And perhaps that's why I called the taxi so early, and why, when Stevens passed out eggnog to the six of us who had ventured out on that bellowing, frigid night, I felt so keenly excited. Nor was I the only one; I saw that same excitement on a good many other faces.

McCarron, old and dry and leathery, sat in the huge chair by the fire with the packet of powder in his gnarled hands. He tossed it in, and we watched the flames shift colors madly before returning to yellow again. Stevens passed among us with brandy, and we passed him his Christmas honorariums. Once, during that yearly ceremony, I had heard the clink of change passing from the hand of the giver to the hand of the receiver; on another occasion, I had seen a one-thousand-dollar bill for a moment in the firelight. On both occasions the murmur of Stevens's voice had been exactly the same: low, considerate, and entirely correct. Ten years, more or less, had passed since I had first come to 249B with George Waterhouse, and while much had changed in the world outside, nothing had changed in here, and Stevens seemed not to have aged a month, or even a single day.

He moved back into the shadows, and for a moment there was a silence so perfect that we could hear the faint whistle of boiling sap escaping from the burning logs on the hearth. Emlyn McCarron was looking into the fire and we all followed his gaze. The flames seemed particularly wild that night. I felt almost hypnotized by the sight of the fire—as, I suppose, the cavemen who birthed us were once hypnotized by it as the wind walked and talked outside their cold northern caves.

At last, still looking into the fire, bent slightly forward so that his forearms rested on his thighs and his clasped hands hung in a knot between his knees, McCarron began to speak.

II.
The Breathing Method

I am nearly eighty now, which means that I was born with the century. All my life I have been associated with a building which stands almost directly across from Madison Square Garden; this building, which looks like a great gray prison—something out of *A Tale of Two Cities*—is actually a hospital, as most of you know. It is Harriet White Memorial Hospital. The Harriet White after whom it was named was my father's first wife, and she got her practical experience in nursing when there were still actual sheep grazing on Sheep Meadow in Central Park. A statue of the lady herself stands on a pedestal in the courtyard before the building, and if any of you have seen it, you may have wondered how a woman with such a stern and uncompromising face could have found such a gentle occupation. The motto chiselled into the statue's base, once you get rid of the Latin folderol, is even less comforting: *There is no comfort without pain; thus we define salvation through suffering.* Cato, if you please . . . or if you don't please!

I was born inside that gray stone building on March 20th, 1900. I returned there as an intern in the year 1926. Twenty-six is old to be just starting out in the world of medicine, but I had done a more practical internship in France, at the end of World War I, trying to pack ruptured guts back into stomachs that had been blown wide open, and dealing on the black market for morphine, which was often tinctured and sometimes dangerous.

As with the generation of physicians following World War II, we were a bedrock-practical lot of sawbones, and the records of the major medical schools show a remarkably small number of washouts in the years 1919 to 1928. We were older, more experienced, steadier. Were we also wiser? I don't know . . . but we were certainly more cynical. There was none of this nonsense you read about in the popular medical novels, stuff about fainting or vomiting at one's first autopsy. Not after Belleau Wood, where mamma rats sometimes raised whole litters of ratlings in the gas-exploded intestines of the soldiers left to rot in no man's land. We had gotten all our puking and passing out behind us.

The Harriet White Memorial Hospital also figured largely in something that happened to me nine years after I had interned there—and this is the story I want to tell you gentlemen tonight. It is not a tale to be told at Christmas, you would say (although its final scene was played out on Christmas Eve), and yet, while it is certainly horrible, it also seems to express to me all the amazing power of our cursed, doomed species. In it I see the wonder of our will . . . and also its horrible, tenebrous power.

Birth itself, gentlemen, is a horrid thing to many; it is the fashion now that fathers should be present at the birth of their children, and while this fashion has served to inflict many men with a guilt which I feel they may not deserve (it is a guilt which some women use knowingly and with an almost prescient cruelty), it seems by and large to be a healthful, salubrious thing. Yet I have seen men leave the delivery room white and tottering and I have seen them swoon like girls, overcome by the cries and the blood. I remember one father who held up just fine . . . only to begin screaming hysterically as his perfectly healthy son pushed its way into the world. The infant's eyes were open, it gave the impression of looking around . . . and then its eyes settled on the father.

Birth is wonderful, gentlemen, but I have never found it beautiful—not by any stretch of the imagination. I believe it is too brutal to be beautiful. A woman's womb is like an engine. With conception, that engine is turned on. At first it barely idles . . . but as the creative cycle nears the climax of birth, that engine revs up and up and up. Its idling whisper becomes a steady running hum, and then a rumble, and finally a bellowing, frightening roar. Once that engine has been turned on, every mother-to-be understands that her life is in check. Either she will bring the baby forth and the engine will shut down again, or that engine will pound louder and harder and faster until it explodes, killing her in blood and pain.

This is a story of birth, gentlemen, on the eve of that birth we have celebrated for almost two thousand years.

*   *   *

I began practicing medicine in 1929—a bad year to begin anything. My grandfather was able to lend me a small sum of money, so I was luckier than many of my colleagues, but I still had to survive over the next four years mostly on my wits.

By 1935, things had improved a bit. I had developed a bedrock of steady patients and was getting quite a few outpatient referrals from White Memorial. In April of that year I saw a new patient, a young woman whom I will call Sandra Stansfield—that name is close enough to what her name really was. This was a young woman, white, who stated her age to be twenty-eight. After examining her, I guessed her true age to be between three and five years younger than that. She was blonde, slender, and tall for that time—about five feet eight inches. She was quite beautiful, but in an austere way that was almost forbidding. Her features were clear and regular, her eyes intelligent . . . and her mouth every bit as determined as the stone mouth of Harriet White on the statue across from Madison Square Garden. The name she put on her form was not Sandra Stansfield but Jane Smith. My examination subsequently showed her to be about two months gone in pregnancy. She wore no wedding ring.

After the preliminary exam—but before the results of the pregnancy test were in—my nurse, Ella Davidson, said: "That girl yesterday? Jane Smith? If that isn't an assumed name, I never heard one."

I agreed. Still, I rather admired her. She had not engaged in the usual shilly-shallying, toe-scuffing, blushing, tearful behavior. She had been straightforward and businesslike. Even her alias had seemed more a matter of business than of shame. There had been no attempt to provide verisimilitude by creating a "Betty Rucklehouse" or whomping up a "Ternina DeVille." *You require a name for your form*, she seemed to be saying, *because that is the law. So here is a name; but rather than trusting to the professional ethics of a man I don't know, I'll trust in myself. If you don't mind.*

Ella sniffed and passed a few remarks—"modern girls" and "bold as brass"—but she was a good woman, and I don't think she said those things except for the sake of form. She knew as well as I did that, whatever my new patient might be, she was no little trollop with hard eyes and round heels. No; "Jane Smith" was merely an extremely serious, extremely determined young woman—if either of those things can be described by such a Milquetoast adverb as "merely." It was an unpleasant situation (it used to be called "getting in a scrape," as you gentlemen may remember; nowadays it seems that many young women use a scrape to get out of the scrape), and she meant to go through it with whatever grace and dignity she could manage.

A week after her initial appointment, she came in again. That was a peach of a day—one of the first real days of spring. The air was mild, the sky a soft, milky shade of blue, and there was a smell on the breeze—a warm, indefinable smell that seems to be nature's signal that she is entering her own birth cycle again. The sort of day one wished to be miles from any responsibility, sitting opposite a lovely woman of one's own—at Coney Island, maybe, or on the Palisades across the Hudson with a picnic hamper on a checkered cloth and the lady in question wearing a great white cartwheel hat and a sleeveless gown as pretty as the day.

"Jane Smith's" dress had sleeves, but it was still almost as pretty as the day; a smart white linen with brown edging. She wore brown pumps, white gloves, and a cloche hat that was slightly out of fashion—it was the first sign I saw that she was a far from rich woman.

"You're pregnant," I said. "I don't believe you doubted it much, did you?"

If there are to be tears, I thought, they will come now.

"No," she said with perfect composure. There was no more a sign of tears in her eyes than there were rainclouds on the horizon that day. "I'm very regular as a rule."

There was a pause between us.

"When may I expect to deliver?" she asked then, with an almost soundless sigh. It was the sound a man or woman might make before bending over to pick up a heavy load.

"It will be a Christmas baby," I said. "December tenth is the date I'll give you, but it could be two weeks on either side of that."

"All right." She hesitated briefly, and then plunged ahead. "Will you attend me? Even though I'm not married?"

"Yes," I said. "On one condition."

She frowned, and in that moment her face was more like the face of Harriet White than ever. One would not think that the frown of a woman perhaps only twenty-three could be particularly formidable, but this one was. She was ready to leave, and the fact that she would have to go through this entire embarrassing process again with another doctor was not going to deter her.

"And what might that be?" she asked with perfect, colorless courtesy.

Now it was I who felt an urge to drop my eyes from her steady hazel ones, but I held her gaze. "I insist upon knowing your real name. We can continue to do business on a cash basis if that is how you prefer it, and I can continue to have Mrs. Davidson issue you receipts in the name of Jane Smith. But if we are going to travel through the next seven months or so together, I would like to be able to address you by the name to which you answer in all the rest of your life."

I finished this absurdly stiff little speech and watched her think it through. I was somehow quite sure she was going to stand up, thank me for my time, and leave forever. I was going to feel disappointed if that happened. I liked her. Even more, I liked the straightforward way she was handling a problem which would have reduced ninety women out of a hundred to inept and undignified liars, terrified by the living clock within and so deeply ashamed of their situation that to make any reasonable plan for coping with it became impossible.

I suppose many young people today would find such a state of mind ludicrous, ugly, even hard to believe. People have become so eager to demonstrate their broad-mindedness that a pregnant woman who has no wedding ring is apt to be treated with twice the solicitude of one who does. You gentlemen will well remember when the situation was quite different—you will remember a time when rectitude and hypocrisy were combined to make a situation that was viciously difficult for a woman who had gotten herself "in a scrape." In those days, a married pregnant woman was a radiant woman, sure of her position and proud of fulfilling what she considered to be the function God put her on earth for. An unmarried pregnant woman was a trollop in the eyes of the world and apt to be a trollop in her own eyes as well. They were, to use

Ella Davidson's word, "easy," and in that world and that time, "easiness" was not quickly forgiven. Such women crept away to have their babies in other towns or cities. Some took pills or jumped from buildings. Others went to butcher abortionists with dirty hands or tried to do the job themselves; in my time as a physician I have seen four women die of blood-loss before my eyes as the result of punctured wombs—in one case the puncturing was done by the jagged neck of a Dr Pepper bottle that had been tied to the handle of a whiskbroom. It *is* hard to believe now that such things happened, but they did, gentlemen. They did. It was, quite simply, the worst situation a healthy young woman could find herself in.

"All right," she said at last. "That's fair enough. My name is Sandra Stansfield." And she held her hand out. Rather amazed, I took it and shook it. I'm rather glad Ella Davidson didn't see me do that. She would have made no comment, but the coffee would have been bitter for the next week.

She smiled—at my own expression of bemusement, I imagine— and looked at me frankly. "I hope we can be friends, Dr. McCarron. I need a friend just now. I'm quite frightened."

"I can understand that, and I'll try to be your friend if I can, Miss Stansfield. Is there anything I can do for you now?"

She opened her handbag and took out a dime-store pad and a pen. She opened the pad, poised the pen, and looked up at me. For one horrified instant I believed she was going to ask me for the name and address of an abortionist. Then she said: "I'd like to know the best things to eat. For the baby, I mean."

I laughed out loud. She looked at me with some amazement.

"Forgive me—it's just that you seem so businesslike."

"I suppose," she said. "This baby is a part of my business now, isn't it, Dr. McCarron?"

"Yes. Of course it is. And I have a folder which I give to all my pregnant patients. It deals with diet and weight and drinking and smoking and lots of other things. Please don't laugh when you look at it. You'll hurt my feelings if you do, because I wrote it myself."

And so I had—although it was really more of a pamphlet than a folder, and in time became my book, *A Practical Guide to Pregnancy and Delivery*. I was quite interested in obstetrics and gynecology in those days—still am—although it was not a thing to specialize in back then unless you had plenty of uptown connections. Even if you did, it might take ten or fifteen years to establish a strong practice. Having hung out my shingle at a rather too-ripe age as a result of the war, I didn't feel I had the time to spare. I contented myself with the knowledge that I would see a great many happy expectant mothers and deliver a great many babies in the course of my general practice. And so I did; at last count I had delivered well over two thousand babies—enough to fill fifty classrooms.

I kept up with the literature on having babies more smartly than I did on that applying to any other area of general practice. And because my opinions were strong, enthusiastic ones, I wrote my own pamphlet rather than just passing along the stale chestnuts so often foisted on young mothers then. I won't run through the whole catalogue of these chestnuts—we'd be here all night—but I'll mention a couple.

Expectant mothers were urged to stay off their feet as much as possible, and on no account were they to walk any sustained distance lest a miscarriage or "birth damage" result. Now giving birth is an extremely strenuous piece of work, and such advice is like telling a football player to prepare for the big game by sitting around as much as possible so he won't tire himself out! Another sterling piece of advice, given by a good many doctors, was that moderately overweight mothers-to-be take up smoking . . . *smoking*! The rationale was perfectly expressed by an advertising slogan of the day: "Have a Lucky instead of a sweet." People who have the idea that when we entered the twentieth century we also entered an age of medical light and reason have no idea of how utterly crazy medicine could sometimes be. Perhaps it's just as well; their hair would turn white.

I gave Miss Stansfield my folder and she looked through it with complete attention for perhaps five minutes. I asked her permission to smoke my pipe and she gave it absently, without looking up. When she did look up at last, there was a small smile on her lips. "Are you a radical, Dr. McCarron?" she asked.

"Why do you say that? Because I advise that the expectant mother should walk her round of errands instead of riding in a smoky, jolting subway car?"

" 'Pre-natal vitamins,' whatever they are . . . swimming recommended . . . and breathing exercises! What breathing exercises?"

"That comes later on, and no—I'm not a radical. Far from it. What I am is five minutes' overdue on my next patient."

"Oh! I'm sorry." She got to her feet quickly, tucking the thick folder into her purse.

"No need."

She shrugged into her light coat, looking at me with those direct hazel eyes as she did so. "No," she said. "Not a radical at all. I suspect you're actually quite . . . comfortable? Is that the word I want?"

"I hope it will serve," I said. "It's a word I like. If you speak to Mrs. Davidson, she'll give you an appointment schedule. I'll want to see you again early next month."

"Your Mrs. Davidson doesn't approve of me."

"Oh, I'm sure that's not true at all." But I've never been a particularly good liar, and the warmth between us suddenly slipped away. I did not accompany her to the door of my consulting room. "Miss Stansfield?"

She turned toward me, coolly enquiring.

"Do you intend to keep the baby?"

She considered me briefly and then smiled—a secret smile which I am convinced only pregnant women know. "Oh yes," she said, and let herself out.

By the end of that day I had treated identical twins for identical cases of poison ivy, lanced a boil, removed a hook of metal from a sheet-welder's eye, and referred one of my oldest patients to White Memorial for what was surely cancer. I had forgotten all about Sandra Stansfield by then. Ella Davidson recalled her to my mind by saying:

"Perhaps she's not a chippie after all."

I looked up from my last patient's folder. I had been looking at it, feeling that useless disgust most doctors feel when they know they have been rendered completely helpless, and thinking I ought to have a rubber stamp made up for such files—only instead of saying ACCOUNT RECEIVABLE or PAID IN FULL or PATIENT MOVED, it would simply say DEATH-WARRANT. Perhaps with a skull and crossbones above, like those on bottles of poison.

"Pardon me?"

"Your Miss Jane Smith. She did a most peculiar thing after her appointment this morning." The set of Mrs. Davidson's head and mouth made it clear that this was the sort of peculiar thing of which she approved.

"And what was that?"

"When I gave her her appointment card, she asked me to tot up her expenses. *All* of her expenses. Delivery and hospital stay included."

That *was* a peculiar thing, all right. This was 1935, remember, and Miss Stansfield gave every impression of being a woman on her own. Was she well off, even comfortably off? I didn't think so. Her dress, shoes, and gloves had all been smart, but she had worn no jewelry—not even costume jewelry. And then there was her hat, that decidedly out-of-date cloche.

"Did you do it?" I asked.

Mrs. Davidson looked at me as though I might have lost my senses. *"Did* I? Of *course* I did! And she paid the entire amount. In cash."

The last, which apparently had surprised Mrs. Davidson the most (in an extremely pleasant way, of course), surprised me not at all. One thing which the Jane Smiths of the world can't do is write checks.

"Took a bank-book out of her purse, opened it, and counted the money right out onto my desk," Mrs. Davidson was continuing. "Then she put her receipt in where the cash had been, put the bank-book into her purse again, and said good day. Not half bad, when you think of the way we've had to chase some of these so-called 'respectable' people to make them pay their bills!"

I felt chagrined for some reason. I was not happy with the Stansfield woman for having done such a thing, with Mrs. Davidson for being so pleased and complacent with the arrangement, and with myself, for some reason I couldn't define then and can't now. Something about it made me feel small.

"But she couldn't very well pay for a hospital stay now, could she?" I asked—it was a ridiculously small thing to seize on, but it was all I could find at that moment on which to express my pique and half-amused frustration. "After all, none of us knows how long she'll have to remain there. Or are you reading the crystal now, Ella?"

"I told her that very thing, and she asked what the average stay was following an uncomplicated birth. I told her six days. Wasn't that right, Dr. McCarron?"

I had to admit it was.

"She said that she would pay for six days, then, and if it was longer, she would pay the difference, and if—"

"—if it was shorter, we could issue her a refund," I finished wearily. I thought: *Damn the woman, anyway!*—and then I laughed. She had guts. One couldn't deny that. All kinds of guts.

Mrs. Davidson allowed herself a smile . . . and if I am ever tempted, now that I am in my dotage, to believe I know all there is to know about one of my fellow creatures, I try to remember that smile. Before that day I would have staked my life that I would never see Mrs. Davidson, one of the most "proper" women I have ever known, smile fondly as she thought about a girl who was pregnant out of wedlock.

"Guts? I don't know, doctor. But she knows her own mind, that one. She certainly does."

A month passed, and Miss Stansfield showed up promptly for her appointment, simply appearing out of that wide, amazing flow of humanity that was New York then and is New York now. She wore a fresh-looking blue dress to which she managed to communicate a feeling of originality, of one-of-a-kind-ness, despite the fact that it had been quite obviously picked from a rack of dozens just like it. Her pumps did not match it; they were the same brown ones in which I had seen her last time.

I checked her over carefully and found her normal in every way. I told her so and she was pleased. "I found the pre-natal vitamins, Dr. McCarron."

"Did you? That's good."

Her eyes sparkled impishly. "The druggist advised me against them."

"God save me from pestle-pounders," I said, and she giggled

against the heel of her palm—it was a childlike gesture, winning in its unselfconsciousness. "I never met a druggist that wasn't a frustrated doctor. And a Republican. Pre-natal vitamins are new, so they're regarded with suspicion. Did you take his advice?"

"No, I took yours. You're my doctor."

"Thank you."

"Not at all." She looked at me straightforwardly, not giggling now. "Dr. McCarron, when will I begin to show?"

"Not until August, I should guess. September, if you choose garments which are . . . uh, voluminous."

"Thank you." She picked up her purse but did not rise immediately to go. I thought that she wanted to talk . . . and didn't know where or how to begin.

"You're a working woman, I take it?"

She nodded. "Yes. I work."

"Might I ask where? If you'd rather I didn't—"

She laughed—a brittle, humorless laugh, as different from a giggle as day is from dark. "In a department store. Where else does an unmarried woman work in the city? I sell perfume to fat ladies who rinse their hair and then have it done up in tiny finger-waves."

"How long will you continue?"

"Until my delicate condition is noticed. I suppose then I'll be asked to leave, lest I upset any of the fat ladies. The shock of being waited on by a pregnant woman with no wedding band might cause their hair to straighten."

Quite suddenly her eyes were bright with tears. Her lips began to tremble, and I groped for a handkerchief. But the tears didn't fall—not so much as a single one. Her eyes brimmed for a moment and then she blinked them back. Her lips tightened . . . and then smoothed out. She simply decided she was not going to lose control of her emotions . . . and she did not. It was a remarkable thing to watch.

"I'm sorry," she said. "You've been very kind to me. I won't repay your kindness with what would be a very common story."

She rose to go, and I rose with her.

"I'm not a bad listener," I said, "and I have some time. My next patient cancelled."

"No," she said. "Thank you, but no."

"All right," I said. "But there's something else."

"Yes?"

"It's not my policy to make my patients—*any* of my patients—pay for services in advance of those services' being rendered. I hope if you . . . that is, if you feel you'd like to . . . or have to . . ." I fumbled my way into silence.

"I've been in New York four years, Dr. McCarron, and I'm thrifty by nature. After August—or September—I'll have to live on what's in my savings account until I can go back to work again. It's not a great amount and sometimes, during the nights, mostly, I become frightened."

She looked at me steadily with those wonderful hazel eyes.

"It seemed better to me—safer—to pay for the baby first. Ahead of everything. Because that is where the baby is in my thoughts, and because, later on, the temptation to spend that money might become very great."

"All right," I said. "But please remember that I see it as having been paid before accounts. If you need it, say so."

"And bring out the dragon in Mrs. Davidson again?" The impish light was back in her eyes. "I don't think so. And now, doctor—"

"You intend to work as long as possible? Absolutely as long as possible?"

"Yes. I have to. Why?"

"I think I'm going to frighten you a little before you go," I said.

Her eyes widened slightly. "Don't do that," she said. "I'm frightened enough already."

"Which is exactly why I'm going to do it. Sit down again, Miss Stansfield." And when she only stood there, I added: "Please."

She sat. Reluctantly.

"You're in a unique and unenviable position," I told her, sitting on the corner of my desk. "You are dealing with the situation with remarkable grace."

She began to speak, and I held up my hand to silence her.

"That's good. I salute you for it. But I would hate to see you hurt your baby in any way out of concern for your own financial security. I had a patient who, in spite of my strenuous advice to the contrary, continued packing herself into a girdle month after month, strapping it tighter and tighter as her pregnancy progressed. She was a vain, stupid, tiresome woman, and I don't believe she really wanted the baby anyway. I don't subscribe to many of these theories of the subconscious which everyone seems to discuss over their Mah-Jongg boards these days, but if I did, I would say that she—or some part of her—was trying to kill the baby."

"And did she?" Her face was very still.

"No, not at all. But the baby was born retarded. It's very possible that the baby would have been born retarded anyway, and I'm not saying otherwise—we know next to nothing about what causes such things. But she *may* have caused it."

"I take your point," she said in a low voice. "You don't want me to . . . to pack myself in so I can work another month or six weeks. I'll admit the thought had crossed my mind. So . . . thank you for the fright."

This time I walked her to the door. I would have liked to ask her just how much—or how little—she had left in that savings book, and just how close to the edge she was. It was a question she would not answer; I knew that well enough. So I merely bade her goodbye and made a joke about her vitamins. She left. I found myself thinking about her at odd moments over the next month, and—

Johanssen interrupted McCarron's story at this point. They were old friends, and I suppose that gave him the right to ask the question that had surely crossed all our minds.

"Did you love her, Emlyn? Is that what all this is about, this stuff about her eyes and smile and how you 'thought of her at odd moments'?"

I thought that McCarron might be annoyed at this interruption, but he was not. "You have a right to ask the question," he said, and paused, looking into the fire. It seemed that he might almost have fallen into a doze. Then a dry knot of wood exploded, sending sparks up the chimney in a swirl, and McCarron looked around, first at Johanssen and then at the rest of us.

"No. I didn't love her. The things I've said about her sound like the things a man who is falling in love would notice—her eyes, her

dresses, her laugh." He lit his pipe with a special boltlike
pipe-lighter that he carried, drawing the flame until there was a bed
of coals there. Then he snapped the bolt shut, dropped it into the
pocket of his jacket, and blew out a plume of smoke that shifted
slowly around his head in an aromatic membrane.

"I admired her. That was the long and short of it. And my
admiration grew with each of her visits. I suppose some of you sense
this as a story of love crossed by circumstance. Nothing could be
further from the truth. Her story came out a bit at a time over the
next half-year or so, and when you gentlemen hear it, I think you'll
agree that it was every bit as common as she herself said it was. She
had been drawn to the city like a thousand other girls; she had come
from a small town . . .

. . . in Iowa or Nebraska. Or possibly it was Minnesota—I don't
really remember anymore. She had done a lot of high school
dramatics and community theater in her small town—good reviews
in the local weekly written by a drama critic with an English degree
from Cow and Sileage Junior College—and she came to New York
to try a career in acting.

She was practical even about that—as practical as an impractical
ambition will allow one to be, anyway. She came to New York, she
told me, because she didn't believe the unstated thesis of the movie
magazines—that any girl who came to Hollywood could become a
star, that she might be sipping a soda in Schwab's Drugstore one
day and playing opposite Gable or MacMurray the next. She came
to New York, she said, because she thought it might be easier to get
her foot in the door there . . . and, I think, because the legitimate
theater interested her more than the talkies.

She got a job selling perfume in one of the big department stores
and enrolled in acting classes. She was smart and terribly determined, this girl—her will was pure steel, through and through—
but she was as human as anyone else. She was lonely, too. Lonely in
a way that perhaps only single girls fresh from small Midwestern
towns know. Homesickness is not always a vague, nostalgic, almost
beautiful emotion, although that is somehow the way we always
seem to picture it in our mind. It can be a terribly keen blade, not

just a sickness in metaphor but in fact as well. It can change the way
one looks at the world; the faces one sees in the street look not just
indifferent but ugly . . . perhaps even malignant. Homesickness is
a real sickness—the ache of the uprooted plant.

Miss Stansfield, admirable as she may have been, determined as
she may have been, was not immune to it. And the rest follows so
naturally it needs no telling. There was a young man in her acting
classes. The two of them went out several times. She did not love
him, but she needed a friend. By the time she discovered he was not
that and never would be, there had been two incidents. Sexual
incidents. She discovered she was pregnant. She told the young
man, who told her he would stand by her and "do the decent
thing." A week later he was gone from his lodgings, leaving no
forwarding address. That was when she came to me.

During her fourth month, I introduced Miss Stansfield to the
Breathing Method—what is today called the Lamaze Method. In
those days, you understand, Monsieur Lamaze was yet to be heard
from.

"In those days"—the phrase has cropped up again and again, I
notice. I apologize for it but am unable to help it—so much of what
I have told you and will tell you happened as it did because it
happened "in those days."

So . . . "in those days," forty-five years ago, a visit to the
delivery rooms in any large American hospital would have sounded
to you like a visit to a madhouse. Women weeping wildly, women
screaming that they wished they were dead, women screaming that
they could not bear such agony, women screaming for Christ to
forgive them their sins, women screaming out strings of curses and
gutter-words their husbands and fathers never would have believed
they knew. All of this was quite the accepted thing, in spite of the
fact that most of the world's women give birth in almost complete
silence, aside from the grunting sounds of strain that we would
associate with any piece of hard physical labor.

Doctors were responsible for some of this hysteria, I'm sorry to
say. The stories the pregnant woman heard from friends and
relatives who had already been through the birthing process also

contributed to it. Believe me: if you are told that some experience is going to hurt, it *will* hurt. Most pain is in the mind, and when a woman absorbs the idea that the act of giving birth is excruciatingly painful—when she gets this information from her mother, her sisters, her married friends, *and* her physician—that woman has been mentally prepared to feel great agony.

Even after only six years' practice, I had become used to seeing women who were trying to cope with a twofold problem: not just the fact that they were pregnant and must plan for the new arrival, but also the fact—what most of them *saw* as a fact, anyway—*that they had entered the valley of the shadow of death.* Many were actually trying to put their affairs in coherent order so that if they *should* die, their husbands would be able to carry on without them.

This is neither the time nor the place for a lesson on obstetrics, but you should know that for a long time before "those days," the act of giving birth *was* extremely dangerous in the Western countries. A revolution in medical procedure, beginning around 1900, had made the process much safer, but an absurdly small number of doctors bothered to tell their expectant mothers that. God knows why. But in light of this, is it any wonder that most delivery rooms sounded like Ward Nine in Bellevue? Here are these poor women, their time come round at last, experiencing a process which has, because of the almost Victorian decorum of the times, been described to them only in the vaguest of terms; here are these women experiencing that engine of birth finally running at full power. They are seized with an awe and wonder which they immediately interpret as insupportable pain, and most of them feel that they will very shortly die a dog's death.

In the course of my reading on the subject of pregnancy, I discovered the principle of the silent birth and the idea of the Breathing Method. Screaming wastes energy which would be better used to expel the baby, it causes the woman to hyperventilate, and hyperventilation puts the body on an emergency basis—adrenals running full blast, respiration and pulse-rate up—that is really unnecessary. The Breathing Method was supposed to help the mother focus her attention on the job at hand and to cope with pain by utilizing the body's own resources.

It was used widely at that time in India and Africa; in America, the Shoshone, Kiowa, and Micmac Indians all used it; the Eskimos have always used it; but, as you may guess, most Western doctors had little interest in it. One of my colleagues—an intelligent man—returned the typescript of my pregnancy pamphlet to me in the fall of 1931 with a red line drawn through the entire section on the Breathing Method. In the margin he had scribbled that if he wanted to know about "nigger superstitions," he would stop by a newsstand and buy an issue of *Weird Tales*!

Well, I didn't cut the section from the pamphlet as he had suggested, but I had mixed results with the method—that was the best one could say. There were women who used it with great success. There were others who seemed to grasp the idea perfectly in principle but who lost their discipline completely as soon as their contractions became deep and heavy. In most of those cases I found that the entire idea had been subverted and undermined by well-meaning friends and relatives who had never heard of such a thing and thus could not believe it would actually work.

The method was based on the idea that, while no two labors are ever the same in their specifics, all are pretty much alike in general. There are four stages: contractive labor, mid-labor, birth, and the expulsion of the afterbirth. Contractions are a complete hardening of the abdominal and pelvic-area muscles, and the expectant mother often finds them beginning in the sixth month. Many women pregnant for the first time expect something rather nasty, like bowel cramps, but I'm told it's much cleaner—a strongly physical sensation, which may deepen into a pain like a charley horse. A woman employing the Breathing Method began to breathe in a series of short, measured inhales and exhales when she felt a contraction coming on. Each breath was expelled in a puff, as if one were blowing a trumpet Dizzy Gillespie fashion.

During mid-labor, when more painful contractions begin coming every fifteen minutes or so, the woman switched to long inhales followed by long exhales—it's the way a marathon runner breathes when he's starting his final kick. The harder the contraction, the longer the inhale-exhale. In my pamphlet, I called this stage "riding the waves."

The final stage we need concern ourselves with here I called "locomotive," and Lamaze instructors today frequently call it the "choo-choo" stage of breathing. Final labor is accompanied by pains which are most frequently described as deep and glassy. They are accompanied by an irresistible urge on the mother's part to push . . . to expel the baby. This is the point, gentlemen, at which that wonderful, frightening engine reaches its absolute crescendo. The cervix is fully dilated. The baby has begun its short journey down the birth canal, and if you were to look directly between the mother's legs, you would be apt to see the baby's fontanel pulsing only inches from the open air. The mother using the Breathing Method now begins to take and let out short, sharp breaths between her lips, not filling her lungs, not hyperventilating, but almost panting in a perfectly controlled fashion. It really is the sound children make when they are imitating a steam-driven locomotive.

All of this has a salutary effect on the body—the mother's oxygen is kept high without putting her systems on an emergency basis, and she herself remains aware and alert, able to ask and answer questions, able to take instructions. But of course the *mental* results of the Breathing Method were even more important. The mother felt she was actively participating in the birth of her child—that she was in some part guiding the process. She felt on top of the experience . . . and on top of the pain.

You can understand that the whole process was utterly dependent on the patient's state of mind. The Breathing Method was uniquely vulnerable, uniquely delicate, and if I had a good many failures, I'd explain them this way—what a patient can be convinced of by her doctor she may be unconvinced of by relatives who raise their hands in horror when told of such a heathenish practice.

From this aspect, at least, Miss Stansfield was the ideal patient. She had neither friends nor relatives to talk her out of her belief in the Breathing Method (although, in all fairness, I must add that I doubt anyone ever talked her out of *anything* once she had made up her mind on the subject) once she came to believe in it. And she *did* come to believe in it.

"It's a little like self-hypnosis, isn't it?" she asked me the first time we really discussed it.

I agreed, delighted. "Exactly! But you mustn't let that make you think it's a trick, or that it will let you down when the going gets tough."

"I don't think that at all. I'm very grateful to you. I'll practice assiduously, Dr. McCarron." She was the sort of woman the Breathing Method was invented for, and when she told me she would practice, she spoke nothing but the truth. I have never seen anyone embrace an idea with such enthusiasm . . . but, of course, the Breathing Method was uniquely suited to her temperament. There are docile men and women in this world by the millions, and some of them are damn fine people. But there are others whose hands ache to hold the throttles of their own lives, and Miss Stansfield was one of those.

When I say she embraced the Breathing Method totally, I mean it . . . and I think the story of her final day at the department store where she sold perfumes and cosmetics proves the point.

The end of her gainful employment finally came late in August. Miss Stansfield was a slim young woman in fine physical condition, and this was, of course, her first child. Any doctor will tell you that such a woman is apt not to "show" for five, perhaps even six months . . . and then, one day and all at once, *everything* will show.

She came in for her monthly checkup on the first of September, laughed ruefully, and told me she had discovered the Breathing Method had another use.

"What's that?" I asked her.

"It's even better than counting to ten when you're mad as hell at someone," she said. Those hazel eyes were dancing. "Although people look at you as if you might be a lunatic when you start puffing and blowing."

She told me the tale readily enough. She had gone to work as usual on the previous Monday, and all I can think is that the curiously abrupt transition from a slim young woman to an obviously pregnant young woman—and that transition really can be almost as sudden as day to dark in the tropics—had happened over the weekend. Or maybe her supervisor finally decided that her suspicions were no longer just suspicions.

"I'll want to see you in the office on your break," this woman, a

Mrs. Kelly, said coldly. She had previously been quite friendly to Miss Stansfield. She had shown her pictures of her two children, both in high school, and they had exchanged recipes at one point. Mrs. Kelly was always asking her if she had met "a nice boy" yet. That kindliness and friendliness was gone now. And when she stepped into Mrs. Kelly's office on her break, Miss Stansfield told me, she knew what to expect.

"You're in trouble," this previously kind woman said curtly.

"Yes," Miss Stansfield said. "It's called that by some people."

Mrs. Kelly's cheeks had gone the color of old brick. "Don't you be smart with me, young woman," she said. "From the looks of your belly, you've been too smart by half already."

I could see the two of them in my mind's eye as she told me the story—Miss Stansfield, her direct hazel eyes fixed on Mrs. Kelly, perfectly composed, refusing to drop her eyes, or weep, or exhibit shame in any other way. I believe she had a much more practical conception of the trouble she was in than her supervisor did, with her two almost-grown children and her respectable husband, who owned his own barber-shop and voted Republican.

"I must say you show remarkably little shame at the way you've deceived me!" Mrs. Kelly burst out bitterly.

"I have never deceived you. No mention of my pregnancy has been made until today." She looked at Mrs. Kelly curiously. "How can you say I have deceived you?"

"I took you home!" Mrs. Kelly cried. "I had you to dinner . . . with my *sons*." She looked at Miss Stansfield with utter loathing.

This is when Miss Stansfield began to grow angry. Angrier, she told me, than she had ever been in her life. She had not been unaware of the sort of reaction she could expect when the secret came out, but as any one of you gentlemen will attest, the difference between academic theory and practical application can sometimes be shockingly huge.

Clutching her hands firmly together in her lap, Miss Stansfield said: "If you are suggesting I made or ever would make any attempt to seduce your sons, that's the dirtiest, filthiest thing I've ever heard in my life."

Mrs. Kelly's head rocked back as if she had been slapped. That bricky color drained from her cheeks, leaving only two small spots of hectic color. The two women looked grimly at each other across a desk littered with perfume samples in a room that smelled vaguely of flowers. It was a moment, Miss Stansfield said, that seemed much longer than it actually could have been.

Then Mrs. Kelly yanked open one of her drawers and brought out a buff-colored check. A bright pink severance slip was attached to it. Showing her teeth, actually seeming to bite off each word, she said: "With hundreds of decent girls looking for work in this city, I hardly think we need a strumpet such as yourself in our employ, dear."

She told me it was that final, contemptuous "dear" that brought all her anger to a sudden head. A moment later Mrs. Kelly's jaw dropped and her eyes widened as Miss Stansfield, her hands locked together as tightly as links in a steel chain, so tightly she left bruises on herself (they were fading but still perfectly visible when I saw her on September 1st), began to "locomotive" between her clenched teeth.

It wasn't a funny story, perhaps, but I burst out laughing at the image and Miss Stansfield joined me. Mrs. Davidson looked in—to make sure we hadn't gotten into the nitrous oxide, perhaps—and then left again.

"It was all I could think to *do*," Miss Stansfield said, still laughing and wiping her streaming eyes with her handkerchief. "Because at that moment, I saw myself reaching out and simply sweeping those sample bottles of perfume—every one of them—off her desk and onto the floor, which was uncarpeted concrete. I didn't just *think* it, I *saw* it! I saw them crashing to the floor and filling the room with such a God-awful mixed stench that the fumigators would have to come.

"I was going to do it; nothing was going to stop me doing it. Then I began to 'locomotive,' and everything was all right. I was able to take the check, and the pink slip, and get up, and get out. I wasn't able to thank her, of course—I was still being a locomotive!"

We laughed again, and then she sobered.

"It's all passed off now, and I am even able to feel a little sorry for her—or does that sound like a terribly stiff-necked thing to say?"

"Not at all. I think it's an admirable way to be able to feel."

"May I show you something I bought with my severance pay, Dr. McCarron?"

"Yes, if you like."

She opened her purse and took out a small flat box. "I bought it at a pawnshop," she said. "For two dollars. And it's the only time during this whole nightmare that I've felt ashamed and dirty. Isn't that strange?"

She opened the box and laid it on my desk so I could look inside. I wasn't surprised at what I saw. It was a plain gold wedding ring.

"I'll do what's necessary," she said. "I am staying in what Mrs. Kelly would undoubtedly call 'a respectable boarding house.' My landlady has been kind and friendly . . . but Mrs. Kelly was kind and friendly, too. I think she may ask me to leave at any time now, and I suspect that if I say anything about the rent-balance due me, or the damage deposit I paid when I moved in, she'll laugh in my face."

"My dear young woman, that would be quite illegal. There are courts and lawyers to help you answer such—"

"The courts are men's clubs," she said steadily, "and not apt to go out of their way to befriend a woman in my position. Perhaps I could get my money back, perhaps not. Either way, the expense and the trouble and the . . . the unpleasantness . . . hardly seem worth the forty-seven dollars or so. I had no business mentioning it to you in the first place. It hasn't happened yet, and maybe it won't. But in any case, I intend to be practical from now on."

She raised her head, and her eyes flashed at mine.

"I've got my eye on a place down in the Village—just in case. It's on the third floor, but it's clean, and it's five dollars a month cheaper than where I'm staying now." She picked the ring out of the box. "I wore this when the landlady showed me the room."

She put it on the third finger of her left hand with a small moue of disgust of which I believe she was unaware. "There. Now I'm Mrs. Stansfield. My husband was a truck-driver who was killed on the Pittsburgh–New York run. Very sad. But I am no longer a little roundheels strumpet, and my child is no longer a bastard."

She looked up at me, and the tears were in her eyes again. As I watched, one of them overspilled and rolled down her cheek.

"Please," I said, distressed, and reached across the desk to take her hand. It was very, very cold. "Don't, my dear."

She turned her hand—it was the left—over in my hand and looked at the ring. She smiled, and that smile was as bitter as gall and vinegar, gentlemen. Another tear fell—just that one.

"When I hear cynics say that the days of magic and miracles are all behind us, Dr. McCarron, I'll know they're deluded, won't I? When you can buy a ring in a pawnshop for two dollars and that ring will instantly erase both bastardy and licentiousness, what else would you call that but magic? Cheap magic."

"Miss Stansfield . . . Sandra, if I may . . . if you need help, if there's anything I can do—"

She drew her hand away from me—if I had taken her right hand instead of her left, perhaps she would not have done. I did not love her, I've told you, but in that moment I could have loved her; I was on the verge of falling in love with her. Perhaps, if I'd taken her right hand instead of the one with that lying ring on it, and if she had allowed me to hold her hand only a little longer, until my own warmed it, perhaps then I should have.

"You're a good, kind man, and you've done a great deal for me and my baby . . . and your Breathing Method is a much better kind of magic than this awful ring. After all, it kept me from being jailed on charges of willful destruction, didn't it?"

She left soon after that, and I went to the window to watch her move off down the street toward Fifth Avenue. God, I admired her just then! She looked so slight, so young, and so obviously pregnant—but there was still nothing timid or tentative about her. She did not scutter up the street; she walked as if she had every right to her place on the sidewalk.

She left my view and I turned back to my desk. As I did so, the framed photograph which hung on the wall next to my diploma caught my eye, and a terrible shudder worked through me. My skin—all of it, even the skin on my forehead and the backs of my hands—crawled up into cold knots of gooseflesh. The most suffocating fear of my entire life fell on me like a horrible shroud, and I found myself gasping for breath. It was a precognitive interlude, gentlemen. I do not take part in arguments about whether or not such things can occur; I know they can, because it has happened to me. Just that once, on that hot early September afternoon. I pray to God I never have another.

The photograph had been taken by my mother on the day I finished medical school. It showed me standing in front of White Memorial, hands behind my back, grinning like a kid who's just gotten a full-day pass to the rides at Palisades Park. To my left the statue of Harriet White can be seen, and although the photograph cuts her off at about mid-shin, the pedestal and that queerly heartless inscription—*There is no comfort without pain; thus we define salvation through suffering*—could be clearly seen. It was at the foot of the statue of my father's first wife, directly below that inscription, that Sandra Stansfield died not quite four months later in a senseless accident that occurred just as she arrived at the hospital to deliver her child.

She exhibited some anxiety that fall that I would not be there to attend her during her labor—that I would be away for the Christmas holidays or not on call. She was partly afraid that she would be delivered by some doctor who would ignore her wish to use the Breathing Method and who would instead give her gas or a spinal block.

I assured her as best I could. I had no reason to leave the city, no family to visit over the holidays. My mother had died two years before, and there was no one else except a maiden aunt in California . . . and the train didn't agree with me, I told Miss Stansfield.

"Are you ever lonely?" she asked.

"Sometimes. Usually I keep too busy. Now, take this." I jotted my home telephone number on a card and gave it to her. "If you get the answering service when your labor begins, call me here."

"Oh, no, I couldn't—"

"Do you want to use the Breathing Method, or do you want to get some sawbones who'll think you're mad and give you a capful of ether as soon as you start to 'locomotive'?"

She smiled a little. "All right. I'm convinced."

But as the autumn progressed and the butchers on Third Avenue began advertising the per-pound price of their "young and succulent Toms," it became clear that her mind was still not at rest. She had indeed been asked to leave the place where she had been living when I first met her, and had moved to the Village. But that, at least, had turned out quite well for her. She had even found work of a sort. A blind woman with a fairly comfortable income had hired her to do some light housework, and then to read to her from the works of Gene Stratton Porter and Pearl Buck. She lived on the first floor of Miss Stansfield's building. She had taken on that blooming, rosy look that most healthy women come to have during the final trimester of their pregnancies. But there was a shadow on her face. I would speak to her and she would be slow to answer . . . and once, when she didn't answer at all, I looked up from the notes I was making and saw her looking at the framed photograph next to my diploma with a strange, dreamy expression in her eyes. I felt a recurrence of that chill . . . and her response, which had nothing to do with my question, hardly made me feel easier.

"I have a feeling, Dr. McCarron, sometimes quite a strong feeling, that I am doomed."

Silly, melodramatic word! And yet, gentlemen, the response that rose to my own lips was this: *Yes; I feel that, too.* I bit it off, of course; a doctor who would say such a thing should immediately put his instruments and medical books up for sale and investigate his future in the plumbing or carpentry business.

I told her that she was not the first pregnant woman to have such feelings, and would not be the last. I told her that the feeling was indeed so common that doctors knew it by the tongue-in-cheek name of The Valley of the Shadow Syndrome. I've already mentioned it tonight, I believe.

Miss Stansfield nodded with perfect seriousness, and I remember how young she looked that day, and how large her belly seemed. "I know about that," she said. "I've felt it. But it's quite separate from this other feeling. This other feeling is like . . . like something looming up. I can't describe it any better than that. It's silly, but I can't shake it."

"You must try," I said. "It isn't good for the—"

But she had drifted away from me. She was looking at the photograph again.

"Who is that?"

"Emlyn McCarron," I said, trying to make a joke. It sounded extraordinarily feeble. "Back before the Civil War, when he was quite young."

"No, I recognized you, of course," she said. "The woman. You can only tell it *is* a woman from the hem of the skirt and the shoes. Who is she?"

"Her name is Harriet White," I said, and thought: *And hers will be the first face you see when you arrive to deliver your child.* The chill came back—that dreadful drifting formless chill. *Her stone face.*

"And what does it say there at the base of the statue?" she asked, her eyes still dreamy, almost trancelike.

"I don't know," I lied. "My conversational Latin is not that good."

That night I had the worst dream of my entire life—I woke up from it in utter terror, and if I had been married, I suppose I would have frightened my poor wife to death.

In the dream I opened the door to my consulting room and found Sandra Stansfield in there. She was wearing the brown pumps, the smart white linen dress with the brown edging, and the slightly out-of-date cloche hat. But the hat was between her breasts, because she was carrying her head in her arms. The white linen was stained and streaked with gore. Blood jetted from her neck and splattered the ceiling.

And then her eyes fluttered open—those wonderful hazel eyes— and they fixed on mine.

"Doomed," the speaking head told me. "Doomed. I'm doomed. There's no salvation without suffering. It's cheap magic, but it's all we have."

That's when I woke up screaming.

Her due date of December 10th came and went. I examined her on December 17th and suggested that, while the baby would almost certainly be born in 1935, I no longer expected the child to put in his or her appearance until after Christmas. Miss Stansfield accepted this with good grace. She seemed to have thrown off the shadow that had hung over her that fall. Mrs. Gibbs, the blind woman who had hired her to read aloud and do light housework, was impressed with her—impressed enough to tell her friends about the brave young widow who, in spite of her recent bereavement and delicate condition, was facing her own future with such determined good cheer. Several of the blind woman's friends had expressed an interest in employing her following the birth of her child.

"I'll take them up on it, too," she told me. "For the baby. But only until I'm on my feet again, and able to find something steady. Sometimes I think the worst part of this—of everything that's happened—is that it's changed the way I look at people. Sometimes I think to myself, 'How can you sleep at night, knowing that you've deceived that dear old thing?' and then I think, 'If she knew, she'd show you the door, just like all the others.' Either way, it's a lie, and I feel the weight of it on my heart sometimes."

Before she left that day, she took a small, gaily wrapped package from her purse and slid it shyly across the desk to me. "Merry Christmas, Dr. McCarron."

"You shouldn't have," I said, sliding open a drawer and taking out a package of my own. "But since I did, too—"

She looked at me for a moment, surprised . . . and then we laughed together. She had gotten me a silver tie-clasp with a caduceus on it. I had gotten her an album in which to keep photographs of her baby. I still have the tie-clasp; as you see, gentlemen, I am wearing it tonight. What happened to the album, I cannot say.

I saw her to the door, and as we reached it, she turned to me, put her hands on my shoulders, stood on tiptoe, and kissed me on the mouth. Her lips were cool and firm. It was not a passionate kiss, gentlemen, but neither was it the sort of kiss you might expect from a sister or an aunt.

"Thank you again, Dr. McCarron," she said a little breathlessly. The color was high in her cheeks and her hazel eyes glowed lustrously. "Thank you for so much."

I laughed—a little uneasily. "You speak as if we'd never meet again, Sandra." It was, I believe, the second and last time I ever used her Christian name.

"Oh, we'll meet again," she said. "I don't doubt it a bit."

And she was right—although neither of us could have foreseen the dreadful circumstances of that last meeting.

Sandra Stansfield's labor began on Christmas Eve, at just past six P.M. By that time, the snow which had fallen all that day had changed to sleet. And by the time Miss Stansfield entered mid-labor, not quite two hours later, the city streets were a dangerous glaze of ice.

Mrs. Gibbs, the blind woman, had a large and spacious first-floor apartment, and at six-thirty P.M. Miss Stansfield worked her way carefully downstairs, knocked at her door, was admitted, and asked if she might use the telephone to call a cab.

"Is it the baby, dear?" Mrs. Gibbs asked, fluttering already.

"Yes. The labor's only begun, but I can't chance the weather. It will take a cab a long time."

She made that call and then called me. At that time, six-forty, the pains were coming at intervals of about twenty-five minutes. She repeated to me that she had begun everything early because of the foul weather. "I'd rather not have my child in the back of a Yellow," she said. She sounded extraordinarily calm.

The cab was late and Miss Stansfield's labor was progressing more rapidly than I would have predicted—but as I have said, no two labors are alike in their specifics. The driver, seeing that his fare was about to have a baby, helped her down the slick steps, constantly adjuring her to "be careful, lady." Miss Stansfield only nodded, preoccupied with her deep inhale-exhales as a fresh contraction seized her. Sleet ticked off streetlights and the roofs of cars; it melted in large, magnifying drops on the taxi's yellow dome-light. Mrs. Gibbs told me later that the young cab driver was more nervous than her "poor, dear Sandra," and that was probably a contributing cause to the accident.

Another was almost certainly the Breathing Method itself.

The driver threaded his hack through the slippery streets,

working his way slowly past the fender-benders and inching through the clogged intersections, slowly closing on the hospital. He was not seriously injured in the accident, and I talked to him in the hospital. He said the sound of the steady deep breathing coming from the back seat made him nervous; he kept looking in the rearview mirror to see if she was "dine or sumpin." He said he would have felt less nervous if she had let out a few healthy bellows, the way a woman in labor was supposed to do. He asked her once or twice if she was feeling all right and she only nodded, continuing to "ride the waves" in deep inhales and exhales.

Two or three blocks from the hospital, she must have felt the onset of labor's final stage. An hour had passed since she had entered the cab—traffic was that snarled—but this was still an extraordinarily fast labor for a woman having her first baby. The driver noticed the change in the way she was breathing. "She started pantin like a dog on a hot day, doc," he told me. She had begun to "locomotive."

At almost the same time the cabbie saw a hole open up in the crawling traffic and shot through it. The way to White Memorial was now open. It was less than three blocks ahead. "I could see the statue of that broad," he said. Eager to be rid of his panting, pregnant passenger, he stepped down on the gas again and the cab leaped forward, wheels spinning over the ice with little or no traction.

I had walked to the hospital, and my arrival coincided with the cab's arrival only because I had underestimated just how bad driving conditions had become. I believed I would find her upstairs, a legally admitted patient with all her papers signed, her prep completed, working her way steadily through her mid-labor. I was mounting the steps when I saw the sudden sharp convergence of two sets of headlights reflected from the patch of ice where the janitors hadn't yet spread cinders. I turned just in time to see it happen.

An ambulance was nosing its way out of the Emergency Wing rampway as Miss Stansfield's cab came toward the hospital. The cab was simply going too fast to stop. The cabbie panicked and stamped down on the brake-pedal rather than pumping it. The cab slid, then began to turn broadside. The pulsing dome-light of the ambulance threw moving stripes and blotches of blood-colored light over the scene, and, freakishly, one of these illuminated the face of Sandra Stansfield. For that one moment it was the face in my dream, the same bloody, open-eyed face that I had seen on her severed head.

I cried out her name, took two steps down, slipped, and fell sprawling. I cracked my elbow a paralyzing blow but somehow managed to hold onto my black bag. I saw the rest of what happened from where I lay, head ringing, elbow smarting.

The ambulance braked, and it also began to fishtail. Its rear end struck the base of the statue. The loading doors flew open. A stretcher, mercifully empty, shot out like a tongue and then crashed upside down in the street with its wheels spinning. A young woman on the sidewalk screamed and tried to run as the two vehicles approached each other. Her feet went out from under her after two strides and she fell on her stomach. Her purse flew out of her hand and shot down the icy sidewalk like a weight in a pinball bowling game.

The cab swung all the way around, now travelling backwards, and I could see the cabbie clearly. He was spinning his wheel madly, like a kid in a Dodgem Car. The ambulance rebounded from Harriet White's statue at an angle . . . and smashed broadside into the cab. The taxi spun around once in a tight circle and was slammed against the base of the statue with fearful force. Its yellow light, the letters ON RADIO CALL still flashing, exploded like a bomb. The left side of the cab crumpled like tissue-paper. A moment later I saw that it was not just the left side; the cab had struck an angle of the pedestal hard enough to tear it in two. Glass sprayed onto the slick ice like diamonds. And my patient was thrown through the rear right-side window of the dismembered cab like a rag-doll.

I was on my feet again without even knowing it. I raced down the icy steps, slipped again, caught at the railing, and kept on. I was only aware of Miss Stansfield lying in the uncertain shadow cast by that hideous statue of Harriet White, some twenty feet from where the ambulance had come to rest on its side, flasher still strobing the night with red. There was something terribly wrong with that figure, but I honestly don't believe I knew what it was until my foot struck something with a heavy enough thud to almost send me sprawling again. The thing I'd kicked skittered away—like the young woman's purse, it slid rather than rolled. It skittered away and it was only the fall of hair—bloodstreaked but still recognizably blonde, speckled with bits of glass—that made me realize what it was. She had been decapitated in the accident. What I had kicked into the frozen gutter was her head.

Moving in total numb shock now, I reached her body and turned it over. I think I tried to scream as soon as I had done it, as soon as I saw. If I did, no sound came out; I could not make a sound. The woman was still breathing, you see, gentlemen. Her chest was heaving up and down in quick, light, shallow breaths. Ice pattered down on her open coat and her blood-drenched dress. And I could hear a high, thin whistling noise. It waxed and waned like a teakettle which can't quite reach the boil. It was air being pulled into her severed windpipe and then exhaled again; little screams of air through the crude reed of vocal cords which no longer had a mouth to shape their sounds.

I wanted to run but I had no strength; I fell on my knees beside her on the ice, one hand cupped to my mouth. A moment later I was aware of fresh blood seeping through the lower part of her dress . . . and of movement there. I became suddenly, frenziedly convinced that there was still a chance to save the baby.

I believe that as I yanked her dress up to her waist I began laughing. I believe I was mad. Her body was still warm. I remember that. I remember the way it heaved with her breathing. One of the ambulance attendants came up, weaving like a drunk, one hand clapped to the side of his head. Blood trickled through his fingers.

I was still laughing, still groping. My hands had found her fully dilated.

The attendant stared down at Sandra Stansfield's headless body with wide eyes. I don't know if he realized the corpse was still breathing or not. Perhaps he thought it was merely a thing of the nerves—a kind of final reflex action. If he did think such a thing, he could not have been driving an ambulance long. Chickens may walk around for awhile with their heads cut off, but people only twitch once or twice . . . if that.

"Stop staring at her and get me a blanket," I snapped at him.

He wandered away, but not back toward the ambulance. He was pointed more or less toward Times Square. He simply walked off into the sleety night. I have no idea what became of him. I turned back to the dead woman who was somehow not dead, hesitated a moment, and then stripped off my overcoat. Then I lifted her hips so I could get it under her. Still I heard that whistle of breath as her headless body did "locomotive" breathing. I sometimes hear it still, gentlemen. In my dreams.

Please understand that all of this had happened in an extremely short time—it seemed longer to me, but only because my perceptions had been heightened to a feverish pitch. People were only beginning to run out of the hospital to see what had happened, and behind me a woman shrieked as she saw the severed head lying by the edge of the street.

I yanked open my black bag, thanking God I hadn't lost it in my fall, and pulled out a short scalpel. I opened it, cut through her underwear, and pulled it off. Now the ambulance driver approached —he came to within fifteen feet of us and then stopped dead. I glanced over at him, still wanting that blanket. I wasn't going to get it from him, I saw; he was staring down at the breathing body, his eyes widening until it seemed they must slip from their orbits and simply dangle from their optic nerves like grotesque seeing yo-yos. Then he dropped to his knees and raised his clasped hands. He meant to pray, I am quite sure of that. The attendant might not have known he was seeing an impossibility, but this fellow did. The next moment he had fainted dead away.

I had packed forceps in my bag that night; I don't know why. I hadn't used such things in three years, not since I had seen a doctor I will not name punch through a newborn's temple and into the child's brain with one of those infernal gadgets. The child died instantly. The corpse was "lost" and what went on the death certificate was *stillborn*.

But, for whatever reason, I had mine with me that night.

Miss Stansfield's body tightened down, her belly clenching, turning from flesh to stone. And the baby crowned. I saw the crown for just a moment, bloody and membranous and pulsing. *Pulsing.* It was alive, then. Definitely alive.

Stone became flesh again. The crown slipped back out of sight. And a voice behind me said: "What can I do, doctor?"

It was a middle-aged nurse, the sort of woman who is so often the backbone of our profession. Her face was as pale as milk, and while there was terror and a kind of superstitious awe on her face as she looked down at that weirdly breathing body, there was none of that dazed shock which would have made her difficult and dangerous to work with.

"You can get me a blanket, stat," I said curtly. "We've still got a chance, I think." Behind her I saw perhaps two dozen people from the hospital standing on the steps, not wanting to come any closer. How much or how little did they see? I have no way of knowing for sure. All I know is that I was avoided for days afterwards (and forever by some of them), and no one, including this nurse, ever spoke to me of it.

She now turned and started back toward the hospital.

"Nurse!" I called. "No time for that. Get one from the ambulance. This baby is coming *now*."

She changed course, slipping and sliding through the slush in her white crepe-soled shoes. I turned back to Miss Stansfield.

Rather than slowing down, the locomotive breathing had actually begun to speed up . . . and then her body turned hard again, locked and straining. The baby crowned again. I waited for it to slip back but it did not; it simply kept coming. There was no need for the forceps after all. The baby all but *flew* into my hands. I saw the sleet ticking off his naked, bloody body—for it *was* a boy, his sex unmistakable. I saw steam rising from him as the black, icy night snatched away the last of his mother's heat. His blood-grimed fists waved feebly; he uttered a thin, wailing cry.

"*Nurse!*" I bawled, "*move your ass, you bitch!*" It was perhaps inexcusable language, but for a moment I felt I was back in France, that in a few moments the shells would begin to whistle overhead with a sound like that remorselessly ticking sleet; the machine-guns would begin their hellish stutter; the Germans would begin to materialize out of the murk, running and slipping and cursing and dying in the mud and smoke. *Cheap magic*, I thought, seeing the bodies twist and turn and fall. *But you're right, Sandra, it's all we have*. It was the closest I have ever come to losing my mind, gentlemen.

"NURSE, FOR GOD'S SAKE!"

The baby wailed again—such a tiny, lost sound!—and then he wailed no more. The steam rising from his skin had thinned to ribbons. I put my mouth against his face, smelling blood and the bland, damp aroma of placenta. I breathed into his mouth and heard the jerky susurrus of his breathing resume. Then the nurse was there, the blanket in her arms. I held out my hand for it.

She started to give it to me, and then held it back. "Doctor, what . . . what if it's a monster? Some kind of monster?"

"Give me that blanket," I said. "Give it to me now, Sarge, before I kick your asshole right up to your shoulderblades."

"Yes, doctor," she said with perfect calmness (we must bless the women, gentlemen, who so often understand simply by not trying to), and gave me the blanket. I wrapped the child and gave him to her.

"If you drop him, Sarge, you'll be eating those stripes."

"Yes, doctor."

"It's cheap fucking magic, Sarge, but it's all God left us with."

"Yes, doctor."

I watched her half-walk, half-run back to the hospital with the child and watched the crowd on the steps part for her. Then I rose to my feet and backed away from the body. Its breathing, like the baby's, hitched and caught . . . stopped . . . hitched again . . . stopped . . .

I began to back away from it. My foot struck something. I turned. It was her head. And obeying some directive from outside of me, I dropped to one knee and turned the head over. The eyes were open—those direct hazel eyes that had always been full of such life and such determination. They were full of determination still. Gentlemen, *she was seeing me*.

Her teeth were clenched, her lips slightly parted. I heard the breath slipping rapidly back and forth between those lips and through those teeth as she "locomotived." Her eyes moved; they rolled slightly to the left in their sockets so as to see me better. Her lips parted. They mouthed four words: *Thank you, Dr. McCarron*.

And I *heard* them, gentlemen, but not from her mouth. They came from twenty feet away. From her vocal cords. And because her tongue and lips and teeth, all of which we use to shape our words, were here, they came out only in unformed modulations of sound. But there were seven of them, seven distinct sounds, just as there are seven syllables in that phrase, *Thank you, Dr. McCarron.*

"You're welcome, Miss Stansfield," I said. "It's a boy."

Her lips moved again, and from behind me, thin, ghostly, came the sound *hoyyyyyy*—

Her eyes lost their focus and their determination. They seemed now to look at something beyond me, perhaps in that black, sleety sky. Then they closed. She began to "locomotive" again . . . and then she simply stopped. Whatever had happened was now over. The nurse had seen some of it, the ambulance driver had perhaps seen some of it before he fainted, and some of the onlookers might have suspected something. But it was over now, over for sure. There was only the remains of an ugly accident out here . . . and a new baby in there.

I looked up at the statue of Harriet White and there she still stood, looking stonily away toward the Garden across the way, as if nothing of any particular note had happened, as if such determination in a world as hard and as senseless as this one meant nothing . . . or worse still, that it was perhaps the only thing which meant *anything*, the only thing that made any difference at all.

As I recall, I knelt there in the slush before her severed head and began to weep. As I recall, I was still weeping when an intern and two nurses helped me to my feet and inside.

McCarron's pipe had gone out.

He re-lit it with his bolt-lighter while we sat in perfect, breathless silence. Outside, the wind howled and moaned. He snapped his lighter closed and looked up. He seemed mildly surprised to find us still there.

"That's all," he said. "That's the end! What are you waiting for? Chariots of fire?" he snorted, then seemed to debate for a moment. "I paid her burial expenses out of my own pocket. She had no one else, you see." He smiled a little. "Well . . . there was Ella

Davidson, my nurse. She insisted on chipping in twenty-five dollars, which she could ill afford. But when Davidson insisted on a thing—" He shrugged, and then laughed a little.

"You're quite sure it wasn't a reflex?" I heard myself demanding suddenly. "Are you *quite* sure—"

"Quite sure," McCarron said imperturbably. "The first contraction, perhaps. But the completion of her labor was not a matter of seconds but of minutes. And I sometimes think she might have held on even longer, if it had been necessary. Thank God it was not."

"What about the baby?" Johanssen asked.

McCarron puffed at his pipe. "Adopted," he said. "And you'll understand that, even in those days, adoption records were kept as secret as possible."

"Yes, but what about the baby?" Johanssen asked again, and McCarron laughed in a cross way.

"You never let go of a thing, do you?" he asked Johanssen.

Johanssen shook his head. "Some people have learned it to their sorrow. What about the baby?"

"Well, if you've come with me this far, perhaps you'll also understand that I had a certain vested interest in knowing how it all came out for that child. Or I felt I did, which comes to the same. I did keep track, and I still do. There was a young man and his wife—their name was not Harrison, but that is close enough. They lived in Maine. They could have no children of their own. They adopted the child and named him . . . well, John's good enough, isn't it? John will do you fellows, won't it?"

He puffed at his pipe but it had gone out again. I was faintly aware of Stevens hovering behind me, and knew that somewhere our coats would be at the ready. Soon we would slip back into them . . . and back into our lives. As McCarron had said, the tales were done for another year.

"The child I delivered that night is now head of the English Department at one of the two or three most respected private colleges in the country," McCarron said. "He's not forty-five yet. A young man. It's early for him, but the day may well come when he will be President of that school. I shouldn't doubt it a bit. He is handsome, intelligent, and charming.

"Once, on a pretext, I was able to dine with him in the private faculty club. We were four that evening. I said little and so was able to watch him. He has his mother's determination, gentlemen . . .

". . . and his mother's hazel eyes."

III.
The Club

Stevens saw us out as he always did, holding coats, wishing men the happiest of happy Christmases, thanking them for their generosity. I contrived to be the last, and Stevens looked at me with no surprise when I said:

"I have a question I'd like to ask, if you don't mind."

He smiled a little. "I suppose you should," he said. "Christmas is a fine time for questions."

Somewhere down the hallway to our left—a hall I had never been down—a grandfather clock ticked sonorously, the sound of the age passing away. I could smell old leather and oiled wood and, much more faintly than either of these, the smell of Stevens's aftershave.

"But I should warn you," Stevens added as the wind rose in a gust outside, "it's better not to ask too much. Not if you want to keep coming here."

"People have been closed out for asking too much?" *Closed out* was not really the phrase I wanted, but it was as close as I could come.

"No," Stevens said, his voice as low and polite as ever. "They simply choose to stay away."

I returned his gaze, feeling a chill prickle its way up my back—it was as if a large, cold, invisible hand had been laid on my spine. I found myself remembering that strangely liquid thump I had heard upstairs one night and wondered (as I had more than once before) exactly how many rooms there really *were* here.

"If you still have a question, Mr. Adley, perhaps you'd better ask it. The evening's almost over—"

"And you have a long train-ride ahead of you?" I asked, but Stevens only looked at me impassively. "All right," I said. "There are books in this library that I can't find anywhere else—not in the New York Public Library, not in the catalogues of any of the antiquarian book-dealers I've checked with, and certainly not in

Books in Print. The billiard table in the Small Room is a Nord. I'd never heard of such a brand, and so I called the International Trademark Commission. They have two Nords—one makes cross-country skis and the other makes wooden kitchen accessories. There's a Seafront jukebox in the Long Room. The ITC has a See*burg* listed, but no Sea*front.*"

"What is your question, Mr. Adley?"

His voice was as mild as ever, but there was something terrible in his eyes suddenly . . . no; if I am to be truthful, it was not just in his eyes; the terror I felt had infused the atmosphere all around me. The steady tock-tock from down the lefthand hall was no longer the pendulum of a grandfather clock; it was the tapping foot of the executioner as he watches the condemned led to the scaffold. The smells of oil and leather turned bitter and menacing, and when the wind rose in another wild whoop, I felt momentarily sure that the front door would blow open, revealing not Thirty-fifth Street but an insane Clark Ashton Smith landscape where the bitter shapes of twisted trees stood silhouetted on a sterile horizon below which double suns were setting in a gruesome red glare.

Oh, he knew what I had meant to ask; I saw it in his gray eyes.

Where do all these things come from? I had meant to ask. *Oh, I know well enough where* you *come from, Stevens; that accent isn't Dimension X, it's pure Brooklyn. But where do you go? What has put that timeless look in your eyes and stamped it on your face? And, Stevens—*

—where are we RIGHT THIS SECOND?

But he was waiting for my question.

I opened my mouth. And the question that came out was: "Are there many more rooms upstairs?"

"Oh, yes, sir," he said, his eyes never leaving mine. "A great many. A man could become lost. In fact, men *have* become lost. Sometimes it seems to me that they go on for miles. Rooms and corridors."

"And entrances and exits?"

His eyebrows went up slightly. "Oh yes. Entrances and exits."

He waited, but I had asked enough, I thought—I had come to the very edge of something that would, perhaps, drive me mad.

"Thank you, Stevens."

"Of course, sir." He held out my coat and I slipped into it.

"There will be more tales?"

"Here, sir, there are *always* more tales."

That evening was some time ago, and my memory has not improved between then and now (when a man reaches my age, the opposite is much more likely to be true), but I remember with perfect clarity the stab of fear that went through me when Stevens swung the oaken door wide—the cold certainty that I would see that alien landscape, cracked and hellish in the bloody light of those double suns, which might set and bring on an unspeakable darkness of an hour's duration, or ten hours, or ten thousand years. I cannot explain it, but I tell you that world *exists*—I am as sure of that as Emlyn McCarron was sure that the severed head of Sandra Stansfield went on breathing. I thought for that one timeless second that the door would open and Stevens would thrust me out into that world and I would then hear that door slam shut behind me . . . forever.

Instead, I saw Thirty-fifth Street and a radio-cab standing at the curb, exhaling plumes of exhaust. I felt an utter, almost debilitating relief.

"Yes, always more tales," Stevens repeated. "Goodnight, sir."

Always more tales.

Indeed there have been. And, one day soon, perhaps I'll tell you another.

Afterword

Although "Where do you get your ideas?" has always been the question I'm most frequently asked (it's number one with a bullet, you might say), the runner-up is undoubtedly this one: "Is horror *all* you write?" When I say it isn't, it's hard to tell if the questioner seems relieved or disappointed.

Just before the publication of *Carrie*, my first novel, I got a letter from my editor, Bill Thompson, suggesting it was time to start thinking about what we were going to do for an encore (it may strike you as a bit strange, this thinking about the next book before the first was even out, but because the pre-publication schedule for a novel is almost as long as the post-production schedule on a film, we had been living with *Carrie* for a long time at that point—nearly a year). I promptly sent Bill the manuscripts of two novels, one called *Blaze* and one called *Second Coming*. The former had been written immediately after *Carrie*, during the six-month period when the first draft of *Carrie* was sitting in a desk drawer, mellowing; the latter was written during the year or so when *Carrie* inched, tortoiselike, closer and closer to publication.

Blaze was a melodrama about a huge, almost retarded criminal who kidnaps a baby, planning to ransom it back to the child's rich parents . . . and then falls in love with the child instead. *Second Coming* was a melodrama about vampires taking over a small town in Maine. Both were literary imitations of a sort, *Second Coming* of *Dracula*, *Blaze* of Steinbeck's *Of Mice and Men*.

519

I think Bill must have been flabbergasted when these two manuscripts arrived in a single big package (some of the pages of *Blaze* had been typed on the reverse sides of milk-bills, and the *Second Coming* manuscript reeked of beer because someone had spilled a pitcher of Black Label on it during a New Year's Eve party three months before)—like a woman who wishes for a bouquet of flowers and discovers her husband has gone out and bought her a hothouse. The two manuscripts together totaled about five hundred and fifty single-spaced pages.

He read them both over the next couple of weeks—scratch an editor and find a saint—and I went down to New York from Maine to celebrate the publication of *Carrie* (April, 1974, friends and neighbors—Lennon was alive, Nixon was still hanging in there as President, and this kid had yet to see the first gray hair in his beard) and to talk about which of the two books should be next . . . or if neither of them should be next.

I was in the city for a couple of days, and we talked around the question three or four times. The final decision was made on a street-corner—Park Avenue and Forty-fourth Street, in fact. Bill and I were standing there waiting for the light, watching the cabs roll into that funky tunnel or whatever it is—the one that seems to burrow straight through the Pan Am Building. And Bill said, "I think it should be *Second Coming*."

Well, that was the one I liked better myself—but there was something so oddly reluctant in his voice that I looked at him sharply and asked him what the matter was. "It's just that if you do a book about vampires as the follow-up to a book about a girl who can move things by mind-power, you're going to get typed," he said.

"Typed?" I asked, honestly bewildered. I could see no similarities to speak of between vampires and telekinesis. "As *what*?"

"As a horror writer," he said, more reluctantly still.

"Oh," I said, vastly relieved. "Is *that* all!"

"Give it a few years," he said, "and see if you still think it's 'all.' "

"Bill," I said, amused, "no one can make a living writing just horror stories in America. Lovecraft starved in Providence. Bloch gave it up for suspense novels and *Unknown*-type spoofs. The

Exorcist was a one-shot. You'll see."

The light changed. Bill clapped me on the shoulder. "I think you're going to be very successful," he said, "but I don't think you know shit from Shinola."

He was closer to the truth than I was. It turned out that it *was* possible to make a living writing horror stories in America. *Second Coming*, eventually retitled *'Salem's Lot,* did very well. By the time it was published, I was living in Colorado with my family and writing a novel about a haunted hotel. On a trip into New York, I sat up with Bill half the night in a bar called Jasper's (where a huge, fog-gray tomcat apparently owned the Rock-Ola; you had to kind of lift him up to see what the selections were) and told him the plot. By the end, his elbows were planted on either side of his bourbon and his head was in his hands, like a man with a monster migraine.

"You don't like it," I said.

"I like it a lot," he said hollowly.

"Then what's wrong?"

"*First* the telekinetic girl, *then* the vampires, *now* the haunted hotel and the telepathic kid. You're gonna get typed."

This time I thought about it a little more seriously—and then I thought about all the people who *had* been typed as horror writers, and who had given me such great pleasure over the years —Lovecraft, Clark Ashton Smith, Frank Belknap Long, Fritz Leiber, Robert Bloch, Richard Matheson, and Shirley Jackson (yes; even she was typed as a spook writer). And I decided there in Jasper's with the cat asleep on the juke and my editor sitting beside me with his head in his hands, that I could be in worse company. I could, for example, be an "important" writer like Joseph Heller and publish a novel every seven years or so, or a "brilliant" writer like John Gardner and write obscure books for bright academics who eat macrobiotic foods and drive old Saabs with faded but still legible GENE MCCARTHY FOR PRESIDENT stickers on the rear bumpers.

"That's okay, Bill," I said, "I'll be a horror writer if that's what people want. That's just fine."

We never had the discussion again. Bill's still editing and I'm still writing horror stories, and neither of us is in analysis. It's a good deal.

So I got typed and I don't much mind—after all, I write true to type . . . at least, *most* of the time. But is horror *all* I write? If you've read the foregoing stories, you *know* it's not . . . but elements of horror can be found in all of the tales, not just in *The Breathing Method*—that business with the slugs in *The Body* is pretty gruesome, as is much of the dream imagery in *Apt Pupil*. Sooner or later, my mind always seems to turn back in that direction, God knows why.

Each one of these longish stories was written immediately after completing a novel—it's as if I've always finished the big job with just enough gas left in the tank to blow off one good-sized novella. *The Body,* the oldest story here, was written directly after *'Salem's Lot*; *Apt Pupil* was written in a two-week period following the completion of *The Shining* (and following *Apt Pupil* I wrote nothing for three months—I was pooped); *Rita Hayworth and Shawshank Redemption* was written after finishing *The Dead Zone*; and *The Breathing Method,* the most recently written of these stories, immediately following *Firestarter.* *

None of them has been published previous to this book; none has even been submitted for publication. Why? Because each of them comes out to 25,000 to 35,000 words—not exactly, maybe, but that's close enough to be in the ballpark. I've got to tell you: 25,000 to 35,000 words are numbers apt to make even the most stout-hearted writer of fiction shake and shiver in his boots. There is no hard-and-fast definition of what either a novel or a short story is—at least not in terms of word-count—nor should there be. But when a writer approaches the 20,000-word mark, he knows he is edging out of the country of the short story. Likewise, when he passes the 40,000-word mark, he is edging into the country of the novel. The borders of the country between these two more orderly regions are ill-defined, but at some point the writer wakes up with alarm and realizes that he's come or is coming to a really terrible place, an anarchy-ridden literary banana republic called the "novella" (or, rather too cutesy for my taste, the "novelette").

Now, artistically speaking, there's nothing at all wrong with the

---

*Something else about them, which I just realized: each one was written in a different house—three of those in Maine and one in Boulder, Colorado.

novella. Of course, there's nothing wrong with circus freaks, either, except that you rarely see them outside of the circus. The point is that there are great novellas, but they traditionally only sell to the "genre markets" (that's the polite term; the impolite but more accurate one is "ghetto markets"). You can sell a good mystery novella to *Ellery Queen's Mystery Magazine* or *Mike Shayne's Mystery Magazine*, a good science fiction novella to *Amazing* or *Analog*, maybe even to *Omni* or *The Magazine of Fantasy and Science Fiction*. Ironically, there are also markets for good horror novellas: the aforementioned *F&SF* is one; *Twilight Zone* is another and there are various anthologies of original creepy fiction, such as the *Shadows* series published by Doubleday and edited by Charles L. Grant.

But for novellas which can, on measure, only be described with the word "mainstream" (a word almost as depressing as "genre") . . . boy, as far as marketability goes, you in a heap o' trouble. You look at your 25,000-to-35,000-word manuscript dismally, twist the cap off a beer, and in your head you seem to hear a heavily accented and rather greasy voice saying: *"Buenos días, señor!* How was your flight on Revolución Airways? You like eet preety-good-fine I theenk, *sí?* Welcome to Novella, *señor!* You going to like heet here preety-good-fine, I theenk! Have a cheap cigar! Have some feelthy peectures! Put your feet up, *señor*, I theenk your story is going to be here a long, *long* time . . . *qué pasa?* Ah-ha-hah-hah-hah!"

Depressing.

Once upon a time (he mourned) there really *was* a market for such tales—there were magical magazines such as *The Saturday Evening Post, Collier's*, and *The American Mercury*. Fiction—fiction both short and long—was a staple of these and others. And, if the story was too long for a single issue, it was serialized in three parts, or five, or nine. The poisonous idea of "condensing" or "excerpting" novels was as yet unknown (both *Playboy* and *Cosmopolitan* have honed this particular obscenity to a noxious science: you can now read an entire novel in twenty minutes!), the tale was given the space it demanded, and I doubt if I'm the only one who can remember waiting for the mailman all day long because the new *Post* was due and a new short story by Ray Bradbury had been promised, or perhaps because the final episode of the latest Clarence Buddington Kelland serial was due.

(My anxiety made me a particularly easy mark. When the postman finally did show up, walking briskly with his leather bag over his shoulder, dressed in his summer-issue shorts and wearing his summer-issue sun helmet, I'd meet him at the end of the walk, dancing from one foot to the other as if I badly needed to go to the bathroom; my heart in my throat. Grinning rather cruelly, he'd hand me an electric bill. Nothing but that. Heart plummets into my shoes. Finally he relents and gives me the *Post* after all: grinning Eisenhower on the cover, painted by Norman Rockwell; an article on Sophia Loren by Pete Martin; "I Say He's a Wonderful Guy" by Pat Nixon, concerning—yeah, you guessed it—her husband, Richard; and, of course, stories. Long ones, short ones, and the last chapter of the Kelland serial. Praise God!)

And this didn't happen just once in a while; this happened *every fucking week*! The day that the *Post* came, I guess I was the happiest kid on the whole eastern seaboard.

There are still magazines that publish long fiction—*Atlantic Monthly* and *The New Yorker* are two which have been particularly sympathetic to the publication problems of a writer who has delivered (we won't say "gotten"; that's too close to "misbegotten") a 30,000-word novella. But neither of these magazines has been particularly receptive to my stuff, which is fairly plain, not very literary, and sometimes (although it hurts like hell to admit it) downright clumsy.

To some degree or other, I would guess that those very qualities—unadmirable though they may be—have been responsible for the success of my novels. Most of them have been plain fiction for plain folks, the literary equivalent of a Big Mac and a large fries from McDonald's. I am able to recognize elegant prose and to respond to it, but have found it difficult or impossible to write it myself (most of my idols as a maturing writer were muscular novelists with prose styles which ranged from the horrible to the nonexistent: cats like Theodore Dreiser and Frank Norris). Subtract elegance from the novelist's craft and one finds himself left with only one strong leg to stand on, and that leg is good weight. As a result, I've tried as hard as I can, always, to give good weight. Put another way, if you find out you can't run like a thoroughbred, you can still pull your brains out (a voice rises from the balcony: "*What brains, King?*" Ha-ha, very funny, fella, you can leave now).

The result of all this is that, when it came to the novellas you've just read, I found myself in a puzzling position. I had gotten to a place with my novels where people were saying King could publish his laundry list if he wanted to (and there are critics who claim that's exactly what I've been doing for the last eight years or so), but I couldn't publish these tales because they were too long to be short and too short to be really long. If you see what I mean.

"*Sí, señor*, I see! Take off your shoes! Have some cheap rum! Soon thee Medicore Revolución Steel Band iss gonna come along and play some bad calypso! You like eet preety-good-fine, I theenk! And you got time, *señor*! You got time because I theenk your story ees gonna—"

—be here a long time, yeah, yeah, great, why don't you go somewhere and overthrow a puppet imperialist democracy?

So I finally decided to see if Viking, my hardcover publisher, and New American Library, my paperback publisher, would want to do a book with stories in it about an off-beat prison-break, an old man and a young boy locked up in a gruesome relationship based on mutual parasitism, a quartet of country boys on a journey of discovery, and an off-the-wall horror story about a young woman determined to give birth to her child no matter what (or maybe the story is actually about that odd club that isn't a club). The publishers said okay. And that is how I managed to break these four long stories out of the banana republic of the novella.

I hope you liked them preety-good-fine, *muchachos* and *muchachas*.

Oh, one other thing about type-casting before I call it a day.

Was talking to my editor—not Bill Thompson, this is my *new* editor, a real nice guy named Alan Williams, smart, witty, able, but usually on jury duty somewhere deep in the bowels of New Jersey—about a year ago.

"Loved *Cujo*," Alan says (the editorial work on that novel, a real shaggy-dog story, had just been completed). "Have you thought about what you're going to do next?"

Déjà vu sets in. I have had this conversation before.

"Well, yeah," I say. "I *have* given it some thought—"

"Lay it on me."

"What would you think about a book of four novellas? Most or all of them just sort of ordinary stories? What would you think about that?"

"Novellas," Alan says. He is being a good sport, but his voice says some of the joy may have just gone out of his day; his voice says he feels he has just won two tickets to some dubious little banana republic on Revolución Airways. "Long stories, you mean."

"Yeah, that's right," I say. "And we'll call the book something like *Different Seasons*, just so people will get the idea that it's not about vampires or haunted hotels or anything like that."

"Is the *next* one going to be about vampires?" Alan asks hopefully.

"No, I don't think so. What do you think, Alan?"

"A haunted hotel, maybe?"

"No, I did that one already. *Different Seasons*, Alan. It's got a nice ring to it, don't you think?"

"It's got a great ring, Steve," Alan says, and sighs. It is the sigh of a good sport who has just taken his seat in third class on Revolución Airways' newest plane—a Lockheed Tristar—and has seen the first cockroach trundling busily over the top of the seat ahead of him.

"I hoped you'd like it," I say.

"I don't suppose," Alan says, "we could have a horror story in it? Just one? A sort of . . . *similar* season?"

I smile a little—just a little—thinking of Sandra Stansfield and Dr. McCarron's Breathing Method. "I can probably whomp something up."

"Great! And about that new novel—"

"How about a haunted car?" I say.

"My *man*!" Alan cries. I have the feeling that I'm sending him back to his editorial meeting—or possibly to jury duty in East Rahway—a happy man. I'm happy, too—I *love* my haunted car, and I think it's going to make a lot of people nervous about crossing busy streets after dark.

But I've been in love with each of these stories, too, and part of me always will be in love with them, I guess. I hope that you liked them, Reader; that they did for you what any good story should do—make you forget the real stuff weighing on your mind for a little while and take you away to a place you've never been. It's the most amiable sort of magic I know.

Okay. Gotta split. Until we see each other again, keep your head together, read some good books, be useful, be happy.

Love and good wishes,

Stephen King

January 4th, 1982
Bangor, Maine